HIGH HURDLES

To Katie
Happy reading

Lauraine Snelling

Books by
Lauraine Snelling

Golden Filly Collection One *
Golden Filly Collection Two *

High Hurdles Collection One *
High Hurdles Collection Two *

SECRET REFUGE
Daughter of Twin Oaks

DAKOTAH TREASURES
Ruby • *Pearl*
Opal • *Amethyst*

DAUGHTERS OF BLESSING
A Promise for Ellie • *Sophie's Dilemma*
A Touch of Grace • *Rebecca's Reward*

HOME TO BLESSING
A Measure of Mercy • *No Distance Too Far*
A Heart for Home

RED RIVER OF THE NORTH
An Untamed Land • *A New Day Rising*
A Land to Call Home • *The Reaper's Song*
Tender Mercies • *Blessing in Disguise*

RETURN TO RED RIVER
A Dream to Follow • *Believing the Dream*
More Than a Dream

* 5 books in each volume

Lauraine Snelling

HIGH HURDLES

Collection One

◆BETHANYHOUSE
Minneapolis, Minnesota

Scripture quotations identified NIV are from the HOLY BIBLE, NEW INTERNATIONAL VERSION.® Copyright © 1973, 1978, 1984 by International Bible Society. Used by permission of Zondervan Publishing House. All rights reserved. The "NIV" and "New International Version" trademarks are registered in the United States Patent and Trademark Office by International Bible Society. Use of either trademark requires the permission of International Bible Society.

Published by Bethany House Publishers
11400 Hampshire Avenue South
Minneapolis, Minnesota 55438

Bethany House Publishers is a division of
Baker Publishing Group, Grand Rapids, Michigan.

Printed in the United States of America

Library of Congress Cataloging-in-Publication Data is available for this title.
LCCN: 2010053030

About the Author

Lauraine Snelling is an award-winning author of over sixty books, fiction and nonfiction, for adults and young adults. Her books have sold over two million copies. Besides writing books and articles, she teaches at writers' conferences across the country. She and her husband, Wayne, have two grown sons and a basset hound named Chewey. They make their home in California.

Editor's Note

Originally published in the 1990s, these books reflect the cultural and social aspects of that time. In order to maintain the integrity of the story, we opted not to impose today's styles, technologies, laws, or other advancements upon the characters and events within. We believe the themes of love of God, love of family, and love of horses are timeless and can be enjoyed no matter the setting.

Book One

OLYMPIC DREAMS

*With love to my brother Don and my sister
Karen, who helped me catch our horse Silver
even when they didn't want to. I am so
fortunate to be in the same family as you.*

Chapter · 1

"One day—the Olympics."

Darla Jean Randall scrunched her eyes shut, crossed her fingers, and breathed her prayer all at the same time. She repeated it for good measure, then opened her green eyes and stared at the poster on the wall above her dresser. Five interlocking gold Olympic rings topped an illustration of a dark mahogany horse flying over a triple jump, its mane braided with red, white, and blue ribbons. The red-jacketed rider, in total control, rode poised over the horse's withers.

One day she would be in that picture. She, thirteen-year-old DJ Randall—well, fourteen minus twenty-one days—would hear the roar of the crowd as she and her mount triumphantly finished the cross-country course. When DJ closed her eyes again, she could almost feel the horse beneath her, the thrust of its powerful haunches sending them flying easily over the jumps. She could hear the cheers of the crowd, smell and taste the victory.

DJ reluctantly pulled her attention away from her daydream and clattered down the stairs. Her best friend, Amy Yamamoto, waited at the bottom.

"What took you so long?" Amy checked her watch. "You've got a group lesson to teach in half an hour. And you know those little kids are champing at the bit."

"Sorry. I got sidetracked." Darla Jean, known instead as DJ since she demanded everyone call her that, hopped on one foot while she pulled on a boot. She grabbed her riding helmet off the peg by the door, clapped it on her head, and instinctively tucked her wavy blond ponytail up into it.

"You be careful now." Her grandmother's voice followed her out the door.

"Yeah, I will." DJ's answer, yelled over her shoulder, was automatic.

The warm Pleasant Hill, California, sun lay golden over the bleached tan hills of Briones Park to the west as DJ and Amy hopped onto their ten-speed bikes and pedaled up the slope.

"How do you plan to ride in the Olympics when you don't even have a horse?" Amy renewed the discussion they had had countless times before.

"Remember when I said I wanted to ride and you said I didn't even know how?"

"I know."

"I got a job at the Academy to pay for riding lessons, and everything worked out."

"Yeah, and how many gazillion stalls have we mucked out since then?"

DJ shifted down to pump up the steep hill ahead. "So now I need money to buy a horse of my own."

"You need to learn to jump first." Practical Amy, riding in front, had to yell to be heard.

"Sure would be super to be training my own horse at the same time." Labored puffs between DJ's words attested to the grade of the hill.

They crested the hill and coasted down the other side. Aluminum pipe fences surrounded the riding rings, open-air stalls, and pasture area of Briones Riding Academy, known simply as the Academy by the working students and the others who rode there. A square white sign informed the public they could take lessons there and stable their horses.

The two girls turned into the gravel drive. "Too bad your mom can't buy you a horse."

"Right." DJ shrugged. "So what else is new? She couldn't afford lessons either, but I got 'em. I can't afford to wait around for her to help."

They parked their bikes in front of the low red barn with an aluminum roof. A raked sand aisle on each side divided the four lines of stalls fifteen box stalls long. Here lived the horses stabled at the Academy by outside owners. Some of them came to ride every day, but most of the animals were cared for and exercised by academy employees.

"I've got a treat for Diablo, then I'll meet you at the office." DJ dug in her pocket for the carrot pieces she always brought for the fiery sorrel gelding and trotted down the right aisle of stalls, calling out greetings to her favorite animals as she passed. She would have needed a bucket to treat all her friends.

"Hi, big fella." DJ grinned at the excited nicker from the restless sorrel. "I brought you something." Diablo lipped the carrot off her hand, rubbing his forehead against her chest while he munched. When he slobbered on her cheek, she inhaled a strong dose of carrot perfume. "You big silly. You act so tough, but you're really a marshmallow inside."

DJ rubbed the red's ears and murmured sweet words all the while. She was sure she couldn't love him more if he really belonged to her. She buried her nose in his thick mane and breathed deep. Nothing in the entire world smelled as good as a horse.

Amy's whistle called DJ back to reality.

"See ya later." She tickled Diablo's whiskery lip one last time and headed back to the entrance, ignoring his pleading whinny.

"Looks like James didn't show up again," Amy said when DJ joined her. "The stalls need mucking, and I was supposed to do the show grooming today."

"We'll be here all afternoon." DJ's eyes lit up. "Extra money for lessons. Maybe there'll even be some to put in my horse fund!"

"Great. And I thought we could go swimming today." Amy propped both their bikes out of the way against the wall and stuck her hands in the back pockets of her jeans. "Come on, let's get going."

Dust puffed up around their boots as they walked across to the combination tackroom and office building. DJ lifted the clipboard with her class roster off the announcements wall and waved at Bridget Sommersby. Owner, trainer, boss, and good friend. Bridget sat working at her desk on the other side of the large square window.

Bridget signaled DJ to wait. "Angie's mother called. Angie caught a bug and won't be here today." She checked the calendar on her wall. "You're reviewing leads, right?"

"And starting figure eights. Shame Angie's missed so much. She's the only natural rider in the group."

"I know. Too bad kids with asthma seem to catch every bug that comes around. Angie's parents have signed her up for the next series of lessons, though. Say, DJ, after you are finished today, do you want to work Diablo? He needs extra attention. His owners called and said they would be out to see him."

"Really? I thought they'd forgotten all about him. Wish I could buy him." DJ shook her head. "Why own such a super horse and then never ride him?"

"Who cares? This way you can pretend he's yours." Amy picked up a bucket full of brushes and combs. "Where do you want me to start today, Bridget? That Quarter Horse's tail needs pulling if he's going to show. James should be here to help out. What happened to him *this* time?"

"I believe he is sick."

"Who called in his excuse, the nanny or the chauffeur?"

"Come on, now, don't be catty. It is not James' fault his father has as much money as the San Francisco mint."

"Well, he isn't learning much about responsibility when he only shows up when—"

"That is enough." Bridget didn't waste words any more than she wasted motions—or emotions for that matter. "I will come with you, Amy, so we can make some decisions." She ushered them out and closed the door behind her. "Oh, DJ, did you check with your grandmother about the show coming up? The entry fees should be sent in tomorrow."

DJ felt the familiar catch in her stomach. She *hated* asking Gran for money. But Mom was never around to ask. She was forever traveling for her job or at one of her graduate school courses. Not that she ever had money to give anyway.

"Yeah, I know. I gotta get to my class. Talk to you later." DJ strolled across the dusty parking lot to the front ring where two girls, ages eight and ten, stood by the gate with their horses' reins in hand.

"Okay, let's go over your gear." DJ spoke in the hearty, confident tone that helped make her a good teacher. No time now to think about money.

She carefully checked each girth, bit, and chin strap. When she had made sure the girls were wearing the required heeled boots, she swung open the gate. "Riders up."

DJ walked to the center of the deeply sanded ring and watched her charges walk their horses clockwise around its outer edge. Heads bobbing, the horses plodded along, well used to the routine. The girls sat deep in their saddles, heels down, eyes focused ahead on the spot between their horses' ears.

"Keep your right hand on your thigh," DJ called to one of the girls. "And don't let him go to sleep on you." After checking riders and horses again, she ordered a trot.

By the time the class was finished, DJ felt sweat beads trickling down her back.

"So how's the new saddle feel, Samantha? It must fit you better—you look more comfortable."

"I like it. It's still kinda stiff in the stirrups though."

"It will be for a while. A little saddle soap will help soften them up."

DJ motioned the other girl forward. "Krissie, you did real well today. Kept him off the rail and on a steady jog like I asked."

"He's a stubborn horse, but my mom says I'm stubborn enough for three people."

"Then the two of you should do just fine. If you could get out here to practice more, it would help."

"I know. Thanks for the lesson."

"You're welcome." DJ watched as her students headed for their stalls to put away their tack and brush down their mounts. Both owned their horses.

DJ ignored the tiny bite of jealousy she felt. *Beginning riders and they are already horse owners. What I wouldn't give*—she canceled the thought and followed her charges to the stables. Some of the academy riders' mothers waited patiently in their expensive, air-conditioned cars; others walked to the stalls to hurry their daughters along.

"DJ, when can our group go trail-riding in the Briones?" Samantha asked. Briones State Park bordered the west edge of the Academy's acreage.

"You guys have done so good! We'll pack lunches and go in two weeks. But, Sam, you need to get over here to practice more. You could be a really good rider if you did."

"I wish, but my mom is expecting a baby. She says she's too miserable to drive me over every day."

"So ride your bike."

The slender girl shook her head. "Too far. And Mom says the road's too dangerous." She scuffed her boot toe in the dust, studying the patterns she drew. "I want to be the best—you know, compete in the shows and stuff." She looked up at DJ, dark eyes serious. "Like you do."

DJ felt a curious knot in her middle. This could have been her at eight. Only her mom wouldn't have been pregnant. Of course, if her mom had ever found someone to marry, maybe there would have been a brother or sister for—DJ slammed the lid on those thoughts. She *never* let them out when other people were around.

"If you want it bad enough, you can make it happen." She knew where the words had come from. She hadn't planned on saying such a thing. But then, she hadn't planned on having this conversation, either.

DJ grinned and tweaked Sam's red ponytail. She repeated her grandmother's words again, "If you want something bad enough, you can make it happen." Of course, Gran said to pray about it, too, but DJ didn't think this was the right place to bring praying up. She ought to ask Gran out here to give the girls a pep talk, like a coach before a big game.

"You better get Soda brushed down, Sam. Your mom is waiting."

DJ joked with the girls while she supervised them caring for their horses. She did the heavy work—lifting the Western saddles down and standing them on their horns in the aisle—but each girl had to groom her own horse and take care of the stall and tack. While some people paid the Academy for these services, other parents felt that caring for a horse was part of ownership. DJ agreed.

She waved them both off, then walked back to the office. Maybe Bridget had time to talk now. Horses nickered for attention when she passed their stalls. She could hear Amy talking to someone over in the other aisle. It sounded like James had finally made it to work.

But when DJ got to the office, the academy owner was busy with another client, so she returned to the barns. There were still three stalls to muck out on this aisle before she could work with Diablo. She snapped the horses on the hot walker, cleaned the stalls, and spread new shavings in record time. Maybe she'd give Diablo a bath after riding him.

DJ wiped the sweat off her face with the hem of her T-shirt. This July day was meeting its earlier promise of being warm to hot. She stopped at the drinking fountain on the north side of the stable and guzzled the tepid water before splashing some on her face. She'd make sure to splash plenty on herself while bathing the big red horse. The day was growing long. DJ wished she'd brought a lunch.

"Hi, fella, you miss me?" She stopped in front of the impatient gelding and slung her English saddle over the stall's half door. Diablo pawed the shavings down to the hard-packed dirt. He snorted, then pricked his ears forward. DJ stroked his long forelock and brushed it off the bright white diamond in the center of his forehead. A cowlick in the center swirled the hairs in a circle. "You're such a beauty. If only I could buy you. Wonder how much I'd need?"

He rubbed his forehead against her, leaving red and white hairs on her light purple T-shirt. DJ tickled the hairs sticking out of his ears. "Let's get going, you old silly." She kept up the easy murmur she used when working with the horses, talking to the sleek Thoroughbred-Quarter Horse cross as if he understood every word—and answered. Once he was bridled and saddled, she led him out to the cement block for mounting.

Today, just for today, she would pretend Diablo really *was* hers. After all, she *would* be showing him in less than two weeks. His owners, Mr. and Mrs. Ortega, seemed to appreciate how well she and Diablo were doing in the English Pleasure and the Trail Horse classes.

DJ spent the next hour and a half taking the gelding through the entire routine for both classes. By the time they finished, both girl and horse wore a sheen of sweat.

"You two looked mighty good out there." Bridget met them at the gate and swung it open. "You have got him in top shape, both condition and training. Sure has improved since he came in."

"Do you think the Ortegas would like him to learn to jump?"

"I will ask. But seems to me *you* better learn first."

"I know. I want to so bad. How much would lessons cost?"

"Are you not earning enough right now? I have been waiting for you to ask. But you will need to start on old Megs. She knows the bars so well, she will be a good tutor for you."

DJ felt sure her face would split. She gave a decidedly unprofessional bounce in the saddle. Diablo threw his head up, and she tightened her grip on the reins. "Easy, boy, sorry about that. When can I start?"

Bridget smiled up at her star pupil. "Is tomorrow at eight all right? I know that is earlier than you usually come, but let us do it before the sun gets too hot." She slapped DJ on the knee and turned to leave. "Oh, I will ask the Ortegas tonight about jumping Diablo. You already have a good seat, so with some experience you could work with him."

DJ could almost see the Olympic rings shining on the wall of the building in front of her. She waved as Amy rode one of the stable horses into the ring. Amy preferred Western riding, so the two of them usually didn't compete in the same classes.

James followed on his dapple-gray Arab filly. DJ shook her head in disgust. If *she* had a horse like that, she'd sure find it easier to smile than he did.

If James had been one of her students, she would have told him to keep his back straight, his chin up, and his heels down. But he wasn't, and the last time she had made a suggestion—well, James had made it clear that he didn't take suggestions—or even orders—from *anyone*. When DJ had told Gran about the situation, she had said James really needed a friend.

"He can find someone else," DJ muttered, turning back to the barn. She could clean tack until Amy finished her lesson. Rubbing saddle soap into the leathers of a saddle required no brain power, leaving her mind free to explore the challenges of the Olympic long course. Cross country was the most difficult. She and Diablo would jump clean all the way around with the fastest time ever clocked. *First the triple jump, then the brush, then over a water jump . . .*

"You ready to go home or what?" The tone of Amy's voice indicated she'd asked the question before.

DJ jerked herself back to reality. The saddle she was soaping up had *some* shine to it.

Her pumping legs slowed when she pedaled from Amy's house to her own. Now she had to ask for money for the class entry fees. Maybe she should take it out of her horse account. But Gran had promised she would pay the entrance fees. All DJ had to do was ask.

DJ smiled. Why not require a signature in blood or a week of hard time digging in the backyard? Maybe she should offer to clean the kitchen every night without grumping. Not grumbling was the key. Even scrubbing toilets was better than doing dishes. DJ parked her bike carefully in the garage. Nothing fried her mother like something out of place.

Gran was so different from her mom. All Gran said to do was ask. She also told DJ to ask God when she needed something. DJ did remember to ask God for the most important things—at least some of the time. Like winning Olympic gold. It just didn't seem fair to bother God with the little things. She chewed on her thumbnail as she walked through the back door.

"Gran?"

"In the studio."

DJ padded through the living room and out to her grandmother's studio. In a normal family's home, it would have been the family room. Gran, a highly successful illustrator, stood in front of her easel, brush in hand and head cocked, studying her latest work.

"What do you think?"

DJ looked from the whimsical forest creatures dancing on the canvas to her grandmother dressed in matching hot pink shorts and tank top, both liberally decorated with bright dabs of paint. "The painting is awesome, like always, and you have yellow paint on your chin."

"No biggie." The artist stepped forward and applied two more brushstrokes to the fawn, bringing his spotted coat to life. "There, I'll leave it till tomorrow. I actually think it's done."

DJ sank into the stuffed rocker, her feet trailing over the arm. "Gran?"

"What, my darling?" The voice sounded vague, as if Gran were still off in the forest with her creatures.

DJ drew a circle around the puckered scar on her left palm. The words wouldn't come. "When's Mom coming home?"

"Tomorrow night. Why?" Gran continued setting her paints in order. Other things might be left scattered around, but her paints and brushes were always cleaned and organized when she finished for the day.

"I need—ah—Gran, I need money for entry fees." The words stumbled over each other in their rush to reach air.

"Of course, why the hesitation? All you have to do is ask." Gran turned around, hands on her rounded hips. "How much do you need and by when?"

The whoosh leaving DJ's lungs set the folded paper swans attached to a twisted branch dancing on their threads. She named the amount.

"Check or cash?" Gran wiped the wisps of salt-and-pepper hair—heavy on the salt—back from her forehead. A puzzled look flitted across her face. "Did you have lunch? I don't think I did. What time is it anyway?" While she talked she dug in her huge satchel-style purse and pulled out a battered billfold. She wrote and handed DJ a check.

"I'll pay you back."

"You pay me back just by being yourself and helping when I ask. Working to pay for your own lessons is a big help. Besides, when was the last time I had to take out the garbage or mow and water the yard?" She threw her arm over DJ's shoulder and squeezed. "I just thank God I have money to give you."

DJ ducked her head, suddenly shy. That was her Gran all right. Always thankful for everything. But she *would* pay her back somehow.

Right after dinner, Gran buried her head in a book.

DJ climbed the stairs to her bedroom. This was the best time of day to draw. DJ's own pictures of horses filled her walls. Charcoal or pencil foals, Arabs, and jumpers surrounded the colored Olympic poster.

She piled her pillows against the headboard, propped her drawing board on her knees, and leaned back, waiting for inspiration to strike. Her pencil began to move as if controlled by some unseen force. Later, her drawing finished, she fell asleep with horses on her mind, the main one a fiery sorrel sporting a startling white diamond in the center of his forehead.

DJ rode out to the Academy by herself in the morning. Amy would be coming later. Her whistle set all the horses nickering as she jogged down the sandy aisle toward the red gelding's stall.

But Diablo didn't answer her whistle. His stall gate stood open, hooked to the side wall. All of his gear had been cleared out. Even the shavings had been swept away, leaving nothing but bare black dirt. DJ felt her happiness escape with a whoosh. Diablo was gone.

Chapter • 2

"Bridget! Diablo's missing!" DJ stopped to get her breath.

"Easy, girl." The trainer pushed her chair back from the desk. She checked the round clock on the wall. "I had hoped to see you before you . . ."

"But you don't understand. His stall is empty, even the shavings are gone. Did you move him?" The words tumbled over each other, picking up speed like rocks in a landslide.

"DJ, I know." Bridget pointed to one of the well-bruised chairs by her desk. "Sit."

"But . . ."

"Sit!" The command cracked through the stillness.

DJ did as ordered. She dug one chewed-off fingernail into the edge of her thumb. Visions of Diablo lying dead in the stall—or running away over the hills—raced through her mind.

"Now, I have bad news for you. You knew the Ortegas were coming last night to see Diablo?"

"Sure, I bathed him and everything so they would see I was taking good care of their horse." The desire to chew on her thumbnail made her raise her hand partway to her mouth. But, instead, she gripped one with the other and glued them to her knees.

"They came with a trailer and took him. They are moving and have a new stable lined up for him."

"Where did they go?" Instantly, her eyes burned. Her heart felt heavy. "Where did they take him?"

"Out of state. Texas, I think."

"So I won't ever see him again?" DJ couldn't have loved Diablo more if he'd been her own. How awful, not to see Diablo, not to ride him again, not to play with him in the corral.

Her shoulders slumped with the weight of the news. "Why didn't you warn me?"

Bridget shook her head. "I didn't know. Usually people give me thirty days' notice—that's what our contract stipulates—but they just showed up. Said they had to move quickly, something about his job." She handed DJ an envelope. "Here, this is for you."

DJ took it and slid her finger under part of the flap. "Ouch." A paper cut opened a red line across the top of her finger. She finished opening the envelope and stuck her finger in her mouth to stop the bleeding. She looked up at Bridget, then dropped her gaze. The compassion in her mentor's eyes was too much for her to handle.

DJ pulled out a folded sheet of paper. Classic penmanship made it easy to read. *Dear DJ, please accept this token of our appreciation for the fine job you've done with Diablo. His conditioning and training show how much you've cared for him. We thank you and wish you the best in your endeavors. Sincerely, Manuel Ortega.* DJ unfolded the check.

"A hundred dollars." She stared at the zeros. Counted them again. "Look." She handed the check across the desk. "They gave me a hundred dollars."

"You earned every penny of it." Bridget handed it back with a smile. "That will help your horse fund."

DJ stuffed the note and check back into the envelope. "I was hoping to buy Diablo from them someday." The thought of never seeing her best friend again roared back.

Before DJ had more time to dwell on the bad news, Bridget pushed her chair back. "You better get Megs saddled and ready for your first jumping lesson. Our time is running out." She nodded toward the clock.

"Yes, ma'am." DJ jumped to her feet, stuffing the envelope in her pocket. "I'll be ready in ten."

She jogged across the dust-caked drive and back to the stables.

Funny, the sun still shone and the birds sang. Maybe it was only her world that had stopped, not the one around her. Somewhere Diablo rode in a horse van, moving to his new home. Did he miss her as much as she already missed him?

She snagged a bucket with grooming gear, along with a jumping saddle and bridle, from the tack room and hustled down the long aisle. At least she didn't have to pass Diablo's empty stall. Megs, now retired from the show circuit but with a wealth of experience to teach her riders, hung her dark head out the stall door. She nickered when DJ came near, as did the other horses DJ ignored in her rush to ready the mare.

"Hi, girl." DJ hung the saddle and bridle on the half door hooked open to the wall, and slipped the mare a carrot piece. She grabbed a brush from the bucket, shoved the handle of the currycomb in her back pocket, and ducked under the web to begin the quickest grooming this side of tomorrow. Within minutes she had the mare brushed down and the tack in place. If one of her students had done that haphazard a job, she'd have made her redo it.

"I'll give you a really good brushing afterward," she promised as she led the Anglo-Arab bay mare down the aisle. "Then I'll turn you out for a while. How does that sound?" Megs clopped along beside her, ears pricked, head down as if hoping for a quick stroke now and then.

Once in the ring, DJ walked the mare around the outside, loosening her up even though they would be jumping only the lowest rails today. One thing Bridget drilled into her students and staff alike was that you could never be too careful with your horse. Not warming up enough led to strains and poor performance. A horse was like any other finely tuned athlete—warm muscles stretched easily and were less likely to suffer an injury.

DJ worked the mare through her paces: walk, trot, and collected canter. The thrill of riding a well-schooled horse sent DJ's mind instantly to the show-ring—and the Olympics. She jerked herself back to the present. If Bridget caught her daydreaming, she'd be grounded for sure.

Just as DJ was about to ask someone to fetch her instructor, Bridget entered the ring. She walked to each of the four jumps and checked the rails, all set at the lowest peg.

"Ready?"

"Yes, ma'am." DJ had watched enough classes and videos to know what was coming. She squeezed her lower legs to guide the mare over to the center of the ring. Even though she'd jumped before, this was her first official lesson.

"I hope you have not learned any bad habits that we have to undo. Let me see you in your two-point trot, keeping the pace over the cavalletti." Bridget motioned to three parallel rails she had placed on the ground, spaced wide enough so the horse wouldn't stumble.

After DJ completed several successful rounds, Bridget moved to the center of the ring. "Good. Now, keeping the same pace, bring her over this jump. Remember to rest your weight in your heels and to lean into the jump. When you settle back, return to the two point."

Again, DJ did as asked, loving even the small moment of being airborne.

While DJ completed several circuits, Bridget lowered the rails on another jump and set the two in a straight line.

"Good, Megs. You're so smooth." DJ patted the mare's neck.

"Now maintain the pace up to the first obstacle, then canter to the next. Count the number of strides and keep her going straight."

Keep her between your hands and legs, DJ reminded herself. She had heard the instructions so many times before that she knew the routine, but making Megs do it exactly right wasn't as easy as she'd thought. Invariably Megs drifted to the right.

"Pay attention, DJ. You are using too much left leg."

DJ nodded but overcorrected, and Megs obediently swung to the right.

"You are trying too hard—just relax and forget we are in a class situation."

DJ tried to smile, but it felt more like a grimace. She set the mare into another round: cavalletti, two point, jump. Going straight was much harder than she'd ever dreamed.

"No, keep the pace. Get yourself in balance before you reach the jump."

DJ returned to the two point and completed the circle. Trot, jump, count one, two, three, four, five, and over. "Fiddle."

"What was wrong there?"

"I needed six strides and I used five."

"And got left behind?"

DJ nodded. Circle again. Jump, count, and jump. By the end of the hour, DJ could feel the pull in both her back and calves.

"You must keep her going straight. She has a tendency to pull to the left."

"I know. I'm using too much right leg."

"I know you know, so don't let her. One more time around and we will call it a day."

DJ concentrated on everything she'd been told. This time Megs jumped once, took six strides at a canter, made another jump, and headed straight toward the arena fence before dropping back to the trot. DJ rode a tight circle and met Bridget at the gate.

"I have always said you have a good seat," Bridget commented when DJ stopped in front of her. "I know you would practice for hours if you could. Just do not neglect your other duties. You know which horses need the work. I will lay out a program for you if you like."

"Thank you. Oh, thank you, Bridget! I can't wait to try the big ones." Visions of triple jumps, water jumps, brush jumps, and in-and-outs flew through her mind.

"In good time." Bridget shared one of her rare smiles with her charge. "Now, you have stalls to clean and horses to work—after you cool out Megs, of course. Oh, and about the show. You know you may ride one of the school horses."

DJ's shoulders slumped. No Diablo to show meant no chance for a decent ribbon. She mentally ran through the stable horses. Only Megs would have a chance, and she was retired. Bridget would never change her mind on that.

"Thanks, but none of them are ready. I'll help coach the beginners." The thought of not competing in the better classes this summer made her groan. If only she had a horse of her own—then things like this wouldn't happen. Now she had to prepare another horse, which also wouldn't be her own. She clenched her teeth as a blaze of anger ripped through her.

Megs jigged to the side. "Sorry, girl." DJ ordered her body to relax. *There must be a connection between my knees and my jaw.*

She looked up to catch a look from Bridget that clearly said, never take your personal problems out on your horse.

"I'm sorry." DJ seemed to be saying that a lot. "I . . . I . . . what if I can't show at all this summer?"

"Is that what is worrying you?" Bridget stepped close to Megs' shoulder. "There will always be a horse here for you to ride. You just need to take the time to prepare one. I will talk with one of the owners. Mrs. Orlando might be pleased to have you show one of her horses."

DJ started to ask which one, but thought the better of it. Early on she'd learned that when Bridget was ready to tell her something, she would. And asking before that would not make her popular with the academy owner.

"Someday I'll have a horse of my own."

"Yes, I am sure you will." Bridget laid a hand on DJ's knee. "I *know* you will. Now, take care of the ones you can." She patted Megs' neck and walked out of the gate. Two people were waiting to talk with her outside the arena.

Feeling as if she were floating on a cloud, DJ nudged the mare into a trot. She had plenty of work to do.

Along with each shovelful of shavings and manure, she tossed out another moneymaking idea. She *had* to buy a horse of her own. But first she had to earn the money. Counting the check this morning, her total now stood at $189.89. If only she didn't have to buy things like presents and give part of her earnings to Sunday school.

"I'm never going to a movie again," she muttered, spreading the clean shavings she'd hauled in.

"What's up?" Amy stopped with her wheelbarrow.

"The Ortegas moved away and took Diablo with them."

"That's why his stall is empty?"

"Yup. At least now I don't have to spend Gran's money for entry fees. I won't be showing."

"Not ever?"

"Don't be dumb." DJ leaned on her pitchfork. "Bridget says I can use school horses to show, but none of them are ready for Saturday."

"You can use Josh." Amy offered her most prized possession.

"Ames, you know that won't work. Our classes are usually at the same time—besides, I've never ridden him in competition." She looked deep into her friend's eyes. "You're the best. Thanks."

"James isn't here—again." Amy rolled her eyes. "I've had to do most of his work."

"Again? What's with him, anyway?"

"Wish I knew." Amy picked up the handles of the barrow. "Gotta finish so I can work Josh. Hey, how did your lesson go?"

"Great. I was born to jump, I just know it." DJ closed her eyes and saw five interlocking rings on the back of her eyelids. She crossed her fingers and breathed her prayer. *Someday, the Olympics.*

"Ames, I *have* to find some ways to earn money this summer. You had any brilliant ideas lately?"

"Sorry." Amy shrugged and trundled her wheelbarrow down the aisle.

That evening when her mother returned home from her latest business trip, DJ had just finished setting the table.

"Darla Jean, how many times have I asked you to put your bike away? One of these days I'm going to run over it, and then where will you be?" Lindy Randall dropped her briefcase on a chair and crossed to the sink to pour herself a glass of water.

DJ clenched her teeth. She'd been so anxious to tell Gran the bad news, she'd forgotten her bike. Fiddle. She slammed the napkins down on the table and headed for the garage. Now she didn't dare mention needing extra money for her horse fund. Double fiddle.

Chapter • 3

"DJ, I'm sorry. I didn't mean to scold you first thing." Lindy stood in the doorway to DJ's room. She had changed out of her business suit and into an emerald lounging outfit.

"I know. It was my fault. I couldn't wait to tell Gran about Diablo." DJ looked up from her drawing. "You look nice." Her mother always looked stylish, dressed in the latest fashion. DJ looked down at her tanned legs topped by the cutoffs she'd put on after her return from the stable. Jeans or shorts and T-shirts—what else did a kid need anyway? Besides her outfits for competition, of course, and Gran made most of those.

"Thanks, can I come in?"

"Sure." Her mother's recent insistence on privacy—both her own and her daughter's—still caught DJ by surprise sometimes.

Lindy looked down at her daughter's drawing of a jumping Thoroughbred. "You're getting to be very good at that, you know. I'm glad one of us got Mother's talent." She sat down on the end of the bed. DJ watched her mother pleat the fabric of her pants. Something was up. But what?

Lindy looked up, her chin-length hair swinging as she moved her head. "What happened with Diablo?"

"They . . . the Ortegas moved to Texas and took him away."

"Without telling you?"

"Even Bridget didn't know. And now I don't have a horse to compete with this summer." DJ wanted to go on to say that if her mother spent less money on clothes, she might have some cash to buy her daughter a horse, but she didn't. She'd heard the argument too many times: "Fashionable clothes help make sales, and if I don't make sales, we don't eat."

"I'm sorry. I wish I could help, but right now my company is talking about cutting back. What little I have saved might have to tide us over if I get laid off."

"You've been their best rep for the last two years, Mom. Why would they let you go?" When would her mother think of something besides her job and getting her next degree? DJ had a whole slew of questions that she kept hidden in a box in her mind. A box labeled *Mother*.

"Well, when I get my Masters of Business Administration, they'll have to take notice. If they don't, I'll find a better job." She nodded as if to convince herself. "So I better get to studying."

"So what's new?" DJ mumbled in spite of her promise to herself not to be a smart mouth.

"Darla Jean, I'm doing this as much for you as for me."

"Right. Sorry." There, she'd done it again. Why couldn't they just talk like Amy and her mother did? Instead, she couldn't keep from giving a smart answer every time her mom said something.

"Well, I am doing this for you. And a little gratitude might go a long way." Lindy flounced out of the room, leaving a trail of expensive perfume.

DJ heaved a sigh and set her sketch pad down on the double bed. This certainly hadn't been one of her better days. She uncrossed her legs and slid to the edge of the bed. Gran would remind her that her mother was under a great deal of pressure. That selling equipment such as guns and flak vests to police departments and sheriffs' offices was usually a man's job. That her mother felt the need to be so much better than the male sales representatives in order to keep her position.

DJ had heard the story too many times to count. She tried to remember the last time her mother had made it to one of *her* events. Her mom had missed the horse shows, the art fair at school—even missed her thirteenth birthday.

DJ trailed a hand on the banister on her way down to Gran's

sunroom that extended from the family room. She knew she'd find her grandmother curled up in her tattered but comfortable wing chair. She'd be reading a mystery, her favorite kind of book. Or else writing a letter. Gran was great about writing letters to her two sisters who still lived where they grew up in Georgia.

But Gran wasn't in her chair. She wasn't hiding behind an easel, sneaking in some extra work hours. She wasn't in the kitchen making their favorite snack—popcorn, slathered with butter.

"Gran?" DJ checked the laundry room and glanced out at the deck.

Coming back through the French doors, she heard the murmur of voices from her mother's room. DJ grabbed an apple out of the bowl on the kitchen counter and ambled up the stairs. She started to tap on the almost-closed door to her mother's room but stopped.

"But I just don't know what to say to her." Lindy sounded depressed.

"She took the news of losing Diablo pretty hard."

"Oh really? She barely mentioned it. She never talks to me, unless it's a smart remark. Was this the way I was at her age?"

A soft chuckle. "No, you were much worse. You were boy crazy by twelve."

"Yeah, and look what it got me."

DJ couldn't hear Gran's answer.

"At least boys aren't a problem—are they?" A pause. "Oh, Mother, I don't know how you stood it."

"The good Lord's grace, that's how. You might find it, too, if you asked."

"I don't need you preaching to me." The tone switched to harsh resentment.

"You asked, I told you. Now about you and DJ . . ."

DJ leaned closer, but the voices dropped to a low murmur. Gran always said that eavesdroppers heard only bad things about themselves. *Ha!* She shrugged. Who knew when stored information could be useful? Another shrug, this one forced. It sure would be helpful if she and her mother could really talk for a change. Then she wouldn't have to go around feeling guilty so often.

DJ meandered back down to the kitchen, tossing her apple core in the compost bin. She and Gran recycled everything possible. Just last week DJ had turned in aluminum cans and made three dollars, all in nickels. But then a dollar was a dollar no matter what form it came in. She stashed it all in her horse box. Every time she reached $10, she made a bank deposit.

She stuck her head in the refrigerator. Nothing to munch, unless you counted the bag of carrots her mother kept. Horse treats. She checked the cupboard. Microwave popcorn, nothing like the kind Gran made from scratch. She pulled a bag from the box.

"I made popcorn if anybody wants some," she yelled up the stairs on her way to the family room and the television set. When nothing caught her interest and no one came to share her popcorn, she dragged her feet back up the stairs to her room.

What a crummy ending to a perfectly crummy day. Other than her lesson, she corrected. The thought of jumping helped her pick up her feet until she entered her room. The eight-by-ten photo Amy had taken of her and Diablo in the ring last summer sent her spiraling again.

She banished the threat of tears with a clamped jaw. Crying was for babies. She ripped the half-finished picture of the jumper off the pad, crumpled it between both hands, and stuffed it in the wastebasket. It wasn't good enough anyway. Something was wrong with the thrust of the back legs.

If she only had a horse of her own, everything would be all right.

———

Morning dawned along with the beginnings of a moneymaking idea. DJ flew to the window and gazed out at the backyard. The hummingbirds were already buzzing. House finches sang at the seed feeders and two bright yellow and black goldfinches hung upside down on the thistle feeder. DJ sucked in a breath of crisp morning air flavored with the scent of the roses that bloomed around the deck below her second-floor window.

This had to be a better day than yesterday. If she hurried, maybe she could get in an hour on Megs before she had to start her chores. She tugged a brush through her long blond hair while she pelted down the stairs. Her mother would already have left for work, so she didn't have to worry about making conversation.

"You have to eat before you leave," Gran called from her chair. As usual, she sat curled with her steaming mug of coffee on the table beside her and her Bible in her lap.

DJ crossed the room to drop a kiss on her tumbled hair. "I will. You want something?"

"I'll make scrambled eggs if you wait long enough."

"No, I can eat a food bar on the way." DJ headed back to the kitchen. "How come we're out of fruit?"

"You ate it all."

DJ sneaked the orange juice container out and began chugging from the pour spout.

"Darla Jean Randall, you pour that into a glass."

DJ flinched and shoved the jug back in the fridge. Taking out the milk, she did as Gran asked. Drinking from the container was certainly much quicker.

"Will you call Amy and tell her I already left?" She returned from the open door and grabbed a second food bar for her pocket. That would be a morning snack.

"Please? Tell her I left for the Academy at—" she checked her watch—"six-thirty, and she should get her b—"

"Darla Jean! Ladies don't use words like that."

"Sorry, Gran. See ya." DJ let a grin stretch her cheeks. What would Gran do if her darling granddaughter ever said a *really* bad word? Like some of the four-letter words she heard every day at school? One thing Gran liked about Bridget, she didn't tolerate swearing, either.

DJ pedaled by Amy's house, wishing she could have called. But Mrs. Yamamoto had made it clear that no calls were tolerated before seven-thirty in the morning or after nine at night. And it wasn't even seven yet.

Was her idea a good one? Could she and Amy pull it off? Would it make enough money for her so she could buy a horse by summer's end?

The hour in the ring with Megs flew faster than they took the jumps. *Squeeze. Lift. Let Megs show you how to judge the distances; she's an expert. Use your knees.* All the commands of the day before echoed in her head. She'd heard them before, but it was different when they were directed at her.

Oh, the feeling of flying! The thrust of powerful hindquarters and then . . . for that brief second, to be free. And these were only small jumps. What must the larger ones feel like?

"Look straight ahead, between her ears," Bridget called from the fence. "That is right. Do not rush. The more relaxed you are, the more comfortable your mount will be."

DJ completed another circuit and rode over to the fence. "You seen Amy yet?"

"No. By the way, James' housekeeper called. He will be in today—"

DJ snorted in what Gran would call a decidedly unladylike manner.

Bridget cut her a glance that said she entirely agreed with Gran. She continued as if there had been no interruption. "—and he will clean one extra row of stalls, down to the dirt."

DJ knew James was getting punished.

"*And* he will spend two hours cleaning tack. Then he will work in the ring for an hour. I do not want to hear about any comments from you and Amy."

That James! On top of leaving most of his work to the other staff, he was a whiner and a tattletale. What she wouldn't like to do to him!

"Understood?"

Why did Bridget stick up for him? She and Amy knew the instructor never played favorites. James deserved a good yelling at. He even neglected his own horse. *If I had a horse like Gray Bar, I'd spend every minute of my life with her.*

DJ quit studying her hands and looked at Bridget. "Understood." She leaned forward and stroked the bay mare's neck. "I better cool her out." She turned Megs back to the ring. They'd walk around twice, and then she'd put the bay on the hot walker so she could muck stalls.

One thing was sure, there was never a lack of work to do around the Academy. Maybe her other dream of someday owning one wasn't such a hot idea after all.

Amy's entrance snapped DJ out of her daydreams. "Hey, thought you were going to sleep all day."

"I called at seven and you'd already left. Why didn't you tell me you were going so early?"

"I didn't know. I just woke up and couldn't wait to get here. Besides, you know your mom says no early calls. But hurry with your stalls, I got a great idea!"

"What?"

"Can't tell you now. But it's a hummer." DJ grinned at the look on Amy's face. Her dark almond-shaped eyes nearly disappeared when Amy glared. And she was definitely glaring.

"You know I hate secrets." Amy planted both fists on her nearly nonexistent hips. Their flat-chested bodies were one of their big-time gripes.

"I know." DJ attacked her stall with a vengeance.

At the water hose an hour later, DJ ran some over her neck and up her arms.

"Okay, what's your idea?" Amy grabbed the hose and mimicked her friend's actions.

"First, look at me." Amy did. "Do I look green-eyed to you?"

"Silly, you always look green-eyed. You *have* green eyes."

"No, I mean the green-eyed monster—you know—jealousy."

"Who would you be jealous of?"

"James."

"James? Why?"

"His horse. What I wouldn't do for a registered Arab like Gray Bar, and he doesn't even take good care of her."

Amy turned off the faucet. "No, you aren't bitten by the monster. But you're going to be murdered by another one—namely me—if you don't tell me what your idea is."

"Pony rides at birthday parties!"

"What in the world are you talking about? We don't even have a pony."

"You want to hear more or not?"

Chapter • 4

"Dumb question. What are you dreaming up now?"

"You know I need money to buy a horse. You also know we need to exercise Bandit. Right?"

"Yeah, his family almost never comes." Amy turned the hose back on for a drink.

"And you like to take pictures."

"I don't just take pictures. I'm a photographer." The glint in her eye warned DJ to tread lightly. "Or will be someday."

"Your family just got a new Polaroid camera, right?" Teasing Amy like this was a privilege given only to best friends.

Amy flicked the hose, sending drops of water at DJ. "If you don't get to the point, you'll get soaked."

"Do I have to draw you a map?" DJ ducked, but her T-shirt darkened with wet blotches anyway.

"All right, come on." DJ sank down on a concrete block against the barn wall and patted the block beside her. "Sit."

Once they were both leaning elbows on knees, she turned so she could watch Amy's face. "The way I see it, we both want and need money this summer—me for a horse, and you for film, so . . ." She paused for dramatic effect. "So we ask the McDougalls if we can use Bandit to entertain kids at birthday parties. The kids get to ride a pony we lead, have their pictures taken in a Western hat on the pony, and the adult in charge pays us. See, with the Polaroid they can take their pictures home with them." By the end of her speech, DJ bounced up from her block and began pacing in front of Amy, arms waving for emphasis.

She stopped. Planted her hands on her hips. Waited. "Well?"

"I'm thinking."

"I can tell." DJ started to say something else but caught herself. Amy always needed thinking time.

"We don't have a pony, a hat, customers, or a camera. We've never done anything like this. How do we let people know about it?" She closed her eyes as if to concentrate better. "And . . . how much would we charge?"

With the final question, DJ knew Amy planned to go along with the idea.

"Super, huh?"

"Yeah, if we can work it all out. I'll ask my dad about using the camera. Maybe he'll have some suggestions for us."

"And I'll ask Bridget for the McDougalls' phone number and call them. My mom knows a lot about selling stuff, so I'll—" she stopped her pacing to point at Amy—"*we'll* talk to her together. That way she won't think this is another of my 'harebrained schemes'—her words."

"You gotta admit you've come up with some wild ones."

"It wasn't my fault the Great Dane got away. How was I to know he didn't understand leash laws?"

"What about breeding hamsters?"

"So they chewed a hole in their box. That guy with the snake was glad to take the ones that didn't get away."

"Snails?"

"They said the restaurants would pay thirty-five cents each. Anyway, the book said to feed them cornmeal; I thought they'd like it."

"Yeah, well, they liked your grandmother's garden better."

"That was still a good idea. If we ever do it again, I figured out how to make a box even a snail couldn't escape."

"And what about selling greeting cards?"

DJ sank down on the block. "So we've tried different stuff. We *did* make some money selling fruit and vegetables door to door."

"Sure, after your grandma grounded us for a week for picking her strawberries without asking."

"I thought she was done making jam."

"Well, one thing we've learned—or at least *I've* learned—you've got to think things through. Ask lots of questions. This time we don't just jump in and . . ."

"I could draw a real neat cartoon for some fliers. We could use it on invitations and . . ."

Amy shook both her head and her friend.

But DJ was off and running. Like a filly with the bit in her teeth, she took off toward the office. "I'll talk to Bridget right now," she called back from halfway across the parking lot. "We'll have a zinger of a time."

"Hey, Cat Eyes, the bogeyman chasing you?"

The voice stopped DJ in her tracks. *James.* Where had he come from? She turned and looked toward the sound. Sure enough, there he stood in the barn door. The little creep. Life around the Academy was so much sweeter when he didn't show up, even though they had to do all his work.

She turned back toward the office. Maybe if she ignored him, he'd go away. She heard a snicker from behind the line of cars. Sure enough, James must have brought a friend along. He always played best to an audience.

"As if anyone would really be his friend." Her mutter carried her into the dark of the building. She blinked in the dimness, but it didn't slow her pace. If only Bridget had a minute right now!

But the office was empty. DJ checked the board. No classes scheduled. Where was Bridget? Should she flip through the file and find the McDougalls' number herself? She gnawed the end of her already chewed-to-the-quick thumbnail.

"Fiddle. Double fiddle." She swung around and charged out the door, nearly colliding with Bridget as she walked in. "Bridget, I got an idea."

"Thank the Lord for small favors." The woman's grin made sure there was no sting in her words. "Just leave me standing vertical, I listen better in an upright position."

"Sorry. Amy and I are gonna give pony rides at birthday parties so we can earn extra money, so can you give me the McDougalls' phone number so I can call them to see if they'll loan me Bandit?" DJ ran out of air.

"Glad you have to breathe occasionally." Bridget crossed the room to her desk.

"We'll take pictures of the kids on the pony with the Polaroid camera . . ."

"Hold it." Bridget pointed at the chair beside the desk. "Let me think a minute."

DJ perched on the edge of the chair. She hastily stuck her hands between her knees so she wouldn't chew her nails. Bridget did not like to see her students chewing their fingernails. She said it didn't look professional.

"I will give you their number on one condition. You give me a signed paper saying your mom approves and accepts responsibility."

DJ could feel her excitement drain out the toes of her boots. "But . . ."

"No *buts*. You are a hard worker and a responsible girl, but you do go off half-cocked sometimes with new ideas. Since Bandit is stabled here, I have to make sure my clients are cared for properly."

"We wouldn't hurt Bandit." The thought that Bridget could think she wouldn't take good care of a horse made DJ's heart pound.

"DJ, I know that. But you cannot control everything around you. Learning to look at all sides of something and making good plans is part of growing up and becoming an adult. I know how bad you want a horse, so I will help you all I can—but I need to cover myself, too. Bring me the signed paper, then you can call them. I will put in a good word for you if they ask."

DJ nodded. "Okay. Thank you." She got to her feet. The ideas that had been swirling and jumping in her brain now lined up with some sense to them. She had to get her mother's permission. Not Gran's, her mother's. It seemed impossible.

Chapter • 5

"Mom's home. Can you come over?" DJ spoke softly into the phone so no one would hear her.

"I'll ask." DJ heard the phone clunk on the counter and noises in the background. With four kids in the family, there was always noise at the Yamamotos'. "Yes, I can. You want me to bring the stuff?"

The two of them had spent the afternoon making lists and writing plans so they could present their ideas in a businesslike way. Both Lindy and Mr. Yamamoto would appreciate that.

"Have you talked with your mom and dad yet?" DJ twirled the cord around her finger.

"No, we said to wait."

"I know, but . . ." Leave it to Amy. She always did exactly as they agreed. DJ had told Gran all about the idea as soon as she got home. Gran said she'd hold judgment until after the conference. But DJ could tell by the twinkle in her grandmother's eye that she approved. As usual, Gran said, "I'll pray we'll be doing what is in God's will for us."

DJ wished she'd have thought of that without the reminder.

"Mom." DJ knocked on her mother's bedroom door. "Can Amy and I talk with you?"

"Sure." Lindy came to the door, pushing her glasses up on her head. "Up here or down in the family room?"

"Well, I'd kinda like Gran in on it, too."

"Okay, give me a sec to save what's on the computer. Fix us some iced tea, all right?"

DJ and Amy pounded down the carpeted stairs. Within minutes they had four tall glasses of raspberry iced tea on a tray. "Grab some cookies." DJ pointed at the sunflower cookie jar. "Gran baked today."

With the treats served, DJ didn't know what to do with her hands. Other than eat and drink.

"So?" Lindy tucked her legs up under her.

DJ started to chew her fingernail but stopped herself. Her mother looked like someone right off a magazine page, and here DJ was still in her shorts. At least she didn't have jeans on. Her mother didn't think horse scent made a good perfume.

She and Amy swapped looks. Amy's clearly said, "Get going."

"Mom, we have an idea . . . a business idea, and . . ." Once she got started, the words rushed like a creek after a winter rain. When she forgot something, Amy filled in. They spread their papers out on the floor and explained each detail.

When her mother joined the girls on the floor and started asking questions, DJ began to hope.

"How about if I buy the Western hat and give you a loan for the printing costs?" Lindy marked some numbers on one of the sheets of paper. Her glasses had migrated back down on her nose.

DJ knew they were home free. Now to get permission to use Bandit.

"What do your parents say, Amy?" Lindy turned to the girl beside her.

"We haven't asked them yet."

"We thought we'd start here," DJ chimed in.

Lindy tapped her chin with the end of a pen. "This can't be run like your other 'businesses.'" The look in her eye said she remembered the hamsters and their progeny. She never had cared for "creepy crawly things," as she referred to them. Along with a few other words and in a more than slightly raised tone of voice.

"We're older now . . ."

"And more responsible." The two girls ran their sentences together. That happened a lot with them.

"I would like to help design the fliers." Gran slid from her chair to join the others on the floor. "And I have a friend who would give you a good price on the printing."

"Now for the important question. Do you know any parents who have kids with summer birthdays?"

"You do." Amy stuck her tongue in her cheek.

DJ gave her one of *those* looks.

"Surely there will be some at church. I'll check." Gran wrote herself a note.

"But the parties have to be within walking distance. We don't have a trailer or anything." Amy leaned her elbows on her crossed legs. "I guess the next thing is for me—for us—to ask my mom and dad. We need to write up a paper . . ."

"An agreement," Lindy put in.

"We'll all sign it and turn it in to Bridget," DJ finished.

"This is gonna take forever." She lay back on the carpet. "Besides all this, we still have no idea how much to charge." She flopped her hands over her head so the backs slapped the floor.

"You showed me a partial cost sheet," Lindy said while searching through the scattered papers. "Here. It'll be about . . ." She neatly penciled numbers beside the items they'd have to purchase. "Now, add them up and divide by—how many parties do you think you can do this summer? One a week, two?"

The girls looked at each other and shrugged. "Many as we can get, I guess."

"No, let's say twelve to start with. See, divide your total by twelve." She handed the sheet back to the girls. "Okay, now that gives you the cost of the party. Whatever you set above that is your profit."

By the time they'd finished, they had an agreement, a budget, a simple business plan, and aching heads.

By the next evening they had the Yamamotos' permission and a phone number for the McDougalls. An answering machine picked up the call.

"Fiddle!" DJ let the phone clatter into the cradle. Amy, upstairs on the extension, sighed as she came down the stairs. Clattering wasn't her style.

"So what did they say?" Gran asked from her chair. She pushed her glasses back up on her nose.

"Answering machine." The two girls sank to the floor at Gran's knees.

"Have you prayed about this venture of yours?"

Both nodded their heads.

"Good. Then if it's supposed to happen . . ."

"The doors will open." Again the two spoke in unison. They couldn't count high enough to number the times they'd heard those words.

Gran grinned and laid a hand on each head. "You've listened well."

"The phone!" Amy and DJ leaped to their feet and charged for the kitchen. When an unfamiliar voice asked to speak with DJ, her heart started beating triple-time.

"Speaking."

"Hi, you called me? I know you, don't I, from the Academy?"

DJ mumbled a response. Amy glared at her. DJ took a deep breath and started again. "Yes, my friend Amy Yamamoto and I take care of Bandit. And that's what we'd like to talk to you about. You see, we would like to earn some money this summer . . ." As she went on to explain their idea, Amy ran back upstairs to listen on the extension.

"What does Bridget think of this?" Mr. McDougall asked.

"She said she'd call and talk with you if you'd like."

"She thinks it's a good idea," Amy added.

"Let me talk this over with my wife—it's really her pony. We'll call you back in a few minutes."

Amy charged back down the stairs. The two of them fished cans of soda from the refrigerator and plunked down by the phone.

"You think they'll say yes?" Amy sipped from her can.

"I hope." DJ checked the clock again. Five minutes! It seemed more like fifteen.

"Your dad sure was nice about us using the camera."

"I know."

The phone rang. The girls looked at each other. It rang again.

"Here goes everything." DJ picked up the receiver.

Chapter • 6

"You will? We can! Oh yes, we'll take the best care of Bandit in the whole world." DJ could hardly keep her feet on the floor.

"But there's one catch. We'd like you to do a party for our five-year-old son, Danny. Without charge, of course."

"Of course." DJ hoped she sounded like a businesswoman. "And what will you charge us for the use of Bandit?" She hoped Amy was impressed.

"Why nothing—the party, that's it."

DJ swallowed a shriek. "Th-thank you. We'll be talking with you later, about the party I mean." She hoped she got all the words in the right order, but she wasn't sure.

"Kiddy parties, here we come!" The two danced around the kitchen, ducking and spinning like Indian braves.

Amy froze in the middle of the floor. "What are we gonna call our business?"

"Pony Parties, of course." DJ danced on. "But will people think we're bringing a bunch of ponies?"

"We'll tell 'em up front. Besides, our flier will say . . ." DJ froze beside Amy. "We better get going on our flier." The two headed for DJ's bedroom, grabbing a sack of pretzels on the way.

DJ was nearly asleep that night when another good idea came

creeping out of the mist and bit her. Long ago she'd adopted her grand-mother's habit of keeping a notebook and pencil by her bed to capture good ideas. She'd learned the best ideas came right before sleep and just before she opened her eyes in the morning. "Offer Western or English pony parties," she muttered as she wrote. She studied the page. Maybe it wasn't such a good idea. She flipped off the light and snuggled back under the covers.

But now her mind wouldn't shut down. Instead, it traveled back to the session with her mother and Gran. Gran could always be counted on to pitch in with a new project, but not her mother. She'd never seen her mother in business action before. If she was this way at work, it was no wonder she usually made top salesperson for the company.

So how come she can never find time to be with me? DJ let the thought peek out of the internal box where she kept things that hurt too much to think about. *Maybe if I wore dresses sometimes* . . . The thought made her gag. *I do look pretty good when I'm dressed for a show.* She had to believe that. Bridget said as much, and she never gave out compliments just to give them out.

It's just me. I know it is. I leave things around, and I can't help the smart mouth. The words leap out before I can stop them. It's probably even my fault my father left. Images floated through her mind. There weren't any of her father. Most of her memories were of her and Gran. She didn't remember much about Grandpa, either. He died when she was four.

"Dear God, I'm sorry for all the stuff I do wrong. Thank you for Gran and for Mom. Help me to do my best. Amen." She flipped over to her other side. Maybe *now* she could go to sleep. "Oh, and, God, please take care of Diablo—wherever he is."

Each day the empty stall reminded her again of Diablo. Where was he? How was he? Was anyone exercising him? Did they give him carrots and brush his flanks carefully? He was so ticklish!

That afternoon when she finally got home, she fixed herself a sand-wich and took it in to watch Gran paint.

"Hi, dear. Say, that looks good. Would you mind fixing one for me?"

"You haven't eaten? It's after three." DJ bit her tongue before she said what she thought. Gran forgot all about eating or anything else when the "creative genius," as she called it, took over.

Gran flinched. "I know, I know better. But I lost track of time."

"I'll fix yours. You want mayo or mustard?" DJ threw the questions over her shoulder on the way back to the kitchen.

"Mayo if it's tuna; mustard with baloney."

When DJ got back, Gran stood in front of the easel studying the forest scene she was painting. "That's a new one. I like the trees."

"Umm." Gran took the plate DJ offered without taking her eyes from the easel. "It needs more depth. I want the reader to feel as if they can't resist that path any more than Tara can." She crossed the room to her wing chair and nestled into it. Tara was the name of the character in the book she was illustrating.

DJ still stood in front of the painting. "Makes me want to go there."

"Darlin', 'go' is your middle name. But thanks for the compliment. So how'd you do this morning?" She took a bite of her tuna. "Who taught you to make such good sandwiches?"

DJ grinned at her. "You did."

"Really?" Gran studied the bread. "But then you do all kinds of things well. Have I told you lately how proud I am of you?"

"Thanks, Gran, I needed that." She started on the second half of her sandwich, trying not to talk with her mouth full but wanting to catch Gran up on everything that had happened. When she told about James calling her "cat eyes," Gran shook her head, sending the tendrils of hair around her face to swinging. "That poor boy. Mark my words, something tragic is going to happen there."

"Yeah, I might pound him into the dust one of these days."

"No you won't. You'll keep on praying for him like we said . . ."

"*You* said," DJ muttered.

"Like we agreed." Gran sent her one of those smiles that made it impossible to argue.

"But if I had a horse like his, I'd . . ."

"Now, child, a horse isn't everything. We'll keep on praying." She leaned forward and tapped the end of DJ's nose. "And I'll pray especially that you can find it in your heart to be kind to James."

DJ groaned. When her grandmother started to seriously pray about something—look out! DJ finished her sandwich and picked up the crumbs with a wet fingertip. "Gran, do you still miss Grandpa sometimes?"

"More than just sometimes, but nothing like I used to. There comes a day when you find yourself remembering something really good, maybe a fun time, with that person. Then it doesn't hurt so much. It takes time, of course."

"I wish it didn't. I sure miss Diablo."

By the end of the next week, with DJ's birthday only three days away, Bridget had the rails up two more notches when DJ came for her lesson. She worked Megs around the edge of the ring, careful to warm the mare up even though she couldn't wait to get going. Post to the trot, collected canter—the horse responded smoothly to DJ's lower leg and hand signals. Megs knew the drill inside and out and seemed to be having as much fun as her rider. Ears pricked and with an occasional snort, she went through her paces.

"All right, take the two low ones on the outside first, then head up the middle for the others." Bridget had taken her place in the center of the ring, the best place to watch for each flaw of DJ's performance.

"No, do not let her rush it. You are signaling her to lift off too soon. A good rider is a calm rider. Now, again."

DJ tried to keep her excitement under her hat, but it wasn't easy. After the next round, Bridget signaled her over.

"Keep your hands like so, and your knees here." With each command she put DJ in the proper position. "Now, again."

By the end of the session, DJ didn't want to hear "now, again" for a long time. One thing about Bridget, you had to have one skill down perfectly before you could go on to the next.

"Okay, work on those the next few days. Remember to picture the perfect jump in your head. See yourself doing it perfectly every time. It is not practice that makes perfect, but perfect practice that makes perfect."

DJ said the same to her young students at the class she taught an hour later. *Perfect practice*—she'd remember that one.

"When are we going on our ride up into the park?" Sam asked at the end of the session.

"You promised," Krissie chimed in.

DJ pretended to be deep in thought. "You really think you can handle your horses well enough to leave the arena?"

At their chorus of "yes-s-s," she grinned. "Then bring your lunches on Tuesday—in saddlebags if you have them. You'll need signed permission slips, and I recommend you pack your sandwiches and chips and such in plastic containers so they don't get squished. My friend Amy will be coming along. Any questions?"

All three girls wore matching grins, the kind that wrapped nearly around their heads.

"Now, take care of your horses. I see at least one mother hanging over the fence. Krissie, aren't you in a hurry today?"

"Hey, kitty-cat." DJ heard the nasty voice after she'd just waved her last student off.

"James, I'm gonna . . ." She spun around but couldn't see him anywhere.

"Meow, meow, meow." Now he sounded just like a cat food commercial.

She looked down the aisle again in time to see him duck into Diablo's stall. Why did he always pick on her? Or did he treat everyone this way? She thought about that, all the while letting his taunting set her on a slow burn.

"Kitty-cat, kitty-cat, where are you hiding at?" Now he'd rhymed it.

DJ started down the aisle, fists clenched at her side.

"Hey, DJ, I need some help over here," Amy called from the other end of the barn.

DJ turned and stomped back the way she'd come. She'd have to take care of James later.

"Don't let him bug you," Amy said after one look at DJ's face. "He's not worth getting all mad over."

"He doesn't call *you* names." Without being told to, DJ held the horse while Amy picked its hooves. Since this one had a habit of reaching back to nip once in a while, they took extra precautions.

"As your Gran says, 'sticks and stones . . .'"

"I know what she says, but words *do* hurt. I can't help my green eyes. Nobody else has cat's eyes. He's right."

"So that makes you special."

"Ames, sometimes you sound just like Gran." The two giggled together.

"So, what are you doing for your birthday?" The two were ready to head home.

"I thought maybe you could come over and we'd go out for pizza and then a movie. Maybe my mom and Gran will go, too."

"You don't want a party?"

DJ shook her head. "Not this year. I think we're going to get enough of birthday parties as it is."

"Hey, Mom and Dad might hire us for Danny's party on August tenth." Amy swung her leg over the seat of her bike. "Great, huh?"

DJ nodded. "Flier is almost done. You want to come eat at my house so we can work on it?"

"I'll ask." The two pedaled hard up and down Reliez Valley Road, coasting down the last hill to their houses.

Sure hope Gran doesn't ask me about James, DJ thought when she braked into her garage. She put her bike away and closed the garage door. She'd been extra careful lately. This was *not* a good time to get her mother mad. But then when was? The thought made her smile. Her mother was due back from another trip tonight. They'd talk about her birthday then.

What if her mother gave her a horse for her fourteenth? Wouldn't that be unbelievable? The thought stopped her from getting a drink at the sink. She closed her eyes, imagining what having her own horse would be like. But when she opened them, reality took hold. The day Lindy Randall bought her daughter a horse would be the day the sky fell.

That evening the girls took their flier to the copy shop and ran off five hundred copies.

"Guess we're in business, partner." Amy stuck out her hand.

"Yup." They shook and grinned at each other. This one would be a winner.

DJ fell asleep that night with twenty-dollar bills flitting through her mind.

Her birthday dawned with gray skies but brightened considerably when James' nanny called to say he wouldn't be at the Academy that day. DJ rushed through her work, cleaning stalls at top speed and grooming horses like a robot set on super fast.

"DJ, can you come here a minute?" Bridget called as DJ finished snapping her last horses on the hot walker.

"Sure." DJ trotted across the dusty parking lot and into the office.

"Surprise!" All the kids who worked at the Academy yelled in unison. A chocolate frosted cake with the words *Happy Birthday, DJ* took up half the desk.

Bridget finished lighting the candles. "All right, everyone. Let us sing! 'Happy birthday to you!'" The song filled the room and traveled down the aisle.

DJ looked from face to face, sure that her grin mirrored those of her friends. Amy stood right beside the cake, singing the loudest.

"Okay, make a wish and blow out the candles."

DJ crossed the room and bent over. Panic squeezed her throat shut. She couldn't blow.

Chapter · 7

For a horrible moment, all DJ could see was flickering fire. Her heart pounded louder than any drum. She couldn't tear her gaze away from the burning candles in front of her.

DJ licked her lips. They were so dry.

One hand curled around the scarred palm of the other to protect it. She remembered the sensation of the fire searing her hand, remembered thinking she would never escape it. She was lost again in the terror of that day.

"DJ! DJ!"

DJ heard a voice. Someone was shaking her. *Bridget!*

"The fire." Her words croaked past a throat burning from smoke. DJ shook her head. It was a birthday party. Just a cake. She was to blow out the candles. She looked down. Only tiny spirals of smoke rose from the green candles.

Happy Birthday, DJ. The letters were green, too. A brown horse jumped a fence below the words.

DJ forced her eyes to blink. To look at her friends. Amy had tears running down her face. Bridget's face was mercifully expressionless. The others were as embarrassed to look at her as she was at them.

"I . . . I'm sorry, DJ, I forgot. I'm so sorry."

DJ could hear Amy's wail, but it seemed far off. As if it were coming from the end of a long tunnel.

Only Bridget's arm around her shaking shoulders kept DJ in place. "No problem. We wanted to surprise you. I guess we did just that." Bridget squeezed again. "Hilary, you cut the cake. Daniel, you serve the ice cream." While the others bustled around, looking relieved at having something to do, Bridget leaned closer. "Are you all right now?"

DJ nodded. "It's never been that bad before."

"You've never had so many candles." Amy clung to DJ's left arm. "I'm sorry, DJ. I should have thought."

"Has it always been like this?" Bridget spoke for DJ's ears alone.

"When I was real little, I was somehow caught in a fire and burned." She held up her hand and showed the scar in the palm. "I've been afraid of fire ever since." DJ looked up. "Dumb, isn't it?"

"No, not dumb." Bridget relaxed her arm. "Here, take my chair, the place of honor. You think you can eat your cake and ice cream now?"

DJ nodded. "Sure." But she felt like crawling under the chair rather than sitting in it. Under the chair, then under the desk, and out the door. At least James wasn't there.

"I just wanted to celebrate your birthday," Amy said later, after the others had left and they'd cleaned up the trash. The expression on her face would have made a Basset hound look happy.

"Thanks, Ames. It isn't your fault I'm such a geek about fires. Even little ones like birthday candles." DJ studied the half-burned green stems of wax. "How could I have freaked like that?"

"Do you have nightmares about the accident?" Bridget asked, elbows on her desk.

"I used to. But I haven't for a long time." DJ straightened a stack of papers on the corner. While her heart rate had returned to normal, the tips of her fingers still trembled.

"Thank you both for surprising me like this. And for the cake and everything. I'm glad I have friends like you."

"Now we're getting mushy." Amy grinned and punched DJ's shoulder. "Let's hit the bikes. We're supposed to hand out fliers this afternoon, remember?"

DJ groaned. "How could I forget?"

"You two be careful now, you hear?" Bridget called after them as they left the building.

Putting a flier on every door in the neighborhood sounded easy but took plenty of time. Amy's two brothers helped, but even so, by the time five o'clock rolled around, they hadn't finished.

DJ eyed the stack she still carried. The sweat from her arm had wrinkled the bottom one. She tossed it in the trash and collapsed on the front steps of her house, along with Amy and her older brother John. Twelve-year-old Dan hadn't returned yet.

"How'd you guys do?"

Identical groans answered her.

"One old man yelled at me," Amy said without opening her eyes. "He accused me of not being able to read."

"Read what?" John asked.

"His 'no solicitors' sign."

"Did you tell him you're in the honors program at school?" John propped himself up on his elbows.

"No, the sign was hidden by a bush. How was I supposed to see it?"

"So, did you give him a flier?" John winked at DJ.

"Yeah, right." She glared up at him on the step above her. "Besides, he was too old to have little kids."

"Maybe he has grandchildren." John tweaked her braid.

"Nah, he's too mean."

"Hey, guys. I have a number for a lady who wants you to call her." Dan pedaled up the street and let his bike drop on the grass.

"DJ, telephone," Gran announced through the screen door.

Within the hour, they had three bookings. DJ and Amy rushed to the door as soon as they heard Lindy's car. "Mom, guess what?"

"You're ready to go for pizza. Please, I need some time off first." Lindy shut off the engine and started to open the door.

"No—well, yes—but even better. We have three parties to give! And we just gave out the fliers today."

"And we're not even finished." Amy waved the paper they'd written all the information on.

"We had to turn a Saturday party down because of our horse show, so the woman said they'd have the party Sunday after church instead. Cool, huh?"

"Cool is right. How about pouring me some cool iced tea. My air-conditioner is on the blink." She brushed her hair off her forehead.

An hour later, Lindy, Gran, and the two girls climbed into Gran's minivan and headed for the Pizza House.

When Lindy asked how the day had been, DJ sank back into her chair. Amy gave her a poke in the ribs.

"Oh, they gave me a birthday cake at the Academy. I freaked at the candles. No big deal." DJ threw in a shruggy laugh and looked up at the faces of her mother and Gran. "Really, it was nothing."

Gran looked at Amy.

Amy looked from DJ to Gran and then to Lindy. "It *was* a big deal. She scared us all half to bits. She freaked. It was as if she weren't even there." She grimaced at DJ and shook her head. "I have to be honest." She looked back at Gran. "She froze."

"Thanks a lot, buddy." The tone said the name meant anything but.

"I thought you'd outgrown your fear of fire." Lindy spoke softly, her comment a question.

"I did, too. So I guess I haven't."

The restaurant loudspeaker crackled. "Number 43."

"That's us." DJ leaped to her feet, nearly toppling her bench at the rush.

When the cupcake came and the waiters and waitresses gathered around to help sing, there was no candle burning bright. DJ didn't know whether to be glad or sad. She caught a wink from Gran. She knew they'd be talking about this later.

"Open that one first." Lindy pointed to a big square box.

DJ tossed Amy the ribbon and tore off the paper. Nested in a crinkle of tissue paper lay a red cowboy hat with white lacing around the edge. "Thanks, Mom." DJ handed it to Amy. "We're in business now."

"Now this one." Lindy handed her daughter a flat box that looked as though it held clothes.

"Wow!" DJ held up a starched white shirt. "And jodhpurs." She caressed the tan twill fabric. "They're perfect."

"I hope they fit. Your others were looking pretty shabby."

"Thanks, Mom."

"Well, I figured when you start jumping, new duds would help." She handed DJ another box. "This one's from both Gran and me together." A black hunt coat with a store-bought label lay folded in front of her.

DJ looked up at both her mother and Gran. "You guys didn't have to do this. It must have cost a bundle." *And with Diablo gone, I won't even get to show.* When she looked at Amy, she could read the same thought on her face. "Thanks, Mom, Gran. Now you don't have to spend your time sewing me a new one."

"A labor of love, my dear. But now that you're so grown up, you deserve a professionally tailored coat."

Amy handed DJ a package wrapped in paper covered with jumping horses. "Here, I know you needed these."

The box contained a new set of charcoal pencils and two thick pads of drawing paper.

"You're right. Thanks, now I don't have to raid my horse fund." DJ closed all the boxes and piled them at the end of the table. "What a super, fantastic, wonderful birthday."

"If we're going to see a movie, we better hustle." Lindy picked up the check. "Come on."

DJ tucked all the boxes under her arm. The next thing she'd need would be boots. Hers were beginning to pinch in the toe. If only she'd quit growing!

She tuned back into the conversation between her mother and Gran.

"But I don't really care to meet anyone," Gran was saying.

"Now, Mother, Joe Crowder is one of the nicest men I've ever met. I think the two of you will get along famously." Lindy held the door open for all of them. "Besides, I invited him over for dinner a week from Sunday. And I know you'll like him, too, Darla Jean. He's head of the horse patrol in San Francisco."

"He's a policeman?" DJ spun around to stare at her mother.

"And a good one. His wife died two years ago. I've known him for a long time, and I can tell he's lonely."

"You invited a policeman to our house? The whole neighborhood will think we're being arrested!" DJ couldn't resist the smart remark.

"He won't come in a squad car, silly." Lindy slid into the front seat of the minivan. "Besides, how would I meet any men outside a police force?"

For some reason, DJ had a bad feeling in her stomach.

Chapter • 8

"Okay, riders up." DJ checked her students one more time.

"Oh, wait, I forgot my drink." Angie withdrew her foot from the stirrup. "I'll be right back."

While she was gone, DJ and Amy checked everyone's cinches for the third time. "All the rest of you sure you have everything?" At their chorus of *yes*'s, DJ signaled Amy to mount while she led Megs and Angie's horse to the front of the barn. She crossed to the gate of the trail to Briones State Park and opened it, signaling them through. While she waited, she checked her saddlebags again to make sure she had the beesting kit. Angie had asthma and was violently allergic to beestings.

Angie rushed up as the last horse trailed through the gate. "Thanks, DJ. My mom says to give you an extra thanks from her. She's looking forward to a day off."

"You're welcome. Up you go now." After leading Megs through, DJ closed the gate, making sure the latch fell into place. One time the gate had accidentally been left open, and a horse had run away.

With DJ in front and Amy bringing up the rear, the group headed single file up the hill. Oak trees dotted the steep hillsides where the trail led along the flank of another rounded hump, then down to the staging area and parking lot for the Reliez Valley entrance to Briones Park. Beef cow and calf pairs roamed the pastureland, along with young steers. One calf with a white face and black body ran off, tail in the air at the sight of the trail horses. Several others followed.

"Watch your horses." DJ kept a secure hand on her reins. "They could spook easily."

Once on the shady trail that followed the creek up into the park, the kids could ride side by side. A stellar jay scolded them from one of the branches, flitting along as if trying to convince them to go back. The curious calves plodded behind, making the girls giggle.

"We're supposed to *herd* cattle rather than lead them," Krissie called. "DJ, you ever tried cutting cows from a herd?"

"No way. Besides, Ames here rides Western, not me."

Once they reached the high meadow, the girls voted to ride up to the Briones Crest Trail. From there they could see the Carquinez Straits and up the Sacramento River to the north. The oil refineries below looked like a toy Erector set with their towers and round storage tanks.

"What are those boxes on the fence?" Krissie asked.

"Bluebird nests. Since so many of their natural nesting spots are gone, people have put these up to encourage them to stick around."

"How do you know so much?"

DJ and Amy swapped grins. "When we rode up here with Hilary, we asked the same question and she gave us the answer. Maybe someday you'll be doing the same for other kids."

"Can we peek in one?"

"If a mother is nesting, you might frighten her off the nest. Would you like that?"

All the girls shook their heads.

"Oh, look!" Sam pointed into the air. A hawk dove straight down, then lifted off again with something dangling from its talons.

"He killed something."

"Yuk."

"No fair." The girls voiced their disapproval.

"Probably a ground squirrel or mouse. That's the way of life. You want him to starve to death?"

"It could be he's taking it home to his family." Amy shaded her eyes with her hand. "He is so beautiful."

After lunch the girls flopped back on the ground.

"I want to come up here every week." Krissie rolled over on her stomach, clenching her lead rope in one hand. They'd removed their horses' bridles and snapped lead lines to the halters. "If we lived in olden times, we could hobble our horses and spend the night."

"The older kids get to take a pack trip up in the Sierra Mountains every summer. You have that to look forward to." Amy tucked her gear back in her saddlebag.

"You ever done that?"

"Nope. Not yet, maybe next summer."

DJ shook her head, too. You had to have your own horse for that trip. And she knew Amy had waited because DJ couldn't go. Maybe by next summer she'd have a horse of her own. Not maybe. When.

"I want to go on the overnight."

"Well, think positive, and you'll make it." DJ wasn't sure if she was talking to herself or to her students.

She breathed a sigh of relief when they rode back into the academy parking lot. They'd had a great time—not a single bee in sight.

"How did it go?" Bridget asked when DJ and Amy stopped in at her office.

"Fine."

"Great."

"Good, because the girls were bubbling over. Oh, DJ, your grandmother called. Said for you to hurry right home."

"Is she all right?" DJ started for the door.

"She's fine. She was laughing, said the phone has not stopped ringing. I think you two are going to be mighty busy young women. Just make sure you keep up with your chores around here."

"We will." DJ pushed Amy out the door ahead of her. Visions of a horse of her own jumped through her mind.

Saturday morning DJ and Amy arrived at the Academy before six to help load horses in the trailers to take them to the show. The first event would be at nine.

"Your mom and dad coming later?" DJ asked.

"Uh-huh. The boys, too. I have four events today." Amy yawned. "Dad's coming to help trailer Josh. Says he's sure glad we don't own a truck and trailer."

At least you have a horse, DJ wanted to say but didn't. Sometimes the little green monster of jealousy got her by the throat.

If only Diablo were here! How can I stand by and watch all the others out in the ring? She'd gone to sleep with that question and woke without an answer.

"Just keep real busy today," Gran had whispered in her ear just before DJ went out the door. "I'll be praying for you."

"God, please help me." DJ added a prayer of her own. *Oh, Diablo, I miss you so!*

By the time the sixteen horses were loaded, DJ had sweat pouring down her face and back. Hilary, the oldest and most experienced of the working students and a skilled rider in dressage, had to drive home to retrieve the duffel bag she'd forgotten. One family overslept. Bridget wore that stern look that said she'd get everyone there on time even if it killed her—and them.

After one longing look at Diablo's stall, DJ hadn't had time to give him another thought. "How come James isn't here to load his own horse?" she muttered as she passed Amy, who was heading back into the barn for another animal.

"Got me." Amy brushed her bangs off her forehead. "Today's gonna be a scorcher."

DJ clucked to Gray Bar, James' Arabian filly. "Easy, girl. You just keep calm and we'll all have a better day." They trotted across the parking lot, Gray Bar dancing along with DJ. But the filly sat back on her haunches as soon as she touched her front feet to the ramp.

"We would have one troublemaker." Hilary's father, better known to the academy kids as Dad, stood beside the trailer. He'd been assisting Hilary since she was seven, so knew a lot about loading horses.

"Come on, girl." DJ tugged on the lead rope. The filly snorted, her eyes rolling white.

"Walk her around in a circle and bring her up again," Dad said in a soft but commanding voice.

DJ did as he instructed, but again Gray Bar balked. When DJ tugged the rope, the filly flung her head in the air and backed up fast. The sliding rope burned through her palm. Repeating the sequence, she followed the horse, this time keeping a tight grip on the lead.

"Let's leave her till last. Why don't you just walk her around and let her calm down."

"Would it be better to wait for her owner?" asked one of the newer fathers. Dad shook his head. "DJ can handle her better than James."

DJ felt a warm glow tiptoe into her chest. Leave it to Dad to always make her feel good. But when she led Gray Bar around the truck, there sat James on the bumper. The look he gave her doused the warm feeling like water drenching a fire.

When DJ offered him the lead rope, James shook his head. "You're so good, you do it."

DJ shrugged and kept walking. When they brought Gray Bar back around a few minutes later, she walked right up the ramp as if there'd been no fiasco. But DJ knew there'd been a problem. Her hand still stung.

DJ kept so busy helping the younger kids, she hardly had time to miss not being in the arena. Lost hair ribbons, making sure the entry numbers were pinned on the right rider, catching a loose horse—it was all part of a show.

Amy won three blues, her best ever.

"Congratulations, Ames. You looked great out there."

"All the hard work with Josh here is paying off." Amy chugged a can of soda. "These chaps are killing me. One more class and I can change to shorts."

"DJ, I can't find my saddle pad." A worried-looking student interrupted their conversation.

DJ turned to find it and caught a glimpse of James in the ring. His horse was refusing the gate in the trail-riding event. Just as she'd done at the loading, Gray Bar backed up fast—so fast she threw James up onto her neck. DJ felt her breath catch in her throat. She didn't wish anyone, even James, a fall in the ring. How embarrassing!

A few minutes later he stormed past her. "If you hadn't gotten her so excited this morning, I might be doing better out there."

The words and their tone caught DJ smack in the middle. "James Corrigan, I . . ."

He gave her a rude gesture and slammed the door on his parents' motorhome.

"I wish you'd fallen!" DJ felt like yanking open the door and pounding him into the carpet.

By the end of the day, the riders from the Academy had garnered a good fifty percent of the ribbons, many of them blue or red. Bridget congratulated everyone while they loaded horses and weary kids.

"Any of you who want to come up to the house for a pool party

afterward are welcome. Mr. Yamamoto and Mr. Benson have volunteered to bring pizza."

A cheer went up. DJ was too tired to care.

Maybe having a stable of her own one day wasn't such a hot idea
after all.

"Tomorrow we have our first pony party," DJ groaned later as she
and Amy lay beside the pool. Most of the other kids were still in the
water.

"I know. But there are only supposed to be five kids at this one.
That should be easy."

"Oh, it should be, all right." DJ shook her head. "But after today,
who knows what could happen!"

Chapter · 9

"No, Jamie, don't feed that to the pony."

DJ spun around at the sound of Amy's voice. The five kids at the pony party now seemed like a squadron. With one hand DJ snatched the pink flower from the little boy's hand, and with the other she set him back five feet. Then she returned to putting the cowboy hat back on the little girl seated on Bandit.

"No, don't want no hat!" The child jerked the Western hat off and threw it on the ground.

Bandit sidestepped, the better to see the flying object. DJ followed, one hand on the pommel and the other holding the little girl in place. Amy hung on to the reins, trying to calm the pony, her camera on a strap around her neck.

"Who ever came up with this harebrained idea?" DJ muttered through the smile she kept in place for the child's benefit. "Okay, no hat. Now hang on to the saddle horn—this thing"—she placed the girl's hand on the horn—"and I'll lead you around. Then smile for Amy and you'll get a picture to take home."

The little girl stuck out her lower lip.

DJ led her around the drive. Bandit stopped at the halfway point to make manure. *Oops, should have brought a shovel.* DJ looked up at Amy, who shrugged her shoulders.

"I'll take care of it in a minute." Amy snapped the photo. The little girl smiled and waved. Afterward.

By the last rider, it seemed as though they'd taken fifteen terrors around the circle. At least no one had fallen off or slipped. Amy went up to the door to ask for a shovel.

"Time for cake and ice cream," the hostess mother called when she answered Amy's knock at the front door. Three children ran right through the pile of manure and into the house.

"Icky," whined the grumpy rider.

"Oh no, my white carpet!" The mother glared at Amy. "I hope this washes out. We just had the carpet installed last week."

"It will." Amy mentioned a brand of cleaner her mother used. "I need a shovel, please."

"You certainly do. And I hope you're not planning on putting that mess in *my* garbage can."

"I could put it on your flower beds, it'll help—"

"I should say not. I'll bring the shovel. And the carpet cleaner."

Amy turned back to DJ and raised her hands.

By the time Amy had cleaned the carpet and DJ the drive, the kids had eaten their treats, opened presents, and were ready to ride again.

"No, dears, the pony has to go home now." The woman smiled brightly as she handed DJ an envelope with their fee in it in exchange for the stack of photos. "Thank you for such a perfect party. I'll be sure to recommend you to all my friends."

DJ and Amy looked at each other, shrugged, and headed for home.

"Go figure." Amy shook her head. "The way she talked at first I didn't think she'd even pay us."

"It must have been her first time giving a birthday party. She was pretty uptight."

"Who wouldn't be with new white carpet? My mom says she's not getting new furniture and carpet till all us kids are grown and gone." Bandit snorted as if in agreement.

"What a good boy you were." DJ stopped to rub the pony's neck. "But you shouldn't take bites out of the flower bed."

"How'd it go?" Hilary asked when they hung Bandit's bridle on his peg in the tack room. She wiped the sweat off her wide brow with the back of her brown hand and pushed back tightly curled black hair that refused to obey a ponytail clip.

"Oh, it went." By the time they finished telling their tale, Hilary had collapsed on the tack box, tears running down her face.

"You poor kids, talk about a party! Now that all the bad stuff has happened, the next one'll be a cinch." She rocked back with her hands around one knee. "You *are* going to keep going, aren't you?"

"We have to. We signed people up." Amy counted on her fingers. "We have eight more parties to go."

"And that's if no one else calls." DJ squeezed her eyes shut. "Next time I have a good idea, someone shoot me, okay?"

"Don't tempt me." Amy grabbed DJ's hand and pulled her to her feet. "I gotta get home. And remember, you've got company coming for dinner."

DJ groaned louder but let herself be led from the building. "Well, at least the next party will be profit."

"Unless we buy a pooper scooper. You know, like the ones they use at parades."

"I think the Academy has one. I'll ask Bridget if we can borrow it." DJ mounted her ten speed. "At least I'll be able to put money in my horse fund after Tuesday."

When DJ got home, the table was set in the dining room with a jade green cloth and matching print napkins—in napkin rings no less. Gran's good china and sterling silver were set for four. Green candles flanked a low arrangement of peach roses.

"Wow, does this look cool or what? What's the name of that man who's coming?"

"Joe Crowder, Captain Joe Crowder." Lindy turned from arranging salad on separate plates.

"Right. He must be something pretty special. It's not Christmas or Easter, is it?"

"You just hustle up and shower. And no jeans. In fact, a dress would be nice."

"That'll be the day." DJ pulled a can of soda from the fridge.

"I don't need that kind of attitude right now." Mom swiped a hair off her forehead with the back of her hand.

"I mean, I don't have a dress to wear." Surely her mother had lost her mind.

"A skirt then."

DJ groaned. "Skirts are gross." After popping the can top, she took

a long drink. "Where's Gran?" Her mother hadn't done all the cooking—had she? That would be bad.

"She's changing." Lindy wrapped the salad plates in plastic wrap
and set them in the fridge.

"What are we having?" Her mother's skill ran to hamburgers or
spaghetti. If it didn't come in a box, she couldn't make it.

"Are you going to get ready or not?"

DJ wanted to say "not" but thought the better of it. Her mother
didn't look as if she was in the mood for any teasing. "I'm going, I'm
going." *She could at least have asked about our pony party,* DJ thought
as she climbed the stairs. *Leave it to my mother not to ask. She's more
worried about a dinner party for a man she hardly knows than about her
own daughter.* If she gave it some effort, DJ knew she could turn this
evening into a full-blown pity party. "Wow, Gran, you look amazing."

Gran spun away from studying her reflection in the full-length
mirror at the end of the hall. "I hope so. Your mother spent a fortune
on this new outfit for me. I feel as if I'm on the auction block or something." She turned so the skirt swirled about her calves.

"That looks like something you might have painted." DJ fingered
the gauze fabric. "All swirly and all shades of blue. Leave it to Mom to
find the perfect thing."

Gran turned and placed her hands along DJ's cheeks. "Thanks,
darlin'. How did the birthday party go?" Gran laughed in all the right
places as DJ retold the story. "Well, I never. And to think she made you
girls clean the carpet!"

"Amy did that." DJ patted her jeans pocket. "But at least all our
bills are paid. Now we can make some money."

Gran took one more glance over her shoulder toward the mirror.
"Well, here goes nothin'." She started toward the stairs. "Oh, my stars,
where's my mind today! DJ, there was another call for you. A lady
wondered if you could come tomorrow. Her clown called with the flu.
I put the number on your dresser."

"Thanks, I'll call her now." DJ dialed, dollar signs dancing in her
head.

She could hear a man's voice in the living room by the time she
descended the stairs. Her skirt had been too tight, so she had improvised
with a pair of dress pants and a striped blouse. No T-shirt and jeans.
She paused at the bottom stair. At least the guy knew how to laugh.

Hearing a man's laugh in their house was sure strange. The pastor from their church had been their most recent male visitor, and that had been ages ago. His laugh hadn't had the deep, happy sound of the man's in the living room.

"Hi, darlin'," Gran said when DJ walked into the room. She beckoned DJ to her side. "This is my granddaughter, Darla Jean. She's a real promising artist, but her first love is horses."

DJ barely kept herself from wincing. *Darla Jean.* Only her Gran, and sometimes her mother, got away with calling her that. She didn't want this stranger calling her that. "Darlin', this is Joe Crowder."

"Well, Darla Jean, I certainly am glad to meet you." The voice fit the man. He took up half the living room, or at least seemed to. Shoulders straight and square like a military man's, a crew cut gone silver, and cerulean blue eyes.

"I'm glad to meet you, too. Mom said you like horses."

"You'll have to meet my best friend sometime. His name is Major. I've ridden him in the San Francisco Mounted Patrol for the last ten years."

"What's he like?"

"Thoroughbred-Morgan cross. Sixteen-three. He has to be big to carry me. White stripe down his face, two white socks. He's a blood bay, the prettiest red you ever saw when the sun glints off his rump. Even has a scar on his right shoulder where he took a bullet meant for me."

"Really?"

"You ever watched the mounted patrol in action?"

DJ shook her head.

"Then I'll have to take you and Melanie to watch one of our drills."

DJ almost looked around the room for the Melanie he'd referred to. "You mean Gran?"

"Dinner's served." Lindy stopped in the doorway.

DJ rolled her eyes so only Gran could see. The look clearly said what she thought of the formality. But when Joe Crowder tucked Gran's arm in one of his and angled out his other elbow for DJ to do the same, she went along with it. Who was this guy, anyway?

She was wondering even more by the end of the meal. He'd had them all laughing at his tales of life in the mounted patrol. And the stories about his family. He had three kids, two sons and a daughter.

The daughter had two children, including a girl who was only a year older than DJ.

"Robert, my oldest, is a widower like me. He has five-year-old twin boys."

"That must have been really hard." Gran reached across the space and laid her hand on his.

"It was. To lose two women in our family in one year." He sighed. "I can't wait for you to meet them. I know they'll like you . . ." He cut off the sentence, but his eyes said the rest.

DJ dropped her fork. She'd read about talking with your eyes before, but now she was seeing it in action. The way those two were looking at each other usually meant a love scene coming up in the movies.

She glanced at her mother. Lindy wore a sappy look that said she was happy with the whole thing.

"Can I be excused? I . . . I'll clear the table." *Anything to get out of here.*

"I'll help you." Mom pushed her chair back, too.

The other two in the room didn't even seem to notice.

A cold hand slipped over DJ's heart and squeezed.

Chapter · 10

"That was disgusting!"

"I don't know, I think they're kind of cute." Lindy opened the dishwasher door.

"Cute!" DJ spun around, catching a plate before it slid off the counter.

"Shhh, keep your voice down or they'll hear you."

"Cute. Gran and a man she just met are making goo-goo eyes at each other and *my* mother thinks it's cute."

"Careful, you said you'd wash the dishes, not break them." Mom took over the sink detail. "You finish clearing the table."

"I can't go in there again." DJ clamped her hands on her hips.

"Darla Jean Randall, for pete's sake, grow up!" Lindy's voice changed from teasing to angry. "We've had a very nice time tonight, and I don't want to see you ruining it. Your grandmother is entitled to a little love in her life."

"She had Grandpa."

"And he died ten years ago. She has spent the last ten years taking care of you and me."

"She has her art, you know. And her garden and books and church and . . ." DJ let the words trail off.

"And you. If I'd been a better mother, she wouldn't have had to spend her life raising her granddaughter."

"You said it, I didn't." The words popped out before DJ could trap her tongue. She headed for the dining room. Sometimes retreating made more sense than fighting.

There was no one there. DJ drifted over to the windows that overlooked the backyard. Gran was showing Joe her roses. The two of them didn't have to stand so close together.

––––––––––

"Stupid birds, you don't have to sing so loud, do you?" DJ covered her head with her pillow early the next morning. But when she closed her eyes again, all she could see was Gran smiling up at that old policeman as though he were the last man on earth. She flung back the covers and stomped down the hall to the bathroom. Maybe things would go better over at the Academy.

"Mornin', darlin', you're up early." Gran sat in her chair in front of the bay window, Bible in her lap and her hair in the normal disarray.

Maybe I'm blowing this all out of proportion. The thought zipped through DJ's mind like the hummingbirds at their feeders. *Gran was just being polite. Southern women are supposed to be polite and gracious. She's trying to show me how to be the same way.* After popping a slice of wheat bread in the toaster, DJ pulled the pitcher of orange juice out of the fridge and poured herself a glass. She spread peanut butter on the toast and took her juice and toast into the other room, where she sat at Gran's feet.

"So, what's on your schedule for today?" Gran laid a hand on DJ's head.

"The usual. Then we have that pony party this afternoon. You want some help in the garden when I get home?"

"Thank you, dear, but no thanks. Joe and I are going to a concert this evening."

DJ jerked out from under the loving hand and twisted around to look up at her grandmother. *What a sappy look!* "You mean you're going out with him—like on a date?" Her voice squeaked on the final word.

"I guess you could call it that." Gran smiled. "He's really a nice man, don't you think?"

DJ gave a decidedly unladylike snort. So much for her grandmother's training. "If you like old men, I guess."

"Darla Jean, why I'm surprised at you." Gran leaned forward and lifted DJ's chin with gentle fingers. "Look at me, child. He's only ten years older than I am."

"But . . . but you're not old. Why, you're not even fifty yet." DJ tried to look at her grandmother as if she were seeing her for the first time. All she could see was the love shining in her grandmother's eyes. "You . . . you're my gran. You're beautiful."

"Why, thank you, but fifty really isn't far off." Gran put her cheek next to DJ's. "I love you more than words can ever say." She straightened up. "If I only had time to sew a new dress."

DJ pushed to her feet. "The one you wore yesterday sure made him look twice—if that's what you want." She left the room, her thudding heels leaving no doubt as to her opinion.

"You're acting like a brat," she scolded herself as she pumped up the hill. "Gran looks happy as a kid with a Popsicle, and you want to take it away from her." The climb made her puff. *You can't get along with your mother, and now you're grumbling at Gran. Grow up!*

After DJ had finished her beginners' class, she entered the office to check the duties board. Bridget called her in for a conference, her expression serious.

"DJ, James said that you took the missing bridle and saddle."

"He's crazy! Why would I do that?"

"That's what I asked him. He said you were going to sell it so you would have more money to put in your horse fund."

"And you believed him?" DJ clenched her hands. *Why would Bridget believe James over her?*

"I did not say that. I just have to follow up on every lead. We have never had a problem with things being stolen before." Bridget leaned forward, her elbows on her desk. "So if you tell me you did not take it, then I will know for sure you did not."

"I didn't take that tack or anything else." DJ forced the words through gritted teeth. *That . . . that lying, cheating, lazy, good for nothing creep!* "Is there anything else?" All she could think of was getting out of there, finding James and—what could she do to him that was bad enough?

"DJ, do not take this personally."

But DJ was already out the door.

"What's the matter, DJ?" Hilary tried to grab DJ's arm and missed. "Where's James?"

"He just left. Said he had a headache." She rolled her eyes. "You know James."

"That lazy little creep, I'm gonna kill him."

Hilary fell into step beside her. "What'd he do now?"

"Told Bridget I stole a new saddle and bridle."

Hilary let out a bark of laughter. "He what? DJ, surely Bridget doesn't believe him. Come on, be real!"

"I think he hates me."

"So what? James hates everybody. Anyway, most everybody—around here at least—returns the favor." Hilary plunked down on a bale of straw. "Here." She patted the bale beside her. "You've just got to develop a thick skin. James is jealous because he's been taking lessons longer and you ride better than he does."

"But he has his own horse. He could ride all the time if he wanted, practice until he gets everything perfect."

"DJ, that's the way *you* do things because you have a goal. Like me with dressage."

"You're good." DJ clasped her hands between her knees.

"I've worked hard to get there. And I'll keep on working hard. Just like you do. So don't let this get to you. James isn't worth it."

DJ nodded. As usual, Hilary made sense. "Thanks. It just seems to me that if you've got your own horse and you can ride whenever you want . . ."

"That everything should be all right."

DJ nodded. "Wrong, huh?" She could feel her grin coming back.

"Wrong is right." Hilary slapped DJ on the knee. "So let's get back to work." She got to her feet. "Okay, now?"

"Okay." But inside, DJ thought only two things. How would she get even with James? And who had taken the tack? A new flat saddle and a good bridle—why, that kind of equipment was worth hundreds of dollars.

DJ and Amy trotted Bandit down the shoulder of Reliez Valley Road. If they didn't hurry, they'd be late. The pooper scooper they had borrowed and tied to the saddle clapped against the pony's side with each quick stride.

"We need a cart for him to pull all of our stuff in." DJ puffed between words.

"Not a bad idea." Amy jogged along, the lead strap in her hands. "Is Bandit used to the harness?"

"Got me! If he was, we could ride, too." Down a hill and around the corner. "If he hasn't been broken to the cart, he will be soon."

"Hey, Mom, the pony's here." A little boy met them in the drive. His shriek made Bandit lay back his ears.

"Here we go again," DJ whispered to Amy.

"No, this party's going to go great. I've been praying about it."

DJ felt a surge of guilt. Why hadn't she thought of that?

"You should have prayed harder," DJ grumbled when a little boy refused to get off the pony. Instead, he let out a scream that brought the mothers running to see who was attacking their kids.

"Now, Robert, honey," the mother said soothingly. "You have to give the other children a turn."

"N-o-o-o! I want another ride." Robert clung to the saddle horn like a flea to a dog.

The mother smiled apologetically. "Maybe you could take him around one more time. I'm sure he'll get off then. Won't you, dear?"

DJ and Amy swapped raised-eyebrow glances. They knew they were thinking the same thing. If Amy's brothers had tried something like that, her mother wouldn't have let them get away with it.

The little girl who was next in line started to cry. The other mothers glared at Robert's mom. DJ led Bandit once more around the circle.

"If you don't get off when you get back, I'm gonna let this pony gallop down the street with you on his back, and you'll go splat on the pavement." She kept her tone low, muttering just loud enough so she knew Robert heard. When she looked at him, his eyes were wide. "I will, too."

Robert jumped right off and ran to his mother, where he clutched at the back of her pants.

The rest of the party went as planned. All the kids rode and smiled for their pictures. The hostess even brought DJ and Amy glasses of icy lemonade.

"Thanks. We needed that." DJ drank half of hers without stopping.

"Would you be interested in bringing the pony to the park one day and just letting kids ride like this? It wouldn't be for a party." The mother looked from DJ to Amy.

The two girls looked at each other and shrugged. "I guess so." Amy spoke first.

"What would you charge for an hour? No pictures."

DJ named a figure and Amy agreed.

"Good, I'll get back to you." The woman handed them an envelope and started to leave. "Oh, I'm sorry about the problem with Robert. He's a bit spoiled."

"He's a *bit* spoiled!" The two girls hooted when they were a block or two away. They took the money out of the envelope and split it. With the bills already paid, this could become a very successful project.

"That much more for my horse fund." DJ stuck the bills in her pocket. "Wish it were twice this much."

"Or ten times." Amy stopped trotting to retie the pooper scooper before it fell off. "You want to talk to Bridget about harness training Bandit, or should I?"

"Let's do it together. There's that harness buried in the tack room. That should fit him fine. I haven't seen any carts around there though, have you?"

Amy shook her head. "Bridget will know of one."

But Bridget was busy with a class when they got back to the Academy, so as soon as they'd given Bandit a good grooming, they jumped on their bikes to head for home.

"Gran? Gran?" DJ wandered through the house, calling. When there was no answer, she headed for the backyard. Gran's minivan was in the drive, so she had to be around here somewhere.

"I'm out here."

DJ followed the voice to the backyard. She could see Gran's pink rear when she knelt to pull weeds from the flower bed. "I'm home."

"Good." Gran straightened up and wiped the back of her gloved hand across her forehead. "Would you like to bring us out some lemonade?"

"I told you I'd help you weed tonight."

Gran rocked back on her heels. "I know. I was just too restless to paint anymore today."

DJ gave her a look that questioned whether they'd better head for the hospital emergency room, but she turned and headed back for the kitchen without commenting. That in itself was a miracle, she reminded herself while pouring their drinks. How come it was easier to keep the lid on her mouth with Gran than her mother? Maybe Gran had changed her mind and was staying home from the concert.

"So, how was the party?" Gran sat cross-legged on the grass and reached up for her drink. Her wide floppy straw hat caught in the breeze and flipped back behind her.

DJ sank down beside her, not answering until she'd poured a few glugs down her thirsty throat. As she relayed the story of her day, she sneaked glances at her grandmother. It was clear that she wasn't hearing a word. *Where is she?*

"And so I bopped Amy on the head to make her shut up, and . . ."

"That's nice, dear." Gran sighed.

DJ tried to follow Gran's gaze to see what was so interesting. Grass. Flowers. Pretty, to be sure, but . . .

DJ tried again. "Then I slapped the little kid upside the head . . ."

"Good." Gran handed DJ back the glass. "You want to finish weeding? I think I'll go take a shower and get ready." The older woman rose to her feet and drifted over to the French doors off the deck.

DJ stared after her for a moment before slamming the glass down on the lawn. Jerking weeds out of the ground was probably better than jerking the hairs out of a certain policeman's head. When she stabbed herself on a hidden thistle, she said a word she was glad Gran wasn't around to hear. Maybe getting a horse wasn't her biggest problem after all.

Chapter · 11

"You lying little—little zit!" At the moment DJ couldn't think of anything worse. "I could pound you so far into the dirt, not even your hair would show."

"You and who else, jerk face?" James stood plastered against the stall wall. Six inches shorter than DJ but snarling like a cornered bobcat, he traded insult for insult. "You think you know everything, cat eyes."

DJ clamped her hands to her sides, knowing that if she touched him, she would pound until . . .

"What is going on here? DJ! James! Both of you, out of that stall this instant."

"But she . . ."

"I do not want to hear it. Up to the office! Now!"

DJ could feel the flames burst from inside and turn her skin to fire. Bridget never tolerated fighting on the grounds. And here DJ had been right in the middle of one! With James. She shot him another murderous glare, spun around, and stomped her way to the office. She could hear James behind her trying to make excuses. It wouldn't do any good. Bridget did not accept excuses. If you blew it, you better admit it. Thoughts raged inside her.

What kind of self-discipline lets a creep like James get through? If you can't control your anger over a stupid thing like this, how can you handle the stress of big-time competition? DJ tried to ignore the question, but the guilt that rode her shoulders felt like a pair of Percherons.

She straightened her spine and crossed her arms over her chest when Bridget walked in, trailed by James. DJ glared pitchforks at him, tines first. "I'm sorry I let him get to me like that." She forced the words from between clenched teeth.

Bridget nodded.

DJ stood even straighter and dropped her arms to her sides. Bridget's look said she'd better try again. *Why is Bridget picking on me? After all, James started it.* DJ dug deeper. She could feel the heat on her face, as surely as if she were standing in front of a roaring fire. "I . . . I'm sorry I fought like that. I should have been able to control my temper." She breathed a sigh of relief. The slight softening of Bridget's mouth meant she'd passed.

"James."

James slouched in a chair, arms across his chest, refusing to look at DJ. Or Bridget. He seemed to be studying a dirt spot on his jeans.

"James." The word cracked like a whip.

"Sorry."

Sure, thought DJ. *You really look sorry.* Instantly her mind flashed to herself. Was she sorry? Truly sorry? Or did she just want to get back in Bridget's good graces? The urge to chew on her thumbnail made her hand twitch. But then she'd get a look from Bridget for that. Instead, she bit on her lower lip.

The silence around her waited as if it were alive.

James squirmed, twitching first one shoulder and then the other.

With a rush of surprise, DJ felt sorry for him. He was having a harder time apologizing than she was—and she had hated every minute of it.

"I'm sorry I started the fight with DJ." The words burst out.

"Then there'll be no more incidents like this?"

Both DJ and James shook their heads.

"Consider yourselves both on probation. Any more such displays and you'll suffer the consequences."

DJ could hardly hear the words, even though she saw Bridget's lips moving. James had admitted he provoked the fight! That took guts. More guts than she'd thought he had. She watched him nod and walk out the door.

"DJ." DJ stopped in her tracks.

"Yes, ma'am?"

"I expected better of you."

"Me too." But Bridget's words cut into DJ's heart.

"Is there something going on that you would like to tell me about?"

DJ shook her head. Why would Bridget care that Gran had gone out with Joe five times in the last week? And that DJ had had a knock-down drag-out fight with her mom? And that Amy and everyone else but her got to ride and show this summer? "I better get back to work."

"If I can help in any way, I would like to." The words followed DJ out of the office. Why was she having trouble seeing the writing on the duty board? She dashed a hand across her eyes. *Must be allergies. There's too much dust around here.*

Gran's minivan was gone when DJ rode her bike up to the house. She dug in her pocket for her key to let herself in the front door, leaving her bike leaning against the side of the house. *Remember to put it away,* she reminded herself. *You don't need to get yelled at again.*

She heard the phone ringing as she finished fiddling with the key in the lock. Why, oh why did she always have trouble with the key? On the fourth ring, she finally opened the door and dashed across the room. The message machine was already asking the caller to leave a message. DJ clicked it off with one hand and lifted the receiver with the other.

"Hi, DJ speaking." She listened for a moment. "No, I'm sorry, my mother isn't here right now. Anyway, I don't think she wants the house painted. Gran and I did it last summer." She hung the phone up and read the message left for her.

Gran would be back late; she'd gone into San Francisco on BART to meet Joe for dinner. BART was the rapid-transit train that linked Bay Area cities by rail.

DJ crinkled up the paper and tossed it in the trash. *Great!* Now on top of everything else, she'd have to cook dinner—unless, of course, her mother wanted to eat out. She checked the calendar. No, Mom would be at class tonight. And most likely, she wouldn't come home first.

She could call Amy and invite herself over there for dinner. Mrs. Yamamoto always said to come anytime. One more didn't make much difference, since there were already four kids. But if someone asked her about her summer . . . well, maybe it was better to stay home.

DJ wandered into the family room. The house wore that empty, forgotten smell it had when both Mom and Gran were gone. DJ lifted the cloth draped over her grandmother's latest painting. She hadn't gotten very far today. DJ shook her head. Gran wasn't thinking too well lately, and it showed.

She ambled back into the kitchen and opened the refrigerator door. There weren't even any good leftovers. Usually when Gran was going to be gone, she made something that could be reheated in the oven or the microwave.

The quiet settled on her shoulders like a heavy blanket. A sigh escaped. She took out a can of soda and, after shutting the door with her foot, filled a glass. The soda fizzed, one side running over, so she had to slurp it quickly. The clock clicked. She'd never noticed it before.

She climbed the stairs to her room, one hand trailing on the banister. "This is a good time to work on my own art." Her voice echoed in the stairwell.

But even with charcoal in hand, her mind kept drifting back to the Academy. Why had she lost it like that with James? Some kind of Christian she was to want to beat up another human being! That is, if you could call James a human being.

DJ rolled over on her back. "How come the harder I try, the worse I get?" She curled back on her side. "God, I really want to be good and gentle, like my Gran. I hate it when someone is mad at me. That jerky James! He makes me so mad. I'll bet you'd get mad at him, too, if you were here." She hugged her knees and waited. It was so quiet. Even the birds were taking a break.

"I should have just walked away. Gran says to be extra nice to people who are mean to you. I really blew it this time. All I do anymore is blow it." She reached for a tissue in the drawer in her nightstand. The box was empty. She wiped the drip from her eye on the edge of her seafoam green bedspread. *If only Gran were here.*

"Darla Jean Randall!"

DJ jerked awake. Night had fallen. Her mother was home. "What?" She pushed herself to her feet and scrubbed her eyes with her fists. She could hear her mother downstairs.

"Your bike, that's what! How many times have I told you to put it away? You know someone could steal it. I should just let that happen—then what would you do?"

DJ flinched as if each word were a switch lashing at her legs. "I'm sorry." She swallowed the *I didn't mean to* and clattered down the stairs. On her way out to the garage, she paused at the dining room where her mother was going through the mail.

"How was your class?"

"Fine. Where's Gran?" Lindy tossed a couple of envelopes to the side.

"Out to dinner with Joe."

"Any messages?"

"No." DJ continued out to the garage. Talking with her mother was a real kick. If Gran had been there, she'd have asked about DJ's day. But not *her* mother. DJ put her bike away and closed the garage door. Her stomach rumbled when she stepped back into the kitchen. She got out the bread, peanut butter, and strawberry jam. Some dinner this had turned out to be.

The lights were out in the dining room. The family room was empty. She could hear her mother moving around upstairs in her bedroom. DJ took her sandwich and milk up to her own bedroom and shoved the door shut with her foot. What a totally crummy day!

Saying her prayers didn't make her feel any better.

———————————

"Mornin', darlin'." Gran greeted her as though nothing had happened. "You want scrambled eggs for breakfast?"

"No. I'm in a hurry." DJ grabbed a food bar out of the cupboard. "See you."

Gran came to the door to the garage. "Joe invited all of us to his house for dinner on Sunday to meet his family."

"I have a show." DJ swung aboard her bike and pedaled away. "Why'd I want to meet his family?" she muttered to herself while pumping up the street. "Who cares? I've got more important things to do than that."

———————————

"Have you been watching Megs' legs?" Bridget joined DJ at the mare's stall.

"Sure."

"Well, check that off foreleg. There's some swelling there. I saw her limping yesterday when I turned her out, so I iced it last night."

DJ stroked the bay mare's nose and squatted down to examine the leg. Sure enough, the pastern was swollen. "Sorry, girl. I'll get the ice packs." She rose to her feet and turned to leave the stall.

"I'm sorry, DJ. You want to ride Jake?"

DJ shook her head. "He'd probably come up lame, too." Now she couldn't even take her jumping lessons. The one thing in her life that seemed to be going right. Angry, she muttered a word her Gran would be shocked at. It only made her feel worse.

Chapter • 12

"I'm sorry, DJ. We're going to have to postpone the party."

"That's okay. You can't help it that your boy has the chicken pox. We'll be glad to bring the pony when he's better." DJ hung up the phone. "That's the second cancellation. We had to run into an epidemic of chicken pox! How am I ever going to earn enough money for a horse at this rate?" She slammed her fist on the telephone stand, making the pencils in the holder jump and spill onto the floor.

"DJ, are you all right?" Gran called from the other room.

"I'm fine! Just fine!" DJ knelt and picked up the scattered pens and pencils. *If I get any more fine, I'll explode.* She dialed Amy's number and waited while Amy's brother went to get her.

"Bad news. Both our parties are canceled for Saturday—chicken pox."

"Have you ever had them?" Amy sounded funny.

"I guess. Why?"

"Because John is breaking out in spots and I never have, that's why."

"Oh, great. So, you sick or what?"

"No, not yet. But Mom says I probably will be in ten to fourteen days. I don't want the chicken pox."

DJ flinched at the wail in Amy's voice. She glanced at the calendar.

Two weeks! That was the weekend of the Danville Saddle Club show, one of the biggest in the area.

"Maybe you won't get them. Come on, Ames, you can pray for that. I will."

"I'd rather get them now than later. Spots all over my face—yuk!"

"Yeah, and you hardly ever even have a zit." DJ twined the phone cord around her fingers. "So, how's John taking it?"

"He's too sick to care. Mom says the older you are, the worse you get it."

Visions of John covered with pussy sores made DJ cringe. "I gotta go. Talk to you tomorrow." She hung up the phone and turned to find Gran standing in the door.

"So you don't have any parties on Saturday?"

DJ shook her head.

"I'm sorry for that, but your new schedule will work out well for Joe and me. We'll have the barbecue on Saturday instead."

DJ watched as Gran lifted the receiver. Her face turned into all-over smiles when Joe answered the phone. Why, she looked as sappy as some of the girls at school who claimed to be in love. If that was what love did to a person, DJ wanted no part of it.

Gran can't be in love. She hardly knows the guy. But there she was, calling him *darlin'*. But then Gran called everyone *darlin'*. Well, not everyone—just her family. DJ and Lindy. And now Joe.

DJ felt like heaving. What was happening to her grandmother? She tried to get Gran's attention. But waving arms and making faces didn't work. Gran just smiled that sappy smile, laid a finger over her lips, and kept right on talking to Joe. Shouldn't he be at work? Wasn't there a law against calling a policeman when he was on duty? DJ stomped from the kitchen and up to her room.

"I don't want to go to a barbecue at Joe's house! I don't want to even *see* the man ever again! I don't . . ." She paused before slamming her fist into her pillow a third time. "I don't want Amy to get the chicken pox!"

How could a summer that started out so great turn into such a disaster? Diablo to ride and show in equitation and dressage. Jumping classes. Ways to earn money for a horse of her own. The best summer ever! Now it was all a bust.

She flopped across her bed and let her arms dangle over the other side. Even sketching horses wasn't fun anymore. How could she ever ride in the Olympics when she couldn't even get through the summer? She pounded her fist on the carpet, keeping time with her swinging feet. What a mess—bam! What a mess—bam! Four beats. Wait—she'd forgotten about James accusing her of stealing the saddle and bridle. What a mess—bam!

"That bad, darlin'?" Gran stood at the door.

DJ swallowed. And swallowed again. Her eyes burned. *Bam! Don't call me "darlin'," not when you call that—that man—the same thing.* But all she said was, "I'll live."

"Guess I didn't realize livin' was in question."

DJ refused to rise to the gentle humor. What a mess—bam! But when she heard Gran make her way back downstairs, she wanted to run after her and bury her head in Gran's lap. To tell her how awful everything was. To let her make everything all right again.

"What's with you today?" Amy planted her fists on her hips and stood, legs spread, as if to keep DJ from running right over her.

"Nothing."

"Right. And I'm Ronald McDonald. Come on, DJ, you've been ugly as sin the last couple of days. This isn't like you, not one bit."

DJ kept on brushing Megs, using long strokes with such a heavy hand that the horse turned to look at her. Dust motes flew in the sunlight from the open doorway. Megs stamped her foot and swished her tail when DJ failed to swirl the hair at her flank.

"DJ, this is your best friend, Amy, remember me? What gives?"

DJ dropped the brush and rubber currycomb into the pail. "You really want to know? Well, tomorrow I have to go to a barbecue at *Captain* Joe Crowder's house to meet his family. Sunday I get to help all of you who own your own horse at the horse show. I don't get to show, mind you—I get to *help*." She unsnapped the crossties and turned Megs around to take her out to the hot walker. "You want more?" She stopped and looked back at her friend.

Amy stood in the same spot, hands now at her side. Even in the shadow, DJ could see two tears leave Amy's almond eyes and spill down her cheeks.

DJ bit her lip. "And now even my best friend hates me. But that's no problem, because I don't like me, either." She dashed away a piece of dirt that was making her eye water. "Come on, Megs. *Someone* around here should get what she wants. And you want to be outside."

What a creep you are! DJ couldn't think of any names black enough to call herself. When she returned, Amy was nowhere in sight.

Since she and Amy didn't have any pony parties on Saturday due to the chicken pox, DJ spent the early afternoon cleaning tack for the show on Sunday.

"Cat eyes," James hissed when he rode by her on the way out to the arena to practice.

While DJ heard him, ignoring him was easy. She had too far up to reach to answer. Once, she'd heard the saying *lower than a slug's belly.* It fit her now.

Amy came, did her chores, and left without saying a word to DJ. Round and round DJ moved the rag, dipping it back in the saddle soap, then round and round some more. One thing was sure, there was always plenty of leather to clean.

"Need some help?" Hilary sat down on the bale beside DJ.

"Sure." DJ nodded to the waiting pile of tack. "I hang 'em up when I'm done."

"I know the drill." They rubbed in silence. They could hear observers commenting on those still practicing in the rings for the show. A horse snorted. Another whinnied.

"How's Megs?"

"Seems okay now." Rub, dip, and rub some more.

"You helping tomorrow?"

"Yep." DJ flexed her shoulders and sat up straight.

"I had a summer like yours once."

That caught DJ's attention. *How does she know everything that's going on?* "Sure you did."

"I broke my arm, my horse went lame, and my mom and dad separated." Hilary stopped rubbing. "I was thirteen; it was a rough time anyway."

"So?"

"So, what?"

"So what happened?"

"My arm healed, my horse recovered, and my parents got back together. We were lucky. Or as my mom says, 'God took good care of us.'"

"You believe that?" Rub, dip, and rub. DJ wanted to watch Hilary's face, but she couldn't.

"Sure do. But it hurt as if I were dying at the time."

. Hilary stood to hang up a bridle. She reached down and took the one DJ had just finished. "When you thank God for what's going on—no matter how bad it seems—it gets easier."

"Thanks?" DJ's voice sounded like that of a cornered mouse.

Hilary nodded. "I know it doesn't make sense, but it works. Try it and let me know what happens." She patted DJ on the shoulder. "Gotta run. See you tomorrow."

DJ checked her watch. Today was not a good day to be getting home late. And she still had to take a shower.

Gran looked as if she'd swallowed the sun—she couldn't quit shining. "You better bring a jacket; it could be foggy in San Francisco."

DJ already had hers lying by the door. Thanks to direct orders from her mother, she wore a long-sleeved green cotton shirt and tan dress pants. It was the nicest outfit she owned. When she'd suggested clean jeans and a new T-shirt, the look she got from her mother quickly changed her mind.

Everyone else would probably be in jeans. Everyone but her mother and Gran, that is.

DJ put on her earphones and plugged them into her portable cassette player as soon as she got in the car. This way she wouldn't have to talk—or listen. Or think, for that matter. One foot bobbed in time with the music. When they parked in front of a two-story house with big bay windows like many San Francisco houses, she shut off her recorder and stared. There was no yard on either side of the house—in fact, there was no place to walk between them, the walls butted right up against each other.

"Nice place," she muttered in as sarcastic a tone as she could dig up.

Her mother pinched DJ's underarm and hissed in her ear. "Shape up!"

DJ clapped her mouth shut. How could she smile and be pleasant when Gran and Joe were kissing in front of everybody? Worse still, DJ was the oldest kid there. All the others were still in grade school or younger.

Gran took DJ's hand. Joe held the other—Gran's, that is. "Come on, darlin', we want you to meet the family."

By the time DJ had met two of Joe's three children and their kids, she felt as though she were caught in a memory game time warp.

The oldest, Robert, had a pair of five-year-old twin boys named Billy and Bobby. *What yucky names,* DJ thought.

"Our mom went to heaven," Billy announced. Or was it Bobby?

"Oh." *What do you say to that?*

"Do you like horses?" Bobby asked. Or was it Billy?

"Yes, I do."

"Good, 'cause my grandpa said you'd take me for a ride."

"Ah, sure." *Come on, DJ, loosen up. They're just kids—you like kids.*

"Grandpa said you ride at an academy." A girl with shy, dark eyes stopped next to DJ.

"I'm Shawna. That's my mom and dad." She pointed to the man burning the meat and a woman holding the platter. "I'm nine."

"Hi, Shawna. I do ride."

"And you teach kids to ride."

"Some."

"Would you teach me?"

What could she say? DJ nodded. "Someday, sure." *Joe sure has been volunteering me for all kinds of things. Who does he think he is, anyway?* DJ shot him a look, but it bounced off the circle of love shining around him and Gran.

DJ rubbed her stomach. She had a really bad feeling about all this.

Shawna sat right across the table from DJ, and the twins parked themselves on either side of her. DJ felt hemmed in by munchkins. She cut into her steak. Pink juice dribbled onto her plate. These people couldn't even cook meat right! She ate around the pink part and tried to make a real meal out of the salad and corn on the cob. When she glanced up, her mother was sitting by the twins' father.

"Okay, everybody, we have an announcement to make." Joe whistled to quiet the crowd. Gran stood next to him wearing a beaming smile. "I know it's kind of sudden, but we aren't spring chickens anymore, so I'll get right to the point. This lovely lady beside me has done me the honor of agreeing to be my wife."

Wife! DJ felt her breath leave in a whoosh. *What was Gran thinking? Now her life was ruined for sure!*

Chapter • 13

"Does that mean we'll have a new grandma?"

"Does it, DJ?" the other twin asked.

DJ pushed back her chair. Not bothering to catch it before it hit the ground, she fled from the scene. Into the house, out the front door, down the street. She ran as if a pack of angry wolves panted at her heels.

Vaguely, over the pounding of her feet and heart, she could hear someone calling her name. Down a hill, up another. Her chest ached. Her side ached. Could a broken heart still beat? *Gran is getting married. Gran is leaving me. Am I so terrible that everyone wants to leave me?*

She leaned against a metal lamppost, her breath coming in searing agony.

"Darla Jean Randall, get in this car immediately."

It couldn't be her mother's voice. She'd left them all behind. DJ bent forward, her strangled breathing beginning to slow. "You hear me?" A person grabbing her arm accompanied the voice.

DJ twisted around and looked into her mother's angry face. Fury radiated from Lindy's eyes, her mouth, the deep lines in her cheeks. DJ noticed these as if from a great distance. She swung around and let herself be hustled into the open door of her mother's car. She sank into the seat, snapped shut the seat belt, and locked her arms over her chest.

"What is the matter with you? You've broken your grandmother's heart. And on a day that should be so happy for her! You ruined it. What a selfish brat you've become! Darla Jean, are you listening to me?"

"Sure I am. You're yelling right in my ear." *You can't make me cry. I won't let you.* The words echoed in her head and helped her clench her teeth tighter, till they felt as though they might crack.

"I think I could beat you within an inch of your life."

"Go ahead. I don't care."

"All these years Gran has cared for you—and when she needs you, you run away like a spoiled brat. And in front of all those people! I was so embarrassed I could die."

"Sure, *you* were embarrassed. Well, I'm *so* sorry. The great Lindy Randall was embarrassed." DJ wanted to stop, but words kept coming. "All those nice people, what will they think? I don't care what they think. I never wanted to meet them anyway." *I won't cry. You can't make me.*

"When we get home, I'm going to lock you in your room until you're sorry or—" Lindy swerved away from a car that she almost cut off.

"You better watch your driving." DJ wished she'd bit the words back before they leaped into the air, but biting back words didn't seem to be her skill at the moment. *I'm a real motor mouth. All this time I've been praying about my temper, and now look at me. What good has it done?* The thought made her scrunch her eyes shut. If she started to cry now, she might never stop. But one lone tear made it past her dam. One tear that slid down her face and dripped off her chin.

DJ refused to wipe it away. If she did, the rest might follow. *Gran, Mom—I'm so sorry.*

"We'll finish this discussion when we get home."

DJ sneaked a peak at her mother; all she could see were white-knuckled hands clenching the steering wheel. The force of the driver's door slamming shut when they finally parked in their garage shook the whole car.

DJ stayed in the car. Maybe if she gave her mother some time alone, she'd calm down. *And maybe a comet will strike us first.* DJ sank lower in her seat. How would anyone forgive her? She'd never overreacted like this before. But when Gran got married, she'd leave them. Or what if Joe decided to move in? The thought sent her rocketing from the car. *He'd* probably just throw her in jail, claim she was a juvenile delinquent or something.

She got out and slammed the door shut. Picking up her feet took an effort. Thankfully, her mother wasn't in the kitchen, or the family room. The sounds of stirring came from upstairs. DJ stopped at the foot of the stairs. They loomed up in front of her like a mountain, and the pack she carried was too heavy to bear.

She started up. *Selfish brat—guilty. Smart mouth—guilty. Terrible temper—guilty.* One for each step of the way. All of them true. How could anyone forgive her for this mess? How could she forgive herself?

Once at the top, she started for her mother's room. She could hear the shower running. A shower was her mom's answer to everything; she said she could think better there than anywhere else.

DJ slunk into her own room and collapsed on the bed.

When she awoke, she could hear voices downstairs. She crept to the head of the stairs and sat down on the first step. The voices carried easily from the family room. Her mother, Gran, and of course, Joe.

Gran was crying.

Each sob was like a nail driving deep into the girl huddled against the wall. *I made Gran cry. I broke her heart.*

"Well, I think we should drag her down here and hash this out right now." DJ could hear her mother's pacing footsteps punctuating her speech. "We've been much too soft on her, Mother. It's my fault, I should have been around more."

"No, no . . . I just never thought she'd take our news like this." Another sniff. "And we were so happy."

"We will be, my dear, we will be. I promise you." Joe's voice rumbled.

"I'm going to get her. Now." Lindy's face appeared at the bottom of the stairs before DJ could disappear. "Good, you heard us. Now get down here."

DJ felt like a little kid caught stealing. Her grandmother had been right. Eavesdroppers never heard anything good about themselves. She rose to her feet and clumped down the stairs. By the time she reached the bottom, she knew she had to tough it out. Whatever they dished out, she could take.

But the sight of Gran's tear-washed face nearly did her in. All DJ wanted to do was run and bury her face in Gran's lap to cry out all the pain and anger. To beg forgiveness.

"I think you should be grounded for life." Her mother's words brought her up short. There would be no lap for DJ, no gentle hands brushing the hair off her forehead for a forgiving kiss. Joe stood beside Gran's chair as if to keep guard. As a policeman, he sure knew how.

"Say you're sorry."

The words stuck in her throat. Sorry didn't begin to cover how she felt.

She looked from one face to the next. Joe hated her. Her mother hated her. And Gran, who never hated anyone, looked as if her heart would never mend.

"Sit." Mom pointed to a chair in the middle of the room.

"I'll stand." DJ didn't know where the words came from. She'd been going to say she was sorry. Instead, she glared down at the chair. Where was Joe's bright light? Cops were supposed to be good at interrogating prisoners. When she raised her chin again, the steel was back in her spine.

"I wouldn't let you go to the show tomorrow, but I know Bridget is depending on you. You'll go to work and come straight home. No lessons. No riding for pleasure. I will leave a list of chores for you to do. There'll be no phone, no television, and no time with Amy—except for the pony parties. You cannot put other people at a disadvantage because of your thoughtlessness."

"Anything else?" DJ forced the words from between clamped teeth.

"Lindy, dear, you're being too hard on her." Gran's soft voice made DJ nearly crack.

"No, Mother, keep out of this. We've been much too soft on her." Lindy turned back to face DJ. "We'll discuss this again in two weeks. Is there anything you'd like to say?"

Does a condemned prisoner get any last requests? DJ squared shoulders already so stiff they ached. "I'm sorry."

Her mother shook her head. "I just wish I could believe you meant that."

"Of course she meant . . ." Gran's voice trailed off at a look from her daughter.

"May I be excused?" At her mother's nod, DJ turned and marched back up the stairs.

She woke in the middle of the night, her face wet with tears. When she got up to go to the bathroom, she paused by Gran's closed bedroom door. From inside she could hear the sounds of weeping. DJ tiptoed back to her own room. Maybe if she weren't here, everything would be better.

The sun was just tinting the sky when she finally threw back the covers and got up. There was plenty to do at the Academy before they'd be ready to trailer all the horses. At least there everyone didn't hate her. Other than James and Amy, of course. Both Gran and Mom were still sleeping when DJ silently let herself out of the house.

She threw herself into the work. She groomed horses, adjusted traveling sheets, and checked off lists to make sure all the tack was included. Loading went like a perfect drill.

She ignored the questioning look Bridget gave her and made sure she was always somewhere Amy and Mr. Yamamoto weren't. When she finally slammed the door on the van Hilary was driving, she settled in for the ride.

"You okay?" Hilary asked just before putting the van in gear.

"Sure." DJ pulled a list of the day's events from her pocket. "How many classes you entered in today?"

If she kept busy enough, maybe, just maybe, she could forget the scene in the living room the night before. Maybe she could forget her grandmother crying in the night. Maybe she could forget the fact that her best friend hadn't even said hello.

But more important, maybe she could turn off the voice inside her head that kept calling her names. Names in what sounded suspiciously like her mother's voice.

The Sunday show ran even more smoothly than the one before, which only gave DJ more time to think.

"DJ, could you look at my stirrups for me?"

DJ whirled around from the rail where she leaned her chin on crossed hands. "Sure. Have you tried?"

The little girl looked up at her as if DJ had parked her brain somewhere and forgotten to pick it up. " 'Course."

"Sorry, just checking." DJ turned and walked back to the line where the horses were tied. "Okay, mount up and face me." DJ scrutinized both sides of the pony. "You sure you checked to see if your stirrups are the right length?"

A shrug was her answer. DJ smiled and shook her head. "Does

the right one feel good? Great, then let's move the left up a notch." DJ followed her words with quick actions.

After patting the girl's knee, DJ glanced over to where Amy had Josh tied.

"Second call for Western Pleasure, class number eleven," came the tinny echo over the loudspeaker.

Amy mounted and trotted down the fence line to join the other contestants waiting by the entry gate.

"Go get 'em, Ames. You can take this one." DJ whispered the words to empty air.

When she watched the English Pleasure class, DJ was certain she and Diablo would have taken first. The pair that won, while competent, just didn't have the flair that she and Diablo had had. Oh, how she missed him! Watching from the sidelines was eating her alive.

"DJ, would you check with the registrar and see if Sondra is listed on the next class? Oh, and make sure James is listed in trail riding. He was trying to back out of it." Bridget handed DJ a list of contestants from the Academy.

"Sure." If James and his filly could back around the rails as well as he backed out of work, they'd win for sure. The thought made her wish she could share the joke with Amy.

The end of the day brought both relief and dread. She'd made it to the end of another show she couldn't compete in—and now she had to go home. She dragged out putting things away as long as she could. All the horses were fed, watered, and hayed. *Cut it out, DJ, you're stalling.* Her frustration goading her, she hopped on her bike and headed for home.

"Well, I hope you're happy." Her mother met her at the door.

"Now what did I do?"

"Because of your infantile actions yesterday, Joe and Gran have called off the wedding."

"But . . ."

"Darla Jean Randall, I am so ashamed of you."

"My name is DJ." *And you can't be any more ashamed of me than I am.*

Chapter · 14

If I ran away, where would I go?

The buzzing of the alarm jolted her wide awake.

The thought hadn't been a dream actually; it felt more like a prodding. Must be pretty serious when even her subconscious thought about it. Maybe that was the easiest solution. They'd all be better off without her to worry about. Gran could get married so she and Joe would be happy. Mom wouldn't have to worry about finding a place to live big enough for the two of them. At least she'd be out of their hair. And there was no horse for her to worry about leaving.

DJ buried her face in her pillow. Where would she go? How much money did she have?

She threw back the covers and crossed the room to her desk. Pulling her money box out of the center drawer, she set it on the desk and lifted the lid. Her bankbook read $345.88. She counted the bills and change. Another $36 and some change. A total of $382 and—she scrambled for the exact count—seventy-seven cents. How long could she possibly live on that?

I can get a job. I look older than I am. She peered at the face in the mirror. *I could pass for sixteen, maybe even seventeen.* But right now she needed to head for the Academy. At least there she had plenty to do and people to talk to. She stuck her bankbook in her jeans back pocket.

But when she pedaled past Amy's house, it felt as if a giant fist smacked her in the gut. Riding up the first hill took more breath than the fist had left her. She downshifted. What about the pony parties? Could Amy handle them by herself? One of her brothers would surely help her.

Catching her breath on the downhill, she pumped like crazy up the next rise. Pump and coast. That seemed to be the story of her life. All ups and downs with few flat stretches. *God, what am I gonna do?* She coasted off the paved road and into the Academy parking lot. After work she would take all her money out of the bank. Tonight was as good a time as any to leave.

"DJ, you have a minute?" Bridget leaned on the fence observing as DJ finished her beginning riders' class.

"Sure." DJ turned back to her students. "Okay, time to walk your horses to cool them out, then head for the area behind the barn. Another class needs the arena." She swung the gate open and smiled up at her girls.

"When are we going up in Briones again?" Krissie stopped halfway through the gate.

"Ah-h-h, soon. I'll let you know next lesson." DJ forced her mouth into a smile. She wouldn't be here to take them up in the park again. Once she closed the gate, she joined Bridget at the rail.

"You really are good with them. One of the mothers told me her daughter keeps her room clean now just because you told her neatness is a key to performing well." Bridget turned so she was leaning against the aluminum rail.

"Thanks. I like teaching." DJ copied Bridget's pose.

"You want to tell me what has been bothering you?"

DJ blinked. She thought she'd been keeping her thoughts to herself, not skywriting them for all to see. "Ah—just home stuff. It'll all work out." She could feel the heat flaming up her neck. One thing Gran had drummed in her head—never lie or cheat.

"Remember, I am here for you when you need me." Bridget hooked a heel over the bottom rail. And waited.

DJ fought the tide of tears that threatened to swamp her. She swallowed, then swallowed again, her hands clenched by her side. *How can I just disappear when she counts on me? How can I stay? This is a mess!* The thoughts burst over each other in a confusing rush. *I can't stay—I messed up Gran's life. I'm so selfish.* She blinked herself back to the arena. "I'm sorry, I didn't hear you."

"I asked if you checked out the new gelding I put in Diablo's stall? I have assigned him to you for exercise. His name is Dandy Son, but he answers to Patches. His family only plans on being out here on the weekends. He needs training so their ten-year-old can ride him. Think you can take care of that?"

"I'll do my best."

"I have every confidence in you, DJ." Bridget started to walk away. "Let me know when you are ready to bring him out. We will see what he knows and set up a program for him." She nodded at a call for the telephone. "I will be right there. Oh, and, DJ, he is trained for Western riding."

DJ checked on her students and sent them all to dismount and groom their horses. None had worked up a sweat, thanks to the cool breeze.

She worked her way down the line of nodding horses until she came to Diablo's old stall. These stalls were supposed to be James' responsibility, but none had been forked out. And as usual, James was not in sight.

DJ shook her head. A dark brown horse, nearly black, but with a splotch of white between his eyes, came forward to sniff her hand. DJ rolled back the barred upper half of the stall door and took hold of his halter. "So, you're Patches, are you?" The gelding snuffled up her shoulder to her hair. DJ stood quietly and let him explore her. "You are a beauty, you know that?" Her soft voice and soothing hands worked their magic, aided by the carrot she dug out of her pocket.

While he crunched, she slid back the lower door and entered the stall. He stood a bit over fifteen hands, with one white sock in front and another on the opposite back leg.

When she bent down to check his legs, he rumpled her hair. "You're a bit of Arab, but what's the rest? Morgan? Quarter Horse?" He pricked his ears and nudged her shoulder. "Yeah, I like you, too. Somebody bought themselves a fine animal, didn't they?" *If only I could be here to train you.*

She felt that even more painfully after the riding session. Patches had a nice gait, easy to sit to, but with only two speeds—walk and run. He seemed willing, but he didn't know much more than simple neck reining. He also tended to get hyper when she asked him to do something unfamiliar, such as backing up or going at a gentle lope.

After she put him away, she decided to write Bridget a letter and leave it in the office.

Amy worked on the other side of the barn, cleaning her stalls and grooming horses. But she never came out to watch the new mount or swap jokes the way she usually did.

When DJ dared to sneak looks at her used-to-be friend, she could tell Amy wasn't any happier than she was. Guess she'd have to write a note to Amy, too.

By the time DJ'd gotten her money out of the bank, it was late. She pedaled like crazy for home, not looking forward to explaining why she was late. The list of chores covered both sides of a sheet of paper.

Gran's minivan was gone again. *Probably off seeing that stupid policeman.* DJ left her bike on the front sidewalk. She'd be gone before anyone could yell at her to put it away.

First she'd write the letters, then pack. She sat down at her desk. Should she write to Gran and Mom? She shook her head. They wouldn't care anyway. Just Amy and Bridget. She wrote fast and stuffed the sheets in the envelopes. Gran could come home anytime.

DJ packed another pair of jeans, two T-shirts, and a pair of shorts in her backpack. By the time she'd added underwear, a sweatshirt and jacket, and her toothbrush and paste, she hardly had room for food. She rummaged in the cupboard downstairs. A box of food bars, a couple apples, matches. She'd camp up in Briones for a couple nights before heading . . . DJ didn't know where. She clamped her hands on the counter. Would she ever see her family again?

She wandered into the family room and lifted the cloth on Gran's latest painting. As Gran would say, it needed work. She let the cloth drop and went to sit in Gran's chair, letting her gaze wander around the room, saying good-bye to everything. When she finally pushed herself to her feet, she might as well have been pushing up the world.

With her sleeping bag tied on the back of her bike, a canteen slung on her shoulder, and her pack on her back, she pedaled out the drive and around the corner. That way no one she knew would see her on the main street, the way they usually came.

Once at the Academy, she parked her bike behind the long barn and dropped her pack beside it. The sun had already set, and long shadows stretched across the dusty parking area. She could hear a class going on in the covered arena and another at the open arena set up for jumping. Most of the adults came in the evening after work. A horse whinnied in one of the outside stalls. Inside the barn, only an occasional snort or the rasp of hay being pulled from a rack broke the silence.

Horses came to the gates and nickered or wuffled when DJ made her way down the line. She knew them all, many of them for the four years she'd worked there. An ear scratch here, a chin rub there—Megs insisted on having her ears rubbed when DJ slipped inside her stall. DJ scratched, then wrapped her arms around the deep red neck, burying her face in the black mane.

You will not cry. "You be a good girl now, you hear?" She tickled the mare's whiskery upper lip. "Thanks for all the good jumps we made." Megs nickered when DJ left the stall.

DJ leaned against the wall. She'd say good-bye to Patches, then get out of there. After she left the letter on Bridget's desk.

Even with her heart pounding in her ears, she detected an unfamiliar sound. She stopped in her tracks, the better to hear. Was there an animal trapped in a stall? A horse down? She made her way down the aisle, past Patches, and stopped again. Nothing. Concentrating, she tiptoed so as not to make a sound, checking each box stall, always moving like a ghost. She stopped and listened again. It was coming from across the aisle. She peered into Gray Bar's stall. The Arabian filly studied her with large, calm eyes. But something light colored was huddled back in the corner.

DJ slid open the stall and slipped inside. With one hand on the filly's halter, she drew closer to the far corner.

"So what are *you* staring at, cat?"

"James!" DJ nearly jumped in surprise. "What are you doing here?"

Chapter • 15

"Nothing. I can come visit my horse, can't I?"

"Well, sure, but . . ."

"But nothing, just get out of here and leave me alone." His voice broke on the last syllable.

DJ stroked the filly's neck and smoothed her mane. *What was going on? James never spent time alone with his horse. He rode, practiced, did his chores, and left.* It had never occurred to her that he even liked the animal, in spite of what a beauty she was. The green-eyed monster of jealousy had attacked DJ more than once because of this superb horse.

"You did pretty good yesterday."

"Yeah, right. Best I got was a red. My dad . . ." He waved her away with a clenched fist. "Go on, will ya?"

DJ kept her attention on the horse. She was sure she'd seen tears on James' cheeks. She could hear them in his voice. She knew how rotten she felt when someone came upon her when she was crying. Crying should be a private affair. But she couldn't leave. James needed someone, that was for sure. And it looked to be her.

"But you placed in the trail-riding class, and the show before, Gray Bar wouldn't even finish the course. All your practice and work with her showed. Your dad should be real proud of you."

DJ thought she heard him mumble, "Too drunk to care," but she wasn't sure. She didn't dare ask him to repeat himself. How could she get him to talk?

God, please help me help James. She went on stroking the filly. "What about your mom? Isn't she proud of you?"

"Why? She's never home."

"Sounds like my mom. She travels for her job and then goes to school nights for her master's degree. She's been in school ever since I can remember."

"My mother says she hates coming home."

DJ felt like James had socked her. "No, she doesn't. She can't. Not really." She wished she could grab the words back and swallow them quick.

"You think I'm stupid or something? I understand English. Especially when she's screaming at the top of her lungs."

"In front of you?" DJ could hear her voice squeak.

"Nah, I listen from the top of the stairs. My dad was drunk again . . ."

Again. This time DJ caught the words before they slipped out.

"And Mom said it was the last time. She was leaving, she'd see him in court."

DJ sank down on the shavings beside him. *What do you say to something like this?* But she didn't have to say anything. It was as though someone had pulled the plug; the words bubbled out nonstop.

"My dad threw his glass into the fireplace then—I heard it smash. He'd been drinking ever since he came home. I tried to get him to stop, but after he hit me, I stayed upstairs." James clenched his hands over his knees. "It's safer that way. If I hide, he sometimes forgets what he was yelling about—at least when he's yelling at me. But Mom said she couldn't take it anymore. I think he hit her once, but she lied and said she bumped into a door."

When he fell silent, DJ cleared her throat. "So what are you going to do?"

"Me? They're gonna send me back East to military school. Dad says I need some discipline to shape me up. Ha! He's the one who needs discipline." He turned to look at DJ. "Why does he do it—drink, I mean? He says he's sorry, but then he just drinks again."

"I don't know." A picture of Gran flitted through her mind. Even if Gran got married, she'd find time for her only granddaughter. Of course she would.

James sniffed again. "I don't want to go to military school. I don't want to leave Gray Bar. I like it here at the Academy." His voice broke. The silence lengthened. "They're going to get a divorce. They say it'll be better for all of us that way." He picked up a handful of shavings and let them tumble through his fingers.

DJ wanted to take him in her arms and hold him as Gran so often held her.

He sniffed and rubbed the back of his hand across his nose.

DJ watched him from the corner of her eye. What could she say? What could she do? No wonder he'd been such a mean kid all summer.

"I'll take care of your horse for you. When you come home next summer, she'll be better trained than ever."

"Dad says he's gonna sell her."

"Oh no!" DJ looked up at the filly, who'd lowered her head to sniff and wuffle in James' hair. "She's so beautiful. You'll never find one like her again."

"I know. But . . ." He slammed his fist into the shavings. Gray Bar threw her head up and backed away. "I hate him! I could kill my dad. And Mom's no help. All she can think about is never coming home again. I hate her, too."

DJ felt her breath leave. It left her hollow, as if she might cave in. "James, you don't mean that . . . about killing, I mean."

"No. But I hate him, I really do."

She could hear the tears running into his words. And she didn't even have a tissue. *I thought I hated Joe, but I don't. Nothing like James and his dad. God, please, I want to go home. I'm sorry I've been so hard to live with.* She crossed her arms on her knees and rested her forehead on them.

The filly made manure in the corner, filling the air with the pungent aroma. Then she came back to nuzzle James.

With one hand James reached up to rub her nose. She dropped her head lower, resting her cheek against James' shoulder.

"She can tell you're sad. Horses know more about us than we give them credit for."

"I know. And I haven't taken good care of her. That's why Dad says he's selling her. He says I don't care. That I never care about anything."

"Little does he know." Right now DJ felt like going over to their fancy house and telling that mean old drunk off.

"Thanks, DJ." James turned so he could look right at her. "I'm sorry I called you names. And about that saddle and bridle. . . . I . . . I hid it." He swallowed the words.

"You did what?" DJ jerked upright.

"I hid them. Everyone likes you, and you're so good with the other kids and the horses. I just wanted you to get in trouble for once. Like me."

"James Edward Corrigan, that was a double dumb thing to do! Why'd you . . ."

"I said I was sorry. I'll put 'em back tomorrow and tell Bridget what I did."

"I'm glad you told me."

"You gonna tell my dad?"

"No way. There is some stuff I'd like to tell him, though. And none of it's very nice." Now she was the one tossing handfuls of shavings.

"How are you going to get home?" DJ leaned back against the wall.

"Call George. He's the gardener, driver—whatever we need. I thought about sleeping here tonight." He rubbed the filly's forehead. "Would you share your stall with me, girl?" She nibbled at his hair and blew gently in his face.

"She'd probably step on you."

"No, she wouldn't. Sure wish I'd worked her harder. My dad's right, you know. I *am* lazy. I'd rather play games on my computer than most anything. But I do like riding—and showing." He pushed himself to his feet and, grabbing a handful of mane, swung up on the filly. "If they don't sell her, would you show her this fall? I know you want a horse of your own, but Gray Bar here loves to jump. She's good. Bridget says she has plenty of ability."

DJ knew her mouth made an O. She could feel her chin smack on her chest. She closed it and shook her head. "James, I . . ."

"Just say yes." James scooted back and leaned forward to rest his chin on the filly's withers. "You could go far with her."

"If you have to sell, I wish I could buy her." She thought about the money in her pocket. It wouldn't even be a down payment on a registered Arabian like this one.

"You can use her. That way it won't cost you anything."

"Thanks. You all right now?"

"Yeah, I'm fine. Just cool."

"Guess I better get home. I'm not supposed to be out past dark."

"Me neither." James slid to the ground. "I'll see you tomorrow. They can't ship me off that fast." He gave the filly another pat and pushed back the lower door. "Uh, you won't tell the other kids about this, will you?"

DJ shook her head. "Nope. You sure you're okay?"

"Hey, I'll live. Military school can't be all bad."

"I'll write to you, tell you about Gray Bar."

"Promise?"

"Promise." DJ ducked back around the barn and hefted her back-pack. She couldn't get her arms in the straps fast enough. Maybe she'd get home before they even realized she was gone.

She climbed onto her bike, hitting the pedals so hard, gravel spurted out from under her rear tire. Would she ever be able to say *sorry* enough?

Chapter • 16

"And just where have you been, young lady?"

"Mom! I thought you were on another trip." DJ knew those were the wrong words as soon as they left her mouth.

"So that made it okay for you to be out after dark? Wasn't there something about being grounded?" Her mother stood in the door, fists on hips, ready to do battle. "Why do you have your sleeping bag? And a backpack? Darla Jean Randall, what in the world is going on?"

Gran ducked past her daughter's arm. "Oh, darlin', what kind of mess have you gotten into now?"

Joe filled what was left of the open doorway.

DJ wished the earth would just open up and swallow her whole. "Why'd you call in the police?"

"He's not the police . . ."

"I'm here only because I care, DJ. No other reason." Joe laid a hand on Gran's shoulder, much as DJ would gentle a horse.

"Where were you going?" Lindy bit out the words as if each one were too hot to contain.

DJ untied her sleeping bag and held it in front of her. "I was going to camp in Briones." She watched the blood drain from her mother's face.

"But there are rattlesnakes up there and . . . and tarantulas."

"Not to mention ticks. Am I right in assuming you were running away?" Joe joined in the accusations.

DJ nodded.

"Oh, Darla Jean, how could you?" Lindy sagged back against Joe's broad chest.

DJ squared her shoulders. Might as well get it all over with. "I figured you'd all be better off without me. I was acting like a spoiled brat. I'm sorry." She raised tear-filled eyes to Gran's. "I love you, Gran, and I don't want you to be unhappy."

Gran spread her arms wide, and DJ dropped her bag to fly into them like a baby bird back to the nest. "How could you ever think we would be better off without you? You've been my life. Caring for you gave me a reason to keep on living after Grandpa died. Darlin', you are my pride and joy."

"But . . . but now you have Joe."

"I wish," the deep voice grumbled.

"There's plenty of love to go around. Why, we'll be living right up the road from the Academy, so you can come to our house after school and when your mother is traveling. We plan to have plenty of room for grandkids."

"Huh?" DJ pulled back to look Gran in the face.

"I made an offer on a place near the Academy yesterday. Looks as though they'll take it." Joe drew the women into the house.

"My bike."

"You can let it lie there for now." Lindy's voice had lost its edge. Now she just sounded tired. "Let's sit down and hash this out." She reached for her daughter and DJ went into her arms willingly. "You scared me half to death. I should ground you for life." She sniffed and continued. "Amy didn't know where you were. Says you haven't talked to her for days. Bridget said you left earlier this afternoon."

DJ groaned. "Did you call everybody?"

"Just about. Hilary said she knew you'd been bothered about something lately."

"I'm sorry, Mom. Please forgive me."

"Oh, I forgive you, all right, but there are some serious consequences here. You could have gotten lost or murdered or kidnapped or . . ."

"I get the picture. Will a promise to never do something so stupid again help?"

Gran and Joe sat down on the couch, holding hands like two kids. Lindy took Gran's wing chair, and DJ folded herself down to the floor.

"Now, then. Start from the beginning and tell us what's been on your mind."

"Easy, Joe. She isn't a delinquent, you know." Gran squeezed his hand and laid her head against his shoulder.

DJ wrapped her hands around her bent legs and did as he asked. By the time she finished, her throat felt as raw as if she'd been running during the hottest time of the day.

"Now it's your turn, Lindy. Let's get this out on the table."

By the time they'd all talked, the grandfather clock bonged eleven times.

DJ's stomach growled in time with it.

"Oh, you poor child! Didn't you have any dinner?" Gran started to rise, but Joe stopped her.

"The three of you keep talking. I'll bring something in for all of us."

When he left the room, DJ whispered, "Is he always this nice?"

"Of course, DJ, when you give him a chance." Lindy leaned forward. "Just like you didn't give any of us a chance to work things out. You panicked. Now you and I'll be living here together, just the two of us. I think learning to communicate will be rather important, don't you?" She held up a cautioning hand. "I know, I'm as much at fault as you—more so since I'm the adult. But we *will* make it."

DJ knew she should say something in response, but words seemed to have vacated her brain. She just nodded.

"I'm glad to see the two of you coming to this agreement. That's the first step. Now we need to leave the rest of it in God's hands." Gran reached out and patted their hands.

DJ scooted over by Gran. "So, when's the wedding?"

"We haven't discussed it again . . ."

"As soon as we can arrange it. Two weeks max." Joe set a plate with ham sandwiches on the table and popped open a bag of tortilla chips.

DJ squirmed at the way he butted into the conversation. But she kept her mouth closed—this time. *You're learning,* she congratulated herself. "Will I have to wear a dress?"

"As one of my bridesmaids, you sure enough will."

"What?"

"Your mother will be the other."

"And my son Robert will be the best man. Bobby and Billy thought they should be included, but we vetoed that idea."

"Sounds as if it's all planned." DJ swallowed quick so she wouldn't get accused of talking with her mouth full. Ham and cheese had never tasted so good. "Oh no!" She leaped to her feet and headed for the garage. "My bike."

"Serves you right if it's stolen," Lindy grumbled.

When DJ returned, she sat at her mother's knee. "What are you going to add to the list in there to punish me for tonight?" She figured knowing was better than guessing.

"I'm not sure yet. Once I get over wanting to strangle you, I'll think better." She leaned forward and wrapped her arms around her daughter. "I sure hope you've learned a lesson. If you do it again—"

"I won't."

"If you do, I'm going to call the police—and I know just where to start." She hugged DJ hard.

DJ snuggled closer. "What can we do about James?"

"Nothing, I'm afraid. Just be his friend. He needs one right now, that's for sure. I'm surprised he hasn't been in more trouble already."

"Military school, ugh." DJ shivered. When a yawn caught her, she covered her mouth with one hand. Even so, it traveled around the room.

"I'll be getting on home. Sure glad we're not putting out an APB on you, kid. Melanie, you want to walk me to the door?"

DJ picked up the remains of the meal and carried them into the kitchen. She glanced out the window to see Joe and Gran kissing by his car.

"Cute, aren't they?" Lindy asked from right behind her.

"Guess so." Tonight *cute* didn't sound quite so bad. As Gran always said, "If ya can't lick 'em, join 'em." Tonight she'd done just that.

Saying her prayers came easy. "Thank you for my room and my bed. Sure beats the rocks in Briones. And for Mom and Gran—and Joe, too. But, God, I'm kind of scared. There are just so many changes happening." She paused to think. "And help James. Amen." She didn't include her nightly request for a horse this time. Not asking was part of her punishment. And in the morning she had to make up with Amy, if Amy was willing.

"God, please help me talk to Amy. Forgive me for the mess I made.

I really want to listen to you. Could you maybe speak a little louder, please?"

She overslept and arrived at the Academy late. James was shoveling out stalls.

"Amy is out in the arena." He leaned on the handle of his shovel.

"How ya doing?" DJ crossed to the other aisle.

"I'll live." He went back to his job. "You can ride Gray Bar later if you want."

"Thanks, but I can't. I'm grounded from pleasure riding."

"What?"

"It's a long story. But thanks for the offer. Later, all right?" At his nod, she turned and trotted out of the barn into the sunlight. She blinked and dodged just in time. Amy's horse stopped before stepping on her.

"Hey, you don't have to run me down." She shaded her eyes with her hand. "Amy, I need to talk to you."

"So talk." Amy crossed her arms over the pommel of her saddle.

"I'm sorry I've been such a dumbbell."

"Me too."

"I've missed you."

"Me too."

"Is that all you can say?" DJ ran a hand down the horse's gray neck. It was easier to study the swirls on the hide than to look up at her friend. "You still want to be my friend?"

"Of course. I just figured you wanted out. I never stopped being your friend." Amy tightened the reins to keep her horse still. "What happened?"

"Can we talk later? I'm way behind. You have no idea how stupid I've been."

"You said it, not me." She nudged her horse forward and into the shadow of the barn. "Bridget wants to see you," she called over her shoulder.

"Okay." DJ started toward the office but turned and trotted down the aisle to see Patches first. At least she'd have him to train and she could jump James' Arab. That ought to give her time to earn some more money for her own horse.

"Hi, fella, you miss me?" She rubbed the gelding's swirled white patch. Digging a carrot out of her pocket, she fed him and told him how handsome he was. "Gotta go. I'll be back to clean your stall in a bit."

"DJ, your mother called me." Bridget pointed to the chair beside the desk. "She said you are grounded from riding for a month but can do your regular chores around here. Is that correct?"

DJ stared at a spot above Bridget's head. "Yeah, but I can still train horses. I'm only grounded from riding for pleasure and classes."

"I see. Well, you know how I feel about self-discipline." She waited for a nod from DJ. "I believe we learn best by accepting our mistakes. So, to help you remember yours so you won't do them again, I have assigned Patches to Hilary for training. Megs will be turned out to pasture for a month. That should give her leg time to heal. Is there anything you would like to say?"

DJ clamped her jaw and shook her head. She *couldn't* say anything.

Chapter • 17

By the time I can ride again, school will start. I won't get to show in the Labor Day Horse show. "What a zero for a summer."

"Tough break?" Hilary fell in step beside her.

"You don't know the half of it." DJ sucked in a deep breath. The rock in her throat made it difficult.

"You'll get through it. I can feel in my bones that something good is coming for you." Hilary turned and walked backward. "And my bones never lie."

Her effort at making DJ smile nearly worked.

By the time she finished her usual work and the extra stalls Bridget had assigned her, DJ longed for a cold soda. But she'd left all her money at home in her box until she could put it back in the bank. The hose would have to do. She ran it until it was cold, drank, and washed off her arms. If only she could go riding, she'd feel better. Right now she understood what jail might feel like.

At least it was old times for her and Amy. They rode their bikes home, promising to talk later.

"Oh, I forgot. I can't!" DJ wailed. "You're on my grounded list. Unless we have a pony party, which we do tomorrow."

"Great." Amy shook her head. "When you mess up, you really mess up."

The next morning James wore a face that dug a furrow in the dirt. "They're not selling my horse."

"That's great!" DJ slapped him on the shoulder.

"They're shipping her back with me to the military school so I can join the equestrian program. I'm sorry, DJ, I was hoping you could train and jump her."

DJ swallowed the disappointment. Maybe God didn't think she needed a horse after all. "That's okay, thanks for the thought." She kicked a piece of crushed rock off to the side. "You know when you leave?"

"School starts the day after Labor Day, so I'll miss the show. You said you'd write."

"I will. I better get to work. Don't worry, James. Hilary said something good is coming my way." *And I just wish it would get here.*

The time before the wedding flew by in spite of the strict rules DJ's mother had laid out for her. Gran painted, cooked, and sewed in a daze. One afternoon she took DJ shopping.

"You need school clothes and a dress. I think a long dress would look lovely on you."

"A dress?" DJ slumped in the car seat. "I hate dresses, you know that."

"For *my* wedding, you will wear a dress. And since Joe is in such a rush that I don't have time to sew one, we'll do the shop-till-we-drop routine."

I'm dropping already. But DJ was learning to keep her mouth shut. After all the trouble she caused Gran, at least she could wear a dress. She didn't have to like it, though. "No ruffles and lace."

"All right. No ruffles and lace." Gran patted DJ's knee. "But that'll probably make for a longer shopping trip."

DJ groaned.

They started at the Sun Valley Mall and ended up at the Broadway Plaza in Walnut Creek.

"My feet hurt." DJ collapsed on a chair in a coffee shop.

"At least your feet are young. What about mine?" Gran propped her elbows on the table. "We're about out of stores, darlin'. If we don't find something at Nordstrom's, we'll have to go down to Stoneridge Mall or into the city."

DJ laid her head down on her crossed arms. "We bought enough school clothes. You know I hate shopping, and I hate shopping for a dress even more." She raised her head enough for a half-hearted grin. "But if I have to shop, going with you is the best. Thanks for my new school clothes."

But even she bit her tongue when she looked in the mirror a while later. It *was* the perfect dress. The deep aqua made her eyes sparkle and the simple lines disguised her flat chest. She looked grown up.

"Wow."

"Darla Jean, I knew you would be a beauty someday. I think some-day is now." Gran smoothed a hand over the gauzy fabric.

DJ could see Gran was fighting back tears. "Come on, Gran. It's just me, horse-crazy DJ." But even she couldn't help taking an extra twirl just to feel the cloth swish about her legs. "Bummer."

"Now what?"

"Now I need new shoes."

Gran laughed in her tinkly I'm-really-happy voice. "Shoe depart-ment, here we come!"

By the day before the wedding, DJ and Amy had given three more pony parties, worked extra hours at the Academy, and tried to keep Gran on track. For the first time in her years of illustrating, she was behind on a deadline.

"Just call 'em and tell 'em you're getting married. You'll finish the book later." DJ sucked in half a can of soda in a single chug.

"I can't do that." Gran peered at the half-finished painting. "I'm just not happy with this one."

"Don't worry, Gran. Being in love makes everyone looney."

"How would you know?" She daubed some darker green on one of the trees.

"Television, movies. Sappy looks go with the territory." DJ hurriedly left the room when her grandmother threatened her with a paintbrush. She returned a bit later with a flat package all wrapped in silvery wed-ding paper. "Here, I can't wait till tomorrow."

Gran sat in her chair and carefully removed the ribbon. "Just rip it." DJ sat in front of her, legs crossed.

Smiling, Gran shook her head. "It's not every day one gets to open wedding gifts. I'm going to enjoy every minute." At last the paper fell away and she held the framed picture in her hands.

"I didn't know what to get you."

"This couldn't be more perfect." The jumping horse and rider was DJ's best picture ever. She'd colored it with pastels. Even all the shading had come out right.

"I'll hang this in a place of honor." Gran held the frame up to catch the morning light. "You chose a perfect mat and frame to set it off. Darlin', you have a real flair for this."

"They helped me over at Frame City." The seventy-five dollars it had cost had sure hurt her bank account. But she'd wanted it to be perfect.

Gran set the picture aside and placed both hands on DJ's cheeks. "Nothing you could give me could mean more. I know Joe will agree with me. Thank you." She brushed away the tears that threatened to spill over. "My, I sure have turned into a waterworks lately. I better get back to my own pictures."

But Gran had her paintings finished, boxed, and ready to ship by the next morning. Her suitcases were mostly packed when DJ came yawning down the stairs.

"Did you sleep at all, Mother?" Lindy folded one more garment into the waiting luggage before zipping them all shut.

"Thank you, my dear." Gran yawned. "I never would have made it without your help."

"This is just terrific—the bride is so tired she's collapsing before the wedding." Lindy looked around the room in case she was forgetting something. "Darla Jean, you need to get a move on. I'll do your hair if you like."

"My hair? I thought I'd wear it in a snood, like I do for the shows." DJ backed away.

"Some curls would be nice, you know. We could pull it back on the sides and leave it in curls down the back." Lindy's hands described the style. "We bought you flowers to wear, too."

DJ groaned. "I think I'm going to be sick."

"Speaking of sick, Mrs. Yamamoto called. Amy broke out this

morning, so she won't be at the wedding. And no, you can't go over there. We don't have time."

DJ felt her face. What if she broke out in the chicken pox today, too? Then she could stay home. She shook her head. No, she didn't want to miss the circus.

But it wasn't a circus. She led the way down the aisle at their brick-walled church. Straight ahead, over the altar, Jesus cuddled a group of children in a stained-glass window that glowed in the sunlight. Lindy followed with Gran on her arm.

DJ looked up to Joe in time to see two tears glisten on his cheeks. Gran took his arm and smiled up at him. As they stood in the golden light from the window, it shone like a special blessing.

"Dearly beloved," the minister began. "We are gathered here in the sight of God and this company . . ."

DJ fought a lump in her throat. This wouldn't be happening if God didn't want it to. Gran had prayed for all of them. DJ added her own request. *God, please make Gran happier than she's ever been. I love her so much.* Crying at weddings was silly—wasn't it?

Gran said her vows in her soft southern accent, all the love of creation shining in her eyes.

DJ heard her mother sniff. She didn't dare look at her. *I am not going to cry.*

"You may kiss the bride." The minister's words brought an end to the ceremony. "I am proud to introduce to you Mr. and Mrs. Joe Crowder." Gran and Joe turned to face the congregation and everyone clapped.

They really did look nice together, Joe so tall and silvery, Gran so small and golden. DJ sniffed in sync with her mother. The music burst forth in applause as Gran and Joe started back down the aisle, shaking hands with friends and relatives as they went. Lindy took the arm of Robert, Joe's oldest son, and smiled up at him through her tears. DJ took the younger son's arm.

"You look like a million dollars, DJ," Andy whispered as they left the sanctuary.

"Thanks to Gran." DJ stood straighter and smiled up at him. Did this make him her uncle? They followed the newlyweds down the aisle and out the door.

The reception was being held in the fellowship room, one building over.

"DJ, we was quiet, wasn't we?" The twins each grabbed a handful of her dress. "Daddy said if we be good, you could take us for a ride on Bandit someday."

DJ stooped over and gave each of them a hug. "I surely will." Funny how she needed to hug someone, as if there was so much love sloshing around inside her it might run out. Is this what weddings did for people?

"Today?" Bobby—or was it Billy—asked hopefully.

"Sorry, not today, but soon." She looked from one beaming face to the other. "How am I gonna tell you two apart? I know, you . . ." She pointed to the one on her right.

"Bobby." He supplied her with a name.

"You have a freckle on the end of your nose."

"Are you sure it's not frosting?" Their father appeared at her side. "The newlyweds are looking for you." He pointed across the room. "Over there."

"Thanks." DJ made her way through the crowd to where Gran and Joe were accepting best wishes, along with bunches of hugs and laughter. Just standing by them made DJ feel bubbly.

"Oh, there you are, darlin'." Gran drew DJ into one of her special hugs and whispered in her ear, "Thank you for looking so lovely and for being my maid of honor. I'm so proud of you."

DJ couldn't disguise a sniff this time. "I miss you already."

"But I'll be back soon. Joe has something to ask you. He was going to wait till later, but he's as bad as I am when it comes to keeping secrets." She wiped her eyes with a tissue and tucked another into DJ's hand.

DJ turned to the man standing behind her. She reached out to shake his hand, but instead put her arms up for a hug. She could hear both her mother and grandmother sniffing now. At the rate they were going, they'd all be in tears soon. Including her.

"Thank you, my dear. You've made your grandmother very happy today." He kept an arm around her shoulders and eased her over closer to the wall. "I have kind of a suggestion, or a . . . a . . ."

DJ looked at him with a question. Surely a police captain wasn't having a hard time saying something? "A . . . ?" She tried to help him.

"Well, you heard me talk about Major?"

DJ nodded. "Your horse on the mounted patrol."

"He's going to retire with me, but he has a lot of good years ahead of him, good working years. I just thought maybe he'd be a good horse for you—if you're willing, that is."

"W-willing? Major would be mine?"

Joe nodded. "Melanie says you'd have to pay for him. Something about learning responsibility."

"I only have four hundred dollars."

"That's right about what I thought would be good."

"Major would be mine."

"As soon as I retire, in another month."

"I will have a horse of my own." If she said the words often enough, maybe she would begin to believe them. Hilary had been right. Something good *was* coming her way. She not only had a grandfather and a whole new family, but a horse of her own. A horse named Major. Get ready, Olympics. DJ Randall was on her way!

Acknowledgments

My thanks to Joanie Jagoda for her expert horsewoman's critique and suggestions.

Book Two

DJ'S CHALLENGE

*To my mentor and friend
Colleen Reece,
who's given me tools
to make writing easier and
encouragement to keep
growing on.*

Chapter • 1

Being grounded was the pits. Even though it *was* her own fault for almost running away, she *had* come back. They hadn't had to call the police or anything. Darla Jean Randall, DJ to anyone who wanted to remain on her good side, stared at the telephone and tried to forget the dumb things she'd done. She couldn't even call her best friend, Amy Yamamoto, since the phone was off limits, too. Amy could be dying from chicken pox for all DJ knew—as if her mother cared.

Now . . . if someone called her, would it be okay to talk? DJ shook her head, her wavy, golden ponytail slapping from side to side. She'd never been grounded like this before. And the few times she had been, Gran, her mother's mother, had been there to clarify the rules. Or bend them.

The thought of Gran turned the ache into a pain, one that seemed to surround her heart and squeeze. Last Saturday—three days and twelve hours ago—Gran had married soon-to-be-retired Police Captain Joe Crowder. Right now they were somewhere off the coast of Mexico, living it up on a honeymoon cruise.

DJ pushed herself out of Gran's winged recliner and scuffed her bare feet all the way up the stairs to her bedroom. She crawled into bed and pulled the covers up over her head. Maybe it was a good thing school was starting pretty soon after all.

Pedaling her bike past Amy's house in the early morning brought on another pang of loneliness, as if the again empty house she'd left behind weren't enough. *Is this what latchkey kids feel like? Am I a latchkey kid?* She fingered the key she wore on a chain around her neck. She snorted and pedaled harder. At fourteen she was pretty grown-up to be called a kid of any kind.

Amy had to get over the chicken pox in the next couple days. Then at least they could talk on the way back and forth to the Academy where they both worked. Maybe if she could shoot the breeze with Amy, she wouldn't miss Gran so much.

The horses nickering down the aisle brought the first smile of the morning to her mouth. She put two fingers between her lips and blew, the whistle echoing off the rafters of the low red barn. The nickers turned to whinnies, and where the stalls' upper doors had been opened, her equine friends nodded to her.

"Hey, you about broke my eardrums." Hilary Jones, one of the older riders whom DJ looked up to, strode out of the tack room, English saddle over her arm.

"Sorry." The grin DJ shot her made the apology an out-and-out fib.

"Sure you are. And so are all your friends. You riding today?"

DJ shook her head.

"Sorry."

DJ dug in the sack of carrots she kept in the stable refrigerator. "That's okay. At least I won't be grounded for the rest of my life."

"Just seems like it?"

"Yep." DJ picked up a bucket of brushes and combs. "I gotta get to work. With Amy home sick, I never get a break."

"I'll help you after I finish practicing. We're still having trouble with the square oxer. Prince keeps dropping his back feet before the second bar, so either he doesn't get it or I come down on him midfence." As Hilary headed for her horse's stall, she called over her shoulder, "Hang in there."

"Right." DJ hoisted her bucket to check to see if it contained a hoof-pick. If only Diablo were here. But the fiery chestnut gelding she'd been training and showing for the Ortegas had moved with them to Texas. There had been too many changes in her life lately.

She started down the line. Each horse got a carrot snack, a heavy dose of loving, and a thorough grooming. DJ clipped them on the hot walker while she shoveled out the dirty shavings.

"Easy, fella," she cautioned a rambunctious school horse. "You'll get your workout in a bit." She snapped him to the crossties since he had a habit of sneaking in a nip or two. "You just think you own the world, that's all." She tapped his foot with the pick. The horse stood there. She ran her hand down the back of his foreleg and pulled at his fetlock. He snorted.

DJ stood upright and clamped her hands on her hips. "You would pick today to be difficult." He turned to gaze at her. She could swear she saw an imp dancing in his eye. He nosed her back pocket. "No way. Bad horses don't get second treats. Now give me that foot."

This time, the horse let her raise the hoof and rest it on her bent knee so she could pick out the compacted manure and shavings. She could feel his breath on her rear. "You bite me, and you'll be dog food for sure."

She moved to the rear hoof. It took three tries before he let her pick it up. "What's the matter with you, get up on the wrong side of the stall or something?" She glanced up to check his ears. Sure enough, they were laid back. "All right, knock it off." She felt him relax. Only now he leaned his weight on her. By the time she finished, she could feel sweat trickling down between her shoulder blades. She trotted the problem horse out to the hot walker and, after snapping him in place, gave him a slap on the rump. "Work off some of that orneriness before your riders come."

"You want to ride Gray Bar?" James, the former academy terror who'd only recently become DJ's friend, stopped her dog trot to the next stall.

"I wish." DJ wiped a hand across her damp forehead.

"Still grounded?"

"Right. You okay?"

James shrugged. " 'Bout the same. I've been accepted at West Virginia Military Academy. Great, huh?" The look on his face said it was anything but.

"When do you leave?"

"I'm not sure. Too soon—or not soon enough if my mom and dad have anything to say about it." He turned and continued brushing his gray Arab filly.

DJ stroked the filly's broad cheeks and dished face. "She is so beautiful." Gray Bar nosed DJ's pocket. "Sorry, girl. I'm all out of treats."

James brushed his way to the filly's rump. "If you wanted to ride her, I wouldn't tell."

DJ could get away with it. Bridget Sommersby, owner of the Academy, wasn't here; she had a meeting somewhere this morning. And none of the other student workers would rat on her. DJ wanted to ride Gray Bar so bad she could feel it like a toothache.

She sucked in a deep breath. "Thanks, James. But I gave my word. Not riding for a couple weeks never killed anyone." She could hear Gran's voice in her ear. *A real lady always keeps her word.* While being a true southern gentlewoman like Gran was not at the top of DJ's priorities, she knew keeping her word was a mark of a Christian, too. And that *was* important.

"See ya, I gotta get back to work." By the time she'd finished, the sun blazed well past the sky's zenith. She could hear Bridget, back from her meeting, giving instructions to a class in the jumping ring—a class DJ would be part of if she hadn't been grounded. Megs, Bridget's mare, now retired from the show and jumping ring, needed a good workout. But jumping classes, like nearly everything else that could be called fun, were forbidden while DJ was grounded. Why, oh why, had she panicked and run like that?

DJ swung aboard her bike and pedaled toward home—and an empty house. If she hadn't been in such a hurry to escape it that morning, she could have packed a lunch. There was always tack to clean. But the rumblings from her midsection nearly drowned out the singing of her tires on the pavement.

How come an empty house even smelled lonely? She checked the machine for messages—none. After tossing a pound of frozen hamburger in the sink to thaw for tonight's tacos, she stuck her nose in the refrigerator. Baloney sandwich? Nah. Tuna? Yuck. Grilled cheese? She pulled the block of cheddar from the door and cut off a chunk. The groan and then hum of the fridge made her jump.

When she ambled back into the kitchen again, evening had fallen. Chores, drawing, and making dinner had used up most of her time. DJ glared at the silent telephone hanging on the wall. *Ring, you stupid machine.* She paced into Gran's studio, which replaced what would have been the family room in most homes. Another silent phone took up part of a lamp table. Silent like the entire house. A house that, until now, had always rung with Gran's chuckles and her hymns on the stereo. Always smelled good from something baking or cooking, and always wrapped comforting arms around those who lived there. Always. Except now. At least the tacos DJ had made for dinner canceled the empty smell. Her mother did like tacos if she hadn't already eaten.

DJ glanced up at the clock. Her mother should be home from class pretty soon. Lindy Randall was on her way to a Master's degree, earned after her day job selling guns, flak vests, and other supplies to police departments. Most of Lindy's life was spent working, traveling for work, studying, and dressing in knockout clothes. She claimed her expensive wardrobe helped her make a better living for her family—or at least that was her excuse for spending so much money on the latest styles.

DJ looked down at her grungy jeans. The horses at the Academy where she worked and rode didn't care if her jeans had a hole in one knee and smelled like a stable. In fact, they liked it. One shoulder of her navy blue T-shirt sported horse slobber to prove it. She glanced in the sink. She needed to put stuff in the dishwasher and wipe down the counters.

"The sprinklers. Gotta get that done first." Even her voice sounded loud in the empty house. Bare feet slapped across the cedar deck to the backyard, where she turned on the sprinklers and stood watching to make sure the lawn and flower beds were getting their needed soaking. Now that evening had come to the Pleasant Hill, California, community, less water would be wasted in the heat. Gran and DJ had spent hours together learning how they could best help the environment.

How come everything pointed back to Gran?

Think of Major! A month after Joe and Gran came back, Joe would retire from the mounted patrol. His horse, Major, would retire with him. But Major wouldn't be put out to pasture. He would belong to DJ. Joe said the $380 she'd saved from the pony parties and all her other money-raising schemes would be enough to pay for him.

DJ hurried back into the house and up the stairs to her horse-decorated bedroom. A picture of Joe on Major, both in uniform, perched in the middle of her desk. DJ flicked on the lamp. The white blaze down the blood bay's face and his two white socks gleamed in the light. Joe said Major was the best horse and friend anyone could have. And he liked to jump.

DJ raised her eyes to the poster on the wall. The five entwined Olympic gold rings shone above the horse and rider jumping a triple. She repeated her daily affirmation. "One day I, DJ, will jump in the Olympics." Grabbing her sketch pad, she flopped down on the bed. Within a heartbeat the drawing she'd been working on that afternoon absorbed her concentration.

"Darla Jean Randall!"

DJ's gaze flew first to the clock—it was after nine—and then to the window. It was nearly dark. Where had the time gone? She leaped off her bed and down the stairs. The kitchen! She'd left the kitchen a mess.

"Hi, Mom."

Lindy Randall stood at the oak dining room table, sorting the mail with one hand and rubbing her forehead with the other.

Uh-oh, that meant a headache. DJ closed her eyes. Not a good night to have left a mess.

Lindy dropped the envelopes onto the table and used the fingertips of both hands to rub her temples. "You'd think you could do the little bit I ask of you without being reminded." The words came out hard and biting.

"But, Mom—"

"No *buts*. You made the mess, you clean it up. That doesn't seem too much to ask."

"I thought—"

"No, you didn't. You never think, you just act."

"I made dinner for both of us." DJ reared back at the word *never*.

"You know how I hate a messy kitchen."

"Yeah, well, excuse me. I thought maybe you'd like something to eat when you got home. Sorry I'm not Gran."

"You don't have to bring Gran into this. Your thoughtlessness is between you and me. I raised you to—"

"You never raised me. Gran did. You're never home—you couldn't raise a flea." DJ spun around and headed for the kitchen.

"Darla Jean, you can't talk to me like that."

DJ threw the pans in the sink, the clatter making as angry a sound as her stomping.

Better cool it, DJ, she warned herself. But the fires raging at her mother's accusations refused to bank.

A glass shattering against the cast-iron skillet in the sink brought her up short. A line of blood trickled from a spot on the back of her hand where a sliver of glass had embedded itself.

Say you're sorry! "I'm not sorry," she muttered into the back of her hand as she sucked the blood out of the wound. She could feel the piece of glass with her tongue.

"If you can't be polite, you can just go to your room."

"I'm cleaning up the kitchen, can't you tell?" DJ let the door of the dishwasher clang open. How would she get the glass out? Blood dripped down over her fingers. Oh, great. What had she done? Cut a vein or something?

Gingerly she picked out the pieces of glass in the bottom of the sink and dropped them in the trash. She couldn't apply pressure to the wound to make it stop bleeding. She ran cold water from the tap over her hand. Pink blood stained the white enamel. Maybe she'd bleed to death—then she'd find out if her mother really cared. At least there'd be no one around to leave a mess.

The cut stung like fury. "Stop bleeding, you stupid thing." All the while she tossed stuff in the trash, put dishes in the dishwasher, and scrubbed the frying pan. "I shoulda just had peanut butter. Why'd I try to make something *she* likes? Never does any good anyway." Her mutterings were drowned out by the running water.

The blood kept dripping.

She wiped up the counters. Each swipe of the dishcloth wiped up watery drops of blood. How long did it take to bleed to death? Could she be so lucky?

Chapter • 2

"Darla Jean Randall, what have you done now?"

"Cut myself, as if you care." DJ leaned over the sink. Wasn't she losing an awful lot of blood?

"Let me look at that." Mom grasped DJ's hand, carefully keeping it over the sink. "How did it happen?"

"Broken glass. There's still a piece in there." DJ wanted to yank her hand out of her mother's, but the warm contact felt good.

"Here." Lindy pulled off several paper towels and bunched them under the dripping hand. "Let's go up to the bathroom where the light's better. Maybe we can see the glass then and get it out with tweezers." Her voice still hadn't lost its hard edge, but at least she wasn't yelling.

DJ bit her lip against the pain. How come such a little cut could bleed so much?

Upstairs in the bathroom with good light, a magnifying glass, and steady hands, Mom lifted the glass sliver free and, with both thumbs holding the cut open, sluiced water over it for several minutes.

DJ squinted her eyes against the sting. She would not complain—no matter what. Letting her anger rule her like that made her feel like sticking her head in the toilet bowl and flushing. *Why can't I control my temper? What's the matter with me? I pray about it and pray about it, and look what happens.* She didn't dare glance up because she didn't want to catch her mother's gaze in the mirror.

"Here, put some pressure on this while I get out the Band-Aids." Lindy looked up just as DJ did, and, sure enough, their eyes locked in the mirror.

"Oh, DJ, what are we going to do?" Lindy put an arm around her daughter's shoulders and squeezed.

"I'm sorry I left the mess and then mouthed off. I hate myself when I do that."

"Join the club. Just because I had a headache was no reason to light into you." She finished drying DJ's hand. "How's it feel?"

"Hurts." DJ lifted her fingers from the cut so her mother could apply antibiotic ointment and a bandage. "Thanks for getting the glass out. I thought I might bleed to death or something."

"Thought it or wished it?"

"Huh?"

"You heard me. I remember being fourteen and fighting with my mother. Sometimes you remind me so much of me that it scares the bejeebers out of me."

"You used to fight with Gran?" DJ couldn't believe her ears. "Gran never fights with anyone. She says a lady never raises her voice."

"Gran wasn't always as genteel as she is now. But then, I really knew how to push her buttons. Kinda like you do mine."

DJ smoothed the ends of the tan plastic strip down with her forefinger.

"When you get a southern woman riled, you've got a real problem on your hands." Lindy rubbed her forehead again. "I need to change and—"

"Mom, you've got blood on your suit." DJ touched the spots on the lower sleeve of the cream silk. "I'm sorry."

"It'll come out. How about getting me a glass of water and two aspirins? If your hand works now, that is."

DJ looked up in time to catch a smile lifting the corners of her mother's mouth. Her mother was teasing her. Actually trying to make a joke. And after a big fight, too. *Maybe miracles really do happen.*

DJ took the stairs two at a time both down and up. She'd finish cleaning the kitchen later.

"Thanks, dear." Lindy swallowed the tablets and collapsed on the bed.

"You need anything else?" DJ stuck her hands in her pockets.

"You wouldn't have a spare million lying around anywhere, would you?"

"Sorry."

"Good night, then. Guess I'll just try to sleep this thing off."

DJ bent down and dropped a kiss on her mother's cheek. The fragrance of expensive perfume filled her nose. "Night." DJ turned at the door. "Thanks for fixing my hand."

"You're welcome." Eyes closed, Lindy waggled her fingers from their place on top of the covers.

DJ fell asleep promising both herself and her heavenly Father she wouldn't lose her temper like that again. One thing she was grateful for, her restrictions hadn't been extended. Was that thanks to the cut? Probably a good thing she hadn't bled to death after all. "When I have kids," she promised herself, "I'm not gonna say 'you always' or 'you never,' like Mom does. Nobody does things 'always' or 'never.'"

In the morning she found a note on the counter.

"Sorry for the way I blew up at you. How about going out for dinner tonight; maybe we can do some real talking. I should be home early. Love, Mom."

DJ read the note a second and third time. *Her* mother apologizing? On one hand she felt she could touch the stars, on the other, an ant belly would be higher off the floor than her feelings. She grabbed a couple of food bars and an apple, stuffing them into her backpack along with a can of soda. At least now she could stay at the Academy longer. The house could stay empty all day.

"Bridget wants to see you," Hilary called when DJ walked into the barn.

"What for?"

"How should I know?"

"Oh, okay, thanks." DJ threw the words over her shoulder, already halfway to the office.

Bridget Sommersby, Academy owner and former Olympic contender, sat at her oak desk behind piles of papers, magazines, file folders, and a frayed girth strap. The pained look on her face and the ledger in front of her said she was working on the books. Her feelings about the bookkeeping end of her business were well known to all who knew her.

"You wanted me?" DJ knew that if she was in trouble, bookkeeping time was not a good time to get called on the carpet. This was worse than the principal's office.

"Hi, DJ, sit down. You saved me." The smile on Bridget's square-jawed face told DJ she was not in trouble. Bridget stuck the pencil she'd been using into her slicked-into-a-bun blond hair. "How are things going?"

DJ sank down into the wooden chair by the desk. "Going."

"That bad, huh?" At DJ's nod, Bridget pulled the pencil back out and tapped the eraser on the desk. "How much longer do you have in jail?"

DJ felt her heavy mood begin to lighten. "A week. Guess I'll live through it."

"Not riding is rough." Bridget leaned back in her swivel chair. She let the pause lengthen while she studied DJ over the tops of her horn-rimmed half glasses. "How would you like Patches back?" She raised a hand to suggest DJ not leap out of her chair. DJ settled back on the edge of her seat. "Hilary has already started classes at Diablo Valley College and just does not have the time to train and work anything but her own mount right now. So, while I agree with your mother on the importance of discipline, as an employer, I need you to work Patches. I take it this would not cause you unhappiness?"

"Not in the least." DJ could respond formally when needed. But she couldn't disguise the bounce of pleasure that rocked the chair.

"Fine, here is the training program I have set up." Bridget handed a sheet of instructions across the desk. "Hopefully Amy will be back soon, because I would like you to work with Patches an hour a day at least—for now. His owners want him ready for their young son to ride. Mrs. Johnson plans to take lessons once a week on him, too, after school starts."

"Wouldn't the boy do better on a pony at first? Maybe like Bandit? Patches is pretty big." DJ sat on her hands so she wouldn't bite her nails.

"True." Bridget nodded. "That is a good suggestion. I will talk to the McDougalls. Maybe exchange some board for using Bandit as a schooling horse." The phone at her right hand rang. "Talk to you later."

DJ was out the door almost before Bridget answered "hello." She got to ride again! It felt as though she hadn't been on a horse for a hundred years or more.

She rushed through her assigned stalls, making sure each horse got its required care, but not spending her normal amount of time scratching ears and giving love pats. She left Patches till last.

"Howdy, Patches, old boy. You ready for some training?" The big dark bay snuffled her hair, then rubbed his forehead against her shoulder. "You're just a sweetie, you know that?" DJ leaned down to retrieve two brushes from the bucket, one for each hand. "Let's get you all shined up and ready to work." She kept up a running monologue, her tongue moving in rhythm with her hands while she brushed, combed his tail, and picked hooves. The white splotch between his eyes gleamed white in the dim light.

"You're going to make a real flashy show horse someday, you know that?" She finished by wiping down his face with a soft brush. She dropped the pick and brushes back in her bucket and set it outside the stall door. Once he was saddled and bridled, she led him out and trotted him over to the ring, to mount inside the gate. Just swinging her leg over the Western saddle and settling into the seat felt like coming home. Even though DJ would rather ride English, her specialty, Patches' owners had requested Western training, at least for now. So Western it was.

She started the neck-reining review, turning him first in circles to the right and then the left, followed by figure eights. Patches let his displeasure at the slow pace be known as they moved from a walk to a jog. Instead of an easy-on-the-rider jog, he wanted to keep up a bone-jarring trot.

"Easy, fella." DJ repeatedly pulled him down. "Until you can manage this, you can't go any faster." When he refused to follow the figure-eight pattern, she brought him to a stop. He wasn't happy with that, either, and he showed it by jigging to the side.

"You know, your manners leave a lot to be desired." The gelding tossed his head, jangling the bit, and stomped his front feet. DJ kept him in place. "I think tomorrow we'll put you on the hot walker so you can work some of this off before our training time." Patches snorted and sighed, as if giving up.

"Good fella." This time he went through his paces without a scolding.

"You are very good with him, DJ." Bridget had stopped to watch without DJ noticing. "I agree, putting a beginning rider up on him could cause some real problems."

"Whoever green-broke him let him get away with murder." DJ brought the horse to a stop in front of Bridget, who was leaning on the aluminum rail.

"He likes to run, that is for sure." Bridget reached out and stroked the gelding's nose. "But he will catch a judge's eye in the ring."

DJ leaned forward and stroked the now-sweaty neck. "That's what I told him. Okay, fella, back at it. Ready for a lope? A nice, easy rocking-chair lope?"

"Good luck." Bridget pushed away from the fence.

Half an hour later, Patches still fought the restrictions. He did *not* want to lope, he wanted to run. DJ dismounted and led him over to the barn, where she reached for a lead shank to snap onto his halter.

"Here, I'll hold him." James took the reins.

"Hey, James, thanks. You see what a pill he is?" DJ entered the tack room and returned with a running martingale. She undid the cinch and slipped the loop over it, settling the leather between Patches' front legs. Then she slipped the reins through the rings and checked to make sure all the adjustments were correct.

"That should help you with him." James stroked the horse's shoulder and helped adjust the leather straps.

"At least he won't be able to toss his head around." DJ patted the gelding's nose. "Sorry, fella, but you asked for it."

"I'll get the gate." James started across the dusty parking area.

"If I didn't know better, I'd say someone new is living in that boy's body." DJ swung aboard while muttering to no one in particular.

"You got it." Hilary led her mount into the sunlight. "You sure did work a miracle with that kid."

"Me?" DJ stopped herself from signaling Patches to move forward. She snapped her jaw closed.

"Well, he was buggin' you the worst, and then you worked at becoming his friend."

"I did?" DJ looked at Hilary as if maybe she'd gotten straw on the brain or something.

"Just a shame he's leaving."

"I know. I wish he weren't. Well, at least he'll be here for the Labor

Day show." DJ thought about Hilary's comments while she rode across the parking lot and into the arena.

"Thanks for helping me, James. You gonna work Gray Bar now?"

"Yeah. After I finish my stalls. You got time to coach me on the V-bend for the trail class? She really hates that."

DJ swallowed a boulder of shock. James was asking for help. Wait till she told Gran! And here she'd laughed and groaned at Gran's suggestion to pray for James.

Patches stopped flat in his journey around the ring. He didn't like the martingale. DJ kept him at a jog, legs firm and whip in hand. Finally, after three circuits, the horse settled down and let out a sigh of defeat. Immediately, DJ nudged him into a lope. At first he tried bolting into a gallop, but the firm hand on his reins wouldn't allow that. And he couldn't get his head up. Sweat popped out on his neck, staining the smooth hide nearly black.

When he finally made two circuits of the arena at a gentle lope, DJ eased him back to a jog, then down to a walk. "Good boy. You might be stubborn, but you'll make it." She walked him around a few more times to help cool him down, then stopped to watch James work the parallel bars laid in a V formation in the center of the ring.

"Don't let her get so excited," DJ called out. "Make her stand in one place until she calms down. When you tense up, she gets tense."

James nodded.

DJ could see him unclench his jaw and his hands on the reins. When he settled down, so did Gray Bar.

"Good. Stay relaxed. Now, easy with your aids on both hands and legs. Use small motions, but be consistent. You can do it."

James backed Gray Bar into the first side of the V. When they reached the point, they stopped.

"Good. Pat her. Tell her she's wonderful. You're doing fine."

With his left leg pressing against her side and the reins signaling to reverse, Gray Bar swung her rump around the sharp turn and continued backing out the opposite leg of the obstacle. When they stood free, James threw his arms around his horse's neck.

"We did it! Didn't tick one pole. First time ever."

DJ felt elation bubbling up. To see James so happy made her want to leap and dance. "I told you you could do it." Her bounce in the saddle made Patches sidestep. "Sorry, guy. Okay, James, now you and

Gray Bar know what it feels like. Do it again, exactly the same." When James settled at the beginning again, DJ leaned forward, hands on her pommel. "You watch this, Patches, 'cause you're going to be doing the same thing pretty soon."

When DJ finally left for home, afternoon traffic was already increasing the car count on Reliez Valley Road. The sun beat down, hot and dry. For a change, the only breeze was created by her moving bike.

"Hey, DJ."

DJ hit the brakes. Amy waved and called from her bedroom window. DJ stopped at the bottom of the upward-sloped drive. "You finally better?"

"I'll be right down."

A moment later, with black hair flying, Amy leaped down the concrete steps and across the lawn.

"Yuk, you look awful." DJ sat with her feet on the ground, holding the bike upright, still on the street. Technically, she wasn't at Amy's house. It wasn't as though DJ had called to her. "When you coming back to work?"

"Probably tomorrow. I'm all scabbed over now—"

"You can say that again." DJ could feel her own smooth skin crawl at the sight of the scabs all over Amy's face and neck. "You had a bad case, didn't you? You gonna have scars?"

"I hope not. I didn't scratch any on my face. Mom gave me gloves to wear at night, and I'm putting Vitamin E on 'em to help stop the scarring. Chicken pox is the pits."

"Yeah, and you never even have any zits." DJ fingered the prize she'd discovered on her chin that morning. "Think you can do the pony show tomorrow?"

Amy shook her head. "Sure, and scare all the kiddies away. I asked John. He said he'd go with you. But we owe him big time—and you know what that means."

"Ugh, paper route some morning when it's still dark."

"You got it." Amy shook her head. "But I didn't know what else to do." She lifted her shirt to show her midriff. "How about this for gross?" Spots covered her tanned skin.

"Pretty bad." DJ put one foot back on a pedal. "I better get going. If I don't get something to drink, I'll faint."

"And I need to get out of the sun. See ya in the morning." Amy spun away and headed for the house. Her little sister, Becky, waved from the doorway.

DJ waved back and pedaled the block to her house. She laid her bike by the garage and unlocked the front door. The empty smell struck her in the face. Not even the refrigerator hummed in the stillness. She sighed, dumped her backpack on the counter, and went out to the garage to put her bike away. There would be nothing out of place tonight to make her mom mad again. They were going out for dinner—and not for fast food, either.

After chugging a glass of water, she nosed in the refrigerator and pulled out stuff for sandwiches. Dumping it all on the counter, she crossed the room to check the answering machine for messages.

"Sorry, DJ, but an unexpected appointment came up, and I have to meet with the client tonight. Not sure what time I'll be home, but it'll probably be late. Let's plan on dinner out tomorrow night." DJ stabbed the Erase button.

If only she could erase the hurt as easily.

Chapter • 3

Wasn't Gran *ever* coming home?

That night, DJ pretended she was asleep when her mother knocked on the bedroom door. She heard the knob turn and the door open, but she lay on her side under the covers as if zonked to the world. *Serves her right*, she thought when she heard her mother sigh. The door closed with a soft click.

In the morning another note lay on the counter. After reading it, DJ crumbled it up and threw it in the trash. Tonight *she* didn't have time to go for dinner. And maybe she'd never have time again.

"You look like you lost your best friend, and I'm right here. What's up?" Amy leaped on her bike to join DJ in the pedal up the hill.

"Nothing." Eating worms was sounding like a possibility. *Fat worms, skinny worms, guess I'll go eat worms.* The song ran through her head.

"Hey, you don't have to bite my head off. I just got out of prison myself."

"You look funny with that hat on."

"Pardon me for living. My mother said that if I wanted to work, I had to wear this straw number out in the sun. My Stetson doesn't have a wide enough brim." Amy shook her head so the floppy straw brim did what it did best—it flopped, then flew up in the wind.

"You'll scare the horses." DJ could feel her good humor coming back. She crested the hill and stopped at the stop sign. "I'm glad you're here."

Amy puffed to a halt beside her. "So why play the grouch?"

"My mother couldn't be bothered to come home in time to take her daughter out to dinner last night like she'd promised, that's all." DJ pushed off again. "No big deal."

The wind felt good on her face when she coasted down the hill to turn into the Academy drive. And now that she'd dumped her gripe on Amy, she could even smile up at a big crow scolding them from a Eucalyptus tree. How come she could be so up one minute and down in the pits the next? Maybe it was PMS. Lindy always blamed half her bad moods on it. DJ coasted to a stop and leaned her bike against the barn in its usual place. Another question to ask Gran—if and when she ever came home.

DJ hurried through her chores at the Academy. Fast brushing and slinging dirty shavings in record time was becoming a habit. She couldn't work Patches until after her class of beginners. "Okay, let's hustle." DJ went down the line, hurrying her girls along.

"DJ, when we going up in Briones again?" Angie, a chronic asthma sufferer, stopped brushing her horse to ask.

"I cleared Friday with Bridget. We'll head out right after our regular class. I told everyone last week."

"I wasn't here."

"Oh, I'm sorry. I should have called." DJ turned to the girl's pregnant mother standing off to the side. "Can Angie come?"

"That'll be fine. Then she can wash her horse in the afternoon to be ready for the show." Angie's mother laid a hand on her big belly. "This baby's due anytime, so we're just going day by day. My neighbor says she'll bring this daughter of mine down to ride if I'm in the hospital."

"Great. Okay, kids, let's get to work." DJ trotted ahead of them to slide the gate open. "Walk to the right please."

All three students grinned at her as they rode into the arena and did as she asked.

"Okay, backs straight but relaxed. Come on, Krissie, keep those reins even. Neck rein to the left—good. Now back to the right." The class proceeded as usual, only this time they were gearing up for a show. DJ treated them just as a judge would, ordering a walk, jog, back to a walk, lope, and reverse and repeat. When they were finished, they lined up in the middle. She walked down the line, inspecting the horses and riders, trying to keep a straight face.

She had them practice picking up their ribbons and leaving the arena. At the end of the hour, she motioned them into the shade of the roof. "You did good. I'm really proud of you. Angie, you gotta keep him on his toes. He'll go to sleep on you if you let him. Sam, remember, when you come up too close on another horse, turn a circle into the ring and come around again so you have plenty of room. Now, all of you, those saddles and bridles need to be so clean they shine. Angie, your horse is due for new shoes."

"Again?" Angie leaned on her saddle horn. "There goes my birthday money."

"The farrier will be here tomorrow. You want me to put your name on the list?"

"I guess." Her sigh could be heard clear into San Francisco.

"Okay, let's get 'em put away. Remember to bring your lunches with you on Friday, packed in saddlebags if you have them, and in smash-proof containers."

"We know."

"Just reminding you. And, Angie, make sure you bring your bee-sting kit." DJ held the gate open and let them file out. Their mothers were already waiting.

Training Patches took up the rest of the morning. She had to fly home to get ready for the pony party. It wouldn't do to go in her grungy clothes. And besides, she needed a shower. Even she could tell the BO wasn't coming from the horses.

When she and Amy's older brother, John, trotted up the street to one of the monstrous new houses at the top of hill on the west side of Reliez Valley Road, they were nearly late. The subdivision was so new, all the trees in the yards still looked like sticks. But the sodded lawns were green and kids played in the street. Some of them even ran after the pony until DJ told them to stop.

Balloons bobbed above the mailbox at the birthday house.

"Oh, I was beginning to worry you weren't coming," the young mother said when she answered the door. "Do you think you could bring the pony into the backyard? We have more room there."

"Sure. You have a side gate?" An image of Bandit traipsing through the garage or the house flitted through DJ's mind.

"Oh, of course, I'm sorry."

DJ could tell the woman was flustered. If she was high-strung, what would the kids be like?

Like crazy is what they were. When one little boy bit him, John glared at DJ.

"Just help him down," DJ muttered under her breath. A little girl tugged at DJ's shirt.

"I wanna ride the pony." The whine would have cut logs.

"You'll get a turn in a minute."

"I wanna ride *now*!" The whine turned to a shriek.

The hostess came running over. "Is she hurt? What's the matter, dearest?"

"She's not taking turns too well." DJ kept the smile on her face in spite of her clenched teeth. If she had her way, the brat would never ride Bandit.

"Did you get that last picture?"

John glared at her. "Of course." He had red Kool-Aid stains on the front of his white T-shirt, thanks to a little boy who had refused to give up his drink. How come the mothers seemed to ignore the entertainment, sitting under a tree and visiting as if their kids belonged to someone else?

"Are *all* the parties like this?" John muttered through clenched teeth.

DJ shook her head, fighting to keep a smile on her face.

"Ow-w-ie! He bit me!" The ear-shattering scream from the vicinity of her left knee made DJ's heart jump. She looked down. A tow-headed boy was running in place and screaming in megadecibels that increased in direct proportion to the speed of his feet. DJ wished she could clap her hands over her ears, but she had to see what was wrong.

Bandit pulled back on the reins, a clump of grass dangling from the side of his mouth. His eyes rolled white, and his ears smashed flat against his head.

DJ didn't know which to work with—the boy or the pony.

"He bit me!" The kid clutched one hand with the other.

The hostess ran out of the house. Another woman came to help her. Both pestered the howling boy with a thousand questions, all the while glaring at DJ, John, and poor Bandit.

DJ couldn't see any blood. Since the others were there to care for the child, she opted to attend to Bandit. John lifted the current rider down from the saddle and set her on the ground. Her face screwed up, ready to wail, in sympathy for the screamer.

It took all of DJ's will to keep calm. "He gave Bandit some grass and his finger got in the way." Her tone sang comfort to the horse while her words filled John in on what had happened.

"You shouldn't bring a horse that bites to a children's party." One of the women now held the sniffling child on her hip.

"I told them not to feed the pony." Again DJ kept her voice calm. Inside, she wanted to scream. *It's not Bandit's fault. It's your fault! Keep a watch on your bratty kid.* This was the boy who had dumped his drink on John's shirt. A real charmer if ever there was one. At that moment, DJ was glad she'd never had younger brothers and sisters—what if they'd turned out like these kids?

She rubbed Bandit's ears and waited for things to calm down.

"Bad pony." The boy scrubbed his cheeks with grubby hands and kicked his mother to let him down.

DJ caught a look from John that made her bite her lip.

"Who's next for a pony ride?" She pointed to a little girl in jeans and a sideways Giants baseball cap. "You haven't ridden yet. How about if we swap our Western hat for yours while you ride?"

"No." The little girl clutched her hat.

John started to say something, but instead just lifted the child into the saddle. "You won't have a Western picture like everyone else," he warned her.

"I don't care. Giddy-up." She slapped her legs against the saddle.

DJ led her off around the yard. This kid was a corker. But from the look on her face, she loved to ride. She leaned forward and stroked Bandit's neck, not bothering to hang on to the saddle horn like the others. "Good pony. What's his name?"

"Bandit."

"Nice Bandit. I'm gonna have a pony someday."

DJ nodded. "I hope you do." Now this was a neat kid. Not a brat—she just knew what she wanted. DJ gave her an extra turn around the yard.

"Okay, that's all for today." DJ checked to make sure all the children had had their turns.

John opened the back of the camera and handed the pictures to the hostess. She gave him an envelope and a frosty "thank you."

DJ made sure they had all their gear and led Bandit toward the gate. Once out on the street, John checked the envelope.

"Just wanted to make sure she paid us. What a pain!"

"That has to be the worst party we've had, worse even than the one where the kids tracked horse manure onto the woman's brand-new white carpet. That's why we bring the pooper scooper now." Just then Bandit lifted his tail and plopped some green offerings onto the asphalt.

John glared at DJ. She held the reins while he untied the metal scooper and did his chore, dumping the manure under a bush when they came to one. "Just don't ask me to help with these parties again— ever." His words matched the narrow line of his mouth clenched over clamped teeth.

"They could at least have offered us something to drink."

By the time DJ and John told Amy all about the pony party, she lay on the floor kicking her heels and hooting.

"John, it's never been *that* bad. You guys are making this up, right?" John glared at her and nudged her with his toe.

"Hee-hee, I love it." Amy sat upright and clasped her arms around her bent knees. "Bandit bit him." This time her giggles infected DJ much like a germ, and when she described the bratty boy dumping his drink down John's shirt, she, too, collapsed against the back of the sofa.

"Th-thanks for he-helping." She glanced at the scowl on John's face and grabbed her middle. This was the kind of laughter that couldn't be stopped. Every time she and Amy looked at each other or John, they laughed till they hiccuped. "I'm going to wet my pants if we don't q-q-quit."

John fought to keep the frown on his face. He gave it his best effort. But the grin broke through. It started with a snort. Then a hoot. He leaped to his feet. "You two can waste your time carrying on like this, but I have better things to do."

"B-b-better th-things to . . ." The two were off again. DJ made a fast charge down the hall. It's hard to run with your legs crossed.

When she came out of the bathroom, Mrs. Yamamoto had brought homemade lemonade and cookies into the family room. "Here, you giggling gerties, you need something to cool you off. John, I hear you really earned your money today." Her smile set DJ and Amy off again. John took his glass and a handful of cookies and left the room.

"You two better never ask me to help again," he called back. "You're totally nuts to do those parties." He stomped up the stairs to his room.

"You two." Mrs. Yamamoto shook her head when she left the room.

DJ could hear the younger kids playing outside on the swing set. She looked at her watch. She should get home. She wasn't supposed to be here anyway—but she just *had* to tell Amy about the party.

"See ya tomorrow." She headed for the door. "You remember we're taking my beginning class up to Briones on Friday?"

"Yep. Mom said I could go." Amy followed DJ all the way to the sidewalk. "When do you get off restriction?"

"Just in time for school. Big deal, huh?" DJ swung her leg over her bike. "I never thought being grounded could be so bad." She shook her head. "Sure wish you could come home with me. I hate it there all by myself."

Another message on the machine didn't do anything to improve the evening. Her mother couldn't make it again.

DJ tried to shrug it off. Who cared anyway? She didn't.

But if she didn't care, why didn't drawing a new horse sketch make her feel better? One fingernail started to bleed, she'd chewed it down so far. Good thing she didn't say the word she thought. That kind of language wasn't allowed in their house. Even an empty one.

Chapter • 4

I wonder what my father was like? DJ lay on her bed, one leg crossed over her raised knee. She swung the upper foot in time with the rhythm of her snapping gum. Snapping gum was another one of those habits that made her mother see red. There were sure a lot of things that set Mom off, especially lately.

DJ started listing them. Her bike left out—anything left out. She could hear her mother's demand. "A place for everything, and everything in its place." She hated that line. On with her list: horse-scented clothes, whether on her daughter or left in the hamper; loud music; mouthing off; any clothes DJ liked; two-fingered whistles in the house . . . DJ sighed. Face it. Nearly everything she did set her mother off now that Gran wasn't around.

But that was enough thinking about her mother. *So, what about my father? What do I really know about my dad?* She wrinkled her forehead, trying to remember anything her mother or Gran had said about him. One thing they'd both said was that she got her love of horses from him. And she must look like him because she sure didn't look like any of her mother's relatives. There had to be some reason no one talked about him. Was he in jail for murder or something? Her mother must have really liked him at one time. After all, babies didn't just come out of the sky.

Her mind followed this new thought. What would it feel like to really be in love with someone? Some girls at school thought they were in love, and they talked about guys all the time. DJ's leg bounced more quickly. In love—fiddle! She'd never even kissed a boy, not really. You couldn't count Raymond's peck on her cheek. But if she'd wanted to, he probably would have—kissed her on the mouth that is.

But you had to feel something pretty special to let someone slobber all over you like actors did in the movies. DJ cracked her gum. "I'd rather have horse slobber any day."

Someday there *would* be someone special in her life. Gran said God had one person in mind for her; she'd been praying for him since DJ was a little girl. And if love was like the glow surrounding Gran and Joe, it couldn't be too bad. Kind of fantastic actually. DJ turned over and wrapped her arms around her pillow. Not having Gran around was a bummer.

Not having *anyone* around was worse than a bummer. Only four more days till she was off restrictions. She was counting the minutes. DJ made sure everything was put away, the laundry done, and the family room picked up—not that it needed much—before she went to bed. She wasn't taking any chances on getting her grounding extended.

Her mother knocked on the door and said good-night when she came home. It made DJ miss Gran even more.

Friday morning, DJ packed her lunch for the picnic, putting a sandwich in a sturdy plastic container just as she'd told the girls to do. She stood at the open fridge door; they were out of fruit. No chips, either. She should have ridden her bike to the store last night. At least there were cookies. She dug a carrot out of the drawer and peeled it. Some lunch. Maybe Amy would grab an apple or something for her.

"Thanks, bud," she yelled over her shoulder when Amy returned from getting a nectarine for DJ.

"You're welcome. Are all three going today?"

"Yep. Unless Mrs. Lincoln had her baby during the night."

The early morning felt crisp, and a breeze blew that made DJ glad she'd put a sweatshirt over her T-shirt. She could see trails of clouds peeping over the hills to the west. When San Francisco Bay was foggy, mornings here by Briones were cool. And wonderful. She sniffed the air, breathing deep in spite of the hill they were pedaling up.

At the Academy she and Amy rushed through their chores. Amy

picked up some of DJ's stalls so she'd have time to train Patches. Once in the ring, the gelding jigged sideways, tossing his head and generally being a number one pain.

"You sure are a stubborn one." DJ leaned forward and patted his neck. "Keep testing me every day, hoping I'll get soft?" Patches flicked his ears back and forth, taking in all the sights and sounds. With a sigh, he settled into an even jog, following her reining instructions without a hitch.

Half an hour later, he stopped immediately when DJ barely tightened the reins. "Well, I'll be." She shook her head. "If you behaved like this every day, I'd say you were ready for your owners. You could enter a Walk/Jog class and come out with a blue." The thought burst like Fourth-of-July sparklers. No, it was too late. The Labor Day show was next week, and she hadn't cleared it with the owners. But Patches sure would look good out there. And they'd find out how he did under pressure.

"You're one smart fella." She dismounted and led him out the gate. "Thanks, Ames," she said when they entered the barn. Patches' stall was cleaned and new shavings spread. "When are you going to have time to work with Josh?"

"This afternoon after the ride. If he doesn't know the routine by now, he never will." Amy leaned on her shovel handle. She started to scratch a spot on her face and instead used the tail of her T-shirt to wipe the sweat away.

"You look lots better."

"Better'n what? At least it only looks like a bad case of the zits now. Sure makes me feel sorry for anyone who has bad skin. I never appreciated mine before." She dabbed her forehead again.

DJ finished putting her gear away and trotted Patches out to the hot walker. She unsnapped Megs and brought her back into the barn.

Two of her students giggled their way to the barn, saddles over their arms. Their mothers brought up the rear with saddlebags and helmets.

"We'll be back about two, right?" Sam asked.

"Angie and Sam need to wash their horses. We did mine last night." Krissie hung her saddle over the door. "And I soaped this thing till my arm almost fell off."

DJ tapped her on top of the head. "Good for you. That arm looks pretty well attached to me."

Krissie giggled. "You know what I mean."

Angie and her mother arrived next. Mrs. Lincoln handed DJ the beesting kit. "I'd rather this was in your saddlebag than hers. You be careful now, dear." She gave her daughter a hug.

Angie rolled her eyes. "Yeah, Mom. See you about five?"

DJ smiled and turned to her crew as soon as the last of the mothers walked away. "Okay, kids, let's hit the arena. Last class before the big show, so let's do it right."

"And only three more classes before school. Yuk." Sam shook her head and made a face. "I hate school, just hate it!"

"I'd rather ride every day like DJ."

"You think I don't go to school?" DJ tugged on Angie's ponytail. "Dream on. Come on, strap on your helmets. You're sure poking along today." She went from horse to horse, checking to make sure each saddle was positioned over the withers and the girths smooth.

"We know how to saddle up by now." Sam stood back so DJ could check.

"I know you do, but double-checking is my job. You wouldn't want your horse to get a saddle sore, would you?"

"No." Sam stroked her horse's nose.

DJ picked up a front foot. "You didn't pick this enough. See the manure caked here by the frog?"

Sam nodded. "It was too dark in there to see good." DJ turned and gave her young pupil *the* look. She'd copied it from Bridget, who was a master at it.

"Don't look at me like that." Sam tied her horse and dug a pick out of her bucket. "You'd think . . ." She looked up at DJ and swallowed whatever else she'd been going to say. Her lower lip stuck out until she bit down on it. She checked each hoof before dumping the pick back into the bucket and leading her horse out to the arena.

"Ya did good." DJ walked beside her. She knew what was going through Sam's head. One time Bridget had caught her trying to rush. She'd never dared to do it again.

By the time the class was finished, the sun had baked any coolness out of the air. The girls got drinks at the fountain beside the barn, slung their saddlebags up behind their Western saddles, and tied them down with latigos.

DJ let them through the gate that led to the trails, Amy going first.

Megs, saddled English for DJ, seemed glad to have a rider. She pricked her ears and picked up her feet to catch up. "Easy, girl. They won't get away from us."

Rising in her stirrups, DJ stretched her legs and hugged her shoulders up to her ears. If—she quickly corrected herself—*when* she had a horse of her own, she'd ride up here every week. Maybe when Joe got his cutting horse, they could ride together. Would Major like trail-riding?

Once inside the park, the shade up the trail felt like a cool blanket. DJ looked up to see a squirrel jump from one tree branch across the trail to another tree. He scolded them as though they'd invaded his kingdom.

"There's another squirrel." Angie, who rode in front of DJ, pointed to a particularly fat squirrel, the sunlight through the branches glinting off his red fur. He dropped bits from the pinecone he rotated in his paws, stuffing its nuts into already fat cheeks.

DJ and Angie let the others get ahead so they could keep watching the squirrel's antics. He dropped the core of the cone and, flicking his tail, ran back up the branch and around the tree trunk.

"We had a squirrel nest in a tree in our backyard. Three babies. The mother yelled at us if we got too close." Angie nudged her horse forward. "They're all grown now. They come down to our deck for peanuts."

"My grandpa used to tame squirrels, but we haven't had any in our yard for a while. The neighbors cut down their tree and the squirrels left." The two girls rode side by side. "You excited about the show tomorrow?"

"Scared. When I get too scared I throw up. What if I throw up tomorrow?" Angie shuddered. "I'll just die. I know I will."

They crested the top of the last hill and rode into the open meadow. Briones Crest Trail stalked the higher ridge off to their left. The green grass of spring had dried to straw, painting the hills in shades of tan and gold. Two black turkey vultures rode the thermals above them, seeming to drift without a flicker of feather.

"We riding to the top?" Amy called back. She and the other riders were trotting the fire road that curved around the meadow and up to the trail.

"'Course. We can eat when we come back down." DJ nudged Megs into a canter. "Come on, Angie, let's catch 'em."

By the time they'd ridden to the top of the crest trail, where they watched a red fox slinking over the top of yet another hill, they were more than ready to eat.

"Wait a minute." DJ hissed the command. "Stop."

When all were silent, she pointed to a gentle hollow in a hill across the small valley. Three deer grazed as if they'd never before seen humans. One raised its head, big ears poised to catch any unusual sound. "Ohhh," Angie breathed a sigh of delight. "They are so pretty."

"The little one must be this year's fawn," Amy spoke softly, moving only her lips.

One of the horses tossed its head, the bit jangling loudly in the silence.

The other two deer raised their heads. With a single motion, they leaped the dirt bank and bounded up the hill. Once they disappeared over the crest, DJ nudged Megs forward.

"Come on, let's go eat."

They dismounted under some trees and, after removing their bridles, slipped on halters and tied their horses to low branches. While two girls used a fallen log for a chair, the rest sat cross-legged in the dead leaves and forest duff.

"Did you check for poison oak?" DJ finished inspecting everyone's tie knots before joining them with the lunch out of her saddlebag.

"Yep, Amy did." Angie leaned back against the log. She took a long drink from her water flask. "I could eat a bear."

"Yuk."

"Better'n eating a horse."

"Angie!" The other girls groaned in unison.

For a time there was only the sound of munching. DJ crunched a carrot stick between bites of her sandwich. She and Amy swapped grins. This was about as good as it got.

"Just think, when you have Major next summer, maybe we can both go on the Sierra trip." Amy leaned back on her elbows. "I think that would be the best thing ever."

"How old do you have to be?" Sam looked up from digging for something in her saddlebag.

"Twelve, unless you have parents who can ride along." DJ swatted at a yellow jacket that was exploring the top of her soda can. "Get out of here, bee."

Angie ducked when it flew by her. "I wish my dad could take me. He says he loves to ride but just doesn't have time."

"Mine too." Krissie put the lid back on her sandwich container. "Just think, riding every day for a whole week!"

"Camping out . . . cooking over a fire."

"Ants in your food." Amy brushed one of the tiny creatures off her hand. "They show up everywhere." She ducked and shooshed the persistent yellow jacket away. "Beat it, buzzer."

"Owww. Oh no!" Angie swatted at her hand.

"Did he sting you?" DJ felt her heart leap.

"Yes. DJ, help." Angie scrambled to her feet. Eyes wide, her mouth an O. "Help me. I won't be able to breathe!"

Chapter • 5

DJ leaped to her feet. She dashed toward the horses, only slowing in time to keep them from shying. Why hadn't she brought the saddlebags with her? Or at least the bee kit. What kind of a teacher was she?

She fumbled in the first saddlebag but came up empty-handed. She could hear Amy cautioning the girls to be calm. *Please, God, don't let Angie quit breathing.* The prayer beat in DJ's mind at the same pace as her thudding heart.

Megs backed away when DJ hurried around her to get into the other saddlebag. "Easy, girl." But DJ could tell her own actions were anything but easy. *Calm down!* She made herself stop and take a deep breath as her fingers closed over the plastic box. But her mind continued to race. *I've never given a person a shot before. What do I do?* A more calm voice spoke gently but firmly. *Just read the instructions. You've seen lots of shots given, just do the same.*

"She's starting to wheeze," Samantha called. "Hurry, DJ."

"It's going to be all right, Angie, take it easy. The more uptight you get, the worse it will be." Amy acted as if they did this every day.

What if the shot doesn't work? The reassuring voice came again. *It will.* Was this what listening to God's voice was like? DJ felt herself calming down. She took another deep breath as she dropped to her knees on the ground beside the wheezing girl.

Angie's chest rose and fell with each struggling breath, as though she were being pumped by a bellows—slowly. Sweat broke out on her forehead.

Angie looked up at DJ. "I don't want to die."

"You won't." Amy wiped the girl's hair back from her forehead. "Come on, you've been through this before. You can tell DJ what to do."

"No, I don't remember." Her breathing sounded like a marathon runner's who'd just crossed the finish line.

In, out, in, out. DJ could feel her own breaths come in time with Angie's, as though she were trying to breathe for the girl.

DJ held the prefilled syringe between her teeth and ripped open the square packet of alcohol rub. She took the syringe out of her mouth. "Easy, Angie—just bend your arm like you do at the doctor's office. Good. Now we'll wipe it . . ." DJ's actions followed her words. She dropped the gauze square on the ground. "And . . ." She closed her eyes. *Please, God.* With a quick jerk, she pulled the cap off and, without giving herself time to think, stabbed the needle into Angie's bicep.

After depressing the plunger, DJ pulled the needle out and sat back on her heels. Her heart raced like a bike going downhill with a tailwind. She put the cap back on the syringe. "Thank you, God." Her whisper blended with the agonized sound of Angie's breathing.

"That . . . didn't even . . . hurt. You're good." Angie leaned back against Amy's knees and chest. Her eyes closed and she tried to take a deep breath. Instead, she coughed.

"Easy, just think about how much fun we've had. Seeing the deer on the hillside." DJ kept her voice smooth and gentle. The singsong worked with horses, why not a sick kid?

"You want me to ride down and get help?" Amy asked, her hands busy smoothing Angie's forehead.

DJ forced her careening mind to stop and think. "Maybe you better. But Mrs. Lincoln said this stuff really works, if we get it into Angie fast enough."

"Do you think we did—get it in quick enough, I mean?"

"I'll go," Sam volunteered.

DJ looked up to see the scared expressions on the faces of the other girls. "No, Sam, but thanks. Amy will get help, if anyone. I can't take a chance on someone else getting hurt." *Why'd I ever let this happen?*

Maybe Angie shouldn't do this kind of thing. But she wants to so bad. Why couldn't the stupid bee have stung me instead?

"I'm getting better, DJ. I can feel it." Angie reached out a shaky hand and stuck it in DJ's.

A rash of relieved giggles broke out from the other girls. Both flopped back on the ground as if someone had just cut their puppets' strings. "Angie, that was the scariest thing I ever saw."

"Man, DJ, you did that just like a nurse." Krissie pointed a finger at DJ. "You are awesome."

Angie sat up on her own. While she was still wheezing, now it was more like a whistle than a freight train. "Thanks, DJ, you saved my life."

DJ blinked her eyes and gritted her teeth. She would not cry now, not in front of these girls. She looked up at Amy to see a sheen of moisture in her dark eyes. A smile trembled at the sides of her mouth.

DJ rolled her lips together, licked them, and took a deep breath. "Well, girls, you all finished with your lunches?" She looked around at heads shaking no. "Okay, then let's do that. If I don't get something to drink, I might faint."

Amy handed DJ her water bottle. "Drink fast. We don't want any fainting up here. We might have to give you a shot . . ."

"A shot of water will do just fine." DJ glugged and felt the boulder stuck in her throat go down with the water.

Krissie picked up the syringe and the leftover pieces of the bee kit. "Here, DJ, we don't want to be litterbugs."

"No way." Sam started to giggle, then Krissie. DJ and Amy tried to keep straight faces.

Angie giggled, wheezed, and giggled some more. "We c-could litter th-the ground with b-bees." She fell back against the log, her laughter growing stronger with each easing breath.

"Dead bees."

"Definitely dead bees." They all rolled on the ground, clutching their stomachs and wiping their eyes.

"Wh-what's s-so funny?" DJ made the mistake of looking at Amy. She knew better.

"G-got me."

Finally the giggles let up.

"I have to go to the bathroom." Angie lay on the ground, the back of one hand over her eyes.

"Pick a tree—any tree." Sam waved her hand. "We have plenty."

"Sure, and get stung on my rear this time."

That did it. The girls fell against one another, their giggles floating up through the branches like a strange kind of bird song. DJ tried to take another drink from the water bottle and ended up blowing the water out her nose.

"Ow. Knock it off. See what you made me do?"

By now Angie could laugh without wheezing. She was making up for lost time. Every time one person calmed down, another started in. Finally they all lay flat on the leaves and dried grass. *Better giggling than crying*, DJ thought, gazing up through the gnarly oak branches above them. Sunbeams outlined the leaves. DJ drew in a deep breath and let a prayer float up toward heaven. *Thank you, God. I couldn't have done it without you.*

"DJ, you want one of my cookies?" Angie nudged DJ's shoulder with her boot toe.

"Sure." DJ pushed herself upright and accepted the offer. Munching and sitting spraddle-legged, she studied her group. While they all had bits of leaves and twigs in their hair and could use a good dusting, no one looked the worse for wear. Her heart had resumed residence in its normal place, and when she held up a hand, it no longer trembled like a leaf in a windstorm.

"Thanks, Angie. Good cookie."

"I made them."

"Wow, you can come bake cookies for me anytime." DJ rose to her feet and dusted off her rear. "You guys ready to hit the trail?"

"No, I'd rather stay up here." Angie finished packing her saddlebags.

"Yeah, well, if one of those mean bees comes after you again, we're fresh outta bee kit." DJ extended a hand to pull the girl to her feet. "And I'm just so grateful you're all right that next time I'll pack a whole case of 'em." She turned Angie around and brushed her off. The girls took turns doing the same for one another. By the time they rode back into the academy lot, the beesting was nearly a forgotten incident, until the girls started telling their mothers about it.

"Should we call your mother and have her take you to the doctor?" DJ stopped by Angie's stall where she was unsaddling her horse.

Angie shook her head. "Once I'm breathing okay again, the doctor can't do anything. I'm just a little tired. Right now I need to wash my horse and soap my saddle. Mom'll be here about five. Don't worry about me, okay? I hate having people worry and watch me."

DJ nodded. "I'd feel the same. Holler if you need help."

She accepted the other mothers' thanks, reminded them of next week's schedule, and headed for Bridget's office.

"I hear you are the hero of the day." Bridget turned from the filing cabinet where she'd been inserting papers into their proper files.

"How'd you know?"

"A little bird. I am really proud of you; it sounds as though you handled yourself in a totally professional and competent manner."

"Bridget, I was so scared. More than I've been any time in my whole life."

"Heroes are not necessarily brave when the chips are down; they just keep on going, doing what needs to be done. You kept your head about you—"

"I prayed hard."

"That helps too. The main thing is, you did not panic. I have always felt I could count on you, and now I know it." Bridget sat on the edge of her desk.

"You should have seen the giggle fit we had when it was over and Angie was starting to breath easy again."

"Natural reaction. To laugh, cry, get mad, giddy."

"*I* felt like crying. So did Amy."

"That would have been normal, like I said."

"But it might have scared the girls."

"Right. That is why I say you are a hero. You got the job done and thought of others first. You can always fall apart later, if need be."

DJ could feel her lower lip tremble. "I hate crying." She swallowed hard and rolled her eyes toward the ceiling. Blinking quickly, she fought back the tears.

"There is nothing wrong with crying. Tears help wash both the eyes and the soul."

"I gotta check on the girls." DJ bolted from the office.

Mrs. Lincoln had tears in her eyes when she told DJ thank you. She wrapped her arms around DJ and hugged her as though she'd invented hugging. And hugging with a baby-big stomach between them wasn't easy. DJ grinned.

"Hey, what was that?" DJ pulled back and stared down at the mound under Mrs. Lincoln's top.

"The baby said thank you, too." Mrs. Lincoln patted her tummy.

DJ's eyes traveled from the huge belly to the woman's face. "Did you feel it?"

"Of course. This one's been kicking like he plans to join a World Cup soccer team tomorrow."

"I never knew it felt like that."

Mrs. Lincoln took DJ's hand and laid it on her abdomen. The baby let loose with a one-two punch that bounced DJ's hand.

"Wow! Didja see that?"

Angie and her mother burst out laughing. "We see it all the time. If this one's as active after it's born as it is now, we'll be chasing him down the street in a couple of weeks."

DJ glanced up for permission and, at Mrs. Lincoln's nod, put her hand back on the woman's belly. When nothing happened, she looked up again.

"Guess we wore him out."

"You know for sure it's a boy?"

"No, so it's a good thing there are girls' soccer teams, too. You ready to leave, Angie? We have tons of things to do."

DJ watched them drive away, waving in return when Angie rolled down the minivan's window to wave good-bye. Babies had never seemed so real to her. And just breathing had never been something she thought to be grateful about. If only Gran were here. What stories DJ had to tell her!

When she walked into the empty house after pedaling home, the light was blinking on the answering machine. She pushed the rewind button.

After a squawk, the machine let loose with Gran's voice.

"Hi, darlin's. We've been having such a wonderful time, Joe and I decided to stay a bit longer."

DJ felt her chin drop to the floor. "No, you can't do that!"

Chapter • 6

"Just teasing! We'll be home Sunday night."

DJ sagged against the wall. "Not funny, Gran. Not funny at all."

The next message was from her mother. "If you get home before 4:30, call me. Otherwise we'll plan on going out for dinner; you choose the place."

"I'll believe that when I see it." DJ checked the clock. It was already 4:45. She looked down at her clothes. If her mother caught her looking and smelling like horse and the woodsy ground she'd lain on, they'd never go out.

She shucked her clothes by the washing machine and threw the shirt and jeans in, along with others in the hamper. Then while that started running, she charged upstairs to shower.

Where should we go? Pizza? Nah. She thought of places and discarded them as fast while the water pounded on her head and shoulders. By the time she wrapped a towel around her stringy wet blond hair, she'd decided on Chinese. If they ordered enough, they could warm it up for dinner tomorrow night. Only two more days and Gran would be home.

For a change, DJ and her mother spent an entire evening together without arguing. They each chose a dish at the restaurant and even tried a new one, Mongolian Beef, which they both loved. And when her mother suggested a movie and ice cream afterward, DJ nearly fainted.

"You . . . you don't have to study tonight?"

"Nope. And I didn't bring any work home, either. We should mark this on the calendar." Lindy flipped the lock so DJ could get into the car. " 'Course I can always find more to do. . . ."

"Who can't." DJ thought of the mess she'd left in her bedroom. She'd made sure the door was closed so her mother couldn't see in.

Later, at the ice-cream parlor, Lindy licked hot-fudge sauce off her spoon and bobbed it at DJ. "You know, about that emergency with Angie. I'm not sure I could have given a shot like that."

"There was nothing else to do. It wasn't much different from giving a horse an injection." DJ twirled her spoon in the fudge sauce. "Making sure to give her the right amount would have been worse. This syringe was all loaded."

"Still, it took plenty of nerve."

DJ watched her mother from under her eyelashes. What was going on? Could this be a peace offering? Lindy never ate ice cream—said there was too much fat in it—let alone a hot-fudge sundae. And after popcorn at the movie and Chinese food?

"I think I'm going to burst." Lindy wiped her mouth with her napkin.

DJ could hear Gran's voice in her ear. *Your mother loves you, she just doesn't always know how to show it. She's been so tied up at work and school, she let motherhood slip right past her.*

They didn't say much on the way home, but what was new? They'd already talked more in one evening than a typical month. And when her mother thanked her for a nice time, DJ's red flags really went up. Danger! Warning! *What's going on?*

DJ left for the Academy in the morning before her mother woke up.

"Get real," Amy shouted at DJ's back when they pedaled up the hill. "Maybe your mom just wants to spend more time with you. You know, that old 'quality time' thing. I think grown-ups get hung up on that pretty easily."

"But she didn't yell at me once. Wouldn't you be suspicious?"

"Nah, I'd be grateful."

After clipping Patches to the hot walker where he could dance off some of his energy, Amy and DJ rushed through their chores so they could take Patches and Josh into the ring at the same time. DJ wanted Patches to get used to having other horses around him when he had a rider.

"All right, settle down, you hyper thing." DJ pulled the gelding to a standstill for the third time. Even after his hot walker workout and four times around the ring, Patches wanted to race whoever else was present. Sweat from his excitement already darkened his shoulders. She watched Amy put Josh through his paces. The two of them looked as though they were welded together. "See, silly, that's what we're supposed to look like. We're supposed to work together."

Patches jigged in place, his front feet raising puffs of dust as they pounded the ground. When he finally relaxed, DJ loosened the reins and let him walk. "And here I thought you were ready for your owners. You'd shake them senseless." When Patches finally managed to make an entire circuit of the ring at a walk, she let him jog. He made it with only one return to a walk this time.

"Looks like he's trying." Amy rode beside her for a circuit.

"Yeah, trying my patience."

"You know what I mean."

"Sure, he's trying to run. He wants to catch up to anyone ahead of him."

"Don't worry about it, DJ. Pretty soon you'll have him obeying just like Diablo did. I know you will."

This time when DJ neck-reined Patches in a circle so he could go back the other way, he minded. "So there is hope for you after all," she muttered.

They had to rush to get ready for their next pony party, but it was worth it. The hostess stayed with them the entire time, making sure all the kids took turns. She brought DJ and Amy punch to drink and offered them ice cream and cake if they'd stay longer and let the children ride again. When she offered to pay them an extra ten dollars, the girls agreed.

"This sure beat the last one," DJ said when they trotted Bandit up the road toward the Academy. "Poor John. He hated it. And those kids were just awful."

"We could tell John about this one and blame him for the other." Amy wore a sly grin. This was her chance to get even with a big brother who thought teasing his younger sister was what he was put on this earth for.

But John wasn't home when they got there; he and his dad had taken a load of yard clippings to the dump.

"Fiddle." DJ plopped down on the curb in front of the house.

"Double fiddle." Amy joined her. "Well, at least the party went well and we made extra money."

"We have only one party to go. You know, I've been thinking—"

"No." Amy shook her head so hard her black hair swished her cheeks. "We're not keeping on with the parties. Once school starts, we just don't have time."

"But . . ."

"No. Nada. Ix-nay."

DJ wrinkled her mouth to one side. "Next summer?"

"Maybe. If we don't come up with a better idea by then. But if we do the pony parties, we are going to train Bandit to pull a cart."

"It's a deal." The two slapped high fives.

DJ entered her house to the sound of the vacuum cleaner and her mother's easy-listening music playing on the stereo. "I'm home." She heard the vacuum shut off.

Even for cleaning house, her mother managed to wear things that matched. The observation crossed DJ's mind at the same time as she registered the scowl her mother sported. A frown of that type caused wrinkles, but DJ didn't feel stupid or daring enough to comment.

"Have you noticed your room and bathroom lately?" The tone matched the face. They were certainly back to normal. The evening before must have been a fluke.

"I know. I was in a hurry."

"It doesn't take any more time to hang up the towel than to drop it on the floor."

The words pricked like a burr under a saddle. "I know, I'll take care of it." DJ bit her lip to keep from answering back and climbed the stairs to her room. Gran would say to count her blessings. Last night had been a blessing—a fun one. She sighed. If only it had lasted.

The next morning revealed another hole in DJ's life. She attended church with the Yamamotos since Gran was out of town. She'd thought of asking her mother to take her, but they hadn't said much to each other the night before. In fact, they hadn't said anything. The house didn't need an air-conditioner with her mother in *that* kind of mood.

DJ looked up at the stained-glass shepherd behind the altar. Jesus looked so kind; He held the lamb as if He really cared. The window made DJ miss Gran even more. She needed a hug, a Gran-type hug. It wouldn't be long now until the newlyweds returned. During the moment for silent prayer, she prayed for a safe flight for Gran and Joe. But the pastor started talking again before she got around to praying for her mother.

Later, at home, DJ asked, "Who's picking Gran and Joe up at the airport?"

"Robert. He'll take them back to Joe's for his car, and then they'll come out here." Lindy looked up from the book she was reading. "I've told you this before."

"I forgot." DJ gnawed on the nub of her right thumbnail. "You don't think they had an accident or something?"

Lindy shook her head. "No. The flight was probably late, that's all. Or maybe there's traffic, or they had something else they had to do first." Her tone said she was losing patience.

DJ headed to the kitchen for a drink of water. "They're here!" She set the glass in the sink and barreled out the front door. "Gran! You're back!" She flew around the hood of the car and threw her arms around the petite woman just emerging from the front seat.

"Oh, my Darla Jean, if you've missed me as much as I've missed you . . ." Gran patted her granddaughter's back and hugged her again. Arm in arm they came around the car, talking nonstop.

"Hi, DJ." Joe leaned his arms on the top of the open car door. "Lindy." He raised a hand in greeting to the woman standing in the doorway.

"Hi." DJ caught herself. She'd almost forgotten about Joe. "Won't you come in?" There, she'd remembered her manners. She stood back to let Gran hug Lindy and Joe do the same. A funny kind of feeling invaded her stomach. Not a ha-ha kind of funny but an oh-oh kind. "You want me to get your suitcases, Gran?"

"No, we left them at Joe's. Come see the things we brought you."

The oh-oh turned to an oh no and left DJ with a new hole in her heart. Gran wouldn't be staying here. She wouldn't be sitting in her chair, Bible in her lap, to tell DJ good-bye in the morning. *She won't be here when I come home from the Academy.*

"Darla Jean, whatever is the matter?" Gran turned and wrapped an arm around DJ's waist. "You look as though you've seen a ghost."

"You're not going to stay here." DJ choked the words out.

"Of course not, but soon we'll move into our new house and we'll only be a mile away." She moved forward, drawing DJ with her. "You knew that, surely."

"Yeah, I just never thought about it." DJ didn't say what filled her heart and mind. *But, Gran, I need you here. Mom and I, we aren't doing so good. I need you.* She studied the raw spot on her thumb cuticle. Gran looked so happy. So did Joe. She couldn't be a brat again—she just couldn't. *Shape up! Don't ruin it for them again by saying something stupid. You want to be grounded for life?*

Chapter • 7

Smiling and saying thank-you when you want to cry isn't easy. But DJ did it. She pasted on a smile, laughed in the right places, and even said something nice to Joe. But inside . . . she was a mess. DJ didn't dare look directly at Gran. She was too good at reading eyes. And from the burning, DJ knew hers must be red. Or at the very least, sad and scared.

She held her new scooped-neck T-shirt up to her chest. Three dolphins leaped and dove across the turquoise fabric. "It's a beaut. And the shorts are perfect. Thanks." She admired the swirly skirt and tank top they'd brought her mother. And oohed and aahed at the pictures. Maybe she should try out for drama when she got to high school. This was turning into an Academy Award performance.

"Someday we'll go back and take you with us to snorkel." Gran handed DJ a picture taken under water that showed fish they usually saw in saltwater aquariums.

"It's a whole new world under the surface." Joe handed her another photo. "Your grandmother was a natural, took to snorkeling like a duck to water. We should call her the diving duck." He reached over and patted Gran's hand. "When we go again, we'll take Shawna, too. She'd love it." He checked his watch. "We better get going, darlin'. I've got first watch tomorrow."

DJ hugged her stomach with both arms. Anything to keep it in place. *Stay here, Gran. Don't leave me again.* But instead, she smiled and waved good-bye from the lighted doorway.

Then she headed for her bedroom at a run.

The next morning everyone hurried through their chores. DJ spent an hour and a half with Patches, making sure she focused on him entirely. He could get out of control faster than any horse she'd known, but when he decided to cooperate, he learned quickly and never forgot the lesson.

"I think the trick with him is to let him work off all his steam on the hot walker. Either that or just take him around the ring until he settles down." Bridget had been watching the last few minutes of the session. "He has too much energy. But you are doing a good job with him."

"I don't want his riders to get frightened at first, especially the child." DJ leaned forward and stroked Patches' mane away from where it had tangled in the headstall.

"The boy is going to ride Bandit at first, like you suggested. Think I will put him in your beginners' class."

"But the others are already riding well."

"He will catch up with some extra coaching. You will have him on Mondays and Wednesdays at first, then right before your girls, then with them. It will work." Bridget turned to leave. "Johnsons are not interested in showing; they want to trail-ride as a family. Or at least that is what they are saying now."

DJ dismounted and led Patches out of the arena. "You get an extra treat today. You've been a good boy." As soon as she stripped the tack off, she fed him a horse cookie, brushed him down, and led him out to the hot walker.

James was just saddling up. "You got him looking good, DJ."

"Thanks. What's happening?"

James finished buckling the girth on his flat saddle. "This is my last day here."

"What?"

"Gray Bar and I both leave tomorrow for Virginia." He ducked his head, fiddling with the stirrups.

"Oh, James, no."

"I gotta get her worked." James kept his head turned toward the horse when he pushed by DJ.

"We'll still be here when you come home for the summer." She tried to sound cheerful, as if leaving for a military academy was the most natural thing in the world.

"You may be, but my house won't. Mom and Dad are selling it. I don't even know who I'm going to live with—or where."

Was that the sheen of a tear on his cheek? She turned away so he wouldn't be more embarrassed. What could she say? "Bridget asked me to tell you to come up to the office as soon as you're finished." DJ crammed her hands into her pockets. Here she'd been feeling sorry for herself because Gran now lived with Joe, and James didn't even know who he was going to live with. Bummer. Double bummer.

"I'll see."

"You better—she sounded determined."

"What did I do now?"

"Got me." DJ turned away again, this time to hide a smile. She knew what Bridget wanted. All the student workers did except for James.

"Surprise! Surprise!" everyone hollered when James walked through the door.

He stopped as though he'd walked into a glass wall. His face turned as red as the helium balloons bobbing on strings tied to the chairs and table legs. He half turned as if to run back out the door he had just come in.

"Come on, James." DJ stepped in his way. She kept her voice low for his ears only. "You can do this."

He turned back. "Th-thanks. How come no one told me?"

Giggles broke out. "It's a surprise party, that's why!"

"Okay, everyone, line up over here for hot dogs, then get the rest of your food." One of the mothers working behind the food table called out, "James, you get to be first since you're the guest of honor."

Hilary nudged James forward. "Come on, we're starved. I didn't have lunch yet because of you, so get with it." The grin she wore lit up her dark eyes. "We really surprised you, didn't we?"

James nodded. He picked up a paper plate and asked for two hot dogs.

Before long everyone had a plateful and had found a place to sit. In between bites, talk of the Labor Day horse show took over. DJ, Amy, James, and a couple of others sat cross-legged on the floor in a circle.

"So you'll be involved in the horse program at your new school?" one of them asked.

James nodded, his mouth full of food. "I want to get on the novice jumping team. And I can ride on fox hunts in the fall."

"Cool." One of the other boys leaned back and thumped James on the arm. "Then you could compete Hunter/Jumper. Just think, riding behind hounds. I watched 'em do it in a movie once. Incredible."

"Yeah, I guess."

DJ studied James from under her eyelashes. Just a few weeks ago he was the biggest pain in her life, and now they were friends. Incredible was the word all right. And she knew who to thank. Only God worked miracles.

After the cake was served, Bridget clapped for order. She brought a wrapped package out from under her desk and handed it to James. "So you do not forget us. You will be a success at that Academy. You are really just exchanging one academy for another. And they will not be any tougher than I am, you can count on it."

"Th-thanks." He tore into the paper and held up a black T-shirt. Inside a circle of white letters that read *Briones Academy*, a white horse and rider cleared a triple.

"You now have the first shirt produced for our school here. The rest of my students will have to buy theirs." Bridget handed him another box. "This one is from everybody."

James lifted a shiny new headstall out of the box. "Thank you." His voice cracked on the words.

DJ leaped to her feet and started picking up dirty plates and plastic cups. "Come on, you guys, put away your mess." She knew how James felt, hating to cry and so afraid he might. And one look at his face told her how close he was.

Saying good-bye when you didn't know if you'd ever see that person again was the pits. "I'll write if you will." She helped James find all his gear in the tack room.

"You got a modem?" James dug a brush with his name on it out of the tack box.

"No, I don't even have a computer. Why?"

"I could send you messages that way." James found an old jacket in the closet. "Faster and easier than the post office."

"Sorry, you'll have to use the mail. Or the phone." She picked up a loaded bucket and lugged it over to Gray Bar's stall. "You learn to jump, old girl, and I'll see you in the ring next year." She stroked the filly's nose and rubbed her ears. "See ya." She turned, gave James a hug, and hustled out the door. What she wouldn't give to tell his parents what a mess they were making of their kid's life. Military school! It was all so stupid.

Tuesday morning her eyes flew open and she leaped out of bed. No more restrictions. She was free! She could use the phone, watch TV, visit Amy. . . . Today she would ride Megs again—and this evening, Joe was taking her to meet Major, her soon-to-be own horse.

"I'm free!" she sang to Amy when she came out the door of her house.

"Do you have to be free so early in the morning?" Amy tried to grumble, but ended up grinning instead. "You get to jump again."

"And tonight I get to see Major. What a day! What a super fantastical, awesome day." DJ raised her face to the sun peeping over the tops of the buckeye and eucalyptus trees. "Nothing can stop me now—I'm on my way. Olympics, here I come!"

"You might want to win a couple local shows and qualify for the Grand National first." The two pedaled side by side up the street.

"Gran always says you need the dream first. Can't you just imagine?" DJ flung her arms straight out, causing her bike to waver from side to side.

"I can imagine you splattered all over the street if you don't watch out."

"Amy Marie Yamamoto, you are the most—"

"Most perfect friend you've ever had."

"Right." DJ's thoughts flitted to James. Wouldn't it be awful to have to move away and leave your friends behind? Especially a friend like Amy. They'd been best friends since preschool. Poor James, his flight left at 7:00 a.m. She glanced at her watch—right about now.

They parked their bikes beside the barn and checked the duty board. Who would take over James' chores? Two new names appeared on the roster. Tony Andrada and Rachel Jones.

DJ and Amy swapped raised-eyebrow looks. "Sure hope they know how to work. We just got James whipped into shape before he left. Is Tony a girl or guy?"

"Got me. I've never met either of them." DJ's gaze scanned the board. "But Hilary is training them, so I don't have to. And look, they're taking some of my stalls. Good deal!"

"So what'll you do?"

DJ shrugged. "Who knows—besides Bridget, that is. But I'm sure she has something planned. Today I have stalls, Patches, my lesson—my lesson!" She threw her hands in the air and jigged around in a circle. "I finally get to jump again!"

"It hasn't been forever, you know."

"Just seems like it." She did another jig step.

"You know, DJ, one thing I like about you is your low-key personality." Bridget stopped just inside the door. The smile on her face made DJ feel as though the sun shone inside the building. "You get Megs saddled, and I will meet you in the arena in ten minutes?"

"I'm outta here." DJ dashed across to the barn and saddled Megs in record time. Once in the ring and mounted up, she wanted to whoop and shout. Even staid Megs caught the excitement and pranced to the side. "Thank you, thank you, thank you, God!" Her words kept time with the slow trot, one hoofbeat per word.

She felt as if she were flying. When Megs left the ground to clear each jump, DJ was sure they were going to take off and circle like Pegasus. They could have easily cleared a brush and pole or a square oxer if they'd been in the arena.

"DJ, that was an excellent performance. I could tell Megs was having as much fun as you were. When the rider is confident, the horse will do far beyond its best. Remember what this felt like and how you feel right now. Dream about it and know you can recapture this feeling. The best riding is as much mental as physical."

"I think this was the most fun I've had in my entire life." DJ leaned forward and hugged Megs with both arms. "You old sweetie. Thank you, Megs."

Her class went the same way.

"That was fun, DJ." Sam stopped her horse by the open gate. "I wish school wouldn't start for months or ever. I love it here." She leaned forward and rubbed her horse's neck. "When are we going back up in Briones?"

"After what we went through, you want to go back?"

"Sure." Angie stopped beside her. "A stupid ol' bee can't keep us away."

"Well, we'll see."

"Now you sound just like a grown-up." Krissie shook her head. "And we thought you were different."

DJ took hold of the girl's bridle. "Get back to the barn before your mother scolds me for taking too long. You want to get me in trouble?"

They shook their heads and headed for the barn, giggles floating back over their shoulders.

After the girls finished grooming their horses and cleaning their stalls, Mrs. Lincoln returned to pick up Angie. She handed a wrapped package to Angie, who brought it to DJ with a smile big enough to crack her face.

"Here, we want you to have this—kind of a thank-you."

"For what?" DJ looked from Angie to her mother.

"For saving my daughter's life."

"Yeah, but . . ." DJ sputtered the words. "You . . . you can't—"

"Yes, we can. Just open it." Mrs. Lincoln clasped her hands on her mountain of a stomach.

DJ tore the paper and let it drop to her feet. Inside the box lay a headstall and reins, along with an envelope. "Wow, what a beauty."

"For your new horse." Angie crowded close. "Open the envelope."

Inside was a gift certificate for a local tack shop.

"We thought you could use that for a bit. We didn't know what kind to buy." Angie looked up at DJ. "Do you like it?"

"Like it. I don't know what to say. Thank you."

"Thank *you*, DJ. Your quick thinking made me feel so much braver about letting Angie out of my sight. The first time she got stung by a bee, we found out she had asthma. Until then, we thought her breathing problems were only allergies." Mrs. Lincoln tried to straighten and twisted her shoulders from side to side. "I have an ache in my lower back that tells me we better get home. We might have a baby tonight."

"Are you sure you can drive?" DJ asked. "I mean—should you? I can call someone."

"No, no. It'll be hours yet, and maybe not till tomorrow. But I probably won't make the show this weekend." She patted DJ on the shoulder. "See you."

DJ watched them get in their car and leave. *What an incredible thing for them to do.* She held the headstall in her hand, running her fingers over the smooth leather. It looked large enough for a big horse, all right. And Joe had said Major was more than sixteen hands tall.

When she took Patches out in the arena, even *he* behaved—for him, anyway. He tried to run away with her only once.

She didn't even mind the empty house when she got home. Joe would be coming soon!

Chapter • 8

"Major, I'd like you to meet my new granddaughter, Darla Jean Randall. She prefers to be called DJ."

"Oh, wow." DJ stretched out her hand so the big horse could sniff her. "Major, am I ever glad to meet you." She smiled at the tickle of his whiskers on the back of her hand and up her arm. He continued his sniffing exploration, up her shoulder, her hair. When he gently blew horsy breath in her face, she knew she was accepted.

DJ dug in her pocket for the bit of carrot and the horse cookie she'd brought along. She held them out, one on each palm. "Which do you like best?"

Major looked at her, intelligence beaming from his large, dark eyes. He nosed each treat, then lipped the carrot first.

"Ah, so you're a vegetable man." He quickly ate the other before she changed her mind and put it away.

"He likes sugar the best, but I keep telling him cubes aren't good for his teeth." Joe rubbed up behind the black ears and down the horse's neck and shoulder. "But you don't agree, do you, old man?" Major leaned into the rubbing, almost purring in pleasure.

"What else does he like?"

"Popcorn, peanuts, candy. When we're out on patrol, he's not supposed to have snacks, but sometimes kids sneak him things. He likes kids, hates guns, and has a heart as big as the Golden Gate Bridge."

DJ rubbed the horse's cheek and stroked the white blaze down his face. When she stopped, Major ducked his head lower so she could reach him more easily.

"He loves parades, especially when the mounted police march as a unit. Crowd control is what he excels at. Not too many people argue when he swings his rump around and moves to the side. See his feet? While he's careful where he puts them, even the roughest, drunkest agitators don't want to get their feet stepped on."

"But he doesn't have big feet for his size."

"No, but he looks as though he could mash your foot, wouldn't you say?"

DJ nodded. "Even a pony stepping right on your toes can hurt."

"Right. And you should see Major when he pins his ears to his head and starts to glare. Could melt ice, he could." Joe stepped back. "He and I, we've been through many a scrape, we have." He retrieved a lead rope off the nail by the horse's stall and snapped it to the blue nylon halter. "Here, I'll take him out so you can see how he moves. Sorry, I can't let you ride him tonight, department regulations, you know."

"That's okay. What breed did you say he was?"

"Morgan-Thoroughbred. Half and half. Nice easy gaits; you can ride him all day and not get tired. I should know, I have." He led the horse down the dirt aisle.

DJ stood and watched the horse's action from the rear. Strong in the haunches, straight in the leg. She tried to remember all the points Bridget had been teaching her. He was a good mover; it showed in knees, hocks, and ankles. Bridget said that was important for a jumper. That and strength in the hindquarters.

"You say he likes to jump?"

"When he's had a chance. We set up some low jumps over a downed tree in Golden Gate Park a couple times for fun. He learns quickly and remembers better'n an elephant. If he gets a treat at a certain place one time, he'll expect it every time."

Joe stopped Major right in front of DJ. He held the gelding at attention, head up, ears forward, feet squared. The white blaze down the horse's face gleamed in the light from the overhead bar.

DJ smoothed her hand down the horse's shoulder and down his

leg. When her hand ran over his fetlock, Major lifted his foot without any hesitation. DJ moved to the rear and checked each of his legs. The horse obeyed the slightest command. "He's had to learn to be handled by more than one person; police horses can't be picky about their riders. It's just he and I've been on the force together for so long, he became mine."

She let Major sniff her shoulder again before working down the last leg. Halfway down his shoulder lay a patch of black skin with no hair. "What happened here?"

"That was a bullet meant for me. He deflected the shot by running into the guy. Not much of a scar left now, but that was too close a call for either of us." Joe smoothed the sleek hair down over the spot. "His badge of honor."

"Wow. When you said he was all heart, you weren't kiddin." DJ stood back to look at the horse face on. Deep, wide chest and balanced on all fours. "He sure looks good to me. How do you get your horses here?"

"We purchase some, but many are donated. A calm temperament is most important. We also like it when we can form a drill with matching horses—bays like Major here are popular. I was fortunate that when I needed a horse, a family was moving to the East Coast and needed a home for their horse." He stroked the arched neck with obvious love. "Major and I've been buddies ever since."

This is going to be my horse as soon as Joe retires. DJ felt like dancing again. Like running up and throwing her arms around the bay's neck, then hugging Joe. Or maybe the other way around.

"Do you like him?" The question caught her short.

"*Like* him? How could I not like him? I just can't understand why you want to sell him."

Joe put the horse back into his stall and unsnapped the lead. "Well, it's like this. I decided to buy him and keep him for my grandchildren to ride. I knew Shawna had horses on the brain, and I thought maybe Bobby and Billy might like to ride someday. That way I could keep my best friend here with me. He's too young to be put out to pasture."

DJ stroked the horse one more time, told him good-night, and followed Joe down the aisle. They waved good-night to the officer on duty and the night watchman.

"So why sell him to me?"

"Are you sure you want him?

"Joe, for pete's sake, what do I have to do—get down on my knees and beg?" DJ shot him a questioning look. What was wrong with the man? Couldn't he see she was already nuts about the horse?

"Okay." He opened the car door for her. "I know he'll be good for you."

"So?"

"All my life I've dreamed of having a cutting horse. Goes back to my love of Western movies, I guess. You know, where the cowboy and his horse are cutting cows out of the herd and the horse saves the rider from an irate bull. That kind of thing." Joe ducked his chin, as if embarrassed to admit his dream.

"Hey, that's cool."

"Since you'll be putting Major to work, I'm going to buy a cutting horse and enter the competitions. Think your grandmother will tag along while I compete?"

"Sure." DJ shrugged. "Long as she doesn't have a deadline. Gran will try anything and have a ball doing it."

"Does Bridget know anything about cutting horses?"

"Some. She knows something about all kinds of horses and lots about showing and jumping. She'll put you in touch with the right people."

Joe eased his car into traffic on the Bay Bridge. "Kind of exciting finally realizing a lifelong dream—my cutting horse, I mean."

"Tell me about it. I've wanted a horse of my own since I was little. I started working at the Academy when I was ten so I could have riding lessons. Mom and Gran thought I'd quit in a couple weeks." DJ couldn't believe she was talking like this with the man who had stolen Gran. It wasn't long ago that she'd decided to hate him.

"Melanie says you want to jump in the Olympics someday."

"Yep, that's my dream." It seemed strange to hear Gran referred to as anything but Gran. Melanie was someone else entirely. "I have a long way to go, so much to learn."

"That's what makes life interesting." Joe checked over his shoulder and changed lanes. "You up for an ice-cream sundae?"

"Sure. There's a good place in Pleasant Hill. I'll show you where to turn." DJ looked over at the man driving the car. Light from the dashboard showed a strong face with an almost permanent smile. Laugh lines crinkled the edges of his sky blue eyes. His thick hair looked more white than gray in the dimness. It was cut short as though he didn't care to fuss with it.

"You think I could compete with a cutting horse?"

"Why not? There are all kinds of local shows. If the horse is really good and you don't feel confident enough, you can hire someone to train and show him."

Joe nodded. "I mentioned to your grandmother that I might be too old to do something like this, and she nearly bit my head off."

"A lot of retired people compete. They've finally got a chance to buy a horse, and they're loving it." DJ pointed to a huge plastic balloon shaped like an ice-cream container. "Over there. Take the next exit."

By the time they finished their ice cream and Joe dropped her off at home, DJ knew she had a friend for life. Of course, their love for horses gave them plenty to talk about. Joe Crowder was an easy man to talk to. No wonder Gran had fallen in love so fast.

DJ fell asleep thanking God for the big horse that had already taken over a large part of her heart. Soon Major would be hers!

She talked nonstop on the way to the Academy in the morning, telling Amy all about the dark bay horse and her evening with Joe.

"And you didn't want Gran to marry him." Amy set the kickstand on her bike.

"I know. Maybe I could go live with Gran and Joe." She'd thought that before, but never said it out loud.

"DJ, you already have a home."

"Yeah." DJ thought back to the empty house she'd gladly left behind. If she didn't get a bunch of housework done today, she and her mother would be at it again. How come one house could get so messed up with only two people living in it?

Patches pranced around the hot walker, his momentum dragging the other horses clipped to it along at a trot. DJ stopped to watch him for a second. He sure was lively today. She hustled back to the barn to clean his stall. Bridget had increased her time with the gelding to two hours on the days she wasn't teaching.

Once in the arena, she trotted him around the circle three or four times, waiting for the signal that he was ready to settle down to business. When he finally agreed to an easy jog, she knew the time was right.

"Boy, whoever rides you is going to have to spend plenty of time in the warm-up arena." She patted his neck and started him into the routine. Figure eights for reining, first at a walk, then a jog, and finally a lope. He learned to dance with her as they practiced lead changes around the ring. Her body swayed with the rhythm—lean left, left lead; lean right, right lead. The movements gentle, the lope a thing of beauty and grace.

"Good Patches. That was the best ever." She reined him to a halt and patted his neck. There was no better feeling in the world than when a horse did what he was asked. She took in a breath scented with dust and the horse beneath her. "Okay, next step. Time to learn to back up."

She dismounted and, with the reins in one hand, tapped his shoulder with the other and pulled back with the reins. "Back, Patches, back," she instructed. Patches shifted from side to side and snorted. DJ repeated the command, voice firm, "Back, Patches, back."

This time he backed away from the pull on his bit. "Good job, Patches." She patted him and rubbed his nose. When she repeated the command, he planted his feet and didn't budge.

"Fiddle. And here I thought you were going to get this right away." She settled him down and tried again. Patches laid his ears back.

DJ took a deep breath, calming herself as much as the horse. The next time, he swished his tail, but he backed up a couple of steps. "Good, fella." This time he got loves and pats. He rubbed his nose against her shoulder.

When he obeyed the command four times in a row, DJ decided it was time to try the same command from his back. She mounted and settled into the saddle. "Back, Patches, back." She gently but firmly pulled back on the reins and leaned forward slightly, leaving the back door open for him to follow the command. "Back, Patches, back." He flattened his ears back and shifted from one foot to the other before he twitched his tail and backed up. DJ thumped on his neck and down his shoulder. "Good fella, Patches. Good." She petted him for a few moments, then gave the command again.

When he had obeyed three times in a row without arguing, she nudged him forward and let him jog around the arena. He let out a relieved-sounding snort.

"I'm with you, fella. But you did good." Just as she leaned forward to stroke his neck, a little kid ran up to the fence and leaped on the rails, his shoes clanging on the aluminum bars.

Patches exploded. Head down, rear feet in the air. Stiff-legged hop and another buck.

DJ grabbed for the saddle horn. Too late. She was off and flying through the air.

She hit the dirt with a *thwump* that vibrated throughout her body.

Chapter • 9

Air. I can't get air.

"DJ, are you okay?"

If I could breathe, I might be. DJ fought the clenching pain in her chest. She wiggled her fingers and toes. Yep, all there and working. It was just her breath. She tried to take little shallow huffs. Getting the wind knocked out of you took some getting used to.

She looked up to find Amy peering down into her face.

"Blink if you can hear me." Amy spoke slowly, as if DJ were hard of hearing.

DJ blinked.

"Hey, you know what? You're supposed to tuck and roll on a fall like that, not land flat out."

DJ's furious gaze made Amy grin.

"Are you really all right?" Amy let her concern show.

"I . . . am . . . fine." The whisper broke through the lock on DJ's chest. "Wh-where . . . is . . . P . . . ?"

"Running around like a wild mustang. Hilary and John are trying to catch him."

"I . . . could . . . k . . ." DJ finally was able to get enough air past her tongue to talk. She pushed herself till she was sitting on one hip, her straight arms propping her up. Her head refused to remain upright without a steel brace, but other than that, she thought she might live. At least live long enough to kill that . . . She halted the thought. Calling him names wouldn't do anyone any good. And at the moment it was a waste of good air.

"You're really all right?"

"I will be." DJ sucked in a deep breath and spit out the grains of dirt that coated her lips. She rubbed them together, then backhanded her mouth. "That good-for-nothing horse, I . . ." She looked around the arena to spot him playing dodge-'em with the two workers.

"I think he's laughing." Amy fought now to keep a straight face.

"Well, don't *you* laugh. I'll find my sense of humor again, after I beat him into the ground." DJ reached out a hand and let Amy pull her up. Standing, her chest still hurt, but she no longer sounded like a leaky bellows. She dusted off her jeans and T-shirt.

"You look like you've been rolling around in the dirt." Amy ducked a left swing. "How you gonna catch Patches?"

"The only way. Get a grain bucket." DJ strode off across the arena and out the gate, calling Patches all the names she could think of and a few she made up as she went along. She included a few for herself, as well.

"That will not help." Bridget met her halfway back across the parking lot.

"The grain won't? Sure it will, he loves treats."

"No, calling yourself names. Getting dumped sometimes just goes with the territory." Bridget kept pace with DJ.

"How'd you know?"

"DJ, anyone can read your face like an open book. Besides, I remember the times it happened to me. You always think you could have done something differently. Maybe you could have. You never know what will happen to spook a horse, so you need to do your best to pay attention, build lightning reflexes, and dust yourself off when you hit the ground. Praying that you do not get hurt is not a bad idea, either."

DJ nodded. "Here I was patting him and telling him what a great job he was doing, and he dumped me. See if he ever gets praise from me again." Her smile said she was teasing.

She let herself into the arena and shook the bucket. "Hey, Patches, how about lunch?"

Hilary and John both gave her a grateful look. The ones they directed at the now-calming horse could have branded him with a big

D for disgusting. Patches trotted over to DJ and stuck his head out to sniff the bucket. DJ poured grain from her hand back into the pail. Patches stepped closer. DJ reached out and snagged his reins with one hand, letting him grab a bite before handing the pail to Amy. "There now, mister, your running days are done."

"Get back on him now and make him go through his paces so he does not think he can get away with this type of behavior." Bridget crossed her arms on the top rail and rested her chin on a closed fist.

DJ did as ordered, feeling some creaks in her body when she swung her leg over the saddle. It might be a good idea to take a long, hot soak when she got home. Shame they didn't have a hot tub.

She kept a careful eye on her horse and worked him through walk, jog, lope, figure eights, and reverses, working about five feet from the rail. The first time he came to the spot where the child had scared him, he tried to leap clear across the arena—without touching the ground. DJ moved right with him, ready and waiting for his antics.

"Good, that's the way. Do not ever let a horse buffalo you. Show him who is in control."

"He's come a long way, hasn't he?" Mrs. Johnson said when she joined Bridget and DJ at the fence a few minutes later. "But I can certainly see why he isn't a horse for Andrew here. I'm glad I'm not the one training him, even though I've ridden in the past."

"Once DJ is finished with Patches, he'll be a dependable horse for you."

"Maybe we should have you watch for a large pony for us, something more like Bandit." The woman smoothed a strand of long blond hair back into the club at her neck. She dropped her hand to the shoulder of the slender boy standing beside her.

DJ watched the boy's reaction. He didn't look as though learning to ride was the thing he wanted most in the world. In fact, he looked scared to bits. *Uh-oh,* she thought. *This could be a hard one.*

"How would you like to pet Patches?" she asked the silent child. While he looked to be about eight, his face had the pallor of a child who spent most of his time indoors. Had he been sick or something?

Andrew shook his head.

"Come on, dear." Mrs. Johnson took her son's hand and reached toward the horse's muzzle with it.

Patches lowered his head and sniffed, then snorted, not even a big snort.

Andrew jerked back.

Patches jerked up.

DJ knew they were in trouble. His lesson today would not be on a horse's back—not even one as gentle as Bandit.

"Let me put Patches here away, and then we'll start our lesson," she said with a smile meant to reassure the child.

Even she could tell the smile had failed. This kid did *not* want anything to do with horses.

When DJ put the gelding back in his stall, he rubbed his forehead against her chest and blew gently, as if he was worn out. "You silly thing. Yes, I forgive you. Just don't do it again, okay?" Patches snuffled her cheek and nosed her pocket, obviously hoping for a treat.

"Sorry, fella, you don't deserve one. I'm fresh out anyway." She slid the lower half of the door in place and headed for the drink machine. She'd earned a can of root beer, that was for sure. Then it was on to Andrew.

But when the boy absolutely refused to leave his mother's side, Mrs. Johnson smiled apologetically and sent Andrew to the car. He scampered off as if shot from a cannon. "I'm sure he'll come around. We'll be back on Tuesday."

"From now on she will not be allowed in the area while you are giving a lesson." Bridget patted DJ on the shoulder. "I will take care of that, and you can help that scared little rabbit learn horses can be good friends."

DJ nodded, but felt doubtful.

Sipping her drink, she wandered back to the tack room and gathered her grooming supplies. Even though she didn't have many stalls to clean, she still had a couple horses to groom.

When DJ got home, a message on the machine from Angie said she had a new baby brother. DJ clapped her hands. "All right!" She found the note her mother had left that morning, including a long list of chores to do. Lindy would be late tonight, and she had to leave on an unexpected trip in the morning. DJ felt her chin bounce to the floor and refuse to return to its proper place. So what was *she* supposed to do? Could she stay by herself? Why not? She wandered around the house, touching Gran's easel, her wing chair. DJ picked up Gran's painting smock and raised it to her nose. The bite of turpentine and the smell of paints were mingled with the floral fragrance that was Gran. DJ dropped the garment back on its hook on the edge of the easel.

She'd better get to vacuuming. The cord was tangled around the broom in the closet, and when she jerked on the handle, a bundle of cleaning rags scattered at her feet. Putting them back caused the mop to fall over.

"This kind of thing only happens in cartoons." DJ slammed the door on the mess and headed for the kitchen. Fixing a snack sounded like a better idea. But her breakfast stuff, along with her mother's, still cluttered the counter.

"How come I have to pick up after her, too?" DJ grumbled at the food containers in the open fridge. She pushed things around until she found the pickle slices, took them out along with the mayo and lettuce, and set them on the counter. After making a ham and cheese sandwich, she added chips to her plate and took it into the family room. She could watch television now that she was off restrictions, so she plunked down in a corner of the sofa, raised the remote, and started flipping channels.

Channel surfing drove her mother nuts. DJ kept pressing the button just for the pure fun of it, even though she didn't really like it, either—at least not when someone else was doing it. Nothing worth watching unless it was Oprah. She tuned it in for a moment, then flicked the Off button. She was done with lunch anyway.

By the time she'd finished the chores her mother had assigned her, the sun had sunk behind the trees. DJ settled into the lounge on the deck with a root beer and her sketch pad, but she couldn't keep her mind on drawing.

Could she stay alone while her mother traveled? Of course. Did she want to? The house seemed so empty in the daylight, what would it be like at midnight? *It doesn't make any difference—I'd be asleep by then.*

Mom would never let her stay alone. She could go to Amy's. If only Gran was living here where she belonged rather than in San Francisco. Here DJ was fourteen years old, and she'd never stayed alone all night.

"Grow up, you can't be a baby all your life." House finches chirped and tweeted in the buckeye tree by the side fence. Mourning doves dug in the seeds at the bottom of the feeder, their wings whistling when they flew. The backyard peace settled around her. A couple of blocks over, the Rottweiler barked, his deep voice announcing his family's homecoming.

"Gran, you need to be here. You're the one who made our backyard so perfect. What will happen to it without you?" DJ knew she should turn on the sprinklers. The lawn needed mowing. How was she supposed to take care of the house, the yard, work at the Academy, and return to school next week? How was she going to make it?

The questions stole the gentle peace and sent her mind into overdrive. She glared at her sketch pad. The horse she'd been drawing while she'd been thinking was off kilter; something was wrong with his shoulders and the way he carried his head. She crisscrossed angry lines right through him.

She looked up to see Lindy standing on the deck. "Did you call Gran and ask if she could come stay with you?" her mother asked as she sorted the mail. Obviously the stack of bills hadn't helped her mood any.

"No."

"Did you ask Amy if you could stay there?"

"No." DJ softened her tone. "I've been thinking, it's only one night, and since I'm fourteen now, I should be able to stay alone."

"Over my dead body."

"M-o-ther. Other people my age stay alone."

"Not my kid." Lindy headed for the phone. "I'll call Gran. I have to be gone two days next week, too. Have to fly down to Los Angeles on Monday night for a meeting at eight Tuesday morning."

DJ may have looked as if she were listening to her mother, but the voices inside her head were arguing so loudly, she couldn't hear anything else. She clamped her teeth together to keep them from coming out.

This was so unfair.

"Gran said she'll come." Lindy returned to the family room where DJ sat crossways in a chair, her legs dangling over the side. She'd chewed two nails down to the quick.

"Great, treat me like a baby. See if I care."

"Darla Jean, what has gotten into you?" Her mother planted her feet in the carpet and her hands on her hips—right smack in front of DJ. "I know you hate being here alone in the afternoon and evening, so why the big push for all night?"

"I have to grow up sometime. You keep telling me to grow up, and then when I try, you call Gran. 'Please, Mom, come take care of our little darling.'" DJ imitated her mother's voice to perfection. The sneer on her face was her own.

"If you can't talk any more politely than that, you may go to your room."

"Gladly." DJ shoved herself out of the chair and stormed past her mother, thudding her fury out on each stairstep. Just in time, she thought the better of slamming her door. She could barely hear the click of the lock over the pounding of the blood in her head.

She locked her arms across her chest and stared out the window, angry with herself for losing her temper again.

This was all so stupid. She really hadn't wanted to stay alone, and now she had made a big issue out of it. Maybe the fall from Patches had rattled her brains, too.

Gran was in the kitchen the next afternoon when DJ returned from her day at the Academy. DJ crossed the tile floor and wrapped both arms around her grandmother, inhaling the wonderful floral fragrance that Gran had worn so long it seemed steeped in her pores.

"I've missed you so, darlin', you just can't imagine." Gran hugged both arms around DJ's waist.

"Try me. Nothing's the same without you here." DJ stepped back and looked her grandmother in the face. "You don't have to do this, you know. I could stay by myself."

"Oh, I think Joe can live one night without me. He has two days off next week, so we'll both stay here then."

"You'll be here when school starts." Joy welled up and splashed across DJ's face.

The two of them spent the evening out in the backyard, pruning the roses, staking the chrysanthemums, and digging out the bent grass that tried to take over everything.

DJ pointed up at two hummingbirds playing buzz tag, each trying to chase the other out of the yard. One perched on a branch of the pink oleander, then rose up clicking his warning when the other returned.

DJ sat on the grass, her arms crossed over her raised knees. This was the way it was supposed to be. Her and Gran.

"Gran?"

"Yes, dear?" Gran looked up from where she was plucking dead flower heads off the red geranium.

"Can I come and live with you and Joe? When you move into your house out here, I mean."

Chapter · 10

"Oh, my dear, is it that bad?"

DJ studied her chewed-off fingernails. "Mom and I just don't get along too well—you know that." She raised her gaze to see her grandmother shaking her head.

"I know. Maybe it's all my fault." Gran sank down on the grass beside DJ.

"How could it be your fault? You're the one who took care of me." DJ crossed her legs and propped her elbows on her knees.

"Yes, and I took over your mother's job. It seemed best at the time, but now I'm not so sure."

"Gran, that's not what I meant." DJ wished she could bite off her tongue. Why'd she ever bring this up? "Don't feel bad, please. I wouldn't hurt you for the world."

"I know, darlin'. I know." Gran reached over and laid a hand on DJ's upper arm. "We'll all just have to pray about this, let God make it better. He will, you know, if you ask."

"I asked. Mom and I really had a big fight then." DJ eyed a hanging cuticle. Her hand automatically rose to her mouth so she could chew it off. A bit of garden dirt came with it. She spit that out.

Gran took DJ's hand in hers and clucked over the mangled fingernails. "Oh, darlin'." Her voice felt as soft as the falling twilight.

DJ pulled her hand back. "I've been praying about my fingernails, too, and look where it's got me."

"I know. Satan seems to jump right in and let us have it with both barrels as soon as we pray for help changing something. But God's Word is stronger, mightier than a sword." Gran rose to her feet. "Come on, we have to find just the right verse for you. Then when you start to chew your nails, you repeat the Bible verse until the need to chew is gone."

"Oh, right, Gran. You won't find a verse about fingernails." DJ got up and, after picking up their gardening tools and dumping the weeds and trimmings in the compost bin, followed Gran into the house.

Gran had settled into her wing chair, Bible on her lap. A pad of paper and pencil lay beside her on the lamp table.

DJ leaned closer to read the writing on the tablet. Psalm 139 stood out at the top of the list. She looked up into Gran's face. The light from the lamp created a halo in the gold-shot fluffy hair. A halo sure did fit Gran. If anyone was an angel, it was her.

DJ took her usual position at Gran's feet, her cheek resting against Gran's knee. Immediately Gran laid a hand on DJ's head and stroked, much like DJ did with her horses. Calming, comforting, and full of love.

DJ's sigh started at her toes and slithered its way to her head. If only they could go back to the way things used to be. She blinked. Did she want to go back? Back before Joe? Before Major? She scrunched her eyes shut.

"Why don't you and Joe live here? Then everything would be just fine."

"I'm glad you want to keep him in the family. He thinks you're pretty special, too, you know." Gran kept up the stroking.

"I had a great time with him on Tuesday. He's real easy to talk to." DJ tilted her head so the stroking hand could soothe a new place.

"I know. He laughs easily, knows how to have a good time, and gives God the glory for everything—including meeting me and my family."

DJ flinched. Thinking back to the way she'd behaved before the wedding made her want to crawl under the rug. Gran stopped stroking to write down another reference.

"I'll give you this list in the morning. How about scrambled eggs for breakfast?"

"Okay." DJ stood up, her yawn nearly cracking her jaw. "Good night." She bent down to give Gran a hug and a kiss. "Think you can get through the night without seeing Joe?" She dropped another kiss in the middle of Gran's halo.

"Oh, you!" Gran gave her a playful swat. "For your information, I was just about to call him."

"Tell him hi for me." Another yawn, this one longer than the first. She headed for the stairs. How come Gran could make such a difference in the atmosphere of the house?

Two days later, Saturday morning dawned. The birds were barely chirping before DJ was out of bed and scrambling for her clothes. Mr. Yamamoto would be driving her and Amy and all their gear to the Academy. He helped to load horses for all the shows.

A car horn honked. DJ finished gathering her things and flew down the stairs. Maybe by the next show, she'd be able to compete again.

"Morning, DJ. You're looking mighty alert for this time of day," Mr. Yamamoto said out the rolled-down driver's-side window. He'd pulled the car into the driveway to turn around.

"Thanks. I love early mornings, unlike someone else we know." DJ opened the rear door and tossed her duffel bag across the seat.

Amy mumbled something from her nest in the front.

"Come on, Ames." DJ settled herself in back. "You can sleep tonight." She thumped her friend on the head.

"Wish there were barns on the showgrounds so we didn't have to trailer the horses every day." DJ pulled a food bar out of her pocket and unwrapped it.

"This is difficult all right." Mr. Yamamoto took a sip from the coffee mug on the dashboard. "I hear you're getting a horse pretty soon."

"Yeah, his name's Major. Wait till you see him. He's huge." She took a bite out of her bar. Three-day horse shows took a toll on everyone, both people and horses.

Loading went without a hitch, unlike the time before when Gray Bar caused a ruckus. The thought of Gray Bar made DJ wonder how James was doing. Would he really write?

Once at the Saddle Club grounds, DJ helped the younger riders tie their horses side by side on the long rope stretched from tree to tree. Together, they organized their gear. Parents who hadn't done this before needed as much instruction as their children. They set out grain, then wedges of hay, and DJ showed the kids where to fill the water buckets. She took care of Angie's horse since the girl hadn't shown up yet.

Bridget came by, clipboard in hand. The board held a list of all the Academy pupils and the classes they'd entered. She handed DJ a matching board. "Just so we can make changes if needed. And so you can look ahead to see who might need assistance."

"Angie's not here yet."

"They did not ring to say not to bring the horse, so they will be here." Bridget answered a shout from across the long string of horses. "Talk to you later. Any questions, you know how to find me."

"Who does all this stuff when I'm showing?" DJ muttered an hour later.

"We take turns." Hilary stopped brushing her horse long enough to answer. "You've just made my life easier. How about not showing ever again?" Her teeth gleamed white against her dark skin.

"Oh, yeah, I'll just go along to make sure none of you prima donnas have to scoop poop." DJ fetched the shovel from behind Hilary's horse.

"Thank you. I am glad you're getting Major soon. I can't wait till we're competing in the same classes. That'll be fun."

"That won't be for a while." DJ waved at one of the fathers who called her name. It was Angie's dad, apologizing for their being late.

Angie was grooming her horse as though she were in a speed competition.

"We had a sick baby last night, and none of us got much sleep." Mr. Lincoln apologized again. "When he finally dropped off, we all did."

"No harm done. Angie, you have plenty of time. Since you're riding Western, you'll be on after noon."

Angie let out a sigh that could be heard clear across the bay to San Francisco. "I want to do good out there, and I can't swallow past my butterflies. Mom was scared I was going to have an asthma attack."

"Oh no. No asthma allowed here. But watch out for the yellow jackets. They come to feast on all the picnic stuff." DJ turned to answer another question. "See ya, Angie. Take it easy."

Angie took third place in her class that afternoon and received a white ribbon to cheering applause from the Academy rooting section. Sam got a fourth, and Krissie a sixth.

"Your girls did well. It shows what a good teacher you are." Bridget stopped DJ long enough to give the compliment.

DJ met her girls back at the tie line. "I can't believe it. You guys did super. Wow!"

Their thank-you's and sighs of relief tumbled over each other. The three dismounted and formed a ring with DJ, dancing and hugging.

"You don't get excited or anything, do you?" Amy led her horse past them on her way to the warm-up ring.

"Not a bit." DJ thumped her friend on the arm. "Go get 'em. You have the Academy's honor to uphold."

"Oh, yuk. Thanks a big fat bunch. Now you're making my insides flop around rather than fly in formation."

"Do *you* still get scared?" Angie asked.

"Of course. Everyone gets scared. That's part of showing." Amy led Josh around the arena where the novice Western class was now showing.

By Monday evening when they returned the final trailer load to the Academy, DJ felt as if she'd been dragged under the wheels of the trailers. The Academy students, both youth and adult, had done very well. Hilary won Hunter/Seat equitation again and took a second in Hunter/Jumper. Amy took the Trail-riding class and won two reds and a white in her other events.

"You get on home now; you have done enough," Bridget said when she found DJ putting tack away. "Thank you so much for all your help. You can be proud of yourself. I certainly am."

"Thank you. We did good, didn't we?"

"About the best ever. Our reputation is really growing, thanks to all of you." Bridget turned to leave. "See you tomorrow after school."

DJ groaned. "Thanks for reminding me."

"Hey, you comin'?" Amy trotted up to the tack room. "Dad's ready to go."

As soon as they got into the car, the girls slumped against the doors. Mr. Yamamoto wore a weary look himself.

"Anybody for a pony party?"

Groans drowned out his chuckle.

"Your dad has a sick sense of humor."

"I heard that." Their groans turned to halfhearted giggles. More like wimpy chuckles, really.

"See you at 7:30, right?" he asked after stopping the car at DJ's house. "I see your grandparents are here."

"See ya." Grandparents—as in two. What a nice thought. DJ slung her duffel over her shoulder and dragged herself into the house.

She almost fell asleep trying to tell Joe and Gran about the show.

"Well, I tell you, if you don't have another one before the first of October, this is the last show of yours I miss." Joe crossed one leg over his opposite knee. "I could hardly keep my mind on patrol, I kept thinking of you Academy kids competing. Major's going to love it. Today some little kid stuck cotton candy up for him to taste. He tasted it all right. Ate every bit in two bites. The poor kid started screaming. After I gave him money for another cotton candy, I had to take Major to a hose and wash off his face."

DJ giggled at the thought of Major with a pink nose. Her giggle turned into a jaw-cracking yawn. "Mom get off okay?" Gran nodded. DJ yawned again. "I'm so tired I don't think I can climb the stairs."

"Do you have your things ready for the morning?"

"You kidding? This is DJ you're talkin' to, remember? I'll get up early; it's easier than working now." She hugged and kissed Gran, then paused for a second. Crossing to the sofa, she gave Joe a hug, too.

"Night, DJ." Joe sounded gruff, as though maybe he had a frog in his throat. "I'll be at school to pick you up, okay?"

"Great."

"There's something for you up on your desk," Gran said.

DJ gave her a questioning look, but Gran only smiled. The stairs could have been Mt. Everest. DJ groaned when she made it to the top. When she finally dragged her feet down the long hall and into her room, she dumped her bag by the bed and collapsed across it. If only she didn't have to move for ten years.

When she roused herself enough to sit up, her gaze fell on the paper on her desk. In Gran's most beautiful calligraphy, the words leaped off the parchment paper. "I can do all things through Christ who strengthens me."

DJ read the verse through a second time, then a third. So this was her verse to overcome nail-biting, smart-mouthing, and everything else that bugged her. She let the paper float back to the desk. This couldn't really work—could it? Would Gran make up something like this?

Sure, their pastor talked about the power of God's Word, but did

God *really* care about Darla Jean Randall chewing her nails? As DJ undressed, she thought about it. If Jesus was really in her heart, and she knew He was, then He cared about every little bit of her. So much He even knew how many hairs were left on her head. Even after she'd left some in the hairbrush that morning.

"You must be awfully smart, God," she muttered as she drew back the covers. "But if you care so much, I'll give it a try. By the way, thanks for taking care of us today. I forget to tell you thank-you a lot. Thanks for Joe—he makes Gran so happy. And please help me in school tomorrow. I haven't told anyone else, but I am kind of scared. First day with new teachers and all that stuff is scary." She flipped over on her side and reread the paper. "So that's my verse, huh? Did you put Gran up to this?"

When Mr. Yamamoto let Amy and DJ off in front of the school in the morning, they looked at each other as if they'd rather climb back into the car and head for home. Each girl shrugged her backpack over one shoulder, squared both shoulders, and started out across the parking lot.

"Bye, Dad." Amy turned to wave.

DJ did the same. "Well, let's get to our locker and pick up our class list."

By the end of the day, DJ knew several new things. She and Amy had only one class together. Art would be DJ's favorite, algebra her least. Literature would be fun because she loved to read, and PE would be an easy A. The rest she wasn't sure about. One thing was sure, how was she going to keep up with everything? There was so much she had to do at home and with Major before she'd be ready for the Olympics. How would she ever do it all?

Chapter · 11

"Who invented school, anyway?" Amy muttered.

"I don't know, but yell at them for me." DJ slumped against the wall by their shared locker. "And if I don't keep my grades up, you know what will be the first to go."

"You always get straight As."

"I've never had algebra and Latin before." DJ hoisted her backpack. "Let's see if Joe is waiting for us out there. Mucking fifty stalls would be better than this."

At the Academy she could tell instantly that Bridget and Joe approved of each other. They sized each other up and both turned to smile at DJ. She left the two of them talking about cutting horses and went to saddle Patches.

By the time she'd worked the gelding through his paces and had him backing up smoothly, she could easily forget school ever existed. And once she flew over the jumps with Megs, she felt alive again. This was where she belonged, on a horse, on target for her dream. After she'd groomed Megs, she noticed Hilary frowning at one of the new workers. She had to think a minute before she remembered his name: Tony. He sure didn't look like a happy camper.

"You know these stalls are your responsibility." DJ could tell Hilary was using every ounce of her tact and patience.

What had he done—or not done?

"I cleaned 'em." His lip stuck out far enough to hang a bridle on.

"Then you'll have to clean them again, and do it right this time."

Oh no, not another James. We need a troublemaker like we need manure. DJ felt like calling for Bridget, but they had their code: Handle everything you can yourself. It made you stronger and promoted better feelings between all the student workers.

She turned in time to see Bridget and Joe pause just inside the door.

"You can't make me!" Tony gripped the handle of his shovel.

"No, I can't make you, but I can report you, and then you won't be able to ride or take lessons until Bridget says you can." Hilary leaned against the stall wall as if she didn't have a care in the world. "It's up to you."

Tony glared. He grumbled. He swore. But he went back into the stall and started tossing out dirty shavings.

"Oh, and that kind of language isn't tolerated around here, either, so consider this your warning. I'll be back to check on your progress in half an hour."

DJ sneaked a look at Bridget. The smile of approval she saw on the trainer's face made her more proud of Hilary than she already was. If only she could learn to be so cool under pressure.

She hung up her tack and straightened the bridles. Hilary came in and sank down on the lid of the tack box.

"You were so cool." DJ sat down beside the older girl.

"Thanks, I felt like taking his shovel and rapping him over the head with it." She shook her head, setting her corn-rowed braids to swinging. "Sometimes I wonder where these jerks come from. Why ask to work here if they don't want to clean stalls?"

"They think it's all show time. The movies don't show how much work goes into caring for horses."

"I guess." Hilary got back up. "Hey, how was school?"

"Don't ask." DJ put on a happy face. "I love my art class, though."

"Sure you do. Let you ride, jump, train, and draw pictures of horses, and you'd be in horse heaven."

"How do you know?"

" 'Cause you're just like me." Hilary patted DJ on top of her helmet. "And if you think junior high takes time, wait till you hit high school."

As usual, Hilary gave her something to think about.

Gran was ready to put dinner on the table when Joe and DJ walked in the door. "Wash your hands, you two. I don't want any horse hair in my salad." She raised her face for Joe to kiss.

DJ felt a blush start about her collarbone.

"We're embarrassing our girl." Gran pushed the big man away with a gentle hand.

The comment turned the heat up. DJ shook her head at them with a grin. "You're as bad as a couple of teenagers."

"How would you know?"

"I got eyes." Her laughter trailed back as she took the stairs two at a time.

Even with Joe there, dinner felt like it was supposed to. She and Gran had spent many nights together with Lindy away on business trips. By the time they'd listened to Joe rave about Bridget and the Academy, Gran tell about a new contract, and DJ fill them in on day one at school, darkness had wrapped the house in its comforting arms.

When the phone rang, DJ jumped up to get it. "Hi, Mom. How's your trip going?" DJ twirled the phone cord around her finger while she listened. "Amy and I only have one class together. We don't even have the same lunch. I know I'll live with it, but I'd rather be at the Academy." She grimaced at her mother's response. She should know better than to tease her mother over the phone. "Sure, Gran's here, I'll get her." She put her hand over the mouthpiece and called her grandmother. "See you Wednesday." She handed the phone to Gran, then stopped in the doorway to listen.

"Say, if it's all right, I'd like to have Robert and the boys to dinner on Wednesday," Gran was saying. DJ stopped in surprise. *How come Gran hadn't mentioned it to her?* She headed for the dining room.

"How come you didn't tell me about Wednesday?" She slumped in her chair when Gran came back to the dining room.

"I needed to check it out with your mother first. If you wouldn't eavesdrop like that, you wouldn't discover so many surprises."

DJ slumped lower. She memorized the pattern on her placemat.

"What difference does it make? I just thought this family needed to get to know one another better, and the boys have been begging to come see their cousin." Gran motioned toward the coffeepot, asking Joe if he wanted more.

He shook his head. "I think we're going to have to buy a pony for the grandkids as soon as we move into our house. One like Bandit would be just right."

"Wish we *did* have a pony; we don't have any stuff here to entertain little kids."

"Oh, Robert will bring something. Anyway, the boys love being read to."

"They can sit still long enough for a story?"

Both Gran and Joe laughed at the skeptical look on DJ's face.

"Well, I better hit my books." DJ started stacking dishes to carry to the kitchen.

"You go ahead, I'll get those." Joe stopped her when she reached for his plate.

"Thanks." She dropped a kiss on Gran's head and whispered in her ear. "You better keep him if he does dishes."

"I heard that."

DJ chuckled her way upstairs. "You two just want to smooch without me watching," she yelled down from the top landing.

"Darla Jean, whatever—" Her grandmother's words were cut off.

———————————

The more DJ hurried the next afternoon, the more behind she got. Patches was never one to be hurried. His crow-hopping on the backing drill reminded her of that.

By the time she'd taken Megs over the course twice, the mare had refused two jumps.

"All right, DJ, what is bothering you?" Bridget called from the center of the arena.

"We have company coming for dinner."

"So."

"So I was hurrying."

"And?"

"And hurrying doesn't work. So now I take a deep breath, relax, and take Megs over the course again, concentrating on what I'm doing."

"Good. I can see that you listen when I talk to you. Now take your own advice and count the strides between each jump. I have spaced them for six. Make sure she is jumping straight. If you get lazy, your horse will feel it immediately."

"Okay." DJ returned to a two-point trot, circled the ring, and cantered toward the first jump again. This time they flew over each obstacle without a pause. She didn't need Bridget to tell her she'd done a good job.

DJ and Joe were the last to arrive for dinner. As they walked in the door, two torpedoes hurled themselves against DJ's legs and clung. Two matching round faces with laughing blue eyes and smiles from dimple to dimple kept their mouths in perpetual motion.

"We been waiting for you. Where you been? How come you didn't come sooner? We comed to see you. Did you bring your horse?"

DJ looked from one to the other, doing her best to tell them apart. No such luck. "Okay, B&B, let me put my stuff down—"

"B&B!" The two shrieked in unison.

"Me's Billy, him's Bobby." The one on the right let go long enough to point.

"Well, how am I supposed to tell who's who?" DJ let a laughing Joe take her bag.

"The same way the rest of us do. We yell 'hey, you' and they both come." Joe grabbed one of the two and, with the giggling body clamped under his arm, headed for the kitchen. The other let loose DJ's leg and pelted after them.

DJ sucked in a deep breath. It was as if those two drained the room of oxygen. She started for the stairs when her gaze snagged on the two people standing by the French doors to the deck. Her five-feet-five mother looked tiny beside a taller and younger version of Joe Crowder. Robert's fair hair and great smile made him look like a movie star. DJ squinted; a tall and blond Tom Cruise filled the doorway. Her mother was laughing, her long earrings catching the light when she shook her head. She wore her hair pulled back on the sides, and, as usual, her clothes looked as if she'd just stepped out of a Nordstrom's window.

DJ looked down at her dirty jeans, a tear in one knee, her T-shirt liberally decorated with horse hairs. She could hear Gran with Joe and the twins in the kitchen. Everyone had someone but her.

Feeling both grungy and unneeded, she made her way up the stairs to take a shower.

"Dinner in fifteen minutes," Gran called after her.

DJ started to take her usual place at the table, but World War III erupted over the chair next to her.

"Me sit by DJ!"

"No." Big shove. "Me!"

"Hey, guys, we can fix this easy. I'll sit here." DJ pulled out the next chair over. "And then there's room on each side." Guess she was needed after all. They reached for her hands when Joe bowed his head for grace. "Thank you, Father, for this new family you have created. Thank you for the food that Melanie has so lovingly prepared. May we all seek to do your will. Amen."

Everyone joined in the amen. DJ glanced from one side of her to the other. The boys were two peas in a pod. When they grinned up at her, she felt her heart flutter and expand. She finally had cousins. And they were pretty cute.

But by the time she cut up their meat, helped pour milk, and answered fifty nonstop questions, she was wiped out. Robert was laughing at her across the table.

"Just tell 'em to knock it off." He put on a stern face. "Okay, guys, DJ would like to eat her dinner, too, you know."

" 'Kay. *Then* will you show us your pictures?"

"Your horse pictures—the ones you drawed." The left side piped up. "Gran said you has lots of pictures."

"We draw pictures, too."

By the time dinner was over, DJ felt as though she'd just spent three hours at a tennis match. While the adults cleaned up, she took the boys upstairs to her room, where they oohed and aahed over her drawings.

"How about a story?" She took them with her to her bookshelf where she'd kept all her favorite books since she was a little girl. "You like Dr. Seuss?" At their enthusiastic agreement, she pulled *Cat in the Hat* off the shelf. She plumped her pillows into a stack, then snuggled against them, one boy tucked under each arm.

When they good-byed Robert and the boys out the door, Robert leaned over to whisper in her ear, "They think you're better than Saturday morning cartoons, and that's really saying something."

"Thanks, I guess. I like them, too."

Robert said good-night to Lindy last. "I'll call you."

"Okay. You guys take care."

DJ watched from her spot by Gran and Joe. If she didn't know better, those were sappy looks her mother and Robert were sharing. The kind of look that lasts forever in the movies. Surely she was reading more into this than she saw.

She looked at Gran and recognized a misty look in her eyes, too. For pete's sake, what was going on here? If romance was contagious, she'd better look out.

"We better get going, too." Joe stepped back, taking Gran with him. "I have to be at the station at seven. Only thirteen more days to go, and I'll be a free man."

"And I have homework." DJ wished she could ask Gran to stay. Couldn't Joe get along without her once in a while?

"Me too." Lindy gave her mother a hug. "Thank you both for coming to our rescue again." When she hugged Joe, she whispered something into his ear.

The grin that split his face told DJ it was a compliment of some kind. "Me too," was all he said.

When the good-nights and good-byes were all said and the door closed, DJ headed for her room. She had a paper to write on a book she'd read during the summer. At the moment, not one title came to mind. This hadn't been a summer with much time for reading.

When she studied her bookshelf, the only thing that caught her attention was the *American Pony Club Manual*. It was definitely American, though she doubted her teacher would call it great literature. She'd been studying that for the last three years.

She pulled it off the shelf, grabbed a piece of paper out of her drawer, and started writing. She wrote fast, covering three pages before she realized it. After reading, rewriting, and copying, she stuck it in her folder. It would have to do.

Their last pony party on Saturday was a breeze compared to some of the others. Only four little kids, mothers who paid attention, and a hostess who gave them a bonus.

"That's my kind of party," DJ said when they trotted up the street on the way back to the Academy. "Makes me think we should continue."

"Think again. We said the end of summer was it. And summer's definitely over."

"I know, but where else could we have made this kind of money doing something we really like?"

Amy stopped and stared at her, shaking her head. "*We* really like pony parties? *We? Dream on.*"

"Come on, you gotta admit we had fun—most of the time."

"Okay, I'll go along with that, but we just don't have time to do this. You said if you didn't keep your grades up, you'd have to quit working at the Academy. My dad said the same."

"You think they've been talking behind our backs?"

"They don't need to. Comes with the territory. And don't change the subject. We are *not* doing more parties."

"Until next summer," DJ muttered the words fast.

"Dream on."

"After I pay for Major, I won't even have two hundred dollars left, and I need a good jumping saddle."

"You can use one of the Academy's."

"Good thing, too. Saddles cost so much. How do those riders on the equestrian team manage? Going for the Olympics must cost a bundle."

"You're just figuring that out? That's why so many riders get sponsors."

They trotted Bandit up to his stall and unloaded their gear. All the while DJ's hands were busy with grooming the pony and putting him away, her mind turned over ideas of how to make money for her dream. She needed thousands and thousands of dollars, not just hundreds. She could barely imagine how she would come up with a hundred dollars, let alone thousands.

Chapter • 12

DJ felt as if she were trapped in a revolving door. Whenever she tried to jump out, it spun faster. Get up, go to school, study, come home, work at the Academy, come home, eat, study, fall into bed, and start all over again. The days that her mother did the cooking gave her a few extra minutes to memorize Latin conjugations.

Only the thought that she was banking hours at the Academy to pay for Major's keep kept her going. Was the entire year going to be like this?

Two days after Joe retired, they trailered Major out to the Academy. When the big horse stepped out of the trailer and looked around as if he owned the place, DJ had to fight the burning in her eyes. Major was hers—as soon as she paid her money, of course. At long last, she owned a horse. A good horse, too, better than she dreamed possible.

She sent a thank-you heavenward and backed Major the rest of the way down the ramp. "Such a good fella. How perfect can you be?"

"He's going to like it here." Joe's eyes looked suspiciously liquid. "Your having him couldn't make me happier."

Major lifted his head and let out a whinny that set DJ's ears ringing. Horses answered him from in the barn and the outside stalls.

"If you'll hold him, I'll go get a saddle. Bridget said to let her know when we got here so she could watch me ride him the first time." DJ handed Joe the lead shank. She'd fit her new bridle later.

While she gathered her tack, she could barely keep from yelling. Instead she whispered, "I have a horse. Major is mine. I'm riding *my* horse for the first time." She felt like tap-dancing through the air.

When she saddled Major, she was instantly grateful for her five-feet seven-inch height. If she'd been a peanut like Amy, she'd have had to stand on a box to put the saddle in place.

She had to let the headstall out to the last notch to fit, but when everything was finally adjusted, she laid a hand over her heart to still its runaway pace.

"Can I give you a leg up?" Joe held the reins with one hand and cupped the other on his knee.

"Sure." Once in the saddle, she checked her stirrups, shortened one a notch, and checked again. This time when she straightened her legs, she felt balanced. And a long way from the ground. She looked down into the face of the man smiling up at her. "Thanks, Joe." She looked deep into his blue eyes, seeing nothing but love and pride shining there. "I have a question." At his nod, she continued. "Do you want to be called Gramps, Grandpa, or Joe?"

He blinked quickly, then cleared his throat. "Do you have a preference?"

"Well, since I'm DJ, you could be GJ—you know, Grandpa Joe."

"Could be." His chuckle invited a like response.

"But I think I'd rather call you Grandpa. I haven't had one of those for a long time, and my other one was pretty special."

"I'm sure he was. I'm honored to be your grandpa." Major gave him a nudge in the back. "I think our boy here is ready to do more than stand and listen to us talk." He turned and walked with them to the arena. "I'll get the gate."

Major moved out in a powerful, ground-eating walk. His smooth, even stride made DJ think about Patches and his spine-pounding hammer step. What a difference training made!

He responded to her aids almost before her thoughts became acts. Two-point trot, posting trot, canter. All controlled and as smooth as floating on a pool. What would he be like over a jump?

Reverse, figure eights, lead changes—he danced down the length of the arena as though they were performing to music. When she signaled him to back up, he did. Going sideways was no problem, either. She was almost afraid to move, in case this was all a dream and she might wake up in bed.

The sound of clapping brought her back to the real world. Bridget, Joe, Amy, Amy's father, and several others lined the aluminum rails.

"Do you bow, too?" Major flicked his ears back and forth at the sound of her voice.

DJ stopped him directly in front of Joe and Bridget. "He knows so much more than I do that it scares me. What if I'm not good enough for him?"

"Then he'll just make you better." Bridget studied the horse's head. "He has the look of a gentleman about him."

"You wouldn't say that if you were causing a disturbance and Major here figured it was his job to convince you differently. He's better than a German Shepherd for intimidating suspects."

"I'll remember that when my students get out of control."

DJ only half listened to them. She stroked Major's neck, reliving the experience she'd just had. Riding Major was like a piece of heaven—her own special piece.

"He's amazing," Amy said reverently.

"The two of you will definitely cause a sensation in the ring," Bridget said. "You look like you were made for each other."

"And to think he's spent all these years wasting away on the San Francisco police force." Joe winked at DJ.

"Those were his working years; now he gets to have fun." DJ motioned for Amy to open the gate. "Come on, I'll let you help me brush him down."

"You'll *let* me? How come I'm so honored?"

"You're my best friend, that's why." They headed for the barn, Amy trotting alongside.

"Does he feel as smooth as he looks?"

"Yup. You can ride him tomorrow if you like." DJ kicked her feet free of the iron stirrups and leaped to the ground. She stroked Major's neck and shoulder, running her hands over him as if memorizing every inch. When she led him to his stall, floored with fresh shavings, he looked around, acquainting himself with his new home. The horse in the stall next to him raised his nose to sniff through the bars. Major ignored him, snuffling the shavings, the hay rack, the full water bucket.

"You can have a drink as soon as we're finished."

Major raised his head, nickered at a horse that whinnied to him, then stood perfectly still for DJ to remove his tack. After she replaced his bridle with a nylon web halter and turned him loose, he drank a couple swallows and again checked out his new quarters.

DJ watched his every movement as if she'd never seen a horse before.

Amy watched both the horse and her friend. "I think you're in love."

"I think you're right. I've been waiting for this day for fourteen years."

"Come on, you didn't want a horse the day you were born."

"How do you know? Maybe I did." DJ gave Major a final pat and closed the door behind her. "You gotta admit it's been a long time."

When they got home, DJ went up to her room and opened her money box. Her bank account was now nearly empty. She lifted out the $380 they'd agreed upon and counted it again. Downstairs, she handed it to Joe.

"I don't know how to say enough thank-you's."

"You don't have to. I got the thrill of my life just watching you with him. And this way, I never have to tell him good-bye." He put the money in his billfold and drew out a folded piece of paper.

"Here's the bill of sale. We need to make this official, so after I sign it, you do the same. Then I'll make a copy for me. You get to keep this one. How's that?"

"Fine." Two thrills chased each other up and down her spine.

They both signed on the dotted lines. Joe reached out, and they shook hands.

"He's all yours." Joe, still holding her hand, patted it with his other. "With both mine and God's blessing."

DJ couldn't think of anything to say. But then, she would have had a hard time talking anyway.

The next afternoon when her students arrived, DJ stopped them before they could saddle their horses. "I have someone for you to meet."

"You got your horse!" Angie clapped her hands.

"Let's see." They grabbed DJ by the hands and dragged her down the aisle. She stopped in front of Major's stall. "Angie, Krissie, and Samantha, I'd like you to meet Major. Major, these horse-crazy girls are my students. You'll be going up in Briones with them some Saturday, so you might as well get to know them." Major arched his neck over the door and let each one of them pat his cheek.

"Wow! He's huge." "He's handsome." "I'm glad for you." The girls all spoke at the same time.

"Okay, back to work. I just had to show him off." DJ shooed them back to their stalls. She gave Major one last pat and followed them. His soft nicker followed her down the aisle.

"He already likes you," Angie said, picking up her saddle.

"Well, the feeling is sure mutual."

––––––––––

Now besides teaching, training Patches, and her other chores, she had to work Major. Had to, as in she'd die if she didn't. Within a week they were working him over the low jumps. He cleared them as though they were a waste of his time.

"Bit of a snob, is he?" Bridget said with a laugh one day.

DJ patted Major's sweaty neck. "He wants to go for the big ones. Like me."

"As soon as you both keep your timing consistent on these, we will talk about bigger jumps. Remember to count your strides between the jumps. You have to get that down to pure reflex. Timing is everything."

DJ nodded. She clamped her bottom lip between her teeth. She hated to have to be reminded of something so simple. But when they were jumping, she forgot everything but the glorious feel of it. She practiced as long as she dared before rushing home.

If this was life in the fast lane, she was keeping up—barely. But she wouldn't trade places with anyone for anything.

One afternoon there was a message from Gran on the machine when she got home from school. "I've called your mother at work and she says yes, so you have to come along. We'll pick you up at 7:00. I'm afraid you won't be able to spend all evening with Major. No jeans!" There was a pause, a giggle, and then her voice again. "And by the way, this includes dinner, so don't eat." DJ punched the Rewind button and listened again. The message still didn't make a whole lot of sense.

She changed clothes and headed for the Academy. Since she had her students today, she'd hardly get any time for Major. As soon as she got to the Academy, she put him out on the hot walker to loosen him up.

Patches loosened her up. He tried to loosen her clear *off*, but DJ had learned to read him and his tricks and was ready for him. He didn't like backing up. Not one bit.

"I know you like to be able to see where you're going, but you just have to learn to trust your rider. It's not as if I'm taking you into quicksand." His ears twitched back and forth as he listened to her. When she finished, he snorted and pawed the ground with one front foot. "Stop that!" Her sharp command caught his attention—fast.

This time he backed hesitantly. At least his ears were up. "Maybe that's what I need to do—yell at you."

"Mrs. Johnson started class with him today, but it did not go very well. Next time I am going to suggest she use one of the school horses until you have Patches better trained. I do not know why someone would go out and buy a green-broke horse for their child, especially for a boy like Andrew." Bridget shook her head. "Makes no sense to me."

DJ fought against the urge to hustle her class along. Every time she looked at her watch, it seemed the hands were racing to reach seven.

By the time she'd worked Major through the flat work, there was no time for jumping. What did Gran want that was so important anyway? Couldn't they do it on Saturday?

Everyone else was ready when she hit the door at 6:55. She held up a hand. "Don't panic, I'll make it." Four minutes and thirty seconds later, she shut the door on her room so her mother wouldn't see the mess. But she was ready. She could rebraid her hair in the car.

"Mother, what in the world is the big secret?" Lindy leaned forward. She and DJ occupied the backseat of Joe's new Ford Explorer.

"This is the first time we've ridden in this car." DJ sniffed in the new-car fragrance. "It almost smells as good as Major."

"DJ!" Lindy's tone had that impatient parent sound.

"I'll take that as a compliment." Joe beamed at her in the rearview mirror.

"You just have to wait." Gran turned in her bucket seat. "In fact, you have to close your eyes. No peeking!"

DJ and Lindy both groaned but did as they were told.

A few minutes later, the car stopped, and Gran said, "Open your eyes now."

DJ looked around. "This is your new house!"

"Mother . . . does this mean . . . ?"

"Yes. It's ours!" Gran dangled the keys with one hand and clasped Joe's with the other. "We're moving this weekend."

"Can we see it?" DJ shoved the car door open as she spoke.

"That's what we're here for. Robert will be here any minute with the boys. Sonja couldn't come today, but she and Andy will be here to help on Saturday." Gran led them on a grand tour as if they'd never seen a house before. DJ lingered in the room designated as hers. There was another guest room for the rest of the kids.

When the boys showed up, they each grabbed one of DJ's hands and made like they were stuck on with Crazy Glue. She could have used some glue on their mouths. Did little kids always ask this many questions?

On Saturday, as soon as she finished her work at the Academy, DJ rode her bike to Gran and Joe's new house rather than riding home. It wasn't any farther and there weren't any hills on the way.

Sonja grinned a greeting and handed DJ a box. "Master bedroom. You and I can start on the kitchen next."

"Where's my mom?"

"She and Robert are at your house packing Melanie's bedroom things. They're going to use that set for your room."

"Oh." DJ thought of the room that had always been Gran's. It would now be empty. And all her things would be gone from the studio, too. An ache started in her middle and traveled to her eyes. She almost stumbled on the front step because she was blinking and rolling her eyes upward to keep the tears from falling. One more chunk was disappearing out of her life.

By the time they finished moving and devouring the pizzas Joe had ordered, the twins were sound asleep on the floor. DJ felt like joining them. She'd never moved in her life, and now she knew why. Moving was the pits.

"Oh, my aching back." Sonja lay flat on the carpet. "Wake me when Monday comes."

Gran rested her head on Joe's shoulder. "Thank you all so much. I don't know what we'd have done without you."

"Called a moving company," Andy, Joe's youngest son, said.

"How about having a housewarming next weekend at the same time as Joe's retirement party?" Gran sat up straight, her eyes catching a sparkle again at the thought of a party.

Groans met her suggestion.

"We'll have it catered. I know someone really good and not too expensive."

"You'd hire a caterer?" DJ jerked totally awake.

"Mother?" Lindy and DJ wore the same shocked expressions.

"You always do everything yourself," Lindy added.

"I know, but I'll probably still be busy putting things away, and with DJ's horse show the week after that, this weekend is our best option."

DJ scooted back to prop herself against Gran's legs. "You'd plan a housewarming around my horse show?"

"Darlin', of course. I can't miss that."

"That's not all. I'll be coming, too. She can't have a retirement party without the retiree there." Joe tweaked DJ's braid. "And I wouldn't miss your horse shows for the world."

DJ felt love wrap itself around her, snuggling into all the cracks and hollows. "Thanks, Grandpa." She reached over her shoulder to take Gran's hand and tilted her head back to wink up at the man on the seat above her. "You know, I think I like GJ better. Then our names nearly match. You now, DJ and GJ. What do you think?"

"I think anything you call me is fine." He cleared his throat in the middle of the sentence.

"Well, we better get going so we can come back tomorrow and help some more." Lindy started to rise and Robert leaped to his feet to pull her upright.

"Your car isn't here. How about if I give you and DJ a ride home?"

"Thanks." Lindy started picking up the leftover trash from the pizza. "Oh, did I tell you?" She stopped in front of the couch where Gran and Joe sat. "There may be a new position opening up in L.A. My boss thinks it's ideal for me, or I'm ideal for it."

Only a huff in the breathing of one of the twins broke the absolute silence.

DJ couldn't breathe. An invisible elephant was squashing her like a bug.

Chapter • 13

Was her mother totally off-the-wall bonkers?

"Thanks for the ride," Lindy said when they arrived home. She prodded DJ.

"Yeah, thanks."

"See you tomorrow?" DJ heard Robert ask, but she didn't wait for her mother's answer. If she never in her whole life spoke to her mother again, it would be too soon. She didn't stomp. She didn't yell. She didn't cry. She unlocked the front door, left it open for her mother, and walked up the stairs to her room. This door she shut. The click sounded loud in the silence.

She crossed the room and stood in front of the window. It was a good thing breathing didn't take thought and effort, because she wouldn't have bothered. How could she ever afford to keep Major in Los Angeles? How would she find a stable? She knew Bridget gave her extra help without charging. Would anyone else do that? And Amy. How could she leave Amy? And Gran and Joe? She couldn't live without Gran.

Gran. The thought stopped the panic like throwing a light switch.

"DJ?" Her mother knocked at the bedroom door. "DJ, I want to talk with you."

DJ crossed the room and opened the door. She stood right in the doorway, making it very obvious that her mother wasn't welcome.

"DJ, don't panic yet. Nothing has been decided. I just wanted to give you time to think about it."

"Doesn't matter. You do what you want. I'll go live with Joe and Gran." DJ crossed her arms over her chest. She met her mother's shocked gaze with a perfectly blank face.

"But, it will be a better job, more money, more . . ." Lindy took a step backward. "We'll discuss this when I know more about the job."

"Fine." DJ could feel one eyebrow twitch as if it wanted to form a question mark of its own. "Good night, Mother." She stepped back and quietly shut the door.

DJ didn't know she could do it—not talk to her mother, that is. Usually she did everything but stand on her head to get back in her mother's good graces. This time she didn't care. She wasn't the one who had decided to move to L.A., no matter what her daughter wanted and needed. *Grown-ups are good at that,* DJ thought. *Always so sure they know best. They don't always—unless they're like Gran and Joe.* "I will *not* give up my dream," DJ promised the face in the bathroom mirror. "I *will* ride in the Olympics someday." She tugged the brush through her hair. "And I will *not* give up Major."

Monday her art teacher announced an art contest for local students. "The entry can be in any medium: pen and ink, charcoal, water colors, tempera, oils, or acrylics. The choice of subject is your own, and you can enter a class project or one you've done at home. Just don't use any outside help."

Mentally DJ flipped through the horses she'd done. She could think of a flaw in every one. It would have to be something new, but she would stick with pen and ink or pencil. She brought her mind back to her classwork with difficulty. She'd much rather start the drawing now.

"Can I see a show of hands of those who think they'll enter?"

DJ's hand was the first in the air.

That evening, as soon as she finished all her home chores after the hours at the Academy, she took out her pad and pencils. She closed her eyes. She could just see Major clearing the triple. She started to draw.

It seemed like only a few minutes had passed, but her scratchy eyes and the nearly complete picture told her otherwise. She glanced at the clock. Midnight. Had she heard her mother come up to bed? Vaguely she remembered a knock at the door and her mother's voice bidding her to sleep well. She fell into bed, asleep before she could pull up the covers.

A noise jerked her out of a sleep so deep she hadn't heard the birds serenade her with their morning song. A car horn. She checked her clock. Seven-thirty! What had happened to her alarm? As she bailed out of bed, she couldn't remember setting the stupid thing. She ran to a window in her mother's bedroom and called down to Amy.

"I just woke up. Can you give me five minutes?"

Mr. Yamamoto waved and nodded.

DJ threw on her clothes, brushed her teeth, gathered her hairbrush and bands, grabbed her backpack, and raced down the stairs. No time for breakfast. She dumped the box of food bars over the counter in her rush to get one.

She felt as though she were an hour behind all day. She dragged from lack of sleep. Still rushing when she got home from school, she fixed a sandwich, grabbed a juice package, and pedaled as fast as she could to the Academy, eating as she rode. When she did think of the mess she'd left behind, she promised herself to get home early to clean it before her mother got there.

She made herself calm down once she reached the Academy. The more you rushed a horse, the longer it took to accomplish anything.

Major greeted her with a nicker, nosing her pockets for the treats she always carried. DJ could tell Joe had been there. The stall was clean, horse groomed, and a note pinned to the outer wall.

See you later. I rode Major this morning, so he's already had some exercise. Bridget found me a Quarter Horse to look at. Want to come along? GJ.

DJ read the note again. Of course she wanted to go along, but when? Major reached out to take a taste of the paper. "What are you, half goat? You can't eat everything! Stop that." She yanked it away, but not before he took a sizable nibble out of one corner.

DJ opened the stall door and, with a hand on his nose, backed him up. She turned and stood with his head over her shoulder, rubbing his ears and his face. He sighed and tipped his head a bit so she could reach another spot.

She could hear people talking in another part of the barn and horses moving around in their stalls, but here, for this moment, she felt peace. It was easy to forget that her mother was considering moving to L.A., that they didn't get along, that she had enough to do to keep three people busy. She turned her face to sniff the best fragrance in the world—horse.

The good feeling remained until she got home. The garage door was open. Gran's minivan wasn't there, so that meant only one thing. Right now she prayed it was burglars. But no such luck. Her mother had come home early.

DJ quietly put her bike away, closed the garage door, and opened the door to the kitchen. Going into the house was like stepping into a meat locker set on deep freeze.

No more mess on the counter. DJ chewed her lip. Her mother had been home awhile. She listened, holding her breath to hear better. Sounds came from upstairs. Water running. She tried to remember. Had she closed her bedroom door? The bathroom was a disaster, too.

"Well, you better get it over with." She dredged up every available bit of courage and climbed the stairs. "Please, God, don't let her ground me again. I don't have time for that right now. What with the show coming and all."

Lindy turned from scrubbing the sink in the bathroom. The counter was neat, the dirty towels in the hamper, and new ones on the racks. The scene registered in DJ's mind at the same time as the scowl on her mother's face. Compared to here, the kitchen had been balmy.

"I . . . I'm sorry. I overslept and—"

"Darla Jean, if you are that tired, then it's time we made some changes around here—"

"No, I just forgot to set my alarm."

"Forgot? Or was too tired?" Lindy gave the sink one last wipe and flicked off the light. She pointed the way to her daughter's room. "Your bedroom looks like a tornado went through there."

"I know."

"Your light was still on at 11:30 last night. Homework?"

"Well . . ." DJ tried to think whether she could call her art project homework.

"You've got too much to do—"

"Yeah, taking care of the house and yard besides school and my work at the Academy *is* hard."

"Are you saying I don't do anything around here?"

"No—well, yes." DJ threw up her hands. "You're never home. Why do you care?"

"That would be one of the good things about the job in L.A. I'd be home more, do less traveling."

"Goody for you. I don't care if you are home. I didn't mean to leave a mess, and I would have cleaned it up. I always do. You don't care about me and what I like at all. You never have." DJ caught herself. She'd used *always* and *never* after promising that when she had kids, she wouldn't use it.

"Go to your room, Darla Jean, I just can't deal with any more of this right now."

"Gladly." DJ spun around and left as ordered. At least she hadn't been grounded—yet.

She threw herself across her unmade bed. Why couldn't she and her mother talk without yelling at each other? It wasn't as though she'd murdered someone or stolen the family jewels. She just hadn't gotten all her chores done. And the day wasn't even over yet. If her mother had come home when she usually did, everything would have been fine. *I shoulda run away when I had the chance.* Her stomach rumbled. You'd think her mother would spend the time to make a meal for her daughter, rather than clean up a mess that wasn't that bad to start with. But no good smells came from the kitchen, unless you liked the smell of polish and disinfectant.

She got up and started putting away her clothes. After making the bed and cleaning off her desk, she picked up the horse drawing she'd been working on last night. It was good, the best she'd done. Now if Gran were here, she'd take the picture to her and they'd discuss the quality of lines, the perspective, the balance of the horse. If only Gran were here.

Maybe she should pray her mother got that stupid job in L.A. so she could live with Gran and Joe. She propped the picture on the top of her chest of drawers and stepped back. Another thought hit her: What if Gran and Joe wouldn't let her live with them? What if they didn't want any kids around? What would happen to her and Major then?

Chapter • 14

"Over my dead body."

"But, M-o-m." DJ immediately erased any trace of whine. This time she would present her idea just as she and Amy had their pony club plan. Businesslike and to the point.

"Mother, please listen to me. I've come up with a way to get more done in my day, and I'd like us to talk about it." She hesitated a moment. "Please?" She kept her hands behind her back so her crossed fingers didn't show.

Lindy started to say something, then changed her mind. "All right. Since you've put so much thought into this, I'll listen. But that doesn't mean I have to agree."

Two days had passed since their last blowup. Nothing more had been said, so DJ knew she would not be grounded. But this morning she had woken up with a gonzo idea. Amy agreed with her. Amy also advised her on how to handle her mother. Now they'd see if this new approach worked.

DJ took a deep breath and made sure she had a pleasant expression on her face. "Mom, you've always told me that it is important to have goals and work toward them."

"Of course." Lindy turned her head a fraction to the side. Her look said, *What's up?*

"Like you do. You know my goal is to ride in the Olympics one day." Lindy nodded. She leaned back against the sofa and crossed her arms.

"So."

"So, most of the Olympic contenders, like the ice skaters and the gymnasts, work out for a couple of hours before school, then again afterward. I never—" she caught herself. She had just overslept. "I *like* getting up early. Morning's a good time for me. If I could work with Major at about six or so, then I'd have more time in the evening for stuff around here."

Lindy was shaking her head already. "You're not riding up to the Academy in the dark. That road is too dangerous."

"You could drop me off on your way to work."

"How would you get home to get ready for school?"

"I could take my clothes and have Mr. Yamamoto pick me up there. I don't think he'd mind."

"Oh, sure. You'd go to school smelling like horse." She made "horse" sound like a dirty word.

DJ bit her tongue just in time. One smart remark would ruin everything. So her mother didn't think horses smelled good. So what? Not everyone had to love horses like DJ.

"Please, just think about it?" DJ clamped her fingers together, hard. *Please, God, make her change her mind.*

DJ now knew what a bug under a microscope must feel like. The look her mother was giving her seemed to see right through her. She'd done her best. Now it was time to wait.

The silence seemed to stretched from then till Christmas.

Was that a smile breaking through? The corners of her mother's mouth had twitched.

"All right, I'll think about it." Lindy held up a hand to stop DJ before she spun into orbit. "I only agreed to think about it. Now you have to agree not to bug me for a decision. I'll tell you when I'm ready."

DJ nodded. That wasn't the answer she wanted, but it sure beat "over my dead body." And they'd managed to talk about something really important without fighting. She should put a star on the calendar.

Lindy still hadn't made a decision by Saturday. DJ now had one week to finish preparing Major for their first show. And today was Gran and Joe's open house. She'd quit thinking about her mother moving to Los Angeles. No news was good news. She had enough else on her mind.

"I'm going right over to Gran's from the Academy," she called to her mother through the closed bedroom door. All she got in response was a "humphf," but she knew her mother had heard.

"Did you finish your drawing for the contest?" Amy asked on their trek to the Academy.

"Almost. I still have some shading to do. I was going to show it to Gran, but she's been so busy getting ready for the party, I thought I'd work some more and then see what she says. So far, it's the best I've ever done—at least I think so." Yelling and pedaling at the same time took all her breath.

They halted at the stop sign and looked back over their shoulders. The sun, with only a rim up over the horizon, painted the scattered clouds in shades of pink and rose with lavender tops.

"Wish I had my camera."

"You always think of that too late."

"I know, I should carry it all the time. Hey, did I tell you my idea?" DJ raised an eyebrow.

"I'm going to take pictures of the party today and put them in an album as my wedding present to Joe and Gran. What do you think?"

"Fantastic, she'll love it. We could make little labels with funny sayings and stick them underneath."

"Perfect. See you at the party."

DJ got to the party by a different mode of transportation. She rode Bandit, who would be the entertainment for the younger set. She managed to get there, take a shower, and dress before the party began.

"Here, darlin', please put these platters on the table."

"Sure. I thought you were having this catered." DJ picked up the round tray of vegetables and dip.

"I did. I bought all these, but I couldn't see any sense in having someone else do the serving."

"That's what we have kids for." Joe took two platters.

"And grandkids." Shawna returned from arranging the napkins.

Robert and Lindy arrived together, along with the twins.

DJ caught her raising eyebrow. Her mother hadn't said she wasn't bringing the car. The thought got buried under the twins' onslaught.

"You brought a pony! What's his name? Can we ride now? I'm first." "No, me!"

"Boys, boys." Robert shrugged his apology. "What can I say, DJ? They like you."

DJ peeled them off her legs. "All right, let's go. Shawna, you coming?"

Andy and Sonja were setting up the volleyball net when DJ got dragged out to the yard by the two Bs.

"Hey, we can use some more hands." Andy waved to them.

"No, we's riding!" one of the Bs informed him.

"Ex-cu-se me."

DJ stopped them before they reached the pony. "You can only ride on one condition."

"What?" They tugged on her hands.

"When I say you're done, you have to get off. No arguments. Understood?" She used the tone of voice that worked best with her students.

They started to frown, then changed their minds and flashed their sunniest smiles. *How'd they do that?* DJ wondered. *They do things at the same time without ever talking about it.* "Now remember, a horse can't see behind him, so when you come up, talk to him, let him know you're there." She suited her acts to her words. "Hey, Bandit, ready to give these guys a ride?" While she talked, she retightened the saddle girth, then untied him and put his bridle back on over his halter. "Sorry, fella, you can eat more later."

She turned to the boys. "Okay, first time around you ride together; then one at a time."

Even though the rides went well, by the time DJ had given every little kid there a turn, she was dragging her wagon.

"I could lead for a while, if you'd like," Shawna suggested softly. "You can go get something to eat."

"I better not leave him. If something happened, it would be my fault."

"Then tie him up and come join the rest of the party." Robert appeared at her side. "Even though you're family, you don't have to be slave labor."

DJ took him at his word. She tied up Bandit, warned the kids to stay away from him, and went in to feed her rumbling stomach. After eating, yakking with Amy, and shooshing Gran out of the kitchen, she wandered out to the backyard where she could hear shouts from the family caught up in a wild volleyball game.

"Come on, DJ, you can be on my team." Robert waved at her.

"No, she can't. Lindy's on your team." Sonja grabbed the bottom of the net, toe to toe with her brother-in-law.

"Lot of good that does." Lindy wiped her brow with the back of her hand. "Athletic, I'm not."

"Robert doesn't care," Andy yelled from the back row of his team. "Come on, DJ. We'll pound 'em into the dirt."

DJ did as they said, but the shock of seeing grass stains on her mother's knees and the seat of her white shorts was too much. *Her* mother, Lindy Randall, playing volleyball?

When it was DJ's turn to serve, she stepped behind the line and drilled an overhand serve right at her mother.

Lindy squealed and ducked. The ball hit her shoulder and went out of bounds. "Not fair."

"Good job, kid. Do it again." Andy clapped his hands and winked at her.

DJ looked straight at her mother. And served to Joe. He bumped it up and Robert spiked it over the net. DJ bumped it to Andy, who set it for her. Jumping up with all her might, DJ spiked the ball. Robert got under it, but the ball spun out of bounds.

"Yes!" DJ grabbed air with her fist and pumped down. Andy slapped her hands. Sonja threw her arms around DJ and jigged her in a circle. "You spiked one down on ol' Robert. You're great at this."

"How come you're not on the volleyball team at your school?" Andy asked. "You're a good player."

"No time. And I'd rather ride any day. But I love playing."

"Well, let's just run this play again. You ready, Robbie, old man?" Their team won 15-5.

"Want to go again?" Sonja yelled.

"In your dreams." Joe leaned over, panting. "I think it's time I leave this game to the younger generation."

"Not on your life." Robert slapped his dad on the back. "You're going to have to do something to stay in shape now that you're off the force."

"Well, I'll tell you a secret, volleyball against those three dynamos isn't it."

"You two probably could have done better without me to fall over."

Collapsed on the ground, Lindy wiped her face with her shirttail. She picked a grass blade out of her hair, then combed it back with her fingers.

"Nah, you were great." Gallant Robert sank down beside her.

"Daddy. Daddy!" The two Bs charged across the court to throw themselves on him. The three guys tumbled over in a giggling heap of arms and legs.

"Sorry, they couldn't sit still another minute." Gran followed them out of the house. "I thought for a few minutes they were going to take an *n-a-p*." She spelled the word.

DJ watched the boys roughhouse with their father. If she'd known her dad, would they have had times like this when she was little? She caught herself in surprise. How come all of a sudden she was thinking of him again—whoever he was?

"I made a fresh pot of coffee, and there's plenty of food left. Come on inside," Gran said.

Everyone lumbered to their feet, pulled the twins off their father, and headed for the house. Once they were all served and seated in the living room, Andy looked over at Lindy.

"So, you heard any more about that job in L.A.?"

DJ's gaze flew to her mother.

Lindy took a long time looking up from her plate. "I have an interview down there on Friday morning."

DJ choked on her bite of ham.

Chapter • 15

"Gran, please, please, can I come live with you?"

Gran smoothed tendrils of hair back from DJ's forehead. "I don't know, darlin'. We'll just have to pray about it and see what God says. It might be that Lindy won't get that job."

DJ humphed. "Not hardly. You know how good she is. They'd be stupid not to hire her. Gran, I *can't* move away now. Everything I want is right here." DJ swallowed, bit her lip, blinked. Nothing was working out. One big fat tear slid down her cheek.

Gran gathered her close. The urge to rest her head on Gran's shoulder and cry until she ran out of tears made DJ pull away. She sniffed any other tears back and made herself stand up straight.

"My Bible verse won't work for this, Gran." DJ shook her head. "There's nothing I can do."

Gran stroked DJ's cheek with the gentle touch of love. "Then I have another one for you to think about. 'Trust in the Lord with all your heart and lean not on your own understanding.' "

"You are awesome." DJ couldn't stop the tiny smile that insisted on accompanying the words. "How do I do that?"

"Just tell Him you're trusting Him to work out this situation for the best for everybody."

"That's hard. I want what's best for *me*." DJ studied the cuticles on her hand. Only one was hanging in shreds. One fingernail had actually begun to grow. Her verse floated through her mind.

I can do all things through Christ who strengthens me. But she hadn't even been working on it—much. She stared at the fingernail. "God, I'm trusting you to work this out for the best for everyone." How come a whisper could hurt so?

"What's going on here?" Joe entered the kitchen but stopped short when he saw DJ's face. He wrapped his arms around both Gran and DJ. "Don't worry, love. It'll all work out."

"I better get Bandit back to the Academy before dark." DJ stepped outside the hug. "I'm glad you're in your new house, and I had a good time at the party." She turned and fled out the back door as if a pack of wolves were on her heels.

Successful at outwitting the other kids, she trotted Bandit up the drive. Off to the left she saw her mother and Robert walking along the rail fence frosted with pink roses. They looked to be having a serious discussion.

"Tell her not to move," DJ muttered.

The empty house didn't seem so bad when she got home. She had a lot of serious thinking to do and the quiet helped. Not talking to her mother was getting easier and easier.

Monday she turned in her drawing. Gran had told her not to change anything when she saw it on Saturday. Tuesday her mother brought home pizza for dinner and insisted DJ eat with her.

"We have to talk." Lindy set out napkins and put the pizza box in the center of the table.

Go ahead and talk. There's no law that says I have to answer. DJ brought two cans of soda from the fridge and took her usual place.

"So, how are things going?"

"Fine."

"Are you ready for the show Saturday?"

DJ looked up from shoving strings of cheese into her mouth. *As if you cared.* She finished chewing and swallowed. "I guess."

"About Saturday . . ."

DJ felt like clapping her hands over her ears. "Listen, you do what you have to do, and I'll do what I have to do." She took another bite of pizza.

"No, *you* listen. I have an interview Friday. Gran has already said you can spend Thursday night there, and I'll be back Friday night. Robert and I will be attending your show."

"*You* are coming to my horse show?" DJ nearly choked on her pizza. Lindy nodded. "With the boys."

"Oh great." *It was bad enough when Joe was coming, now the whole family was going to be there.* And she had thought the butterflies were bad before.

"Have you thought more about my taking the job down there?"

DJ looked at her as if she'd left her brains in her purse. *Had she thought about it?* Only repeating her Bible verse kept her from going totally looney.

"You don't have to be sarcastic."

"I didn't say a word."

"You didn't have to."

Lindy tossed the tough end of the crust in the box. "I'm just trying to do what's best."

"I know."

Wednesday DJ let the jitters for the up-coming show get to her, and Major refused a jump. She calmed herself and him down and tried again. No problem.

"Come on, DJ, you know better than to let a show get to you." Bridget waited in the middle of the arena for DJ to complete another circuit.

"But this is the first time on my own horse. Not to mention entering a jumping event."

"I think it would be better if you did not enter the jumping event this first show. You and Major need to get more accustomed to each other first. See how you do."

It was as though someone had turned off the sun. Bridget didn't think they were ready yet. She could enter anyway. But maybe this was for the best. "Can we leave this open to change if we're really doing well?"

"Of course. Is anything else bothering you?"

Oh, nothing. It's just that my mother might be leaving, and there'll be a big fight if I have to go along. That and we don't even talk to each other anymore. "No, I'm fine."

"I do not believe you." A smile took the sting out of the words. "Do not worry about this weekend. You will do fine."

Thursday night was the first time she stayed over at Joe and Gran's. Joe met her at the Academy and helped her give Major a bath. By the time they finished, the big horse shone as if they'd waxed him.

"You have time on Wednesday to go take a look at that cutting horse Bridget found?"

DJ thought a minute. "Sure. I don't teach that day."

"I know. That's why I chose it."

DJ leaned her forehead against Major's shoulder. Only two more days to go. One, actually, because they showed Saturday morning. Any time she swallowed, it seemed the swallow went only so far down before it twanged around like a ball on the end of a rubber string.

"DJ, can I help?" Joe spoke softly, all the while keeping his hands busy grooming Major.

"I wish. I just have to get through this first show." Her chuckle sounded hollow in the dimness. "I tell my students not to let the butterflies bother them, but look at me. I'm a basket case."

"I think it's more than just the show."

"I think you see too much." DJ retrieved her new show sheet from off the door and laid it over Major's back. Together she and Joe adjusted all the straps and buckles. "You stay clean now, Major. You gotta look your best on Saturday."

Friday she had a surprise quiz in Latin. It was a surprise all right. More like a shock, actually. For the first five minutes her brain refused to function. *Please, God.* She shrugged her shoulders up to her ears, took a breath, and reread the first question.

She wrote fast and finished answering the questions just as the teacher called time. She handed in her paper with a sigh of relief. That was one way to take her mind off the weekend.

Joe picked her up at the Academy and they drove to his house for dinner.

"You think butterflies are contagious?"

DJ looked at him, eyebrows questioning. "You're not the one entering."

"I know, but I think being a grandparent may be even worse in this case. I remember feeling this way when Robert played basketball. When he went to the free-throw line, I almost threw up."

"Come on, it wasn't that bad."

"Almost. You ask him sometime."

"Well, if you ever run out of butterflies, I'll gladly share some of mine."

"I've got good news and bad news," Gran said when they walked into the kitchen.

DJ started to shake her head. She knew what was coming.

"Lindy called."

"I knew it. She isn't coming home tonight and won't be at the show tomorrow. Now, what's the bad news?"

"The good news is you get to stay here again so I can make sure you get off all right in the morning."

"You're right, Gran. That part is good news."

"She said she'd come straight to the showgrounds. Robert and the boys are meeting her there."

"Great." *Maybe my events will be over by the time they get there.*

Having someone to help her in the morning gave DJ an extra boost. Joe joined forces with Mr. Yamamoto, and together with the other fathers, they had horses and riders loaded in record time.

"Now, all of you have your tack and riding gear?" Bridget stuck her head in each vehicle and asked the question. When everyone was ready, she waved to the driver in the first truck. "Let's go." The Academy parade had begun.

"Don't even think about it!" DJ gave herself such a stern order that Amy, who had tied Josh next to Major, turned to look at her.

"What are you mumbling about."

"Hunter/Jumper."

"I thought Bridget told you not to enter that."

"She suggested it."

"Yeah, and Bridget only makes suggestions. Come on, there'll be another event in less than a month. Just wait."

"I've been waiting all my life."

"You know what I mean."

The loudspeaker crackled and a tinny voice echoed from the tree right above them. "First call for English Pleasure."

"Well, Major, old man, you and I better head for the warm-up ring." She unbuckled his halter, slipped it off his nose, and rebuckled it around his neck, just for safe keeping.

"You need some help?" Joe stopped right beside her. Major nickered, his nostrils barely moving. "I know, old son, it's time for you to earn your keep. Now you do everything DJ tells you, hear?"

DJ could have sworn the horse understood every word Joe said. She finished buckling the chin strap on the bridle and checked the reins.

"I hardly recognized you." Joe gave her a look full of approval.

"First time I've worn my new clothes. I got them for my birthday." DJ knew she looked good because she felt it. The black jacket, tan pants, and white stock looked put together and very professional.

"Between the two of you, you'll catch the judge's eye for sure."

"Good luck, DJ. Go get 'em." Her students wished her well.

"You can do it." Amy added her encouragement.

"Sure we can." DJ tried to smile but her mouth wobbled instead. "Come on, big fella, let's do it."

Joe walked with her on the dirt trail around the ring. "I have cloth in my back pocket," he told her. "To take care of all this dust."

DJ managed a smile, a small one, but a smile nevertheless. She looked over at the bleachers. Gran sat by herself. "If you want to go sit with Gran, you can. Major and I will be fine."

"I will, soon as you go in the ring."

DJ let him give her a leg up, checked her stirrup length, and smiled down at him. "Thanks, Joe, for all you've done."

"How's your stomach feeling now?"

"Better. When we enter that ring, I'll be having too much fun to think about butterflies." Just then a couple of them did flips and invited their friends to join them. DJ looked up in time to see Robert and the twins sit down beside Gran. How'd her butterflies know?

Major turned his head to nuzzle Joe's shoulder.

"Knock 'em dead, you two." Joe gave each of them a pat and crossed the dirt staging area to the log seats that made up the viewing stands.

DJ worked Major easily through his paces, letting him take his time while she exchanged remarks with other riders. She could feel herself relaxing. This was what she loved to do. Like actors loved the camera or the stage, she loved horse shows.

"English Pleasure to the ring. English Pleasure to the ring."

DJ trotted Major the remaining distance around the warm-up ring and out the gate. Joe stood there, cloth in hand. He wiped off Major's nose, legs, and hooves. With a soft brush, he ran quickly over the horse's rump. "Okay, now you really are ready."

DJ blew him a kiss. She entered the ring, third in line. Major acted as if he'd been showing all his life. Ears pricked forward, taking in everything around him, he did everything DJ asked. Walk, trot, canter, reverse. When she came too close to a rider in front, she turned him in a circle into the ring and back in line. He changed gaits smoothly and on command.

The judge motioned them into line in the center of the ring. The horse on their left refused to stand, and the rider had to take him out of line and bring him back. Twice.

Major never moved. The big horse could have been carved in granite.

The judge started with the lower ribbons, and the spectators gave each rider a burst of applause. When she handed DJ the blue, cheers and whistles broke out—mostly from the Academy line-up.

DJ tried to be cool about the whole thing, but the smile she gave the judge for the ribbon and the sack of feed donated by a local feed store could have warmed Alaska.

"Congratulations. It's good to see you back in the ring."

"Thank you. This is his first time out." She patted Major's neck.

"Well, you certainly couldn't tell by that performance. Good luck with him."

DJ looked up to the stands. Her mother sat beside Robert, and she was clapping harder than anyone. Anyone but Joe, that is. When he met her at the gate, she could have sworn he'd had to wipe away moisture from his eyes—tears maybe?

DJ dismounted so they could walk together. After his congratulatory hug, he strolled beside her, letting the silence be. For a change DJ felt no need to fill the silence. "I'm really proud to own him, Joe. Thank you so much for making this part of my dream come true."

"I can see we're going to do a lot of dream building together, darlin'. You are a real pro."

The next class didn't go as well; DJ and Major only got a white.

"You were the best out there." Angie looked ready to take on the judge.

"You got ripped." Krissie was all ready to join her.

"Thanks for the vote of confidence, but the judge didn't see it that way. Being a good sport is a part of the game."

DJ's mind flitted back to the question she'd been asking herself all day. *Should I, or shouldn't I?* One minute she was all ready to register for the Hunter/Seat jumping class. The next she remembered what Bridget had said. But Major wasn't acting like a new trainee. He loved it out there.

She left the horse area and went to sit by her family.

"The boys are ready to start riding tomorrow." Robert kept them corralled, one under each arm. "Did you hear them hollering for you? If the judge hadn't given you a ribbon, they were ready to attack."

Bobby and Billy looked up at her, their faces serious for a change.

"Can I hold your ribbon?"

"Me too?" They didn't even yell.

Joe leaned closer. "I think it's your outfit. They aren't one-hundred percent sure it's really you in there."

DJ looked over at her mother, sitting on the other side of Gran. The two wore matching grins of pride. "Thanks for coming, Mom, Gran." To her own surprise, DJ realized she meant it. Having her mother here for the first time to see a horse show made the day even better. "I better get back to work. See you later."

Should she, or shouldn't she?

"What do you think, Ames?" The two of them spent the lull between entries leaning on the arena fence in front of the horse line.

"I think you should do what Bridget suggested." Amy made "suggested" sound like ordered. She raised an eyebrow when DJ groaned.

"DJ, come help me." The cry came from one of her students.

Sam's horse had kicked his neighbor.

DJ ran a hand down the kicked leg. She wiped away a dirt smudge. "He just grazed it. Let's put some more space be—no, let's move him to the end of the line." She assisted the transfer, and when she got back to the fence, she'd decided.

If one of her students went against her advice, she'd be peeved. What if Sam had said no to the move? DJ carefully hung her jacket on a hanger in the tack box. She placed her helmet in a plastic bag to keep it clean.

Amy gave her a thumbs-up sign.

"We'll jump another day," she whispered to Major's flicking ears. "By then we'll be so good, they'll beg us to jump." She tickled his whiskers and slipped him a horse cookie.

"Last call for novices on the lead. Hunter/Seat will follow."

DJ swallowed—hard. With one last look at the riders coming into the arena, she turned and headed down the line to see if Hilary needed any help.

"I'm fine, thanks. I was hoping you'd be in the ring with me." Hilary rechecked the girth on her saddle.

"So was I. Next time."

"Major looked really great out there. He was having fun, wasn't he?"

"Yep, me too."

"Everything all right here?" Bridget stopped beside them, her clipboard a natural extension of her arm.

"How come DJ's not entering Hunter/Seat?" Hilary asked.

"Do you want to?"

Dumb question. Did kids like ice cream? "B-but you said—"

"I said our discussion was open to change. You and Major have done a fine job. He appeared comfortable out there—in fact, I think he likes to show off, so I . . ." she glanced down at her list. "I entered the two of you. Joe is coming over to help you get ready. Any questions?"

DJ shook her head.

"Then what are you waiting for?" Bridget tapped DJ on the shoulder. "Don't rush—and concentrate."

"And count his strides." DJ touched her finger to her forehead in a salute and dog-trotted back to where Joe was already saddling Major.

"I'll get my jacket." Her heart thundered in her throat. They were ~ing to jump. Granted the jumps were low and easy, but this was it. ~ first time.

~lajor was scheduled to jump last, but waiting didn't seem to ~ him at all. "Remember, he's used to patrol. A lot of nothing ~ for hours. He learned years ago that getting excited only raises ~ Joe wiped the beads of moisture off his forehead. "Hot here ~ it?"

~ed at him to see if he realized what he'd said. His wink let ~ did. "You're the best, GJ."

~ a run for their money, DJ." He boosted her into the ~."

Major trotted into the arena, ears forward, seeming to float above the ground. He took the jumps like a veteran, never a hesitation, at a perfect pace. Each time he leaped into the air, DJ reminded herself to count.

The judge conferred with another when all the entrants had jumped. DJ and Hilary kept their horses at a standstill.

"For a first-timer, that was wonderful." Hilary gave DJ a smile to match her compliment.

"You'll get the blue, just watch." Even while DJ said what she felt to be true, she wished—oh, how she wished—for the blue.

Again the judge started at the lower end. She worked her way up, leaving Hilary, DJ, and one other rider for the three remaining ribbons.

"Number 43, a white ribbon goes to . . ."

DJ didn't hear the rider's name and horse. The blood pounded through her ears and out to her fingertips.

"The red goes to . . ." The judge paused. DJ couldn't find any spit to swallow.

"Number 61, DJ Randall on Major."

DJ pasted a smile on her face and trotted forward. She leaned over to accept the ribbon and thanked the judge.

"Hilary Jones, also of The Briones Riding Academy, earned the blue today, along with a halter donated by Pleasant Hill Feed Store."

DJ clapped along with the rest. "Next time, Major. You keep your eye on that ribbon because we want two blues next time." She leaned over to slap high fives with Hilary.

"I am very glad I was not the judge." Bridget met them when they left the arena. "You can both go home proud of what you accomplished."

That kind of compliment from Bridget was better than a ribbon any day.

By the end of the day, weary riders and fathers loaded weary horses. When they had all the animals back in their stalls and the tack put away, Joe reminded DJ that Robert was taking them all out for dinner.

"I'd rather go home." DJ didn't want to sound ungrateful, but beat didn't begin to describe the way she felt.

"We won't be late."

"Did Mom say anything about her trip?" Now that the excitement was over, reality crowded back in.

Joe shook his head.

"Where are we going?" DJ looked over at Joe when he turned into his own driveway.

"The boys voted for fried chicken." He winked at her. "It was supposed to be a surprise."

"I'm surprised."

When everyone had dished up their plates in the kitchen and found places to sit around the long dining-room table, DJ and her two shadows sat directly across from Robert and Lindy. *So what did they decide? To hire you on the spot? Have you already found a place to live?*

DJ kept her mouth under tight rein. Answering the boys' questions gave her no time to ask any of her own.

Robert clapped his hands for attention. "Lindy has something she'd like to say." Silence blanketed the table.

Lindy gave DJ a tiny smile. She got to her feet. "My trip to Los Angeles was very successful."

DJ froze, her fork halfway to her mouth.

"I have a new position."

"Tell 'em your title," Robert prompted from beside her.

"I am now the district manager in charge of sales."

DJ started to push back her chair.

"The district covers Northern California."

Northern California. We live in Northern California. "I thought the job was in L.A." The words burst out before she could stop them.

"I said the trip was successful. They created a matching position for this area."

DJ let out a whoop and scooped both of the twins up in her arms. They giggled and threw their arms around her neck. "No more changes. You hear that, guys? We're staying right here."

"Right here."

"No changes." The two sounded like parrots.

DJ looked over to see the sun shining on Gran's face. Gran mouthed the words, *I told you so.* "Well, I for one am in favor of no more major changes for this family. We've had enough challenges lately." She gave Joe that special smile she reserved for him.

"Oh, I don't know about that," Robert said under cover of the hub-bub.

DJ heard him. What kind of changes could he be talking about? Oh-oh. His face was lit with the same kind of smile Gran gave Joe.

Maybe there would be more changes ahead—but then, changes, challenges, both were good. Weren't they?

Book Three

SETTING THE PACE

To Joanie Jagoda,
who shares her horse expertise
and her heart with me.
As is always the case with true friends,
my life is richer because of her,
and my books are better thanks to her input.
One day she'll be giving me riding lessons.
Yes!

Chapter • 1

"Do not rush the jump!" Bridget ordered.

Straight ahead between Major's pricked ears, DJ Randall watched the brush jump draw closer with every thrust of her horse's haunches. *Now!* They lifted and flew over the jump, clean and perfect, before her mind could finish the command. Major came down on his front feet, his rear landing in perfect timing.

DJ kept her focus on the three rails of alternating height before them. Silently counting, she leaned forward, heels down and eyes straight ahead.

"Come on, boy." Her murmur was lost in the shush of hooves in the sand, the grunt of a horse giving his best effort. For a split second, they hung suspended in air.

That was the moment DJ lived for.

The clack of a back hoof on the rail sounded as loud as a cannon shot.

"Concentrate, DJ—you lost your concentration." Bridget Sommersby, trainer and owner of Briones Riding Academy, called from the center of the ring. "You got left behind."

"Fiddle."

"Come on, go around again."

DJ did as she was told, this time forcing herself to forget the glory and count the paces.

They finished the circuit with the in and out, a jump that looked more difficult than it actually was. If horses could laugh, Major was—both he and DJ. In her case, the laugh was one of pure delight.

"Well done." DJ's mentor leaned her elbows against the aluminum rail fence. "That was as close to a perfect round as you have ever ridden, in spite of the tic." Bridget pushed her glasses farther up on her nose with one finger. Her smile made DJ feel as though she'd just won the Grand Prix.

Or at least she thought it would feel that way. Since DJ had never won the Grand Prix in her fourteen years, or even been to one for that matter, she held on to the feeling for as long as she could.

She wanted to squeeze Major's neck in a hug to end all hugs, shout hallelujah, and . . . and how could she possibly act professional, as Bridget expected? Her huge smile splintered her cheeks and her jawbone.

"Thank you." There, DJ had managed to keep the lid on her excitement.

"Wow!" Amy Yamamoto, DJ's best friend, rested her arms across her saddle horn as she and her half-Arab gelding, Josh, rode up. Josh tossed his head and nickered as if he agreed.

After shooting a raised-eyebrow look at Amy, DJ stopped Major in front of Bridget. Cheers would come later.

"We will raise the poles for your next lesson, but you must concentrate. You have a tendency to get so caught up in the thrill of the jump that you leave too much up to Major. If you were riding a horse that was not a natural jumper, you could get into difficulties."

DJ listened attentively and nodded. "Will that feeling go away with more practice?"

"I hope not." Bridget smiled up at her student. "That joy is what makes you a good rider and is why you are learning so quickly. Major feels it, too, so he gives you his best."

"I'm not sure I understand."

"The more you concentrate and focus on what you are doing, the more joy there will be for you in riding. You will understand what I mean in time." Bridget smiled again.

DJ felt the warmth of the smile encircle her and bring an answering grin to her own face. "Thanks." No other word came to mind that began to describe what she was feeling. *I'm finally jumping, I have a super-fantastic horse of my own, and if I don't get to move soon, I'm afraid I'll explode!*

"I better put Major away and get home. See you tomorrow." At Bridget's nod, DJ lightly squeezed her lower legs. Major responded immediately by heading for the gate.

"You know, horse, if I didn't know better, I'd think you understood English better'n I do." DJ patted the sweaty neck of the sixteen-hand bay. Major paused so she could swing the gate open, then walked on through, stopping again to allow the gate to be closed. "And if I didn't want to jump so bad, you'd be a sure winner in the Trail class."

"You two were awesome." Amy dismounted at the same time DJ did, and together they led their horses into the red-sided pole barn. The two friends were about as opposite as could be. Amy, tiny at five feet, had flowing dark hair, almond-shaped eyes, rode Western, and thrived on hot, spicy food. At five feet seven, DJ was as long-legged as a colt, had sparkling green eyes, felt English was a far more comfortable ride, and hated peppery food. Both girls shared one major complaint—their bodies had about as many curves as a plank. Many times, DJ had sighed and noted, "Some *boys* have bigger chests than we do." Amy had to agree.

"Ames, pinch me so I know I'm not dreaming." DJ held out her arm to her friend. "Ouch! I was only kidding."

With the reins draped over one arm, she reached up to remove her helmet and tighten the band holding her wavy blond hair in a ponytail.

Major sniffed her hair, then her jeans pocket, nosing for the treat she saved for his reward.

"Sorry, old man, you ate it earlier."

Major blew in her face, slobber and all.

"Yuck." DJ wiped the wet drops off her tanned face with the hem of her T-shirt.

The horse rubbed his nose against her chest, leaving white hairs, slobber, and sweat on the dark blue fabric.

"Now you did it. Mom will insist I change clothes before dinner."

"Well, you better hurry then. We won't be home before dark at this rate. And I have tons of homework. Besides, you don't want your mother yelling at you." Amy stripped off her Western saddle and the thick pad underneath it while she talked. Always practical, Amy did her best to keep DJ out of trouble.

"Okay, okay." DJ followed suit, setting her English saddle on one of the two-by-four bars that made up the saddle rack on the wall of the tack room. Her name was written on a three-by-five card to remind everyone that this was her private property. Most horse boarders took their gear home with them, but since DJ and Amy usually rode their bikes to the Academy, they kept their tack there.

"You *did* do your chores before you came?" Amy peered around Josh's neck when DJ didn't answer. "Didn't you?"

DJ kept quiet.

"*DJ!*"

"Well, I was in a hurry, and—"

"We'd really better hurry now. What time did your mom say she'd be home?"

"Seven." *And I sure hope that means eight, as usual. I don't know where the time goes.* DJ's thoughts kept pace with the two grooming brushes she wielded with such skill. Grooming a horse had become second nature to her.

If only Gran . . . DJ clapped a lid on the thought. Gran didn't live far away, but on nights like this, her house might as well have been on the other side of the moon. She wasn't living with DJ and her mother now that she'd met and married Joe Crowder. She wouldn't be in the kitchen cooking dinner or out in her studio putting the final touches on one of her paintings for illustrated children's books.

"Earth to DJ. Come in, DJ." Amy waved her hand in front of DJ's face.

"Oh, sorry. Did you say something?"

"No, not really. I was just talking to Josh here about his homework." Amy wore a disgusted look that said she'd been expecting an answer.

"Sorry." DJ gave Major's now-dry coat a quick once over, checked the hay in the hay net, and grabbed the water bucket. "I'll be right back." While water gushed into the bucket from the spigot, she looked up toward the hills of northern California's Briones State Park. While the hills still wore the gold of fall, soon winter would bring rain and, with it, tender shoots of green grass. The oak trees were turning shades of rust and gold, the color deepened by the setting sun. Down in the hollows, the trees already looked black.

DJ shut off the water. Black trees meant black skies, and black skies meant a black mood on her mother's face and over the entire house if

DJ wasn't home before dark. DJ knew she'd better put herself in gear, but she'd rather be at the Academy than anywhere else on earth.

Amy and DJ signed out on the duty roster, DJ gritting her teeth at the signature right above hers. *Tony Andrada*. He was even worse than his predecessor, James, whom she used to think was the biggest pain alive. But thanks to her grandmother's counseling, DJ and James had become friends. Unfortunately, Tony outdid James in rottenness a hundred to one.

"Have you heard from James?" As usual, Amy seemed to know what DJ was thinking.

"You blow me away."

"How?" The pair swung their legs over their bikes at the same moment, as if the move had been choreographed by a dance instructor. "How did you know I was thinking about James?"

"I didn't." Amy shot a grin over her shoulder as they turned onto Reliez Valley Road. "So answer the question."

"So I haven't heard. You know he'd rather send e-mail than a letter, but since I don't have a computer, he has to do things the old-fashioned way. Why is it so hard to type up a letter on the computer and stick it in the mail?"

"Don't ask me, I'm not a computer nerd."

"No, you're just a horse nerd—like me." DJ panted. The second hill always made her huff.

They turned and coasted down their own street. Coming home was always easier than going to the Academy, at least as far as peddling was concerned. DJ groaned. Her mother's car sat in the driveway.

"You have company."

"Hey, you're right." DJ's groan changed to a grin. "Robert's here."

Amy turned up her drive and stopped to wave. "See ya in the morning."

"Okay." At least now, with company in the house, she wouldn't get a lecture till later. And sometimes when her mother and Robert had been swapping gooey glances, trouble disappeared altogether.

DJ dismounted and entered the front door to press the button that raised the garage door. Tonight she would make sure her bike was put away. No need to make matters worse.

"Mom, I'm home." No answer. DJ stashed her bike in the garage and reentered the house.

"DJ, is that you?"

"Who else do you suppose it would be?" DJ was careful to keep the mutter just that. "Yeah." She raised her voice to be heard outside. Obviously they were out on the deck.

"You're late."

"It's not dark yet." DJ grabbed a soda out of the refrigerator and crossed the family room, no longer Gran's studio, to the French doors leading onto the redwood deck. Robert and her mother turned to greet her.

DJ stopped as quickly as though she'd run into a glass wall. A diamond ring glinted on her mother's hand.

"Robert has asked me to marry him." Lindy looked up at the man standing just behind her, his arm around her waist.

DJ felt as if she'd been kicked in the chest by a feisty horse.

Chapter • 2

"Have you nothing to say?"

DJ looked from her mother's hand to her eyes and up at Robert. "I . . . I . . ." She cleared her throat. What was she supposed to say? Hurrah and congratulations? This was her life they were planning so glibly! "I . . . ah . . . that's great." Even to her ears, the response sounded weak.

"I know this comes as a surprise to you."

Yeah, you could say that. About a hundred times over.

Robert's deep voice drew DJ's attention back from her mindless study of the ring to his face. The two lines that cut between his straight eyebrows looked deeper than they had the moment before. His gray eyes had darkened.

"I better get something to eat so I can get started on my homework." *Ask 'em when the wedding will be, bozo.* DJ headed for the kitchen. *Why would Mom take his ring if she didn't want to marry him, yo-yo brain?* DJ felt as though she had another person in her head, arguing her mother's case.

I'd have a father. Someone else to boss me around. And if Mom married Robert, those two human dynamos would be here all the time. DJ shuddered. The five-year-old twin boys, Bobby and Billy, would make St. Peter wish for a new assignment. Her smile at the thought felt stiff, like a pair of shoes left out in the rain and then dried too quickly.

She dished up food from all four take-out containers and stuck the plate in the microwave. How come two minutes of waiting for the microwave timer to beep and two minutes in the show-ring passed at such different rates of speed?

Carrying her plate up to her room, DJ stopped in the family room. "Does Gran know yet?"

Lindy shook her head. "We hoped you'd be happy for us, DJ."

"Oh, I am." DJ started up the stairs. "I am." She hurried upstairs, half worried they might chase her and shake the truth out of her. She was proud of herself for not slamming the door to her room. But then, she wasn't mad—was she?

She sat on the edge of the bed shoveling food into her mouth as if that could shut out the thought. Beef with broccoli, sweet-and-sour prawns, egg foo yong, chicken chow mein—it all tasted the same. She set the plate on her desk and cracked open her fortune cookie. *Great money is coming into your life.*

She read it again. Wouldn't that be incredible? Money she needed in spades. Money for a new saddle and a horse trailer would be nice— and, of course, a new truck to haul the trailer with. She let the piece of pink paper flutter into her wastebasket. So much for the wisdom of fortune cookies.

She nibbled one half. Stale. She spit it into the wastebasket and tossed in the other half behind it. *There should be a law against giving out stale fortune cookies, let alone stale fortunes.*

She crossed to the window and looked out at the yard she and Gran had worked so hard over. The roses wore their October finery, blooming again after a slowdown in the heat of summer. Pink and red begonias lined the bed at the back of the yard. Carrots rose their feathery plumes in front of the squash, and pumpkins sent tendrils snaking everywhere.

I suppose I could have fun carving jack-o'-lanterns with Bobby and Billy. The Double Bs. They and Robert and Lindy always laughed whenever she called them by the name she had given them.

DJ pushed away from the window, full of memories, and slumped into the chair in front of her desk. "Like they really care what I think. Grown-ups don't consider kids at all when they make changes in their lives." She hung her head in her hands. If only she could call Amy, or better yet, Gran. But Gran wasn't home, and Amy's mother had a rule against phone calls after eight.

Could this be defined as an emergency? DJ shook her head, defeat setting around her shoulders like a lead cape. Opening her algebra book to the assigned page, she began her homework. "If x equals blank and y is twenty-four, what is . . ." DJ snapped her pencil in two. What did it matter? She slammed the book shut and stuffed it into her backpack.

Taking out her drawing pad and number-three charcoal pencil, she crossed to the bed and made a nest against the headboard with her pillows. Finally, with the pad propped on her knees, she closed her eyes. That way, it was easier to picture Major.

After a few moments of concentration, she began drawing. Five minutes later, she tore off the first sheet. The sketch looked more like a camel. The next one closely resembled an okapi. She dumped the pad onto the floor before she wasted any more paper.

Once in bed, comforted by her Mickey Mouse nightshirt, she tried to pray. Gran had always said to pray when you were stuck—it was even better if you prayed before you got stuck in the first place. But then, Gran found it easy to ask God for things. He really answered her.

DJ thumped her pillows into submission and turned onto her side.

"God, help! I don't want a new father—I don't even know the one I've got. Please, please, *please* don't let Mom and Robert get married. Mom and I . . . we . . . well, we're just starting to get along as it is. What am I gonna do now?" She waited. There was no answer. She heard footsteps coming up the stairs, so she shut off the light and rolled onto her side to face the wall.

"DJ?" Mom tapped at the closed door. When there was only silence, her feet padded down the hall to her own room.

DJ heard her mother's bedroom door click shut. Lindy was a strong believer in privacy, both for herself and her daughter. Right now, the daughter felt . . . DJ tried to figure out how she felt.

Lost seemed as good a word as any.

––––––––

"Close your mouth, Ames, you'll catch flies."

"But you say your mother and Robert—?" Amy stopped, heedless of the students milling around them. She ignored the one who bumped into her and kept her attention riveted on DJ.

"Bummer, huh?" DJ kicked her sneakers against the curb.

"Well, maybe not."

"Where's your head, girl? I'm counting on you to help me break this fast romance into a thousand pieces."

"What does Gran say?"

DJ kicked again. "I don't know. I haven't talked with her. She was gone last night." She raised her head. "There's the bell. We'll have to discuss this later. Try to come up with a really creative idea in the meantime. A plan—you know, the kind that's so good they'll think they thought of it."

"Right." Amy's groan rose clear from her ankles. "You know what happens to our good ideas."

"Not this time. This time I'm desperate." DJ slung her backpack over one shoulder and headed for the doorway.

"When aren't you?" Amy had to take three strides to DJ's two.

"But this time . . . this time could mean the difference between . . ." DJ wrinkled her brow. Life and death sounded too—well, *normal* would do for lack of a better word. She skidded into her homeroom just as the final bell rang.

———————

The house smelled empty, the same lonely smell that greeted DJ every day now. Would she never stop missing Gran? As she climbed the stairs to her room, she remembered the way fresh-baked cookie perfume had floated out to the street to greet her. If Gran had been too involved in painting to bake, a familiar turpentine and oil scent had said she was hard at work. The easel set up in the corner of the family room had always exhibited the artwork for the latest children's book Gran was illustrating, the stereo playing one of Gran's "uplifting" tapes.

So many times, DJ had teased Gran about her music when they both knew DJ enjoyed listening to the contemporary Christian singers as much as her grandmother.

DJ reminded herself that Gran lived only a mile and a half away and she could drop in to experience all those things if she wanted to. Frequently she did—but only after her work at the Academy and only on nights when her mother said she'd be home late.

DJ did her usual quick-change routine and clattered back down the stairs, leaving the memories behind. The answering machine winked its red eye at her. She pushed the play button to hear her mother's voice.

"Please be ready to go to dinner by 7:15. We will be going someplace nice, so make sure you are presentable."

DJ read between the lines. Presentable meant "take a shower so you don't smell like horse." But who did the "we" refer to? Would it be just the two of them? The entire family? Was Robert coming? The tone said her mother had a long way to go before she would be happy with her one and only daughter.

If DJ was going to be clean and dressed by 7:15, she'd better hit warp speed right about now. She grabbed a soda and an apple from the refrigerator, a food bar from the cupboard, and stuck her cereal bowl and glass from that morning in the dishwasher. No sense adding fuel to her mother's fire. Everything had better be put away.

DJ rushed out the door and hopped onto her bike. "Put a move on it," she called as she coasted past Amy. "Her highness called and said to be ready tonight for dinner out."

"Well, at least she won't yell at you while you're in public." Amy pedaled up beside her friend.

"Hope not. She read somewhere that restaurants are perfect for having heavy discussions—people are on their best behavior." DJ alternately munched and sipped as she pedaled until they reached the steep part of the hill where she needed two hands to steer. "You come up with any great ideas?"

"For what?"

"Getting this wedding canceled, of course. What did you think I meant?"

"DJ, I hate to remind you, but all our great ideas flop, remember?" Amy halted at the stop sign. "Besides, Robert is a nice man. And personally, I think having a father around is the best."

"Yeah, but you've got a good one."

"I know. Anyway, I think you should let nature take its course."

"Nature what? Are you out of your mind?" DJ skidded in the loose gravel, then dismounted. They both parked their bikes in the shade of the long barn containing four rows of stalls. DJ finished her soda in a gulp and dropped the can in a recycling barrel as they trotted across the dusty parking lot to the office. Once inside the dim interior, they looked up at the roster, a shiny white board with names and duties written in erasable marker.

"Yuck." Amy pointed at the name Tony Andrada. Recently relocated from the South, Tony had already made a name for himself as one of the most disliked student workers at the Academy. He gave a new and deeper meaning to the term *redneck*.

"Well, at least I don't have to work with him. James was bad enough."

Together they turned and entered Bridget's office. A stack of bills, invoices, magazines, and advertisements teetered on the edge of the desk, nearly hiding the woman working at a pullout board.

"Just do not sneeze in here, and I will remain calm." Bridget looked up from glaring at a ledger. "Is either one of you skilled enough on a computer to enter all this information for me so I can finally get organized?"

Both girls shook their heads. "Sorry."

"Me too. Oh, DJ, Angie's mother called. Angie had another bad asthma attack last night, and they kept her overnight at the hospital. She will not be here for her lesson today."

"Fiddle." DJ rubbed a finger over the scar from a childhood burn on her right palm. "She's the best rider of the group, and the one with real natural talent. If only she didn't have to miss so much."

"Actually, we are fortunate to have her at all. Many parents would say riding is off limits to an asthmatic child due to the dust. The Lincolns trust us a lot to let her ride here."

"After she got stung by the bee up in the park, I'd want to keep her in sight all the time." DJ flinched at the memory. "Seeing her gasping for breath like that and having to give her a shot scared me half to death."

"You did well." Bridget cocked her head and studied the two girls. "You all right, DJ?"

"Sorta."

"Well, if you need a friendly ear, I have two." Bridget paused as if giving DJ a chance to add something. "Okay, this is not written on the board, but since Angie is not coming to care for her horse, could you find a few minutes to ride him or at least put him on the hot walker? And, Amy, Tony got here late, so he needs some help grooming the horses along the north wall. Hilary will not be coming, so I would like you to supervise him." Bridget raised a hand to forestall any groaning on their part. "I know Tony is a bit of a pain, but he will become accustomed to our ways. He *is* a good rider."

But if he treats his horse like he treats us, it doesn't matter how good a rider he is, DJ thought. *He'll be out of here. And it won't be a moment too soon.* "Anything else?" DJ fingered the scar again. She'd found herself doing that more often lately—at least it beat chewing her fingernails.

Bridget looked up at the clock above the duty board. "I have a new client coming in a half hour. I might be late for your jumping lesson, DJ, but feel free to start without me."

"Sure." DJ bit her lower lip. "I have to leave at 6:30 so . . ."

"So you may have a shorter lesson today. We will make up for it later." Bridget glanced at the stack before her. "If a wind came through here, we would have a paper snowstorm. Something has to be done about this." She bent her head to her task, one yellow pencil stuck above her ear in her slicked-back hair.

DJ and Amy trotted back across the parking lot and into the tack room for grooming buckets. "Go ahead, say it, Ames." DJ's chuckle had just the right amount of fiendish glee.

"My mother would wash my mouth out with soap."

"I'm not your mother."

"But once I got started, I wouldn't stop. That . . . that . . ."

"Yes, go on." DJ made beckoning motions with her hands.

" . . . that absolute jerk!"

"Hmm . . . not good enough—or bad enough, in this case. We called James 'The Jerk,' remember? We need to be a little more creative around here."

"Beat it, DJ, I've got work to do." Amy flipped another soft brush into her bucket and headed down the sandy aisle between rows of box stalls.

DJ checked her watch. Only a half hour till the students in her beginners' class arrived. She grabbed a bridle that she knew would fit Angie's horse and hurried across the middle lane to where the gelding was stabled. Within minutes, she had him groomed, tacked, and out in the ring. He was an easy-gaited horse, and DJ enjoyed the exercise as much as he did. She put him through his paces, all the things she'd been teaching the girls: walk, jog, lope, reverses, figure eights, back-ups, and stops and starts.

"How come you have Angie's horse out here?" Krissie, a bubbly little blonde, rode into the arena.

"Angie had a bad attack." DJ reined her mount to the center of the ring. "How about if I teach from horseback?"

"Fine with me."

15

"Me too." Sam, short for Samantha, followed Krissie into the ring. They both walked their horses to the left and stayed just off the rail like they'd been taught.

"We're going to be adding another rider to this class soon," DJ announced, keeping her reins steady and patting the gelding's neck. At their unison groans, she raised her voice. "Hey, let's give the poor guy a chance when he comes.

"Now focus. Jog, please."

By the time the lesson was done, the gelding was tired of standing still. DJ rode over to the gate. "You did fine. Krissie, what do you think about working toward entering the trail-riding class? Both you and your horse are calm enough for that." She turned. "Sam, you have to keep an even pace. You move fast one minute, then slow the next—makes me wonder who's giving the orders."

"My horse is. He's bigger."

Sam and Krissie laughed but cut it short when DJ frowned at them.

"I'm trying—really I am." Sam looked sheepish. "I will do better. I'll practice between now and next week. We'll do it right. You'll see."

"That's better. No 'trys' allowed here." DJ let her smile return. "You done good."

How many times had she had to replace "I'll try" with "I will" back when she was first beginning? Everyone started out saying "I'll try" at first. And trying wasn't good enough at the Academy. "Now hustle. I see your moms waiting."

While the girls took care of their horses, DJ put Angie's horse up and groomed Patches, the gelding she was training for the Johnsons. The horse had come in green broke, and the owners had no idea how to make him mind. Now Mrs. Johnson was finally able to take riding lessons on Patches.

Fortunately, Bridget had talked the Johnsons into giving their son riding lessons on a pony at first. The boy, Andrew, acted scared to death of horses in general and Patches in particular. Soon he would be DJ's private pupil every Wednesday. So far, he hadn't been on Bandit yet, but at least he was grooming him. DJ already felt like she was winning.

Just as she'd suspected, her own riding lesson was cut short, but she almost didn't mind because she couldn't keep her mind on jumping. As dinnertime grew closer, DJ fought to think about something else—anything other than her mother and Robert and their crazy engagement.

Bridget made her repeat the lower jumps over and over.

"I know, I know—my focus is shot to pieces." DJ stopped herself at Bridget's sharp look. Grumbling would do no good.

Chapter • 3

"DJ, I'm speaking to you." Lindy wore the tight-lipped look that meant trouble lay just over the horizon.

DJ looked up from the circles she was drawing on the white tablecloth with the tines of her fork. "I know. I heard you."

"Then why didn't you answer?"

"I don't know what to say."

"You have to admit that was an honest answer." Robert placed a hand on Lindy's arm.

Lindy jerked her arm away and brushed a strand of hair from her cheek.

DJ saw hurt in Robert's eyes.

Mister, you ain't seen nothin' yet. Wait till she has PMS. DJ had to fight to keep a grin off her face. She didn't need a creative idea to break this romance up, she just needed to keep quiet.

A woman dressed in a black evening gown played a harp by the velvet curtains.

"Can I get you something else, sir?" A white-jacketed waiter appeared at Robert's elbow.

"No . . . ah . . ." Robert looked from Lindy to DJ. "Would either of you care for dessert?"

DJ started to shake her head, then changed her mind. "Could I see the dessert tray, please?" She made the request as smoothly as if she ate at places like this every other Tuesday. She tried to ignore the withering look from her mother, but she could feel it digging into her scalp.

Robert had discarded three different conversational topics by the time the New York cheesecake with blueberry topping arrived.

"Want a bite, Mom?" DJ offered with a smile.

"No, thank you." The *k* could have cut glass.

"So, Robert, what do the twins think of this idea of yours?" DJ ventured.

"The twins?" Robert had obviously resorted to polite smiles that hid his real thoughts.

"You know, Bobby and Billy." DJ savored the last bite of cheesecake. She felt as though she was going to be sick. She hadn't eaten this much at one time since who knew when.

"They think that having a new mom and a big sister would be the best thing since ice cream."

"If you are finished, Darla Jean, I would like to go now." Lindy shot DJ an icy look.

"Yes, thank you. I'm done." DJ carefully folded her napkin and set it on the table. "Thank you, Robert, for the awesome dinner."

Robert pushed back his chair and stood to pull out Lindy's for her. "Honey, are you all right?"

Honey? Gag time again. DJ followed her mother out the door, Robert bringing up the rear. By the time the valet brought the car around, Lindy was rubbing her temples.

Headache—big time. DJ recognized the signs. An itty-bitty twinge of guilt waved to get her attention, but DJ deliberately faced the other way. She hadn't said one wrong thing. In fact, she'd hardly said anything at all. But if looks could kill, she'd been skewered.

So that was the new rule: Don't answer even when spoken to—until the third time or when the tone took on a real bite. Ignore, ignore, ignore.

But when DJ crawled into bed after faking polite good-nights, all she could think of was how disappointed Gran would have been with her that night. DJ rolled over and tried counting horses instead. She thought about the Olympics and being on the Olympic team. But when she finally fell asleep, the feeling that she had somehow let down Gran still troubled her.

"How come I'm more tired now than when I went to bed?" DJ's grumbles received no answers. There was no one to hear them. DJ was beginning to think she was going loony, all this talking to herself. Maybe she should get a dog. At least then there would be someone to listen to her.

Yeah, just like you listened to your mother last night. Where had that thought come from?

The car honking outside told her Mr. Yamamoto and Amy were waiting to take her to school. Wait till Ames heard the plan DJ had come up with before dropping off to sleep. It was destined to work.

"You're going to what?" Amy and DJ hadn't had time to talk in the car without Amy's father overhearing. Now, that afternoon, they were on their way up the hill to the Academy.

"You heard me." DJ took another bite of her apple, tossed the core into the bushes, and pedaled to catch up.

"Yeah, but you—keeping your mouth shut? Gimme a break." Amy's grin took any sting out of her words.

"You'll see." DJ tried to forget today's message on the red-eyed answering machine at home. Her mother had said, *Tonight, we talk.* Her voice had sounded about as friendly as that of a wounded wolf.

Lindy's headache must have gone away. Or maybe she had gone to work in order to avoid remaining at home with her daughter.

DJ set to grooming her horses for the day, whistling so she didn't have to think. Tonight Gran would be back. That was one thing to put on her things-to-thank-God-for list. Gran and Joe were returning from her yearly trip to New York to talk with her publishers.

DJ stopped picking hooves when a loud voice broke into her reverie.

"I don't have to listen to you." The nasty edge said it could be none other than Tony Andrada.

The answer came as a soft murmur.

DJ listened hard. It had to be Hilary. Why didn't she just tell him to shape up or she'd ship him out to Bridget? He had to listen to Hilary; Bridget had assigned them to each other. Didn't Tony understand that the older student workers trained the new ones? And that they all worked as a team?

The angry voice came from farther away. Tony was heading out to the arena.

"Hilary?" DJ left the horse she was working with and went hunting for her mentor and friend. Hilary Jones had always been one to encourage the younger members, DJ included. Through the years, watching Hilary's graceful riding in the jumping ring had given DJ pure pleasure—and, depending on which day it was, a bad case of envy.

No answer.

"Hilary?" DJ stuck her head into the empty stall. At least she thought it was empty until she saw Hilary sitting in the far corner, her hands between raised knees. A tear meandered down her cocoa-colored cheek.

"Hil, are you all right?"

Hilary wound one corn-row braid around her finger. "I don't think so."

DJ slumped down the wall until she was sitting beside her friend. What could she say? "It's Tony, isn't it?"

"Umm."

"When are you going to talk to Bridget about him?"

"I'm not."

"What?" DJ turned to look the college freshman in the face. Hilary kept her gaze forward. She let the tear drip off her chin.

"DJ, if I tell you something, do you promise not to tell anyone else?"

"Not even Amy?"

"That's up to you." Hilary sighed. "I'm thinking of moving my horse to a different stable."

"Hilary Jones, whatever is the matter with you? You know Bridget is the best coach around. And not only is this the best-run stable, but it's also the one closest to your house."

"I know. But, DJ, this situation with Tony ... it's a racial thing. He called me a ... a black ..." She couldn't finish the sentence.

"You don't have to say it, Hil. I know Tony is a real creep." DJ stared at her hands. This couldn't be happening in Pleasant Hill, California. "But if you move your horse, you let Tony win. You can't do that."

"What else can I do?"

"I don't know, but Amy and I'll think of something. I'll talk to Gran, too." DJ held up a hand. "Don't worry, I won't tell her any names.

But you can bet she'll be praying for you, and Gran's prayers always get answers. You wait and see."

"I'll give it till after the fall regional show in the beginning of December. If he doesn't come around by then, I'm out of here." Hilary pushed herself to her feet. "Sorry, DJ, that's the most I can give. I can't let this keep getting in the way of my schoolwork like it has been."

"The show isn't very far away."

"I know." Hilary extended a hand to pull DJ to her feet and stepped out of the stall. She turned back. "You better get out there. Your little student is coming down the aisle looking for you."

DJ groaned. "Hang in there, Hil. We'll turn things around, we will." *I could beat that stupid redneck into the ground if I had to. But I can't do that. What are we gonna do?*

DJ met Andrew halfway up the aisle. "You looking for me?"

Her small pupil tried to smile, but fear darkened his eyes, the same fear she'd seen each week during the time she'd been working with him. Whatever could have happened to make him so afraid? She'd asked his parents, but they insisted that no horse had ever run away with him or lunged at or bitten him or any such thing. DJ and Bridget were both stumped by the situation.

Right now, it was DJ's job to get the boy over his fear since his parents wanted the family to ride together regularly.

"You been to see Bandit?"

Andrew shook his head. He reached for DJ's hand and glued himself to her side. At five feet seven, DJ wasn't a giant, but she felt like one next to this little boy who looked more like eight than ten—and a small eight at that.

"Bandit's waiting to see you. He likes the way you brush his legs."

"Really?" Two huge blue eyes looked up at her.

"Sure, I think you're going to be a very good horse groomer." DJ felt like swinging him up into her arms and hugging his skinny body. She'd always been a sucker for big blue eyes. "How about combing his mane today?"

They stopped in front of the stall, where Bandit pushed his nose over the web gate and nickered silently, his nostrils wide to sniff for treats.

"See, I told you he likes you."

Andrew made like a mollusk and clung.

DJ stroked Bandit's nose, then dug in her pocket for a horse cookie. "You like cookies, Andrew?"

He nodded.

"So does Bandit. These are made especially for horses. Why don't you give it to him? Like this." DJ held part of the cookie on the flat palm of her hand and let Bandit lip it up. "See, it tickles." She took Andrew's hand and tickled the palm. "Feels funny, huh?"

Andrew nodded. A smile almost peeked out of one side of his mouth.

"You want to try?"

He shook his head vigorously, setting the dark hair that flopped over his forehead to swinging. Then he reached down into the grooming bucket and picked up a brush. With a sigh that shook his entire body, he looked up at her. "Please tie him."

"You are one gutsy kid." DJ gave him her most reassuring smile. "What makes you think Bandit will bite you?"

"Horses bite. I've seen it."

"Really?" DJ snapped both crossties to Bandit's halter and opened the web gate. "Where?"

"On TV." Andrew ducked under the ropes, keeping a careful eye on Bandit's head. Standing as far away as possible, he brushed down the gray shoulder.

"Oh, really? What happened?" DJ picked up the other brush and moved to Bandit's far side.

"A horse bit a boy and made him bleed. I saw one trample a lady, too. Horses are mean."

"Do you think Bandit is mean?" Andrew shook his head and kept on brushing. Bit by bit, he edged closer so he could brush more easily.

DJ kept up a line of chatter, telling Andrew about the times Bandit did well in the show-ring and took children on trail rides. She even got a laugh when she told him about the kids tracking in green horse manure on a woman's brand-new white carpet at one of the birthday parties. The more she got him to talk, the closer he moved to the pony.

After a while, DJ asked, "How about feeding Bandit a treat?"

Silence. Then a soft, "All right."

She reached into her pocket and pulled out a mutilated horse cookie. "Here. If you like, I'll keep my hand right by yours."

Andrew nodded. He held his hand out flat and watched DJ place the cookie on the palm. She put her hand under his and squatted down beside the boy. "Anytime you're ready."

She kept the other hand on Bandit's halter just in case he moved too quickly. "Easy, Bandit. Go ahead, Andrew, talk to Bandit and tell him what you are going to do. Horses like to hear our voices."

"B-Bandit. I have a c-cookie for you." Andrew stepped closer and held the treat out just like DJ had shown him. Bandit opened his eyes, blinked, and lipped the goodie, his whiskers scraping the boy's palm.

"He tickles." Andrew's grin could have lit the entire barn on a gray day. But just at that moment, Bandit stamped his foot and flicked his tail to chase a pesky fly.

Andrew leaped back, tripped over the bucket, and sprawled in the straw. He scrambled to his feet and was out of the stall before DJ had time to blink. She could hear him crying as he went.

"Bummer. Double bummer." She untied the pony and picked up the brushes scattered in the fall. *Better luck next time—if there is a next time. Poor kid.*

Later when she told Mrs. Johnson about the conversation, the woman shook her head.

"I had no idea. Why, Andrew knows those things on television aren't real. We've certainly talked about it often enough."

DJ just looked at her.

"But that's why he's so afraid, huh?" Mrs. Johnson sighed. "Guess I better pay more attention—he's such a sensitive child. Thanks, DJ."

The rest of the day continued the downhill slide. Patches acted as though he'd been snacking on loco weed. DJ had to return to the basics of stop, start, walk, and jog. She refused to let him tear around the ring like he wanted. And Angie's horse had to be worked again, too. The poor girl was still in the hospital.

"They are trying out a new routine," Bridget said when DJ questioned her. "They are hoping it could stop some of the attacks."

"I sure hope so." DJ resolved to create a card for Angie that night. She knew how down she would feel if she were in that hospital bed.

Major behaved in his usual easygoing manner, but as dusk fell, DJ's thoughts kept returning to what was waiting for her at home. After less than an hour of working Major, she finally put her horse away. It wasn't his fault she couldn't concentrate. It was a good thing tonight wasn't a lesson night because DJ knew she would have been scolded. She was doing a pretty fair job of that herself.

You know better than this, DJ. Now concentrate. A true rider puts everything out of her mind but the horse and the jumps. But the reminders didn't help. Telling herself that all she had to do tonight was keep quiet didn't help, either. Staying silent in a restaurant with Robert present was one thing. But one-on-one with her mother was something else entirely.

The clipped voice on the answering machine replayed itself in her head. *Tonight, we talk.*

Chapter · 4

Her mother's car sat in the driveway.

Thanks a bunch, God. Why didn't you make her work late tonight? I hoped you were on my side. DJ parked her bike by the driver's side of the car and opened the door so she could push the garage opener. The garage door did its usual moaning and groaning routine on its way up. It would have been nice for it to be quiet this one time. Then maybe DJ could have sneaked in, parked her bike, and tiptoed up to her room without her mother knowing.

"Yeah, and maybe the sky will fall." She grumbled at her bike when the kickstand didn't go down on the first flip.

The back door squeaked when she opened it. Her boots sounded like hammers on the kitchen floor no matter how lightly she tried to step.

"I'm in the living room."

Uh-oh. Trouble! DJ felt herself freeze. Here it came. She peered around the corner. Her mother sat in a corner of the sofa, her legs crossed over the middle cushion. She'd changed from her work suit into an emerald lounging outfit. A half-empty glass of sparkling water dripped moisture on the coaster protecting the oak end table.

Her mother had been home for some time.

"Come on in."

"You want me to change first?" DJ knew the rules. Jeans scented with horse were not allowed in the living room.

"Of course."

On the way upstairs, DJ tried to decipher her mother's tone. Angry? She shucked off her jeans and tossed them into the hamper. Furious? Her T-shirt followed. Hurt? She grabbed a pair of shorts from the drawer and a clean T-shirt, this one with a leaping dolphin on the front. Gran had bought it for DJ on her honeymoon cruise.

If only Gran were here. Of course, she'd want me to apologize. But this isn't my fault.

DJ could hear Gran's voice as clearly as if she were right here in the room. "Any time you hurt someone else, you must ask forgiveness and apologize." Then Gran would follow her pronouncement with a Bible verse. How could DJ argue with the Bible?

She reminded herself again that this whole mess wasn't her fault. All she'd done was keep her mouth shut. Hadn't she been told to do that a million times by now?

She entered the darkened room and took the wing chair across from her mother. Silence reigned. The light from a crystal lamp on an end table made a halo around Lindy's head. Her mother appeared to be studying the painting on the wall, one of Gran's.

DJ knew it by heart. Gran had painted it of DJ in the garden when her granddaughter was five and loved sniffing the roses, especially the pink ones. The picture had won an award at the county fair. The judge had said the painting had the luminescent quality of French Impressionism. DJ had been wearing a floppy straw hat and a polka-dot sunsuit that Gran had sewn for her granddaughter's fifth birthday. Gran had kept the sunsuit, and DJ had proudly pinned the hat to her bedroom wall.

The silence between mother and daughter stretched like a rubber band pulled to its limit.

DJ sat on her fingers to keep from chewing her nails. *Just holler at me and get this over with,* she wanted to say.

"What are we going to do, Darla Jean?" Her mother's voice held all the sadness of a wounded puppy.

"Mom, I didn't murder anyone or anything." The hoped-for light tone fell flatter than a flour tortilla.

Lindy looked across the space between them, a space that at that moment seemed to measure the width of the Pacific Ocean.

"Mom, it's not my fault. All I did was . . ." The words trailed off. If only DJ could make like a slug and slime her way out of the room. Her thumbnail ached to be chewed on.

"No, it's not your fault. But you hurt someone who doesn't deserve to be hurt."

DJ immediately knew who she meant. "Robert?"

"Yes." Lindy kept her gaze trained on her daughter's face.

If DJ concentrated on not chewing her fingernail, maybe she could make it through this tortured conversation.

"He had the silly idea that we would make a good family. He says he fell in love not only with me, but with you." Each word dropped like a tear.

Why couldn't they yell at each other like they usually did? DJ felt as if a giant hand was shoving her deep into the chair. "I . . . I'm sorry."

"I know. I can tell. Sometimes sorry just isn't enough." Lindy leaned forward. "Listen to me carefully, Darla Jean. You keep saying you want me to treat you like an adult, that you are growing up. Well, I tried to do that, and you blew it. You blew it big time." She sighed. "Robert says we'll work this out in time. But I don't know." Her mother shook her head. "I just don't know."

DJ curled her feet under her and tried to disappear into the back of the chair. She couldn't think of a thing to say.

She went to bed feeling like she'd kicked a floppy-eared puppy.

The next night, since her mother had to attend a graduate course, DJ waved good-bye to Amy and turned left toward Gran and Joe's. She'd have dinner with them, then Joe would drive her home. If you could call the icebox she'd left behind home, that is. Even with the air-conditioner off, the temperature must have registered only thirty degrees. There had been no message from her mother.

DJ pedaled up to her grandmother's new house. She and Joe had lived there little more than a month and already she could tell it was Gran's house. Roses bloomed by the door, and a flowering bougainvillea vine painted the adjoining garage brilliant purple. Best of all, the smell of fresh chocolate chip cookies met DJ's nostrils as she mounted the three concrete steps. Pots of pink begonias were in a race to outbloom one another on each step.

"Gran?"

"In here, darlin'." All the years of living in California still hadn't erased Gran's soft Southern drawl. Like Gran's gentle hands, the accent meant love in DJ's mind. Her Gran always loved everyone, no matter what.

DJ followed her nose into the kitchen. "You have green paint on your chin," she teased as she gave her grandmother a hug and snitched a cookie off the counter. She turned to greet the man sitting at the round table in the bay window overlooking the backyard. "Hi, Joe." She grinned around the cookie-crumble greeting. "I was beginning to think you guys were never coming home."

"Hi, yourself. Hand me one of those, will you? Melanie's been keeping me on diet restrictions." He tried to sound abused and failed miserably.

"After all we ate in New York, I shouldn't be baking at all." Gran slid the last cookies off the sheet and set it in the sink. She turned off the oven, arranged cookies on a plate, and brought it with her to the table. "Do you want anything to drink, DJ?"

DJ shook her head. "Might spoil my dinner."

Gran laughed and poked DJ on the shoulder. "Fat chance. So, do you want to tell me what's going on?"

Leave it to Gran to get right to the point.

"Nothing much. Major and I are getting better every day, and school—well, school is school."

"Have you heard anything about your drawing yet?"

"Nope. In another couple of weeks. How come it takes so long to judge a bunch of drawings?"

"Depends on how many entries they had." Gran took a bite of cookie and leveled one of her let's-get-to-the-point looks at her grand-daughter. "What else?"

"Well, Robert wants to marry Mom."

"And . . ." the soft voice prompted.

"Do *you* think it's a good idea?"

"Not my place to say."

"Did you know about it?" DJ moved her gaze from Gran to Joe and back again.

"It seemed like a good possibility." Joe joined the conversation.

"Why didn't someone warn me?" DJ slumped in her chair. "I *hate* surprises." She stuck one finger in her mouth and bit off the cuticle. With a guilty look at Gran, DJ picked up another cookie. "I have been doing better—about chewing my fingernails, that is." She sighed. Gran was much too good at waiting for answers. "Gran, this thing between Robert and Mom isn't my fault. All I did was—well, nothing."

"That's not like you."

"I know. It drove Mom crazy. Me too, nearly. I wanted to yell at her." DJ studied the bloody spot on her chewed cuticle. Nobody moved. No one said anything. "You should be proud of me for not losing my temper."

"Are you?"

DJ grimaced and shook her head. "But think about this: My mother is having enough trouble taking care of me—what will she do with twin boys?" She looked up. "You could always come home."

"I *am* home." Gran smiled across the table at Joe and reached for his hand.

Joe leaned forward. "DJ, you didn't ask for my opinion, but I'm going to give it to you anyway. Now, I might be prejudiced a bit, but my son Robert is a fine man." He looked to Gran for agreement. At her nod, he continued. "You could do far worse for a father than him." He leaned forward. "In fact, your life might be a lot easier."

"With the Double Bs?" DJ's look of horror made both adults laugh.

"They are a handful, I admit, but Robert makes them mind. And I know he cares deeply for your mother."

"Don't you think it's time she had a man's love in her life?" Gran stood and rested a hand on her granddaughter's shoulder. "You need to do some praying about this."

"I knew you'd say that." DJ flopped back and crossed her arms over her chest. "And if I know you, you're going to find me a Bible verse to learn, too. One I can't even argue with. That's just not fair."

"Maybe it's time you found your own verse." Gran leaned against Joe's solid shoulder. Her eyes twinkled, and the smile on her face made DJ yearn for the mornings she'd come down to the family room to find Gran in her chair, Bible on her lap and a ready smile for a sleepy girl. There had already been so much change in DJ's life. How could she stand any more?

DJ propped her elbows on the table. "Maybe. Are we going to eat soon? I'm starved."

"Not enough cookies?" Joe raised his hands in horror. "Melanie, quick! Feed the child."

It still seemed so strange to hear Gran called by her first name. Everyone else called her Gran or Mother. DJ got to her feet. "You want me to help?"

By the time they finished off the meatloaf and baked potatoes, DJ knew she had to hurry to her homework. When she mentioned it to Joe, he rose to his feet right away.

"And here I thought we could have a relaxing evening, just the three of us. I found a couple of ads in a horse magazine about a cutting horse." Joe took his jacket out of the hall closet as he spoke. "Maybe this weekend we can go look at a couple of them."

"Where?" DJ set her dishes in the sink and wrapped an arm around her grandmother.

"Up by Redding. Melanie said she'd like to go. We could make a day of it."

"We could leave after I'm done working at the Academy. I need to spend some extra time with Patches. He's been a brat lately. Ever since Mrs. Johnson started riding him, he thinks he can get away with murder." DJ dropped a kiss on Gran's cheek. "Thanks for the yummy dinner. Maybe we could stop on the way at that gourmet olive place and get a couple of jars. Mom loves their spicy ones."

"Buying your way back into her good graces?" Gran patted DJ's cheek. "God will work this all out, you'll see, darlin'."

That night DJ didn't have to worry about arguing with her mother. The frosty message on the machine said she would be home late, well after DJ's bedtime. Her mother was finally near completing her master's degree in business administration. The last assignment, to write a thesis, already had her tied in knots, and she hadn't even decided on a topic. DJ didn't know what it would be like to have her mother *not* going to school.

She wished she'd asked to spend the night at Gran's.

Why is it that when you're bummed about one thing, it makes other things bummers, too? DJ forgot her assignment at home, and when she called to see if Gran or Joe could bring it into school for her, they were out. More than once she envied kids who could call home for something and have their mothers bring it. It used to be that way at her house, too—even though Gran had promised only one errand a quarter. That way, DJ had learned to be responsible for her own things. Until today, anyway.

She glared at her reflection in the mirror. Add a bad hair day on to that and a pop quiz in history and now, by the end of the day, she felt like crawling under a rock, or at least the covers. DJ looked longingly at her unmade bed. All she could remember of her short-on-sleep night was a nightmare where her mother had kept calling her. The voice had faded away every time DJ tried to find her.

She jerked the covers in place, changed clothes, and straightened her bathroom. No sense in adding fuel to a fire ready to burst into flame any time now.

By the time DJ had groomed four horses and cleaned Major's stall, she felt more like herself. "We'll ride in a while," she assured the rangy bay who loved to decorate her T-shirts with deep red and white hairs by rubbing his forehead on her chest. DJ gave him an extra bit of carrot and, with another hug, slipped out the gate. Work before pleasure—and Patches had definitely become more work than pleasure.

"You know, you are the most stubborn horse I've ever met." DJ kept the showy dark brown horse to a walk. She'd let him work off steam on the hot walker, then trotted forty-six times—at least it felt that way—around the arena. Still he couldn't seem to mind. Slow jog wasn't in his plan for the day, and his trot left her less than pleased since she was riding Western. Posting made for a less pounding ride. Was Patches picking up on her bad day, or was he just born ornery?

She pulled him to a stop for the umpteenth time. When he finally quit shifting from one foot to the other, she signaled him forward again. Four paces of pounding front hooves, and he was back to a stop. And until he behaved and did as he was told, she couldn't put him away.

"What'd you feed him, Jose?" She reined the snorting gelding over to the fence, where the head stable hand leaned on the aluminum bar watching her. Jose Guerrera, who blamed the gray in his black hair on the antics of the Academy kids, had worked at the Academy since long before DJ joined the student workers.

"Just the usual. I put him on the hot walker when I cleaned his stall this morning and left him there a good, long time. He needs a lot of exercise, that one. Pretty hyper."

"Tell me about it." DJ kept the reins taut but stood in her stirrups to stretch her legs. She could see her girls gathering for their class. "Did Mrs. Johnson show up for her lesson?"

Jose shook his head. "Not that I know."

Jose pretty much knew everything that went on around the Academy.

"Okay, rotten horse, once more around. And this time, do what I say."

For some reason, Patches finally minded her. With his ears pricked instead of flat against his head, he walked, jogged, and was eventually allowed to lope. DJ extended the time to several circuits around the ring since both of them could enjoy it now. By the time she'd returned the gelding to the barn, unsaddled him, brushed out the sweaty area under the saddle, and given him half a horse cookie, her girls were already in the ring.

"Hey, Angie, glad to see you back." DJ locked the gate behind her and strode to the center of the arena.

"Thanks. I'm glad to be here."

"Is the new routine helping?"

"Got me. But the hospital is the pits. I kept thinking of you guys out here riding and felt like sneaking away."

"I know the feeling." DJ greeted the others and ordered the lesson to begin. Today if all went well, they would work on backing up.

She led Angie to the middle to show her what she'd already taught the others. Suddenly, a girl let out a shriek.

DJ spun around just in time to see Krissie catapult through the air and land flat out in the sand.

Chapter • 5

Out of the corner of her eye, DJ saw a cat streak across the arena.

Krissie lay without moving while her horse tore around the ring.

DJ dropped to her knees beside the fallen girl. With one hand, she smoothed back the gritty hair that straggled from under her student's riding helmet.

Krissie groaned and rolled over, clutching her stomach. "I . . . I can't breathe." The words came in jerks, so soft DJ could barely hear them.

"Do you hurt anywhere else?" DJ did a visual check. No twisted limbs. Body had landed flat out. She knew what was wrong. "You ever had your breath knocked out of you before?"

"Is she okay?" Bridget appeared at DJ's side and knelt by the fallen rider.

"Wind's knocked out of her." DJ kept a gentle hand on Krissie's now rising and falling rib cage. "You're gonna make it, kid. Now you know what a real fall feels like."

"Yeah . . . awful." Krissie's eye's widened. "Where's my horse? Is he okay?"

"Spoken like a true horsewoman." Bridget sank back on her heels. "Jose will have caught your horse in a few minutes. You did not by any chance feed him before riding? Jose is trying to lure him with grain."

"No." Krissie sat up with a little help from DJ. "Whew, that scared me."

"I bet it did." DJ stood and pulled Krissie to her feet. "Now you know why I keep telling all of you to pay attention to your horse and what's going on around you. If you'd seen the cat before your horse did, you'd have grabbed the reins and the horn and been ready to move with him."

"Instead of smacking the ground." Sam had been the one to dismount and dash across to the office for Bridget. She stood now with her horse's reins in one hand, the other patting her mount's neck. "Boy, I thought you were a goner."

Krissie brushed sand off her stomach and chest and spit out still more. "This ground felt mighty hard for being soft sand." She took a couple of steps and spit again.

"Here's your horse, missy." Jose handed Krissie the reins. "He likes extra feed as much as anyone."

"Thanks." Krissie glared at her horse and started leading him toward the gate.

"Where are you going?" DJ asked.

"To put him away." Krissie looked back over her shoulder.

DJ shook her head. "Not yet. We have a lesson to finish. Mount up and join the others." She made a circling motion with her hand, letting the girls know they should ride to the left.

"But . . . but . . . I still have dirt in my teeth." Krissie glanced down at her dirty clothes. "I . . ." She glared at DJ. "I want to go home."

"You'll be home soon enough. Now get back on your horse, and let's finish this lesson. Your mother isn't even here yet." DJ's tone allowed no room for argument.

Krissie looked at her now quiet horse. He stood still, head hanging. She sucked in a deep breath as if gathering courage, glared at DJ one more time, muttered something, and took the reins. She slipped a booted foot into the stirrup and swung aboard.

"Congratulations, I'm proud of you."

"For what?" Krissie adjusted the reins and squeezed her heels into her horse's sides. He moved forward as though nothing had happened.

"For getting right back on. Tomorrow it would have been harder." DJ turned to the others and signaled for them to change directions. "Okay, move into a lope."

DJ sucked in a deep breath.

"Good job," Bridget's voice startled her. DJ had forgotten her teacher was still watching behind her. "You are an excellent teacher for one your age. Besides being a fine rider."

DJ felt as if she'd been given an Olympic gold medal, Bridget's compliments were so rare. "Thank you. I was scared spitless. She could have really gotten hurt."

"Accidents happen, but falls are one of the reasons we keep the sand worked frequently. If one has to learn to fall—and you must admit, no one becomes a good horsewoman without falling a few times—a soft arena is the best place to do it."

"Getting your wind knocked out of you sure is scary."

"It is. But the only student here that would be a real problem for is Angie. It might send her into an asthma attack." Bridget touched DJ's arm. "See you later."

After the lesson, DJ stopped the girls at the gate before allowing them to care for their horses. "Today, you all had a good lesson on how important it is to concentrate on what you are doing. Horses will shy at the littlest things, sometimes even a shadow. You've got to be alert. You'll get better with time. The more you ride, the more ready your body will be to move with the horse when he startles."

"Instead of falling off, like me." Krissie could already laugh about it.

"That's right. And if you take gymnastics at school, you'll learn the safest way to fall. Tucking your head and rolling is better than landing flat out. Now get moving, your moms are waiting."

DJ opened the gate. "Oh, I'll need entry forms for the show next Tuesday. I expect you all to enter three classes this time."

After checking their gear and horses, answering their mothers' questions, and praising Krissie to her worried mother, DJ felt as if she'd earned a lesson on Major. On her way to the gelding's stall, she paused. The words coming from a stall in the other aisle burned her ears. Who was Tony cussing at now? Instead of going to investigate, she quickly saddled Major and mounted outside the barn door. She sat for a moment, not believing what she had just heard. People didn't talk that way around the Academy. Hilary hadn't been making Tony out to be worse than he was, that was sure.

As DJ rode out to the jumping arena, she promised herself that she and Amy would come up with a plan—a plan to make Tony leave the Academy.

That made two plans for her to carry out: One to get rid of Tony, and one to keep Robert from marrying her mother. She and Amy certainly had plenty of work ahead of them. She forced the problems out of her mind and concentrated on her horse. It wouldn't be too cool if she got dumped like Krissie had just because she wasn't paying close enough attention.

DJ warmed up Major so he wouldn't sustain an injury. At the same time, she reviewed his show-ring skills so she could enter him in equitation classes. Like her students, she wanted to be able to enter a minimum of three classes—and at least one of those would be in jumping. DJ had yet to take a first, even in the training shows they sponsored here at Briones Riding Academy. They had one more training show here before the big show in Danville in December.

She focused on keeping Major's strides as even as a metronome's tick, no matter what gait they were in. Walk, trot, canter—all at a controlled pace that showed beautifully. "Good boy." She patted Major's neck and smoothed the lock of mane that insisted on flopping to the left. It wouldn't matter in the ring. She planned to braid his mane with ribbons for the big show.

DJ wished she had someone else to work with so she could see how Major would do with other horses in the ring. But because her horse had learned to ignore distractions during his time on the mounted police force, she knew he would be fine. He had been last time, his first time out.

"Are you ready?" Bridget passed through the narrow gate into the jumping arena.

"Sure am." DJ wanted to tell Bridget what she'd heard Tony say but tattling wasn't allowed. Anyway, DJ had never been a tattler. She set Major into a two-point trot around the ring and over the cavalletti. Every class began with a review of the basics. Sometimes DJ wondered if she'd ever move beyond them.

Bridget adjusted the bars on the two middle jumps. "Now remember—all your aids work as one. Do not rush the jumps."

DJ did exactly as Bridget told her not to.

"Fiddle." She'd been practicing just this, and as soon as Bridget walked into the ring, her hard-earned skills disappeared.

"Good job, DJ," Bridget said at the end of the hour. "I can tell how hard you are working, but remember, people do not learn to jump in a month or a year. Be patient."

DJ replayed the advice as she rode back to the barn. *Be patient.* Easily said—hard to do.

"What an afternoon!" Amy met her by their bikes.

"Did you run into Tony?"

"No, but I heard you made Krissie get right back on after she went down." Amy slung one leg over the seat of her blue ten-speed.

"Yeah, right. You know Bridget's rule: Always get back on unless you are broken or bleeding."

"Hurts bad enough getting the wind knocked out of you."

"Don't I know it."

Together they pedaled up the road to Reliez. At the stop sign, DJ planted both feet on the ground. "Ames, we have to come up with some plans."

Amy groaned. "DJ, you know what happens when we make plans."

"We need two of them. Two big-time plans."

"Do I dare ask what for now?" Amy turned to look at her friend.

DJ frowned. "Tony Andrada, for one. My mother and Robert, for two. We need to force Tony out of the Academy and stop the wedding."

"Not asking much, are you?"

"Ames, this is really important."

"Darla Jean Randall, you remember what happened when you last tried to stop a wedding."

"That was different." DJ started peddling.

"Yeah, right."

When they reached Amy's house, DJ hesitated at the curb. "I mean it, Ames. I need help."

Amy sighed. "When do you want to talk?"

"Tomorrow night. Maybe you can sleep over. Then we'll have lots of time to make plans. Remember to ask if it's okay."

When Amy finally nodded, DJ gave her a thumbs-up sign and pedaled off.

Her mother was home, or at least her car was. DJ went through her usual routine, but when she roamed through the house, it had an empty look. Faint traces of her mother's perfume lingered in the air.

DJ climbed the stairs. Passing her room, she knocked on her mother's closed door. When no answer came, she opened it a crack, then wider. Immaculate as always, the room was empty.

DJ returned to the kitchen and checked the machine. No messages. No notes on the board. *Strange.* DJ grabbed an apple out of the bowl of fruit on the counter and ambled out the French doors to turn on the sprinklers. They were going to have to hire someone to take care of the yard work if things didn't change around here. Now that Gran was gone, there were weeds in the flower beds and the grass needed mowing. Maybe DJ could get that done on Saturday before Gran and Joe took her with them to Redding.

Back in the house, DJ dished up the remains of the leftover Chinese food and put the plate in the microwave.

When the bell dinged, DJ took her dinner into the family room, curled up in Gran's chair, and picked up a mystery she'd left on the lamp table and began reading. Lost in the adventures of teen sleuth Jennie McGrady, she didn't hear the door open.

Before she could draw into a defensive position, the Double Bs grabbed her knees.

"DJ! We been missing you." The two spoke as one. Two round, identical faces grinned up at her—even their curly blond hair waved the same direction.

"So, how are you two?" DJ set her plate aside and gave them both a hug at the same time.

"Daddy brought pizza."

"You like pizza?"

"How come you's already eating?"

"Daddy, DJ didn't wait for us!"

"Didn't you read the note I left?" Lindy, in jeans, looked like a model. DJ shook her head. "I checked all over."

"I left it on your bed so you would be sure to see it."

"On my bed? I haven't even been in my room. Why didn't you put it by the phone?"

"DJ. DJ!" The twins pulled at her hands. "Show us your horse pitchurs."

"Can we color?"

DJ tried to answer them, listen to her mother, and greet Robert all at once. She felt like clapping her hands over her ears.

"That's enough, boys." The quiet authority in Robert's voice seemed to penetrate the twins' excitement.

They swiveled around. "But DJ . . ."

"No buts. Come and take your places at the table. In fact, you can help DJ set it."

DJ shot her mother a look. She got to her feet, smiled at the boys, and led them into the dining room. Since when was Robert giving the orders around here? And why should she have to eat? She thought of her plate of Chinese, only half eaten. She *was* still hungry—but that wasn't the point. This wasn't Robert's house.

She dug some paper plates out of the cupboard and handed them to the boys. "One plate each."

"What's to drink?"

"Got me. Ask your father. He seems to know better'n I do what's going on around here."

"Darla Jean Randall!" The hiss came from directly behind her.

DJ felt as if she'd been stabbed. Her mother only called DJ by her full name when she was really angry. Lindy knew how much her daughter hated the name.

"You will be polite, you hear?"

DJ nodded. She reached up for the glasses. "Did you bring soda to drink?"

"No, Robert says the boys can have milk." Lindy leaned over to check the open fridge. "Oh, we're out."

"Yeah, we're out of lots of things. No one's been to the store."

Lindy planted her hands on her slim hips. "Did you mark it on the list?"

DJ pointed out the check marks on a computerized grocery list stuck to the door with an apple magnet.

"Oh" was all Lindy said.

DJ took down the container of powdered lemonade and began mixing it. "If it's sugar he's worried about, tell him we drink diet stuff." She held up the can. "Sugar free."

DJ took the napkins and forks and headed for the dining room. Knowing her mother, she would probably forget the drinks.

"I'm sorry, DJ, I should have called." Robert took the forks and set them around the table. The Double Bs perched on either side of an empty chair.

"That's okay. I'm always ready for pizza." DJ eyed the two giant-sized pizzas, one loaded with everything, the other topped with Canadian bacon and pineapple. "And you got my favorites."

"Mine too." He dropped his voice. "Left off the anchovies."

DJ felt the beginnings of a smile tug at her mouth. DJ had never shared her mother's love for anchovies. "Thanks."

"DJ, sit here." Both boys patted the empty seat. "We saved it for you."

"What can I say?" Robert lifted his hands in a shrug. "They think you're the next best thing to Santa Claus."

Robert waited for all to clasp hands and bow heads. "Bobby, your turn to say grace."

Bobby scrunched his eyes closed. "God is great, God is good . . ."

DJ said it along with him under her breath. Since Gran left, the Randalls hadn't said much grace. Her mother had only done it to appease Gran.

Billy chimed in loudly on the "Amen."

Neither DJ nor Lindy could stay mad through dinner. Laughter erupted, calmed, and erupted again between Robert and the boys. DJ felt as though she was in the first car on a roller-coaster.

"Daddy's gonna buy us a pony."

"No, two ponies."

DJ wished she could tell which twin was talking when. "Can anyone tell these two apart?"

"Most of the time," Robert answered. "But not always. At least, not immediately. I watch for certain clues. I'll teach them to you when we have a few minutes."

There he goes again, as if there are going to be many nights like this. She carefully refrained from looking at her mother. Lindy couldn't tell the twins apart, either, and she didn't like using B&B. The pair got full giggle mileage out of her mistakes.

By the time they'd cleaned up after dinner, DJ excused herself. "I've got a bunch of homework to do." She fended off four small, clutching hands. "Later, guys. Next time we'll draw and color." There she went, acting as if this would become a common occurrence, just like Robert.

Help, Amy, we need a plan—and quick!

Chapter • 6

"But, Ames, this time'll be different. I promise."

Amy shook her head and sighed. "That's what you always say."

The two girls rested propped up with pillows on the floor of DJ's bedroom, frequently dipping into a giant bowl of popcorn. The item of the evening: plans.

"I know what we can do about Tony. If everyone ignores him and we all pretend he isn't around, pretty soon he'll quit the Academy. And then Hilary won't have a problem anymore." DJ rolled over to her belly, the better to reach the popcorn. "It's got to work." She stuffed a handful of popcorn into her mouth and licked her buttery fingers.

"But we can't tell Hilary." Amy sat up. "She'll be furious—Bridget too."

"I know, that's the hard part."

"How are we going to let all the others know without them finding out?"

"I'll take care of that."

"Now *that's* a scary solution." Amy ducked to escape the pillow DJ threw. "Let's go to bed—I'm beat."

"No way. Now we need to work on the major plan." DJ twisted her mouth from side to side. "The plan of all plans—to keep my mother from marrying Robert."

"You know how cruel that sounds?"

"You've got to be kidding. You should have seen the way Robert took over the other night. 'DJ, set the table. DJ, entertain the Double Bs. DJ . . .' You'da thought I was the nanny or something." DJ ignored the twinge of guilt she felt. Even she could recognize exaggeration.

"So . . . could be worse." Amy dug a hull out from between two teeth.

"Whose side are you on, anyway?"

Amy shrugged. "I like Robert. But more than that, I know you do, too. And it's obvious what your mother thinks. Who knows? It could be fun to have him for a dad."

DJ stared at her friend. Had Amy read her mind again? "It's a matter of principle."

"You talked to Gran?"

"Sure, I was there the other night, remember?" DJ tried to find a comfortable position. She smacked the pillows behind her into a new shape and then repeated the effort. But when she leaned back, something poked her.

"I mean about the wedding."

Ignoring Amy, DJ punched her pillows again. "You want something else to drink?"

Amy sloshed her can. "Nope." She got to her feet and picked up her sleeping bag. "How about we sleep out on the deck? Pretty soon it'll be too cold."

A few minutes later, stretched out in their sleeping bags on the lounges, they stared up at the black sky. A jet winked its way east. The sliver of moon hung above the tallest eucalyptus trees, as if tethered like a kite.

A dog barked. DJ recognized the Rottweiler from two doors down. From a distance came the muted roar of the freeway. The light from the master bathroom clicked off, leaving the house dark except for the lamp in the family room.

"We'd have to leave this house if Mom and Robert go through with it." The breeze carried DJ's soft voice.

"The house isn't the same anyway without Gran."

"Do you have to have an answer for everything?" While meant as a joke, DJ felt like slamming her fist on the redwood deck. "I don't *want* to move. I don't *want* a new father. I don't even care about the one I do have." Quiet for a minute. " 'Course I might if I knew my real dad, but I don't. And I most especially don't want . . ."

A cricket answered her, and a soft snuffle told her that Amy had fallen asleep.

I don't know what I want anymore. DJ turned over and replayed her pillow-thumping routine. It didn't help any more now than it had earlier. What was she going to do?

The next morning, both girls hurried through cleaning their required stalls and grooming at the Academy. Amy and her family were going into San Francisco, and DJ was going with Joe and Gran to Redding to look at a couple of cutting horses for Joe. With Tony nowhere in sight, they didn't have to worry about putting their plan into action.

Saturday mornings were usually spent riding and practicing. Sometimes DJ taught a class. This Saturday, the plan added an extra task. Every time DJ saw one of the other student workers, she pulled that person aside and explained the plan. "Don't talk to Tony Andrada" became the password of the day. DJ told each person to pass it on but to make sure Tony, Hilary, and Bridget didn't hear about it. By the time she'd worked both Major and Patches, the hands on her wristwatch were already close to eleven.

Amy had finished and gone home an hour earlier.

DJ rode into Gran and Joe's drive just as they were loading things into his green Ford Explorer.

"You're just in time." Gran turned from packing the fishing tackle box that held all her paints.

"I thought we were going to look for horses." DJ dropped a kiss on her grandmother's rose-scented cheek.

"You're dropping me off at the Viano Winery so I can paint, then picking me up on the way back." Gran gave DJ a quick one-arm hug. "I haven't gotten to do a landscape for a long time, and the hills covered with grape vines are so beautiful this time of year."

"You're busy 'cause you keep getting more contracts for books." DJ rubbed her stomach. "Anything to eat? I'm starved."

"So what's new?" Joe came out of the house with a cooler and picnic basket in hand. "I brought plenty so you can start munching immediately if you need to."

"Thanks. How come you already know me so well?"

"I raised three kids, that's why." Joe set the food boxes on the floor. "And teenagers, whether male or female, are always hungry. It's a universal law."

"You should know, Mr. Policeman." DJ leaned in and flipped open the cooler to extract a soda and an apple.

"Mr. Ex-policeman, you mean." He held the front door open so Gran could climb into the Explorer. "Last call for anything you've forgotten."

As soon as they were on the road, DJ dug a bologna and cheese sandwich out of the cooler and a bag of chips from the basket. "Anyone else want anything?" she asked just before sinking her teeth into the sandwich. Gran had even baked bread.

"No, thanks."

After they dropped Gran off to paint, DJ moved to the front seat and propped her knees on the dash. "I think you should buy Gran a horse, too."

"I offered, and she said no thank you but we could buy one for the other grandkids if I liked."

"That's like Gran. I know she would love riding up in Briones. She could find some neat places to paint. You know, if you want to ride Major up there, I can always take Megs. She's feeling left out since I got Major." Megs belonged to Bridget and had been retired from showing.

"We'll see. I might have a horse of my own after today."

But that was not to be. DJ took an instant dislike to the first horse they looked at. "I don't care if his bloodlines go clear back to Spain, his back legs are bad. As he gets older, they'll just get worse." The Bridget-like comments rolled off DJ's tongue.

Joe gave her a smile. "I saw that, too, but he is well trained."

"You can train one just as well."

The second horse required more deliberation. Joe rode the chestnut gelding around the ring, putting it through what paces it had. The ad had stated the horse was green broke, and it wasn't kidding.

"He'll grow some." The owner leaned on the board fence beside DJ. "His sire has taken awards up and down the coast. We'll be entering him in Nationals next year. And his dam has produced two Nationals winners already."

DJ listened to his sales pitch and watched Joe on the horse. "He'll take a lot of training." The gelding was refusing to switch leads or stand still.

"True, but he hasn't learned any bad habits, either. I broke him myself, so I know he's a willing learner."

Joe rode the horse up to the fence. "What do you think, DJ? He's fairly easy gaited. You ride him and see what you think."

DJ adjusted the stirrups on the Western saddle and swung aboard. The horse reminded her of Patches, all go and no brains. What would Bridget say? The bloodlines were good, the confirmation okay—near as she could tell—and the price wasn't too bad for a three-year-old registered Quarter Horse.

Joe thanked the man and promised they'd get back to him in a day or so. They discussed the pros and cons of the horse on the way back to pick up Gran, but still had reached no decision by the time they got home.

"Well, my darlings, I say if you have to talk about that horse this much, then he isn't the one to buy. When you see the right one, I think you'll know right away." Gran carefully lifted her easel out of the car so she wouldn't smear the still-wet oil paints.

"Sort of love at first sight, you mean?" Joe handed DJ the cooler and hamper while he retrieved the remainder of their gear.

"Y'all could call it that."

"But, Gran, there are so many things to consider."

"You'll see."

DJ and Joe swapped there-she-goes-again looks.

But DJ had learned through the years that when Gran gave her opinions, they were usually right. "Have you been praying for a horse for Joe?"

"Of course, child. Why wouldn't I?" Gran stopped with one foot on the bottom step. "There is nothing so small that God doesn't want us to talk it over with Him. Why, I even talk to Him about what to serve for dinner."

DJ followed her into the house. The delicious smells of garlic and tomato sauce greeted them.

"And what did He say today?" DJ sniffed appreciatively.

"Lasagna. The salad's all tossed, and the garlic bread's ready for the oven." Gran glanced at her watch. "Lindy and Robert will be here with the boys any minute now. Thank goodness for ovens with timers."

DJ groaned. "Why didn't anyone tell me they were coming?"

"Why, what difference does it make?" Gran looked at her as if she'd grown horns or something.

"I didn't bring clean clothes. You know how she hates it when I smell like horse."

"Do you want me to take you home to change?" Joe dropped a kiss on the back of Gran's neck as he walked by.

"You needn't worry—I washed the jeans and shirt you left here last time you spent the night." Gran gave DJ a gentle shove toward the bedroom. "You can shower, too, if it would make you feel better."

"There's the car. I'll keep the Double Bs busy until you're ready." Joe winked at DJ. "They think grandpas are *almost* as good as a big sister." He ducked away from her fake punch.

"I'll just ignore them all and hide out in here," DJ muttered to the pounding water. But she knew that wouldn't work. Her stomach was growling in anticipation of the lasagna. Besides, she knew her mother would threaten general destruction if she tried such a thing. Anything too obnoxious, and she might be grounded again. Now *that* was a fate worse than death. Last time—actually the one and only time it had ever happened to her—had nearly done her in.

DJ turned off the shower and dressed quickly. The laughter from the other room beckoned almost as persuasively as the lasagna and garlic bread.

The Double Bs' giggles were more catching than poison oak.

DJ forced her lips to stay in a straight line at their first elephant joke. Baby stuff.

She couldn't remember the answer to the second. It had been a long time since she'd heard an elephant joke.

But she knew the answer to the third. When Robert paused for someone to answer, she couldn't resist. "Footprints in the Jell-O."

"Huh?" The B on her right looked up at her.

"You can tell an elephant's been in the refrigerator by the footprints in the Jell-O." Left B started to giggle, then right B got the joke and the giggles turned to hoots. Very contagious.

DJ glanced up to see Robert smiling at her. Gran and Joe were chuckling with the boys. DJ sneaked a peek at her mother. Lindy had *never* appreciated stupid jokes. But growing up, DJ hadn't much minded because Gran had always been there to laugh with her.

When the giggles subsided somewhat, Robert asked, "How can you tell if there's an elephant in a cherry tree?"

"How?"

DJ had to bite her tongue. The silly answers were coming back to her.

Oh, fiddle. DJ leaned to her right and whispered in that B's ear. "Because elephants always wear red tennies."

" 'Cause elephants gots red pennies."

DJ rolled her eyes. She tried again. "Tennies, B, *tennies.*"

" 'Cause the tree gots tennies."

The other B laughed so hard he fell off his chair.

"You okay?" DJ leaned down and helped him up.

"Tennies in the tree! Elephants wear red tennies in the cherry tree so we can see 'em." He looked up at her to make sure he had gotten it right.

In shifting from one twin to the other, DJ caught a glimpse of her mother's face. Lindy wore a half smile, the polite kind, the kind that DJ knew meant her mother was only half there. The rest of her was probably selling more guns to the police departments or planning her thesis.

What she wasn't doing was having fun.

"Can I be excused?" DJ pushed her chair back from the table. "Come on, guys. I'll race you to the road and back."

DJ hoped the breeze in her hair and on her face would blow away the anger she felt toward her mother right now. Why couldn't she laugh at a little joke? Just to be part of the group. It wasn't as if her mother didn't know how. *Maybe she didn't get the joke. Or maybe she's a snob.* The thoughts raced through DJ's mind as her feet pounded the gravel.

Careful to keep even with the running boys, she reached down for their hands, and together the three sprinted the last few yards.

"I won."

"No, me!"

"Hey, guys, we all won." That was the way it was supposed to be, wasn't it? Everyone winning?

DJ tickled one twin and then the other. "Race you back to the house." They darted off and she followed, this time letting them win by a jump or two.

Before falling asleep that night, DJ looked up at the poster of the Olympic rider and horse clearing the jump and prayed, "God, I really need a way to stop my mom and Robert from getting married. A plan with a capital *P*." She tacked another line on to her prayer to cover all the bases. "And, God, please help my mother to laugh. She wouldn't even smile at the elephant jokes."

Did God really have a plan in all this?

Chapter • 7

Two weeks passed and still DJ had no plan.

Worse yet, Tony Andrada continued making life at the Academy miserable for all of them. DJ felt as though something in her life wasn't working—like everything. On top of all that, she'd been notified that she had received only an honorable mention in the art contest.

"What's so great about an honorable mention?" she sighed to Amy.

"Most people would be pumped about an honorable mention." Amy shook her head. "But not *my* friend. *My* friend likes only blue ribbons."

"No, I'd take a purple rosette, too." DJ licked the other side of her mocha almond fudge ice-cream cone. The two girls had bicycled down to the local shopping center for "some real food," as DJ called it. Her mother was on a low-fat kick again and had only rabbit food in the house. Or at least, that's what DJ called all the vegetables.

"Mom wants to lose weight, so I get to starve." DJ took a bite of her sugar cone and closed her eyes in bliss. "Why don't we go to the exhibit and see what kind of illustration took grand prize? I thought my horse was pretty good, and even Gran said I'd done well. You know what a perfectionist she is about artwork."

"Okay, but how are we going to get there?"

"Bus. I could ask Gran, though. Maybe she'd like to see it, too—of course, she would, my picture's hanging there," DJ thought aloud.

"What about your mom?"

"Ha! You know she's been to only one—no, make that two—of my horse shows since I began showing. What kind of a mother is she, anyway?"

"A busy one." Amy finished her cone and tossed the wrapper into the trash.

"Your father goes to every show, and your mom makes most of them." DJ leveled a look at her friend that dared her to get out of this one.

"I know. But my mom says it's easier to make it to things like that when you're a stay-at-home mother."

"Yeah, *you* never have to come home to an empty house."

"Sometimes I'd like to." Amy shoved up the kickstand on her bike.

"Feel free to visit mine any day."

"Mom won't let me—there's no adult there." Amy tipped her head and licked her lips.

DJ knew the gesture meant Amy was trying to keep from laughing.

"See what I mean?"

"You know what it's like at our house. You have to shout to make yourself heard. With four kids, I have to lock the bathroom door for some privacy—then John always has to go."

DJ often dreamed of becoming a member of the Yamamoto clan. Having brothers and sisters around had always sounded neat.

Until now. Now brothers and sisters meant the Double Bs.

"You're lucky to have an older brother."

"You want him, you can have him." Amy slung her leg over the bicycle. "You ready? I have to clean my room. With the show next weekend, I promised I'd do it today."

DJ glanced up at the fading light. "You better hurry, the day's about gone."

"I know. You could come help me."

DJ thought of the quiet house that awaited her. Lindy was off doing research to help her decide on a thesis topic. The note she'd left said she'd be home by dinner. She didn't mention who was cooking it or eating it.

"Sorry, but I better not. I think I'm supposed to be at home or Gran's."

"You think?" The two pedaled side by side up the residential street.

"Well, you know . . . Mom and I haven't been communicating much lately, at least not speaking. She writes me notes or leaves messages on the machine. Easier that way."

"Is she coming to the horse show?"

"Dream on. It's no big deal. When she is there, my butterflies invite all their friends in and have a party—at my stomach's expense." DJ kept pedaling and stretched her arms above her head. "Gran and Joe will be there, and they're the ones who count."

"You going to church with them in the morning?"

"Yep."

"You could ride with us if you want."

DJ sometimes wished her mother would come along, too, but Lindy used Sunday mornings to study. She said Gran could take care of the praying and churchgoing for their family. Lindy didn't want to be bothered with it.

The message light blinked on the machine. "DJ, I'm at Robert's. I'll be home late. Robert would like us all to go to church together tomorrow, so tell Gran you'll be going with us."

"With us where? I don't want to go to some strange church in the city. I like our church." DJ slammed the replay button. The message sounded no better the second time.

I think I'll go sleep with Major, that way I won't have to go with anyone. What about my Sunday school class? Doesn't my mother ever think of anyone but herself? Since when does she go to church? Just because Robert asked her? DJ fussed and fumed until she climbed into bed.

"Great, she didn't even mention what time we're leaving." DJ debated going downstairs and leaving a message on the machine herself, but instead she set her alarm for an early wake-up. She had to feed Major no matter what.

———

It wasn't hard to pull off the silent act the next morning. By the time she returned from the Academy, Lindy was in a fit. DJ had barely ten minutes to get ready.

"And don't you dare make us late," Lindy yelled above the sound of the shower.

DJ soaped and rinsed as quickly as if she were a four-handed alien. There wasn't time to wash her hair; she'd have to braid it in the car. Half dry, she dashed into her bedroom and into her underwear. Putting on a bra with a wet back wasn't easy, but the real problem hit when she opened her closet: no dress pants. She'd forgotten to put her laundry in the dryer again.

"Mom, I'm gonna have to wear jeans," she called, hunching her shoulders against the tirade she knew was coming, at the same time buttoning a teal blouse and adding a vest.

"Why can't you at least dress up for church?" Lindy stopped in the doorway. "Where are all your good pants?"

"In the washing machine."

"I can tell your chores are getting to be too much for you. You'll just have to—"

The doorbell rang.

"We'll discuss this later." In her ivory silk suit and matching hat and shoes, Lindy looked as if she'd just stepped out of a Macy's display window.

DJ grumbled under her breath, grabbed her suede shoes, and pounded down the hall. She snagged a brush and a hair band from the bathroom before leaping down the stairs. So she didn't have dress pants on—she looked pretty good as far as she could tell. Jeans were always in style.

But they certainly weren't her mother's idea of a fashion statement.

The day went downhill from there. While the boys squirmed only a little during the opening prayer, they both let out soft whoops of joy when it came time for the children's sermon and then children's church.

Although the San Francisco church had beautiful stained-glass windows and a neat folk choir, DJ missed her Sunday school class.

At the restaurant where they went for brunch, Bobby—or was it Billy?—spilled his orange juice. While Lindy said it didn't matter, the stain showed up bright orange on her silk skirt. DJ kept herself from laughing only through sheer strength of will.

As Robert scolded the culprit, DJ dropped her fork. Bending to retrieve it, she bumped her plate—which bumped her water goblet. The goblet tipped, and water spread across the tablecloth. For the second time that morning, Robert called the waiter for assistance.

"I'm sorry." She didn't dare look at her mother. The vibes coming across the table told her enough.

"Accidents will happen." Robert tried to smooth things over.

Bobby sniffed on the chair beside DJ. Billy acted as though he'd been scolded, too.

As DJ had thought, silence was the best defense, or offense, as the case may be—in this case, anyway.

———————

Telling Amy about it the next day, DJ couldn't help but laugh. "My mother does *not* like scenes in restaurants or church or anywhere."

"Did you drop your fork on purpose?"

"Gimme a break. Even I wouldn't dare do something like that."

"Did you ask her about the jumping clinic at Wild Horse Valley?"

"Fiddle. How could I forget something like that?" DJ shook her head. "I'm losing it, I tell you." They hopped off their bikes as they arrived at the Academy. "I'll ask tonight. We're having dinner at Gran's."

"Mrs. Johnson wants you to show Patches next weekend," Bridget informed DJ when she and Amy stopped in her office to say hello. "I said it was up to you."

"You think he's ready?" DJ picked at her fingernail.

"It would be good experience for both of you."

"Sure then. Why not?"

"Joe found his cutting horse yet?" Bridget asked.

DJ shook her head.

"I got a call from a friend who has been keeping an eye out for one. I missed Joe when he was here today taking care of Major. I will give him a call."

DJ flashed Amy a grin. "He'll be thrilled. Where is it?"

"Sacramento." Bridget shooed them out the door. "You two have work to do."

Tony was already in the ring practicing when they walked past. The two girls stopped for a moment to watch. The boy and horse moved as if they were welded together.

DJ felt a surge of envy. Tony and his horse were already at level two in dressage, and she had barely begun. The horse floated around the ring, each leg extended and then placed with precision. Tony didn't seem to move a muscle.

"It's just not fair," DJ muttered, turning to the barns. "Tony is such an excellent rider, and yet he's meaner than a—"

"Rabid skunk?"

"Yeah, and twice as smelly." DJ picked up her grooming bucket and headed for Patches' stall. She had plenty of work to do if they were going to show.

"Major, you must be the most willing horse in the world," DJ said later after putting the big bay through his paces. She leaned forward and rested her cheek on his mane, wrapping both arms around his neck. "You are so easy to love."

"Now that's as nice a picture as I have yet to see. Wish I had a camera so Melanie could paint you."

"Hi, Joe." DJ straightened to see her grandfather leaning against the aluminum fencing of the jumping arena. "You hear the news?"

"Sure enough. Think we could go over there and look at him this evening?"

In her mind, DJ flashed to her backpack at home. All she really had to do tonight was read a chapter for history, and she could do that in the car. "Sure." Then her excitement drooped. "I should ask Mom first. I thought we were having dinner at your house."

"That was the plan. Lindy called and asked if we could put dinner off till tomorrow. Something came up at work she had to deal with right away."

On one hand DJ thought, *Figures, her work always comes before the rest of us,* and on the other, she was thrilled to have the evening free. "Why don't you ask her while I finish my lesson. Is Gran coming, too?"

"Yep. We'll stop for dinner after we see the horse." He held up one hand. "I know, I know—bring food, you'll be starved."

DJ grinned and blew him a kiss. "See ya."

Her lesson with Bridget was a challenge. Bridget claimed that if you learned the finer points of jumping right the first time, it saved hours of relearning. But sometimes the first time meant weeks of drilling and redrilling.

And DJ loved every minute of it. Neither she nor Major resented the repetition. Jumping was jumping. Each moment they spent airborne, DJ felt like yelling for pure joy. One time around, she became aware of Joe watching from the sidelines, but she kept her focus on her hands, her feet, her seat, her posture, and Major. After each jump, she looked forward to the next—the height, the length, and the timing. At last, some things were becoming enough of a habit that she could concentrate on others.

"Very good." Bridget met her at the gate when the lesson was over. "You can be proud of your granddaughter, Joe. And your horse."

"Oh, I am. No doubt about it." Joe stroked Major's sweaty neck. "God gave me a gift here"—he laid a hand on DJ's knee—"that I'll never be able to thank Him for enough. That was some ride, kid."

"Thanks, GJ." DJ wanted to hug her horse, her grandfather, and even the fence post. For the first time in a while, Bridget hadn't had to call her on concentration.

"By the way, DJ." Bridget looked up at the rider. "Is there something you would like to tell me about Tony Andrada?"

DJ swallowed. She cleared her throat. "Ah . . . no, not really." What was Bridget referring to? Had someone blabbed about the silent treatment? "Why?"

"Oh, a little bird told me about something going on in the barns, and I have a feeling the hand of DJ Randall is all over it."

DJ swallowed again. She couldn't lie. *Please, Bridget, don't ask me any more. Especially not now with Joe here.*

"I will leave it for now, but make sure no one gets hurt."

DJ nodded.

"What was that all about?" Joe asked after Bridget left for her office.

"Tell you later." DJ nudged Major forward. "If we're going to Sacramento, we better get moving."

Joe brought up the subject of Tony once they were on the road to Sacramento. DJ had already put away a soda, six chocolate chip cookies, and an apple.

She tossed the core into the garbage and wrinkled her nose, hoping that would help her think better. "Well, you've heard me say what a creep Tony Andrada is."

"I gathered that he wasn't your favorite student worker."

"With good reason. He called Hilary a . . . ni—"

"DJ." Gran's gentle reminder made DJ stop midword.

"Well, that's not the worst thing he's called her, either. Is everyone from the South like him?"

"Darlin', I'm from the South."

"I know, that's why I'm asking." DJ thought about what she'd said. "But I don't mean you, of course. Just boys. Come on, Gran, you know what I mean."

"I do. And to answer your question, there are some people in the South—and other places, mind you—who think people with dark skin are of less value. It's that old slaveholder mentality. Sometimes I wonder if discrimination will ever end." She shook her head and turned to look at DJ. "But, darlin', I know you don't feel that way, and if more young people can grow up colorblind like you, our world will eventually become a better place."

"In the meantime, what have you cooked up?" Leave it to Joe to bring the subject back to DJ.

"Well, Amy and I have a plan to deal with Tony."

Gran groaned. "Heaven help us."

"Gr-a-n!"

"You have to admit some of your *plans* haven't worked out quite like you hoped." Gran's smile let DJ know she was teasing.

"I know, but this time . . . this time it *has* to work or Hilary will move her horse to another stable. That'll mess up her whole life."

"And your plan?"

"To ignore Tony. No one's supposed to talk to Tony. We pretend he isn't even there."

"And Hilary?"

"She doesn't know anything about it." DJ took a bite of the cuticle on her right pinkie as she waited out the silence in the front seat.

"So, how is it working?"

"Don't know. I haven't talked to Hilary lately, and the only time I see Tony is in the ring. Since he goes to a private school, his hours are different from mine." DJ clenched her hands in her lap. Why did she always want to chew her fingernails when she was uptight? She leaned her arms on the back of the front seat. "And you know what? *Amy* thinks he's cute!"

"So?"

"So how can anyone be cute when he talks like Tony?"

Gran chuckled. "That's one of the many things I love about you, darlin'. You look to the inside of a person, not just the outside."

"You know, your plan does have a sound basis." Joe caught DJ's eye in the rearview mirror.

"Really?"

"Sure. Ignoring bad behavior is a good way to make someone change. But to make the program really effective, you have to go one step further."

DJ unbuckled her seat belt so she could lean on the front seat without cutting off her circulation. "I hear you."

"You have to compliment him for doing the right thing."

"Right. The dinosaurs will return before I catch Tony doing something good."

Joe smiled at her. "I'm sure if you try, you'll find a way. And you better explain this addition to your plan to the others."

DJ thought about phrases like *a snowball's chance in that hot place reserved for people like Tony* and *when cows have wings,* but she kept them to herself. She did need to talk to the rest of the student workers, that was for sure.

She was still thinking about what Joe and Gran had said when they turned into an entrance arch with *Denison's Quarter Horses* painted in white across the top. Board-fenced fields lined the drive, and a barking border collie met them at the gate to the low, rambling house off the circular drive. A man donned his felt Western hat as he came down the steps toward them.

"You the fellow who wants to see my young cutting horse?" He extended a hand. "I'm Hank Denison."

After the introductions, he showed them where to park, and they followed him down to a shiny white barn. Horses blinked and nickered as he flicked on the light. "Rambling Ranger is right over here. I kept him in tonight when you said you were coming." He took a lead shank off a hook on the wall and led the way to the third stall on the left. A bright sorrel head with a perfect diamond between the eyes and another smaller one between flaring nostrils bobbed in greeting. The horse wuffled, his nostrils quivering as Denison snapped the lead shank onto the blue nylon halter.

"He's sixteen hands and three years old, as I told you on the phone, so he may grow a bit more. He'll fill out, anyway." As he spoke, Hank led the horse out of the stall. Both front feet had white socks nearly to the knees.

DJ fell in love. She looked up at Joe. His eyes were shining, too.

The horse moved with the natural grace of good confirmation and a style that came from excellent bloodlines. When Denison trotted, the gelding followed, his hooves clopping a steady rhythm on the hard-packed dirt.

"Let's go over to the covered arena, and I'll saddle him up for you. Now, remember he's only begun his training. I haven't worked him with cattle yet."

Joe and DJ walked around the horse, studying him from all angles as Denison saddled him. DJ couldn't find a thing wrong. How much was the man asking? She looked up at Joe. The silly grin on his face said it all.

"I'll take him around a few times so you can watch him. Then you can try him out." Denison mounted as he spoke.

DJ and Joe watched without a word, sharing a glance of pure excitement. When the man returned to the rail and dismounted, he offered the reins to DJ.

"You better ride him first, GJ," DJ whispered.

Joe nodded. He stroked the horse's nose, then mounted when Denison handed him the reins.

DJ watched as her grandfather moved the horse through his gaits, reined him from side to side, and tried to get him to back up. Only then did Rambling Ranger balk for the first time.

"He don't like backing too much yet, but he learns quick." Denison rubbed the cleft in his chin with one finger.

DJ was doing her best to control her excitement. After all, when you bought something, you were supposed to be cool about it, not scream, "Yes! Yes! Yes!" like she wanted to.

"You want to ride, kid?" Joe stopped the horse in front of her.

"Sure." DJ changed places with her grandfather. She rode the horse around the ring, doing all the same things Joe had. "You're a dream come true, you know that?"

The horse twitched his ears, but he still didn't want to back up. DJ made him stand and then pulled firmly on the reins. Ranger shook his head but finally he backed—one step, then two. He sighed and kept on backing up until DJ let off the pressure. She patted his neck. "Good boy."

Rambling Ranger was perfect, but could Joe afford a horse like this?

Chapter · 8

"You bought him? Just like that?"

"He really did." Gran shook her head. "I knew I married a man who could make split-second decisions, and now I've seen him in action." Gran patted Joe's arm. "I'm glad for you, darlin.'"

"Why don't we look for a horse for you while we're here?" Joe covered her hand with his. "You have no idea what you're missing when you can't ride up in Briones with us."

DJ watched several expressions flit across her grandmother's face before a slight dip of her chin indicated she disagreed.

"But, Gran, you've never ridden around here. Have you ever ridden at all?" DJ asked.

"When I was younger." Gran reached up to stroke the gelding's nose. "I'm just glad you two can have your dreams of showing. I'll come along to cheer you on."

DJ and Joe swapped looks. They were going to have to work on this. If they were to become a horse family, Gran would have to join in.

"So, when can you deliver him?" Joe turned to Denison and took out his checkbook. "I need to have a barn built, but in the meantime I'll stable him at the Briones Riding Academy where my granddaughter works and rides. The owner, Bridget Sommersby, gave me your name."

"Day after tomorrow soon enough?" Denison led Rambling Ranger back to his stall and removed the tack.

"That'll be just fine."

DJ felt as though she'd been struck by lightning. Any time she'd wanted anything, there'd always been a big discussion, a plan to earn or save the money, and then usually a big "no" from her mother. Horses and horse things weren't high on Lindy's list of priorities, unlike school and fashionable clothing and—DJ cut off that line of thought as she rubbed down the horse's shoulder. Ranger sure was a beauty. He and Joe looked wonderful together.

She was still bubbling when she walked in the door at home and found Lindy and Robert looking through the photo albums DJ and Gran had spent so many hours putting together.

"Mom, you won't believe it. GJ bought his horse!" She grinned at Robert, who sat beside her mother. "You got some dad there. Wait till you see him—the horse I mean. His name is Rambling Ranger, but we're gonna call him Ranger." DJ didn't take time to breathe.

"Sounds like my dad all right." Robert stretched his hands above his head. "I better get going. Full day ahead."

"Hey, Mom, I forgot to ask. There's a jumping clinic coming up at Wild Horse Ranch in Napa, and Bridget thinks it would be good for me and Major to go. What do you think, can I?"

"Can you afford it?" Lindy let Robert pull her up from the sofa. She smiled up at him with one of those gooey looks DJ was coming to expect from the two of them.

"Well, I'm trying to save for a Crosby—that's a good make of jumping saddle. I was kind of hoping maybe you could swing this." DJ clamped her bottom lip between her teeth.

"You know the rules." Lindy adjusted her slacks. "You can go only if you can afford the time and the money."

"How much is it?" Robert looked from mother to daughter.

When DJ told him the amount, he reached for his wallet. "Why don't you let me get this one?"

"No." One word from Lindy stopped him in the act.

He turned to her, surprise written across his handsome face. "But why?"

DJ bit her tongue to keep from telling him how she felt. *Because my mother always has money for her things, but mine don't count. Get it?*

"Because *I* can't afford it, and I'm raising my daughter to be a responsible person who earns her own way."

Robert started to say something and stopped.

"DJ understands."

Yeah, right! Sure I understand. DJ felt like yelling. She had no time now to earn extra money. Other kids baby-sat. She and Amy had given pony parties for kids' birthdays during the summer, but now her time was all taken up with school, the Academy, and home chores. Her mother was the one who didn't understand.

Or maybe she doesn't care. The thought shocked DJ into continued silence.

"Well, why don't you let this be my gift to DJ?"

DJ felt a stirring of hope.

"That's very nice of you, but no thank you. DJ, don't you have homework to finish?"

"No, I'm done." DJ knew that had been the signal for her to leave the room, but instead she dug in her heels. She still might have a chance if she played it right.

DJ sneaked a peek at Robert. His smile had disappeared along with his wallet. Questions pounded in her head. What was wrong with Robert's giving her a present? Lindy had already accepted several gifts for herself: a bracelet, a designer scarf, and a program for her computer. So why was it okay for her mother to get presents, but not her? A hangnail on DJ's right thumb itched to be chewed off. She dug at it with her finger.

"Say good-night, DJ."

DJ did as she was told, barely holding back from stomping up the stairs.

This was one of those nights when she wished with all her might that Gran was still living in the same house. Gran would be able to explain her mother's actions to her—they made no sense at all to DJ. She knew she could call Gran and talk about it, but somehow the phone wasn't the same as sitting at Gran's feet. She *needed* Gran's gentle hands on her hair and the smell of roses and Gran saying, "Well now, darlin', I think we should pray about this and see what God has to say about it."

DJ tried. "Heavenly Father, I don't understand my mother at all. Sometimes I don't even like her." She stopped. She shouldn't say such things even though she thought them a lot. But her Sunday school teacher had said God knew people's thoughts even before they spoke them.

DJ shuddered. Some of her thoughts sure weren't the kind she wanted God listening in on.

What was the Bible verse Gran had given her recently? She wrinkled her forehead, hoping that would make her remember. Something about God answering our prayers. She'd have to ask Gran because DJ sure needed some answers right now. She moved on to all the "blesses," including Robert and the Double Bs. "And, God, thank you for finding Grandpa Joe such a neat horse. Amen."

How on earth was she going to earn the money for the clinic?

Both DJ and Amy were out of breath when they spun into the Academy parking area the next afternoon. They spied Joe's Explorer immediately.

"Is he here yet?" DJ pelted into Bridget's office. "Where's his stall?"

"Should I ask who 'he' is?" Bridget looked up from her charting with a smile. She raised a hand to cut off DJ's questions. "Outside stall, next to Major. I figured since Joe feeds both of them in the morning, we should make it as easy as possible."

"What do you think of him? Didn't we do great?"

"He is everything Denison said he was. Now Joe has to decide if he will train Ranger himself or hire a trainer." Bridget waved the girls toward the door. "Go on before you wear a hole in the floor."

The girls dashed across the lot and jogged down the sandy barn aisle. Horses nickered on either side, and one slammed a hoof against the wall with a squeal.

When they found them, Joe had one of Ranger's hooves propped on his knees to pick out any compacted manure and dirt. The crosstied sorrel stood quietly, showing that he'd been trained in being handled.

"He's beautiful, Joe." Amy and DJ stopped at the stall opening.

Joe stood up and, stroking the gelding as he walked, joined the two girls.

"I'm pretty pleased myself." He rubbed up behind Ranger's ears and down his neck. "He and I are going to get along just fine, aren't we, boy?" Ranger reached his nose out to sniff the girls, who stood still for his inspection. Ears forward, he sniffed at DJ's extended hand. She turned it over to palm a horse cookie for him.

"Now you've made a friend." Joe continued to stroke the horse as he talked. "Denison said Ranger has a weakness for sugar lumps, but cookies and carrots are definitely better, right, fella?" Ranger nosed DJ for another treat.

"Have you ridden him yet?" Amy asked.

"Nope, he arrived not more than an hour ago. I figured I'd let him get accustomed to the stable first and ride tomorrow morning when the arenas aren't taken up by you kids." He picked up a brush and stroked down the already gleaming shoulder.

Next to them, Major nickered and tossed his head.

"He's jealous." Joe nodded to his former horse. "I kept telling him you'd be by pretty soon, but he didn't believe me."

DJ switched her attentions to the bay. Major nosed the pocket where she always kept his treat. She dug out a cookie and let him munch. "See, that wasn't your treat I gave away. That young sprout may be getting all the attention right now, but that's because he's new."

"And pretty." Amy moved to Major's side and stroked his dark neck.

Major whiskered DJ's cheek and made her giggle.

"You just wait a bit, and I'll be back to get you." DJ gave her horse one last ear rub and stepped back. "Got work to do. Behave now." The horse tossed his head and nodded as if he understood everything she said. "See ya, GJ."

"You going to braid his mane and tail for the show?" Amy asked.

"No, not for the training show. But for the one in December I will. Just think, that will be our first big show. Mine and Major's, I mean."

"You think Joe will enter that one?"

"He could, in halter class at least. Even halter showing would give Ranger a feel for the crowds and activity."

They stopped in the door of the barn when they heard an angry voice coming from the south side stalls.

"I don't have to listen to you, you stupid jigaboo! My dad is going to talk to Bridget and get me assigned to someone with some real horse sense. Everyone knows niggers don't have no sense a'tall."

"Listen here, Tony, I have my assignments, and I do them. You have been assigned to me, and that places me in charge. Now get back there and redo that stall. We don't allow people to pitch fresh shavings on top of dirty ones."

"If you're so all-fired worried about doing things right, *you* do it."

DJ and Amy peeked around the corner just in time to see Tony shove the handle of the manure fork at Hilary. She wasn't prepared, and it knocked her on the shoulder before she could stop it.

"I have better things to do." Tony made a rude gesture and strode down the aisle to where his horse stood looking over the gate of its stall.

DJ debated. Should they go to Hilary, or was it better to let her friend handle this alone? In the end, she signaled Amy, and they headed back to their side of the barn.

"Well, that sure shows our plan isn't working." DJ slammed her hand against the wall. "How can we help Hilary?"

"Short of dumping a ton of hay on that . . . that creep. Why'd he ever choose to come here anyway?"

"Because Bridget is such a good teacher, that's why." DJ rubbed the palm of her hand to remove the sting of slapping it on the wood. "Why didn't Hilary shove the handle right back at him? I would have. I'd have picked it up and bashed him over the head with it. Nobody but nobody's ever gonna get away with calling *me* names like that. Should we tell Bridget?"

Amy shook her head. "I don't know."

"You know what? I talked about this with Gran and Joe, and Joe said just ignoring Tony wasn't enough. He said we need to *compliment* him when he does something right. Can you beat that?"

"Yeah, as if he's going to do something good. Get real." Amy picked up a grooming bucket. "I've got to get going, or I won't have time to work Josh. DJ, something's got to get better around here, or Hilary will leave—and I wouldn't blame her a bit."

By Friday, DJ's butterflies were in full flight. All she could think of was the show coming up the next day. Even though it was only a schooling show, this would be only the second time she showed Major, and she was going to enter Patches, too. All that plus coaching her three students and helping wherever Bridget needed her.

"Would you like to join us in class, DJ?" Her history teacher eyed her curiously over her glasses.

DJ could feel the heat begin at her collarbone and race up her face. "I . . . I'm sorry." If only she could slither down under her desk and out the door.

"Please join us on page ninety-three and read from the second paragraph."

"Yes, ma'am." DJ found the place and rose to her feet. She heard someone snicker behind her. Now even her ears burst into flame. Reading aloud forced her to keep her mind on the lesson.

"Thank you," the teacher said when DJ reached the end of the section. "Next?"

DJ sank into her desk. At least she hadn't been asked a question on top of the reading. How embarrassing! If Bridget caught her daydreaming like that, she'd have had to do extra stalls.

The barns were in a flurry that afternoon with everyone bathing the show horses, then grooming them till they could nearly see their faces in the shiny hides. With two horses to prepare, DJ felt as if her arms would drop off by the time she finished. The white blaze on Patches' face shone like new-fallen snow when the sun struck it.

"You know, if you could behave as well as you clean up, you'd have it made." She slapped his rump to keep him from leaning on her while she picked his hooves. "You know all kinds of tricks to make my life miserable, don't you?"

The gelding snorted and twitched his tail, catching some hairs in DJ's mouth. She spit them out and brushed others off her head. "Sometimes I wonder about you, and other times I *know* you're rotten clear through."

"I really should be helping you so I learn how to do all this," Mrs. Johnson said from her position at the gate.

DJ flinched. Here she'd been saying bad things about the horse, and the owner was standing right there. *Stupid horse, why didn't he warn me?* She finished with the hooves and came around to drop the pick into the bucket. "You could keep brushing him and comb out his mane and tail."

"Sure." The woman ducked under the gate, picked up both brushes, and set to work. "We bought a leather halter and lead shank for tomorrow. He looks real good in it. Maybe next time I can show him—in halter at least."

"Sure thing." DJ started to leave. "You'll be here in the morning for loading?"

"Wouldn't miss it." Mrs. Johnson stopped brushing. "DJ, I keep meaning to ask. How is Andrew coming with Bandit? Is he getting over the fear? We've been talking about it a little, but he doesn't say much."

"He's doing better. I guess sometimes it's hard to talk about."

"I would love to see him entered in a show, and I just know he would enjoy riding up in the hills."

"Yes, ma'am." DJ had her doubts about Andrew ever wanting to show, but she wouldn't voice them now. "See you in the morning."

DJ headed for Major's stall. Joe had washed the big gelding earlier in the day, so he only needed grooming. She glanced up to see clouds of red reflecting the setting sun. How could the time pass so quickly?

"You go check on your students—I've got everything under control here." Joe paused in his brushing of the big bay as DJ walked up. Major leaned against his ties, half asleep.

"Thanks." DJ turned and headed back to the barns. The girls should be in soaping their saddles by now. The three had all gotten soaked on the wash racks but helped each other so all the horses were clean and blanketed. They reminded DJ of her and Amy back when they were younger, all excitement and giggles.

"My arm's gonna fall off." Krissie groaned when she saw DJ. "This saddle is so big."

"Not really. It just seems that way when it's soaped up." DJ checked the carved designs on the skirts. "You better get the soap cleaned out of here. It'll show up white in the daylight."

Krissie groaned again. "I'd rather wash my horse any day."

Angie looked up from her bridle. "DJ, do you feel sick the night before a show?"

DJ nodded. "I got yelled at in school today because I was thinking about the show instead of history."

The three girls giggled. "Did you get detention?"

"No way. I wasn't *that* bad." DJ inspected the work of all three. "Looks pretty good. You need to be here by 6:30 A.M. to load your horses." More groans. "Sorry, but that's part of showmanship. And make sure all your clothes are ready tonight, too." It felt like a century since DJ had started showing, but it had only been three years. "Shine your boots, and—"

"Get plenty of sleep!" The three shouted in unison.

DJ tapped Krissie on the head. "Smart mouths. Any questions?" When they shook their heads, she glanced over at the cars where their mothers waited. "Good, then you better hustle. See you in the morning."

DJ headed back toward Major's stall. Tony Andrada appeared in the side aisle.

"Hi, DJ."

DJ looked the other way and kept walking.

Chapter • 9

"Stuck-up!"

The name-calling hurt, but DJ kept right on going. No way would she say anything to Tony—not after the way he had treated Hilary. No matter what Joe said. Besides, DJ sure hadn't seen him doing anything right. If only she could shut off the part of her that made her feel lousy when she was being less than honest. Tony hadn't been mean to her. He only had this thing against Hilary because she was black. Had he been mean to Maria, a girl with a Hispanic heritage? And what about Amy? She was a Japanese American.

She shut off the thoughts, said good-night to Major, and after snagging Amy from the tack room, headed home. Would her mother be home or out with Robert? She sure was spending a lot of time with him.

"You want to ride over to the show with us in the morning?" Amy asked when they reached her house. A discussion about Tony had kept them occupied all the way home. As usual, there were no solutions, only more problems.

"If your dad doesn't mind."

"That's a silly thing to say. Why would he mind?"

DJ shrugged. "Okay, see ya."

No car in the drive, no lights on—obviously no one was home. Was that good or bad? DJ put her bike away, checked for messages—none—then wandered up to her room. Maybe her mother had left a note on the bed again. No such luck. The phone rang just as she was getting sandwich fixings out of the refrigerator.

After a greeting, Gran continued. "Lindy phoned to say that Robert called her and asked if the two of you would take care of the twins for the weekend. Robert was called out of town unexpectedly, and the boys' nanny already had plans. Lindy's gone into the city to pick them up."

"But I have the show tomorrow."

"She knows that. I'll help tomorrow if needed."

"I thought you and Joe would be at the show, too."

"We will. Maybe we'll bring the boys along with your mother. We'll work something out. I said the boys could come here, but Lindy thought this might be a good idea. This way, you can see how you all do together."

DJ felt a shudder start at her toes and reach her ears before blowing out the top of her head. Robert wouldn't be there to calm them down. And her mother's patience level lately had been nonexistent. Some weekend this was going to be. After saying good-bye to Gran, she wished she'd asked to come spend the night there. At least it would be quiet.

She ate, then wandered up to Gran's old room. Since the bedroom set had moved to Gran's new home, the room was empty. DJ got two sleeping bags down from the storage closet and two pillows from the linen closet. After spreading them out on the floor, she tried deciding what would help the boys feel at home. A radio? No, too old. Stuffed animals? Sure. She took a couple of bears and a pony off the shelf in her room and set them on the sleeping bags.

In spite of her best intentions, the boys ended up on the floor in DJ's room.

"Okay, knock it off. I have to get up early."

"Us too. We help you."

DJ groaned at the thought. She hung over the side of her bed to watch the two boys, still bright-eyed and wired. "Do you two ever wind down?"

They shook their heads as if strung together.

"Well, you better now. No more giggling, no more talking, and don't snore."

At that, the giggles erupted again. DJ had used her sternest voice, but making them laugh made her feel giggly, too. How could she resist?

"You said your prayers yet?" She watched them shake their heads again. How could they do things in such perfect sync? "Okay, who's first?"

"We say them together." Both boys folded their hands on their chests and closed their eyes. "Dear God, bless Daddy, and Mommy in heaven, Grandpa and new Grandma, DJ, our maybe new mom, and Bandit. Please give us a new family soon and a pony—two ponies. Amen." Their eyes popped open. "We always say bless DJ. Is that okay?"

"You bet, I need as many blessings as I can get. Good night, guys."

"Good night, DJ. We love you." Both voices sounded as one.

DJ turned out the light and flipped over on her back. If the twins were praying for Lindy to be their new mother and she was praying that the wedding wouldn't happen, which prayer would God answer?

She closed her eyes and pictured the jumps at the show. Bridget always said to picture what you were going to do in your mind first and always to imagine yourself doing it perfectly. Imagining was easy. In her mind, DJ had jumped the entire Olympic course many times. She'd jumped in a Grand Prix and at the Cow Palace, too. She'd made every jump with room to spare and basked in the thunderous applause.

Now if only her butterflies would go to sleep along with the rest of her.

"What's wrong, DJ?" Joe asked in the morning at the Academy.

"Too many things on my mind."

"I always find that when I get in a situation like that, prayer helps more than anything else."

"Yeah, well I prayed last night and this morning. The boys woke up when my alarm went off, and let me tell you, there was no way I could concentrate. They were so noisy! I left them watching cartoons after promising them Mom and Gran would bring them later. You suppose I had that many questions when I was little?"

Joe nodded. "From what Melanie remembers, yes. Come on, let's get this guy loaded." Ranger pawed the shavings in the next stall. "Sorry, fella, you have to stay home today."

DJ led Major out to the trailer and walked him right in. Josh and Amy followed, then Hilary with her horse. Next they loaded Tony's Thoroughbred and the other jumpers since the jumping events were always held first. Equitation classes came later, in the afternoon. As soon as the first load of horses departed, they started on the other students' horses.

Finally, Joe called the jumpers to ride with him. DJ cringed. Would Tony join them? Sure enough. And Joe waved the creep to the front seat.

DJ felt as if she'd been smacked with a two-by-four. What was the matter with GJ? She and Amy swapped looks and made a place for Hilary. With five kids, the Explorer was full.

When Hilary slammed the side door, Tony opened his. Joe put a hand on the boy's arm. "You're riding with us." He spoke in his police-man's stern voice. Tony slammed the door and snapped his seat belt. He hugged the door as if he might be contaminated by the others.

Joe tried to make conversation, but all anyone answered was "yeah" or "no" or even a shake of the head.

DJ's butterflies invented new stunts.

They pulled into the showgrounds right behind the long trailer.

"You'd think he was afraid of catching something from us," DJ muttered when Tony bailed out before the truck had finished moving.

"Yeah, as if you could catch black skin," Hilary said in the same undertone.

"*We're* the ones who might catch something," Amy added. "And I sure don't want what he's got."

"Me neither."

By the time they had the rope strung between trees and the horses spaced out, the second trailer arrived, and with it, the younger students.

DJ decided that if she heard her name called one more time, she would freak.

"Concentrate, DJ." Bridget accurately picked up on DJ's panic. "I will take care of the young ones until you are finished showing. Besides, their parents are here to help. They must learn what to do, too."

DJ nodded. "Thanks." But even when Joe put a hand on her shoulder to stop her mad scurrying, she felt like yelling. What was the matter with her? She'd never been this uptight before, not even the first time she showed.

DJ changed into her tan stretch pants, white turtleneck, and black tailored jacket. She tied her stock, watching the material drape in the mirror. After dusting off her velvet-covered helmet, she left the RV used as a dressing room and headed back for the lineup.

Joe waited with Major, who was polished to a super sheen.

"You're looking good, kid." He gave her a leg up and left one hand on her knee. "Come on, let's see a smile. This isn't the Olympic finals, you know."

"I know." DJ let out a deep breath. "I keep telling myself to focus, then someone calls my name and I'm off again."

"Well, let's get over to the warm-up ring, and you'll be fine."

Hilary rode in front of them, and Tony fell in behind as they followed the trail around the ring to a separate area where riders were already warming up their horses. DJ settled in her saddle, straightened her back, and reminded herself to always look ahead. She smiled at Joe and signaled Major to walk forward.

After several turns around the ring at a two-point trot, she eased him over to the cavalletti, the bars laid out parallel on the ground. She kept Major going straight and bending smoothly in the turns. All the hours she'd worked on the basics seemed to be paying off. He moved better than any well-oiled machine, his gait smooth and collected.

DJ could feel herself become more in tune with the movements, aware of the horses around them yet blanking out the rest of the world. She made a visual check, her body over her pelvis instead of settled back in the saddle like she used to ride. Sure enough, there was a straight line from her elbows to Major's mouth. Heels down and looking straight ahead, she glanced down—right away, Major changed the beat. Back around again, over the cavalletti, one and two, relaxed and aware. She kept giving herself mental orders, sounding just like Bridget had for so many sessions.

When the announcer called for Hunter Seat, she joined the lineup at the gate. There were four entries from Briones Riding Academy in a class of ten. DJ waited her turn, keeping her mind on the horse beneath her and the class ahead.

Until Tony walked his horse up beside her and hissed out the side of his mouth, "Nigger lover."

DJ felt her body tense as if she'd been struck. "Why, you . . . you . . ."

Tony touched his whip to his helmet and trotted into the ring.

"Next." The ring assistant waved her forward.

DJ now understood the meaning of the phrase "seeing red." A brilliant haze seemed to separate her from the rest of the world. She signaled Major into a trot but let him stumble as they entered the ring. The judge was staring right at her.

Concentrate! Come on, DJ, don't let him get to you. She swallowed and forced herself to look straight ahead, focusing on Major's ears and the direction they were going. All around the ring she gave herself instructions, but too many times she called herself names at the same time. When they placed sixth, she knew it was her own fault. Major could have done better—all by himself. Hilary took the first, and Tony the red.

DJ had to smile at the look on the boy's face. He didn't like being beaten, and he sure didn't like being beaten by Hilary. There was justice in the world after all.

"What happened?" Joe confronted her as soon as she exited the ring.

DJ wanted to tell him. After all, he'd invited the creep to sit in front on the way over. But tattling had never been her style. And she resolved she wouldn't start now. But she *would* get even. If only she could figure out how.

Calling herself names had become a habit halfway through the Hunter/Jumper class. She knew she was jumping ahead of Major, but she couldn't seem to stop. As soon as he left the ground, she knew she'd signaled him to jump too soon. Up and nearly over, and—the tick reverberated through her head. The last fence. She held her breath, but the pole didn't fall. She finished the circle to a round of applause, but in her head, the names continued.

"I don't deserve a horse like you when I mess up like this," she told Major as she left the ring.

"Self-talk is for building up, not tearing down." Bridget stopped to check on DJ with clipboard in hand. "Sometimes we learn by our mistakes. But good riders, even when they make mistakes, do not waste time calling themselves names. Let it go and learn from it. You will do better next time."

DJ nodded. It was good advice, but could she figure out how to take it? She and Major still had a chance to show in English equitation that afternoon.

She looked up when she heard someone call her name. Two matching pairs of arms waved wildly from the log seating off to the side. Gran and Lindy had the twins corralled between them. DJ waved back and rode off to the lineup. Now she had to answer to her students and remind them not to commit the same mistakes. Yuck!

"Tough luck, DJ." Angie turned from wiping her horse's face with a soft cloth. "I thought you had it."

"I wish." DJ remained on Major to watch the final round. Hilary jumped cleanly. She and her horse looked as though they were having a party out there. *How can she handle the pressure?* DJ thought. Tony and one other person had already completed perfect rounds.

The other rider ticked on the next round with the jumps raised two inches. DJ held her breath and let it out with a shout when Hilary made another perfect round. So did Tony. DJ swallowed a groan. The young girls around her didn't need to know about the problem between them, so she kept her thoughts to herself.

"He's so cute," Krissie whispered to Sam.

DJ shook her head. If only he were as nice as he was good-looking.

The poles went up again. DJ sent a prayer heavenward for her friend.

Hilary jumped first, another perfect round.

"This is your day, buddy, keep it up." DJ and Amy stood shoulder to shoulder with Major on the outside, head drooping over DJ's shoulder so she would scratch his cheek.

Only a nicker broke the silence as Tony entered the ring. His horse seemed to fly over the jumps. The oxer, a double, triple uneven poles, crossed poles and a double oxer, and the final, a square oxer. A hind foot rang on the pole. The pole wobbled but remained in place.

The crowd groaned.

"And the winner of our Hunter/Jumper class today is Hilary Jones on her horse, Prince. Hilary is from the Briones Riding Academy. Come on over here, young lady, and accept this well-earned blue ribbon and a coupon for a sack of horse chow from the Concord Feed and Seed Company."

The arena assistant gave out the ribbons while the announcer continued. "We'll take a few minutes to clear the arena, then start the equitation classes. Let's give Hilary Jones and Tony Andrada, our second-place winner and also from Briones, a well-deserved hand."

"He's not a happy camper," Amy said with a shake of her head.

"You suppose that's his dad?" DJ looked over at the man talking with Tony just outside the ring entrance.

"Got me. I haven't seen him around the barns. Tony's mom picks him up."

DJ turned at familiar shouts from the Double Bs. Joe had one on each hand pulling him along. He stopped them before they could run into the horses. DJ turned Major and walked back to them so they could pet the horse.

"I wanted you to win. How come you hit the pole? Don't you like blue ribbons best? Major's the best horse, isn't he? I was scared you was gonna fall off. Can I ride now?"

DJ looked up to see a grin on Joe's face. "Kinda make you tired, don't they?"

She switched her attention back to the matched pair, who were dancing in place. "How can I answer anything when you don't give me a chance?" She looked back at Joe. "Put them up on Major, and I'll walk them around. Major's tired of standing still anyway." She wiped the smile off her face and gave orders once they were aboard. "Now, no yelling or banging your legs. You have to sit still. Grandpa Joe will walk beside you so you won't fall."

"We wasn't gonna fall off." They looked at her as if she'd said a nasty word.

"No, of course not. Now hang on. Front B, grab the mane, B in back, the saddle cantle." She pointed to the places as she spoke. Life would be a lot easier if she could tell them apart well enough to call them by name.

When they returned, it was time to help her students and get Patches ready for the Halter class. Mrs. Johnson had been grooming him till he gleamed. DJ was wishing she had entered him in the Walk/Jog class, too—anything to give him experience.

The twins had gotten restless, so Lindy took them home after DJ placed third in equitation for fourteen-and-under riders. She didn't feel too badly about the results—she and Major still had a lot of work to do on form and pacing.

"You could have brought Ranger for the Halter class," DJ told Joe as she snapped the lead into Patch's show halter.

"I know, but I'd rather get to know him better first. I'll watch you now, and then you can coach me," Joe responded.

"That goes for me, too." Mrs. Johnson fell into step beside them as they walked the path around the arena. "This is so much more fun than riding up into the hills. You think I could show Patches?"

"Why not? Halter class is a good place to start, then Walk/Jog. These training shows make it really easy to begin."

"Not like the big one after Thanksgiving, huh?"

DJ felt a flurry of butterfly wings in her stomach. She *had* to do better at that show, and the competition was tougher there.

Patches loved the show-ring. He strutted as though he'd been showing for years.

"You big show-off," DJ whispered as the judge gave the flashy gelding the blue ribbon. "Now if you only minded this well when you were under saddle."

By the end of the day, DJ felt as if she'd been run over by a six-horse hitch—with each hoof hitting her twice. Besides that, her belly felt like it hadn't been fed in a week.

She hit the front door wanting nothing more than food and bed.

Instead, she had two tornadoes wrapped around her legs before she could close the door.

"We been waiting for you. Grandma baked cookies. Lindy made us take a nap. Did Patches win? How come you took so long? You said next time we came we could color. Dinner's ready, and you get to sit by both of us."

DJ felt like burying her head under her pillow. "Put a cork in it, guys." At the frown on her mother's face, DJ stopped trying to walk and peeled each twin off her leg and set them in front of her. "Now, give me a minute, okay?" At their nods, she continued, "No more questions."

They nodded again—in unison.

"Get to the table, boys. Joe, you and DJ want to wash up? Dinner is ready." Gran lifted a covered dish out of the oven. She set it on the counter and handed DJ a peanut-butter cookie. "That'll hold you till you get to the table."

At least it was quiet in the bathroom. DJ decided she'd never gripe about a quiet house again. She washed her hands and wiped a smudge off her cheek. Must have been a kiss from Major. Back down in the dining room, the boys patted the empty chair between them in case DJ didn't know where to sit.

Joe led the grace. "God is great, God is good, and we thank Him for our food." At the "Amen," one of the boys started to say something, but a look from Joe stopped it.

DJ promised herself she'd ask him how he did that.

———

Sunday after church, they all picked up Amy and went to the gallery where DJ's drawing hung on display.

"How come you didn't get the purple ribbon?"

"I like it better."

"So do I, guys, but an honorable mention isn't too bad." DJ studied the artwork around hers. She had to keep telling herself that.

"I like yours the best," Amy finally said after looking around. "All this other stuff is . . . is . . ." She turned to Gran. "What would you call it?"

"Modern art is as good a term as any. They were obviously looking for something unusual here." Gran stopped to study a sculpture.

"What do you think it is?" DJ whispered.

"It isn't what it is, but how it makes you feel." Gran turned to her with a smile.

"It makes *me* feel hungry."

"Oh, great—all my artist friend here can say is that it makes her hungry." Amy danced away from DJ's threatening look.

"I think we'd better leave," Lindy said. "The boys are about to knock something over, and then where will we be?"

"Apologizing, most likely." Gran put two fingers in her mouth and whistled. Other visitors looked at her kind of strangely, but the boys came running back.

"You better teach me how to do that." Lindy curled a lock of hair behind her ear. "Or get me a leash."

"Well, I think you can be very proud, darlin'. Your drawing stands out among the rest of the works hanging here." Gran gave DJ a hug.

"She means yours is the only one that makes sense," Amy whispered with a giggle.

By Sunday night when Robert came for the twins, Lindy was the one who looked like she'd been caught under the six-horse hitch—and dragged.

Chapter · 10

"Did the boys behave?"

"We was good, Daddy. Wasn't we?"

"Yes, of course." Lindy pushed back a strand of hair that had fallen across her forehead. She didn't even have any lipstick on, and she still wore the jeans she'd put on when they went to the park to play on the jungle gym. They'd stopped for hamburgers on their way home, and a smear of ketchup decorated one pant leg.

DJ hung back and watched as Robert kissed Lindy, then bent down to hug and kiss the boys, who by now had glued themselves to his legs.

"Did you bring us a present, Daddy? Did you? Did you?"

"Shh, boys—in a minute." He looked at Lindy. "Sorry I'm late. We've been stacked up over northern California waiting for something to clear at the airport."

"Daddy!"

"No problem." Lindy swiped the hair back again.

DJ watched as the boys grew louder and her mother's lips tightened. Soon Robert took on the same harassed look Lindy wore.

"Well, see you guys. I got homework."

The twins threw themselves at DJ for hugs and kisses before returning to their father.

"What did you bring us? I want to go home. Will Nanny Jean be there?"

On one hand, DJ wanted to see the rest of the scene, and on the other, she had to leave before she burst out laughing. She didn't need a plan to prevent a wedding between her mother and Robert. All she had to do was let the twins loose. A short time later, she heard the front door close and Robert's car start and leave.

Her mother turned out the lights and made her way up the stairs and down the hall. She tapped on DJ's door. "Thanks for your help, dear. I never could have done it without you."

"Come on in." DJ lay flat on her bed, algebra book and notebook spread in front of her. *Dear.* Since when did her mother call her or anyone "dear"? *Things they are a'changing, that's for sure.*

"Are you behind on your homework?" Lindy leaned against the doorjamb.

"Not too bad. I worked ahead since I knew this weekend would be busy."

"Wish I could have done that."

"You decided on your thesis yet?" DJ found herself fishing for something to say. This was worse than being in a group of adults asking, "how's school?" or, "what do you want to do when you grow up?"

"I've narrowed it down to two projects. One might interest you."

DJ looked up from tracing the pattern in her bedspread.

"I'm thinking of focusing on teenage entrepreneurs, like you and Amy with the pony parties. I want to zero in on how kids start their own businesses and manage them. What do you think?"

"Your advisor would approve something like that?" DJ swung her feet to the floor.

Lindy nodded.

"Then I think it's cool."

"Do you know any other teens who've started their own businesses?"

DJ crossed one leg over her other knee and rested her elbows on her leg. "Not right off the bat, but I can ask at school. In fact, you could put an article or something in the school paper and let the kids contact you."

"If I did that at your school, maybe I could at others."

"I've seen articles in papers and magazines about kids and their businesses." DJ slid back on her bed and sat with her legs crossed. She patted the bed beside her. "You could check *Scholastic* or *Seventeen*. That would help you tap into kids from other areas."

"Do you read those magazines?"

"Sometimes."

"Hmm. And I thought you read only horse stuff." Lindy scraped at the ketchup stain on her jeans. "You know, you're really good with the twins."

"Thanks."

"They like you."

"They like anyone who answers their questions." *Where is this conversation going? What am I supposed to say now? They like you, too?*

"Well, I better get to bed. I'll set up a search on the Internet tomorrow and see if I can find more kids who have businesses of their own. I can use you and Amy for a case study, can't I?"

DJ nodded. "Sure."

"And some of your other attempts, too?"

"M-o-m, get real."

"No, I'm serious. I need failed attempts, too, and yours are good examples of learning by trial and error."

"Yeah, mostly error." DJ looked up at her mother, one eyebrow raised. "You're kidding, right?"

Lindy shook her head. "And if the thesis works out well, I'm thinking of using the research to write a book. What do you think of that?"

"Wow. That's really cool."

"That's also just a dream. Thanks for all the help." Lindy started to walk out. "Oh, DJ? I'm sorry you didn't do better in the show. I hope having the twins there didn't affect your performance."

"Yeah, well, I have to learn to deal with distractions and the unexpected. At least that's what Bridget keeps drilling into me. I'm glad you came."

"Me too." As Lindy left the room, a breath of her perfume lingered on the air.

DJ sniffed. How come Gran's roses still smelled so much better? "Night, Mom."

Later, as she lay trying to go to sleep, DJ thought back over the conversation with her mother. DJ and Amy in a thesis? What would Amy say?

When DJ got home from school on Monday, the house was still a shambles from the weekend. She wandered out to the backyard that used to be such a showplace. Now dead flowers and seed pods covered more of the plants than blossoms. The roses needed pruning. She tried to pull a carrot to munch, but the ground was so dry the top broke off.

"Fiddle." She dug down into the dirt and yanked out the carrot. She washed it under the faucet and turned on the sprinklers. They needed to get automatic ones at this rate. Now DJ couldn't leave till the yard was soaked. She shook her head. She'd have to remember to turn them on when she got home and off again.

"Even the hummingbird feeders are empty. Just like me." She shook her head. Here she was talking to herself. And yesterday she'd been praying for quiet.

Joe and Ranger were in the ring when she and Amy arrived at the Academy. Tony had the jumping arena. His horse wore the dark sheen of hard work, and Tony's face wore a frown.

"Did you hear what his father said to him yesterday?" Amy asked as they ambled toward the tack room.

"Nope." DJ picked Patches' bridle off the peg.

"Well, let's just say I know where the kid gets it."

DJ stopped before picking up a grooming bucket. "Gets what?"

"The way he talks to Hilary." Amy dropped her voice. "If my father talked to me that way, I'd . . . I'd . . . I don't know what I'd do, but it would be bad."

"Ames, quit yakking in circles and tell me. What did the man say?"

"He yelled at Tony for letting a—you know, the n word—beat him. He said if Tony couldn't do better than that, they'd sell his horse and he could go play Pogs with the little kids."

DJ sank down on the bench. "How come you didn't tell me sooner?"

Amy shrugged. "No time. And you weren't in a very good mood, if you remember. That man used more four-letter words than the creeps do at school. If I talked like that, I'd be grounded for life."

"Me too." DJ gnawed on her lower lip. "All I know is that if things don't change soon, Hilary will leave. If anyone's gonna leave, it ought to be Tony."

They both picked up their buckets and started down the aisle.

"DJ."

She turned to see Bridget coming toward them. "What's up?"

"I need to know if you are going to the jumping clinic at Wild Horse Ranch. The registrations need to be in the mail today."

DJ rubbed her bottom lip with her tongue. "I guess not. I really need a saddle, so I'm saving all my money for that."

"Sorry to hear that. It is not often one is given the opportunity to work with someone of this instructor's caliber."

"I'd just like to meet the man. Seeing a former Olympic rider in person—that's better than meeting any movie star."

"Well, maybe next time."

"Maybe next time what?" Joe, leading Ranger, walked up to the trio.

After DJ explained the situation, Joe just shook his head. "I'll pay the fee. Why didn't you tell me? You know Gran says all you have to do is ask."

"I know, but Robert volunteered and Mom wouldn't let him. I figured I better leave well enough alone."

To go or not to go. The choices warred in DJ's head. So what if her mother got mad at her—it wouldn't be anything new. Was the jumping clinic worth a fight? Lindy hadn't exactly said DJ couldn't go—she'd just said Robert couldn't pay and that DJ needed to earn the money. This wasn't exactly earning the money, but she had found it another way. And Joe was right, Gran *had* said she'd pay for DJ's showing fees, but that was when she lived in the same house. Did the offer still stand?

"DJ, let me worry about Lindy, okay?" Joe dug his wallet out of his pocket. "How much is it?"

"Thanks, GJ. I'll pay you back somehow."

He pulled out several more bills. "How about if I go, too? I'm sure I could learn plenty since I'm such a novice. This way, I'll know what you are talking about."

"Good idea." Bridget nodded. "You will find there are clinics for cutting horses, too, in case you decide to train Ranger yourself."

"I better get going. Thanks again, GJ, and you, too, Bridget." DJ picked up her gear and danced down the row until she came to Patches' stall. The gelding nickered when he saw her. "Hey, that's a first." She dug in her bucket for a couple of horse cookies. "Here's your treat. I better remind your mother to bring them to you since you're such a sweetie today." The horse tossed his head, spraying her with slobber and bits of grain. "And then again, maybe not." She wiped her face and set to work with the brushes.

By the time she'd worked Patches' energy off so he could get down to business, she'd used up half of her time with him. Obviously his owner hadn't been out to ride him today. DJ couldn't get used to the idea that people who owned horses didn't ride them every day. In fact, some of the stabled horses were never ridden except by Academy employees.

"Why have a horse if you don't ride him?" Patches shook his head. He pulled at the bit as if hoping DJ had forgotten to let him run.

"No, you have to mind. Then we can play." She kept her aids firm, insisting that he move away from the pressure of a leg. Every time he obeyed, she rewarded him with pats and praise. "Remind me to tell Mrs. Johnson to lunge you or let you at it on the hot walker before she gets on. No wonder you can buffalo her—you just have too much energy."

By the time she'd put him away and taken Major out, she felt like she'd been sitting on a jackhammer. When she put Major into an easy trot, it felt as though she were sitting on a pillow. What a difference a well-behaved horse could make!

"He learned to conserve his energy when he was on the force," Joe said from the sidelines. "He knew there was a long day ahead."

"He's smart all right. That's why he's learning so fast." DJ rode over to the side and stopped. "You on your way home now?"

He nodded.

"Give Gran a hug for me. Tell her the cookie jar is empty."

"Yeah, sure. The one at my house comes first, kid."

DJ watched for a moment as he strode across the lot to his Explorer. While she was glad Joe and Gran were so happy, she sure wished Gran would be at home for her like she used to, with dinner waiting and a clean house. The comforting smell of turpentine and oil paints was almost gone, and it had been far too long for the delicious smell of cookies to linger.

"Back to work, big fella." She spoke to cover the lump that blossomed in her throat.

Lights on meant Lindy was home. DJ pedaled faster and parked her bike in the garage, then closed the automatic door. "Hey, Mom?"

No answer. The kitchen wore a half-clean look, and the family room could stand a clutter check. DJ reminded herself to turn on the sprinklers. Then she ambled up the stairs. A glance in her mother's bedroom told the story. Lindy lay with a cloth over her eyes—a sure sign of a migraine headache.

DJ tiptoed to the edge of the bed. "Can I get you anything?"

"No, thanks." Lindy spoke without moving her lips.

DJ knew then that it was a bad one. She sighed and reached over to unplug the phone.

"Robert has something to show us. He'll be here Saturday morning about ten."

"I won't be here. I've got that jumping clinic up in Napa. I told you about it."

"Oh."

DJ hoped her mother would let it go at that.

"Call him, then, so we can make other arrangements."

"Sure." DJ took a deep breath of relief. "I'll check on you later in case you want some soup or something."

"Thank you."

DJ closed the door gently and made her way downstairs. After slicing a piece of cheese, she dialed Robert's number. "Hi, Mom said to call you. I'm going to that jumping clinic in Napa on Saturday, so we—or at least, I—won't be here."

"Good, I'm glad you're going. Decided to take money out for it, huh?"

"Well, no. Joe paid for both me and him." *And please don't tell my mother,* she wanted to say, but then . . . things were becoming a tangled mess.

"Oh, okay. How about Sunday after church? The boys and I could go to your church, and then we'll have brunch out before I show you the surprise."

"Ah . . . well . . . you know my mom doesn't like surprises. I think I take after her."

"Well, I think she'll like this one—at least I hope so. Tell her I'll call her tomorrow. Oh, DJ, does she get headaches like this very often?"

DJ thought a moment. "Maybe once a month or so. I guess I never paid much attention to how often." After hanging up the phone, she thought about the surprise Robert had in store. He sure sounded excited. She hoped her mother would like it.

She'd just finished making tomato soup and a grilled-cheese sandwich when the phone rang.

It was Gran. "DJ, I have a problem," she began. "I need some horses for a new book I'm working on, and your horses are usually better than mine. How about drawing some for me, then I'll paint them in?"

"Sure, but when do you need them?"

"Yesterday. I took this project knowing it would be a tight deadline. The artist they originally hired took sick, and they need it as soon as I can get it to them."

"I could come over each night after I work at the Academy." Without touching the floor, or at least it seemed that way, DJ danced across the room after hanging up the phone. She was going to help Gran out. Her horses would be in a children's book! If only she could call Amy, but it was too late.

She took her tomato soup and grilled-cheese sandwich up to her room so she could look through her sketches. Maybe one or some of them might work. Or maybe she could make them work.

The house was still a mess when she came down in the morning. She'd planned to straighten up, but she'd gotten so involved in the drawings, she'd gone to bed late. A horn honked from the drive. Amy was already here. She'd have to take time to do it before she headed for the Academy.

The light was blinking on the machine. That would wait, too. Out the door she flew.

DJ's art teacher stopped her before she left class.

"I was really pleased to see you got that honorable mention at the art show. Have you thought of taking some extra art classes after school or on the weekends? You have real talent."

"Thank you, but all my time is taken up at the Academy where I work and stable my horse. I really don't have any spare time right now." DJ fidgeted from one foot to another. Mrs. Yamamoto was waiting for her.

"I think horses are great, but art classes could make a difference in what you choose to do with the rest of your life. Why don't you have your mother give me a call?"

"Sure, thanks. I'm late for my ride." DJ took the slip of paper and dashed off to her locker. She had so much to do, and now she was already late.

She listened to the waiting message while she got out peanut butter and jelly for a sandwich.

"DJ, you left the sprinklers on all night. You know what that will do to our water bill?"

DJ groaned. And she didn't have time to do her chores, either. She threw the dishes into the dishwasher, then grabbed the books, crayons, and paper in the family room and stuffed them under a cushion—the rest would have to wait. Out the door. Back inside. Upstairs to get her drawings for Gran. Out the door. Back inside. She needed a sweat shirt. The clouds were already edging the tops of the Briones hills.

"You're late," Amy scolded.

"Don't I know it." The girls pedaled as though they were in a race.

Joe met her at the tack room. "DJ, was Major limping last night?"

"No, why?"

"There's some swelling in his right front leg. I've been icing it, but you better not ride him for a few days. He must have pulled a muscle."

DJ felt her stomach thud down to her ankles. What had she done now?

Chapter • 11

DJ charged out to Major's stall. "Hey, fella, what's happening with you?" She ran her hand down his leg. Sure enough—hot to the touch and puffy. "Do you think we need to call the vet?"

"No. I have some liniment, and with that and the ice, he'll be fine," Joe said.

"You're sure? Did Bridget see him yet? Oh, Major, I'm so sorry." The horse snuffled DJ's hair and searched her pockets for treats. He blew in her face when he found nothing. "Sorry, no time to stop for cookies. Joe here scared the thought right out of me."

"I'm afraid it means no jumping clinic on Saturday."

"But what could have caused it? He didn't hit a pole or anything."

"Did he stumble?"

"Not that I can think of." DJ squatted down to inspect the swelling again. She ran gentle hands over the area. "Joe, I wouldn't hurt him for anything."

"I know. These things happen. Maybe he just figures he needs a rest. It's not your fault."

"I should have checked him more carefully when I put him away. Didn't I cool him down enough? Is that it?"

Joe lifted her up and set her on her feet. "DJ, look at me. Watch my mouth move. It is not, I repeat—*not*—your fault. No matter how hard you try, you can't take care of the entire world. Or take responsibility for it, for that matter. Now, go about your chores and we'll leave early for a scrumptious dinner. You earned a break as much as Major did."

"A break? Could it be a stress fracture?"

"Help!" Joe shook his head. "I won't even dignify that with an answer. I'll see you in a while. You go practice concentration with your students and Patches."

"But I . . ."

"Go."

"Maybe I should spend the night here so I can ice him again."

"Go."

DJ started to follow his instructions and stopped. "If you talk to Bridget right away, maybe you can get your money back for the clinic on Saturday. Or you *could* go without me."

"No chance. I'll talk to her—now get."

DJ managed to check on Major three times over the afternoon, and each time the leg looked the same. She wrinkled her nose at the smell of the liniment. The last time, Joe had applied the ice boot again, and Major looked as though he wore a padded sleeve over his leg.

The big horse stood contentedly munching his evening ration of grain and hay. She gave him another hug and a kiss on the soft skin of his nose.

"See you tomorrow. You be good now." She turned to Joe. "Maybe I should—"

"Get in the truck. Gran is waiting dinner on us."

DJ and Gran lost themselves in planning the horse drawings for the book. They didn't even look up when the phone rang.

"DJ, it's for you." Joe held out the receiver.

"Oh no." DJ knew she was in trouble. "I forgot to leave a message for Mom about where I'd be." She held the phone away from her ear to soften the cutting tones of her mother's voice. "But, Mom—" She couldn't get a word in edgewise as she was reminded again about how irresponsible it was to leave the water running all night.

Joe stood when she hung up. "I'll take you home."

"I'd rather stay here." DJ could feel her anger burning as fast as a fire built with dry kindling. "It's just not fair. No matter how hard I try, it's never good enough. Gran, I miss you so much." She dropped to her knees by her grandmother's chair and laid her head in the soft lap.

"I know, darlin'. But you and your mom have been doing pretty well lately." Gran stroked the wisps of hair back from DJ's forehead.

"Yeah, we get along really well when we never see each other." DJ could feel the anger dwindling with each stroke of her grandmother's hand.

"Lindy will do better once her thesis subject is approved. She's worked long and hard for this degree. It means a lot to her."

"More than I do."

"No, that's not true. I know you feel that way sometimes, and I understand. But your mother loves you—she just doesn't know how to show it."

"Yeah, well, yelling at me sure doesn't cut it." DJ looked at the folder of drawings resting on the table. "I better get home. I didn't get my homework done, either, so I hope she doesn't ask."

"That's my fault. We were having too good a time." Gran dropped a kiss on DJ's hair. "I'll tell her we need to do this all week. She'll understand—she was just worried about you."

"Where else would I be?" DJ got to her feet. "Thanks for dinner. Sorry I didn't help with the dishes."

"Oh, that's nothing. Our art was far more important." Gran walked DJ and Joe to the door. "I can always do the dishes."

"Or I can." Joe winked at DJ. "I *do* do dishes, you know."

Lindy was on the phone by the time DJ walked in. She could tell Robert was on the other end by the soft sound of Lindy's voice, not at all like the one she'd used to call DJ.

"Night, Mom." DJ waved and got a nod back. Too tired to do any homework, she crawled into bed and fell asleep on the *a* of amen.

———

Because she couldn't train Major, DJ had extra time that week to work on the drawings Gran needed. Each night they sketched, erased, and finally transferred the illustrations to stretched canvas so Gran could paint them. DJ particularly loved one they'd done of a young foal with furry ears and a brush of a mane.

Lindy left a message that they'd be going with Robert to see the surprise on Saturday since DJ didn't have the clinic.

DJ was spending Friday night at Gran's, and the two of them were working in the studio. "Why can't Mom ask me about *my* schedule before she plans things for *us* to do? Joe said I can ride Major again tomorrow, but only at a walk. He did fine on the lunge line tonight."

DJ studied the horse's head they were pairing with that of the little girl who was the heroine in the story. It made an attractive logo. If this book did well, the publisher was considering turning it into a series. "I really like this. I wish I could draw people as good as you do."

"And I wish my horses had as much life as yours." Gran held up the last drawing. "You have a real gift, darlin'."

"Well, I got it from you. Did I tell you my teacher said I should take art lessons?"

"No. That's exciting news."

"I said no. I don't have time right now." At the sad look on Gran's face, DJ added, "You know riding is more important to me than anything. I just can't do one more thing. If I mess up again, Mom will ground me forever."

"Just remember, if you decide you might like to take art classes, the money will be there."

Joe looked up from the book he was reading. "The same goes for riding clinics, shows, and riding lessons should you need training beyond what Bridget can offer you."

DJ blinked a couple of times to dry her eyes. "Thanks. You two are the best."

Gran turned back to the drawings spread across the table. She lifted one of a month-old colt. "I think this one needs some work on that off hind leg, then we can use him for page eight. What do you think?"

DJ picked up her art-gum eraser. "You're right. The ears need some work, too." The quiet of concentration came to rest on the room.

Some time later, the phone rang.

"It's for you, DJ." Joe held out the receiver. "Your mother," he mouthed.

"I just wanted to remind you to be back home and cleaned up by eleven tomorrow."

"I know." DJ held the phone away from her face and stared at the receiver, shaking her head. "She hung up. She must still be upset." DJ returned to the table. *That I can do without.* She could feel the resentment bubble. *Who needs her?*

She caught the look that passed between Joe and Gran.

"Do you know what's going on?"

"Robert wants it to be a surprise. We won't spoil it for him." Gran shook her head when DJ started to interrupt. "Nope, I won't even give you a hint."

"Ah, come on, Gran." DJ put her best wheedle into her voice.

"No way."

DJ hurried through Saturday morning chores so she had plenty of time to walk Major around the soft sand of the arena.

"You act as if you never had a problem at all," she said, leaning forward to stroke his neck. Major moved smoothly beneath her, not favoring the injured leg in the least. DJ thought about the clinic going on up in Napa. Both Tony and Hilary had gone up for it, along with a couple of the adults who stabled their horses and rode at the Academy.

The sun was breaking out of the early morning fog, and DJ lifted her face to its warmth. "I'd rather be riding up in the hills, wouldn't you?" Major snorted and lifted his feet a bit higher, as if hoping she would relent and let him trot.

"Sure would." Joe rode up beside her. Ranger didn't appreciate walking any more than Major.

"Then let's. The trail wouldn't be too hard and . . ."

"And you have to be ready at eleven. You know that if we got started, we wouldn't want to turn back."

"I know. Am I gonna like the surprise?" DJ clutched her reins, willing herself to remain calm. She deliberately loosened her fingers and relaxed her wrists. With the release of a deep breath, she turned her head to look at her grandfather.

"I hope so, DJ, I surely hope so."

DJ kept his words in mind as she put Major away and climbed onto her bike to ride home.

Robert and the boys were already there. "No, you're not late," he reassured her when she glanced at her watch. "We're early."

"DJ, we's gonna see—" Robert clapped his hands over both twins' mouths.

"Remember, this is a secret. A surprise." Robert squatted down so he was on eye level with the bouncing Bs. "You promised not to tell."

They both nodded, blue eyes bright above his fingers. When he removed his hands, they flung themselves at DJ's legs.

She bent down to hug them. How could anyone resist the adoration shining in their faces? "I'll be ready in a few minutes." She headed for the stairs. When they started to follow her, she sent a pleading look at Robert.

"Come on, guys, we'll wait here while DJ dresses. She's not used to an audience."

"We can help."

"I'm sure you can, but we'll read a story instead while we wait." Robert took them by the hands and over to the sofa.

DJ fled up the stairs as they clamored for their favorite story. Strange, her mother wasn't downstairs pacing the floor, making noises like DJ should hurry. Did Lindy know what the surprise was? Was she unhappy about it? Questions, questions.

Robert herded the boys to the car as soon as DJ leaped down the stairs. She looked at her mother but saw nothing other than a gracious smile on her face. The headache lines were gone. With the boys buckled into their seat belts, DJ sat back and tried to unwind. She knew she could get the twins to tell her about the surprise, but that wouldn't be fair. Robert wanted to surprise them.

He stopped at the stop sign and turned right, the same way DJ rode every day to the Academy. They drove past the Academy, then passed Gran and Joe's. DJ looked down to see the Double Bs with their hands clapped over their mouths. What was going on?

A quarter of a mile beyond Gran's house, Robert turned into a tree-shaded driveway. They stopped beside a white house with brick halfway up the front and friendly windows.

"What do you think of it?" Robert shut off the ignition and turned to Lindy.

"It's a nice house, I guess." Lindy looked up at him. "Pretty yard."

"Let's go see the inside."

The boys threw off their seat belts and exploded out the door. At a shake of their father's head, they ran in place until they could grab DJ's hands and pull her toward the front door. A fan-shaped window over the door caught her eye.

Instead of knocking, Robert unlocked the door. Strange. One didn't go unlocking someone else's house. They obviously weren't coming here to visit someone.

They entered an empty living room with vaulted ceilings—a

fireplace ran clear to the ceiling on one wall, and an abundance of windows let in the outdoors.

"What do you think?" Robert had his arm around Lindy's shoulders.

"It's beautiful." Lindy stood very still, her eyes trained on the wide stair that curved up to the second floor.

"I thought so, too—that's why I bought it. The place has five acres and a barn with horse stalls. Though the house isn't large enough now, it will be by the time my men get finished with it. I figure we could move in by March . . . that is, if you think a February wedding would be about right?"

"Robert, I . . ."

"Let me show you the rest of the place." He took Lindy's arm and led her through an arch to another room.

DJ felt as though she'd been kicked in the head by a one-ton draft horse. Robert had bought them a house! *He* certainly was convinced they could become a family. But her mother hadn't said yes yet—had she?

DJ could ignore the dynamos tugging at her arms no longer. She let them pull her up the stairs, down the stairs, out to the kitchen, and to the backyard, but she needed no encouragement to visit the barn. Four stalls, a board-fenced paddock, and a field for grazing. She turned and looked at the house. Robert wanted to make it *bigger*?

"Daddy said we could have two ponies, and Major can live here, too." The boys ran from stall to stall, opening each half door and chasing each other inside and out again.

DJ tried to tune them out so she could think clearly. Had her mother agreed to this? She shook her head. No, Lindy had been as surprised as her daughter, DJ realized, remembering the shocked look on her mother's face.

"Come on, guys, let's go see what's happening at the house." She turned and headed out of the barn, sure they would follow.

"Daddy said we could have a dog here, too. Two dogs, even. You want one? I want a pony now." The two overlapped comments as usual. "When we gonna move, DJ? You're the best sister in the whole world!"

DJ sensed the icy chill the moment she stepped through the sliding-glass door into the breakfast area. Uh-oh, her mother was not happy. DJ put a finger to her lips to shush the boys before they charged into the house.

"But, Robert, I didn't say I'd marry you."

"But you've said that you love me. This just doesn't make sense."

"I know, but marriage is a big step. It's a lot to think about, and it's not fair to pressure me by buying this house."

"Lindy, honey, this isn't pressure. I'd have bought this house even if it were just for the boys and me. It's near Dad and Gran, the boys can have a dog and ponies, and I'm building more houses out in this area now. I can move my office out of the city and not have to commute."

DJ put her hands over the twin mouths about to erupt beside her. She shook her head and whispered, "Be quiet, okay?" The boys nodded, so she removed her hands and took theirs. Together, they tiptoed back outside and sat down on the redwood steps.

So many things to think about. She stared out at the barn. She could have Major right at home with her. She wouldn't have to work at the Academy all the time to pay for his board and keep. She'd ride over there for lessons. There was room in the field for jumps. The boys could ride in the paddock until they got good enough to ride up in the hills.

And DJ would have a father—and two brothers. She watched the boys kneeling on the ground, studying something in the grass.

"DJ, come here." One of them waved to her.

"DJ, boys, come on. Let's go eat." Robert stopped in the doorway.

DJ got to her feet. Robert sure did have a knack for surprises. When DJ found her mother in the living room, traces of tears still glistened in her mother's slightly red eyes.

What had her answer been?

Chapter • 12

"What do you think, DJ?"

"What do you mean, what do I think? About what?" DJ stalled for time. She knew her mother was talking about Robert. *It's not fair. Don't ask me. I'm just a kid, remember—that's what you're always telling me.*

Lindy sat curled up in Gran's wing chair, one hand propping up her head. The lamplight glinted on the auburn tints in her hair and made it shine blood bay.

The phone rang, and DJ leaped to her feet. "I'll get it."

"If it's Robert, tell him I'm not home."

"Sure, she's right here." DJ leaned around the corner. "It's for you."

"Who is it?" Lindy mouthed. DJ shook her head and shrugged.

DJ left her mother talking and headed for her room. How could she give her mother an answer when she had no idea what she thought? And asking her daughter to lie for her? Of course, it had been Gran who had always insisted on telling the truth. Lindy had never been home.

DJ got out her sketch book and pencil box, taking time to sharpen each tip to perfection. After building her nest on the bed, she soon lost herself in a world of lines and shading. The foal she and Gran had been working with slowly appeared on the paper. Trying to get the ears just right, she erased one and started again.

A loud knock at the door finally got her attention. "Yeah?"

"May I come in?"

"Sure." DJ heaved a sigh. Why couldn't she be left alone to draw? Life was so much easier when all she had to think about was sketching and shading. Draw and approve or erase. No major decisions.

"That was my boss. I'll be leaving tomorrow morning for a three-day trip to Los Angeles. Mom said it was okay for you to stay there."

"Great."

Lindy paused, as if waiting for DJ to say something else. "Fine, then. I better get packed. Good night."

"Night, Mom. Have a good trip." When the door closed again, DJ thumped her fist on the pillow. "Yes!" Three days with Gran and Joe—and without her mother.

Tuesday morning Robert called before DJ left for school. She answered the phone with a questioning look at Gran, who shrugged in return. What could Robert be calling *her* for?

"You want to take *me* out to dinner? Why?"

"I'd like to get to know you better. We never get time to talk when all the others are around."

DJ tipped her head to the side. "Well, I guess."

"Good, I'll pick you up at seven, if that's all right."

DJ hung up the phone and turned to Joe and Gran, who were sitting at the breakfast table. "What'll we talk about?"

Joe laughed. "I think you'll find Robert is an entertaining companion, if you give him a chance."

"There's a message there, darlin'." Gran took another sip of her coffee.

DJ picked up her backpack and slung it over one shoulder. "We gotta go, GJ, or I'll be late."

Monday was the day she got to spend the most time with Major, but since his leg prevented them from jumping yet, they worked on the flat instead. DJ posted till she felt her legs turn to cooked spaghetti. She concentrated on each of her aids—hands, legs, and feet—but especially on how she held her head. She'd never realized how often she looked down or off to the side. Keeping Major going straight was one problem, but the more crucial one was her concentration.

They crossed the cavalletti so many times she felt pole happy. Major seemed to enjoy every minute of it, striding with ears forward, neck arched, and snorting every once in a while.

After walking him out, DJ checked the leg to make sure there was no swelling. "You're a trooper, you are." She stroked the horse's neck and rubbed his ears. "We'll probably be able to jump on Wednesday. What do you think?"

Major snorted and bobbed his head. She checked his hay net and the water bucket, then got his grain. "I'd much rather stay here with you than go to dinner with Robert. Why doesn't he just come to Gran's for dinner?"

Joe appeared at the stall opening. "Because he wants time with you, not us. You ready to go?"

"Where would you like to eat?" Robert asked once they were in his car heading for the road. "What kind of food do you like?"

"Chinese, Italian, Mexican—pretty much anything but Thai, it's too spicy." DJ looked over at the man driving. "I'm not particular. What do you like?"

"All of the above. How about we go somewhere you don't go often?"

That won't be hard, DJ thought. *We never go out except for hamburgers or pizza.* "Italian then?"

"Fine. How about Giannini's?"

When they were seated in a booth with a white tablecloth and their hostess had lighted the low candle, DJ looked around. Robert had good taste in restaurants—now if only the food lived up to the decor.

"I know the ravioli is delicious, and the pastas are superb. They make their own." Robert smiled at the waiter, who wore a black tie and spoke with a heavy Italian accent. "What do you want to drink, DJ? I'm having iced tea."

"That'll be fine." DJ looked up when the waiter lifted the crown-shaped napkin from her plate, shook it, and laid it across her lap. "Ah, thank you." She glanced over to catch a smile on Robert's face. She raised her eyebrows and smiled back.

By the time they'd ordered, she couldn't begin to explain why she'd been uptight about dinner with Robert. He made her laugh and got her to tell him all about her early days at the Academy—and the disastrous times she and Amy had tried to earn money.

"And the hamsters got loose in the garage?"

"Actually, some of them were in my bedroom. One even got into Mom's." DJ rolled her tongue in the side of her cheek. "She can yell pretty loudly when a creepy critter gets too close."

Robert went from a chuckle to an outright laugh, a deep sound that made other people turn to see who was having such a good time.

"Did you catch them all?"

"Finally. I sold them to a friend whose brother had a six-foot boa constrictor. He was always looking for snake food."

Their dinner was everything Robert had promised. DJ knew that from then on, she'd be partial to ravioli. The dessert tray looked like an artist had been painting dreams. She chose something called chocolate decadence and wished she could eat such creamy chocolate every night.

When Robert ordered coffee, she leaned back in her chair and gave serious thought to unbuttoning the waistband of her twill dress pants.

"Tell me about your dream of being on the Olympic team."

"That's what I'm trying for." DJ leaned her elbows on the table.

"No, I mean, what will it take? I have no idea how a person ends up on the U.S. equestrian team."

"Well, you need to qualify, just like for all the other sports. I'd have to be known for winning shows—the big shows where you earn points. Olympic riders have really top-notch horses—hot bloods like Thoroughbreds—and both the horse and rider undergo tremendous training."

"Sounds expensive."

"It is. It's also one of the few events where age doesn't count. In fact, rarely is someone under twenty-five admitted to the team." DJ moved her spoon around. "I know I can do it, though. Gran says that if you want something bad enough and pray hard and work hard for it, you can do it. I've been working and praying as hard as I can, so I figure God will help me. At least, that's what Gran says. She teaches me Bible verses so I know where to turn for encouragement."

"Well, I'd like to be one of those who helps you, too. You have a big dream, DJ, and I admire people who are willing to work hard for their dreams."

"Thank you."

Once back in the car, Robert asked, "What did you think of my new house?"

"It's nice."

"Did Lindy tell you what I plan to do with it?"

DJ shook her head. "Mom and I haven't talked a lot since then."

"She's upset, isn't she?"

DJ shrugged. How was she supposed to answer that?

"Look, DJ, I know you weren't exactly pleased at first with the idea of me marrying your mother. I'm hoping that's changed, because I really want us all to be together. I love your mother, and I know she loves me. If we all work at it, we'll make a wonderful family. And after I finish the remodeling, that house will be a great place for all of us. You can have what is now the master bedroom and bath for your own, and the boys will share the other. The new wing will have a master-bedroom suite, an office for me, and probably a playroom. I'm not sure yet."

He looked over at DJ. "I'm trying to give you a sales job, aren't I?"

"You didn't mention the horse barn yet." DJ grinned at him. "The boys already told me they were going to take riding lessons."

"Yeah, ponies and dogs are all they think about." He turned into Gran's driveway. "Sometime I'd like to hear what you think about this wedding. Thanks for the date. I really enjoyed myself."

"So did I." DJ climbed out of the car. "Tell the boys hi for me. And thank you for the yummy dinner."

"Did you have a good time?" Gran asked as DJ stepped in the door.

"Yeah, I did. He's a really nice person." DJ yawned. "I better get to bed. Gran, I've been thinking—if I could work Major mornings before school, I'd have more time in the afternoon and evening for all the other stuff I have to do. What do you think?"

Gran shook her head. "I think that's asking too much of yourself."

"Other Olympic contenders do it—why not me?"

———

"But why not?" DJ carefully kept any trace of a whine out of her voice. She had asked her mother to discuss the idea of early morning workouts again, and acting like a little kid wouldn't help her cause. While her mother had said no several months before, maybe now would be different. DJ certainly hoped so.

"DJ, you have too much to do already." Lindy paced the family room. "You'd have to ride up to the Academy in the dark, and I won't permit that."

"You could give me a ride on your way to work."

"But you'd go to school smelling like a horse. No, that just won't work."

"Please, Mom. Just think about it, okay?"

"DJ, no. I haven't changed my mind. I cannot give you permission to ride in the morning, and that's that. You are only fourteen, and you need your rest. You'd have to be in bed by eight to keep going, and you know how you like to stay up late."

"I can change." DJ bit her lip to keep angry words from spilling out.

"We won't discuss this anymore. Just keep up your chores and your grades—that's all I ask. Your life at the Academy is your choice. You have your horse now, can't you be satisfied?"

"No, I can't. You always have money for the things you want, like school and another degree. Just because I don't want the same things you do, you won't help me. You don't care."

"Darla Jean Randall—"

"Don't bother to say it. I'm going." She spun away and dashed up the stairs to her room. Just in time, she kept from slamming the door. She flung herself across the bed and pounded her fists on the mattress. Her eyes burned and her throat closed. She *would not* cry. She would not! Only babies cried.

How come her mother could be so selfish? She didn't care about anything but herself. DJ thumped her fist again in rhythm with her thoughts. *Why? I know she hates me. She isn't like a mother—Gran is more my mother. It isn't fair!*

After a time of thumping and muttering her angry thoughts, DJ rolled over onto her back and stared at the ceiling. Why couldn't she stay cool and calm like she'd planned? Fighting never did any good.

She could hear the water running in her mother's bathroom. Lindy was brushing her teeth. What would happen if DJ went in there and demanded she be allowed to ride in the morning?

Dumb idea.

What if she went in and said she was sorry? But sorry for what? For asking for what she wanted? That's what Gran had said to do—ask. Of course, Gran had meant she should ask God and Gran; she never mentioned asking Lindy.

DJ chewed on the cuticle of her thumb. What if her mother came in here and kissed her good-night and said I love you, like Gran used to do? She brushed the sides of her eyes and swallowed—hard.

The next afternoon at the Academy, she was back to square one with Andrew. Suddenly, he didn't want to brush Bandit, he didn't want to feed Bandit, he didn't even want to be in the stall with the pony.

"What's happened, Andrew? I thought you were beginning to like Bandit."

"No. I want to go home."

Short of dragging him into the stall, DJ didn't know what to do. "You want to come see Major?" A head shake. "How about saying hello to Patches? We could stand back a ways." Another shake. The boy's lower lip stuck out, and his chin wobbled. DJ sank down against the wall and patted the shavings next to her. "Come sit here with me. We have to talk."

Keeping one eye on the pony who stood in front of the hay net pulling out wisps of hay and munching, the little boy joined DJ, copying her cross-legged pose.

"Now, the way I see it, your job is to groom Bandit here. He's never hurt you."

"But, he scared me."

"I know, but it wasn't on purpose. He was swatting flies. I need to put fly spray on him so the flies don't bother him. How would you like flies crawling on your legs and in your eyes?"

The boy shuddered. "Yuk."

"So let's get with the program and get this pony groomed. Then we can put fly spray on him." She got to her feet and extended a hand. Andrew let her pull him up.

With a look that said he thought she was killing him, he took the brush and started brushing.

Please, God, don't let Bandit frighten him again. Help this kid get over his fear and please show me how to help, too. DJ kept brushing, praying, and teasing Andrew until he finally laughed at one of her jokes.

By the end of their session, they had one clean pony and one boy who'd overcome enough fear to keep going.

"You know, Andrew, you are one brave guy." DJ held the bucket while he filled it with grooming gear.

"Why?"

" 'Cause even though you're afraid, you keep on trying. That's pretty neat, don't you think?"

"I guess."

His mother met them with her arm in a sling.

"What happened to you?" DJ asked.

"Andrew, why don't you go get in the car. I'll be right there." Mrs. Johnson sent her son on the way with a pat on the shoulder. She turned to DJ. "I fell off Patches and wrenched my shoulder. Andrew was scared again today, wasn't he?"

DJ nodded. "But we got through it. Tough about getting hurt. Falls happen a lot with horses. Did Patches act up?"

"He spooked at something, and I just wasn't ready. I probably wasn't paying close enough attention."

"Too bad. Well, take care of your arm, and I'll make sure Patches gets the steam worked off. You're putting him on the hot walker or lunging him first, aren't you?"

"Usually, but that time I didn't. I was in a hurry." Mrs. Johnson shook her head. "I had to learn a lesson, I guess. See you."

DJ wandered back into the barn. She could hear raised voices coming from the south aisle of the barn. She stopped to listen. The drawl and the words being used indicated one voice could only be Tony Andrada's. DJ felt like a rampaging mother bear whose cub had been attacked. What right had he to talk to Hilary like that—Hilary, who wouldn't hurt an ant?

DJ stormed down the aisle, but by the time she reached the stall, Tony had made it out the door and Hilary had disappeared.

DJ checked all the stalls. No Hilary. She looked in the tack room and trotted across to the office, but it was locked. Even Bridget was gone. Back in the barn, she thought for a moment. The haystack!

Hilary was wiping away her tears when DJ approached.

"I swear, I could hit him over the head with a shovel." DJ sank down on a bale of hay.

"It wouldn't do any good. He's as hardheaded as they come. It isn't just that I'm black, either—he thinks all women should do his work for him. I bet his mother still butters his toast."

"And picks up his dirty socks."

"Makes his bed. She'd probably breathe for him if she could." The two girls shared a bit of a smile at their jokes.

"Have you said anything to Bridget?" DJ rested her arms on her knees.

Hilary shook her head. "But I don't think I can put up with this much longer. I've found another stable that will take my horse, and their trainer is okay." She straightened her back and took a deep breath. "If I could only keep him from getting to me. My father says to ignore him, and, DJ, I try. I really try. But he just won't quit. And to make matters worse, he doesn't finish his chores and tries to get by without doing a good job. You know Bridget trains us all to do everything correctly. We don't allow slipshod work here."

"Until Tony." DJ swung her clasped hands. "James wasn't always the greatest worker, either, but he was younger and he came around. And he didn't have a father who hammered racist garbage into his head."

"You heard Tony?"

DJ nodded. "I guess I didn't really want to believe people think like that anymore, let alone teach it to their kids."

Hilary rose to her feet and pulled a tissue from her pocket to blow her nose. "Thanks, DJ, you're a true friend. I just wish we could find a way to deal with Tony."

"You could tell Bridget and get him kicked out of here."

"Yes, I could do that."

"Or I could."

Hilary shook her head and stared up at the hills in Briones. "No . . . if anyone tells, it will be me."

That evening at Gran's, DJ told them what had happened. "Tony Andrada is creepo of the creepos. I don't blame Hilary for wanting to leave. Some plan Ames and I had—it didn't work at all. We've been ignoring him, but the only one he picks on is Hilary. And me, 'cause he knows I'm her friend."

"Changing someone's behavior can take a lot of time and effort." Joe set his paper down so he could see DJ.

"Our time is running out."

"You know, darlin', there's a Bible verse that says—"

"Gran, with you there's *always* a Bible verse!" DJ was getting exasperated.

Gran winked at her and continued. "This one fits perfectly. Jesus tells us to pray for our enemies, and so heap burning coals on their heads."

"Burning coals will work for Tony's head just fine. I'll help with the heaping."

"So, how about praying for him?"

"Gran, that's impossible. I can't do that."

"Would you pray for Tony if it could help Hilary? Keep her at the Academy?"

DJ stared at her grandmother. *Could* she pray for Tony? "I don't know."

"Then you need to pray another prayer first."

DJ sighed. "What's that?"

"A pastor friend of mine once told me that when you know you should do something and you can't, you should pray, 'Lord, make me willing to be willing.' Works every time."

"How about, 'Lord, make Tony willing'?" DJ shook her head at the look on her grandmother's face. "All right, I'll try." She sighed.

Gran shook her head.

"I'll do it, okay?" What had she gotten herself into this time?

Chapter • 13

The prayers weren't working.

"I'm sorry, DJ," Hilary said. "Even my dad said we should go somewhere else. We'll stay till the show and then I'm out of here."

"Oh, Hil, I don't want that to happen."

"Me neither, but we'll still be friends. I'll see you at shows and stuff."

"It won't be the same. I still think you should tell Bridget. She has a right to know."

"Dad says to write her a letter after I leave so it won't look like I'm asking her to make a choice. Besides, what can I say? 'Tony calls me names and such.' I should be tougher than that."

After the girls went about their work, DJ couldn't get Hilary's sad face out of her mind. *God, I thought you were going to work on this. I've been praying for Tony—sort of—and nothing's happening. Time's running out.*

She saddled Patches and prepared for a rough workout since he hadn't been on the lunge or hot walker. She needed the fight as much as he did.

———

Since it was the Tuesday before Thanksgiving and they were having company, Lindy had just finished making the bed in the spare room and setting out towels when DJ arrived at home. "Do you mind if the girls bunk down in your room? I thought they could choose between the family room, their parents' room, and yours. What do you think?"

"Whatever." It seemed strange that they were preparing to meet family for the first time. Robert's sister, Julia Gregory, her husband, Martin, and their two children were coming for Thanksgiving because Gran and Joe had invited everyone to their house for Thanksgiving dinner. The Gregorys lived in Connecticut and hadn't been able to come to the wedding.

"You've already stabled Bandit at Joe's so we can give the kids pony rides?"

"No, not till Friday. Joe and I thought we'd take everyone over to the Academy to look around. Mom, calm down. It isn't like the president of the United States is coming."

"Easy for you to say." Lindy stopped in the doorway with her hands on her hips. "At least it looks nice."

Looked nicer when Gran lived here. But DJ kept her thoughts to herself. She didn't want to shatter the truce that existed between her and her mother. Besides, Gran wasn't coming back, and DJ needed to live with that.

Lindy glanced at her watch. "Robert and our guests will be here any minute, so hurry up and change. Then we're going to Gran's for pizza."

"Mom, I already know all that. You've been over the weekend schedule sixty-five times." DJ ducked her mother's fake swing and headed for her room. Wouldn't it be nice if they could tease each other like this all the time?

Six-year-old Allison decided immediately that DJ belonged to her. She oohed and aahed over the pictures on DJ's bedroom walls and voted that her sleeping bag should definitely be spread in there.

Meredith, a year older than DJ at fifteen, looked bored with the entire thing. When she did take her earphones off, she acted as though she still had them on and ignored everyone. She chose to sleep in the family room—by herself.

When DJ entered Gran's house with Allison on one hand, Bobby and Billy wore matching thunderclouds on their faces. They glared at their cousins and parked right in front of DJ.

"Hi, guys. Do you remember Allison? You were still in diapers the last time you saw her." She nodded to each of the girls as she said the names. The twins eyed Allison suspiciously, as if sizing up the competition.

"I'm Bobby." The right twin pointed a thumb to his chest.

"I'm Billy, and DJ's our sister." They stepped forward, shoulder to shoulder.

"She likes us best."

DJ looked to Robert for help. All the adults were laughing and talking as if they'd forgotten all about the kids. Meredith had disappeared. If something didn't happen, they were going to have a war on their hands. Allison's lower lip stuck out as far as those on the twins.

"Hey, that's enough, I—"

"And we get to ride Bandit first." The Bs each grabbed one of DJ's legs and looked up. "Don't we?"

"No ponies for kids who don't share." Robert scooped a twin under each arm. "And that includes sharing DJ." He regarded his sons seriously until they each nodded and then put them down. "You guys show your cousin where the games are, or we can put a video on."

"Or I could read a story." DJ thanked Robert with her eyes.

"Or you could take a break," Robert said over his shoulder as he carried the twins into the other room.

"That's right," Julia said with a smile. "You are not the designated entertainment for the weekend or the baby-sitter. Come get something to drink and catch your breath."

"Thanks." DJ could tell she was going to like this relative. Julia gave you the feeling that she'd known you all her life and you were best friends. How'd she end up with a daughter like Meredith?

Andy and his wife, Sonya, along with their daughter Shawna, entered with armloads of pizza boxes. Andy was Joe's youngest son. Even nine-year-old Shawna carried a pizza box.

"Hi, all. Food's here." Andy led the way to the dining room and they spread the boxes out on the table.

"Everyone help yourself. The paper plates are over there," Gran pointed to a stack of wicker plate holders. "And the—"

"Drinks are in the kitchen," Joe finished for her. "Little kids get to eat at the breakfast table."

"DJ, come on!" One of the twins grabbed her hand and pulled.

"Nope, DJ is not one of the little kids. She can eat wherever she chooses." Robert saved the day again.

DJ took slices of the Hawaiian special and gourmet delight and wandered after the others into the family room. She sat down next to Andy and Sonya on the floor.

"So, how are the horses and riding coming?" Sonya asked around a mouthful of pizza.

"Good. Now that I have Major, it's even more fun." DJ took a bite of the topping-heavy pizza cradled in her hand. "You playing much volleyball?"

The conversation swirled around her with everyone laughing, talking, and teasing one another as if they'd been together the weekend before. It would have been easy to feel left out, but Andy made sure she was part of the conversation. When the twins charged back in, Sonya grabbed them and wrestled them to the floor.

"Run, DJ. Run for your life!"

DJ ran, but only as far as the dining room for more pizza. She was just scooping a slice onto her plate when she heard someone ask, "So, Robert, when's the wedding?"

DJ froze in midaction. She looked up just in time to see Robert flinch.

"I . . . ah . . . we haven't set a date yet."

DJ glanced at her mother. She wore a smile that almost disguised her tight jaw. But DJ knew her mother too well. Lindy didn't like being pressured.

"We decided we needed to get to know each other better before marriage." Lindy's words were true, but DJ wasn't fooled.

"DJ, we was missing you." The twins glommed to her like magnets. DJ sighed and smiled down at them. "Where is Allison?" She didn't bother asking about Meredith. That cousin had made it clear she had no time for people who rode horses.

"Watching *The Little Mermaid.* Can you give us horsey rides?"

"No, she can't, but I can." Andy grabbed the gigglers up and dropped to the floor. Both boys climbed onto his back and away they went. Hearing the laughter, Allison clamored for a turn. Within minutes the Bs were riding Robert and Joe while Andy carried Allison. The "horses" raced down the hall on hands and knees. The riders shouted "giddy-up," the men cried, "outta my way," and the women laughed till the tears came.

In bed that night, DJ caught herself giggling again at the thought of the inside race. Allison was already sound asleep after her telling of "The Three Bears," complete with voices to suit the characters. DJ crossed her arms over her stomach. What a crazy evening. Even if Robert didn't marry her mother, they were still a part of this wacko family. *Bet Grandpa Joe's knees hurt tomorrow.*

That was the first thing she asked when he stopped by for her in the morning.

"Oh, some. But I beat out Robert and Andy. Not bad for an old guy." Gray fog had lightened as they fed the horses and cleaned the stalls.

The chill made DJ shiver.

"You should have worn a jacket, child." Joe tossed out the last of the dirty shavings.

"It'll burn off. If shoveling this stuff doesn't warm you up, what will?"

"You recovered from all the attention last night?"

"You mean the kids?" DJ leaned on the handle of her fork. "I wasn't the one giving horseback rides."

"To be honest, someone should have shot me and put me out of my misery. My kneecaps!" He shook his head with a laugh.

They were both laughing when they saddled up and headed for the arena.

"Hi, Tony." Joe lifted a hand in greeting.

DJ shot her grandfather a startled look.

"Hi, Joe." Tony reigned his horse to ride on Joe's other side. "How's the cutting-horse training coming along?" He didn't say anything to DJ, and she squeezed Major into a trot.

She didn't hear Joe's answer. She didn't want to. Here they'd been having a perfectly good time together and that . . . that—no, she wouldn't ruin Thanksgiving Day by calling anyone names.

DJ worked Major on the flat until a sweat rose on his shoulders, then the pair transferred out to the jumping arena. *Concentrate,* she ordered herself over and over.

Following Bridget's advice, DJ tried to keep her self-talk positive. That way, she couldn't think of Tony—or Hilary, or anything besides jumping. She stayed with the low jumps, focusing on her posture, her hands, and, as always, her head and eyes.

Major lifted off as if he were floating, each jump effortless as they moved in perfect sync. The sun peeked through, melting away the remaining fog. Around they went, back across the ring and over the jumps.

DJ heard another rider enter the arena. She looked up. Tony!

"Guess that's enough, fella." She put Major to the final jump. He pulled to the right and ticked the pole. The words she muttered to herself were not positive as they rode back to the barn.

After cooling Major out and putting him away, she bridled and mounted Bandit to ride him to Gran's. You'd have thought she brought Santa Claus the way the little kids greeted her.

"Okay, I get breakfast before anyone rides. That's the rule." She tied the pony to the fence with his lead shank, removed the bridle and saddle, and headed for the back door.

The smell of roasting turkey wafted through the house. DJ sniffed and closed her eyes to better appreciate the fragrance. How come turkey smelled best on Thanksgiving? She followed the sounds of laughter into the kitchen, where most of the family was gathered, either drinking coffee at the table or preparing food at the counters.

"Good morning, darlin'." Gran turned from the dough she was kneading to give DJ a kiss.

"Homemade rolls?" DJ snitched a bit of dough. "Anything for breakfast for a starving granddaughter?"

Orange juice, a cinnamon roll, and a bowl of mixed fresh fruit appeared on the table at the same time she sat down.

"You want some hot chocolate, too?" Julia asked. "The other kids sure enjoyed it."

DJ nodded around a mouthful of cinnamon roll.

"Maybe she'd rather have coffee. She's almost an adult now," Andy added.

"No thanks, hot chocolate will be fine. But you could put a drop of coffee into it."

"Ah, we have a mocha lover here." Martin leaned forward. "I knew it yesterday when we met—a girl after my own heart."

DJ grinned back and kept on eating. Each of the Bs had already been in the house asking when she would be ready.

"Where's Mom?" She looked at Gran. "And Robert?"

"They're over looking at the new house." Gran winked. "I think they wanted to be alone."

Uh-oh, that might not be too good. DJ sipped her hot mocha. She could feel the warmth circle around her belly. Was Lindy over her grump of the night before?

———

By the time DJ had given each kid three rides, settled forty-two arguments, refereed thirteen fights, and heard "DJ" one thousand times, she was ready to turn in her cousin badge.

What she really wanted to do was eat dinner in the garage, on the condition that no one under five feet follow her. Maybe Meredith was the smarter of the two, always disappearing.

"No, DJ and Meredith are eating with the grown-ups. They'll be in here just for grace," Joe settled firmly. "Andy and Sonya are hosting this table." He parked the twins on phone books so they could see better. "Now we're all going to say grace together."

He took a hand of each twin and raised his voice. "Okay, everyone! God is great, God is good, and we thank Him for our food. Amen."

DJ headed to the dining room with a sigh of relief. The kids were fun, but oh, she was ready for some peace and quiet.

By the time everyone had eaten their fill, the kids were ready to ride again.

Robert shook his head. "No, DJ is off limits. You can watch a video or play a game or go play outside, but no pony and no DJ."

DJ sent him a silent thanks and went to find Joe. They needed to go feed Major and Ranger, and she needed some peace and quiet. Her ears were still ringing from the kids' endlessly calling her name.

———

By the time Sunday evening rolled around, DJ enjoyed the quiet of her own house. She'd been sad to see the Gregorys, except Meredith, leave for Connecticut and had really had a fabulous time like everyone else. Everyone, that is, but her mother. DJ could tell something was bothering her mom. The twins were still at Gran's, and Robert and Lindy were off someplace together.

DJ flipped the channels on the television until she found a mystery movie and settled in to watch. She'd already finished her homework, and with the bowl of popcorn on her lap, she didn't have to get up for anyone or anything.

A car pulled into the driveway.

"I don't think so," her mother said in the doorway. "Good night, Robert."

DJ flinched. She knew that tone well. She huddled deep into the security of the wing chair, wishing she were up in her room and sound asleep in bed. Her mother entered the room.

"I suppose you'd like to know that I told Robert I wouldn't marry him. I know that's what you wanted. Now you can finally be happy." With that, Lindy marched up the stairs, down the hall, and slammed her bedroom door.

DJ started to get to her feet, but the shock of the news pushed her back. "Fiddle. Double and triple fiddle."

Chapter • 14

"No school tomorrow. What do you want to do?"

"We should spend the day getting ready for the show." Always practical Amy.

"How about taking a lunch and heading up into Briones? We don't have to stay too long." DJ closed her eyes. "Just think—trees, trails, hills. I'm so tired of flat arenas I could croak."

"Right." Amy shook her head. "The day DJ Randall turns down a chance to ride just because the ground is flat is—"

"You know what I mean. Come on, Ames, we'll work extra fast and then go. We can give the horses baths when we get back." DJ rested one foot on the curb to prop up her bike. She sent Amy a pleading look. "You don't want me to go without you, do you?"

"I'll ask and call you. Mom's got the Cub Scouts here right now." Amy waved and pushed her bike into the cluttered garage. With four kids, there were always toys and sports gear, school books, and other stuff lying around.

DJ walked into an empty house. As usual, she answered the blinking light to find out where her mother was. "I'm going to dinner with Robert. We won't be late."

DJ shook her head. You had to give the man an *A* for persistence.

Even after Mom said she wouldn't marry him, he kept coming around. They'd been on the phone every night, and he'd come to visit on Tuesday.

DJ thought about the wedding that wasn't going to be while she heated some leftover soup and made a sandwich. Her plan had been to keep Robert and her mother apart. Well, they weren't apart, but the wedding was off. And her plan had nothing to do with it, even though it was obvious her mother halfway blamed DJ. But now DJ found herself rooting for Robert.

What would life be like with the Bs around all the time? Noisy, but they could learn to stay out of her room when she needed some space. What about Robert?

She took her tray into the family room and settled into the wing chair. He wasn't too bossy. Actually, he was a pretty nice guy. And rich. Well, not really, but he sure had more money than she'd ever seen in her life. And he said he'd help her go for her Olympic dream. Was that the only reason she now thought the marriage might be a good thing?

That would be really creepy of her. One thing was sure: She wouldn't come home to an empty house anymore. He'd even said he'd keep the nanny so Mom could continue her career.

DJ swung one foot and tucked the other underneath her. Robert was right—this house wasn't big enough for that many people.

She shrugged and turned on the television. What did any of this matter now? Her mother had decided against the wedding.

But that night in her prayers, DJ changed her request. "God, my plan sure doesn't seem to be a good idea anymore. Now that Mom and Robert aren't getting married, I don't like it." She stopped to think. "Gran always says we should ask for what we want and then thank you for doing what's best. Is that what's going on here, or did I mess up big time?" She waited, hoping for an answer.

She heard Lindy come up the stairs. Was her mother crying?

It wouldn't be the first time this week.

DJ tried to return to her prayer. "So, do you have a plan that's better than mine?" She could still hear sobs.

She threw back the covers with a sigh. Her mother's bedroom door was closed. Obviously she didn't want any company. DJ turned back toward her room, then with a shrug, tapped on the bedroom door. All Mom could do was yell at her or tell her to go away. So what?

"Yes."

"Can I come in?" When there was no answer, DJ pushed open the door just a crack and peeked in. Lindy sat on the edge of the bed blowing her nose and looking as if she'd been crying for hours. Red eyes, mussed hair, and a mound of crumpled tissues on the bed gave her away.

"Can I get you something?" DJ paused in front of her mom. "How about some tea or hot chocolate?"

"That would be nice." Lindy sighed and wiped her eyes. "I don't know what's come over me. All I do is cry lately." She rubbed the spot where the diamond engagement ring had been, then flopped back on the bed, one hand on her forehead.

"I'll be right back." DJ clattered down the stairs and set the teakettle to heating. She took out a box of tea bags and one of cocoa packets and got out two mugs. By the time she had the tray set, the teapot shrilled. She fixed the hot chocolate, topped it with miniature marshmallows, and carried the tray back upstairs.

What could she say? If only Gran were here. She always had the perfect words.

Lindy had changed into a pair of silk pajamas and folded back the covers of the bed. The tissue pile had disappeared, but the box sat on top of the nightstand, within easy reach.

"DJ, I don't know what I did right to deserve as good a kid as you." Lindy accepted the steaming mug with a nod of thanks. "I sure haven't been the kind of mother who helped make you that way, that's for certain." She set the mug down and swung her bare feet up onto the bed. Scooting toward the middle, she patted the edge for DJ to sit down.

"That's okay, you were busy. I had Gran." DJ sipped after blowing on the hot liquid. The screen-saver images on the computer flashed different colored patterns in the corner. Outside, a dog barked.

"DJ, I'm just so scared." The words sounded small in the stillness.

"Scared? You? Hey, you're not afraid of anything." With one leg up on the bed, DJ turned so she could see her mother better.

Lindy pushed her hair back with a shaking hand. "Yes, I am. The thought of marriage makes my stomach hurt. And look what kind of a mother I am. I yell at you or don't talk to you. I expect you to be the adult around here when you're just a kid. You shouldn't have to bring me hot chocolate and listen to me cry." She snorted. "That's my job."

"Well, I'm not the one who's sad right now. You can do this for me when it's my turn." DJ watched as another tear brimmed over and ran down her mother's face. If only she dared reach over and wipe it away. Instead, she handed her mother a tissue.

"See what I mean." Lindy took it and wiped before the next one could fall. "A waterworks, that's what I am." She tossed the tissue toward the wastebasket, but it missed and floated to the floor. "I've even prayed about this. I pleaded with God to tell me what to do, but there's been no answer. I know Gran gets answers all the time. She must have an inside track or something."

"She's been praying for you."

"Oh, I'm sure she has. Robert has, too—look where it's gotten him."

"Gran says God can't guide you unless you're already moving."

"What's that supposed to mean?"

"I don't really know—it just came to mind." DJ wished she knew what to say. *God, please help me.*

"So what do you think? Should we marry Robert?"

"We?" DJ's voice squeaked on the words. "*I'm* not the one getting married."

"No, but you're my family." Lindy reached over and patted DJ's knee. "I know how you feel. You've made your opinion abundantly clear. Don't worry, DJ, love isn't fatal. I'll get over it." Her voice cracked on the words.

"But, Mom . . ."

"Good night, dear, and thank you for the comfort."

"Good night." DJ picked up the tray and left. How *did* she feel? She wasn't sure anymore.

"What can I do, God?" she asked later just before falling asleep. "We have to come up with a new plan." Or had her plan been the reason everything was so messed up? Scary thought.

DJ woke in the night to the sound of her mother's crying again.

"How about if we ask Joe to go with us?" DJ gave her saddle one last swipe with the polish rag.

"Fine with me." Amy held up her headstall. All the conches shone in the sunlight. "But my mom said I have to be home by five."

DJ leaped to her feet. "Then we better get out of here." She trotted through the barn and out to the stalls where Joe was brushing down Ranger. "You want to ride up in Briones with Amy and me?"

"Sure, when?"

"Now. I'll even share my lunch." DJ gave Ranger a rub on his nose. Major nickered in the next stall. "Come on, guy, let's get saddled." She led the big horse out and tied him in front of the tack room. By the time she'd answered fifteen questions from her students, found a missing brush, and finished saddling Major, twenty minutes had passed.

Amy met her at the gate. "Where's Joe?"

"Coming. If I don't get out of here, the munchkins will snag me again. They're so jealous about our trail ride, they're turning green." DJ opened the gate. "Let's wait up the trail a bit."

Just then Joe rode up, followed by Tony Andrada. "Hope it's okay. I asked Tony if he'd like to come along."

DJ stared at Joe. What could she say? Tony Andrada, the creep of all creeps. What a way to ruin a so-far perfect day.

"Fine, why not?" She could tell from the look on Tony's face that he understood her sarcastic comment. He didn't look as if he wanted to be with them, either.

DJ and Amy trotted their horses up the tree-shaded trail. Off to the right snaked a gully that ran with water during the winter. Squirrels scolded the riders for invading their territory, and scrub jays squawked their own brand of insults. When they could ride side by side, DJ and Amy hung on to the lead. Single file, DJ went ahead. She didn't want to be any closer to Tony than she had to, and right now she wasn't at all happy with her grandfather. The nerve of Joe, inviting Creepo along. He knew how she felt about the guy.

The ride wasn't nearly as much fun as she'd thought it would be. It was all Tony's fault.

Once they reached the open meadows, she nudged Major into a canter. "Come on, Ames, let's go." The two galloped along the fire road that curved around the meadow and up to the Briones Crest Trail. Sunlight, blue sky, even a puffy cloud or two. The day was definitely improving. Horse hooves pounded the packed dirt road, a steer bellowing at their interruption. DJ laughed—without Tony, it would have been perfect.

At a shout behind them, DJ turned in the saddle to see Tony galloping across the meadow. He was not keeping to the fire road.

"Oh, fiddle. That stupid—" Before she could finish her sentence, Tony's horse stumbled. Tony yelled and flew through the air, landing crumpled on the ground.

Horrified, DJ reigned Major around, and she and Amy pelted back to the fallen boy. Joe rode up at the same moment, dismounting in a fluid motion and throwing the reins to DJ.

At the look on his face, DJ shook her head. "It's not my fault. I never thought Tony was stupid enough to ride through the gopher holes."

The sternness in Joe's eyes silenced her.

He thought it was her fault.

Tony hadn't moved. His horse stood, head hanging, one hoof barely touching the ground.

God, please don't let him be really hurt. I'm sorry. Please.

DJ and Amy dismounted, keeping their gaze on Joe, who was examining Tony for broken bones.

Tony groaned. "I . . . I can't breathe." A whisper. He raised his head. "My horse?"

"Do you hurt anywhere?" Joe rested back on his heels, his hands gentle as they unbuckled the boy's helmet.

"Everywhere." He wiggled his hands and feet. "But I'm not broken anywhere." With Joe's assistance, he sat up. When he held up his head, the bruise that was fast turning purple shone bright. He lifted a hand to touch it and flinched.

"Are you dizzy? Feel like throwing up? Sharp pain anywhere?"

Tony shook his head at the questions. "Just got knocked out, that's all. Y'all needn't worry about me." He looked up at Amy. "Thanks for catching my horse."

"He didn't run off. His leg is hurt too bad."

DJ hunkered down and inspected the already swelling foreleg. "I don't think it's broken, just sprained. He can put his weight on it but is limping pretty bad."

Tony let Joe help him to his feet. At the first step, he nearly fell. "Ow!" He grabbed his leg. "Talk about sprains." He pressed against the side of his boot.

"Don't take it off—the boot will help keep the swelling down."

"Should we go tell Bridget to bring up the van?" Amy asked Joe. "If fire trucks can make it up here, she can, too."

"Let's give it a moment and see how both Tony and the horse feel." Joe turned to his saddlebags. "I brought cans of soda for everyone. Tony, you sit there and prop your foot on that rock. DJ, Amy—you brought food, right?"

Joe still hadn't looked at DJ. She felt like spraining her leg just so he would look at her with all the concern he was wasting on the creepo. And now she was supposed to share her lunch. Could things get much worse?

They could. After the food was gone, Joe helped Tony to his feet again. "Well, you can't walk your horse out, that's for sure. How about if I lead him?" He turned to look at DJ. "DJ, Major can ride double."

"Tony can ride Josh. I don't mind walking." Amy stepped forward.

"No, thanks for volunteering. DJ?"

"All right." Why should she have to give Tony a ride—the fall was his fault. He'd ruined their whole day. "Get on," she hissed, her back to Joe so he couldn't see her.

"I'd rather walk."

"Well, I'd rather you walked, too, but when Joe says to do something, it's best to do it." She stabbed a finger in his direction. "Now, get on."

Once Tony was mounted, DJ accepted Joe's assistance to get in the saddle. Still, he said nothing more to her. She felt like giving the rider behind her an elbow in the gut.

"You're the biggest snob I ever knew." He made sure his whisper didn't carry to Joe's ears.

"Redneck."

"How would you know?"

"I heard the way you talk to Hilary. She's gone out of her way to help you, and you keep on making her life miserable. If she wasn't so nice, she'd have told Bridget about you weeks ago, and you'da been out on your can."

"I suppose you're one of those do-gooder Christians." The tone of his voice said what he thought of those who followed Christ.

"Sure am. So's Hilary—that's why she puts up with you."

"You okay back there?" Joe called from the front of the line.

"Fine, sir," Tony answered.

"You may be fine, but I'm sure not. I'd rather dump you in the creek."

"Just let me off, Miss Christian. I can walk."

DJ nudged Major into a trot.

Tony groaned and hung on for all his worth.

In a few steps, DJ ordered Major to walk again. Where had she gotten such a mean streak? Was this the way Jesus wanted her to act?

What would Gran say if she knew what was happening? Joe knew, and that meant Gran would hear about it.

They were halfway down the trail when Tony asked, "So why hasn't Hilary told Bridget?"

"Because Bridget wants us to learn to handle things on our own. Each student worker is assigned a new person to train. You got Hilary, the best trainer of all." DJ wanted to add, *And if you don't knock off the racial slurs, Hilary will leave,* but she'd promised not to say anything. "You're lucky—you really are."

Hilary was the first to see them ride back onto the Academy grounds. She ran up the hill and took the reins of the injured horse. "What happened?" She looked up to see Tony behind DJ. "Are you hurt?"

"Take his horse to the stall and get some ice while we unsaddle these horses. DJ can ride Tony over to the office. When will your mother be here, son?"

"Six."

"Then we better call her. You probably should get that ankle looked at." Joe dismounted at the barn door. "Go on, DJ, take him over while I put Ranger away."

DJ did as he said. How could Hilary take care of Tony's horse like that when he'd been so mean to her? Let alone be polite to him?

In front of the office, DJ slung her leg over Major's neck and slid to the ground. "If you scoot up the saddle . . . no, that won't work." She stepped closer to the horse. "If you slide off carefully, I can catch you so you don't put all your weight on that foot." Between them, they got Tony sitting on one of the chunks of log kept there for that purpose.

"If you'll hold Major's reins, I'll go call your mom." DJ got his phone number and dialed. After telling his mother what happened, she returned to the shady spot where Tony now had his injured leg propped on another wood block. "She'll be here as soon as she can. You want me to get you some ice while we wait?"

Tony looked up at her as though he didn't trust what he was hearing. "Y'all sure you want to do that?"

"Yes or no."

"Yes, please."

DJ returned with two plastic bags filled with ice cubes. She helped stack them around the ankle of his dusty boot. "Sorry you won't be in the show tomorrow."

"Me too." He stared at the ice bags. "Thanks for the ride."

"You're welcome." DJ headed back to the barn, Major trotting behind her. Joe and Hilary were working with the injured horse, and Amy was brushing Ranger and Josh down. DJ put her tack away. "You ready to wash?"

Together, they bathed their horses, brushed them, and fastened on coolers. By the time they were finished, Amy dashed for her bike to head home. "See you in the morning," she called over her shoulder.

DJ fed both Ranger and Major before ambling back to the stall where Joe had just finished. "He going to be all right?"

"With some rest. Lucky he didn't break it."

"Joe, I'm sorry." DJ looked up at him. "Please don't hate me."

"Hate you?" Joe shook his head and laid a hand on her shoulder. "Never. I was disappointed in you, though. Riding off like that was thoughtless."

"But everyone knows to stay on the trails. You'd think . . ." She stopped. The thought that they might have had to destroy Tony's horse made her heart pound. If that had happened, she never would have forgiven herself. If today had been part of God's plan for answering her prayers, she sure didn't understand Him.

"I better get home. Show mornings always come earlier than others." At the thought, her butterflies took a practice flight. After a day like today, who knew what tomorrow would bring?

Chapter • 15

Show time—two days' worth.

"This is our day, big guy. I can feel it." DJ tickled Major's upper lip, loving the whiskery feel on her fingertips. She could hear the sounds of other riders readying their horses for transport. Horses nickered, and a whinny came from off to the right, floating through the fog like a phantom song.

DJ shivered in the chill. One good thing about summer shows, she didn't freeze getting to the site. But then, today, even after the sun came out, she wouldn't be sweating bullets, either. She forked out the dirty shavings while Major ate his breakfast, then brought up a cart of clean bedding to dump in as soon as he was out of the stall. That way, he wouldn't get more dust on him.

DJ picked his hooves. She probably should have had him shod first, but it was too late now. She always put it off as long as she could because it made such a dent in her bank account. At this rate, she'd never get a new saddle.

"Mornin', kid," Joe said with a grin.

"Overslept, did you?" DJ dropped the last hoof.

"Now, none of your smart remarks. I'm supposed to be retired, you know."

"Plain tired's more like it." DJ hid a snicker. Giving Joe a bad time was almost as much fun as teasing Gran. "By the way, I fed your starving horse for you. *He* shouldn't suffer because you can't get out from under the covers." It wasn't as if Joe didn't feed Major every morning, but laughing at the menacing look on his face made her feel lighter and less nervous.

She jogged past the other riders to find Bridget.

"We will send the jumpers first load, as usual," Bridget said, consulting her clipboard. "Mr. Yamamoto is in charge. By the way, DJ, Tony called to say he would not be showing today but that his ankle is only sprained. They had the vet out to check on his horse, and he will be out of commission for a couple of weeks. What happened up there?"

DJ's first racing thought was *Tony didn't tell her.* The second: *Please don't ask me any more questions about it.* "Ah . . . Tony's horse tripped and threw him." That much was the truth.

"Were you racing?"

DJ stared at Bridget as if she'd left some of her marbles at home. "No way!" A swift knife stab of pain that Bridget would even think that, and another of guilt. Technically, it could have been called racing by an innocent bystander.

"Well, then, I am glad no one was injured worse. It is a shame that Tony has to miss the last big show of the season."

"Yeah, right." DJ headed for the trailer. *I'm sure we'll all miss him terribly.*

DJ trotted over to where the slight man wearing the Academy sweat shirt was letting down the ramp to the six-horse trailer. "Who you want first, Dad?" Mr. Yamamoto told all the student workers to call him Dad—he claimed it made life easier.

"If Major is ready, let's start with him, then Prince. Have you seen Hilary yet?"

DJ shook her head. "I'll go see if he's been fed. Maybe something happened to make her late."

With a swift dash by Prince's stall to see that he was eating, DJ told Amy to get a move on readying Major. The barns were bustling as she dodged horses, kids, adults, and a baby in a stroller. Life at the Academy was definitely a family affair.

"Major's first." DJ slipped under the tie across her stall opening and snapped the lead shank to her horse's halter.

"I'll throw those shavings in as soon as you get going." Joe checked the buckles on the sheet and gave Major an extra pat. "You're out of here, kid."

"Thanks." DJ swallowed her resident troupe of butterflies and clucked to Major. Was there any more exciting place on earth than a barn preparing for a show? Her broad grin brought forth answering smiles and greetings from everyone she met.

Major walked into the trailer as if he did it every weekday and three times on Sunday. Josh followed while DJ went to get Prince. That was the rule: If riders weren't there to take care of their horses, whoever was would do it for them.

She stopped by Tony's stall to see the gelding. The horse turned from his grain pan and nickered. "At least *you* know how to be polite." DJ looked around to make sure no one else heard her.

She opened the web gate to Prince's stall and snapped a lead shank to his halter. "Hey, guy, come with me, okay?" The rangy Thoroughbred snuffled her shoulder and followed docilely.

If DJ let herself think ahead to the show-ring, she wouldn't be able to keep her feet on the hard-packed dirt.

But where was Hilary?

For the first time in DJ's memory, the horses were loaded with no fireworks on the loading ramp. Even Patches walked right in as if he'd been doing this all his life. Mrs. Johnson clapped her hands like a little kid. DJ's students wore grins that nearly chased the sleep from their eyes. But still no Hilary.

"You want me to call her?" DJ asked Bridget.

"If you want." She handed DJ a slip of paper. "Here's her number."

DJ let the phone ring and ring. No answer. "They must be on the way."

"Maybe she slept through her alarm," suggested Krissie from her place glued to DJ's right hip. The little blonde had been bouncing like a tennis ball all morning.

DJ shook her head. "Not Hilary. The show means too much to her." DJ felt a little worm of fear wriggle in her belly. *Please, God, don't let anything have happened to Hilary.*

They loaded students into the vans and cars with their waiting parents, and the caravan eased out of the drive. DJ rode in the front seat of Joe's Explorer. Last time Tony had been riding in that spot—and

Hilary had been in back with her. Things sure were different today. DJ didn't like it one bit.

"Gran will be coming with Lindy, and Robert will meet them there with the boys." Joe looked over at her with a smile.

DJ groaned. "Now you tell me. Do they have to come?"

"Why, child, I thought you'd be pleased."

"I am—I think. But when my family's around, the butterflies act as if I'm performing for the president of the Olympic games or something. Joe, you have no idea what I feel like inside."

"Sure I do. When I was a member of the force's mounted drill team, I had worse butterflies than when I faced an angry crowd. The anticipation gets to you."

Even after they had the horses tied to the rope stretched between trees and the announcer had made the first call for Hunter/Jumper, Hilary wasn't there.

"Should we saddle her horse?" DJ and Amy looked at each other.

"Yeah, she'll be here." Amy turned to leave. "You saddle Prince, and I'll go ask Bridget to make sure Hilary is last on the program."

"Good idea." DJ had already changed into her riding gear, but, with Joe's help, she managed to stay neat.

God, please, please, please *make Hilary all right. Help her to get here in time.* The prayer kept pace with her hands as she brushed the tall sorrel horse. Hilary usually braided Prince's mane—DJ should have done that.

She looked over at Major. She and Joe had finished his braid just a few minutes before. The red ribbons made Major look like a professional show horse. Having someone to help her sure made a difference. A nice difference. What would it be like when the boys and Shawna started showing? The thought made her gasp. What a circus that would be!

"DJ, we's here."

"Good luck, DJ. Now stay back, boys. You can hug DJ later." Robert grinned at her. "We just wanted you to know you had a rooting section."

"You look pretty, DJ. Major too." The boys couldn't move. Robert had them in a steel grip.

"Say good-bye. See you later."

As they left, the squawk boxes announced the second call for Hunter/Jumper.

DJ mounted Major, and Joe unsnapped Prince's lead line. Together, they started around the track to the warm-up ring on the other side of the huge covered arena. The Black Diamond Riding Center sprawled over ten acres and looked like a place out of the movies. Tubs of blooming plants, white-board fences, a shaded picnic area, and an enclosed plot with swings and climbing equipment for bored children. With stalls for over a hundred horses and four rings beside the covered area, the place made DJ drool.

But where was Hilary?

Riders loosening up their horses circled the open arena, big enough to equal the two at Briones combined.

"Hilary's on last. You're in the middle," Amy said with a rush. "How about if I warm up Prince?"

"Good idea." Together, the two girls entered the arena and joined the circling throng. If all of these riders were entered in Hunter/Jumper, the class would take hours. DJ's heart sank. She didn't have a chance.

She put that thought out of her mind and focused on Major, slowly warming him up and concentrating on the event ahead of them.

The announcer called the first entrant. She could hear the applause and then a groan from the spectators.

The next time around the arena she saw Joe flag Amy. Hilary stood by his side. DJ trotted over to join them. "What happened?"

"First our car wouldn't start, then it stalled halfway here." Hilary adjusted her stirrups and mounted as she spoke. "I can't thank you enough for taking care of Prince for me." She held out a hand. "See, I can't quit shaking."

"Take a deep breath and let it all out." Bridget had joined them. "You will be fine. Relax your shoulders and breathe deeply again." Bridget's voice held all the calm of a summer lake. "Now, Hilary, you know how to concentrate, so get out there and do it. Forget what has happened and do your job."

"Thanks, Bridget. How is Tony's horse?"

"He will be okay in a week or two. Thank you for all the extra time you put in with him last night."

DJ looked from Hilary to Amy and gave a brief shake of her head. What was Hilary, a saint or something? Amy raised an eyebrow. It was obvious she wondered the same.

"Two more and you're on." Bridget nodded toward the gate to the show-ring. "Do your best. That's all anyone can ask."

DJ waited her turn, Joe standing beside her.

"I think it's worse being your grandfather than showing myself." He looked up at DJ with a smile. "Know what I mean?"

"Yep, that's how I feel when my students are in the ring. I want them to do well so badly." DJ stroked Major's neck. "You know, nothing seems to bother this guy. He's calm as a sleeping dog, but I can tell he's ready to go."

"His years of police training in action. Sure wish it worked for me." He wiped a bead of sweat from his forehead. "Okay, kid, do it. I'm going up into the stands where I can see better."

The announcer called DJ's number. She took a deep breath, let it out, and trotted into the ring.

"Go, DJ! Y'all can do it."

The Southern accent. She didn't dare look. Tony Andrada was in the stands and cheering for *her*.

DJ put everything out of her mind but the jumps ahead. She signaled Major and away they went. Plain fences, an oxer, three jumps of varying heights, an in and out, a brush. DJ thrilled to being airborne. She and Major were one. The rhythm of canter, thrust, fly, and land echoed in her heart. Perfect. Yes! This was what she wanted most in life.

They completed the round to a burst of applause. Two small voices screamed, "DJ! DJ!" A glance up at the stand told her the entire family was there, even Andy and Sonya with Shawna.

DJ bit her lip. They had *all* come to see her and Major. She rode out of the ring to their enthusiastic cheers.

"Way to go." Tony, on crutches, was the last to congratulate her.

"That was some jumping, kid, and, Major, you didn't look too bad yourself." Joe met her outside. He clapped one hand on DJ's knee and slapped the horse's shoulder with the other. "I'm so proud of you I could pop."

Amy trotted up. "That was great, DJ. And did you notice who is here?"

"I know. Tony. I can't believe it."

"And he was cheering for you—man, was he ever cheering. What do you think happened?"

"Got me." She stopped to listen. "Hilary's up next. I want to go watch."

"I'll take Major, you go on." Joe reached for the reins. "I already saw the jumper most important to me."

DJ blew him a kiss as she dismounted and ran for the arena.

Hilary jumped a flawless routine.

Tony Andrada shouted and cheered as if they were best friends.

"God must've done a miracle." DJ looked at Amy and shook her head. "I can't believe it."

Five people made it into the second round, DJ and Hilary included.

"I thought last time was bad—this is worse." Even under her gloves, a hangnail tempted DJ to chew it. She wouldn't make it around the arena again. She had to go to the bathroom.

The first entrant knocked a bar down. The second jumped clean.

DJ rode in third position. "Okay, fella, this is the test." With each clean jump, she felt more like she was flying. Up, airborne, and down. Major kept his ears forward and grunted with each landing. "One more." Thrust, fly, and—the tick echoed in her mind. She finished the course and exited to cheers, Tony one of the loudest.

DJ glanced up at her cheering sections—one made up of family, the other of academy riders.

The fourth entry's horse refused a jump. That left only Hilary.

Joe again held Major so DJ could watch. She stood with her hands behind her back, fingers crossed and prayers flying heavenward. Amy, right beside her, did the same.

Hilary and Prince jumped a clean round to the roar of the spectators. She'd have to go another. While the attendants raised the poles another two inches, DJ dashed outside.

"Don't worry, I'll stay here." Joe waved her back to the arena.

DJ felt as though she'd chew all her fingernails down to the quick. But with her fingers locked in a prayer, that would have been hard.

The first entry, a man, trotted into the ring. But, with a perfect round, he rushed the last jump. The pole wobbled and fell.

"Come on, Hilary. Even a tick will take it now. Do it, Hil, do it."

Hilary Jones jumped a perfect round.

DJ and Amy stamped their feet, pounded their hands together, and screamed at the top of their lungs.

"You've got to get your ribbon." Amy jabbed her friend with her elbow.

"Oh, right." DJ flew back out to mount Major. She followed the others back into the ring and accepted the third-place white ribbon. This time she didn't feel bad about not placing higher. A white ribbon in a group this size was fantastic.

When she stopped Major in front of Joe, she grinned at him. "Thanks for the horse, GJ."

"You're welcome." He let out a sigh as if he'd been swimming under water. "Let's go put this animal away, and I'll treat you to—I don't know, whatever they have over at that food room that looks good. I feel like I've been jumping those hurdles myself."

"DJ, I can't thank you and Amy enough. I'd have had to cancel without you." Hilary stopped her horse on the edge of the group.

"No problem. You'd have done the same for us."

"You did the same for me." Tony leaned on his crutches. "Bridget told me how you worked with my horse last night."

"It was nothing. That's the way we do things at Briones."

"Yeah, well . . . thanks."

DJ watched him hobble back to the arena. She shook her head. "Can you beat that?"

———

That afternoon after lunch, DJ took a breather from her showing and teaching duties. She joined her family in the stands and propped her elbows on the bench seat behind her.

"Want a cookie, darlin'?" Gran leaned over Joe to offer DJ a chocolate chip cookie.

"Yes, thank you." Joe took it and bit into it.

"Not you, you big galoot." Gran thumped him on the arm.

"You said darlin'." He winked at DJ and looked soulfully at Gran. "How was I to know which darlin' you meant?"

Gran dug in her box for another cookie. She shook her head at the clamoring Bs and handed it to DJ. "You'd think these characters hadn't already eaten half the box."

"Thanks, Gran." DJ munched and watched as Gran opened the box and let the boys each have another cookie. "You're a soft touch." She looked at Shawna sitting quietly on her other side. "Did you get any?"

The girl nodded. "DJ, you were awesome. You think I'll be able to ride like that someday?"

Andy groaned. "Next I suppose we'll have to buy a house out here, too."

"Really, Daddy?" Shawna's blue eyes lit up as if someone had just turned on a Christmas tree. "When?"

"We'll just send her to live with Robert and the boys." Sonya reached over Gran's shoulder and helped herself to a cookie. "How's your house coming?"

"Plans are finalized, now I just need approval from Contra Costa County. As soon as the permits are in my hand, my men'll go to work." Robert stretched his long legs over the seat in front of him. "Boys, no running." He snagged one of the Bs by the back of his shirt.

"Hey, Lindy, did you get approval for your thesis?" Sonya turned to ask.

"Probably Monday. It looks pretty safe."

DJ glanced at her mother. How come she hadn't told her daughter? You'd think that was good enough news to share. But DJ remembered back to the scene in the bedroom the night before. Probably her mother hadn't been thinking much about her thesis when she was crying over Robert. Grown-ups were so strange.

A shriek, cut off by a thud, derailed the thought. DJ leaped to her feet. But not before Lindy, who was closest to the edge of the bleachers. She was over the side and on the floor before anyone could blink.

By the time DJ got there, Lindy had the twin who'd taken a header off the bleachers cuddled in her arms, a gentle hand smoothing back hair already slick with blood.

"There now," she murmured, rocking him at the same time. "You'll be okay."

When Robert tried to take Bobby into his own arms, the little guy clung to Lindy.

Joe put a folded handkerchief on the streaming cut and held it in place, in spite of Bobby's turning away. "Robert, go get some ice. Don't worry, son, head wounds always bleed like crazy. He's all right—or will be once we get this stitched up."

Robert did as he was told, and DJ put her arms around Billy, who was crying just as hard. "Hey, you're not hurt."

Lindy carried the now hiccuping twin to the bleachers and sat with him on her lap. Blood stained her silk blouse and pants. She had a smear of blood across her cheek and more on her hands. When the ice came, she put the Ziploc bag against the wound and held it in place with her other hand.

DJ and Gran swapped grins. This was the woman who thought she couldn't be a mother?

"I knew she had it in her all along." Gran wrapped an arm around DJ's waist, patting the twins' legs in the same motion. Both twins had taken the same position, legs wrapped around the Randall who held them, cheeks into chests and arms around necks.

Later when DJ returned to the horse line, she thought about the look Robert had given Lindy and her charge as they'd gotten into his car to go to the emergency room. Gooey looks for sure.

———————

The next night, after the entire show was finished and the horses were all back in their proper stalls, the family gathered at Gran and Joe's for dinner. Bobby proudly showed everyone his five black-thread stitches.

Billy moped around, his lower lip stuck out.

"Come here, B, I have a surprise for you." DJ took his hand and led him into Gran's studio. She set him up on the table and picked up a drawing pencil. With deft strokes, she drew lines in the same spot as Bobby's.

He giggled.

"Now, let's check that out." She carried him into the bathroom so he could see himself in the mirror.

"I gots stitches, too." He smacked a kiss on her cheek. She set him down, and he dashed off announcing the change as he ran.

The look Robert gave her made DJ feel warm inside. It had been such a little thing. But then, little things were important to kids. She ought to know.

She strolled back into the living room and looked over at her mother. Lindy was just reaching up to hand Robert something. The diamond ring twinkled on her left hand.

DJ crossed the room and leaned over the back of her mother's chair. "So, is there something you need to tell all of us?"

"I wanted to tell you first." Lindy looked up over her shoulder. "Is it okay?"

"Fine with me. But what about being scared?"

"I learned that thinking about something that's coming is always worse than the actual event. With God's grace and a lot of love, I think we'll make it."

"Me too." DJ took her mother's hand. "Oh, and I better get a plan started if we're going to have a wedding."

She looked up to catch the twinkle in her grandmother's eyes and the slight shake of the white-crowned head. *That's right, Gran, no more plans. At least not for other people. Let them make their own.* She made an *O* with her thumb and forefinger and showed it to Gran.

Gran smiled and nodded.

But, then again, maybe just a teeny *little plan.*

Book Four

OUT OF THE BLUE

To Angie Ingalsbe,
my friend and encourager.
Someday I'll be reading your books
starring horses and kids.

Chapter • 1

Even in California, winter can be cold and wet.

DJ Randall sneezed, tempted to wipe her nose on her sleeve. Why hadn't she thought to bring a tissue? It would be nice if she could warm her frozen hands in her pockets, but that was tough to do when your horse's reins required two hands. Of course, it helped if the hands weren't shaking.

She glanced around to see if anyone was watching and quickly swiped her sleeve under her nose.

"Gross."

"Where'd you come from?"

"I was hiding behind the posts. What do you think?" Amy Yamamoto, DJ's best friend for all of their fourteen years, reined her gelding, Josh, next to Major. Tall DJ on the rangy bay and petite Amy on her compact sorrel kept alive the Mutt and Jeff nickname the two had earned.

Amy dug a tissue out of her jacket pocket. "Here."

"You're just like my mother."

"Hey, dweeb, you need a mother. How come we're working horses in the rain instead of home making fudge or something?"

"Popcorn sounds good."

"Fudge is better. Right now anything chocolate would be better."

Amy played turtle in her collar to stop the drips from her helmet from running down her neck. "Make that *hot* chocolate."

"It's not raining now." DJ glanced up at the dark gray sky hanging one story off the ground. A fat raindrop splattered in her eye. "So I was wrong. I'm going in—got more horses to groom."

"Lucky."

DJ signaled her Morgan-Thoroughbred, Major, to trot and circle the arena again. "Come on, fella, let's get this right so we can quit." She'd been working on rhythm to stride so that they would be more controlled in approaching jumps. She'd rather jump any day than work the flat, but today the outside jumping arena would be slippery, so flat work it was.

Flat is what DJ felt. Flat and wet. She gritted her teeth, ignored a shiver, and kept the beat of the trot. Major wanted to go to the barn as badly as she did. He snorted and picked up the pace every time they neared the gate.

"You want to stay out here all night?"

Major shook his head, and the droplets that had gathered on his mane sprayed her face.

DJ tightened the reins to bring him to a stop. She wrapped the reins around her wrist, dug the tissue out of her pocket, and blew her nose. Major's ears twitched at the honk, and he shifted his front feet. "Major, stand still." Her tone cut like a P.E. teacher barking orders. Major laid his ears back and twitched his tail. But he stood. They circled the ring once more, this time the beat perfect—no gaining, no slowing. Controlled.

"Why couldn't you do that fifteen minutes ago?" DJ leaned forward to open the gate. Major raised his head and nickered at the male figure just coming out of the barn door. "Oh, sure, say hi to Joe and spray me. Some friend you are." While she grumbled, DJ swung the gate open, kneed Major through, and swung the gate closed again. All the while, Major kept his eyes on the approaching figure.

"How you doing, kid?" Joe Crowder, recently married to DJ's widowed grandmother, stopped in front of them and stroked the bay's nose. "How you doing, old buddy? Did I see you giving DJ a hard time? You wouldn't do that, would you?"

"Yeah, right. Sure he wouldn't." DJ leaned forward and stroked her horse's neck. Joe had sold her Major when he had retired from the San Francisco mounted police, taking his horse with him.

Joe rubbed Major's ears, then down the white blaze. "He never did care much for rain all those years on the force. Can't say I blame him." Joe turned and walked beside them back to the barn. "You and Amy want a ride home?"

"Do dogs bark?"

"A simple yes would be fine." His smile crinkled the skin around his blue eyes. "You look like a drowned rat."

"Gee, thanks." DJ kicked her feet from the stirrups and dropped to the ground. "Ouch."

"Cold, huh?"

"Y-e-s." She caught her upper lip between her teeth. With the easy motions of long habit, she ran the stirrups up, unbuckled the girth, and swung flat saddle and pad off in one smooth swoop. Then, grabbing a grooming bucket, she led Major out to his stall in the covered but open pens. Joe's sorrel Quarter Horse, Rambling Ranger, nickered a greeting, as did Josh.

"Get a move on," Amy said from Josh's stall. "We're supposed to be home by dark, remember?"

"Joe's giving us a ride." DJ slipped the bridle off and fixed the blue web halter in place. "Thanks, GJ." She nodded toward the filled hay sling and the measured grain in the feed bucket.

"Any time, kid." Joe picked up a brush and began grooming Major's other side. "Your mother getting home tonight, or are you coming to our house?" DJ's mother, Lindy, sold bulletproof vests, Glock guns, and other supplies to law-enforcement agencies around northern California. When she wasn't doing that, she was working on getting her master's degree. Lately, though, much of her time went to Robert, Joe's son— and DJ's soon-to-be stepfather. The thought of having a father around seemed strange to DJ because she'd never met her birth father, didn't know who he was, and didn't care to. After the wedding, she'd have brothers, too—five-year-old twin dynamos named Bobby and Billy. She had yet to tell them apart.

"Mom said she'd be home, but I never know for sure until I see her or check for messages on the machine. Sure would be nice if she had dinner ready." Only since Joe and Gran had married and Gran moved to a new home had DJ learned what it was like to be a latchkey kid. Often she cooked the evening meal for both her and her mother.

Major munched his dinner with enthusiasm, sharing some with DJ through a slobbery snort in her face.

"Ugh." DJ brushed him away. "I love you, too, but sheesh." She sneezed and clamped her brush between her knees to retrieve her tissue. "I should have brought a box full." She blew her nose again and wrinkled her face. "If I'm catching a cold, I'll—"

"Don't say that. Say, 'I'm catching a healing.'" Amy slammed her gate closed and, bucket in hand, stopped at Major's stall.

"What?"

"My mom heard a former Miss America talk about catching a healing instead of catching a cold. She said it works."

"Oh, sure. When my eyes run as fast as my nose and I sneeze till I can't catch my breath, I'm supposed to say I'm catching a . . . a what?"

"Healing, darlin'. Makes perfect sense." Joe took the brushes out of her hands and dumped them into the bucket. He slapped Major a good-night and took DJ by the arm. "Hey, it's worth a try. Of course, prayer is the first defense, but the two might work well together."

"Now you sound like Gran." DJ let him lead her out of the stall. "Night, Major." The big horse followed them and hung his head over the gate. DJ gave him a last pat before trotting off to catch up to the others. "AACHOOO!" The sneeze nearly blew her head off.

"Repeat after me, 'I am catching a healing,'" Amy chanted.

"I ab cadching a coad," DJ insisted. She wiped her eyes and breathed through her mouth. At least that part of her face worked like it should.

"Stub-born," Joe said as he joined the girls at the wide doors leading to the front of Briones Riding Academy's long, low pole barn. The rain had turned to drizzle that sparkled like falling fireworks in the glow of the mercury yard light.

"You two get your bikes, and I'll bring the truck around." Joe gave DJ's shoulders a squeeze. "Hang in there, kid, and we'll get you and your healing home."

Amy chuckled beside her. Her black hair, held back in a scrunchy like the one in DJ's wavy blond hair, glistened in the light. "You sound worse all the time."

"Thank you, Dr. Yamamoto. How am I supposed to 'catch a healing' with you telling me how yucky I sound?"

"Sorry. It slipped out. Hey, I'm just telling you what my mom said."

DJ felt like slugging her but knew it would take too much effort.

With Joe's help, they loaded the bikes into the back of the Explorer. Both girls climbed into the front so they could share the seat and the heater on the short ride home. After dropping off Amy, they drove three houses down and into the empty drive. The kitchen window showed dark.

DJ groaned. Why couldn't her mother live up to her promises for once?

"Come on, let's go see if there's a message." Joe got out and retrieved DJ's bike from the back. He wheeled it up to the closed garage door. "Go open the door and let me in."

"All right." DJ forced herself to leave the warmth of the car and head up the walk to the front door. The wind blew right through her Windbreaker and sweat shirt, knifing into her chest. The shock made her cough, which made her sneeze. By now, the tissue was too worn out to be any use. She jammed the key in the door, but it wouldn't turn. "F-fiddle. D-double fiddle." DJ sniffed, retried the key, and wished she could call her mother a few names. Why couldn't she come home like she'd said? She shoved the key at the lock again. It wouldn't even go in the slot.

"Hey, hurry up over there."

"I'm trying." DJ turned the key over. This time it slipped right in, the lock turning as smoothly as if she'd just oiled it. *Always helps if you put the key in right.* She brightened as she stepped over the threshold. Since her mother wasn't home, she could go home with Joe and Gran. That would make her feel better. She trotted across the kitchen and punched the garage door opener by the back door. The blinking red light on the answering machine caught her attention as the garage door groaned its way upward.

She punched the button on the machine. "Sorry, DJ, but I had an unexpected appointment. I know you won't mind going to Gran's. Call Joe and he will come to get you."

"No need for that, I'm right here." Joe's voice sounded loud in the stillness.

"Let me change, and I'll go home with you."

"Bring your school clothes and books, too, just in case you're spending the night."

"Right." DJ leaped up the stairs to her room and gathered her things.

Amazing how much better she suddenly felt. She bounded back down to meet Joe at the front door.

"You got everything?"

"I think so." They stepped out and as DJ turned to pull the door closed, the phone rang. "Ohhh." She sighed and went back into the house.

Picking up the phone, she tried to sound as pleasant as her mother had drilled her. "Hello."

"Hello, I'd like to speak to Darla Jean Randall, please."

"Speaking." DJ cradled the phone on her shoulder. Who would be calling her? It was a man's voice after all. And he certainly didn't know enough not to call her Darla Jean. Only her mother could get away with that—and then only when she was mad.

There was a pause, then, "Darla Jean, my name is Bradley Atwood. I am your father."

Chapter • 2

A horse kick to the stomach couldn't have shocked DJ more.

"DJ, darlin', what's wrong?" Joe put an arm around her waist.

When did Joe learn to sound so much like Gran? DJ leaned against him gratefully. She shook her head and tried to speak. *Come on, DJ, this has got to be some sort of prank.* She cleared her throat.

"Wh-who are you really? Is this some kind of twisted joke?"

"I am who I said. Bradley Atwood. Your mother and I . . . ah . . . went together when we were in high school."

"*Went* together?" The words blurted out before she could stop them.

"Well . . . I guess it was more than that." Whoever he was, he sounded uncomfortable. He sighed. "Look, Darla Jean, is your mother there?"

"My name is DJ." She wanted to shout at him, scream, slam the phone down. Instead she clipped each sound as if he were hard of hearing.

"Oh, okay . . . DJ." Now he sounded like an adult humoring a kid. He paused, waiting for an answer.

DJ's hand cramped from its death grip on the phone. She looked up to see Joe, questions written all over his face, along with concern. He mouthed, Can I help? She shook her head.

"DJ, is Lindy there?"

"So you remember her name." The smart remark didn't help DJ to feel any better.

"Darla . . . ah . . . DJ, please."

"No, sir, she's not here. I will tell her you called, though. Please call back later." DJ set the receiver back in the cradle as if it were made of the finest eggshell. Only the focused action kept her from flinging it across the room.

"DJ, who was that? Talk to me." Joe clutched her shoulders in shaking hands.

DJ looked up into his eyes. "That was my *real* dad—or so he said."

"Oh, Lord above, be with us now," Joe breathed the prayer, then gathered her close.

DJ leaned into his strong chest. Good thing he was there, or she would be a puddle on the floor. *My dad.* Shock made her shiver.

Joe soothed her like he did the twins when one came to him with an owie. Gentle hands patted her back. "It'll be okay," he murmured. "DJ, it's going to be all right."

Suddenly she pushed herself upright. "Who does he think he is, calling like that? Just like we saw him yesterday. The jerk!" She stamped her way around the kitchen. "I don't need him. Mom doesn't need him. He didn't ever call or visit or anything. Why now? Who does he think he is, anyway?" She balled her hands into hard fists and pounded the counter. Feet stamping, arms waving, she circled the room again. "I don't need a dad now." She turned to Joe. "He didn't care for fourteen years, for pete's sake! Why now?"

"I wish I knew." Joe's voice introduced a note of calm.

DJ slammed the palms of her hands on the counter and stayed there, elbows rigid. "Why, Joe?" She raised stark eyes to his face. "Why?" she whispered again.

"How about you let your mother deal with that? Any idea when she'll be home?"

DJ tried to remember. She *had* listened to the phone messages. *Get with the program,* she told herself.

"Take it easy, kid, you've had a pretty major shock."

"Ain't that the truth." She sucked in a deep breath and let it out. Leaning back against the counter, she absentmindedly chewed on the cuticle of her forefinger. When she realized what she was doing, she jerked it away. "Fiddle. Double, triple, and . . . and ten times fiddle!" Her hands cried out to do something. Slamming counters hurt. So instead, she rubbed the scar in the palm of her right hand.

"Keep talking to me, darlin'."

"You say 'darlin'' just like Gran."

"You mind?"

DJ shook her head. "I like it." She sighed again. "Guess there's nothing I can do about this, is there?"

"Pray. That's all I can do. It's the only thing that keeps me from finding out where this man lives and going there to beat the tar out of him."

Startled, DJ looked up. "You'd do that?"

"Gotta use the skills I learned at the police academy in some way." He grinned at her, then grew serious. "No, DJ, I wouldn't touch him, no matter how much I think he deserves it. But I want you to know that anyone who hurts my family has me to deal with." He jabbed a thumb at his chest.

DJ studied the big man across the kitchen. "You know what? I'm glad you're on my side."

"And I'm glad to be on your side. But let's listen to your mother's message again."

DJ shook her head. "I erased it, but I know she said she wasn't sure when she'd be home. I guess my mind's starting to work again."

"Okay, leave her a message, then let's head for home. Melanie will be getting worried."

It still caught DJ's attention when he called Gran, Melanie. All she'd ever been to DJ was Gran. "Gran will know what to do." DJ paused. "Won't she?" On the way out the door, she wrote her mother a note and attached it to the bulletin board with a stickpin.

But Gran didn't know what to do, and when Lindy finally came to pick up her daughter, the fireworks began.

DJ watched her mother do much the same as she had—pace, yell, wave her arms. Now, sitting on the floor at her grandmother's feet with Gran's hand stroking her hair, she felt as if nothing could get to her. She leaned against her grandmother's knees and sighed.

"Do you have to call him back?"

"Not in this lifetime." Lindy clamped manicured hands on slim hips and spun around to face them. Her dark blond hair, each chin-length strand in perfect order, swung across her cheek. She hooked the curve of it over one ear, sparks flashing from her emerald eyes. The frown lines she fought so diligently deepened. "Well, Mother, what do we do now? You were the last one to talk with him."

"That was over thirteen years ago." Gran kept her hand on DJ's hair.

"I know. And I thought the agreement was that I would never ask him for support and he would never ask to see his daughter."

"It was. You both agreed to that. You were two kids who'd made some less-than-perfect choices; you each wanted to get on with your life, to move forward without any anger between you."

"I remember."

"I know you do, darlin', I just want to refresh your memory." Gran looked to Joe, who nodded at her. "I think we got the better end of the deal by a long shot because we got Darla Jean. Brad's missed out on a lot."

"Whose side are you on, Mother?" Lindy crossed to the sofa and sank down on it, resting her elbows on her knees. She still wore a cream-colored silk suit she had dressed in for work. "You aren't saying I should call him back, are you?"

"I'm saying we need to look at the whole picture and all the people in it. We should always treat others with the respect and love with which we want to be treated. You desperately loved Brad at one time, and he loved you the same."

"I know." Lindy rubbed her temples with her fingertips. "We were so young."

DJ watched and listened as if this were the best movie ever filmed. And she was a part of it. This was her father they were talking about. Now she understood why she'd never heard about him.

"And now you're adults."

A silence, heavy with meaning, filled the room.

DJ tried to decide what she was feeling. Angry? Nope—or at least, not any longer. Scared? A bit. Curious? Big yes. She flashed a look up at Gran and received a loving one back.

I am so lucky. The thought floated into her mind and took hold. She looked up to see Joe watching her. A nod accompanied the gentle smile that barely turned up the corners of his mouth. DJ knew down deep in her heart that he wore the look of love. And it was for her.

"DJ, did you write down his number?"

DJ jerked back into the conversation and stared at her mother. *Number? Whose number?*

"Did you get Brad's number, darlin'?" Gran whispered.

DJ shrugged. "Ah . . . no. I asked him to please call back later. Sorry, I just wasn't thinking straight."

Lindy started to say something, then just shook her head. "Guess I wouldn't be thinking too clearly in a situation like that, either."

DJ looked at her mother as if she'd left a marble or two at work. *A few minutes ago, she was yelling all over the place. Now she's actually being nice. What's up?*

"That answers it, then. We wait until Brad calls back." Gran gave DJ a last pat and got to her feet. "Good thing I turned off that oven, or we'd all be eating peanut butter and jelly sandwiches for dinner." She took DJ's hand and pulled her up. "Come on, you can set the table."

After dinner, DJ and her mother drove home without saying a word. When they got to the house, Lindy checked the answering machine, but the red light lay dark. She sighed. "I'm going to call Robert. Darla Jean, I know this is hard for you. I'd give anything if Brad hadn't called, but he did, and we'll deal with it. Please don't worry about it, okay?"

DJ nodded. She kept thinking of the verse Gran had whispered in her ear as she went out the door. Gran had shared it before. It was one of those in Romans DJ had underlined. *In all things God works for the good of those who love him, who have been called according to his purpose.* She'd never quite understood the last part, but the first seemed pretty clear: God could bring good out of everything.

DJ eyed her mother, who still looked pale and upset. "Don't you worry, either, Mom, okay?"

"Easier said than done," Lindy muttered. "Night, DJ. If he calls again and you answer the phone, try to get his number."

It was DJ's turn to nod. How could she have messed up like that?

When she finally snuggled under her covers to say her prayers, everything was fine—until she tried to say "amen." The word wouldn't come. She lay thinking, *God, what is it?* Often she wished He would talk to her like He had to Moses in the Old Testament. Loud and clear. But, as usual, He was silent. She sighed and flipped over. A thought trickled into her mind. *Pray for your father.*

DJ shot up so quickly, her covers flew off. "Pray for my father—you have *got* to be kidding!" She flopped back down and stared at the ceiling. Why would she do a stupid thing like that?

Why not?

She gnawed on her lip. So maybe it wasn't a big deal. She could just say "bless him" and "take care of him" and—she thought of Gran. Gran would laugh at her right now, that loving laugh that made DJ feel good.

"Godblessmyfather." It was hard to talk through gritted teeth. She sucked in a breath. "But I want to remind you, God, I really don't need another father. I'm going to have Robert, remember?" DJ bit her lip again. "Amen." Why couldn't she say that before?

She woke up crying in the middle of the night.

Chapter • 3

Someone was screaming.

"DJ, what is it?" Lindy entered the room in a rush. "Are you all right?"

"Huh?" DJ pulled herself out of the fog of sleep. Her throat hurt.

"You were screaming. Are you okay? What's wrong?"

DJ shook her head. "Someone was chasing me—I couldn't see who. I fell off the road and just kept falling." She clutched her aching head with both hands. Her heart felt like it would leap out of her chest. She sucked in a deep breath, but it didn't stop the pounding.

Lindy sat down on the edge of the bed. "Can I get you anything?" With one hand, she stroked DJ's shoulder.

"My head hurts." How come she felt like throwing herself into her mother's arms and bawling like a baby? DJ never did anything like that—crying was for babies.

"Let me get you some pain reliever." Lindy got up to leave, and just the movement of the bed made DJ feel like heaving. Was this what her mother's migraines felt like? How did she stand them?

But when she lay down again after her mother's ministrations, DJ felt herself drifting back into the freaky dream. It wasn't supposed to work that way. She forced her eyes open and turned on her bedside lamp. The five gold Olympic rings on the poster above her dresser gleamed in the light. *That* was the dream she lived for. Someday, she, DJ Randall, would jump in the Olympics. She would go for the gold as a member of the U.S. Equestrian Team.

DJ reached over and turned out the light again. This time, horses, horses, and more horses, all with her aboard, mastered the jumps with flying tails and happy grunts.

Rain sheeted her window when she awoke. She slapped off the alarm and sat up, leaning her head first on one shoulder, then the other. She still had the feeling that if she moved too quickly, the headache would return.

"Yuck." She hauled herself from her bed, feeling sticky and heavy. Once in the bathroom she knew why. Her pajama bottoms wore splotches of dull red. Her heart quit thundering in her ears as she realized she wasn't bleeding to death. Her first period. One more thing to deal with! She groaned. As if yesterday's events hadn't been enough.

She stared at the pale face in the mirror. Her shoulder-length blond hair hung in strings about her face. Someone had painted black circles under her green eyes, and a zit beaconed on her chin.

"I'm going back to bed." DJ fumbled under the sink for the box of pads her mother had forced on her months ago. If this was growing up, someone sure had screwed up the program. She reached to turn on the shower. If she didn't go to school, she wouldn't be going to the Academy, either. That was the rule. Since DJ was almost never sick, that hadn't been a problem very often. She'd only stayed home when Gran insisted.

Instead of turning off the hot handle, she added the cold and stepped under the needle spray.

It could have been the shortest shower on record. Calling Joe for a ride to school because she'd missed the Yamamoto bus would be embarrassing. She fixed herself up, donned her one pair of black jeans, and grabbing a food bar, headed out the door on the second honk.

"Gross," Amy said with a wrinkled nose when DJ filled her in on the morning's happenings. The two sat in the second seat of the station wagon since Amy's brother, John, said the front seat was for those about to learn to drive. They didn't mind—that way, if they talked low, they could catch up on all that happened without the others hearing.

"Yeah, and that's not the half of it." DJ filled her friend in on the cataclysmic call of the night before. By the time she'd finished, they were at Acalanese High School, where they were both freshmen.

"Thanks, Dad." DJ waved as she slammed the door. Mr. Yamamoto, head of the volunteer parents for the Academy, told all the kids to call him Dad. Insisted it was easier that way.

DJ pulled her jacket over her head to keep dry and dashed after Amy. It looked like it would rain forever.

The day didn't improve much. Her history teacher finished the far from perfect morning by calling a pop quiz.

"Think I'll go eat worms," she muttered when she met Amy at their locker at lunchtime.

"Now what?"

"No lunch money."

"So share mine. I'll grab an extra salad."

"I'm starved."

"Ask if you can charge."

"I'd rather eat worms."

"Fine, be a grouch, but that's not like you."

"Maybe it's my turn." DJ dumped her books on the bottom of the locker and slung her backpack in on top. She felt like slamming the metal door and banging her fists on it. Instead she let Amy shut it and followed her friend into the lunchroom.

Thanks to Amy sharing her food, DJ's stomach quit growling. By the end of classes, she felt almost human again. Of course, the thought of Major and the Academy had nothing to do with that. Even if it was pouring, they could ride under cover.

"What are you going to do?" Amy asked as they waited outside under the overhang for Joe to arrive.

"About what?"

"Your father, silly."

"Got me. I don't have to do anything till he calls, and maybe he won't." She waved at the man driving the hunter green Explorer. "I hope he doesn't."

She answered Joe's questioning look with a shake of her head. But while it was easy to pretend to shrug the whole mess off on the outside, inside the questions raged. *What kind of man is my father? What does he do? Is he married? Do I have half brothers and sisters?*

She changed clothes in record time and hopped back into the car to go to the Academy. All the way there, the temptation to chew on her fingernails burned like a hot curling iron. To keep from giving in, she sat on her hands. *I can do all things through Christ who strengthens me. I can do all things.* Gran had given her the verse to help her overcome chewing her fingernails. They'd made a pact that if Gran could find a verse that could apply to chewing fingernails, DJ would try to stop. So far it was working. DJ even had to file her nails once in a while.

At the Academy, she checked the white erasable duty board and saw that the outside rings were unusable—too wet. That was no surprise, the way the rain had been coming down. Since the outside work was curtailed, the Academy employees had cleaned stalls and groomed the boarded horses.

"Yes!" She pumped her right arm. That meant more time to work with Major. But first she had to spend her hour working Patches, the green broke gelding she'd been training for Mrs. Johnson.

"I should put you on the hot walker," she told the fractious gelding. He rubbed his forehead against her shoulder, leaving white hairs on her black sweat shirt. "I know, you're just trying to soften me up." But she couldn't resist his pleading and gave him an extra carrot chunk from the stash she kept in the tack room refrigerator. Patches lipped the carrot from her palm, munched, and blew carrot breath in her face.

DJ attacked his heavier winter coat with brushes in both hands. By the time she had combed the tangles out of his tail and picked his hooves, she'd been over the questions in her mind for the umpteenth time. She tacked him up and led him to the wide open front door of the barn. The rain blew in sheets across the parking area.

"You sure you want to go out in that?" David Martinez, one of the older student workers, asked from the tack room. "You'll get soaked just crossing to the covered arena."

"I know." DJ led her mount to the door of the tack room. "Hand me that slicker up on the nail, would you please?"

David did as asked, shaking his head. "I skipped my workout, put my horse on the hot walker, and called it good."

"I thought about it but . . ." She finished buttoning the yellow slicker and placed her foot in the stirrup. "Okay, fella," she said, swinging into the Western saddle. "Let's do it."

Patches balked at the gate. "You sure aren't Major," DJ muttered as she dismounted to open and close it when he finally consented to go through. Mounting into a wet saddle seat did nothing to improve her humor. "You know, Patches, if I didn't like you, I'd have left you in the barn." The gelding's ears flicked back and forth as he listened to her and checked out the arena. The rain had brought on an early dusk, so the overhead lights cast deep shadows in the corners.

DJ kept a firm grip on the reins and paid close attention to her horse. He felt like a coiled spring. She walked him around the ring, letting him get used to the arena. At last, he let out a breath and played with the bit, a sure sign he'd settled down. DJ could feel her shoulders and spine relax along with him. They settled into a jog, and for a change, Patches minded, keeping the even pace he usually fought so hard.

"What's with you today? You finally decide to be a trained mount instead of an ornery one?" Patches snorted and kept the pace. DJ nudged him into a lope, and after a few pounding steps, he settled into the rocking-chair rhythm that was such a pleasure to sit. When she pulled him back down and turned him counterclockwise, he tried to move to the center of the ring, but at DJ's insistence he went back to the rail.

So what if Brad never calls? The questions started again. DJ laid the reins over, shifted her weight, and Patches danced up the ring, changing leads like a ballroom dancer.

"DJ?"

Without warning, Patches exploded beneath her. One stiff-legged jump, as if the horse was starring in a rodeo, and DJ catapulted right over his head.

Chapter • 4

Thought one: *Patches, you're dead meat.*

Thought two: *When I can breathe again, that is. If I can ever breathe again.*

"DJ, are you all right?" Krissie, one of her beginning students, knelt in the dirt beside her.

DJ spit out a chunk of dirt and rolled to a sitting position. One knee burned, and her chest hurt—getting the breath knocked out of you did that. Most of all, though, her pride felt like she'd landed squarely on it.

"I'll be fine." She leaned her head from side to side and sucked in a deep breath through her mouth. She gagged and choked on another chunk of dirt—at least, she hoped it was only dirt. Pulling a tissue from her pocket, she blew her nose, smearing more dirt in the process. The mess showed on the soggy tissue.

Krissie let out a wail. "It's all my fault. If I hadn't called to you . . ."

DJ shook her head. "I know better than to take my mind off Patches. He was just waiting for a chance to—that no-good, rotten hunk of horse meat. Where is he?"

"Running around the arena like he lost his mind." Krissie put a hand under DJ's arm to help her up.

Keep cool, DJ ordered herself. *How could I let that fool horse dump me? This has got to be the worst day of my life.*

DJ brushed the dirt off her jeans and turned to look for Patches. Good thing the gates had been closed, or he'd be out loose in Briones State Park or on the road by now. She gingerly took off her helmet and glanced at Krissie. Fat tears welled in her eyes, and her chin quivered.

"Hey, forget it. Remember the day you took a header?" The girl nodded. "Did you get really hurt?" Krissie shook her head. "It can happen to any rider, no matter how long you've been working with horses. You have to be careful all the time." DJ tried to keep the grumble out of her voice, but she wanted to scream and pound the fence. Or Patches.

"Go get ready for your lesson. I'll get that crazy horse."

Krissie hesitated as though she had more to say, but at DJ's frown, she trotted off.

DJ strode across the arena. When she got close, Patches threw up his head and charged past her. She tried to grab his reins but missed. Calling him every name she could think of and a few she invented, she stomped across the parking lot, the rain dripping down the neck of her slicker.

In the tack room, she found a can and scooped some grain, then rushed back across the lot to the arena, her jeans sticking to her legs. By now, Patches was having a grand time evading David.

"Patches!" DJ rattled the feed can.

The horse skidded to a halt, ears pricked. She walked toward him as he tentatively moved toward her, nose extended so he could sniff to check that she wasn't tricking him. DJ knew better than to scold him before she had a hand on his reins, so she called him names in a gentle, wheedling tone. "You stupid beast. I could brain you, you know. If I have to get someone else to help me, you are going to be very, very sorry."

Patches stopped just far enough away that she couldn't reach his reins. Good thing she'd knotted them for Mrs. Johnson, or he'd have stepped on one and broken it. That could have hurt his mouth—and all because she wasn't paying attention. DJ shifted the name-calling to herself.

"Hey, DJ, having trouble with your horse?" Tony Andrada, his drawl proclaiming his Southern ancestry, leaned crossed arms on his horse's withers. For a while, she and Tony had really mixed it up over the rotten way he had treated her friend Hilary Jones. But lately things had been at least civil.

Except for now.

The daggers DJ shot him should have knocked him bleeding from his horse. "Why don't you go find a canyon and fall into it?"

"Whoa." Tony raised his hands and leaned backward. "S-o-r-r-y." He turned his horse away. "Just thought I could help."

DJ stood still and shook the can to rattle the grain. Patches sniffed as she dug out a handful and held it out to him. He snorted, stepped forward, lipped the grain, and reached for the can.

DJ clamped a firm hand on the reins and handed the can to David. "Here, you take this. A hammerhead like him doesn't deserve a treat." Without offering pats or soft words, she swung aboard and ordered Patches into a slow jog, the gait he hated the most. Once around the ring and she reversed, made him back up, ran through some figure eights, and headed for the gate. "Good boy." Her compliment didn't sound any friendlier than her name-calling had been.

Good thing Bridget Sommersby was gone for the day. Telling her later wouldn't be nearly as humiliating as having her watch. The owner of Briones Riding Academy had become DJ's mentor.

DJ's three girl students—Krissie, Angie, and Samantha—were riding their horses around the arena at a walk when DJ returned after putting Patches away.

DJ was in no mood to give a lesson, but since no one was asking, she gritted her teeth. On top of feeling like she'd been slugged, a case of cramps had hit in full force. Add a headache on top of that, and DJ felt like chewing nails and spitting them out machine-gun style. She rubbed her forehead. Add to the mess a new—or rather old—father, a rambunctious horse, and students who were looking at her as though she'd sprouted horns. She felt like she was trapped in the picture book Bobby and Billy, the Double Bs, loved so much—this was truly a terrible, no good, awful, very bad day. Or something like that.

She sucked in a deep breath and winced. Her ribs hurt. "Okay, kids, let's pick up the pace. Take a lesson from me and keep your concentration on what you're doing. Let's see a good ride." She watched them closely.

"Come on, Angie—back straight, relax your shoulders. Krissie, who's in control over there?" The criticisms came a little too easily. "Samantha, keep those reins even. You're confusing your horse."

By the time the lesson was over, the girls looked like whipped puppies. They quickly filed out of the gate into rain that hadn't let up an iota.

"Boy, were you hard on them or what?" Amy reined up beside DJ. She'd been circling at the far end of the arena for some time.

"Oh, knock it off. I wasn't either."

"Ex-c-u-s-e me." Amy looked closely at her friend. "You're a mess."

"Thanks a big fat lot." DJ turned and stomped through the puddles to the barn. Maybe riding Major would make her feel better. When she walked by the girls unsaddling their horses, they peeked at her out of the corners of their eyes. No playful chatter, no teasing.

DJ stopped. "Look, I get the feeling I've been a grouch. I'm sorry. You all did fine out there."

It was as if the sun came out right there in the barn.

"Are you feeling all right?" Angie asked, always sensitive to other people's pain since she managed so much of her own.

DJ shook her head. "But that's not your problem."

"Did you get hurt hitting the ground?" Krissie's blue eyes were still troubled.

"No. Unless you call smacked pride hurt. Come on, kids, your mothers will be here soon and you need to wipe your saddles." DJ mentally added guilt to the load she was lugging around like a full feed sack.

Major greeted her with a nicker that could be heard the length of the roofed stalls. Rain drummed steadily on the corrugated fiber glass sheets overhead. Only the lights strung along the ceiling beam kept the dusk out of the stalls.

"Hi, fella. Sure glad someone is happy to see me." She dug half of a horse cookie out of her slicker pocket. "I saved this for you." She sneezed and hunted for a tissue.

Major took his treat and munched, nosing her face and shoulders at the same time. Alfalfa grain mixed with molasses smelled good to DJ, but horse smelled even better. She inhaled the horsey perfume and leaned her forehead against Major's neck. Joe had already cleaned the stall and given Major a good grooming. *If I hadn't fooled around with Patches, I would have been here doing my own work. That dumb horse. I better remind Mrs. Johnson to put him on the hot walker.* DJ sighed and rubbed her head again. If this was what migraines felt like, no wonder her mother was a bear at times.

"Come on, fella, let's get going." She snapped the lead shank on to his blue nylon halter and, unhooking the gate, led him through.

Joe met her halfway down the aisle as he returned from working Ranger. "You okay, kid?"

"I will be."

"Heard you took a fall."

"Yeah. Later, okay?"

She could feel Joe's gaze drilling into her back as she led Major to the tack room. The girls were gone and the evening hush that came just before the adults arrived had settled on the barn. DJ put her arms around Major's neck and leaned against him. His warmth felt wonderful as it penetrated through her clothing. "What would I do without you? You big sweetie, you."

Major turned and nudged her shoulder as if to say, Come on, let's get riding. DJ hugged him again and went to get her tack. If riding Major didn't make her feel better, nothing would.

"You want to talk about it?" Joe asked on the way home.

"I'm fine." DJ dug at the snag on her cuticle.

"Sure, and I'm Madonna." Amy gave her a sour look.

"Just bug off, will ya?" The moment she said them, DJ wished she could snap the words back into her mouth. She could feel the looks Amy and Joe were swapping. No one dared to say anything more to her. Amy thanked Joe as she quickly hopped out of the truck.

"You want to come home with me?" Joe asked.

DJ shook her head. The dark house would fit the way she felt. "No, I think I'll just go to bed."

"DJ, did you get hurt out there?"

She shook her head. *How could she tell him that she felt like yuck?* She could feel the heat on her cheeks. He was a guy, for pete's sake. She needed Gran or her mother, and neither one of them was here. She felt like bawling. How stupid!

"I'll be fine. Thanks for the ride." She bailed out and dashed up the sidewalk, waving over her shoulder. She entered the kitchen to find the red eye on the answering machine blinking.

Did she dare ignore it? Habit and her mother's drilling made her punch the button. Message one: "I'll be home later, I have a pile of paper work to clear up here." Message two: "Sorry you're not there, Darla Jean and Lindy. I will call back later." DJ recognized the voice immediately. This time, Mr. Brad Atwood gave a phone number and invited them to return his call.

"I don't need you," she growled at the phone. She punched the Save button hard, as if trying to poke a hole in the machine. "You didn't need me all these years, and now I don't need you."

DJ stormed up the stairs and, after downing some ibuprofen in the bathroom, shucked her clothes and crawled into bed. Her wrist throbbed. If she never had another day like today, it would be too soon.

Chapter • 5

DJ's pride turned out to be the only lasting injury. Having to apologize for being a jerk the day before didn't make it better.

Amy shrugged. "Forget it. I knew you weren't your usual self. You were crazy." She sat her Western saddle down on its horn by her stall and gave Josh a pat on the nose. "See you in the ring."

"You nut!" DJ called over her shoulder. One good thing about riding English, the saddles were lighter. She opened the door to Major's stall, pushing him aside so she could squeeze in. "Hi, guy. Looks like Joe's been here." Major nuzzled her pocket. "I know, you need a treat." She dug out a carrot and stroked his forelock while he chewed. "You are so cool."

"He is, isn't he?" Joe stopped at her stall. Ranger nickered in the next box. "I'm coming, buddy."

Joe saddled the gelding and rode into the covered arena with DJ. Major pricked his ears, aware of everything around him, and settled into an easy trot that didn't even require posting. DJ could feel herself relax. Riding or even working with Major was as different from her time with Patches as birds from bumblebees.

"You've really been working with him," DJ said with a nod toward Ranger.

"Every afternoon. Except today."

"What was today?" DJ leaned forward and stroked Major's neck.

"I . . . ah—well, I checked up on Bradley Atwood."

"You what?" Major snorted at DJ's shift in position. "Easy, fella."

"I had a friend look him up in the computers, that's all. He has a clean record, owns quite a bit of land up in Santa Rosa, and has a sizable bank account."

DJ stopped Major so she could focus on what Joe was saying. "You really ran a check?"

Ranger sidestepped, wanting as always to be moving. "Yes, and your grandmother is not happy with me—or at least, that's what she claims."

"I bet. Why'd you do it?"

"Just to be safe." Joe nudged Ranger forward.

"Well, I'll be." DJ stroked Major's neck and loosened her reins. Joe was watching out for her. Major settled back into his trot, and they circled the ring. When he was warmed up, she signaled a canter. If only they were riding up in Briones. Since the rain had begun—a hundred years ago, it seemed—she and Amy hadn't ridden up in the hills.

DJ slowed the pace and rode with Amy awhile, then with Hilary. "This is like warming up before a show," DJ said with a grin.

"Yep, only without the pressure. You missing jumping as much as I do?" Hilary asked.

"Yeah, but have you looked out at that arena? Pure slop in spite of all the sand."

"I know. Maybe we could move the jumps in here. At least a couple of them."

"Bridget won't go for that."

"She did one year when it was like this. I'll ask her tomorrow. How's the dressage coming?" Hilary ran a loving hand over her horse's mane, smoothing an errant strand.

"Haven't started. Bridget's been gone and now that we're without any extra arenas, she asked if I would wait to begin. I've been working Major on the flat. He sure learns fast. Faster'n I do."

"You'll get it eventually, but it's not like jumping. Dressage takes lots and lots of drilling."

"Sounds like what I'm doing with jumping, only without ever being airborne."

Hilary's teeth showed extra white against her dark skin. "You and

I like the same things. But, hey, I've got to get home. Tests tomorrow." She lifted a hand in a wave. "See ya."

"Yeah, later." DJ took Major down to the far end of the arena and began working him in a tighter circle. She might as well work him on bending. You could never do too much of that.

"See you tomorrow," Joe said when they reached her house. "I see the boys are here."

DJ groaned. "That means I'm late." She glanced at the clock on the dashboard. "Or they're early."

"Have fun."

Each twin glommed on a leg when she entered the house. DJ reached down and hugged first one, then the other.

"We was waiting for you." "Daddy said you could come help us pick out the pizza." "I want to ride." "How's Major?" The boys had a habit of talking on top of each other. Even after all these months, DJ still couldn't tell Bobby and Billy apart. Blond, curly hair topped both round faces, identical blue eyes smiled up at her, and they never stood still long enough to see if one was taller or not. To save time, DJ had nicknamed her soon-to-be brothers the Double Bs.

"Okay, guys, give DJ a chance to breathe." Robert Crowder, a slightly taller and good deal younger version of his father, Joe, came to her rescue. "I thought maybe we would just eat out. What do you think?"

"Fine with me. Where's Mom?"

"She called from her car—should be here in a minute or two." The cellular phone in her mother's car was a gift from Robert. He said he liked knowing she was safe, especially with all the time Lindy spent on the road.

"Good, I'll change then."

"We help you." The boys took her hands. "Hurry, we's hungry."

"Nope, guys, young ladies don't need little boys to help them dress." Robert tucked a squirming body under each arm and headed for the family room. "I know there's a favorite book of yours here."

"We want Arthur and his terrible, awful . . ."

DJ shut the bedroom door on their unison voices. What would it be like after the wedding when they all lived in one house? How would she put up with them underfoot all the time?

She changed with amazing speed—her mother didn't appreciate the rich stable smells that clung to DJ after a day at the Academy. She picked up her boot and checked the bottom. Sure enough, that's what she'd been smelling. She should have known to leave her boots in the garage. Probably left bits of horse manure all through the house.

But nothing was said when Lindy arrived home, and they had a great time at the pizza parlor. DJ took the boys to watch the cooks make pizza, then fed quarters into the horse for them. She'd rather get them up on Bandit again so they could learn to ride a real horse. If only they could buy Bandit. She'd borrowed the Welsh pony several times for the little kids to ride when they had family gatherings. Robert had promised the boys ponies and dogs as soon as they moved into the house he was remodeling over by Gran's. While it wouldn't be ready before the wedding in February, it would be soon after.

"The pizza's here." Both boys dashed back to the table. They bowed their heads and said grace before digging in.

DJ sneaked a peak at her mother. While they'd always said grace when Gran lived with them, Lindy didn't much care for it. She said she'd leave the praying to Gran—she had enough to worry about.

With one twin on either side of her, DJ didn't have time to think during the meal.

"DJ, when can we ride Major?"

"When you are bigger."

"We's bigger now. Can we ride tomorrow?"

"I don't think so." She took a bite of warm pizza and caught the thread of cheese with one finger. As she wound it around and stuck it into her mouth, she glanced at her mother. And flinched. Caught in the act. How come her mother was always looking when DJ did something silly?

Bobby and Billy both stuck their fingers in the cheese and did the same.

"Hey, guys, don't do that."

"You did."

DJ could feel her mother's withering look. And it didn't feel good.

Chapter • 6

"I think you should see your father," Lindy said two evenings later.

"You gotta be crazy! Why would I do that?" DJ could feel her jaw hit her chest. "You said I wouldn't have to."

"I know. I've changed my mind." Lindy sank back against the sofa as if she could no longer hold up her head. She rubbed her forehead, and the telltale gesture warned DJ that her mother was bordering on a migraine.

DJ watched her mother, hoping for a change of heart. "I talked with him on the phone. Wasn't that enough?"

"For thirty seconds?" Her mother's eyebrows lifted slightly, and she gave a minute head shake.

DJ clamped her mouth shut on all the things she wanted to say. Granted, she'd prayed for *him*, but only because the Bible said to. After all, she'd told Gran, wasn't she supposed to pray for her enemies? Gran had chuckled when DJ turned that verse on her.

But was Brad Atwood an enemy?

"So, will you?"

"Will I what?" DJ brought her mind back to the present.

"Darla Jean, please pay attention. This is extremely important."

DJ nodded.

"I am asking you to agree to see your father. He would like to come here to visit."

"I don't have to go to his house?"

"No, not until you want to."

"What if I don't ever want to?" The urge to chew her fingernails made DJ bite her bottom lip instead.

"I don't know yet what the legal ramifications might be. The way the laws read today, Brad could force the issue." Lindy rubbed her head again. A lock of hair swung forward on her left cheek, and she absent-mindedly pushed the wayward hair back over her ear.

"Mom, he never paid any attention to us all these years. How come he can just drop in and make me see him?"

"I don't know." Lindy looked her daughter full in the face. "DJ, have I ever said anything to make you hate your father?"

DJ shook her head. "We never even talked about him. I guess I figured he died or something. I liked our life the way it was—Gran and you and me. I never needed a dad."

"But didn't you question why we never mentioned him?"

"Once or twice I wondered, but it was no big deal." DJ sank into the soft wing chair that had always been Gran's. "Guess I thought more about getting a horse than getting a dad." She studied the cuticle on her right forefinger. *I will not bite it off. I can do all things.* "What does Robert say about all this?"

"He's the one who suggested you see Brad."

"Tell him thanks a big fat bunch. I thought he wanted to be my dad."

"He did and he does. Nothing has changed there. He and the boys are coming over for dinner tomorrow as a matter of fact." When DJ groaned, she added, "Robert's bringing the dinner."

"Oh, good, then. I don't have time to cook and neither do you. And if this rain doesn't let up, I'll be so far behind in jumping Major, I'll have to start all over again."

"So you'll see Brad?" Her mother hung on to the subject like a starving dog to a bone.

"All right!" DJ wrinkled her forehead and thumped her hands on the arms of her chair. "But I don't have to like him."

"But you'll be polite." It wasn't a question.

DJ stuck her finger in her mouth and bit off the troublesome cuticle snag.

"DJ."

She made a face. Now her finger stung, and she could see blood rising to the surface. She sighed. "Yes, Mother, I will be polite. When is he coming?"

"Sunday afternoon."

"Sunday afternoon! Why didn't you check with me first? If it's not raining, I want that time to work Major."

"This is slightly more important than one workout."

"That's what you—" DJ clamped her mouth closed.

"I'm not asking you to sell your horse, for crying out loud. As important as this is, it will only take a couple of hours to do. Gran and Joe will be here, too."

"So Joe can beat him up?"

"Darla Jean Randall, if you would be so kind—"

"I'm leaving. I'll be in my room studying if you decide this is all a horrible mistake."

"Good night, DJ."

DJ climbed the stairs, feeling like she was dragging the world behind her. She glanced out her bedroom window and grew more discouraged. Rain pocked the miniature lake in their backyard and roared in their downspouts. Was this what Noah had felt like? How'd he handle forty days and nights like this?

She thought of an idea and barreled out of her room and down the stairs. "How about if I just call and talk with him? I could do that."

Lindy nodded. "That's a start. Then you can decide if you want him to come on Sunday or not."

"No question there," DJ muttered under her breath.

———

The next afternoon in English class, DJ groaned along with the rest of the kids.

"You want us to do what?" one of the boys moaned.

"You are all going to begin keeping journals. The purpose of this assignment is to write something every day to get in touch with what is going on inside of you."

"My insides want food."

The class snickered.

DJ felt like putting her head down on her desk and groaning, too.

How was she going to write in a notebook every day? She had too much to do already. She tuned back in to what the teacher was saying.

"There are many ways of keeping journals. Famous people all through history have kept journals—it is one of the ways we know what life was like way back when. Thomas Jefferson kept a journal, as did Ben Franklin."

"How about some women?" asked a girl.

"Many did. There are collections of journals kept by the women who traveled the Oregon Trail. Abigail Adams never failed to write in hers. However, the one I want you all to read is more current than those and was written by a young girl about your age. When you read her journal, you will get an intimate picture of a Jewish girl hiding from the Nazis during World War II. There's a new version out now that contains entries not published in the earlier. Have any of you read *The Diary of Anne Frank*?

DJ raised her hand. Not too many others did.

"How many of you have seen the movie?"

DJ kept her hand up.

"Good." Mrs. Adams turned to the board to add some more instructions. "You will need a three-ring binder or a spiral notebook. I prefer to use a binder because I can add more pages as I need them, but a spiral-bound notebook is fine. Put your name on the front of the book and date each entry. I'll expect an entry for each day."

"How long do they have to be?" someone asked.

"As long as you want, just so you write more than one sentence a day. It's important that you write down how you feel about the day's events or anything else you might be thinking about."

"Right now I feel tired," the boy behind DJ whispered.

"But what if someone reads what I wrote?" another student asked.

"Hey, yeah. Are you going to read them?"

"Only if you want me to. I'll have you turn in your journal once a week at first, then if all is well, twice a month. All I am interested in is making sure you wrote every day." She looked at the girl who had brought up the privacy issue. "A journal is a very personal thing. I would not leave mine out for anyone to read, and if that's something that worries you, you may store your journal here in the bottom drawer of my desk and insert your pages as you go."

Great, how am I ever going to keep up with this assignment? I don't have anything to write about. DJ propped her forehead on her hand. What a bummer. *I can't keep track of all I'm doing already.* She swapped looks of disgust with the girl across the aisle. *What a stupid assignment.* She broke into her internal complaining long enough to listen to what the teacher was saying.

"I have copies of the older edition of *The Diary of Anne Frank,* but if you want to read the new one, you'll have to buy that for yourself at the local bookstore."

Fat chance. While DJ enjoyed reading, it usually took a backseat to riding and drawing. While other kids read, she drew horses.

"Now, I'd like you to take out your notebooks and begin your first entry. Place the date in the left-hand margin and your name up in the right." Groans echoed around the room, but the class did as asked. "Good. Now, think of something that's been bothering you today. Did you have a fight with your brother or sister? Someone say something that ticked you off? Bad hair day?"

Giggles and raised eyebrows greeted her small joke.

"Whatever you feel like writing about, start in."

More groans.

DJ stared at her paper. What to write about? Her pencil began to move as if it had a mind of its own. *Last week I heard from my dad. I never even knew his name before, and now he wants to see me.* Before she knew it, the teacher called time. DJ looked down—she'd written three-quarters of a page.

By the time DJ turned her lights out that night, she'd covered four pages, both sides.

She didn't need her mother's questioning look to remind her that she'd said she would call her father. Every time she decided to pick up the phone, the butterflies in her midsection would go into a grand free-for-all. About the time she felt them halfway up her throat in a full-blown flight for freedom, she'd chicken out and they'd go back to roost.

What would she say? *Hey, come on down and let's be best buds?* Or *You come down, but I'll be gone.* Or better yet, *Gee, been a while since I saw you—if I ever did.* DJ knew none of those would earn points with her mother. Or Gran, for that matter. When she tried praying about it as Gran suggested, it was like talking into a phone when the other person had already hung up. There wasn't so much as a dial tone.

"Just do it and get it over with," Amy said, hands on her board-flat hips.

"Easy for you to say, you saw your father this morning." DJ held out a carrot to Josh, who took it daintily, as the sorrel Arab cross did everything. He and Amy were just right for each other, both small and neatly put together.

"What's that got to do with it?" Amy stopped brushing. "My mom says to just do the hard stuff first and get it over with. Then you'll like yourself better."

"At least your mom is married to your father." DJ rubbed the spot near the tip of Josh's ears that made him act half asleep.

"Yeah, I know." Amy started brushing again, the dust flying as she used both hands. "But you've been snorting over this for what seems like forever. Wouldn't it be easier just to get it over with?"

"What do I call him? Mr. Atwood? Bradley? Brad? And what if his wife answers the phone—if he even has a wife."

"You could call him Dad."

"He's *not* my dad." DJ's raised voice made Josh pull back against the crossties.

"Oh, really now?"

"Come on, Ames, Dad is for someone you like." She chewed on her bottom lip. "I'd rather say, 'hey you.'"

"DJ, I don't care what you call him, just do it quickly so you can concentrate on riding again—and school and drawing and anything else but this." Amy threw her brushes into the bucket. "Major's waiting for you."

"No, he's not. He doesn't want to go out in that downpour any more than I do." DJ glanced at her watch. "Yikes, I better hurry. Patches has been out on the hot walker long enough. Maybe the rain washed some of his orneriness away."

DJ had been scheduled for her first dressage lesson that afternoon, but Bridget had left a note asking DJ to forgive her; she had an unexpected appointment. They'd reschedule it for Saturday morning. Since she wasn't particularly looking forward to a dressage lesson—jumping was what she loved, not boring dressage—the postponement didn't hurt DJ's feelings. And when Patches semi-behaved himself, she actually dared to look forward to some play time with Major. Shame they couldn't ride up in the hills, but getting drenched had never been her idea of a great time.

DJ spent her time working at keeping Major bending and yielding to her legs as Bridget had shown her. He showed his impatience with the repeated drills by swishing his tail every once in a while. DJ wished she could do the same.

When Joe dropped her off at the dark house, she hunched her shoulders to keep her neck dry and dashed to the front door. The dark windows were no surprise. She wondered whether her father would be home yet. Did he work late, too?

Inside, the house smelled stale and silent, as if bemoaning the fact no one was home.

DJ flicked on the lights, turned on the stereo, and crossed the kitchen to the phone. The red light was blinking on the answering machine. She listened to the message for her mother and hit the Save button. The light continued to blink.

DJ got a glass of water to wet her parched mouth. You'd think it was a hundred degrees outside, she was so thirsty. Then she had to make a run to the bathroom.

"All right, you're obviously just putting this off." She crossed again to the phone and dialed.

A deep male voice answered on the third ring. "Brad Atwood here."

DJ swallowed hard. She couldn't make any words come.

"Hello?"

Chapter • 7

DJ dropped the phone back in the cradle, her heart hammering like she'd run a mile without taking a breath. She dashed to the sink for another glass of water. "You idiot! What's the matter with you?" She stared at the reflection in the kitchen window. No help there. The face looked about to cry. For pete's sake!

She took in a deep breath and, letting it out, crossed to the phone again. Summoning every bit of resolution she owned clear up from her toenails, she dialed the number.

"Brad Atwood here."

"This is DJ."

"DJ, how wonderful." She could hear warmth spreading over his words like hot fudge on ice cream. "I'm so glad you called."

"Yeah, well . . ." *What do I say next?* She twirled the cord around her finger. "I . . ."

"I know this is awfully hard for you and a tremendous surprise. Maybe it would help if I told you some about me, then you tell me a little about you."

"Okay."

"At least you know my name," he said with a hint of a chuckle. "I live near Santa Rosa, and I'm an attorney. I don't have any other children, but I'm married and my wife's name is Jacqueline—Jackie to her friends. We both love horses. I raise and show Arabians for my hobby, and Jackie shows fourth-level dressage on her Hanoverian-Thoroughbred gelding named Lord Byron."

DJ sighed. "Wow."

"I hoped that might interest you. Your mother says you love horses, too."

"Gran said once that I got that from my dad."

"Yes, I think you did. So . . . now tell me about you."

DJ slid down the wall and crossed her legs at the ankles, the phone propped on her shoulder. "Where do you want me to start?"

"Wherever. I'm interested in everything."

"Like you said, I've always loved horses—started working at Briones Riding Academy when I was ten so I could take riding lessons. Just this past summer, I got my own horse, Major. He's a retired police mount. I'm a freshman at Acalanese High School, I love to draw like Gran, and someday I want to ride in the Olympics."

"Dressage, eventing, or jumping?"

"Jumping." DJ could hear the interest in his voice. "I've always wanted to jump."

"You have a trainer?"

"Yep, Bridget Sommersby. She used to ride for France till she got hurt and couldn't jump anymore. She owns the academy where I work and train."

DJ heard a car pull into the drive and the garage door go up. "Mom's home, you want to talk with her?"

"I'd rather talk with you. I'm hoping you will let me come to see you."

"When?"

"Whenever. Your mother had mentioned Sunday, but I'll leave it to you to set the time and day."

DJ nibbled on the side of her lower lip and let out a breath she didn't realize she'd been holding. "How about three o'clock a week from this coming Sunday?"

"That's nine days from now. Good—we'll be there. Can you give me directions?"

DJ gave him the address and started to add directions.

"No need," Brad said. "That's the house your mother always lived in. We'll see you a week from Sunday, DJ—and thanks."

DJ hung up the phone as her mother walked into the kitchen. "That was Mr. Atwood."

Lindy stopped short. "Brad's father?"

DJ shook her head. "No, *my* father. You're always telling me to call adults mister and missus." DJ twisted the phone cord again. "What *am* I supposed to call him, Mom?" She glared up at her mother. "I don't know who he is or what he's like or anything. What am I supposed to do?" She rose to her feet, hot anger rising with her. "He wants to come see me. What do I say? 'Hi, Daddy, so nice to meet you'? Do I shake his hand? And his wife—I . . . I forget her name." DJ choked on her words.

Lindy stepped forward and wrapped her arms around her daughter. "It's okay, Darla Jean. I promise it'll be all right. You don't have to see him right now if you don't want to." Her voice sounded so much like Gran's that DJ snuggled closer.

"They're coming in nine days." She muttered the words against her mother's shoulder. Never in her life could she remember her mother comforting her like this. Gran had always been there first.

DJ inhaled the fragrance imbedded in the fabric and her mother's skin. It spoke of class and success and beautiful people in fascinating places, but her mother's arms and tone spoke only of love. "Is that okay?"

"If that's what you feel you're up to."

"Gran could make cookies." DJ didn't feel ready to step back from the comfort surrounding her.

Lindy nodded. "Brad always was a sucker for her chocolate chip peanut butter cookies."

"Gran doesn't make chocolate chip with peanut butter." DJ raised her head.

"She used to, and I'm sure she'd do it again. Guess she quit making that particular recipe after . . . after . . ."

"After he went away?"

Lindy clasped her hands on her daughter's upper arms. "I think we need to have a long talk." She sighed. "A long-overdue talk."

"Like about my dad?" DJ tried on a smile and found it still fit.

"Yeah, I kind of blew that one." Lindy put a finger under DJ's chin and lifted it so they were eye to eye. "Darla Jean Randall, I know I haven't been the kind of mother you needed and I should have been, but I promise you, I will try to do my best from here on in. I am just eternally grateful Gran was always there for you. She raised a young woman I am proud to call my daughter." Lindy's words caught in her throat. She cleared it and added, "So proud." The tears pooling in her eyes spilled over and matched the ones on DJ's cheeks. Her mother sniffed and smiled, a wobbly smile, but a smile nonetheless. "I love you, DJ, more than I can ever say." With gentle fingers, she wiped away the tears slipping down DJ's face.

"Oh, Mom." DJ tried to say more, but the words wouldn't come. She sniffed, too. "I smell like horses."

"That's okay—for now." Lindy reached behind her for a paper towel to wipe her eyes. "How about we both change clothes, and I'll order in." She stopped. "You want Chinese or pizza?"

"Pizza. With everything."

"Even anchovies?" Lindy raised one eyebrow.

DJ scrunched her eyes closed. She sighed as if making a big sacrifice. "How about on half?"

"Deal." Her mother extended her hand. DJ took it, and they shook once. "How about you order and I'll pay?"

"Deal." As Lindy climbed the stairs, DJ felt the laughter of pure joy swirl around her ankles and work its way upward. Pushing bubbles of thanks ahead, it burst out in feet-tapping, hand-clapping giggles and spins. "Wow!" If only Gran could see them now.

DJ phoned in the order and raced up the stairs. She had twenty minutes to shower and get dressed. A bit later, still damp from the pounding water, she stood in front of her closet. If only she had a lounging outfit like the ones her mother wore so easily. And beautifully.

"What?" She couldn't stop talking to herself. The energy had to come out somehow. "You want to dress up?" She shook her head. "DJ, you're slipping and slipping bad." She dug out her Snoopy nightshirt, a bathrobe that was now too short in the sleeves, and shoved her feet into fluffy Snoopy slippers. At least she'd be warm while they talked. And man, oh man, did she have questions to ask!

With the pizza box between them, they curled into the corners of the sofa in the family room.

"So how do I start?" Lindy asked after eating half a piece of pizza.

"Gran always says to start at the beginning." DJ scooped up a string of cheese and plopped it back on the pizza.

"She's right." Lindy took a sip from her soda and leaned back. "I had a crush on Brad Atwood from the first day I saw him in high school. He was so handsome, every girl in the hall drooled when he walked by. The first time he said hi to me, I nearly dropped my books." A gentle smile lifted the corners of her mouth, and her eyes wore the dreamy look of good memories. "And when he asked me to go to a movie, I about flipped."

"How old were you?"

"Fifteen."

"Gran let you go out on a date at fifteen?" DJ couldn't believe it.

"It wasn't really a *date* date—a bunch of kids were going." Lindy reached for another piece of pizza. "But *I* was going with the BMOC."

" 'BMOC'?"

"Big Man On Campus."

DJ stifled the *huh?* and took a sip of her drink. *They did talk kinda funny back in the old days.* When her mother seemed lost in her day-dreams, DJ prodded, "And then?"

"Well," Lindy shrugged. "We started going together. Mom and Dad had a fit when they learned I was going steady with Brad. He was too old for me, too fast for me. I was too young, couldn't think of anything but boys . . . but you need to remember, I was only interested in one boy—Brad Atwood." Her face sobered. "Even though my mother and father did their best to keep their little girl safe, Brad and I—well, we were in love, and eventually we . . ." Her voice trailed off.

DJ waited, not daring to say a word.

Lindy sat up straight and crossed her wrists on her knees. She stared at a spot on the rug in front of her. "Let's just say we went all the way."

"You mean you had sex?"

"We thought we were making love, and what we made was a baby. Two kids too stupid to use birth control and too much in love or lust to keep away from each other." Lindy's voice ground to a halt. The ticking clock on the mantel sounded loud in the stillness. Out on the street, a car swished through the water drenching the road from the continuing rain. "If only I had listened to my mother." The words were almost lost behind her fall of hair.

"When I told him I was pregnant, Brad said he'd marry me—said he loved me and he'd stand by me." Lindy shook her head. "His father thought I should have an abortion. Can you beat that—he thought I should kill the baby?" She stared at DJ out of haunted eyes. "He would have had me kill *you*." She raised a trembling hand to DJ's cheek. "I couldn't do that. My own dad thought I should give you up for adoption so I could get on with my life. But when I decided to keep you, he and Mom said there was always room for one more in this house. We were a family that stuck together. So we did."

She kept her gaze locked on DJ's. "When I held you in my arms and you looked up at me, that was it. I'd been talking to you for weeks, and suddenly you were real and I couldn't let you go."

"What happened to Brad?" DJ could barely get the words past the lump in her throat.

"You've got to give him some credit—he paid the medical bills. But while I was taking care of a newborn baby and trying to go to night school, he played football and basketball and tried out for track. Back then, they wouldn't let you attend high school if you were pregnant or had a baby. When he left for college, he said we'd be married as soon as he graduated. . . ." Her voice trailed off again.

But did he care about me at all? Did he play with me? Was he a dad? DJ kept the questions to herself. And waited.

Lindy shook her head. "I was so mad at the whole world, I can't believe my family put up with me. My friends were out having a good time—the dances, the dates—and me?" She shook her head again, so gently now her hair didn't even swing. "DJ, I was so young, I didn't know how to be a mother. I was just a kid myself. So I went back to school to learn a skill so I could get a job, and Gran took over with you. We didn't do welfare then like kids do now."

"I know a girl who had an abortion," DJ volunteered.

"Yeah, and she may not know it now, but it will haunt her for the rest of her life." Lindy turned so she could look directly at DJ. "I know I made mistakes, but keeping you was never one of them. I'm sorry Brad missed out on your growing-up years, but that was his choice. He just faded out of the picture."

"And now he wants to come back in."

"I know."

It was DJ's turn to lean forward. There were so many questions she wanted to ask. *Did you ever wish I wasn't here? Did you hate Brad? Do you hate him now?* "You weren't much older than me." The stunning thought swung her around.

"I know. And I hope you never get boy crazy like I did. Poor Gran, it about drove her nuts. Looking back, all I could think about, talk about, and dream about was Brad Atwood."

He could have come to see me—at least once. It wasn't as if we'd moved to New York or something. We still live in the same house my mother grew up in. He even remembers where it is.

"Do you have any pictures of him?"

Lindy shook her head. "I burned them all one night when I heard he took some other girl to the prom."

Silence fell again, this time more like a warm blanket. Lindy gathered up the napkins and closed the pizza box on the remaining piece. "You want this?"

"For breakfast." DJ slumped against the sofa back. "You know what bugs me the most?"

Lindy shook her head.

"Why now?"

"Guess you'll have to ask him that."

"Are you still mad at him?"

"I wasn't until he crashed back into our lives. Now I'm angry with him at times—more times than I want to admit."

"Me too." DJ rubbed the scar in the palm of her hand and sighed. "Thanks, Mom."

"You're welcome, DJ. Sweet dreams," Lindy said as they climbed the stairs to their bedrooms.

"You too." DJ stepped into her mother's embrace just like they'd been hugging all her life. "Night."

But for the second night since DJ had learned of Brad Atwood, she awoke in the dark of the night, panting hard—running from a faceless man.

Chapter • 8

Seven days till D-day, but who's counting? DJ stared at the words she'd written in her journal and chewed on the eraser of her pencil before writing some more. *Sometimes I think I hate him and hope he doesn't show up. Then I'm scared he won't come. What if I don't like him, or he doesn't like me? Then what?*

Her fingers itched to draw instead of write, but she forced herself to keep at it. She flipped back a couple of pages. She'd written all she could remember her mother saying about her early life. One section in particular caught her attention. *"My own dad thought I should give the baby up for adoption so I could get on with my life, but when I held you in my arms and you looked up at me, that was it. I'd been talking to you for weeks, and suddenly you were real and I couldn't let you go."*

DJ felt a shiver ripple up her back. What if she'd been given away?

She forced her attention back to the current entry. *I wonder what he looks like one minute, then the next, I'm so scared. Scared one minute and mad the next. I think I'm having a nervous breakdown. Do crazy people think like this? Gran says to pray about it like she is, but it's so hard. And what about his wife? What if she doesn't like me? Fourth-level dressage—major wow. And if they are horse people, how can I not like them? Dear God, please help me.*

Oh, and please make Bridget change her mind. Today she said I should take two dressage lessons a week and no jumping lessons for a couple of months. I mean, jumping is what I want to do. I understand learning dressage can make me a better rider, but can't I jump, too? It's not like I plan to show dressage or anything. Please, God, you know Bridget—only you can change her mind.

DJ finally put away her journal pages and took out her drawing pad. After sharpening her pencils, her fingers seemed to take on a life of their own as they shaped a horse on the paper. She held the sketch of the jumping horse up to the light when she finished. Definitely Major. She'd gotten his head just right, but his rear legs were slightly off. When would she draw him right?

She rubbed a hand across her forehead. Mom was out with Robert. They'd gone over to look at the new house and see how the remodeling was coming. It was too late to call Amy, and Gran and Joe were at a meeting. She picked up her journal again.

THIS JUST ISN'T FAIR!!! DJ underlined the capitalized words three times, pushing so hard the lead on her pencil broke. She stuffed the pages in her folder and slipped the folder into her backpack. Dumping the thing on the floor, she reached to turn out the light. But when sleep came, the faceless man came with it.

They finally had sunshine the next afternoon. DJ checked the jumping ring. Still wet but not sloppy. She ached to jump a round—or ten.

"I know, ma petite, but your time in the ring is so short now that winter is here that I believe dressage is best."

"Whoa, you scared me." DJ turned to find Bridget Sommersby at her shoulder. "How'd you know I'd be out here?" Even scarier, how did Bridget know what she was thinking?

Bridget just smiled. With her ash blond hair in a neat bun at her neck and her glasses resting a bit above her hairline, she looked the picture of the neat horsewoman. Blue eyes, crinkles at their outer edges, smiled along with the instructor's lips. "You will like dressage eventually, and even if you do not, you are enough of a horsewoman to see the value in it. Go ahead and finish your work. I will join you and Major in the arena."

DJ nodded. So much for God answering that particular prayer with a yes.

By the time she'd groomed and worked Patches, given her student Andrew his lesson, and saddled Major, she still hadn't mustered any more enthusiasm for her dressage lesson—especially after seeing Tony Andrada taking the jumps. *I should be out there.*

"Come on, Major, let's get warmed up. I don't think you are going to like this any more than I am." The bay snorted and tossed his head, jigged to the side, and struck out with one front foot. "You like the sun, too, don't you? We could have gone up into the hills today. Oh, why didn't I think of that?" DJ stroked his neck and leaned over to open the gate. "Maybe it'll be nice Saturday so we can go."

"Go where?" Amy jogged by on Josh.

"Up in Briones."

"I'm ready." She stopped her mount so DJ could close the gate. "You ready for your lesson?"

"Don't remind me. I could be out jumping—it's the first time in weeks the ring is dry enough."

"Bridget knows best."

"Thanks for taking her side." By the time DJ had circled the arena three times, Bridget had opened the gate and walked to one end. DJ nudged Major into a trot and, following Bridget's beckoning hand, stopped in front of her.

"All right, DJ, we will begin. First, I want to remind you that our goal is to make you a better rider and Major a more athletic horse. I can promise you will become a better jumper because you are willing to work with dressage. Understand?"

DJ nodded.

"Good. Then let us start with the basics. First, you must learn to sit straight. You are used to leaning forward, which is right for Hunter/Jumper. But you will sit straight for dressage." She looked up at DJ.

DJ straightened her shoulders and tried to visualize a straight line from her ear to her heel.

Bridget reached up and pushed her upper body back even more. "I said straight."

"I was."

"Non." Bridget shook her head. "Straight till you feel you are leaning backward. Now, do not let your leg swing forward."

DJ bit back the *I am straight* and tried to sit even straighter. She felt like she was leaning so far back her head rested on Major's rump.

"That is better. Now, signal Major to walk and hold your position."
DJ obeyed, stiff as a board and off balance.

"Now, relax."

Oh, sure, relax. Easy to say, impossible to do. DJ gritted her teeth.
How was she supposed to watch where she was going when she couldn't
even turn her head?

"Now then." Bridget beckoned DJ back to halt in front of her.
"Take your feet out of the stirrups." DJ did as told. With swift motions,
Bridget pulled the leather buckles of the stirrups' down straps and laid
the irons over the front of the saddle, right first, then left.

"What are you doing?"

"You have to learn to feel your horse in three places, your two seat
bones and in front in the crotch. When you are sitting so straight and
deep that you can feel your mount move beneath you, you will come
along quickly." Bridget smiled up at DJ. "Feeling comfortable yet?"

"No, not at all."

"Walk, please."

Yeah, sure—walk. This feels totally weird. Major twitched his ears.
"Sorry, fella."

"And trot sitting."

If this was what a sack of grain felt like, DJ figured they could call
her "oats" for short. What had happened to her balance? She felt herself
slip from side to side. She was riding more clumsily than the first time
she had gotten on a horse.

Major swished his tail and stopped. A dead stop. The only problem
was DJ didn't. Until she hit the dirt, that is.

At least she had the presence of mind to release the reins so she
didn't jerk Major's mouth. He looked down at her, then nuzzled her
shoulder as if to apologize.

"Of all the stupid—"

"It is all right. You are learning." Bridget came over and gave DJ a
hand to pull her to her feet.

"I fell off—just like some little kid. He didn't dump me." Major
nuzzled her again. "Sorry, guy, it wasn't your fault." She rubbed his
ears and smoothed his forelock, then turned to Bridget. "Okay, so what did
I do wrong?"

"Nothing. Major stopped because you were doing what I told you
to do. Without even knowing, you were sitting deeper. Now, if you

would have used your legs to drive the horse forward, you would still be on him."

DJ grumbled to herself as she pulled her left stirrup down so she could mount. Once aboard, she flipped the stirrup back in front of her. *I will do this!*

"Let us keep to the walk."

By the end of the lesson, DJ ached in places she'd forgotten she had. Besides being dumped on her rear, her seat hurt from the constant contact with the saddle. Her inner thighs hurt from trying to keep them flat against the saddle skirt. And her pride hurt from jouncing around like a bag of horse feed.

"You did well." Bridget patted DJ's knee.

"Yeah, sure."

"And you will practice?"

"Of course." DJ gave her a who-you-kidding look.

"Good. You might try a hot bath when you get home. Helps the sore places." Bridget opened the gate and waved her through.

"You okay, kid?" Joe asked when she and Major arrived back at the stall.

"You saw?"

Joe nodded. "Looked to me like she was trying to torture you."

"That about fits it. Think I'll change to Western." DJ slid to the ground and leaned against her horse. Major turned so he could rub his head against her shoulder. "Easy, fella, you'll knock me over."

She stripped off the saddle and pad and hung them on the top edge of the lower stall door. Then, after hooking the halter around Major's neck, she removed the bridle and laid it over the saddle. How come even her arms ached?

"Here, let me help." Joe unhooked the web gate, picked the brushes out of the bucket, and began a two-handed grooming job that would leave Major shining in no time.

"But, GJ, you already cleaned the stall and put out the feed," DJ tried to protest. She was glad for the help. How come she could jump or even do flat work for hours and not feel drained like this? What was she going to say when her father's wife, whatever her name was again, asked about the dressage lessons? *Just great. I only fell off once.*

"DJ, don't take it so hard. You know that riders fall off plenty of times. It's all part of the sport." Joe grinned at her. "Or at least that's what I heard you telling your students."

"I know. It's just so embarrassing. I wasn't even galloping or jumping or anything—just trotting. The kids I'm teaching stay on better than I did." DJ finished buckling Major's halter after giving him the last chunk of carrot.

"It'll get better." Joe dropped the brushes in the bucket and took her arm. "Come on, I know Melanie was baking cookies when I left. I think you could use a good dose of cookies and Gran."

———

By the time DJ wrote about the disastrous lesson in her journal, she was able to laugh, although barely. She probably had looked pretty silly, grabbing for the air and collapsing like a rag doll. Even Major had looked at her as though he wondered what he'd done wrong. As Gran had said, "Someday you'll laugh when you tell your children about this first dressage lesson."

But would she ever be able to laugh about the day she met her father?

Meeting him is always in the back of my mind now, she wrote. *I can't wait until that day is over. I know Mom is pretty uptight about it, too. I heard her talking to Robert, and she was crying. I don't know why she's so worried. This won't change her life much, just mine. But then again, maybe we'll meet and he'll go his way and I'll go mine.*

But is that what I really want? She tapped the eraser of her pencil against her chin. Always more questions.

———

"So what are you doing about Christmas presents this year?" Amy asked one afternoon. They were riding their bikes to the Academy for a change since it wasn't raining. In fact, it hadn't rained for a couple of days.

"I don't know. My saddle fund keeps shrinking—at this rate I'll be fifty before I can afford a decent, all-purpose saddle, let alone a good jumping saddle. What are you going to do?"

"I'm thinking of enlarging some of my photos and framing them. John said he'd help me make frames in wood shop."

"Must be nice sometimes to have an older brother."

"Yeah, sometimes. Other times I'd give him away in a heartbeat."

"I already gave Gran and Joe one of my drawings for the wedding, so I can't do that again." They stopped at the top of the hill and waited for several cars to go by.

"You could for some of the others."

"I guess, but frames cost a bundle, and I don't have John to help me out. One thing about having more family now, I've got more presents to buy."

"I still think you ought to be able to do something with your drawings."

"But what?"

"I don't know. Ask Gran."

"Oh, sure, 'Hey, Gran, what do you want me to make you for Christmas?'" They propped their bikes against the barn wall and headed over to the office to check the duties board. Since neither of their names were down for cleaning stalls, they heaved a collective sigh of relief.

"Have you two drawn names out of the bowl for the Christmas party?" Bridget called from her office.

DJ groaned. "Another present. I think I'm going to get a job at the Burger House."

"Yeah, in your spare time." Amy put her hand in the glass fish bowl and drew out a slip of white paper.

DJ did the same and groaned again.

"Now what?"

DJ held out the narrow strip for inspection. "Tony Andrada. Fiddle and double fiddle. Who'd you get?"

"Sue Benson. No problema."

"Bridget, can I trade this name for another?" DJ put on her most imploring look. "Please."

With a slight smile, the academy owner shook her head. "You know the rules. Oh, and, DJ, Andrew will not be in for his lesson today. He has a bad cold."

"Probably got it so he wouldn't have to groom Bandit. I'd hoped to get him mounted today."

"Did you tell him that?"

"You kidding? But he's no dummy. He's learned to tack the pony up and lead him around. He might be driving a car before I get him on that horse."

"I know you work hard with him, and his mother appreciates the care you have shown. Shame he is so frightened."

"Shame they don't let him play soccer or something instead."

"Facing your fears is very important and part of growing up."

"Yeah, well, *I'm* afraid I won't have presents for Christmas." DJ stuck her hands in her Windbreaker pockets. "See ya later." She turned and headed out the door, knowing full well that she hadn't mentioned what she was really afraid of—meeting her father.

———————

That night, she took out her portfolio of her best pencil and charcoal drawings and studied each one. While many of them were of Major, she had foals, yearlings, and horses jumping, walking, grazing, and lying down. The one of a horse rearing wasn't quite right, and she flipped past it quickly. She also flipped past the drawings she'd added riders to—she was better with horses than people. While she'd been tempted to throw out the sketches from her early years, Gran had told her to keep them so she could see how she'd grown. Her growth as an artist was obvious, even though the subject matter was limited to horses.

DJ turned out the light. Only three days until D-day. And only fourteen more days to figure out Christmas presents.

Chapter • 9

"Are you okay?"

DJ looked up at her mother waiting in the doorway. "Yeah, why?"

"You've been so quiet lately." Lindy motioned to ask if she could come in, and DJ patted the edge of her bed. "Is it about your dad?"

"Sorta." DJ pushed away her art pad, flipped over on her back, and studied her mother. As always, Lindy looked like she'd just stepped out of a fashion magazine. Her emerald green silk lounging outfit whispered secrets as she sat down and turned to rest one knee on the comforter.

"What do you mean by 'sorta'?"

DJ sighed. "For starters, what do I call him?" She crossed one ankle over her other knee.

"Mr. Atwood seems kind of weird, doesn't it?" Lindy said, nodding. "And you can't call him Brad because Gran and I would have a fit."

Lindy laid a comforting hand on DJ's shoulder, sending shock waves through her. "I can see why this would be a problem for you." More shock waves. *Is this my mother?*

"I guess if it were me, I'd be pretty mad at him sometimes, even might think I hate him." Lindy's voice had that gentle quality DJ used with Andrew when she was trying to get him over being afraid of Bandit. "You been thinking that?"

The question caught DJ by surprise. "Yeah, I guess so."

"Gran thought you might, but you haven't really said much." Lindy's hand continued to stroke DJ's shoulder. "Robert and I talked about it, you know. He wondered what you were thinking and feeling." Silence. "You care to talk about it?"

The words came in a whisper. "I'm so scared, Mom . . . so scared."

"Makes sense. Me too."

DJ stopped in midthought. "Why are you scared?"

"You first."

"Well, I . . . I don't know. It's just all so sudden. I mean, we were fine without him, and now all of a sudden he's there and wants to be a part of my life—at least I think so. Sometimes I get so mad at him." DJ flipped back over on her stomach. "Why can't things stay the way they've always been?"

"That's life, honey—change and more change. Lately more than ever—and mostly because I met this neat man I thought my mother would enjoy being with." Lindy clasped her hands around a knee. "Shoulda just kept my mouth shut."

"Gran's really happy being married to Joe." DJ toyed with her pencil. "I wouldn't want to change that."

"Even though you miss her?"

"Yep. I get along okay." DJ drew circles on the comforter with her finger. "And I really like Joe, you know that."

"So change isn't always so bad?"

DJ let the question sink in. Growing up was change. She'd always wanted to ride and draw better—that was change, too. And Robert and her mother getting married, now that would be the biggest change of all. With the Double Bs around, nothing would ever be the same again. Did she not want that to happen?

She curled onto her side so she could see her mother. Her mother had sure been different lately—softer, more smiling, and even open to talking with her once in a while. Would she want that to go back to the old way? "Guess not, at least not all the time." DJ thought a minute. "Do you want to see him again?"

"Who, Brad?"

DJ nodded.

"Not particularly. That part of my life is like a book I closed a long time ago. I like looking ahead." Lindy rumpled DJ's hair. "We'll get through this, and Christmas isn't far away. How you coming with your presents?"

DJ was glad for the new topic. "I'm stuck. We have so much more family now."

"Ain't that the truth." She leaned forward and picked up DJ's drawing pad. "You mind?"

DJ shook her head. She watched her mother's face as she flipped through the sheets. Lindy smiled, chuckled at the colt illustrations, and nodded once or twice.

"DJ, you sure inherited your grandmother's talent. Some of these are really good. You ever thought about choosing one or two and reducing them down to card size? These would make neat note cards."

"I could make up a package of six or eight." DJ felt her brain spring to attention and start working. "They wouldn't have to all be different." DJ took back her drawing pad and started flipping through. "This one, I think." She pointed at the side view of a foal. "And this one." A cameo of Major, ears pricked, made her grin.

"You have plenty to choose from." Lindy leaned forward. "Good night, DJ. Time to hit the sack." She dropped a kiss on her daughter's head and stood to leave. "Don't worry about meeting your biological father. Things are always worse when you are anticipating them."

DJ nodded. "Sure, Mom."

The next morning when she told Amy about the cards, Amy lit up like a neon sign. "I could do the same with some of my photos. Shame it's too late, we might have been able to sell some of these."

"You're right." The wheels began to turn. "We could buy the envelopes and—"

"You two going to make another business flier?" Mr. Yamamoto asked as he braked for a stoplight.

"Flier?" DJ looked at Amy. "We don't need more fliers—we did that last summer."

"No, I mean a new venture. You've had some good ideas in the past, they just—"

"D-a-d," Amy moaned. "You don't have to remind us."

"Good thing those hamsters didn't get loose at *our* house is all I've got to say." John sank down in the seat. "Mom would've gone ballistic."

"My mom about did." DJ grinned at Amy. "At least with cards, they can't escape or track horse manure on someone's brand-new white carpet." That had happened during the Pony Parties venture, when DJ and Amy had used Bandit to give kids rides at parties. "Gotta admit, though, those Pony Parties were our best idea of all. Ames, we should do that again."

"Count me out." John gathered his gear. "I'm not helping with something like that ever again."

DJ and Amy exchanged grins. "Thanks for the ride, Dad," DJ sang out as they exited the car. John disappeared into the throng of teenagers. "So, Ames, when you want to go to the Copy Shop?"

Sunday afternoon arrived faster than anyone was ready for.

"I can't stand it—I think I'm going to be sick." DJ made a puking motion toward the sink.

"Darla Jean Randall, act your age."

"Now, dear, you know she's only teasing." This was already the third time Gran had acted as peacemaker.

"No, I'm not teasing. I've got butterflies on my butterflies. This is worse than a competition any day." DJ opened the refrigerator door and studied the contents. Nothing looked appetizing, and Gran had already smacked her hands away from the cookie platter with a stern warning.

"Close the door, you'll cool the entire house." Lindy's voice said more than her words. It said, Knock it off, DJ, I'm losing my patience. But then, Lindy hadn't had much patience for the last two days.

DJ felt as if she were dancing on the end of a low-voltage wire. Even Gran couldn't calm her down.

Maybe the Atwoods won't come. Maybe they won't find our place after all. And maybe DJ ought to go for a forty-mile run. She opened the fridge again and this time retrieved a can of soda.

"DJ, I said to stay out of there." Lindy whirled from where she was starting the coffee maker. The *kerthwunk* of an open coffee can hitting the floor caught everyone's attention.

"Lindy Lou Randall!" Gran only used that tone when her daughter resorted to the kind of language that had just turned the air blue. "Get a hold of yourself."

"Look, you three women go about your business, and I'll clean up the coffee." Joe gently laid a hand on Melanie's shoulder.

"Thank you, darlin'." Gran placed her hand over his. "I'll go check the table." She glared at her daughter, shot her granddaughter a lesser glare, and headed for the dining room.

"Lindy, come here a minute, please," Robert called from the family room.

DJ watched her mother fix a smile on her face and, after one last laser look leveled at her daughter, leave the room.

"Where's the broom?" Joe asked, picking up the now half-empty coffee can. Dark brown ground coffee covered a sizable portion of the kitchen floor.

"I'll get it." DJ opened the door to the garage and snagged the broom off its hook. All this because she'd gotten a soda? Gran never got mad, or rarely, anyway. But she'd definitely been mad a couple of minutes ago. DJ handed the broom to Joe and went back for the dustpan.

After they'd cleaned up the mess, he winked at her. "Don't take it too hard. Everyone's under pressure here."

"Why are they so worried? It's me who has to meet him. At least they know the guy," DJ whispered back.

"There's a lot at stake here, that's why." Joe leaned against the counter and crossed his arms over his chest.

"Yeah, well, I'd rather be at the barn. What a waste of good riding time."

"It'll be dark soon."

"There are lights in the arena."

"But you never ride after dark."

"Not in the winter, but I would if I could." DJ copied his pose.

"It's pouring again."

"So what's new? Maybe God's trying to wash California off the map."

The doorbell rang.

DJ could feel her heart pounding somewhere down near her knees.

"This is it, darlin'," Joe whispered with a light brush of his knuckles across her cheek. "Knock 'em dead."

DJ listened to her mother cross the room, her heels clicking on the entry tile. The door squeaked when she opened it. Lindy's voice sounded as if she'd just put on her best company manners for someone she didn't like at all.

"Hello, Brad, won't you come in?"

DJ shot a pleading look at her grandfather, who gave her a gentle push forward.

The voices continued. A man's voice, deep and smooth. Would Brad be as nice as his voice? He introduced his wife, Jacquelyn, and Lindy introduced Robert as her fiancé. Gran returned to the kitchen and, wrapping a comforting arm around DJ's waist, began walking her toward the group in the entry.

"Hello, Bradley, so good to see you again." Gran kept her one arm around DJ while she extended her other hand.

"Mrs. Randall, you haven't changed a bit." Bradley Atwood took her hand in both of his.

DJ sucked in her breath. Her father looked like a movie star. Hair a bit darker than hers, waved back off a broad forehead, and a male version of the determined jaw she saw in the mirror every morning. On him it looked good. His smile reached his eyes, the kind of smile you couldn't help but return. While he wasn't as tall as Joe, DJ had to tip her head back to look up at him.

"And this is Darla Jean, but if you want her to like you, call her DJ." Gran's soft voice interrupted DJ's study.

"Hi, DJ, I'm right glad to meet you." His voice cracked, then smoothed out. Light from the fixture above made his eyes sparkle— or was it tears that threatened to choke both his throat and his eyes?

She couldn't have answered if her life depended upon it.

He dropped his gaze and, turning slightly, said, "I'd like you to meet my wife, Jacquelyn."

Come on, yo-yo brain, say something. DJ could still feel Gran's arm around her waist, strong and comforting.

"H-hi, I'm pleased to meet you." Her voice came breathy, as though she'd been running. She hoped the smile she'd ordered had arrived. She wanted to run, to jump, to yell. She wanted to go hide in her closet and not come out till they left.

"Come, we don't need to stand here. The coffee's ready, and we can visit much more easily around the dining room table." Gran motioned everyone toward the dining room and hung back for Lindy to lead the way.

Later, when DJ had played the scene over for the umpteenth time, she could see the look in her mother's eyes. It hadn't been very friendly. And Joe hadn't been his usual self, either. In fact, without Gran, everyone would have been terribly uncomfortable—DJ especially. But Gran had been Gran, asking questions, telling stories of earlier years, passing around the chocolate chip peanut butter cookies that Brad praised to the skies.

As her mother had said, "I guess it went okay."

As far as DJ was concerned, the best part was talking about horses. Brad had asked about Major and what she did at the Academy, then told her about their Arabians and some of the places they'd showed.

Man, oh man, did she have a lot to tell Amy in the morning! DJ dug out her journal and began writing. She wanted to be sure to remember every little detail. *At least Bradley Atwood and I have plenty to talk about,* she finished writing. *That's for sure.*

She was just dropping off to sleep when she remembered something she'd overheard her mother saying to Gran. What was it again? Something about silver-tongued lawyers always getting their way. What was that supposed to mean? All he'd said was that he'd call her. What on earth was bugging her mother now?

Chapter • 10

"If you had Tony Andrada to buy for, what would you buy?"

"I wouldn't have Tony Andrada for all the money in the world." Amy licked chocolate pudding from the back of her spoon as a crumpled milk carton whizzed by her left ear. She turned and glared over her shoulder at the guys at the table behind them. "You'd think the teachers could keep better control in the lunchroom."

"Ames, you're not helping."

"Give him a packet of your note cards."

"Oh, sure. The Neanderthal probably can't even write." DJ dug the last chip out of the sack. "I hate buying presents when I don't really know the person."

"You hate to *buy* anything. You put every dime in your saddle fund."

"I wish. My fund just gets flatter."

"Be glad you're buying a flat saddle then."

DJ groaned. "Now that's a real knee slapper." She smashed her lunch refuse together. "Just for that, you have to go shopping with me."

"If he was a little kid, you could give him a box of Lifesavers or something. That's what I gave Sue."

"I suppose you have all your Christmas shopping done, too."

"Of course." They dumped their trash into the container and headed for their lockers.

"Sometimes you make me sick." DJ pointed at her open mouth and made a gagging motion.

"I don't like leaving things to the last minute, not like some people I know."

"How far are you on your term paper?"

"Set to rewrite."

DJ groaned. "I just started writing. The research took up till now." DJ leaned her forehead against the tan metal locker. "Sometimes I hate school—it just takes away from the time I could be riding or drawing. And now I gotta go shopping, too."

"You better get on it because the party is Saturday night."

The bell rang. "Don't remind me," DJ muttered.

When Mrs. Adams returned DJ's journal that afternoon, she had written, *Glad to see you are racking up the pages. It shows this is helpful for you. Keep going.* DJ looked up to catch Mrs. Adams's eye and shared a smile with her. Now, if she could only get her term paper done on time.

That afternoon at the Academy, Andrew made it for his lesson. They had Bandit all groomed, and DJ was mentally preparing herself for the challenge of actually getting the ten-year-old on the pony.

"Okay, Andrew, this is the big day." DJ turned to the boy she'd been working with for the last few months. His mother, Mrs. Johnson, owned Patches, and she wanted Andrew to get over his fear of horses so the family could ride together.

"I guess." He sighed and brushed a lock of straight brown hair back from his eyes.

"Did you bring a helmet?"

"Uh-huh." Andrew stopped brushing Bandit and looked up at DJ. "Do I have to?"

"Yup. This is the day. We've put it off long enough, and I think you're ready. Everything should go great. Remember how well it went when you sat on him?"

"I guess."

DJ forced herself to keep a smile on her face and make the boy do what he'd agreed to. "Okay then, let me see you tack him up." She stroked the pony's nose to keep him calm. If Bandit so much as twitched right now, Andrew might head for the hills of Briones.

Andrew set the pad in place and looked up to see DJ's nod. He turned to take the saddle down—and stopped, taking in a deep breath and letting out a sigh that tugged at her heart. While DJ couldn't understand how a kid could be afraid of a horse, she also couldn't understand a mother forcing her child to do something he so obviously disliked. What if her own mother had made her take dance lessons, in a tutu no less?

"You're doing great."

Andrew nodded and set the saddle in place. Keeping a wary eye on Bandit's back feet, he reached under the pony's belly for the girth and buckled it.

"Okay, now check to make sure it's tight enough." DJ waited for Andrew to slide his fingers behind the webbing before doing the same. "Never hurts to double-check."

Andrew unlatched the halter and slid it off Bandit's nose, then reattached it around the pony's neck. All the time he slipped the bit into place and the headstall over the ears, he looked strung as tightly as a new wire fence. When he was finished, he turned to DJ.

"Okay, get your helmet." DJ nodded to the brand-new helmet lying in the corner. Andrew put it on and buckled it in place. He didn't say a word, but his eyes accused her of child abuse.

"Very good. Now, let's lead Bandit out to the arena, just like you did before." DJ snagged a lead shank off the wall when they passed the tack room. She looked around, hoping against hope that Andrew's mother hadn't stayed to watch. Bridget had counseled against it, but the unease persisted. Mrs. Johnson so wanted to see her son riding.

They led Bandit around the arena once, then stopped by the fence, keeping a careful distance from the other riders.

Andrew's Adam's apple bobbed up and down, and he chewed his bottom lip.

"We've gone through these motions before, but this time you will swing your leg over the saddle and sit down. Ready?"

He nodded.

"Okay, facing Bandit, put your left foot into the stirrup iron." She kept the lead shank steady and used her other hand to assist her student.

"Now, grip the pommel with your left hand and the cantle with your right, and pull yourself up. Use your leg muscles."

Andrew did as she said and, with her assistance at the last moment, swung his right leg over the saddle and sat down. The look he gave her tightened her throat. A grin tickled the corner of his mouth, and his eyes brightened.

"I did it."

"You sure did." She patted his knee. It was only with superwoman strength that she kept herself from hugging him.

"I did it all myself." Andrew kept one hand on the pommel, using the other to stroke Bandit's neck.

"Let's make sure your stirrups are the right length." She stepped to the front to see that they were even. "Good. Now I'm going to lead you around the arena while you take up the reins and just hold them." She handed him the leather reins and rechecked his feet in the stirrups. "Ready?"

At his nod, she stepped out, Bandit moving gently beside her.

"S-s-stop."

They did. "Good boy," she whispered to the pony and gave him an extra stroke. "What's up?"

"I-I'm scared."

"Okay. Are your feet in the stirrups?" Andrew nodded. "And your seat is in the saddle?"

"Yeah, 'course."

"So you didn't fall off?"

"DJ, I'm sitting here, aren't I?"

"So what's there to be afraid of?"

"I might fall off."

"I'll make sure that doesn't happen, okay?" She checked the reins again and settled his feet back into the stirrups. "Ready?"

"I guess."

She led the pony halfway around the arena before stopping him. "How you doing?"

"Are we done?"

"Soon. You're doing fine."

"Hey, Andrew, way to go!" Tony Andrada waved and called from across the ring.

Andrew waved back. The smile got wider.

DJ could have danced around the arena. She even felt like shaking Tony's hand. By the time they'd circled the ring twice more, other riders had stopped to congratulate the little boy. Andrew wore a grin big enough to hold a wedge of watermelon. Joe and Bridget applauded from the rail.

"He will do fine from now on, ma petite," Bridget said after DJ had given the boy back to his beaming mother. "You have done a good job with him."

"I didn't think I'd ever get him on that pony." DJ shook her head. "And now I'm so proud of him, I could bust."

"That is the mark of a true teacher—one who receives as much of a thrill from watching a student master something as from doing it oneself."

DJ clutched the compliments to her heart.

———————————

That evening over at Joe and Gran's, Joe and DJ shared every detail of the afternoon with Gran.

"It was awesome," DJ said with a sigh and a shake of her head. "Hard to believe." She cocked her head to one side. "But you know, GJ, I still have one major problem."

Joe turned from where he was rinsing the dishes to put in the dishwasher. "What's that, darlin'?"

"Well, you're a guy, right?"

"I certainly hope so." Gran's chuckle made DJ smile.

"You know that's not what I meant, but . . ." She sighed. "I drew Tony's name for the gift exchange at the Academy Christmas party."

"So?" Joe leaned against the counter and wiped his hands on a dishtowel.

"So I haven't a clue what to get him."

"What's the spending limit?"

"Five dollars. And I don't have that, either, but since I already have to take money out of my saddle fund for Christmas, I guess that's that. But what do I buy him?"

Gran leaned back in her chair. "I think you ought to give him a drawing of his horse. That would please anyone. You have to admit, he does love his horse."

"You really think I should?"

"Why not? You draw wonderfully well."

"Yeah, but . . ."

"I'll help you with a frame. I know someone else who would be really pleased to have one of your pictures—Robert. He'd take ours off the wall if we'd let him. Even though you're not really his daughter yet, he already brags about your accomplishments at work."

"He does? Wow."

Gran nodded. "And you know that story you were telling Bobby and Billy last time they were here?"

DJ propped her elbows on the table. "I was making it up as I went along."

"I was thinking you could write that down and do the drawings for it. They'd love it." Gran leaned forward and patted DJ's hand. "You have so much talent, darlin', and you have no idea."

"I have an idea I'm going to be totally swamped between now and Christmas. My term paper is due before vacation starts, too." DJ sent her grandmother a pleading look. "You think I could skip school till then?"

"Don't even think about it."

The next afternoon, DJ ambled over to Tony's stall and looked more closely at his horse. The Thoroughbred stood and watched her, his head over the web gate, tossing his head now and again in a way that made his forelock bounce. The white blaze was distinctive, like a star between his eyes with a long string down to a diamond-shaped patch of white between his nostrils. A blood bay, he had two white socks and a white stocking that came clear to his knee.

As DJ studied the bay, she worked out the other details. Should she draw him in the stall or in the ring? She finally settled on a head sketch since her time was so limited. Anyway, drawing Tony in the saddle would be too hard. She still had a tough time getting the proportions right on people.

When she heard Tony's voice in the tack room, she scuttled back over to her own side of the barn. Her fingers were itching to take pencil in hand and begin drawing the lines that would bring the horse to life.

That night at home when the phone rang, she kept on sketching, leaving it for her mother to answer. Lindy came into the family room where DJ sat curled in Gran's wing chair.

"It's your father. He would like to come over again on Sunday."

DJ looked up, pulling her thoughts together. "Why?"

"He wants to see you again."

"Oh." DJ shook her head. "I can't Sunday. I plan to ride awhile and then we're going to decorate the tree. Robert and the Bs are coming, remember?"

"Guess we'll just have to do that in the evening."

"Why don't you tell him we've got other plans? That's what you tell me to say." DJ picked up her gum eraser and gently took out a couple of stray lines.

Lindy stood in the doorway a moment longer before returning to the kitchen. "That will be fine, Brad. We'll see you about two."

"M-o-t-h-e-r!" DJ catapulted out of the chair. Lindy was just hanging up the phone when her daughter hit the kitchen. "That's no fair! I need to ride, and the weather report said we are supposed to have a nice weekend. I haven't been up in Briones forever."

"Sorry. That was the only time he could come, and he's bringing you something."

"Fine, he can drop it off and leave."

"Darla Jean." The note of warning was lost on DJ.

"How come you guys make all the decisions, and I'm just supposed to smile and agree?" She stomped across the floor to the fridge. "I'm so far behind with everything already, I'll never catch up. . . ." She caught herself. Whoa, not the time to bring that up.

"Then it's a good thing you won't be taking time to go riding, isn't it?" Icicles dripped from the tone.

"You're not being fair. I'll go riding anyway."

"Darla Jean Randall, I think that is quite enough."

DJ clamped her mouth shut, grabbed her soda, and just managed to keep from slamming the refrigerator door. "If anyone else calls with plans for me, I'll be in my room." The only bad thing about carpeted stairs was that she couldn't stomp loudly enough, but DJ gave it a good effort. She knew better than to slam her bedroom door, however.

When she looked at the drawing in her hand, she shook her head and ripped the page off the tablet. Why would Tony want one of her lousy drawings, anyway?

————————

At the party Saturday night, that same question troubled DJ. When it was Tony's turn to open his gift, she squeezed her eyes shut and clutched Joe's arm. What if Tony hated the picture?

Chapter • 11

"Hey, look at this." Tony held up the framed drawing for everyone to see. "Thanks, DJ." He looked at the illustration again and then at her. "Did you draw this?"

She nodded.

"Cool, it looks just like him. I didn't know you were an artist."

"Most people don't," Joe muttered, just loud enough for DJ's and Amy's ears.

"They will now." Amy poked DJ with her elbow. "You want money? Tell people you'll draw their horses—for a fee, of course. Hey, I'm a poet, too!"

"And you're a pain in the neck, but I don't go around telling everybody."

Tony passed the picture around amid oohs and ahs and "Wow, do you think you could do one for me?"

"How much would you charge, DJ?" Angie Lincoln's mother asked.

"I don't know."

Amy leaned around DJ. "She'll talk it over with her business agent and get back to you."

"Who?" DJ sent Amy a glare fit to fell a tree.

"Your business agent—me, of course. You've been getting me in trouble for years with your money-making schemes, and now I'm going to make sure you earn enough money that I don't ever have to do a pony party or raise hamsters again." She ended on a triumphant note.

Joe nearly fell off his chair laughing. Gran pushed him upright and winked at DJ. "See, darlin', I always told you your drawing would be a hit." She turned to her husband. "What's so funny?"

"Wish I had been in on the hamster hullabaloo. Knowing how much you like small, furry critters, that must have been a hoot."

"Mom's worse." DJ grinned at her grandmother. "You can bet they didn't try to help with the hamster roundup. And when John's friend volunteered to bring his boa constrictor over to hunt for his dinner, they really freaked. Mom yelled that hamsters in the garage were bad enough, but she would *not* permit a monster snake, too."

"I saw her freak at a garter snake once. 'Bout scared me half to death," Amy joined in.

"Who, Gran or Mom?"

"Your Mom. Gran can handle garter snakes."

"Thank you, Amy Yamamoto, you just made my day." Gran's smile could melt a block of ice at six paces.

"Attention, please." Bridget, list in hand, stood at the front of the room next to a table of trophies. "We have now come to the most important part of the meeting—the annual awards. Keep in mind that while not all awards are the Olympic gold, every person here deserves an award for his or her conscientious work, dedication to riding and improvement, and contributions to life here at Briones Riding Academy. I want to thank you all. That said, remember that many of *our* awards are of a different sort."

Applause broke out and died again.

"We will commence with the youngest and work our way up." Groans greeted the announcement. "You can wait your turn." Bridget's smile brought forth grins and squirming. "Emily Guerrero, please step up."

A five-year-old with dark hair and sparkling eyes got up from her place on the floor with the other little kids and came forward.

Bridget squatted down to be at Emily's eye level. "You might be our youngest rider, but, Emily, you are all heart." She pinned a heart-shaped badge that read *All Heart* on Emily's chest.

Applause and whooping continued as the younger kids paraded up for their awards. A hush fell when Andrew's name was called.

"Andrew, for your courage in overcoming your fear of horses, I crown you, Chief Courage." She placed a gold paper crown on his head that said *chief* and handed him a box of Lifesavers. "Whenever you need more courage, just think of your crown and eat one of these."

DJ shared a wet-eyed look with Gran. Amy nudged her and grinned.

"Thanks to you," Amy whispered.

Angie received a ribbon-tied fly swatter to chase yellow jackets, Amy got the golden hoof pick for her ability to pick even the dirtiest hoof clean, and David got the beribboned pitchfork for cleaning stalls. The cheerleader-of-the-year pompon went to a blushing Tony for his most improved attitude.

"And DJ," Bridget beckoned.

DJ scrunched her eyes closed for a moment, wishing she could hide behind Joe. *What will she give me?* She stood and went forward in spite of her dread. She hated being in the spotlight like this—they could turn off the lights and her red face would make the room light as day.

"This award is not presented very often," Bridget smiled at the kids on the floor, "because we try hard here at the Academy not to make a practice of flying through the air—unless it is on the back of a horse. DJ, you have the honor of receiving a seat belt for your saddle. I crown you Queen of the Dumped."

DJ tried hard not to laugh, but she had to join in as Bridget placed a ribbon around DJ's neck with a gold-foil medal proclaiming her new title. The heat blazing on her face made her long for a fan as she fingered the medal on the way back to her seat. Someday she'd wear a real gold medal, and it wouldn't be a joke. Perhaps it was a good thing her mom and Robert had to go to his company party and miss this crazy award.

"And last, but not least, we have an award for Joe Crowder." Bridget held up a coffee mug with a rickety cartoon horse on it. "For the oldest new rider here."

After Joe returned to his seat, Hilary stood. "And now it's our turn." She carried a package to the front. "Bridget, for all your hard work and effort on our behalf, we give you this with our thanks and appreciation."

Bridget took the slender box and carefully slit the paper ends.

"Just rip it!" yelled one of the little boys.

Bridget winked at him and slit open the taped seam. When the box opened, she drew out a gift certificate, along with a picture. "A new sign for the pickup." She held up the artwork featuring the academy logo in blue, circled by the name and address. The phone number was at the bottom. "How perfect. Thank you."

"You have to take the truck into a shop to be painted," Emily informed her.

"Thank you," Bridget replied.

"We all gave money," Emily continued, until someone put a hand over her mouth and whispered in her ear. "But I was just—"

"And with that, won't you all come and help yourselves to dessert," Bridget said above the laughter.

Several people stopped DJ and commented on the picture she'd drawn. Before she realized it, she had promised to do several, but made sure they knew it would have to wait until after Christmas.

"Told you so," Amy whispered on her way back from a refill at the punch bowl.

"If you're so smart, why didn't you have a price list drawn up?" DJ hissed back. She turned to field another interested parent.

"I really don't do people very well—"

"Don't believe her, you can recognize her riders, too."

DJ felt like clamping a hand over Amy's mouth like someone had with Emily.

On the way home, she and Gran discussed fees and more about the drawing commissions.

"The fee should depend on the size of the picture." Joe swung the truck into DJ's driveway.

"Wonder how the company party is going for Robert? Shame he and your mother couldn't have been in two places at once. They'd have been proud of you."

"Oh, sure—Queen of the Dumped." DJ fingered the medal she still wore. "Did you see the look on Andrew's face tonight? And to see him up on that pony the other day—that was primo."

"You could come over to our house." Gran reached up to give DJ a half-hug over the seat.

"I know, but I need to work on some stuff here. If only the Atwoods weren't coming tomorrow, Joe, we could go riding. Look." She pointed at the star-filled sky. "Clear and supposed to stay that way."

"There'll be another day. We'll wait till you get in." Joe gave her a pat on the shoulder. "Good night, kid."

DJ worked on the book for the twins until her eyes refused to stay open any longer. When she turned off the lights and snuggled down under the covers, the medal she dreamed of gleamed with the luster of real Olympic gold.

————————

The sunny morning, just cold enough so DJ could see her breath, did nothing for her sense of humor. If she skipped church, she could go riding. Maybe if she dawdled long enough over caring for Major, she would have an excuse. She *could* say she overslept. How would her mother know? Lindy had still been asleep when DJ left the house.

She propped her bike against the barn wall and trotted down the aisle and outside to Major's stall. Her whistle set half the barn to nickering, but Major outdid the others. He tossed his head, his forelock covering one eye. When she got close enough, he sniffed her pockets, finally finding his treat in the pouch of her hooded gray sweat shirt.

"Think you're pretty clever, don't you?" DJ teased as she dug out his carrot.

"He'd take your sweat shirt apart if you didn't give in." Joe stopped the wheelbarrow by Ranger's stall and began forking out dirty shavings.

"What would you say to going for a ride?" DJ let Major lean his forehead against her chest so she could rub the tips of his ears.

"Nice try, kid, but you know the rules."

DJ gazed up at the hills in Briones State Park. This would be such a perfect riding day. "We could hurry and be back in time for church."

"Washed and dressed by nine-thirty?" He looked at his watch. "Give me a break."

DJ muttered her way through feeding and stall cleaning. She gave Major a halfhearted grooming and dumped her gear back into the bucket. Why did grown-ups always have to mess up kids' lives?

When she got home, her mother was vacuuming the family room. From the looks of her outfit, she planned on doing some major cleaning.

"Aren't you going to church?" DJ asked.

"Not if we're going to be ready for company all afternoon. You and Joe are picking up the tree on the way home. Your father is supposed to be here about two, and Robert will come out with the boys at four. Now, tell me when I have time to go to church."

"I could stay home and help you." *And go riding when we're done.*

"No, one of us better get some religion today, just in case it helps to keep the peace around here."

DJ headed for the kitchen to get some breakfast. When her mother was in *this* kind of mood, disappearing was the smartest move. And besides, if she couldn't go riding, she wasn't about to stay home and do housework.

While she dressed, DJ let her mind roam to Christmases past. Up until last year, it had been only the three of them—Gran, Mom, and her. Simple. They had decorated the tree the Sunday before Christmas, attended the midnight service on Christmas Eve, and opened presents on Christmas morning. Of course, Gran had baked lots of goodies, and DJ had helped when she could. But *this* year Gran was married and living in a different house, they had family all over the country, and suddenly DJ had a father.

She jerked the brush through her hair and made a face at the one in the mirror. Wrapping a scrunchy around her ponytail, she headed back to her room. The roar of the vacuum came up from downstairs. With a flinch, she returned to the bathroom, put the towels in the hamper, wiped out the sink, and hung new towels. A last-minute check told her the room passed muster and she wouldn't get yelled at. If she ever wanted to ride again, keeping on her mother's good side was a smart move.

She was just heading for her bedroom when she heard the car honk—Gran and Joe were there. No time to make the bed or pick up the clothes strewn on the floor. She quickly closed the door, promising herself she would do it first thing when she got home.

———————

DJ tried to stay tuned during the service, but she was only partly successful. When the choir sang "Prepare Ye the Way of the Lord," all she could think of was not being ready for Christmas. Would she have her presents completed in time? Her unfinished term paper was due Tuesday, the last day before vacation.

The pastor's sermon was on helping those less fortunate. DJ grimaced as she thought about what she'd done to help needy people this Christmas: nothing. When a special offering plate was passed to buy food baskets for poor families, she dug into her pocket and hauled out the ten dollars she had left for her Christmas shopping and dropped it in. Monday she'd have to go back to the bank, but knowing she'd contributed even that much made her feel better.

The light went on in DJ's head as the pastor went on to relay a story about a boy who gave coupons for lawn-mowing. She could do something like that! The rest of the service flashed by in a nanosecond.

On the way home, she kept thinking. What could she put in coupon booklets for her mom and Gran?

"See you guys later." DJ waved as Gran and Joe drove off. She trotted into the house, only to hear the vacuum running upstairs. Visions of her messy room made her close her eyes. So much for good intentions.

"Darla Jean Randall, it doesn't seem to me to be too much to ask that you keep your room reasonably neat. Look at that pigpen."

"You tell me never to go into your room without an invitation; why did you go into mine?" DJ wished she could snag the words back as soon as she said them. *Why can't I learn to keep my mouth shut?*

"I thought I'd do you a favor and vacuum for you." Lindy brushed her hair back behind her ears. "But not now. You know how I feel about messes, and they'll all be here before you know it."

"I'll get right to it," DJ promised through clenched teeth. Why was her mother so upset about company coming? It was just the usual crowd—plus Bradley and Jacquelyn Atwood. *That's what's bugging her.* "Would have saved a lot of hassle if you'd have just let me go riding this afternoon."

"That's the thanks I get." Lindy snapped off the vacuum and trundled it to the closet. "You can do the dusting when you get done with your room."

"As if I don't have enough to do." DJ yanked the covers up and jerked the comforter into place on her bed. With the stuff on her desk crammed in the drawer and her clothes in the hamper, the place looked pretty good. Of course, she hadn't vacuumed, but then . . . "Who cares." DJ clomped down the stairs to begin her dusting, well aware of how noises like stomping feet irritated her mother.

By the time the Atwoods arrived, the house was immaculate, Lindy wore an indelible white line around her mouth, and DJ's jaw ached from clenching it. When the doorbell rang, DJ had to force a polite smile on her face before opening the door.

Her father stood there with a huge box wrapped in shiny green paper and a big matching bow. "Merry Christmas, DJ."

Beside him stood Jacquelyn, her arms filled with a decorated basket filled with all sorts of odd-shaped things. "From me, too."

"Merry Christmas . . . please come in."

She eyed her father, half hidden behind his gift. What in the world could be big enough to need a box like that?

Chapter • 12

"If you show us to your tree, we'll just put these under it."

"Uh, we don't have it up yet. We're doing that tonight, though this afternoon would have been better." DJ wished she hadn't added that last bit. Even to her ears, she sounded like a grinch.

"How are you, DJ?" Jacquelyn asked. "All ready for vacation?"

DJ led them into the family room. "No, I have to finish a term paper first." *How come they brought presents? We don't have anything for them. I never even thought of such a thing.* As her thoughts screamed in her head, she politely motioned them to seats and sat down in the wing chair, where she could face them.

"Sorry to be late." Lindy came down the stairs, her cream silk blouse and matching slacks set off by an emerald braided belt and emerald green earrings. She looked poised and relaxed—nothing like a few minutes before. "Coffee will be ready in a minute. Oh, what lovely gifts! How about if we put them over there for now?" She pointed to a spot by the wall at the end of the sofa.

DJ felt a giggle coming on. Her mother was incredible. DJ fingered her jeans—at least they were clean. And anything went with them, including her T-shirt, which showed a horse and said, *I'd rather be riding.*

"DJ, I brought pictures of our farm, some of the horses, and a few shows. Thought you might enjoy them." Jacquelyn patted the sofa between the two of them. "I'll explain who's who."

DJ joined them and, with the book spread out on her lap, got a glimpse of a life she'd never even dreamed of. The farm looked like something out of a magazine—all white fences, green pastures along a river bottom, and white buildings shaded by huge oak trees. While Arabs had never been her favorite breed, her father sure owned some beauties.

"That's Matadorian," Brad said, pointing to an obviously professionally done photo, "by Matador. Mares come from around the country to be bred by him. He's been national champion three times, and his get, or his offspring, take trophies wherever they go." Her father's pride was evident.

"He's a beauty."

"And smart." Jacquelyn shook her head. "You don't have to teach him something more than once. I wish my Hanovarian learned as quickly." They showed her photos of futurity shows and of dressage events.

"No jumpers?" DJ asked when she closed the book.

"Nope. It's never been an interest for either of us. That might have to change, though." His friendly smile made her think he planned to be around a lot. All these years of no one but Gran cheering her on, and now look at all the people on her cheering squad. That would mean butterflies at shows, big time.

"DJ, would you bring the plate of cookies?" Lindy asked as she entered with steaming cups of coffee on a silver tray. A glass of soda took up one corner.

"You don't drink coffee?" Brad asked DJ.

"She's only fourteen," Jacquelyn and Lindy said at the same time. They smiled at each other with a look that said, *Men!*

"Sorry, guess I forget. Seems I always drank coffee."

"You did, but I felt DJ needed to grow up before getting hooked on the stuff." Lindy set the tray on the coffee table. "DJ, the cookies."

DJ had been watching the exchange. She hadn't wanted to drink the bitter stuff yet—it had nothing to do with Lindy saying no. At another look from her mother, she headed for the kitchen, hurrying so she wouldn't miss anything.

After Brad had finished his coffee, he held the cup between his hands and stared at it a moment. "I have a favor to ask."

"Oh." Lindy settled deeper into the wing chair.

"Jackie and I would really love to have DJ come spend a couple of days with us during her Christmas vacation." He turned to include DJ in his range of vision. "If you want to, that is. I thought maybe you could bring a friend, if you'd like. I'd come pick you up and bring you back. I—*we* would so appreciate the time with you."

DJ glanced at her mother. Lindy's mouth wore faint traces of the white line again.

The silence that fell on the room made DJ itch.

"How about if DJ and I discuss this and get back to you?" Lindy crossed her knees and tented her fingers. "We'll let you know in the next day or so?"

Do I want to visit, or do I want to stay? I won't go without Amy . . . it would be exciting to see their place. The thoughts chased each other through DJ's mind like kittens skidding down a waxed hall.

"One other thing, we are leaving tomorrow to visit Jackie's family for Christmas, so if we've already left, just leave a message on the answering machine. I'll check in and get back to you right away."

"Fine."

DJ could tell Lindy's answer meant anything but.

They visited a bit more, then Brad patted DJ on the shoulder. "Well, we better be going. If what's in that box isn't to your liking, we can always exchange it." He got to his feet. "Thank you, Lindy, for the coffee and dessert. Hope you have a merry Christmas."

Jackie stood beside him. "Lindy, I do hope you will be willing to share your daughter with us. We promise to take good care of her. She's a fine young woman—one you can be proud of."

DJ felt the heat flame in her face. Why did grown-ups sometimes talk about you as if you weren't even there? As soon as all the good-byes were said and the door closed, she headed for the kitchen and the phone.

"Who are you calling?" Lindy leaned against the doorjamb.

"Amy, to see if she wants to visit them with me."

"I haven't said you were going yet."

At the tone of her mother's voice, DJ set the receiver back in the cradle. "Oh."

"Do you want to go? I thought you'd spend all your time riding, and you do have obligations at the Academy."

"I guess I want to go, if Amy can go along. Besides, I don't give lessons during vacation—Bridget knows working students are gone sometimes during holidays. All we have to do is let her know first." DJ stared at her mother. "You don't want me to go, do you?"

Lindy sighed and shook her head. "I don't know. Yes and no."

The doorbell rang and Robert's voice could be heard, calming the twins.

"We'll talk more later. Don't say anything yet, okay?"

DJ scrunched her face in a questioning look and shrugged. "Guess so. I better get the Bs before they batter the door down." She flung open the door to be bombarded with two high-power torpedoes. "Hi, guys."

"DJ, we was missing you! Christmas is almost here. You got any toys?" The two ran their sentences together as usual.

"I missed you, too. But sorry, no toys."

"How come? Gran has toys." Each of them had grabbed on to a leg and sat on a shoe, waiting for DJ to try to walk. With grins that split their cheeks, the Double Bs looked up at her with puppy-dog devotion.

DJ gave them their ride into the family room and collapsed on the floor, puffing as if she'd run a mile. "You guys get any bigger, and all rides are off." She let her arms fall to the sides and her tongue hang out.

One of the boys knelt next to her ribs and stared down into her eyes. "You okay, DJ?"

"No, I'm dying, can't you tell?" She let out a resounding groan.

The little one lay his head on her chest and an arm across her ribs. "Don't die, DJ. I likes you." The other one followed suit from the other side. "You our sister."

DJ wrapped her arms around both boys. "You two are the best brothers I ever had." She hugged them, then her hand crept into tickle position. Two jabs and they were writhing around, giggles exploding like firecrackers.

"I can tell you found DJ." Robert stood above the squirming pile and caught DJ's eye. "You need a break?"

"DJ likes us." More giggles and guffaws.

"I can tell." He turned at the sound of the doorbell. "Any time you've had enough, DJ, you let them know."

When the boys heard Grandpa Joe, they bailed off DJ and headed for the door.

Robert gave DJ a hand and pulled her to her feet. "I hear you received a very special award at the party."

DJ groaned. "Does the whole world have to know about my getting Queen of the Dumped?"

Robert ruffled her hair. "Nope, just family." He dropped an arm over her shoulders. "Sorry we couldn't be there. Next year you can bet I'll check everyone's calendar before I schedule the company party."

DJ moved just a bit closer, and he tightened his arm. His hug felt good—nearly as good as one from GJ. She looked up in time to catch a sheen on Robert's eye.

"I've never had a daughter before, and now I'm about to have one who's nearly full grown. You've got a special place in my heart, kiddo, and don't you forget it." He hugged her again.

"Should I bring down the boxes of decorations?" Joe asked, lifting each twin-clad foot with difficulty.

"I'll help." Robert grabbed Bobby and Billy, tucked a boy under each arm, and crossed to dump them giggling on the sofa. "You two get out a book and read. Or go help Lindy set the table."

"Are we putting the tree in the living room where it's always been?" Gran asked after dropping her parcels in the kitchen.

"Where else?" DJ looked at her as though she'd wrapped her mind in one of the boxes.

"Well, it would look good in the corner of the family room where my painting mess used to be." She looked over at DJ when she didn't answer. "What is it, darlin'?"

"I miss your painting things, and I never thought they were a mess. This room just hasn't looked right since you left."

"Mel, you going to help us find things, or you just want us bulling around up there?" Joe called from the top of the stairs.

"I'm coming." Gran hurried after the two men. "Can't have you rearranging the attic on such short notice, or we'll never find anything again."

DJ rubbed a sore spot on her chin with one finger. Oh, sure, a new zit. She studied the corner. The tree really would look nice there.

"Come on, guys, you can help me to move stuff." Together, they lugged the magazine rack to the living room, temporarily moved the plants to the dining room until they could find a better place, and shoved a chair over to the other wall.

"What are you doing?" Lindy asked.

"Putting the tree here." DJ laid a hand on the curly head beside her.

"But I already arranged the living room." Lindy rubbed the inside of her cheek with her tongue. "Hmmm . . . you know, the tree would work really well in here." She stopped DJ and pointed to a spot on the floor.

"Oh no." DJ slapped her head with her hands. "A dust bunny."

"Bunny, where's a bunny? I don't see no bunny." The boys hit the corner running.

Lindy threw an arm over DJ's shoulders. "Shall we tell them?"

DJ shook her head. "Nope, keep 'em looking. Besides, one of their knees picked up the dust bunny, so now we won't have to haul out the vacuum." Thoughts of the earlier fracas flitted through her mind.

"Whose present?" The boys had found the big box left by Brad.

"Mine."

"What is it?"

"How should I know? It's a Christmas present, sillies."

"Open it and find out."

"Not on your life, guys." Lindy swooped down and snagged the twins by the bands of their pants. "We don't open presents until Christmas morning. Come on into the kitchen, I think I hear a cookie calling you."

"One calling DJ, too?" They grabbed her hands and all trooped out to the kitchen.

———————

By the time they had the tree decorated, dinner eaten, and the house put back together, DJ felt like she'd been run through a cement mixer. Life wasn't easy with a twin Velcroed to each hip. When they all trooped out the door, DJ headed upstairs to work on her term paper. This promised to be a long night. And she hadn't even gotten to call Amy yet.

Sometime later, on returning from the bathroom, she heard her mother talking on the phone. In spite of all the years of both Gran and her mother cautioning against the evils of eavesdropping, DJ paused outside the door.

From the conversation, she knew Robert was on the other end.

"I know that, but what if he petitions for custody? You know that could happen."

DJ's heart hit her hip bones.

Chapter • 13

Custody! I'm not leaving here. No way. DJ leaned closer to the partially open door.

"I know she's level-headed, Robert, but you've read about all those cases in the newspaper. I just don't want to go through any legal battles. But most of all, I don't want to lose my daughter."

You won't, Mom, you won't. DJ chewed on the tip of her finger. She shouldn't have listened. *What can I do? God, do you see what's happening? Please help us.* She tiptoed back to her bedroom and noiselessly closed the door.

"I'm not going to visit them if that's what's going to happen." She paced to the window and back. "But is Mom worrying about something that's never going to happen? I need to talk to Gran and Joe." She sank down onto her bed and worried her bottom lip between her teeth as she gathered up her term paper. All she had left to do was to rewrite it in decent handwriting. How come every time she thought things were going smoothly again, something messed things up? Was that the way life always was?

That night DJ dreamed she was being chased—again. It was the first time in a while now. She jerked awake, heart pounding, mouth dry. Who was the man chasing her? And why? She turned on the light and headed for the bathroom. Surely by the time she went back to bed, the nightmare would be gone.

But it wasn't. She ran and ran, trying to scream, but no sound would come. Dark behind her, a light far ahead—would she make it in time?

———

Her alarm saved her. She woke up feeling as though she'd hardly slept.

"You look like you've been zapped by the Death Star," Amy said as DJ threw her backpack in the Yamamotos' car.

"Thanks for nothing. I can't help getting a zit."

"Not the zit, silly, you've got huge bags under your eyes and notebook paper has more color than your skin. You sick?"

"I didn't think so, but now I'm not so sure. You stay up half the night working on a term paper and see how you feel."

"That's why I always do my stuff early. I turned it in Friday." Amy ducked when DJ swung at her.

"One more day, just one more day and no school for over two weeks. I can get through it." DJ leaned her head against the back of the seat. "Oh, I almost forgot. Brad—"

"Your father?"

"What other Brad do I know? Anyway, he invited me to spend a couple of days at his house over vacation and said I could bring a friend. You want to go?"

"Do *you* want to go?"

"I'm not sure. Mom's all upset." DJ went on to tell her friend about the scene the night before—and her mother's worries. "You'd think I was moving out tomorrow the way she carried on." They'd reached their locker and the bell was about to ring. "I don't know, Ames, I just don't know."

"Well, I'll ask my mom if I can go, if you want. Sounds like a primo place."

"I wanted to at first—I mean, all their horses and Jacquelyn doing dressage—she said she'd show me stuff and that I could ride one of their horses." The warning bell rang. "See ya."

DJ had a tough time keeping her mind on the rivers of the world in geography class. What was her mother going to say?

But Lindy didn't mention the invitation at all that night. In fact, her mother hardly mentioned anything. She wore the green look of a migraine headache when she came in the door and headed to bed as fast as she could climb the stairs. When DJ offered to bring some soup, Lindy groaned and refused.

"Just leave me alone, and maybe I'll be human again by morning."

DJ spent the evening rewriting her paper and working on the book for the Double Bs. Gran had a meeting and wouldn't be home till after nine. She'd nearly talked with Joe about the whole mess while at the Academy, but they hadn't had enough uninterrupted time. Concentrating on what she had to do took every bit of willpower she owned and some borrowed besides. If only she could have gone to Gran's after riding.

She chewed on the end of her pencil. They were supposed to call Brad. If only that phone call from Mr. Bradley Atwood had never come—and if only she hadn't eavesdropped. She wished she could go riding up in Briones to forget everything. She looked up to see rain rivulets running down the window. Fat chance!

When Gran hadn't answered the phone by ten, DJ gave up. Her final message said, "I'll talk with you tomorrow. I'm crashing."

School let out at noon. DJ let out a whoop and danced all the way to Joe's truck. "I'm free, I'm free! Free at last."

Amy followed behind her, shaking her head at Joe's grin. "Don't blame me that she's gone freaky. I'm just her friend."

At the Academy, DJ worked Patches without incident, to the surprise of both her and the owner. Mrs. Johnson had stayed to watch how DJ handled the horse so she could learn to ride him better. But when it was time for Andrew's lesson, she went to sit in the car and read a book like she always did.

Andrew mounted Bandit with only slight hesitation, grinning at DJ's words of praise.

"You won't make him go fast so I fall off?" His question caught her by surprise.

"Why would I do that?"

"You went fast, and you fell off."

DJ shook her head. "Andrew, my boy, you get some of the screwiest ideas. Falling off isn't such a big deal. Patches dumped me because he had too much pep and he likes to do his own thing. But Bandit is not like Patches—Bandit has known how to behave for years. Patches is just learning. Don't worry, buddy, you aren't going to fall off today. Okay?"

"Promise?" He looked at her from under long lashes.

"Near as I can." DJ snapped a lunge line on to the pony's halter. "Now, are your legs in the right place? Back straight? Tuck in your elbows, hold your chin up, and you are ready to ride." She moved him into the proper position as she talked. "Now, today you get to see what making the pony move feels like. You turn him with the reins, kind of like riding a bike, and you make him walk by squeezing with your legs." She pulled first one rein and then the other, then pressed his legs against the sides of the horse. "So when I say turn right, you pull the . . ." She waited for his answer.

"Right rein. Not hard, though."

"That's right. And to go forward?"

"Squeeze my legs, but not hard."

"Right. We don't do anything hard here. Horses like a gentle touch." DJ led Bandit out to the arena, through a gentle mist. The air smelled clean and fresh. Oh, to be riding herself! And not around the arena.

She closed the gate and led the pony onward, giving Andrew right turn, left turn, stop, and go commands. Little by little she could see him relaxing, and a smile begin to curve his lips. At the stop, she turned again to face him. "Now, see this lunge line?" She held up the coiled rope. "You are going to start going in a circle around me. While you do that, you'll give Bandit his orders just like I did you. Got that?"

The smile flickered, and Andrew gritted his teeth. "I . . . I guess so."

DJ stepped back three paces, letting out the line as she went. "Okay, make Bandit go."

Andrew gripped the reins and squeezed his legs. Bandit walked forward like he always had. The boy turned to DJ with a grin wide on his face. "He did it. I made him go."

By the end of the lesson, his smile was a permanent fixture.

So was DJ's.

She understood much more how Andrew felt when Bridget refused to let her use stirrups during her dressage lesson later. "You remember how Major stopped the other day?" Bridget asked.

"How could I forget?"

"Your seat is much better, so I am sure that will not happen again. Remember what I said—when you pushed down with your pelvis, you pushed his backbone down, and that stopped him. Now, you must continue to drive him forward with your seat and legs. You did not have enough leg before."

"I know, balance between hand, leg, and seat. It sounds so easy in the book."

"You are right, it does sound easy. But nothing of value is ever easy, and you will be a much better jumper because of your willingness to work at this."

So you've said. DJ kept the words to herself—Bridget didn't care much for smart answers. By the end of the hour, her thigh and calf muscles were screaming and her back ached horribly. She was sure she'd hear the words "more leg" in her dreams.

When they finished the lesson, DJ surprised herself by asking Bridget a question. "Do you know of a woman named Jacquelyn Atwood?"

"Sure, she is a fourth-level rider from up north—Santa Rosa, I believe. Why?"

"Nothing much. Is she good?"

"To ride at that level you have to be. She has a wonderful horse, too. I cannot remember the name of the farm, but I believe her husband breeds Arabs."

"Atwoods' Arabians."

"Yes, that is it. Why all this interest in a dressage rider? You thinking of going on?"

"Me? Give me a break!"

"Sorry I asked. Keep practicing, though, DJ. You are doing well." Bridget waved and trotted through the mist to the office.

DJ watched her go, then used her legs to put Major into forward motion. If Andrew could learn new skills, so could she.

———

"Can we go to your house first?" she asked Joe on the road out of the Academy.

"Of course. I'll drop Amy off, and we'll be on our way. Your mother know this is the plan?"

"I left her a message." Now that the fun of riding was over, the questions came hurtling back.

Once at their house, she told Gran and Joe about eavesdropping on Lindy's conversation, then slumped back into her chair. "I don't know what to do."

"You can't do anything at this point, except talk with your mother. The two of you need to come to some kind of agreement." Gran drew a casserole dish from the oven and set it on the ceramic trivet on the table. "Would you please get the salad out of the fridge?" she asked Joe.

DJ sniffed appreciatively. "You baked bread, too."

"DJ, darlin', how many times have I told you not to eavesdrop?" Gran rested her hands on DJ's shoulders. "You wouldn't have so much to stew about if you hadn't overheard that conversation."

"I know, but I couldn't help it." DJ flinched under Gran's steady grip. She knew the look of disappointment that must be in Gran's eyes. "Don't tell, please? I won't do it again." She drew lines on the tablecloth with her fork tines. "But how else am I supposed to know what's happening? No one tells me—they just go ahead and do stuff. It's my life they're messing with."

"I know it must seem that way." Gran sat down, took Joe's hand, and reached for DJ's. "Let's say grace."

"Dear heavenly Father," Joe prayed, "bless this food so lovingly prepared for us. Thank you for the blessings you have given us, one of them sitting right across the table. You know what needs to be done for DJ and Lindy, and we thank you that you are working it all out in your good time. We thank you and praise you. Amen."

"Doesn't seem like He's working it all out. Just seems to be getting worse."

"Might look that way, but it's always darkest before the dawn." Gran held out her hand for DJ's plate. "That's where faith gets a chance to grow, in that dark before dawn. So let's just thank Him in advance for the answers and go on about our business." She looked up to catch DJ's eye and passed her plate back.

"I guess."

"God sees the whole picture, kid, not like us who get only glimpses."

Joe took his filled plate back. "Oh, Mel, this smells like something right from heaven."

"We're lucky it doesn't smell like turpentine or oil paint." She glanced down at the multi-dotted painting smock she still wore. "I had wanted that painting done in time to dry for Christmas, but it doesn't look like I made it."

"What are you working on?" DJ forked chicken and noodles into her mouth.

"A surprise for Robert. Thought he might like it for his new house."

"So it's for mom, too?"

"Will be, after they are married. I don't like to give a mutual present when they aren't exactly mutual yet. A lot can happen between now and February."

DJ stopped chewing on the bread heel she'd just buttered. "You think they won't get married?"

"No, it's just a kind of a superstition I have." Gran gave Joe a quick glance. "I know, I know—Christians aren't supposed to be superstitious, but old training is hard to break. My mother threw more salt over her shoulder than went in her soup. So I'll give Robert this painting, and Lindy something else. Then they can enjoy both gifts together."

"Gran, you blow me away."

"Oh, darlin', you and I both know our heavenly Father is first and foremost in my heart. And we'll all keep praying that He becomes so for Lindy, too."

They ate in silence until DJ said, "So . . . what do you think I should do about going to visit the Atwoods over Christmas break?"

"The Atwoods?" Gran arched one eyebrow.

"I don't know what to call him—them." DJ shook her head. "I hate making decisions."

Gran looked at DJ over the rim of her violet-banded coffee cup. "I think you need to go see him—if not right away, then soon. You have a right and a need to know your biological father if it's possible, and in this case, it certainly is. Between Brad and Robert, you are one mighty blessed girl to have two such fine men in your life."

"Three."

"Three?" The eyebrow went up again.

"GJ. I've got him, too."

"Funny you should say that." Gran patted Joe's hand. "And he even does dishes." The twinkle in her eyes brought an answering one from the man beside her.

"Flattery will get you everywhere. I suppose that was a hint so you could go back to painting?"

"Right."

"Good. You do that and DJ will help me with the dishes so we can make time to work on her frames. Right, kiddo?"

DJ groaned and made a face. "Think I like dishes?" But she began gathering the plates to take to the sink. "Maybe tomorrow you can help me with the Double Bs' book, huh, Gran?" She elbowed Joe away from the sink. "And if it's nice, Joe and I can ride up in Briones."

"More rain predicted."

"You sure know how to make me happy." Their banter continued as they rinsed dishes and stacked them in the dishwasher.

When her mother hadn't come by for her by ten, DJ climbed into bed in her bedroom at Gran's. At least this way she and Joe could get going early in the morning. As she closed her eyes, she thought a moment of the big box waiting at home. Whatever could be in it?

Chapter • 14

"I'll never get this thing right!"

"Just ask that cute guy over there for help. That's why he works here." Amy looked up from the photocopy machine at the Copy House to grin at DJ. "You just have no patience."

"With horses, yes. Machines, no." DJ made her way past the busy machines, most manned by people using red or green paper to make Christmas letters, up to the desk.

"Hi, can I help you?"

Amy was right, he *was* cute, but right now DJ needed brains. "I can't get that machine to print on both sides. I think we're following the directions." DJ pointed to the machine that she was sure was sticking its tongue out at her.

"I'll be there in a minute, okay?"

"Sure, thanks." She felt like stomping back to the machine. Why did everything seem to go wrong when she was in a hurry? At this rate, the cards would never be printed, and DJ was anxious to get going as soon as Joe got back. Today they were finally heading for a ride in Briones.

Amy finished printing the backs of her cards and moved on to the paper cutter. The photos had turned out beautifully clear: one of a rose from her mother's garden, another of her little sister eating an ice-cream cone, a view of fog over San Francisco Bay, and one of a goose swimming in a pond. Each packet would hold two of each card, for a total of eight.

DJ's horses probably wouldn't appeal to as many people, but she knew her family would be pleased. Bridget had said she'd carry them in the tack shop, too, so DJ was running off twenty sets.

The young man flipped a couple of buttons, checked on the card stock paper, slammed the machine closed again, and pushed the green button. Her page came out as clear as could be.

"Thanks."

"No problem." He held up the sheet of card stock. "Hey, that's really cool. Did you draw that?" At her nod, he studied the drawing of the foal again. "My sister would love something like this. She's nuts about horses. You making note cards?"

"Yeah, for Christmas presents." DJ stopped, caught the nod from Amy, and continued. "And we'll be selling them, too."

"Could you get me a set or two? How much are they?"

DJ stumbled over her tongue. On the second try, she answered, "There are eight to a pack, and the packs cost four dollars. My friend Amy has reproductions of her photos on hers." She pointed to the paper cutter table.

"Cool. Are the two of you in business or something?"

"Sorta."

He stopped for a minute, studying the growing stack of four-by-five ready-to-fold cards. "Could I buy two sets from each of you? Makes my shopping easy."

Amy looked up. "Sure, we'll package them and bring them back here tomorrow. If you've got any friends here who might like them, let them know we'll bring extras."

DJ rolled her lips together to contain a grin. *Leave it to Amy not to miss a trick.*

When the Copy House employee walked off to help someone else, the girls swapped high fives. "That'll at least help pay for the envelopes." DJ removed her sheets from the machine and took over Amy's place at the cutting board. "If we sell enough, we'll have free Christmas presents to give. Why didn't we think of this a long time ago?"

Amy folded her cut cards. "You know, maybe we should charge five dollars instead. I checked at a stationery store, and note cards were priced all the way up to $7.95 for a package of ten."

"You know what my mom says, you've got to price stuff according to what the market will bear."

"Woowee, listen to the big business woman over here!"

As soon as they finished cutting the cards, they paid their bills and headed out to the truck where Joe waited.

"You can see if you promise not to tell anyone." DJ couldn't wait to show him.

"Promise."

Each girl handed Joe samples of her cards. A hush fell as they waited for his opinion.

"These are really good." He shuffled through them again. "I'm impressed. Are these Christmas gifts, or your latest money maker?"

"Both. We sold two packs each to a guy who works at the Copy House." DJ bounced on the seat in her excitement. "Now we can go riding. Hurry up, GJ, the horses are waiting." She and Amy took their cards back and carefully put them into their bags. No bent corners or smudge marks would do.

Amy gently tucked the package into the glove compartment. "Hey, I forgot to tell you. My mom said I could go to your father's farm with you, if you still want to go."

"That's the question, isn't it?" DJ slid her fingers up and down the seat belt crossed over her chest. She nodded. "Yeah, we'll go. I'll call him and make the final plans."

Joe patted her knee. "I'm proud of you, DJ. You'll make it."

DJ flashed him a grin. "Promise?"

"Promise."

While clouds crept over the hills as they saddled, DJ refused to give in. The three of them were going riding, and that was that. If they got sprinkled on, so be it. The wind picked up, and they could feel the temperature dropping as they rode up the hill and out of the Academy. Through one more gate, and they were on park land, hills now covered with the green of winter thanks to all the rain they'd had. One hillside had been so rain soaked it had given way and slid downward, leaving a bowl of exposed dirt and rumpled ridges of grass-covered dirt below. The cattle that had free range in the park ran before them as if they were being chased when they made their way down the path to the staging area, a parking lot for park visitors. During the busy park season, a ranger took fees in a small building at the entrance to the parking lot.

Since mountain-bike riders and hikers loved the trails as much as horse riders did, the park was always well used. Today, however, the parking lot was empty.

DJ nudged Major into a canter as they took the main trail under the trees and followed a creek that now held plenty of frothing water. In the summer it was only a trickle.

"Come on, GJ, doesn't that young pony of yours know how to enjoy a real ride?"

"Just watch and you'll see." Joe kept a careful hand on the reins.

Ranger whinnied as the other two horses disappeared around a curve.

"I love riding right before a storm," DJ shouted.

"Me too." Amy kept Josh at the same even gait as they climbed the well-kept fire road trail.

DJ glanced over her shoulder. "Hey, look who's catching up!" What fun it would be to really run, to race up the hill and across the meadow, to let Major have his head and just go.

Major snorted and tugged at the bit. He wanted the same thing.

DJ was tempted, but she kept the easy rocking-chair canter that ate up the miles. Not only was it easier on her horse, but it was safer should the trail be slippery. They rounded another corner, and she signaled a halt, this time with seat and legs instead of just pulling on the reins. Major obeyed instantly.

A washout had dug a three-foot wide and half as deep ditch across the trail. If they'd been galloping, they'd have had to jump over or stumble through it. Sloppy mud all around made footing treacherous.

DJ looked at Amy and shook her head. "Sure glad we weren't racing."

"Me too. That could have been a bad one."

Ranger stopped beside them, front feet dancing while he pulled at the bit and tossed his head. Joe leaned forward and, keeping one hand snug on the reins, stroked his mount's neck.

"Easy, fella." He looked around. "These hills must be soaked for the runoff to be this bad. You'd think that was a regular creek. Well, guy, guess you are going to get a lesson in crossing water. Lead on, DJ. Major will be cautious, but he'll go."

DJ squeezed her legs, and Major, placing his feet with utmost caution, negotiated the two-foot drop, splashed in the ankle-deep water, and headed up the other side. Josh followed suit, snorting all the way.

Ranger, however, would have none of it. He snorted and backed up fast. When Joe brought him up to the water again, he let the horse put his head down and sniff.

Major nickered, as if encouraging the younger animal.

Ranger put one foot forward, then the other. Joe talked to him gently, but when the gelding put his foot into the water, he sat back on his haunches and whirled around. Had Joe not kept a firm hand on the reins, Ranger would have headed for home.

"Easy, fella," Joe kept up the murmur as he dismounted. "Guess we'll do it this way. You'll have to learn someday. We should have made you go through water before—a good trail horse does all this stuff." Joe led him down and stopped at the edge of the running stream. "Now, you *could* just jump over this thing if you had a mind to, but we're going to walk it." He pulled on the reins.

Ranger snorted and he rolled his eyes. He moved to back up, but the steady hands on his reins and Joe's gentle voice kept him coming forward.

DJ watched the process, swapped concerned glances with Amy, and found herself praying, *God, please get that fool horse through this safely*.

Ranger splashed water with one foot and leaped forward. If Joe hadn't been prepared, he'd have been run right over. The gelding now stood trembling on the other side.

Joe patted him and told him how great he was.

DJ breathed a sigh of relief. "You know, you really should make him go back and forth a couple of times to get him comfortable with it."

"I know." Joe grinned up at her. "Want to trade horses?"

"Not me. Just think what this would be like with Patches. I know Mrs. Johnson wants to ride up here. Soon it'll be time for me to get him used to things like this."

Joe led Ranger back and forth across the stream, then mounted to cross a last time and head up the trail. Ranger snorted but stepped down and through the water as though he'd never thought of charging or refusing.

"Good boy," Joe said, stroking the horse's neck and grinning at DJ and Amy. "Well, we had our excitement for the day, wouldn't you say?"

"He's going to be a good horse," DJ said, a smile now chasing the worry away. "I thought maybe that was the end of our ride."

"Nah, I knew he'd do it."

"Just not when, right?" Amy patted Josh's neck. "I remember the first creek he crossed. He wasn't a happy camper."

When they crested the trail and reached the meadow, low clouds cottoned the hilltops and sent tendrils exploring the valleys. Off to the right, the river flowing through the Carquinez Straits lay molten gray. The smokestacks of the refineries in Martinez puffed steam clouds that plumed due east, and the trees above them whipped in the wind, small limbs and dead leaves scurrying before the onslaught.

The air hung heavy with the promise of rain.

DJ sucked in a deep breath and turned to grin at Amy. "Don't ya love it?"

"It's going to get wet out here pretty soon. Think we better turn back?" Joe stopped beside them.

"We should, but let's ride up to the saddle where the bluebird houses are. I hate to turn back."

When the others agreed, DJ nudged Major back into a canter and they followed the road around the curve and up the hill. Cattle grazed the slopes and watered at the pond that now looked like a small lake. She wanted to keep going, down into the valley and around the other hills. Even with all the riding she'd done in the park, she'd never followed all the trails. There was never enough time.

Reluctantly, DJ turned back. Soon, she promised herself. Soon she'd follow that trail around the north side of the hills, the one that didn't look as well used as the others.

They were drenched by the time they made their way back into the stable yard.

Back at Gran and Joe's after DJ had taken a shower to warm up, she and Joe finished the last of the framing and Gran helped her assemble the book for the twins.

"That's it, then," DJ sighed when she tied the last bow on the packages. "My Christmas presents are finished."

"And none too soon, with Christmas Eve tomorrow night." Gran set a plate of cookies on the table. "Try these and see if we should make more of them. I made up a plate of goodies for you to take to the Yamamotos. You want to drop it off on your way home?"

"Sure." DJ grinned around a mouthful of cookie. "You better start mixing, Robert's gonna clean these out." She plucked a chocolate kiss off the top of the round peanut butter cookie. "How come we never made these before?"

"I didn't have the recipe before." Gran poured coffee for her and Joe and set a mug of hot chocolate in front of DJ. "You want a drop of coffee in that?"

"Mocha? You bet." DJ took a swallow. "Thanks, Gran, you're the best."

"After Christmas we'll have to invite Shawna to stay over." Joe leaned back in his chair. Shawna, who dreamed of taking riding lessons someday, was the only daughter of Joe's son Andy.

As he proceeded to impress Gran with tales of their ride, DJ felt locked on the words "after Christmas." After Christmas—next week to be exact—she would be going to her father's house for the first time. Three days away from Major, and three days with a man she hardly knew. Could she stand it?

Chapter • 15

Having lots of relatives sure made a difference at Christmastime.

Early in the afternoon, DJ gave Major his gift—extra horse cookies and a new halter. She gave Patches a treat and then went to see Bandit and Megs. The mare greeted her like a long-lost friend, making DJ feel guilty for not paying the retired jumper more attention since she got her own horse. She'd begun jumping lessons on Megs, Bridget's show horse of many years.

"See you tomorrow," she told Bandit. "You'll have plenty of kids to entertain." Bandit snuffled in DJ's pocket for more treats and was rewarded with a carrot piece. "You're too smart for your own good." She gave him an extra pat, and after making sure Major had fresh water and hay and had finished his grain, she trotted out to ride her bike home. Sun peeked through the patchy clouds, and while the weather announcers said storms were lining up out on the Pacific, tomorrow was supposed to be nice.

Since Amy and her family had already left for the weekend to visit her grandparents, DJ rode alone. Joe had offered her a ride, but as he and Gran were hosting everyone for dinner, she'd done his chores at the Academy, too. Tonight would be like Thanksgiving had been—one long slumber party.

"Hurry up or we'll be late," Lindy called from her bathroom as soon as DJ mounted the stairs.

"I'm hurrying." DJ draped her horsy jeans and shirt over the back of a chair. They weren't dirty, just full of horse hair and stuff. She'd wear them for chores in the morning. Honestly, if her mother had her way, the smell of horses would never pass the kitchen door. What was going to happen at their new house when the twins had ponies and she had Major? How would her mother stand it?

DJ climbed into the shower. Thoughts like that always gave her the shivers. Life had changed so much already, and as far as she could see, it was changing big time in the months ahead.

Her mother gave her a didn't-you-have-something-nicer-to-wear-than-that look when they met downstairs. DJ shrugged. Compared to her mother, she looked casual. But at least she wasn't wearing jeans and a T-shirt. She had on navy corduroy pants and a real shirt with buttons up the front. She'd even ironed it. If she could have found a belt, the outfit would have looked more put together, but she was running late. As usual, the look from her mother said.

DJ picked up the last box of presents and followed her mother out to the car. They'd already taken over most of the wrapped packages, including the big one from her father, the day before. Once in the car, DJ thought again about the big box. More than once, she'd been tempted to open it very carefully, peek in, and wrap it back up.

She glanced at her mother. What would she have done if she caught her daughter sneaking a peek at Christmas presents? DJ grinned. It wasn't worth the chance of being found out, so she'd left well enough alone. Whatever it was sure felt heavy when she shook it—accidentally, of course.

Every light in Gran and Joe's house was on, and the outside looked like a fairyland with small white lights around the windows, doors, trees, and along the roof peak. DJ had helped Joe and Robert put them up two weeks earlier.

"Isn't it lovely?" Lindy breathed. "Robert said next year we are going to do our house." She leaned on the steering wheel. "You know, we haven't put up outside lights since Grandpa died. Do you remember the way he used to decorate?"

DJ shook her head. "I was just a twerp, Mom. The only thing I remember was that the tree was always in the living room corner." She gathered the shopping bags and presents and opened the car door. Gran had carols playing on an outside speaker.

"O Holy Night, the stars are brightly shining . . ."

DJ looked up. The carol was right.

They were the last to arrive. Andy and Sonya with daughter, Shawna, greeted them in the doorway and led the way to stack the remaining presents under the tree, now nearly hidden by gaily wrapped packages.

After dinner at warp speed, the entire family trooped off to the Christmas Eve service. This year, they hadn't waited for the midnight service because of the younger children. They all accepted their white candle with its cardboard shield at the door, and with one twin on each side, DJ followed Robert into the pew. The church glowed with candlelight, and the organ swelled with the age-old carols.

DJ breathed in the scent of evergreens, shushed the boys, and closed her eyes for just a moment. This was her favorite service of the year. A hush fell as if the entire roomful of people stopped breathing at the same instant.

A violin sang the opening bars of "What Child Is This?" joined by a flute and finally the piano. Times like this, DJ wished she'd taken time to learn to play an instrument. She could feel the music tugging at her throat, making the backs of her eyes burn. The words crescendoed in her mind: "This, this is Christ the King . . ."

She put an arm around each of the twins and hugged them to her.

As the verses told the story of the Christ child's birth, she thought of the shepherds, smelled the hay in the stable, and imagined a cow lowing. It was easy to be there in her mind. Her fingers itched to draw the scene.

"Come, see where He lay," the pastor announced from the pulpit. "He came for you and for me, giving up all His godly powers—He who was at the beginning of creation. Think of it! He did this for you, for me, for all people. Think what it would be like if you left all your human qualities and took on being a grasshopper. He who brought us into being gave up being God—for us."

DJ leaned forward, elbows on her knees. Bobby and Billy did the same.

"He loves us that much."

She flashed a glance at her mother, sitting on the other side of

Robert. Were those tears shimmering in her eyes? The burning behind her own eyes grew more insistent.

"No matter what we do, no matter how hard we try to run away, even when we try to ignore Him, He loves us."

At the end of the sermon, when everyone stood for the hymn, DJ felt like hugging everyone who stood around her. The choir sang during the offering, then the lights dimmed. The altar candles were extinguished, and the tree darkened.

The pastor walked down to stand directly in front of the congregation, a tall, thick candle in the hands of one of the teenagers beside him. "We read from the first chapter of the gospel of John, 'In the beginning was the Word, and the Word was with God, and the Word was God. He was with God in the beginning. . . . In him was life, and that life was the light of men.'"

Two more teens came forward, lit their candles at the pastor's, and one by one the light moved down the center aisle and then out into the rows. "Silent night, holy night . . ." When each person had lit a candle, then he could begin singing.

The boys fidgeted beside DJ. When the candle came to their row, DJ watched as each member of her family lit a candle from the one beside. The Bs bounced in their excitement. Gran held her candle steady and the first twin dipped his, oohing at the light he now held. DJ lit hers, sharing her flame with the second twin, who shared his with Robert.

DJ felt an uneasy flutter in her stomach as the sea of flames around her grew. She took a deep breath. Both boys proudly held their candles up to her face to show her the flames. A fist seemed to grab her throat as hot wax dripped onto her hand. *Fire!* She felt the familiar fear take hold. Was someone screaming?

Chapter • 16

"DJ, you all right?"

"Please, DJ!"

The boys' cries sounded as if they were a mile away.

"I . . . I'm fine." DJ blinked and took a deep breath. Robert held her hands in his, and Gran wrapped her arm around her granddaughter's shoulders. "Wh-what h-happened?"

"The fire, darlin'. You know how the memories can affect you. I suppose all the candles . . ." Gran's whisper in her ear brought DJ back to the moment. What had she done? Gone all kooky again? How embarrassing.

DJ looked to see tears pooling in the big blue eyes of the Double Bs. "Hey, guys, you didn't do anything wrong. It's just me . . . and . . . and fire. We don't get along too well." She forced the words past the desert in her throat. All around them, people were extinguishing their candles as the lights came back up. The pastor gave the blessing, and the organ broke into "Joy to the World."

DJ stood with the rest of them. She rubbed the wax off her wrist and covered the scar in the middle of her palm with the other hand. *All because of a couple silly little candles. What kind of a weirdo am I?*

The boys glued themselves to her side, shooting her anxious looks when they thought she wasn't looking. On the ride back to Gran's, the conversation flowed around her as though she were a rock in the middle of the stream. And like a rock, she had no voice—except inside her head, where several voices argued about how stupid she was. She rubbed the scar again as if the action would bring back the memory. One day she would have to ask Gran again how it had all happened.

"It's okay, darlin," Gran said, pulling DJ close as they walked up the sidewalk to the house. The luminaries they'd made out of brown sacks with a candle and sand in them lit the way.

"I spoiled the service for everyone."

"No, no one around us even noticed."

"Was I screaming?"

"Of course not. Did you think you were?"

DJ nodded. "I heard someone screaming, but now that I think about it, it sounded like a little kid." She took a deep breath. "Well, that's over." She grabbed one of the twins by the back of his jacket. "First one into the house gets to turn on the tree!"

Later they hung all the stockings from the fireplace mantel and stood back to admire them.

"Santa's got a big job there," Robert said. "You think he's up to it?"

"Santa's going to bring me a pony," one of the twins announced.

"Me too." The other looked up at their father. "That's all I asked for."

Robert groaned. The other adults snickered.

"Okay, bedtime." Robert clapped his hands. "Santa can't come till you're asleep."

DJ debated whether to stay up longer, but the look in Shawna's eyes made her decide to hit the sack. She and Shawna were sharing the bed, and the boys had sleeping bags on the floor in the grandkids' room. She heard her mother leave with Andy and Sonya while Robert headed for the other guest room. Slowly the house settled down. She shushed the boys again, and Shawna giggled softly.

"Daddy!"

"What now?" Robert came to the door.

"I wanna drink of water."

"Me too."

Robert brought two plastic glasses. "Last time. I hear one more peep from you two, and no Santa."

More giggles. Quiet again.

"Tomorrow we get to ride," Shawna whispered. "I can't wait."

"You want to spend a couple of days of your Christmas vacation out here with me?"

"Really?"

"If it's okay with your mom," DJ whispered back.

"That would be the best Christmas present ever."

DJ fell asleep hearing the violin and flute soar with the notes of "What Child Is This?"

"DJ, wake up. It's Christmas!" Four small hands tugged at her blankets and patted her cheeks.

"Go 'way," she mumbled, scrunching her eyes closed.

"Come see the presents."

"Now, DJ." A giggle, then another.

DJ opened one eye. "It's still dark out. You can't get up till it's light." She covered her head with the quilt.

"We can *turn* on the lights."

"Nope. No Christmas till it's light outside. Hit the sack, guys."

"Go get Daddy," she heard one whisper.

"No, you don't. Let him sleep. Let *me* sleep—just till light."

Shawna smothered a giggle beside her.

DJ closed her eyes and tried to go back to sleep. All she could see was that big box. Today she'd find out what was in it! She could hear the boys turning over and over. They whispered about as quietly as a train whistled.

"Okay, fine—go get your poor daddy up."

They erupted from their sleeping bags with matching shrieks and streaked down the hall.

"Quietly," DJ sighed. "Come on, Shawna, we don't want to miss anything."

"No presents until everyone gets here," Robert decreed when he met her in the hall. "And until the adults get their first cup of coffee." He rubbed his eyes and winked at DJ. "Thanks for keeping them down for a little while longer."

"You heard?"

"Of course." He gave her a one-armed hug on his way to the kitchen, where the tempting smells of coffee and cinnamon rolls beckoned. Gran even had the table set already.

DJ sat cross-legged on the floor with the boys, who were eagerly digging in their stockings, spreading their treasures all around. Tiny packages were tightly bound with tape to slow their nimble fingers. When they reached the sock toes, each held up a shiny silver dollar.

Shawna and DJ joined the excitement and dug into their stockings. By the time DJ had unwrapped each small treasure, she had new drawing pencils, erasers, hair scrunchies, a booklet of coupons for the local hamburger place, gum, mints, a popcorn ball, a tangerine, and a pomegranate.

"What's that?" The boys abandoned their socks to come examine hers.

"A pomegranate."

"What do you do with it?"

"Eat the seeds. I'll show you later." She dug down to the toe of her stocking and retrieved her silver dollar.

"We gots those in our banks."

"Daddy said not to spend them—they special."

"You are, too." She ruffled their curls and set them to giggling with tickles. Her eye kept wandering back to the big box set to the back of the tree.

By the time everyone finally congregated in the living room, the boys were wound tighter than a twister.

"Shawna, you want to play Santa Claus?" Robert asked.

"I thought that was my job," Andy moaned.

"I get to help."

"Me too." The twins bounced in front of the tree.

"Okay, okay." Shawna sat by the tree, dug out the gifts, read the names, and handed the boxes to the boys to deliver. With everyone waiting to watch each person open a present, DJ could tell this would be a long process. Should she ask for the big box first? If only it hadn't been stashed behind the other presents!

Soon brightly colored paper and ribbons decorated the floor in spite of Gran's continual folding. Robert wore a wobbly smile when he thanked DJ for the framed drawing, and the note cards were a huge success. The pile of gifts beside DJ continued to grow. She'd never have to buy clothes again—or drawing paper.

It took both boys to carry the big box to her. She split the paper open with trembling fingers.

"Who's it from?" Bobby asked. DJ had pinned name tags on the twins earlier, saying, "I'm going to figure out who's who or bust."

"My . . ." What to call him? "My father." She glanced up to catch a frown streak across her mother's face.

"Hurry, DJ, I wanna see."

"So do I, guys, so back up!" She grinned and tickled the little boy to make him scoot back. Slowly she unfolded the flaps and got up on her knees to look into the box. Pushing aside the packing material, she stopped breathing. "Oh." Her breath came back on a sigh. "A saddle." She looked under the saddle leather for the brass nameplate. "A Crosby."

DJ lifted out the saddle, scattering foam peanuts in the action. She stroked the fine leather. Never had she dreamed of having such a fine saddle. She'd been saving for a used one. A Crosby all-purpose saddle, she could use this one for jumping, for dressage, and just riding. She looked up to see Robert and her mother exchange meaningful glances.

"There's more." Billy lifted out a new headstall.

Her father wouldn't have known she already had a new one, given to her by Angie's family after the beesting incident.

DJ opened the card attached to the stirrup. *I hope you can use this,* her father had written. *If you need something more, or if the saddle doesn't fit just right, we can always exchange it.*

"Sit in it, DJ!" a twin squeaked.

"No, can't do that unless it's on a horse, or you can break the tree."

"What tree?"

Joe saved her explaining. "Well, that is some surprise." He broke the silence that had fallen on the adults. "I know you'll get a lot of good use out of that. Shawna, there's another box for DJ behind the tree."

This one held a new blue blanket for Major. It even had his name sewn in the corner. The card read *With all our love, Gran and GJ.* DJ leaped from the floor and threw her arms around them both. "Thank you. You knew mine was pretty ratty."

Shawna came over and stroked DJ's new saddle. "Sure is pretty."

Robert and Andy slapped their knees and rose in sync. "Far as I know, there's still one more present." Robert looked at Joe. "You ready, Dad? This is kind of a present from the whole family."

"I guess. What did you young pups get into now?" Joe got to his feet, ribbons and bits of paper slipping to the floor.

"Hmmm. How are we going to do this?" The two brothers grinned at each other.

"I say we blindfold the bunch and lead 'em out," Andy suggested. "Gran, you got any extra dish towels?"

"How many do you need?"

"Ummm..." Robert counted. "Joe, DJ, Shawna, the twins... five'll do it." As soon as all the blindfolds were in place, they led the staggering, giggling parade outside.

"Where are we going?" DJ blew the corner of her blindfold off her lips.

"You'll see. Step carefully now." Lindy had DJ's hand.

DJ shuffled her feet. How strange to be blinded like this. What was going on?

"Okay, what's up?" Joe asked ahead of her.

"You'll see."

"Hey, Billy, no peeking."

"Are you ready? Now, on three, you can all take off your blindfolds. One, two, three!"

DJ whipped the dish towel off her head and gasped.

"Well, I'll be!" Joe let out a roar. "You, you . . ."

DJ looked at Shawna with a grin.

"But I don't have a horse." Shawna looked to her father. A sudden grin lit her face like a megawatt candle. "But I get one, don't I?"

"As soon as we find one we all like."

She ran and threw herself into her father's arms.

DJ let herself be pulled forward till she stood next to the shiny silver four-horse trailer. A huge red ribbon was tied in a bow on top of the roof.

"Look at that. Dual wheels." Joe placed a hand on DJ's shoulder. "And a changing room."

DJ opened the door and peeked inside. Two tiny whirlwinds zipped around her and began exploring.

"How come for us?"

" 'Cause we gets ponies!"

Shawna ducked under her arm. "DJ, I'm getting a horse—you heard him." The light still shone in her face.

"Who do we thank?" DJ turned to the rest of the family, all lined up watching and laughing at the new trailer owners.

"Check the card." Robert pointed to an envelope fastened to the ribbon streamer.

DJ opened it, and Joe read. "To our horse people, with love from Robert, Lindy, Andy, Sonya, and Gran."

"How did you manage to get this here without me noticing?" Joe asked.

"We'll never tell." Robert had his arm around Lindy's shoulder. "Besides, if Lindy and I get horses, we'll need a larger one."

DJ felt her jaw hit her chest and bounce back up to snap closed. Her mother? On a horse? That would be the day. She crossed to the group and, starting with her mom, gave them all hugs and thank-yous. What a day. What an incredible, four-star, awesome, wonderful day! A saddle *and* a horse trailer.

Bobby and Billy jumped on the tailgate and chased each other around the rig.

DJ looked at her mother. She could tell something was bothering her, even though she was laughing at something Robert had said. The tiny furrows between Lindy's eyebrows were a dead giveaway. Was it the saddle?

DJ chewed her lip. *I bet it is,* she thought, *I just bet it is. Now what's going to happen? She won't make me give it back, will she?*

Chapter • 17

DJ lost every video game.

"Don't feel bad, darlin', they beat me every time, too." Joe patted her on the head as he walked by.

When the twins asked her to play the game again, she shook her head. "Not with you two sharks. Get your uncle to play." She heaved herself to her feet. It had been at least an hour since brunch—surely there was something out there to eat. She snagged a candy-cane cookie off the silver three-tiered platter on the dining room table and meandered into the kitchen. Lindy, Gran, and Sonya sat at the kitchen table drinking coffee.

"Where's everyone else?" DJ dunked her cookie in Gran's coffee cup.

"If you mean the big, strong men, they crashed." Sonya lifted her cup in salute. "I hear the monsters mangled you out there. Don't feel bad—Shawna's the only one who can hold a candle to them. They're better with that joy stick than I'll ever be."

"But they're not even six years old yet. Scary." DJ leaned against Gran's shoulder. "Sure smells good in here."

"Is that a hint?" Gran wrapped her arm around DJ's waist.

"Could be called that. I mean, if you had something to offer a starving child, she wouldn't turn it down." DJ tried to make her voice and face pitiful.

"Cinnamon roll?"

"Are there any left?" DJ's voice dropped to a whisper.

"Enough to last until dinner. Check the bread box."

"You make the best cinnamon rolls in the whole world." DJ set the gooey roll on a paper plate and put it in the microwave.

"You know, it's not fair—if I ate like my kid does, I'd weigh three hundred pounds," Lindy observed.

"I know how you feel." Sonya reached over and snagged a bite off the roll when DJ set her plate on the table.

"You want one? I'll fix it." DJ looked from one to the other. Sonya nodded and Lindy shook her head. "Take that one, and I'll make me another."

"You mean just because I peeled off the best part, it's mine?"

"Something like that." DJ grinned at the teasing and flinched when she heard the thunder of the twins' feet. "Quick, bar the door!"

"DJ, can we go riding now?" The twins glanced at the food set out and flung themselves at DJ's legs. "We was good forever. We beat Shawna, too."

"That makes you the champs. Go ask your grandpa. If he says yes, it's okay with me."

"Me too?" Shawna leaned against her mother. "They beat me."

The boys charged out at top speed. These days, that seemed to be their only speed.

"Walk, please. No running in the house," Gran called.

The thunder turned to soft patters, but giggles floated back.

"Just think, Lindy," Sonya said after licking the caramel goo from her fingertips, "in a couple of months, you'll hear that all the time."

"I know, and it sometimes scares me to bits."

DJ looked up and watched her mother's face.

"How do you direct all that energy? I've never been around little boys—in fact, I've hardly been around small children at all. The times they've been at our house, no matter how good they've been, they're just always so busy." Lindy sneaked a bite of cinnamon roll. "Wears me out."

"You'll get used to it. It's good that Robert plans on keeping the nanny."

"Yeah, at least for a while, until I decide if I'll quit my job or not."

DJ nearly choked on the last bite.

Lindy looked over at her and smiled. "Shocker, huh?"

"Really?"

"We've been talking about it. My professor is so interested in my thesis on entrepreneurial kids that he keeps encouraging me to turn it into a book. He says I write well enough. Maybe my mother and my daughter aren't the only ones with all the talent." She looked over at Sonya. "Actually, DJ and Amy gave me the idea."

DJ rolled her eyes. "Yeah, as if all our tries to earn money worked."

What would it be like to have her mother home all the time?

"Well, some better than others. Look at your note card sales. You cleaned out your inventory before Christmas."

"I think they're wonderful. If I'd have known you were selling them, I'd have bought enough to give to the people in my office for gifts," Sonya said.

"I'll always have more." DJ winked at her. She could feel her insides go all warm and fuzzy at the compliment. All those she'd left at the Academy sold, too. And she now had three commissions to draw member horses. Crazy, here when she finally had an actual way to make money, she already had a saddle. Now maybe her saddle fund could go for clinics and stuff. Of course, Major needed new shoes. . . .

Giving the kids rides at the Academy an hour later reminded her of the pony parties. But with Joe taking the twin who wasn't riding Bandit with him on Ranger, and Shawna on Major, DJ had much more fun. She caught the twins' giggles and passed them back.

Shawna had stars in her eyes for the rest of the day after riding Major all by herself.

The next two days flew by like the seconds in a jumping ring. Shawna would have ridden all day and night if allowed. She helped DJ saddle soap her new saddle and chattered nonstop about her dream horse.

Since it was a weekend, Robert and the boys were about. One day they all headed for Marine World Africa USA in Vallejo less than an hour away. By the time they'd seen all the shows, including two visits to the killer whale show, had a butterfly sit on Shawna's shoulder in the butterfly house, and sampled all the food items, they could barely make it back to the car. Only once did DJ wish she could have spent the sunny day riding.

"He's here," Lindy called up the stairs late Monday morning.

"I know, I'm zipping my bag." DJ took one last look around the room and slung the canvas tote over her shoulder. She had packed her boots, rain gear, everyday clothes, and, at her mother's insistence, an outfit dressier than jeans and a sweat shirt. She'd had a hard time closing the zipper. With her other hand she picked up the package wrapped in Christmas tree paper and headed down the stairs. Joe had helped her frame another of her drawings as a gift for Brad and Jackie. As Joe had said when she'd worried over whether they'd like it: if they didn't, that was their problem, not hers. Easy to say, harder to live with.

"Now, remember, if you want to come home early, all you have to do is call," Lindy whispered in DJ's ear as she gave her a good-bye hug.

"I know. *She must think I'm a baby or something.* DJ hugged her mother back. "See ya."

"I promise to return her safely," Brad said with a smile.

"I know. And thank you for the lovely basket of goodies." Lindy crossed her arms over her chest. "You have fun now. And behave yourself."

DJ rolled her eyes. "M-o-t-h-e-r."

"That's okay, I'm paid to say that." Lindy tried to smile. "Comes with being a mother."

"Thank you for letting her come with me," Brad said. "Jackie and I really appreciate it."

"You're welcome."

DJ felt like running in place. Did everyone have to be so . . . so polite? It wasn't as if she was going to the moon, for pete's sake. "Bye, Mom." Would she get the hint?

Once in the car, Brad asked, "Would you like to show me your horse before we go?"

"Sure." DJ slammed the heel of her hand against her forehead. "Sorry, I meant to tell you thanks for the awesome saddle first thing."

"You like it then?"

"Like it? Does the sun rise every day? I couldn't believe it. And a Crosby, to boot."

"I wanted to get you a Hermes, but Jackie said no, you'd be afraid to use it."

"A Hermes?" her voice squeaked. She swallowed. "I would have kept it under lock and key in my bedroom. What if someone stole it?"

"Then this is better. Does it fit you and Major okay?"

"Same size I already use—only so much better. I was saving for a used saddle." DJ pointed at Amy's drive. "Stop here."

By the time they'd picked up Amy, stopped to see Major, and were finally on the road, Brad asked if they were hungry. "Because if you can hold out, Jackie will have lunch ready."

"We can wait."

"Okay, then I'll just get us drinks." He swung into a fast-food place.

Talking with Brad was a lot like visiting with Robert, DJ decided by the time they reached Santa Rosa. Comfortable and easy. Of course any time she could talk horses, that made conversation easy.

He told her how he'd gotten interested in Arabians and begun breeding them back when the breed was rising in value astronomically. Jackie did most of the training and showing, but her true love was dressage. A few years later, they had bought her Hanovarian, Lord Byron.

"She's looking forward to helping you if you want," he continued. "I thought you might like to ride Matadorian. He's a real sweetheart."

"Your stallion?" DJ couldn't believe her ears.

"Sure, why not? And, Amy, there's a mare with your name on her. You do ride English, don't you?"

"Not usually, but I can. DJ made sure I learned," Amy answered.

"Amy thinks Western is best. She and Josh—he's half Arab—do really well."

When they drove into the curving, oak-lined drive, DJ couldn't take in everything quickly enough. White board fences checkerboarded the rolling pastures, where horses grazed knee-deep in grass. The stone house was set off on a rise, and the road curved on around to the type of barn she'd seen in pictures of Kentucky. On the roof two cupolas topped by horse weather vanes stood etched against the blue sky. White siding matched the fences, setting off the window and door trim painted a hunter green. A covered, open-sided arena shared one wall with an open ring that looked at least an acre in size.

"Oh, my." DJ couldn't think of anything else to say.

"I think I've died and gone to heaven," Amy whispered.

Inside the house, after greeting Jackie, DJ gravitated to the wall-to-wall and floor-to-ceiling bank of windows that looked out over the pastures backed by the rocky coastal mountain range. Rows of grapes, now barren for the winter, threaded the lower slopes. A couple of yearlings raced across their pasture, tails flagging in the Arabian way. A flock of ducks came in low over the pond at the end of the manicured lawn and slid their way onto the smooth water.

"This is one of my favorite places, too." Her father came up to stand beside her. "I never tire of watching the land change with the seasons. We'll go down after lunch and I'll introduce you to my other kids." At the question on her face, he added, "The horses, my dear. Not human relatives."

DJ shot him a grin and turned back to the scene. "Sure is beautiful out there."

"I think you and I have even more in common than I dreamed." He took her arm. "Come on, I'll show you to your room and then we'll have lunch. Amy, you want to share a room with this long drink of water or you want one of your own?"

"We'll share. I just wish I'd brought my camera. I can't believe I left it at home."

"You didn't!"

Amy nodded. "I know, you can hit me later."

"You're welcome to use one of ours. You can take your pick." Brad showed them up a curving stairway graced by framed pictures of Arabians in all stages of show and growth. It would take hours just to see them all. An oil painting of a chestnut stallion, wind whipping his mane, held the place of honor. The wide gold-leaf frame brought out the gold in his coat.

"That's Matadorian, my pride and joy, when he was three. He's heavier now that he's mature, so he looks even better. And the foals he sires—winners all." He pushed open a door and ushered them in. "Here's your room. Hope you like it." He glanced at his watch. "I have one phone call I have to return, so I'll meet you in the kitchen. Jackie said to tell you the drawers are empty if you want to put your things in them. Bathroom's through there."

DJ flopped down on the queen-sized bed. "This has enough pillows to start a store. Can you believe this place?"

"Makes you wonder, huh?" Amy flopped beside DJ.

"About what?"

"About why he never wrote to you or anything? It isn't like he couldn't afford it."

"Yeah, I thought of that. Maybe sometime I'll ask him." DJ bounded back to her feet. "Let's go eat. I want to ride Matadorian." She picked up her wrapped package and headed out the door.

When they were all sitting at the round country table surrounded by bay windows, she handed her father the gift. After seeing all the paintings and portraits around the house, she felt silly even giving it to him.

Amy handed her packet of note cards to Jackie. "To say thanks for inviting me."

"DJ, did you really draw this?" Brad held the enlarged picture of the furry-eared foal up to get more light, then handed it to Jackie. DJ nodded. "I know you said you liked to draw, but this is better than something a hobbyist would do. You're a real artist. You taken any lessons?"

"From Gran—sorta. And I'm in art class at school." DJ shrugged. "I just like to draw horses. Been doing it ever since I can remember."

"Amy, are these your photos?" Jackie had looked at the back of the unwrapped package.

Now it was Amy's turn to squirm a bit. "Uh-huh. DJ and I made packets of note cards using some of her drawings and my photos. It's our latest business."

"They're lovely." Jackie smiled across the table. "You mean there have been other businesses?"

By the time they'd all laughed at Amy and DJ's tales of business mishaps and devoured their lunch, clouds had set in.

"Let me go set this on my desk and change clothes so we can all go riding. We'll show you the rest of the farm—especially down by the river. Better hurry before the rain hits." Brad pushed back his chair. "Thank you for the drawing, DJ. You have no idea how much this means to me."

That night Amy and DJ curled up on the bed after saying goodnight to Brad and Jackie. The girls plumped pillows under their chins and waved their feet in the air.

"I cannot believe that horse," DJ whispered. "Riding Matadorian was like . . . like . . ." She couldn't think of anything to compare it to.

"I know." Amy's voice held the same tone of reverence. "I could get used to living in a place like this, with plenty of awesome horses to choose from. Poor Josh would get jealous." She laid her cheek on the pillow and looked at DJ. "To think your dad let me ride his stallion, too. Go figure."

My dad—the words were becoming more familiar. DJ sighed. Tomorrow she could ride Jackie's dressage horse, Lord Byron, if she wanted. Shame they didn't have a jumping setup, too—then the farm would have been complete. She had a feeling if she asked, the jumps would appear as if by magic.

Once home, DJ chattered nonstop about her father's horses, his farm, his trophies, his house, his wife, and what fun he was. When she finally ran down, she noticed the two creases between her mother's eyebrows now looked more like ditches.

"And he said to tell you thank you for letting me visit. He hopes we can do this more often."

"I'm sure he does. I'm glad you had such a good time. Joe said he'll be by about eight." Lindy rose from her curled position in the corner of the sofa. "I have to leave for work early in the morning, so I'm going to bed. You'll stay at Gran's tomorrow night because I'll be in Los Angeles. My number's on the message board." She stopped with one foot on the stair. "I'm glad you're home, Darla Jean, and that you had fun."

DJ looked after her. *Yeah, right—you look thrilled to bits.* What was bugging her mother now?

Chapter • 18

You know you're not supposed to be listening. Look what happened last time.

The battle waged back and forth in her mind. *But if I don't listen, I won't know what's going on. Nobody ever tells me anything.*

DJ sat on the stairs. It wasn't her fault they were talking so loudly she could hear. She'd been on her way to bed when the noise stole her attention. She wrapped both arms around her knees and propped her chin on them.

"You should have heard her, babbling on about how wonderful the Atwoods are. All the things they have, the house, the horses . . . you name it, the Atwoods have it—in spades. Along with a little diamond dust."

"Lindy, she's just a kid. Sure she's impressed. We'd probably *all* be impressed. Sounds like Brad has done really well for himself."

DJ strained to hear. Her mother mumbled something.

"Oh, Lindy, darling, he isn't trying to take her away from you. You've been a good mother and—"

"No, I haven't, Robert. Gran raised DJ, not me. We might as well have been sisters for as much responsibility as I took. I went to work, to school, came home, and studied. Seems I've been doing that all of my life. Then it was on to more school, traveling with the job, climbing the corporate ladder—for what?"

"Hey, take it easy on yourself. You can't tell me that your income wasn't important around here. You did the best you could. Anyone can tell this family's offered up a lot of prayers."

"That's due to Gran, too. I . . . I kind of gave up on prayer, on God, a long time ago. He didn't seem to answer any of my prayers, so I quit praying and left it up to my mother like I did everything else. How can I blame Brad for not accepting his responsibility when I didn't accept mine, either?"

"Oh, Lindy, if you didn't have faith, we wouldn't be getting married."

"Well, I'm not a heathen, you know."

"That's what I said. And now our faith will grow together and our families will blend with God's blessing. It's going to work out—perhaps Brad and Jackie will just become a part of our extended family. We can make room for everyone in our lives—you can never run out of love because it just keeps growing to encompass more people. Instead of worrying about Brad taking DJ away, we can share our lovely daughter with him. We'll all be richer for it."

There was a silence long enough for DJ to think she'd heard it all, but as she started to move, her mother's voice came again. "I wish I could forbid her to see him. I just have a feeling something horrible is going to come of all this."

DJ felt her stomach clench. "Something horrible? Come on, Mom, give me a break," she whispered the words as if hearing them might remove the yucky feeling in the pit of her stomach.

"Well, since that's not possible, we'll just take this one day at a time. We'll get through it." Robert again. At least *he* didn't think her father was a monster from outer space.

"How come you're so wise?" Lindy's voice no longer wore the edge of panic.

"I prayed for wisdom—and keep on praying for it. I think I'm going to need it even more in the months ahead, don't you?"

"Are you sure you still want to marry me?"

When they started to get mushy, DJ went to bed. *Good thing I never told her that Brad said there was always a room for me at his house if I felt I needed to leave here.* She sighed. But that wouldn't happen. Not in a million years. Even though he'd said she could bring Major.

"God, please help me to be really nice to my mother. I want us always to get along like we have lately. Thank you for such a wonderful Christmas and all the family you've given me. Amen."

Before she turned out the lights, she took out her journal and, propping herself against the head of her bed, began to write. And write. There was so much to think about, to wonder over, and to look forward to. The pages filled quickly.

"Well, that ought to impress Mrs. Adams even though I didn't write every day." She slapped the notebook closed and stuffed it back into its drawer. Maybe tomorrow she could go riding up in Briones.

A thought DJ hadn't had for a long time floated through her mind just before she fell asleep: Maybe they would all have an easier time if she weren't there to mix things up. She turned over. Well, if she ever needed a place to run to, she had one now.

DJ's first wish in the morning was to fire the weather reporters. Instead of clear sky as they'd promised, heavy rain washed her windows again. She pulled the covers over her head and tried to go back to sleep, flipping first one way, then the other. The wind and rain sounded as though they were coming right into the house.

She flopped around again. A ringing sound floated down the hall. "The phone?" She bailed out of bed and dashed to her mother's bedroom, home to the closest phone. "Hello?"

"DJ?"

"Who'd you think?" She sank down onto the already-made bed, her gaze traveling around the room. You'd think no one lived in her mother's room, it was always so disgustingly neat.

"Come on, darlin', you can wake up more chipper than that."

"I was already awake, Joe, but it's pouring out."

"That's why I'm planning to give you a ride. You suppose Amy wants a ride, too?"

When everything was set for their trip to do morning chores, DJ hung up the phone and got busy. Joe had said he'd be there in fifteen minutes, and he was never late. Food bars for breakfast again. She should have stayed up when she first awoke. Grumbling at herself, she dressed and headed down the stairs. No time to straighten her room now.

All the early riders at the Academy were as sick of rain as DJ. A couple complained of leaks above their stalls, and the outside stalls had water running through them. Several maintenance men were digging trenches on the hill above the stalls to divert the runoff.

DJ looked longingly up at the hills she knew lurked behind the sheeting rain. "Major, I want to ride up there again s-o-o bad, don't you?" He obligingly nuzzled her shoulder and whuffled in her ear. "Hey, that tickles!" DJ scratched the crisp hairs on his upper lip and made him twitch, then nibble at her fingers. When he licked her palm, she threw her arms around his neck. "You are the best horse in the whole world."

"Then get him out into the arena and make him earn his keep." Joe was grooming Ranger in the neighboring stall.

"Sheesh, what a slave driver. Don't you know I'm on vacation?" She picked up her brushes and went to work on Major's thick winter coat. "How come you get so dirty just standing in a stall? What would you be like if you were on pasture?"

"He will be soon, if Robert has his way. That house of his is shaping up fast. He's already got the fences repaired and a new roof on the barn." Joe raised his voice. "Hey, Amy, you sleeping out there?"

"In this weather? Give me a break! I've got to work fast—we're going to visit my other grandparents this weekend. I thought we were going tomorrow but—"

"So you won't be here to go up in Briones with me?"

"DJ, have you looked outside lately?"

"It's going to stop—I know it will. You can go with me, can't you, Joe?"

"Nope. Since it's raining, Mel and I are going into the city to the new art museum and then to the opera."

"Opera?" DJ made the word sound disgusting.

"That's exactly why we didn't invite you, though Gran said you could do with some artistic training."

"In opera?"

"Don't act like it would kill you. You can thank me for saving you from that fate worse than death."

"Thanks, Joe. I'll feed Ranger for you." DJ retrieved her saddle from the half-door and set it atop the pad. How she would love to be using her new saddle, but she wasn't about to let it get rained on . . .

yet. "Guess I'll just give Patches an extra-long workout and catch up on some tack cleaning."

"Not if you want a ride home." Joe led Ranger out of his stall and swung aboard. "I'm leaving at eleven."

———

Later DJ wandered around the house, feeling as if her last friend had deserted her. The place felt clammy, so she started a fire in the fireplace, turned on the Christmas tree lights and music, and, after fixing herself a ham and cheese sandwich, brought her sketch pad down to go to work. Now was as good a time as any to get started on those three commissions.

Sometime later, she looked up and let out a whoop of joy. Sunshine—watery for sure, but real sunshine—beamed in the windows. She ran to the French doors and studied the sky. Even the Western sky shone blue instead of the all-too-usual gray or black.

She dashed off a quick note to her mother, *Gone riding in Briones*, grabbed her rain gear, just in case, and pelted out the door. Her rear wheel threw up enough water to soak an elephant on the speed-breaking ride, making DJ glad she'd put on the slicker. She tacked Major up with the same lightning speed and trotted up the trail before anyone could find something else that needed her attention.

It took great force of will to ignore the nagging voice that reminded her it was always wiser to ride with a buddy. In fact, buddy trail riding was rule of the Academy. *It's not my fault all my buddies are gone. I'm not about to waste the sunshine.*

The washed-out stretch on the fire road flowed deeper and wider, but Major splashed right through it. Birds twittered and chirped in the trees overhead, and high above the hill she could see a pair of turkey vultures catching the thermals on broad wings. Cows bellowed for their offspring, and the creek played bass in crescendo power. DJ hummed along, the words running through her mind: *And Mary's boy child, Jesus Christ, was born on Christmas Day.* She liked the song's catchy Latino rhythm.

When they crested the hill to the meadow, she groaned. Clouds were sneaking peeks over the tops of the Western hills. "Too bad, you can just hold off. We're taking a new trail today, and a little more rain won't stop us."

Major snorted as if he agreed. When she turned off before climbing to the bluebird saddle and angled along the side of the hill on what looked more like a cow path than a trail, he trotted willingly along. Ears flicking back and forth, he kept track of all the sounds around them.

DJ left off the humming and started singing. She sure wasn't an opera star, but with no one to hear her and make faces if she wasn't exactly on key, she felt free to really sing. From here, DJ could see more of the straits. She stopped once to watch an oil tanker make its way upstream, and the breeze kicked in. It was beginning to feel a little wild.

They came around a corner and Major stopped. Some of the hill had slipped and covered the path.

"We should go back, huh, buddy?"

Major's ears flicked. He lowered his head to sniff the trail.

"But look, it's only a few feet. We'll go down and around." She turned Major off the track, and watching for ground squirrel holes, they made their way back up to the track. DJ stood in her stirrups. They should meet up with one of the main trails again pretty soon. They'd take that one back.

The clouds seemed to be racing to the east. While the sun was putting up a battle royal, it was definitely losing.

They rounded another curve, and the hillside below dropped off. Major stopped. DJ nudged him forward.

"Come on, fella, what's the deal?" She squeezed her knees again. He quivered.

Major took two more tentative steps forward—and the hill dissolved around them. Panicked, DJ slammed her legs into his sides. Major leaped forward, but the moving mud carried him with it.

Too scared to scream, DJ kept a firm hand on the reins to help hold her horse upright. He leaped again, trying to slog their way out. A young oak tree quivered on the lip of the cliff.

DJ grabbed for it. Rough bark bit into her hands.

She clung and felt the saddle slip out from under her. Quickly, she kicked her feet free of the stirrups. There was nothing more she could do.

Major screamed as he slid over the edge of the cliff.

Chapter • 19

"Major!"

All DJ heard in response was the ominous rumble of sliding, saturated clay.

"God, please help me." She kicked against the face of the cliff, searching for a toehold—anything. Her arms felt like they were being pulled right out of the sockets. She tried to look down, but that put more pressure on her shoulders. She looked up instead. The lip of the cliff wasn't so far away. If only she could get a toehold. . . .

She dug into the hard clay with the toe of her boot. Finally she came into contact with a round, solid piece. Sandstone. Praying, whimpering, the pain growing more unbearable, she dug with her foot around the top of the stone.

Keep a cool head. She could hear Bridget's voice in her ear. "I can do all things. I can do all things." She sobbed out the verse. "God, please help."

How far down was the bottom? How was Major? *Get a toehold!* With one more kick, she could feel enough solid foundation under her foot to stand—with the toe of one boot. The relief from even that small help brought tears to DJ's eyes. She took in a deep breath. "Thank you."

Kicking with the other foot created enough space for her to balance on. She let go of the oak with one hand and looked down. The cliff fell away beneath her to a ledge, then fell away again. She could see no farther.

"Major!" She tried to whistle, but her lips couldn't manage it. Besides, you had to have spit to whistle.

The clouds rolled over the hill like a puffy gray waterfall, sending tendrils down to drip in her face.

Her right foot cramped, sending pain shooting up her leg. She shifted the weight to the left and clamped harder on the tree. Stretching her right leg, she tried to release the cramp but failed.

How to escape her trap? Could she go down? Sideways? Mountain climbing had never been one of her aspirations, but she'd watched rock-climbing on TV. How did they do it?

She reached out with her right hand, searching for anything to grab on to. A chunk of dirt broke away. DJ's heart leaped back into her throat, racing as if to burst out of her chest. Back to the oak. She sighed in relief as she grasped it with her left hand. The cramp let up. If only she hadn't tied her slicker on behind her saddle—so what if it hadn't been raining.

"Major!"

Was that a nicker she heard? She called again. Only a crow answered, his harsh caw anything but comforting.

No one knows where I am. The thought sent her heart into over-drive again. "Come on, DJ, keep a cool head." Talking out loud helped. "Okay, now start with the left hand." She looked to the left, imagining this hand move over the surface of the cliff.

Giving up on her hands for the moment, she began kicking a broader shelf for her feet to rest on. She focused all her concentration on her feet. The slippery wet clay clung to her boot, threatening to make her lose her balance, but DJ kept on kicking.

The wind blowing up the river cut through her sweat shirt as though it wasn't even there. She shivered and kept on kicking until she could finally stand on both feet. DJ breathed a sigh of relief. Her legs shook. Her arms ached. She shivered again, this time more like a shudder.

The mist grew heavier, turning to rain. The sky darkened and wind whipped the trees.

"Help!" she screamed as loud as she could. What other idiot would be out in the park late on a day like today? DJ screamed again. And again. Until her throat closed in pain.

Who would look for her? Her mother wouldn't be home from work yet, and Gran and Joe weren't coming home till late. No one knew where she was. Tears joined the raindrops sliding down her cheeks.

I know where you are. DJ sucked in a breath. Of course—God knew where she was. "Then how about telling someone else? Please, please, make someone come. And please, please let Major be okay. Please keep him from suffering, God." The thought of her horse in pain made the tears flow again. "Please."

Should she just let go? How far down was down? What was below her? She tried to figure out the landscape, but this was new territory.

"Bridget'll kill me for letting myself get caught in a situation like this after all the years she's drummed safety in our heads." Talking out loud helped drive the darkness back. "Okay, God, what do I do?"

The smell of wet clay filled her nostrils as she hugged the cliff. What a way to spend an evening.

As soon as she stopped talking, panic stalked her. Panic that made her stomach roil, like it would leap out of her throat. Panic that set her heart to pounding and made her weak knees even weaker.

"So sing." She forced the words past the huge lump in her throat. "The Lord liveth, and blessed be the rock . . ." That one came easily since she was sort of standing on a rock, more grateful for a piece of solid earth than she'd ever dreamed possible. She continued the verse and found another song, then another—each like a friend come to comfort her. DJ set her verse to music. "I can do all things, I can do all things . . ." The tears streaming down her face made singing hard. "I can do all things through Christ who strengthens me."

When she could no longer force the words and tune past her parched throat, she sang them in her mind.

Huddled by herself on the face of a cliff in the dark and pouring rain, DJ could sense that she wasn't alone. Not really. How much time had passed? How long since darkness fell? She had no idea.

What was that? A horse whinny? "Major." What she thought would be a yell barely went farther than the face of the cliff.

"DJ!" A voice came from far away, then a whinny again—this time from the same direction as the voice. And then an answering one from below her.

Major was alive!

"D-e-e-e J-a-a-ay!" The voice sounded closer.

"I'm here." She gathered all her strength and tried again. "Here, over here! Thank you, God. Thank you, Jesus. Oh, thank you!"

A light pierced the darkness coming around the side of the hill. Whoever it was must be on the trail she took earlier.

"DJ!" The shout again.

Another whinny from someplace below her.

"Keep at it, horse, you can make more noise than I can. Please, God, give me strength to holler." She sniffed and wriggled her dripping nose. "I'm here. Down here!"

The light stopped above them. "DJ?"

"Joe! I'm down here . . . on the cliff."

"Easy, kid, I'm coming for you." Never had a voice sounded more like love in action.

A chunk of dirt broke away and went crashing past her. "Stay back—the bank will give again." More dirt and clumps of grass cascaded by her left shoulder. The oak tree trembled. "Stay back!"

"Can you hang on, darlin'?" His voice came from farther away this time.

"I'm okay—now. Major is down below me somewhere. He heard you first and whinnied."

"I know, that's what brought us here. Are you hurt?"

"No."

"Thank you, God! Okay."

She heard the crackle of a radio and someone else giving instructions.

"DJ, we've got a rope here that we can send over the side. Can you get the loop over your head and down under your arms, or do you need one of us to help you?"

"I can do it. I've got a little piece of rock cleared to stand on."

"Okay, here it comes."

She could hear movements overhead and another voice or two. She watched the glare of the lights, and slowly a looped rope came into view.

DJ reached with her left arm and tried to snag it. "More to the right." The rope swung closer. DJ grabbed the loop and slipped her left arm into it. Then, depending on the rope for support, she let go with her right and pulled the loop over her head. "Ready."

"Okay, now, if you can lean back in the rope and walk up the cliff, it will be easier on your arms. Think you can do that? Just brace your feet against the cliff and walk up it."

DJ gripped the rope with both hands, and with the loop holding her secure, she did exactly as Joe instructed. She walked up the cliff and right into his arms. The men with him cheered.

"Oh, DJ, I . . . thank you, Lord." He held her closer and rubbed her back. "You're soaked and frozen clear through."

One of the men handed her his jacket. "Here, put this on."

DJ slid her aching arms into the sleeves. "Joe, how'd you get here? I thought you went to the opera with Gran?"

"Something told me to go home." He zipped the jacket for her since her fingers couldn't. "I'll never question God's prompting again."

"How'd you find me?"

"Ma'am," replied one of the other men, his Southern drawl obviously put on, "I learned trackin' back in the Boy Scouts. We just followed yo tra-il."

"In the dark?" DJ's voice squeaked past her sore throat.

"Let's get her out of here," another ordered.

"What about Major? I can't leave without Major."

"Here, put this around you." Another man held out a heat-trapping emergency blanket. "This will trap your body heat and warm you even more."

"Joe, I can't go yet. What about Major?" DJ grabbed the front of his jacket. "I won't leave him." She stared up at his shadowed face, the light catching the raindrops on his slicker.

"Joe, ETA for the chopper is five minutes."

"No!" DJ clutched the blanket around her. "I can't leave Major."

"DJ, listen to me. I will go down there and check on him."

"No, let me, Cap'n. I've got fewer years on my carcass," one of the younger officers said with a grin. "Besides, we do these all the time—you've been out to pasture."

Joe snorted, but keeping one arm wrapped tightly around DJ as if she might run away from him, he agreed.

The younger officer wrapped the rope around his waist and between his legs, then gave the thumbs-up signal.

"Belay on," someone called from above—and over the cliff he went.

DJ shuddered at the thought of Major down in the darkness over the edge. The warmth of the blanket and Joe's arm around her helped to keep her steady. "I know he's alive, Joe."

"He's a tough old horse—wise, too."

"But what if he's hurt . . . bad?" She stumbled over the words.

"That could be. But since these hills are all clay with so few rocks and trees, that old horse has a good chance. We'll just have to have faith that God is in control. He will lead us through whatever is ahead." Joe hugged her again. "He led us to you, didn't He?"

The walkie-talkie crackled in his hand.

"Joe here."

"Yeah, Captain, we got a problem down here. This horse is stuck in the mud halfway up his rib cage."

"See any injuries?"

"Only dirt and more dirt, but I can't see his legs."

"How's his breathing?"

"Seems to be okay. He looks alert, just stuck."

"Come on up. We'll talk about what to do."

DJ could hear the *thwunk, thwunk* of an incoming helicopter.

"Over and out."

"Cap'n, that chopper can't put down here, so I'm having him land in the meadow. We can all ride out there to meet it. You want her to go home on it, right?"

"Right."

"No! Joe, I'm staying with Major." DJ flung herself at Joe's chest. "Please, Joe, *please.*" She could feel herself spinning out of control. "I can't leave him!"

"No, you aren't staying, child. That hill could give way again."

"But then Major . . ." The horror of what could happen to her horse was too terrible for DJ to contemplate.

Chapter • 20

"Let me go down there to see him, Joe. Please!"

"No, darlin', I can't."

Fury, burning, raging fury, made DJ shake. She bit her lip till she could taste blood. "He's my horse." With every ounce of control keeping her from plunging back down the hill to Major, she whispered it again. "Major is my horse."

"And you're my granddaughter." As Joe swung aboard Ranger, DJ darted to the lip of the hill. An officer grabbed her around the middle and carried her kicking back to Ranger. With a shake of his head, Joe offered her a hand to swing up behind him. "DJ, I've been a policeman all my life, and I will *always* put a human life ahead of an animal's. Even more so when I love that stubborn girl as much as life itself."

DJ settled herself behind him and looked over her shoulder to see the younger officer that had gone down to check on Major standing with the others.

"Don't worry, DJ," the younger man called. "We'll get him out in the morning when we can see to dig. He's okay for the night."

Unless the hill slides down over him. She forced herself to call back, "Thank you."

"DJ, I know you are absolutely furious with me, but that's the way it is. Melanie is waiting at the staging parking lot. The rescue team might decide to take you in to the hospital for observation."

I don't think so, DJ argued back inside her head. She refused to answer Joe. Somehow she had to get back up to Major.

They bundled her aboard the helicopter and wrapped her in more blankets. While she'd felt the warmth of the one, she still shook from the cold. Someone else handed her a mug of hot, sugared coffee.

"Sorry, we didn't bring hot chocolate. Can you drink this?"

DJ nodded, but her teeth clanked on the cup rim when she put it to her mouth.

A television station van was set up in the parking lot—she could see it as they came in for a landing. Her mom and Robert were there, too.

DJ felt the tears burn behind her eyes. *Don't you dare cry*, she ordered herself. But that was easier said than done. When Gran, her mom, and Robert wrapped their arms around her, she couldn't live up to her orders.

"Major is stuck in the mud, and it's all my fault." Deep, tearing sobs ripped through her. "If he dies, it's all my fault."

"How about if we check her over?" a young female emergency medical technician asked.

"I'm not going in any ambulance, and I'm *not* going to a hospital."

"Darla Jean," her mother said firmly, "you will do what is needed."

"Can we ask you a couple of questions?" A tape recorder appeared in front of DJ's face as if by magic. A reporter held the other end.

"How about I answer questions while the medical personnel attend to her." Robert turned DJ over to the medical crew with one arm and the reporter away with the other.

The young woman sat DJ down on the rear edge of the ambulance and popped a thermometer in her mouth and a blood pressure cuff on her arm.

"I'm fine—just cold." Talking with the thermometer in her mouth wasn't easy, but DJ managed.

"Sure you are, kid. You want us to be out of a job? If we don't check you out, my boss'll yell at me. You don't want that to happen, do you?"

DJ glared at her.

Once the plastic thing was out of her mouth, DJ took in a deep breath. "Look, I'm not hurt. I ache all over, but what do you expect?"

"Your temp is subnormal, but not down to dangerous hypothermia levels. Pulse is fine, too. I guess you can go."

"I told you so."

"I know you did. Let's just hope and pray your horse comes out in as good a condition as you."

"Thanks." DJ ran her tongue over her chewed lip. "Sorry I was a brat."

"Don't blame you a bit. Take care now."

The ambulance and the TV van left at the same time. DJ climbed into Robert's car with Gran on one side of her and Lindy on the other—they acted as if she needed guarding or something. Could they read her mind, trying a million ways of going back for Major?

———

Later after a long soak in the bathtub, and wearing sweats and her heavy bathrobe, DJ returned to the family room.

"How you doing, darlin'?" Gran brought a tray from the kitchen. She handed DJ the steaming mug of hot chocolate and offered coffee to the others.

"I'm fine, thanks."

"I put a bit of coffee in that."

DJ knew Gran was trying make things right for her. Leave it to Gran, she could still read her granddaughter like a book. "Where's Joe?"

Silence fell. The adults exchanged looks.

"Is Major all right?" Panic clawed at her middle again.

"DJ, Joe is camping right by Major. He said to tell you that you can go up there first thing in the morning."

"He can but I couldn't."

"Well, he has a few more supplies than you did," Lindy noted, the furrows obvious between her eyes. "And people there to help him if he needs it."

"Face it, DJ—he couldn't leave his old buddy up there alone any more than you could." Robert raised his coffee mug in a salute. "That's my dad."

———

They started digging as soon as it was light, Joe told her later. It took four men two hours to dig around Major enough to slide a sling under his belly. DJ arrived when they were digging his legs free so the helicopter could airlift him out.

"Hey, big guy." She threw her arms around his neck, kneeling in the mud in front of him. Major whuffled and nosed her pockets. "You knew I'd bring you something, didn't you?" She looked over at Joe, who looked like he'd been sunk in the mud himself.

"He's okay, darlin'." His nod gave her as much assurance as his words.

"Th-thanks." She opened a canteen she brought and gave Major a drink, then rationed the horse cookies she'd stuffed in her pockets. Another couple of hours passed, the sloppy mud slowing the digging. All through it, Major never floundered around or fought their efforts. He stood perfectly still, only quivering at times.

Joe finally ordered the helicopter to return. It hovered above them, the rotors drowning any talking. A hook descended on a cable, and the men worked together to hook it to the sling.

DJ kept up a running monologue in Major's ear, stroking his neck and face to keep him calm.

"Okay!" Joe yelled, at the same time giving a signal to the man in the chopper door. "Tighten her up."

"Oh, God, please make this work." DJ held her breath as the sling tightened around Major's belly. With a gigantic sucking, the horse's legs came free, and he swung into the air. DJ dropped to the ground to keep from being hit by Major's dripping, muddy legs as the chopper lifted the horse higher and higher. Major whinnied, but even then remained still, as if he understood the importance of not flailing around.

"That's some horse," Joe said, dropping a mud-caked arm over DJ's shoulders.

———

"He's some horse." Brad Atwood stood by DJ as the helicopter gently set Major down in the parking lot at the Academy.

"Yeah, he is. Thanks for helping pay for the helicopter and all."

"My pleasure. I couldn't believe it when I heard your name on the news. You and that horse of yours are having your moments of fame."

"I never thought much about the reporter there last night, but wow, they filmed the airlift and everything." DJ stepped forward and took the lead shank from Joe, who'd helped hold Major while the crew unbuckled the sling. "Good fella." She wrapped her arms around Major's neck in spite of the caked-on mud. He nuzzled her pocket. "Bet you're still starved. Thirsty, too, huh? That little sip you had was a long time ago." He nudged her again till she handed him a whole horse cookie. She turned to see the television camera aimed right at them.

"You got anything you'd like to say?" the person filming asked.

"Yeah, thank you, God, for saving my miracle horse. And thanks to all those who worked so hard to get him loose, especially my grandpa Joe who spent the night in the mud with our horse."

The man gave a thumbs-up sign and clicked off the camera.

DJ ran her hands down Major's legs, checking for any strain. One front leg and one back leg felt hot. "Let's get you fed and then washed down so we can doctor you, okay?"

Major nudged her and blew gently in her hair. He rubbed his forehead on her chest and nuzzled her pocket again.

Munching on the last cookie, he followed DJ through the barn and up to his stall.

"I put warm water in for him," Tony said. "And there's molasses in his grain. My grandpa always said molasses gives extra energy."

"Thanks. He'll like that."

"I'll help you wash him. I've never seen such a muddy horse in my life."

"I can't believe you're both okay." Hilary stopped at the bars. "Over a fifty-foot cliff and still walking. Not even a real limp. He must be made of steel."

"They both are," Tony said.

Major drained one bucket, and Tony took it to refill.

DJ looked after him and then at Hilary, both of them raising an eyebrow.

"He's been real nice since—"

"Since he sprained his ankle that day. Never would have believed it if I didn't see it with my own eyes." DJ took a rubber currycomb out of the bucket, and Hilary another. They set to work combing the worst of the mud off.

Much later with Major wearing ice boots on both hot legs, DJ allowed Joe to take her home to Gran's. Brad and Jackie were still there—she could tell by their car in the drive. Robert's car was there, also.

"Life sure can change fast, can't it?" She looked over to Joe as he turned the key and pulled it out of the ignition.

"Yeah, sometimes things happen out of the blue. All you can do is get through."

"Joe, I felt Jesus with me up on that cliff."

"I know He's the one who set a bug in my ear to skip the opera. I just knew we had to get home." He shook his head. "Any other woman would have made a fuss, but not your grandmother. She just said, 'Can't you drive faster, darlin'?' And to a retired policeman—can you beat that?"

"Well, I'm sure glad you were listening." DJ glanced up to see the twins come barreling out the door. "Uh-oh, better go."

They each glommed on to a leg. "DJ, we was missing you! You okay? Is Major okay?"

"He'll be okay in a couple of days, and you can see I'm fine." She bent over and hugged each of them. "Now, hang on."

She groaned as she lifted each loaded foot.

"DJ, you gonna be our sister for real?"

"Soon, guys, soon."

A wedding coming up. Not out of the blue, but another big change nonetheless. DJ stopped her straddle walk and grinned.

"Race you to the door!"

Book Five

STORM CLOUDS

To Aunty Bobby and my mother,
who read to me when I was little,
thus beginning a lifelong love of words,
reading books, and now writing.

Who ever knows how God
will use our efforts!
Thank you—
small words that convey
a lifetime of gratitude.

Chapter · 1

"Major, I'm so sorry you got hurt." DJ Randall leaned her head against her horse's dark neck. The blood bay turned his head to nose her shoulder. "Yeah, I know *you* forgive me. It's forgiving myself for doing stupid things that's hard."

Major snorted and pushed his head farther into her ministering fingers, making it easier for her to reach his favorite places. At five feet seven, DJ had no trouble reaching to scratch his ears or his white blaze, but Major had clearly learned that the simpler he made it for his human friends, the more often they obliged him with a rub.

"You're going to spoil that horse rotten." Joe Crowder, DJ's grandfather now that he had married her widowed grandmother, leaned on the aluminum bars separating his horse's stall from Major's. Grandpa Joe, whom DJ had fondly nicknamed GJ, stabled his new cutting-horse-in-training, Rambling Ranger, next to Major, his old friend from the police force.

"Hey, you scared me! I didn't know you were here." DJ straightened up so fast, she clipped Major's muzzle with her shoulder. The horse threw his head back, returning the favor by knocking her across the stall. She grabbed the stall bars with both hands to keep from smashing her face into the wall. DJ glared at Joe, who was trying not to grin. "Thanks for nothing."

"Far as I'm concerned, it was a good show." He reached out to stroke Major's nose. "Hey, big fella, you sure are easy to spook today." Joe had taken his aging Thoroughbred-Morgan horse with him when he retired from the San Francisco Mounted Police Patrol. Learning how badly DJ wanted a horse, he had offered to let her buy his friend.

"You don't seem too concerned about your granddaughter's health." DJ rubbed her shoulder and made a face at her grandfather. A second look was directed at Major, who was enjoying his nose rub so much that he completely ignored her.

"Hey, you two, remember me?" She planted her fists on slim hips. At fourteen, DJ was stick straight and flat in both front and back, to quote one of her frequent complaints. Her sun-shot honey blond hair waved past her shoulders when it wasn't in a ponytail—which was almost never. This rainy mid-January day, she wore long jeans with both a sweat shirt and a Windbreaker—unusual garb for a girl living in supposedly sunny California.

"You think she'll go away if we ignore her?" Joe asked Major in a stage whisper.

"Fat chance." DJ grinned up at him. "Unless *you* want to teach Andrew to ride. He's supposed to go on the lunge line today, but you know him—he backtracks more than he heads forward."

Andrew, an eight-year-old with a belly-deep fear of horses, was one of DJ's newest students. Slowly but surely, thanks to her patient coaching and Bandit's gentle manner, the shy boy was coming around. She'd led him around the arena on the dapple-gray pony for their last lesson to the cheers of everyone around. That major accomplishment had taken six months.

DJ stroked Major's shoulder and down his injured leg. Every minute of every day, she wished she had never gone riding up in Briones State Park that terrible afternoon. A mud slide had carried her and her horse over a cliff. It was a miracle they'd survived. Her Gran said it was the grace of God that had protected them, and DJ fully agreed. She'd pleaded for God to send help, and He had. Now they were both well and healthy—well, at least one of them was healthy. Major's leg was taking its own sweet time healing.

She chewed on her lip and shook her head as she felt the heat that persisted in spite of ice packs, massages, and liniment. It had been ten days since she'd ridden him, and it might be ten more. Sighing, DJ rubbed both hands up and down over the swollen muscles of his leg again, feeling him flinch when she went too deep.

"I'm going for the ice boot." She gave Major a pat on the cheek. "Go back to your first love, you big fake." He nuzzled her ponytail before she got away.

"He loves you, too, you know," Joe called after her.

"Right! See if I come back with any carrots for him." DJ trotted down the aisle to the room set aside for the ice machine, the locked medicine cabinet, a sink for washing wraps, and other equipment needed for the health of the horses stabled at the Academy. She scooped out a bucket of ice, grabbed the canvas wrap that covered shoulder to hoof on an injured horse, and headed back to the stalls.

"You riding today?" Amy Yamamoto, petite as DJ was tall and her cohort in hundreds of escapades since they were five, called from her gelding's stall.

"Later. Bridget had an appointment and won't be back as soon as she'd thought." Bridget Sommersby, who owned the stable and riding school, was also DJ's coach, mentor, and encourager. DJ owned a solid case of hero worship for the former Olympic competitor from the French National Equestrian Team, who never accepted excuses or sloppy work from her students. To DJ's unending excitement, Bridget agreed with her that, a few years down the road, there might be a place on the U.S. Equestrian Team for a girl with big dreams.

DJ marched back to Major's stall, which was housed in the open stalls with corrugated roofing at the west end of the long red barn. Academy boarders could be kept inside the barn, in the outside stalls, or on pasture, depending on how much their owners wanted to spend.

DJ stopped a moment at Patches' stall to palm him a carrot piece. "You put on your willing hat now, you hear? I don't want any surprises." Patches nodded as if he agreed and searched her pocket for more. In truth, Patches would be better known as Trouble. A smart rider never took her mind off the sneaky gelding when riding him. As his trainer, DJ had learned that the hard way.

Back in Major's stall, she wrapped the boot around his leg and Velcroed the straps in place before pouring in the flat ice cubes. As the cold penetrated the boot, Major wrinkled his skin, as if shrugging off flies. "I know it's freezing, but you're tough—you can stand it."

"If that's the worst that ever happens to him, he's home free. Let me tell you, when he took a bullet meant for me and the vet threatened to put him down, I lived in his stall for days." Joe shook his head. "That was a bad time."

DJ stroked the shoulder scar that had never regained its hair covering. She wrapped her arms around her horse's neck and squeezed, and Major sighed as though he liked hugs as much as she did. "You big sweetie, you." She inhaled. "And you smell so good, too."

Life according to DJ meant horses were the best smelling creatures on God's green earth. Unfortunately, her mother did *not* agree.

"You better hustle, kid. I just saw Bridget pull in." Joe ran his rubber currycomb over his brush and banged the two together to clean them. "You want a ride home later?" He raised his voice because DJ had ducked under the web gate across her stall door and was heading up the aisle.

"Yes, please." DJ dogtrotted to the far corner of the building to Megs' stall. Bridget had ridden the Thoroughbred-Arabian in world-class dressage competitions, retiring the horse two years earlier. DJ felt privileged that Bridget allowed her to ride the well-trained animal, even though dressage was not her idea of fun. It was jumping that made her heart beat faster and her dreams soar.

Lessons on Megs were a sign that Bridget believed in her.

"Okay, girl, let's get you groomed and out there to warm up." DJ took her grooming bucket in the stall with her and, after giving the dark bay mare a carrot, took out her brush and rubber currycomb. Using both hands and the flick of the wrist she'd learned from Bridget years before, she had the horse groomed in record time. She picked the hooves with the same quick motions and had Megs tacked up and walking toward the arena in minutes. On the way past the tack room, DJ snagged her helmet off the rack, then mounted up and trotted across the puddle-pocked parking area to the covered arena.

The outdoor arena looked like a small lake in spite of the tons of sand that had been dumped in the ring. Most of the jumping lessons were held in the outdoor arena, so it was DJ's favorite of the Academy's two arenas. In spite of the landslide, her most favorite place in all the world to ride was still up in the hills of Briones State Park.

She walked the horse one circuit of the covered, lighted arena, then trotted, her posting as natural as breathing. They spent the next twenty minutes at a walk, trot, canter, and reverse, repeating the maneuvers before working large circles and figure eights, half halts and halts, all to limber up both horse and rider.

When Bridget, wearing a yellow rain slicker, opened the gate and entered the arena, DJ turned Megs and trotted over to stop in front of their trainer.

"You reviewed your last lessons?" Bridget asked after greeting both horse and girl.

"Yup. Working on the bit is so easy on her. Makes me aware how much training Major and I need."

"Good. I am glad you finally agree with me." Bridget stepped back. "Next time you will not argue, right?" Her arched eyebrow said she was teasing. DJ had been as excited about learning dressage basics as she was about math. As a freshman at Acalanese High School, studying algebra never made it to even the bottom of her fun list, while anything to do with horses or art flew to the top.

DJ nodded. "I'll try not to."

"Try?" The eyebrow disappeared under Bridget's Australian hat brim.

DJ flinched. She knew better than to use that word. "I won't argue." Try was not an acceptable answer around Bridget. You either did or did not. You didn't just *try*. All Bridget asked was that her students do their best—at all times.

"Go on now. Review for me."

DJ took Megs through all she'd already done, making sure her transitions from gait to gait were smooth.

"Deeper in the saddle." Bridget called when they cantered past. "Use your seat and legs to drive her into your hands and onto the bit. Shoulders. Elbows. Eyes."

DJ checked each area of her body that Bridget mentioned. Looking straight ahead and sitting perfectly straight with relaxed shoulders, so deep in the saddle that she felt the horse's movements with her seat bones, should have been natural by now. At least that's what DJ told herself. Since she usually leaned forward slightly for jumping, sitting deep and straight took concentration.

She ignored the others using the arena and focused on both her own body and what Megs was doing. Around and around she went, obeying the commands of her trainer, rejoicing in the round feel of the horse under her. She glanced over at a shout from one of the other riders, and Megs faltered. DJ winced, hoping Bridget had been looking the other way.

Hope wasted. The trainer motioned her over. "Now, what did you do wrong?"

"Broke my concentration and looked off to the side."

"And?"

"And relaxed my seat and legs so I was no longer driving her forward. Megs felt it and slowed."

"Right. Now go again. Same routine."

DJ nodded. When she started to yell at herself, she cut off her words. Bridget stressed positive self-talk—no one was allowed to get on anyone's case, including her own. DJ squeezed Megs into a canter, and the driving power of the horse's hindquarters lifted Megs' head and neck right up into DJ's hands.

By the time the lesson was over, both girl and horse wore drops of sweat in spite of the chilly, damp weather.

"Good. You are improving daily."

"*Merci.*" DJ and Amy had started using some French phrases to get ready to take French classes at school next year.

Bridget smiled up at her. "You have Andrew on the lunge next?"

"Hope so. With him off for two weeks, you never know." DJ patted Megs' shoulder. "Thank you for letting me take lessons on her."

"*De rien.* You are welcome."

———

Back in the arena half an hour later, with an extremely reluctant rider on Bandit, DJ prayed nothing would happen to spook the pony and scare the boy. His lower lip already stuck out about as far as the end of his nose. With Andrew, the fear wasn't pretend. She admired him for working hard to overcome it so he could someday ride with his family.

"Okay, Andrew, how does the horse feel beneath you?" She kept her voice gentle and a soft smile on her face.

"Big."

"But you remember your last ride, don't you? How great you did?"

He nodded, still not picking up the reins. When his head moved, his helmet slid forward.

Resisting the urge to help him, DJ said, "You better tighten your helmet so you can see where you're going."

He shot her a questioning look, but at her encouraging nod, he let go of the mane and lifted his hands to tighten the web straps.

DJ stood poised to grab him if he started to slip but felt a glow of pride when she watched his heels go down in the stirrups. "Good going, Tiger. I'm proud of you."

He picked up the knotted reins. "Ready."

"Okay, we'll walk around once with me leading, and then I'll let out the line, a bit at a time. Gather your reins." He did. "Good. Now, how will you make Bandit go forward?"

"Squeeze my legs."

"Good."

"And to stop him?"

"Pull on the reins gently and say whoa."

"Very good. And what else?"

"Sit straight, keep my heels down and elbows in, and look between his ears toward where we are going."

"You have a good memory. You sound just like a parrot."

He looked at her, a smile tugging at his mouth.

"You ready?" He nodded. "Okay, tell Bandit to move forward."

As soon as the pony moved, DJ did, too. She kept one eye on Andrew and watched Bandit, the ring, and the other riders. All of them gave the boy plenty of space.

"Good going." At the end of the circuit, she patted the pony and cheered Andrew on. "Just keep doing the same thing and we'll move to the center of the ring, out of everyone's way."

By the end of the lesson, Andrew had exchanged "the lip" for a wide smile. He patted Bandit's gray neck.

"You did good, Tiger." DJ led him back to the stall. "Now let's see you untack him and brush him down."

"You did good, too, kiddo," Joe said after DJ had joined him in the green Ford Explorer. The warmth from the heater felt good.

"Thanks. I never know what's gonna happen with him. But at least we didn't go backward."

When Amy jumped in the backseat, Joe drove the two girls home.

Since she had stayed longer at the Academy than usual, DJ hoped her mother had to work late. That way she could still get her chores done and dinner started like she was supposed to. The closer they got to her house, the more she dug at the cuticle on her right thumb with the next finger. She should have cleaned her room, dusted the downstairs, emptied the dishwasher, and loaded the dirty breakfast things, but she had ignored the mess in her rush to get to Major. *Please, God, don't let Mom be home. I promise to do that stuff first off tomorrow.*

No such luck. Light beamed from the windows of the two-story house. DJ groaned—she was in for it now.

Chapter • 2

"Oh good, Robert's here!" DJ felt the weight lift.

"You didn't do your chores before heading to the barns, did you?"

DJ shook her head. "You think I'll ever learn?" She leaned across the console and kissed her grandfather's cheek. "Now, don't you need to come in and save your favorite granddaughter's hide?"

"Try to, you mean." Joe gave her a one-arm hug. "Tomorrow, kid, you will do your home chores first. I'll take care of the Major fella. You get grounded, and you won't be fit to live with." He patted her shoulder. "Tell that son of mine hi for me and that he could come by and see his old father since the house he's working on is only three steps from mine."

"Thanks. I will." She slammed the door behind her and headed for the front door. Joe's son Robert Crowder had fallen in love with her mother. Now there was a wedding planned for Valentine's Day, which was also Gran's birthday. DJ had yet to figure out something special for that.

In the meantime, she was about to become the big sister to a set of five-year-old twins, Bobby and Billy, better known as the Double Bs. At times, though, she called the energetic pair things like tornadoes or motormouths instead. Quiet was not a word in either of their vocabularies.

Robert owned a construction company and had purchased a house near the one Joe and Gran bought. Now he was remodeling the house to bring it up to size for his family, which was scheduled to nearly double overnight. Three weeks and five days until the wedding—but then, who was counting? Robert had apologized that the house wouldn't be done in time for the wedding, thanks to bad weather and the snail-minded city planners who awarded permits for building or remodeling houses. Soon after, though, he had promised.

DJ opened the front door quietly in the hopes she could sneak upstairs and change her clothes before meeting up with her meticulous mother. Lindy Randall dressed like a person well on the road to success. She worked hard at her job of selling equipment to law-enforcement agencies and, in her spare time, was studying to earn a master's degree in business. While she didn't *hate* horses, she also didn't understand DJ's love of "the huge, smelly beasts"—her mother's words.

Gran said DJ's passion for horses came from her biological father, the man DJ had met for the first time in her life just before Christmas.

"DJ's here!" The dual shriek killed any hope of sneaking away to change. Robert had brought the Double Bs along.

DJ braced herself. Two matching towheads with identical grins threw themselves at her legs and squeezed hard. Gazing up at her with adoring, round blue eyes, they giggled and said at the same time—a trick they did so well—"We was missing you."

The one on the right, probably Bobby, though DJ still couldn't tell the boys apart, added, "How come you came home so late?"

DJ groaned. "I'm not late, I . . ."

"She's late." Lindy's voice held the flat tone that said she would be polite—for now. That she was speaking from the kitchen did nothing to hide the fact that DJ was in for it as soon as their guests left. The sound of stainless-steel pans clattering against each other underlined her mother's frustration.

"Let's just order in Chinese or pizza." Robert's voice also came from the kitchen. Leave it to him to work to calm her mother down with an easy dinner solution.

DJ hugged each of the boys, trying to ignore what was happening in the other room. "How you guys doing?" she whispered.

"We's good," they whispered back.

"I gotta go change. I'll be right back." She disengaged their grips and headed up the stairs. No matter if Robert helped her mother relax now or not, later tonight would be miserable for DJ. She dumped her muddy jeans in the hamper, frustrated with herself for messing up again. Why couldn't her mother understand how worried she was about Major? It wasn't as if she skipped out every day. Most of the time, or rather mostly lately, DJ did her chores first, even getting up early sometimes to get some things finished before school.

Life hadn't been the same since Gran married Joe and moved out. It was a lot more difficult.

"Get your coat, DJ, we're eating out." Robert met her at the bottom of the stairs. He had a twin by each hand, their jackets already on. "Climb in the car, fellas." As they darted out the door, he took Lindy's coat from its hanger. "Come on, honey, this is better all around anyway. You didn't expect company tonight." He held the coat for Lindy and dropped a kiss on her hair when she put her arms in the sleeves.

"I know, but I should be able to whip something up for supper. Gran always could."

DJ ducked out the door. Robert and her mom wore that sappy look again that seemed to attack those in love. Even Gran had worn that silly look before she and Joe were married—still did. The pause before the two adults joined the three kids in the car told DJ there'd been some kissing going on, too. The melting look Lindy gave Robert when he helped her into the front seat confirmed it.

Sure would be nice if she stays this way, DJ thought. *Melting is better than mad any day.*

Robert got ready to leave soon after they returned from dinner, saying he had to get the boys to bed so they would be wide awake for kindergarten in the morning. He gave DJ a hug. "How are the portraits for the Academy folks coming?" he asked.

"Slow. But I have to get busy on them. Mrs. Johnson wants the one of Patches for her husband's birthday." Ever since she'd penciled a portrait of Tony Andrada's horse for his Christmas present at the Academy Christmas party, she'd had commissions from other families. Next to riding horses, she loved drawing horses best.

"You guys be good now." She scooped each boy up in turn and, after rubbing noses with them, which always made them laugh helplessly, gave them a hug and a tickle before setting them back down.

"Are you our big sister now?" one asked hopefully.

"Soon. Bye, guys." While her mother walked Robert and sons out to the car, DJ took the stairs three at a time. She could hear her home-work calling her.

"Thank you, Father, that Mom didn't yell at me," she said later in her prayers. Her mother had wished her good-night and floated on to her own bedroom. "Please heal Major faster, and help me get all the stuff done that I have to do." She blessed her family, which took much longer than it used to since Robert also had a brother and sister with families of their own. All of them planned to come to the wedding. The wedding!

"We're having a meeting at Gran's tonight," Lindy's voice said on the answering machine when DJ pushed the Play button the next after-noon. "She'll make dinner, so don't start the spaghetti."

"Good deal." DJ pushed Erase and listened to the next message.

"This message is for DJ." She recognized the voice of Brad Atwood, her father, immediately. "I was wondering if, since you don't have school on Friday, you might want to come up to the ranch for the weekend. Jackie says she'd love to give you a couple of lessons on Lord Byron, if you'd like. She's getting ready for a show in a couple of weeks—maybe you could go along with us. Give me a call." She didn't need to write down the number. She hit Erase and dialed her mother's number at work.

"DJ, I can't talk right now," Lindy said when she came on the phone. "Can't this wait until I get home?"

"I guess, but Brad called and asked if I wanted to go up there for the weekend." She heard her mother's sigh. "Please, Mom, I would like to."

"We'll talk about it when I get home."

"But we're going to Gran's."

"DJ, I have to go. Bye." The phone clicked almost before the final word.

DJ thunked the receiver down and stomped up the stairs. Up one minute, down the next. Her life felt like a roller coaster, and the hills were getting steeper. Why couldn't her mom just say yes? It wasn't as if DJ went up there every weekend. In fact, she'd only been there once. Visions of the white-fenced horse ranch up by Santa Rosa floated through her mind as she changed clothes. Purebred Arabians grazed the green fields, and there were several mares due to foal sometime soon. Riding Lord Byron, Jacquelyn Atwood's Hanovarian gelding, would be awesome.

She rushed through her chores, finishing just as a car horn honked in the drive. Holding her slicker over her head, she dashed out the door.

"You got your chores done?" Joe asked as DJ settled into the car. With the rain still falling in sheets, DJ's and Amy's bikes, their normal mode of travel, remained stowed in the garage.

"Yup." DJ slid her arms into her yellow slicker. "I'm sick of the rain, how about you?"

"Yup."

"Guess who called? Brad! He wants me to come up there this weekend." She continued without waiting for an answer. "Cool, huh?"

"You going?"

"I don't know. Mom said we'd discuss it when she gets home. You know how she is." DJ clamped her arms over her chest.

"You want to go?"

"Yeah, I do." She told him the entire conversation.

"With all the rain we've been having, he'd better hope the levees hold."

"Don't say that to my mom, okay? She'll never let me go if she starts to worry about flooding."

Joe nodded as he braked to a stop for Amy. "All the rivers are rising again north of here. Some of my police buddies are talking about volunteering to fill and set sandbags—if it comes to that. Pastor said some of the people at church are thinking along the same lines," he added as Amy opened the car door.

"I'd go help," DJ offered.

"Go help what?" Amy shook her head, splattering droplets on DJ.

"Fill sandbags if the rivers flood again."

"They'd never let us out of school for something like that."

"We could help on the weekends." DJ looked over at her friend. "You know, if you don't want to go, no one is twisting your arm."

Amy gave her a raised-eyebrow look. "What's with you?"

DJ shook her head. "Nothing."

"I know what it is. You want to get away from all these pre-wedding jitters that are going around." Joe nudged her arm with his elbow. "I take it you aren't looking forward to the meeting tonight?"

DJ mumbled something under her breath.

"Speak up, the rain is making so much noise, I can't hear you." Joe cupped one hand around his ear and leaned closer.

"I said I wish they'd run off to Reno—elope or something. I hate weddings."

"You seemed to have a good time at mine."

"You weren't all over everyone around you, though. My mother—"

"Your mother has every right to be uptight, and besides, you ask any of the guys at work and they can tell you how *I* was before my wedding." Joe shook his head. "Maybe I *should* tell Robert to elope."

"Yeah. I could go visit Brad while they're gone."

But later that night at Gran's, when DJ brought up the message from Brad, Lindy shook her head. "I just can't think of that right now. Let's get these wedding plans finalized, then discuss it."

DJ swallowed, glad her mother couldn't read her mind. She slowly took her place at the table with the others. When would it ever be her turn? If it hadn't been for Gran's good fried-chicken dinner, she'd have been tempted to walk home, in spite of the rain.

Later that evening, when Joe teased Robert and Lindy about marrying the easy way and eloping, Gran rolled her eyes, Lindy nodded, and Robert said "no way." He said he wanted all of his family around to help them celebrate.

Figures, DJ muttered to herself. The least they could do is get this meeting over with in a hurry—she had homework to do.

"So let's see how we're coming on this wedding." Gran flipped through the pages of a yellow legal tablet and picked up a pen. Since Lindy had so little free time between work and her thesis, she'd asked all of them to help with the planning. Gran read the first item on the list. "Wedding dress."

"Done," replied Lindy. "They said it would be ready next week, plenty early. Oh, DJ, how about if I pick you up after school tomorrow so you can come with me to be measured for your dress? That way all of the dresses will be ready at about the same time. I don't want any of us to cut it close."

"I teach my beginners' riding class tomorrow after school." DJ looked up from the horse she was doodling on the tablet in front of her.

"Is there any time you *can* go?" The sarcasm rippled across the table.

DJ set down her pencil. "After five, I guess, unless you want me to leave school early."

"Sure, and go for a dress fitting smelling like a horse."

Robert gently laid his hand on Lindy's shoulder. "How about if I pick up DJ and meet you over there?"

DJ answered him with a shrug. "Fine with me. Then I can change before I go."

Lindy nodded. "All right. But we should have gotten you shoes before now so we could get them dyed to match the dress. There might not be time."

"If we can't, they won't show much under a long dress anyway." Gran ran the fingers of her right hand through her still mostly golden curls. "By the way, I looked for a dress for myself today and had about as much luck as the sun shining tomorrow."

"Wait a minute! Time out!" DJ used the two-handed sports signal. "What's this about a long dress and dyed-to-match shoes? You know I don't wear things like that." DJ kept from shouting only with a supreme effort.

The look on her mother's face turned from puzzled to purple. "DJ, this isn't *your* wedding. I can't believe you'd be so selfish as to . . . to—" Lindy cut off the thought as she shoved her chair back from the table and went to stand by the window overlooking Gran's roses, her back to them.

DJ sank in her chair, guilt smacking her upside the head. *Good going, DJ. You've really messed things up now!*

Chapter • 3

"You know, DJ Randall, if you'd learn to keep your mouth shut, you'd do a lot better."

The face in the mirror, mouth foamed in toothpaste, grimaced but didn't answer.

DJ waved a blue toothbrush for emphasis. "If you want your mother to do something for you, it'd help if you'd first do what she wants." She shook her head. Not only was there a pin-slim chance of her going to her father's horse ranch for the three-day weekend, she was still booked for a dress-fitting and shoe-buying trip. Who cared if the shoes matched, for crying out loud?

She jabbed her toothbrush at the face in the mirror. "Now what would really look good walking down that aisle would be my jumping boots. I bet no one would notice them under my stupid dress." She snorted, and a gob of toothpaste hit the mirror. Several others decorated the faucet.

She spit and rinsed her mouth. When would she learn to think before spouting off? The hurt look in her mother's eyes still hung before her face. Even when DJ closed her eyes she could see it—only more clearly. Of course she would wear whatever dress her mother picked out for her. After all, Lindy would only get married once.

DJ thumped her fists on the countertop. "When will I get my act together?" She rinsed her toothbrush, then the sink. Glaring once more at the face in the mirror, she dried her hands and headed for bed.

But even after her prayers, sleep wouldn't come. Finally, she threw back the covers and padded down the hall to her mother's bedroom door. "Mom?" DJ tapped softly. If her mother was asleep, waking her wouldn't be too helpful, either.

"Come in." The tone of Lindy's voice pierced DJ to the core.

Her mother stood in front of the window, back to the door. She didn't turn.

"Mom, I'm sorry. Please forgive me for being such a selfish brat. I'll wear anything you want me to—dyed shoes, even a hat and gloves." *Please, Mom, please turn around. Say everything's okay.*

The silence stretched till DJ felt like a rubber band about to snap.

Lindy rubbed her forehead, a sure sign a migraine was brewing.

Lord, please. DJ could think of no other words. *Please help me.*

Lindy turned, her face shadowed since only the small lamp by the bed was on. "Darla Jean, I want this wedding to be really special for everyone. I know I get carried away sometimes, and I forget to communicate, to fill people in. But you have to do what I tell you. I'm your mother."

DJ nodded. "I know." *Please say you forgive me.* She clasped her hands behind her back so she wouldn't pick nervously at her cuticles. "I'm sorry."

Lindy shook her head. "Maybe this wedding, this marriage, really isn't meant to be."

"Oh, Mom! Don't say that. You're in love with Robert—anyone can see that. And he loves you. For pete's sake, don't quit now." DJ crossed the space separating them. "Not because of me. Please."

Her throat closed.

"It isn't just you. It's me." Lindy tucked a strand of sleek hair behind her ear. She shook her head. "Well, this is my worry, not yours. I have a lot to think about." She straightened her shoulders, and her sigh sounded like it came from the soles of her feet.

DJ shifted from one foot to the other. She still hadn't been forgiven. "How can I help you? I mean . . ."

Lindy shook her head again, her hair swinging across her cheek. "Just be patient with me." She reached out, and DJ stepped willingly into her mother's arms. As they shared a hug, Lindy whispered, "And,

DJ, I forgive you. All these years, we've been more like sisters, with Gran acting as our mother. So forgive me when I forget I'm the parent now, will you?"

DJ swallowed hard, but the lump stuck. "I . . . I will—I mean, I do." She swallowed again and leaned her head on her mother's shoulder. "Gran says we need to learn to pray together."

Where had those words come from? DJ started to pull away, but her mother's arms held firm.

"I'm working on praying myself first. Guess I finally met something too big for me to handle on my own."

DJ wished Gran could hear those words. She'd been praying for her daughter all through the years—and for DJ, too.

The silence between mother and daughter now felt like a warm blanket. DJ took a deep breath, her mother's perfume filling her nose. "You always smell so good." The whisper didn't disturb the blanket a bit.

"Thanks, at least I get the image right. That has always been so important to me." She shook her head. "But I get the feeling that succeeding in business isn't the most important thing in my life now." Lindy stepped back and cupped her hand around DJ's jaw. "You are far more important to me than beating a sales goal or finishing school."

"And Robert?"

"Definitely Robert, too. Along with two busy, funny, loving little boys." She kissed DJ's cheek. "Good night. You get some sleep now."

"Night, Mom." DJ left the room with the warm blanket of love still snuggled securely around her shoulders.

"Your father called again," Lindy said when DJ got home from an evening meeting at the Academy two nights later.

DJ searched her mother's face for the tense lines that usually arrived with such a phone call, but her mother looked relaxed. Was that a smile lurking in her eyes?

"Yeah?" DJ hoped against hope that everything was going to work out.

"He asked if you could spend the weekend up at the ranch . . . and I said yes."

DJ flew across the kitchen and into her mother's arms. "Thank you, thank you, thank you!"

"I take it this is something you'd like to do?" The raised eyebrow meant her mother was teasing—as if DJ hadn't picked up on that already.

"Only this much." DJ spread her arms wide. She turned her head to look at her mother out of the corner of her eye. "But why?"

"Why what?"

"Why are you being so nice about this? I mean, I know you don't really want me to go."

"You remember how agreeable you were last night, with no smart remarks about the dress or shoes? And when the woman doing the fitting said you'd need to return to try the dress on you didn't even moan. That's why."

DJ nodded. How could she forget, with the still-sore tooth marks on her tongue from keeping her mouth shut? Much against her principles, she admitted, "We did have fun, huh?"

Instead of Robert driving DJ, Gran had picked her up and been there, too. Since Gran was working under another deadline, she didn't have time to sew her own dress, let alone DJ's. The three of them had gone out to dinner at DJ's favorite Italian restaurant, something they hadn't done together for a long time. Her mother had seemed like a new person. Never once did she suggest they needed to hurry home because she had to work on her thesis.

"Brad said he'd be here for you Friday about noon, so you can get your chores done both here and at the barn first. You don't have any lessons to give on Saturday?"

DJ shook her head. "Bridget decided that since so many parents might take advantage of the three-day weekend, we wouldn't have lessons." She had thought to spend extra time with Major, but she knew Joe would take over for her. "You're sure you don't mind if I go up to Brad's?" DJ cocked her head to one side, studying her mother. Where had the lines on her forehead gone? And the tight jaw?

Lindy shook her head, then halfway shrugged and raised her eyebrows. "Okay, that's a fib. I do mind. I'd rather you stayed home." She took in a deep breath, nodding slightly as she released it. "But Brad *is* your biological father, and as Robert pointed out, the man should have a chance to get to know the neat kid he created."

DJ nibbled on her lower lip. "Thanks, Mom." She thought a

moment, then decided to add a question that had been bugging her. "You ever sorry you didn't marry him?"

Lindy shook her head again. "We were too young, too caught up in ourselves. And now," she paused, "now, if he's as different a person as I am from when we were young, we'd never get along. Besides, can you see me helping to run a horse ranch?"

DJ laughed along with her mother. One thing for sure, Lindy Randall was *not* a horsewoman. Other than riding a horse once as a teenager, she preferred to view them from the edge of the arena.

"You might like riding if you tried it."

"That's what Robert says."

"I know. And don't forget that he promised the twins ponies as soon as we move into the new house." DJ clasped her hands around a raised knee, deciding to take advantage of this time while they were actually getting along. "You ever think what it's going to be like, living in that house all together?"

"Living in that house doesn't scare me half as much as all of us in this one, even for a month."

"Who's going to take care of the twins between school and when you get home?"

"Gran and Joe said they would. The boys' nanny will take a vacation until the new house is ready, then move in with us." Lindy leaned forward and patted DJ on the knee. "That will make your life easier, too, you know. She does housework and even cooks."

"I hadn't thought of that." DJ could feel a grin spread from her heart to her face. "I won't have to start dinner." The grin grew bigger. "I can spend more time with Major." She slapped her knees. "Yes!"

"Let's not get carried away."

DJ looked up to catch the teasing light in her mother's eyes, a light she was just getting to know. *If only we could always talk like this.* DJ wrapped her arms around her knees again and rocked back. "It will be super strange to be part of a family with a dad and brothers and all. Better say good-bye to peace and quiet with the Bs around all the time."

Now it was Lindy's turn to clasp her knees. She rested her chin on one knee and looked at DJ from under her eyebrows. "We've got a lot of changes ahead of us." The silence fell softly between the two of them as they sat in the dimness.

"You think we'll be ready for them? The changes, I mean?"

"Well, one thing I learned in my thirty-some years of life: Changes don't wait until you are ready. They just come." Lindy reached out a perfectly manicured hand to tousle DJ's hair. "You better get to bed, love. Morning always comes too soon."

DJ kissed her mother on the cheek and headed for the door. She stopped just before stepping into the hall. "You told Brad I could come?"

Lindy nodded. "He said for you to call him in the morning. Leave a message for me on the machine so I know what's going on."

"I will. Night, Mom."

DJ rushed through brushing her teeth and washing her face. Sure enough, another zit. Would she ever get lucky and find a flawless face smiling back at her? She dug the anti-zit cream out of the medicine cabinet and applied it to the red spot, making a face at the girl in the mirror. The temptation to pop the thing made her fingers itch. She inspected the spot again. Not ready for popping. She could hear her mother's frequent lectures on popping zits as clearly as if she stood right behind her. DJ sighed, spun around, and headed for her bedroom. Studies called, but her bed screamed for attention.

Her final thought floated heavenward. *Please, God, keep it from raining tomorrow.* Friday! Her father would be there at noon to pick her up for the weekend.

While God hadn't answered that prayer in the morning, He had answered another. For the first time since the accident, Major's leg was cool to the touch and free of swelling. "Thank you, Father," DJ murmured over and over as she rubbed liniment into the muscles and tendons. Major nosed her back and nibbled at her jacket.

"I know, I know. You need hugs and loves, but I'm in a hurry this morning. You know I'm not even supposed to be here, don't you? This is Friday, a school day, normally. And I'm going home with Brad for the weekend, so you better be good for Joe, you hear?"

Major snorted and shifted his weight so he leaned into her. "Get over there, you big goof." DJ straightened and brushed back a lock of hair his nosing had released from her ponytail. She dug the last carrot piece from her jacket pocket and presented it to him. "Now, I'm going to tie you in the aisle while I clean up your mess. Don't go messing out there." She tried to sound stern, but she giggled when he whiskered her cheek.

Joe laughed at them both from the next stall. "You two doing a comedy routine?" He leaned on his pitchfork. "I'll clean the stalls later if you need some time to get ready."

"Thanks, GJ, but I'm fine. Thanks for the ride, too—I'd have been soaked riding my bike. Wish Amy had been ready when we stopped."

"I'm sure sleeping in for a change was welcome." Joe stroked Major's nose. "Let me know when you want to head home. Maybe we could do McDonald's for breakfast. Melanie is already hard at her painting."

It was still strange to hear someone call Gran by her given name. At the thought, DJ could see Gran in her old wing chair, open Bible on her lap and cup of steaming tea on the table beside the chair. That had been the sight that greeted DJ on her first trip down the stairs every morning for as far back as she could remember. Some mornings, she still caught herself looking for Gran, wanting the feel of Gran's gentle hand on her hair as DJ knelt beside her knees, leaning her head into Gran's lap.

DJ sighed at the memory. Big-time changes had zapped the Randall house in the last year. And there would only be more!

One of the biggest changes pulled up into the driveway a couple of hours later. Handsome as a movie star and with a voice as smooth as warm caramel, Brad Atwood greeted her when she answered the doorbell.

"Hi, DJ, you about ready?" A smile much like her own lighted his blue eyes and deepened the creases in his cheeks.

"Almost." She motioned him in. "Joe said the rivers are getting high up north. You okay?"

"For now." He shook his head, scattering droplets of rainwater from his sun-lightened hair. "If this keeps up, though, we could be in trouble. Weatherman said we would get a break this afternoon. Even showed a smiling sun on the screen."

DJ reached inside the closet for her slicker. "I hope so. I'll get my duffel, and we can go."

As she headed up the stairs, he called after her. "Why don't you bring your drawing pad? I've got a scene or two up there that will set your fingers to itching."

"Okay." DJ grabbed her portfolio and gave a last glance around her room. Everything in place, the bathroom shiny and kitchen in order to boot. Amazing how quickly she could finish her chores when she had to.

An hour later, as they drove to Santa Rosa, DJ glanced out the rain-streaked window of the Land Rover at the swollen Napa River, which had spread across the lowlands below Highway 29. The area looked suspiciously like an extension of San Francisco Bay. The Petaluma River was also edging dangerously toward the tops of the levees. Rain pounded the windshield, the wipers wapping at high speed.

Chapter • 4

"Oh, what a baby!"

The little filly peeked out at DJ from behind the safety of her mother. The mare's tail acted as a screen for her foal, draping across the tiny dark muzzle and furry ears. Mother stood quietly, leaning into the hands of Brad, who was stroking her cheek.

"She sure is a cutie. And that's her favorite position. I thought you might like to draw it." Brad shifted to stroking the mare's neck. "This old girl was my first mare to foal, back before I had a barn like this and could afford the stallion that sired this baby. I thought last year might be the last foal from her, but she took again. The vet said she's still in good shape, so we may get another."

DJ leaned her chin on her hands on the top of the stall door. "The mare doesn't seem to mind a stranger here."

"No, she's an old hand with humans, but I once saw her drive a coyote out of the field. That critter ran like he had the devil himself breathing fire on the tip of his tail."

The filly snorted and stamped one tiny hoof.

"She thinks she's pretty hot stuff."

"I can tell. She should." DJ held out a hand. The baby took a step back under the protective veil, but extended her nose, nostrils quivering.

"She's a smart one, too. Of course, with her breeding, she should be."

"Have you named her yet?"

"Nope, thought I'd let you do that. I wanted to give her to you, but Jackie says you will need a bigger horse for jumping, probably one with some Thoroughbred blood. Arabians are good jumpers, but they are better known for their endurance."

DJ tried to swallow. Her dry throat ignored her command. "M-m-me?" The stutter barely got past the desert of her mouth.

"Of course, Jackie also reminded me that you'll need an intermediate horse when you've grown beyond Major. We'll have a friend watching for one in a year or two. Jackie was glad to know you're taking dressage lessons, too. Any and all the training you can get will be a help."

DJ finally located her voice. "Ah." *Now that's intelligent. Come on, say what you think!*

Brad turned to look at her. "You all right?"

DJ swallowed again. "I would be if you slowed down some. You can't just go giving horses away. And . . . and . . . Major will be good for a long while and . . ."

"And what?" Brad leaned against the stall, still stroking the mare's neck with one hand. "Darla Jean Randall, I've got news for you. Since I am your father, I can give you something if I want to."

"S-s-something isn't a purebred Arabian filly worth who knows how much and a h-horse for competition jumping and a . . ." She stammered to a close.

The filly stamped her foot again, dragging DJ's attention back to the baby. *What would it be like to have a horse like her for my very own? A baby to raise and train from the very beginning.* A lump formed in the back of her throat and burned behind her eyes.

"Besides, Mom would have a cow."

"She'd do better with a horse." The twinkle in his eyes brought a smile to DJ's lips. "Come on." He threw an arm around her shoulders. "Let's go have lunch. Jackie is waiting for us, and if we don't hurry, she'll claim I've been hogging you. Let's show her just how generous I am."

Cows, horses, hogs—DJ felt like a herd of each of the named animals had run right over her. She thought about the incredible Crosby saddle her father had given her for Christmas. While she'd spent time rubbing saddle soap into it, she had yet to put it on her horse. Not with the yucky weather they'd been having. That saddle she planned to save for the show-ring.

As she and her father matched step for step out to the truck, she put the thought of horses out of her mind and enjoyed the warmth of his arm around her shoulders. If this was what having a father felt like, maybe having two of them wouldn't be so bad after all.

"So what do you think we should name the filly?" Brad asked as he eased the Land Rover toward the driveway up the easy rise to the house. While both house and barns were on a gentle hill, the house crowned the top. The three barns and the covered arena lay halfway down to the flat pastures that spread to the riverbank.

"I don't know. What are her parents' names?"

"Dam is Wishful, out of My Wish. Shenanigans was her sire. Stud is Matadorian. The foal has a two-year-old full brother and a yearling sister. Matadorian and Wishful have great offspring, so I went for a third. The two-year-old was a futurity winner last year, and the yearling's competitors will have to work hard to beat her, too. I'm getting her ready for halter classes this season."

He parked off to the side of the huge house, built of rust and ochre slate from northern California. Camellias in every combination of pink and white bloomed along the house walls, azaleas flaming at their feet. The riot of color was brightened even more by clumps of red and white primroses. It nearly took DJ's breath away.

She and Gran had worked hard to create a lovely summer garden, but their roses looked pale beside this show. "Wow! How beautiful."

"Thanks, it is, isn't it? Jackie loves flowers almost as much as she loves horses." He laughed and shook his head. "Not really, but they are her second love. She takes care of most of the landscaping around here, especially since she cut back on the hours she spends at the clinic. Says she'd rather show horses now than try to straighten out kids who have been given too many things and not enough time and love from their parents."

He held open the heavy front door for her. "Jackie, we made it."

"I'm in the kitchen." The voice floated from the back of the house, along with a tantalizing fragrance.

"She made focaccia bread," Brad said, sniffing, too. "All we have to do is follow our noses. We'll leave your things here, unless you want to put them in your room first."

"Whatever." DJ propped her portfolio next to the duffel bag Brad had set by the wall. "I do need to wash my hands, though."

"In there." Brad pointed to the half bath off the hall to the kitchen.

"Hi, DJ, glad you could come." Jackie greeted her with a hug and a huge smile when DJ entered the gourmet kitchen. Brass pots hung from a rack over the center island stove, and bunches of dried herbs dangled from hooks above the butcher-block work counter beside the stove. Light oak cabinets, some with backlit stained-glass fronts, lined the walls. Beyond the small table set for three, the full wall of glass bayed out to a redwood deck that led in descending steps to a small pond. Pots of blooming pansies mixed with golden daffodils and bright primroses took the gray from the day, in spite of the rain.

"I love this place." DJ stood shaking her head, admiring everything around her.

"Thanks. I hope you're hungry." Jackie opened the oven door and pulled out a pan of flat, herb-topped bread. "I heard you like Italian food, so I made lasagna and foccacia bread. How does that sound?"

"Heavenly." DJ trailed a finger over the marble countertops. "Can I help you?"

"Sure, cut this bread into rectangles about this big"—Jackie spread her fingers about two inches by three inches—"and put some in that basket. Brad, how about pouring the ice water? You want milk, DJ?" While she talked, Jackie removed a ceramic casserole dish from a second oven, its contents topped by slightly browned cheese and meat sauce. "We'll serve from right here," she said, setting it on the hot pads on the table.

"You've done yourself proud, lady. That smells divine." Brad sniffed the air. "Come on, let's eat."

When they were all seated, Brad reached for DJ's and Jackie's hands. "Let's say grace." He bowed his head. "Heavenly Father, thank you for this food that Jackie has so lovingly made for us. Thank you, too, for prompting me to find my daughter—and for all the blessings you give us every day. Amen."

DJ raised her head and took in a deep breath. She felt so welcomed and at home here in this house, with these people, it was almost scary.

By the end of lunch, she felt like she had done almost all the talking, they had asked her so many questions, especially about the Academy. She helped Jackie load the dishwasher and then the three of them headed back to the barns.

"If you look over your shoulder very carefully, you may catch a peek at the sun." Brad dropped his voice to a whisper on the last word. He held a finger to his lips when DJ started to say something and pointed over her shoulder.

"Shhh, don't scare it away," Jackie whispered.

DJ tried swallowing her giggles and coughed instead.

"You did it." Brad shook his head. "See, you scared it. Now we'll have forty days and nights of rain."

"I thought it was forty more days of winter, like with the groundhog."

"Same difference." Brad winked at DJ and shrugged at his wife. "Groundhog, schmoundhog, rain, drain. All parts of winter. And here I thought we might enjoy at least a moment of sunshine."

"Sorry." DJ hoped her face looked suitably apologetic. When Brad shook his head, she fought the giggles again. "You want me to do a sun dance?"

"No thanks. Then we might not see it again for weeks. If a look or a giggle could scare it away, what would a dance do?" He parked by the barn, and they all climbed out.

"Forgive this man I live with," Jackie said to DJ. "Sometimes I think he is certifiably nuts." She waited for Brad to pull open the sliding barn door. "You want to ride Lord Byron first or Herndon, the horse I used before him?"

"We have a jumper we'd like you to try, too." Brad caught up with them.

He reintroduced her to all the horses in the stalls lining the long barn. "Some of the young stock is out on the pasture, since I figured they needed the exercise. While you two go play, I'll put the rest of these guys out on the hot walker. Matadorian and I will join you in the arena later. You can take a turn on him again, too, DJ, if you like."

"So many to choose from, I can't decide." DJ stopped in the middle of the aisle. Dish-faced horses with large, dark eyes and curving ear tips watched them from every stall. Some nickered, some stamped a foot. DJ wanted to hand out carrots to each and every one. Brass nameplates on the varnished wood doors gleamed in the light from long bulbs overhead. "This looks more like a movie set than a real barn. How do you keep it so nice?"

"Hired helpers," Brad answered. "Most of them have worked for us for the last five years or so. Ramone is the head of the barn crew. He helps us with showing and in the breeding barn. Ramone's been working with horses since about the time I was born, so we are really fortunate to have found someone like him. He took today off, but you'll meet him tomorrow."

"I do most of the breaking of the young stock," Jackie offered. "Then Brad takes over the training. When he's out of town, Ramone and I split the work. I spend two to three hours both training and conditioning Lord Byron most days, and my trainer comes twice a week."

"Wow." DJ shook her head. "I had no idea." She turned to Brad. "You travel a lot?"

"Depends on the case."

"He has quite a reputation as a legal attorney. But he tries to schedule his work around the big shows so we can do them together." Jackie paused while Brad walked one of the most persistent nickerers out of her stall. "See how heavy she is? Due to foal within the month. That should be a real good baby, too. By Matadorian again."

"You sell more fillies or colts?"

"Depends on the year. Matadorian's sons are doing real well in the ring, and this year, we will have the first get from Matson, the oldest. We kept him for ourselves, at least for a while."

"How many horses do you have?"

"Thirty-five—no, six with the little filly you get to name." Jackie took her arm. "Come on, let's go saddle up. If the sun does come through, I think we'll ride down to the river when Brad joins us."

If DJ thought riding Megs was a treat, Lord Byron took her breath away. Even with her limited use of aids, he responded like a dream come true. Following Jackie's instructions, she rode the extended trot that seemed to float above the ground.

"You ride well for someone with so little dressage training." Jackie held the big Hanovarian while DJ dismounted. "I think you must have a good trainer."

"I do. Bridget rode for the French National Team a few years ago, but when she decided to live in the United States, she forfeited her place. She says she'd rather teach now, but I think something happened that she never talks about. At least not with us kids. She's really a great teacher, though. One thing about her, you don't ever try to make excuses or not do your best." DJ gave a mock shudder. "I won't ever make that mistake again."

"I'm glad you have someone like that. Too many people give up when the going gets tough. You have to set your goals and work toward them." Jackie stroked the near-black gelding's arched neck. "This boy here was one of my goals. I wanted a horse with the capacity for Grand Prix levels. He can do it, too—but I'm still learning." She smiled. "Boy, am I learning!"

"He's a dream to ride, that's for sure." DJ adjusted the stirrups back to the shorter length. "Thanks for giving me the privilege."

"I'm just trying to brainwash you to switch from jumping to dressage—at least that's what your father says. Mount up on Herndon here, and I'll give you the lesson I promised. Then you can take him over the jumps in the middle. He loves to jump and doesn't get the chance very often."

"I didn't think you had jumps," DJ said.

"We do, but they were in storage since no one was using them. Brad brought them out for you."

As if in a dream, DJ took the reins Jackie handed her and led the dark bay gelding forward a couple of steps. She adjusted the stirrup leathers out for her longer legs, mounted, and checked to make sure they fit. Sliding her right leg back, she tightened the girth and tested again. Now comfortable with the fit, she deepened her seat in the saddle, checked all the points Bridget harped on, and signaled a walk. Herndon obeyed as if they'd been riding partners for years.

"Have you worked on bending yet?" Jackie asked when DJ had Herndon sufficiently warmed up.

"Some but not much."

"But you understand what it is?"

DJ nodded. "Keep the horse bent around my inside leg and ask him to come down on the bit. Keeping Megs down on the bit is mostly what I've been working on."

"Good, then this is the next step. You will work a serpentine pattern down the arena, so you'll need to bend each way as you turn. This increases the suppleness of your horse." She positioned DJ's left leg just behind the girth. "Now for turning left, keep this leg here, shorten your left rein, and hold your right leg behind the girth just a bit. Keep your contact with the horse snug." She looked up. "Do you understand?"

"Sure—until I try it."

Jackie smiled. "That's the way it is, all right. Herndon knows what you want, so relax. Let him teach you."

DJ immediately dropped her shoulders.

"Good girl, now go for it. And remember, sit to the trot."

By the third time through the serpentine, DJ was bending to the left consistently.

"Don't drop your inside shoulder," Jackie called. A few more times, and the right came more easily. Back and forth, up and down the arena. She totally lost track of time, finally picking up the pace. Bending at a walk was the most difficult.

"You did terrific work," Jackie said when she called a halt sometime later.

"Thanks." DJ leaned forward and petted the gelding's sweaty neck. "He sure is willing. How could you bear to give him up?"

"Pure ambition." Brad joined them on Matadorian, who snorted when brought to a standstill. "She wants a chance at the top, and poor old Herndon wasn't good enough. Not the athlete Lord Byron is. We got him from a breeder and trainer in the Netherlands. Another year or so of experience, and Jackie and Lord Byron might make it."

"Might?" Jackie raised an eyebrow. "Might?"

"Sorry. They *will* make it to the big time." Brad shot his wife a teasing glance.

"I'd say level four is pretty big time."

"Me too. It certainly took long enough to get there." Jackie brushed Lord Byron's mane to one side. "You want to jump now, or should we take advantage of the momentary sun to ride down to the fields? You can always jump later."

DJ looked longingly at the series of jumps set up in the middle of the ring. But riding outside drew her like a magnet, especially when the weather had given her so few opportunities lately. "Let's go outside."

A mockingbird greeted them and the sun with an aria of joy. Two of the yearlings raced each other across the green pasture, tails flagging in the distinctive Arab way. Brad leaned forward and swung open the gate, Matadorian responding like a well-trained trail-riding horse. He backed on command and, once through, sidestepped so Brad could latch the gate again.

DJ watched appreciatively. While Major allowed her to do the same, Patches absolutely refused to cooperate yet. "Is there a trick to getting a horse to work with a gate like that? The gelding I'm training for the Johnsons would sooner jump the gate than let me open it."

All the way along the field, they discussed horse training and tricks they had learned to get a spirited horse to obey.

"Calling that clown Patches spirited is like saying a lion is a house cat. I think he's pure ornery and out to prove it to anyone who gives him the tiniest chance. You've got to watch him every minute—he gets bored easily."

California oak trees with naked branches lined the river, giving promise of cooling shade in the summer. Every once in a while, a euca-lyptus raised gray-leafed branches, its trunk littering the ground with shredded bark. Broken branches scattered about gave mute testimony to the latest windstorm. Just beyond the trees, the Petaluma river flowed high up the diked banks, brown with runoff soil.

The trunk of a willow tree floated downstream, its roots waving sadly to the sky. It caught on a fallen tree from the opposite side of the river and hung there before swirling on down toward the Bay.

"At least the river is falling today. That's good." Brad reined his mount to a stop. "If the storms let up, we'll be okay. The Petaluma doesn't usually get it as bad as the Russian River north of here."

DJ watched the willow tree float away. It was moving pretty fast. A cloud covered the sun, sending shivers up her back. The river looked like a swollen brown snake between the banks of green. She never had liked snakes much.

"You want to jump now?" Jackie asked when Brad rode on ahead. "He'd rather patrol the perimeters of his camp, like a good commander. We'll ride back here again during the summer when we can walk the horses right into the river, just around that bend."

Within minutes, Jackie had the jumps adjusted for DJ's training level. She moved off to watch, Lord Byron's reins looped over her arm.

DJ felt a thrill shoot through her. Jumping again! It felt like she hadn't jumped in months, maybe even years. She set Herndon into a canter and toward the first jump. He lifted off at just the right moment and landed so lightly, she felt like she was still flying. She could hear Jackie's applause and Brad cheering her on as he rejoined them. The second jump, the third, and the fourth—each one renewed the thrill. This was what she lived for, those brief moments when she was airborne. There was no feeling like it anywhere else on earth. At least nothing she had ever felt.

DJ finished the sixth and continued the canter to where Brad and Jackie sat on their horses.

"That was great!" Brad's face shone with his excitement.

Jackie nodded. "You did well. Shall I raise them?"

"Okay, but not much. Bridget says to keep the jumps low enough for a good workout, yet high enough to learn something. What I learned this time is that Herndon loves to jump. You see his ears? Forward the whole time." She patted the horse's neck. "Herndon, old boy, you've got a permanent friend in me."

This round, they ticked on the fifth jump, and the pole came tumbling down. "Rushed that one, fella, and I got left behind. Sorry. Let's go again." She cantered back around to jump one and began the circuit again, this time concentrating on her timing. Bridget always said to count the beats between jumps, and DJ had skipped doing that on the tick round. When DJ finished with a clean slate this time through, Jackie asked if she should raise the poles again.

DJ hesitated. If this were a jump-off like those Hilary had to ride in almost every show, the poles would go higher. Should she do it?

She nodded, and Brad set the fifth jump higher than she had ever jumped.

They cantered forward, Herndon's ears forward, joy in his every step. They cleared the first four with space to spare. DJ felt like she was part of a flying machine.

"Okay, fella, let's do this one, too."

They cantered toward the jump with three poles, the bottom two in an X-crossed pattern below the top one. DJ leaned forward, but Herndon swerved to the right.

DJ went airborne.

Chapter • 5

DJ could feel something warm and sticky running down the left side of her face.

"DJ, are you all right?" Brad reached her as she gingerly sat up. "Oh my word—you're bleeding!"

DJ raised a hand to her cheek and came away with blood on her glove. "Other than this scratch, I'm fine, I think." She wiggled her toes, flexed her knees and ankles, and put a hand back on the ground to lever herself up. She looked up into her father's face. If she was as white as he, she must look a sight. Red blood, white skin. *Oh, great. Just great!*

"Thank God for helmets," Jackie said as she knelt by DJ's side. "You must have hit the base of the standard." She reached over her shoulder for the folded handkerchief Brad handed to her. "Let's get this on that cut before you bleed to death." Her smile reassured DJ that bleeding to death wasn't really an option.

If all the heat in her face originated with the cut, that would be fine. But feeling like an idiot usually brought its own hot skin. What a dumb thing to do—let Herndon dump her just because he didn't want to jump the fence. She'd ridden other horses who had refused a jump. You had to be ready, that's all. "Where's Herndon? Is he all right?"

"That fool horse is fine. It's you I'm worried about." Brad knelt at her other side.

"I shoulda been paying better attention. To let him dump me like that . . ." She shook her head.

"DJ, falls happen to the best riders. Hitting the ground goes with the territory." Jackie pressed harder on the pad.

"I know, but . . ." DJ kept herself from flinching away. The cut was beginning to burn.

"No buts." Brad extended a hand to pull her to her feet. "Let's go get that cleaned up and see if you need a couple of stitches."

"Stitches!" DJ could feel her mouth drop open. "I won't need stitches." She looked at Jackie. "Will I?" Her voice squeaked. *The wedding!* Would her face heal in time for the wedding, now only three weeks away? "Mom's going to kill me."

"Why? She should be glad you're not hurt any worse." Brad still wore a white ring around his mouth. "Thank God you aren't hurt any worse. Or are you? Can you walk? How's your shoulder? I should never have raised the jumps that last time. It's all my fault."

"Huh? What's this fault garbage? I took a header, that's all. It wasn't my first, and I'll bet anything it won't be my last."

Jackie smiled up at her husband. "Listen to your daughter, dear. In spite of getting clobbered by Herndon, she has her head on straight." She turned back to DJ. "Come on, let's see if anything else hurts. You'll most likely get a black eye from this, too, since it's right on the cheekbone."

DJ groaned again.

"You hurt somewhere else?" Brad stopped her with a hand on her arm.

"No, but I probably will hurt in all kinds of places tomorrow. Can you just see a wedding where the bridesmaid has a black eye?"

"Oh no." Now it was Brad's turn to groan. "I forgot all about the wedding." Brad turned from them at the arena gate. "You take her on up to the house, Jackie, and I'll put the horses away."

"I should make Herndon go back and take that fence." DJ started to turn back.

"I don't think so." Brad shook his head. "You some kind of masochist?"

"No, she's just like her father—thinking of the horse before herself." Jackie took DJ's arm, as if to keep her from turning back. "Come on, DJ, let's see what we have here. See you in a few minutes, Brad."

The warmth from the Land Rover's powerful heater felt good since the sky had reverted to gray while they played in the arena. DJ shivered a bit and caught herself before she called herself any names. She could hear Bridget's voice reminding her to let it go. *Don't beat yourself or your horse.* How many times had she heard that bit of wisdom?

"I think we better take you in to the urgent care clinic up in Santa Rosa." Jackie tilted the light in the bathroom so she could see better. "That cut looks deep and long enough that a butterfly bandage might leave you with more of a scar than stitches would."

DJ groaned. "I hate going to doctors. They take forever."

"I know. But your father will feel better about it. So will I." She handed DJ a sterile pad. "Hold this in place while I get some ice. Let's get that swelling down, if we can." When she returned with ice in a zipped plastic bag, DJ applied that to the pad.

"I'm going to call the clinic and tell them we're coming."

"How long since you've had a tetanus shot?" the doctor asked as he examined the cut.

DJ shrugged. "I don't know. Can't remember when."

"Why don't you call her mother and ask?" the doctor said to Jackie.

"Can't you just give me one? My mom gets kinda uptight about stuff like this."

"It's better to check." He turned and gave instructions to the nurse.

As Jackie started to leave, DJ said, "Call Gran instead. She's the one who kept track of stuff like this. And please ask her not to tell Mom. Beg if you have to. Telling Mom now would ruin everything."

"I'll try." Jackie wiggled her fingers as she went out the door.

"You want to tough this out, or would you rather have a bit of Novocain?" The doctor looked at her over the tops of his half glasses.

"How bad will the stitches hurt?" While she didn't mind giving shots to a horse, needles puncturing her own hide had never been a real favorite of hers. Not even close.

"I think the shot hurts as bad as the stitches, but that's only my opinion."

"No shot then," DJ said, eyeing the needle. The last time she'd had stitches was when she'd fallen out of a tree, years ago now. She'd ripped her knee on the branch that had cracked on the way down, but at least she hadn't broken any bones. Gran always said DJ had fallen on a guardian angel. She even claimed she'd heard an extra *oof* when DJ hit the ground.

"Ready?" The doctor smiled at her.

DJ nodded. This time she wouldn't be able to watch.

She told herself to relax when she lay against the pillow. She felt the nurse's hands cupping her head to keep her from jerking away.

Jackie reentered the room just before the doctor began. "Her grand-mother says it's been five years since her last tetanus shot. And, DJ, she promised to let you do the talking when you get home."

DJ started to nod, then stopped. "Good."

Within minutes, she was stitched, bandaged, inoculated, and walking out the door. Brad leaped to his feet in the waiting room. "You okay?" At DJ's nod, he turned to Jackie. "They stitched it?"

"Yes, worrying father, and your daughter is a trooper. Stitches without Novocain even."

"Stitches, as in with a needle?" At DJ's nod, he continued. "And you didn't faint?"

"Faint?" She changed from a grin to a straight face when the bandage crinkled. "Ouch."

"Don't mind your father. He faints when a needle gets near him."

"Not quite. Only when it pokes me. I just get dizzy before that." He reached a gentle hand to touch the bandage. "I'm so sorry, DJ."

DJ rolled her eyes and made Jackie laugh. Rather, she rolled one eye. The left one was now swollen halfway shut.

Once in the Land Rover, DJ leaned back and put the ice pack back on her face.

"The seat tilts," Jackie said. "And remember, the doctor gave you some pain pills in case it starts hurting too badly. You don't need to tough it out—the body heals faster when it isn't fighting pain, too."

"It hurts, but let's try some Tylenol first. I hate that fuzzy feeling from pain-killers."

They stopped at a convenience store and bought her a bottle of water to take the Tylenol with, so by the time they got back to the ranch, DJ was feeling pretty good again. But when she suggested she would like to go back to the arena and make Herndon take the jump, Brad looked at her as if she'd cracked her mind in the fall.

"I don't *think* so." He looked to Jackie as if for support. She just shrugged. "Maybe you better lay down for a while."

DJ returned his cracked-mind look. She knew how to raise her eyebrows in just the same way he did, but she'd never dreamed that it was a trait she'd gotten from her father.

"Okay, how about coming with me to check on the mares? You could try out some names for the baby."

DJ turned to Jackie. "I could help you with dinner if you like."

"Thanks, sweetie, but I already made soup. You go with your dad and have a good time."

It was the first time in her life someone had called her "sweetie," but DJ didn't mind a bit. From Jackie, it sounded just right. She followed her dad out to the truck, trying to duck between the raindrops since she had left her slicker down at the barn. "Do you always drive back and forth?" she asked when he had the truck in motion.

"Pretty much. Unless it's really a nice day and I'm not in a hurry. Those days come few and far between, I'm afraid."

"What is your work like?" She turned so she could see him better out of her one good eye.

"Not like what you see on television or the movies. Most legal work involves tons of reading, writing, and talking on the phone with clients. Since I'm not a trial attorney, I don't spend a lot of time in court. I have some really sharp associates for that end of the business. They like the spotlight, and I like having a life besides the law." He motioned to the farm around them. "If I could, I'd retire tomorrow and go full time into horse breeding."

"You can't?"

"Nope, I keep my practice going to support my horse habit. Since the bottom fell out of Arabian breeding, it's hard to get ahead. Plus, we like to show, and Jackie is serious about wanting to compete on the Grand Prix level. International shows take a lot of time and money."

"Local shows are bad enough." DJ leaned back against the seat. "Mom always said having a horse was too much for our budget. Thing is, she's right. If I didn't work for Major's board and then some, I couldn't keep him."

"DJ, are you short on money?"

"No. Why?" She thought back to what she'd said. "Oh no, don't get the wrong idea. I didn't mean—I mean—" She took a deep breath and sighed. "I like working at the Academy, even mucking stalls when I have to. I like training Patches and will take on another when he is ready to leave me. Sure, vet bills are spendy and shoeing costs more than I'd like, but that's part of owning a horse. Major is my responsibility."

"And you're a responsible person?"

"Yeah, I am."

"I can tell. You make me so proud I could pop." He clasped his hands along the top of the steering wheel and turned his head to look at her. "Take today, for example—the way you handled the fall and getting stitched up—not to mention your riding ability, the wonderful way you draw, your sense of humor." He gave her a smile that showed his feelings of pride and love. "Your mother has done a fine job with you."

"Gran did most of the work." DJ immediately wished she'd kept her mouth shut. The comment bordered on being less than nice.

"Well, then I can thank Melanie, too. She always was a woman of wisdom."

DJ picked at a cuticle. When her courage grew strong enough, she said, "Can I ask you a question? One that's been eating at me?"

He nodded. "Ask away, and I'll answer if I can."

DJ kept her gaze on his face. "Why did you never write or call me?"

Silence swelled in the truck cab, the rain on the roof sounding like a drum roll.

DJ wished she had kept her mouth shut.

Brad nodded slightly. "I could give you all kinds of reasons, most of them valid, but the bottom line is I was chicken. I had bowed out of your life, and I was afraid Lindy hated me and had made you hate me, too."

"Mom never said a word about you—ever. Once or twice I wondered, but since I was happy, I figured I didn't need a dad—not when I had Gran and Gramps and Mom. Even after Gramps died . . . our little family felt like enough. I sure missed Gramps, though—for a long time." DJ spoke slowly and softly, exploring the ideas herself as she shared them with her father.

"I missed out on a lot."

"Gran says everything happens in God's timing."

"Yes, I'm sure she does. Melanie always did have a strong faith. She's an example to all of us. No way I'd hear such talk from my family."

"But you believe now?"

"Thanks to Jackie. Still, I might never have contacted you if we had been able to have children. Maybe this is God's way, after all." He reached out and stroked a gentle finger down the curve of her cheek. "I am just so eternally grateful that I know you now. 'If onlys' aren't worth the time it takes to think about them." He patted her hand. "Any more questions?"

"One more?"

"Shoot."

"What do I call you? Before long, I'm going to have two dads or whatever, and I don't know what to call either one of you."

"Let me think on that one, okay? Who knows, maybe you'll come up with something that you feel comfortable with on your own. Eventually, something will work out. Just please don't ever introduce me as Mr. Atwood."

"I won't."

"And, DJ, if Lindy and Robert can handle it, I really want to be a part of your life. Jackie and I both do."

"Things like school and stuff, too?"

"Yep. All of it. Shows, school events, birthdays. Whatever."

"Cool."

Together they walked into the barn and over to the only foaling stall in use at the moment. The filly darted behind her mother and peeked out just like before as the mare hung her head over the low wall to soak up the attention. When Brad obliged by scratching up behind her ears and down her cheek and neck, the mare sighed and let her eyelids close. When he stopped, she tilted her head to coax him to keep going.

DJ leaned over the gate, extending her hand to the filly.

The curious baby reached out her muzzle and leaned toward the hand. But she refused to move a foot closer.

"You should call her Elusive. Ellie for short."

"That's a great name. And it sure fits her temperament—at least what we've seen of it so far. If you want to go inside the stall and just sit in the corner, this old girl won't mind. You'll be able to make friends with Ellie there. I'll finish my chores and come back for you."

"You sure my face won't scare her?"

"DJ!" He dug in his pocket and pulled out pieces of horse cookies. "She won't take these yet, but I know her mother loves them."

DJ opened the stall door very slowly and slipped inside. The filly disappeared behind her mother. The mare wandered over and lipped the cookie bits from DJ's palm, then, munching, gave DJ the nose test. Up her arm, her hair, and finally her jacket pockets.

"You found 'em, huh?" DJ gave the mare another treat while scratching her ears. "Why don't you tell your kid to come visit with me, too? You mind if I sit here in the corner?" As she talked, she slid her back down the wall and crossed her legs to sit comfortably. The mare lowered her head and, after sniffing some more to check out the bandage, blew horse-cookie breath in DJ's face.

"Thanks a big fat bunch." DJ wiped away a bit of slobber. While she paid attention to the mare, she kept her eye on the baby, who hid behind her mother's tail again, peeking out from the veil.

"Curiouser and curiouser, aren't you?" At the low, singsong hum of DJ's voice, the baby ears flicked back and forth. One step at a time, she edged around her dam until she was standing clear, a strand of the mare's long tail still caught on one fuzzy ear. DJ kept herself from laughing out loud only through sheer effort of will.

"Such a charmer, you are. How could anyone resist you? How can you keep from coming over here to see what is pleasing your mom so much?" The mare stood, eyes at half-mast, her nose even with DJ's shoulder.

The filly finally stood within a foot of DJ, her body poised to flee at the slightest mismove. DJ kept playing with the mare.

When she worked her arm up to rub behind the mare's ears, the baby reached out and sniffed DJ's sleeve. When nothing happened, she took a step closer. The mare whuffled DJ's hair, and DJ slipped her another treat. Loud munching filled the stall.

DJ could feel her right foot going to sleep. Soon, she would have to move. "Come on, baby, make it all the way over here. Let me touch you the way I am your mother. I promise you you'll like it."

Ellie sniffed DJ's hair, then darted back one step. She reached again, brushing DJ's hand with the whiskers on her upper lip. At last, she sighed and let DJ touch her nose. Ears pricked, eyes wide, little Miss Elusive huddled closer to her mother's shoulder and let DJ stroke her furry cheek and under her chin.

"What a baby you are . . . so soft." DJ wanted to shout for joy. She'd done it! She'd petted Elusive.

"You really have a way with horses, my dear," Brad spoke softly from above her head.

The filly darted behind her mother again, so DJ pushed herself upright. Needles stabbed her awakening right foot, and she grabbed on to the stall door. "I didn't even hear you come up."

"You were too busy. Such patience that took. No wonder you are able to win even Patches over."

DJ limped out the stall door when Brad swung it open. "Thanks for the treat. What a honey she is."

"Let's go eat, then talk about you drawing her."

Before she left for home Sunday afternoon, DJ had ten drawings scattered over the table. She'd also ridden again, working Herndon until he cleared all the jumps nicely. Another ride on Lord Byron after a dressage lesson on Herndon reminded her again of how much there was ahead to learn.

When DJ called home, Lindy said they would all be over at Gran's, so she should be dropped off there.

"Do you want to come in?" DJ asked when Brad stopped the Land Rover in Gran's driveway.

"Not this time, unless you want me to." He motioned to her face, which at least was no longer swollen.

"Nah, it's no big deal. Thanks for the wonderful weekend. You'll call me when that other mare is about to foal?"

"If it looks like it will happen on a weekend." He squeezed her shoulder. "Take care of yourself, kid."

DJ leaped from the car with all her gear and, after one more wave, trotted to the front door. She had so much to tell everyone!

"Hi, I'm back," she called from the entrance.

The two torpedoes hit her at the same time, but she was braced and ready. She reached down and hugged them, one arm around each. "Hi, guys."

They looked up, their mouths going round as their eyes. "DJ, what did you do?"

She put a finger over her lips to shush them. When she looked up, her mother and Robert stood before her.

"Darla Jean Randall, whatever happened to your face?" Lindy's face matched the shock in her voice.

Chapter • 6

"It looks worse than it is." DJ put a hand to her bandaged cheek.

Lindy's horrified question brought Gran and Joe to the hallway. When DJ looked at her grandmother, Gran shook her head. No, she hadn't mentioned anything about the accident.

Robert put an arm around Lindy's shoulders. "Okay, DJ, fill us in."

DJ set her things out of the way and joined everyone in the living room. With all eyes on her, she swallowed and related what had happened. "So it's just a couple of stitches. I know I have a black eye, but it's getting better." She blinked both eyes for good measure. "Most of the swelling is gone already."

"So you were jumping with a horse you didn't know?" Lindy leaned forward, away from Robert.

The boys had glued themselves to DJ's side as if assigning themselves as her protectors. Every once in a while, one would moan, "Poor DJ."

By the third "poor DJ," she nearly burst out laughing. But she could tell her mother was in no mood for laughter.

"Come on, Mom, it's no big deal. I'm not broken anywhere. If I never get hurt any worse than this, I'll be blessed." *Oops, not the right thing to say*. The frown deepened between her mother's eyes, and DJ sent Joe a pleading glance.

"She's right, Lindy. She's not seriously hurt, and we'll all keep praying that she never will be." Joe smiled at DJ. "Besides, Gran has been sending guardian angels DJ's way for fourteen years now. I'd say they're doing a pretty good job."

"I just don't want Brad Atwood being irresponsible with my daughter."

DJ bit her tongue.

"No one was irresponsible. Accidents happen." Robert rubbed Lindy's shoulder and drew her back into the circle of his arm. "Remember when Bobby took a header off the bleachers? Was that my fault for not watching him better? Or yours? Or DJ's? Or Dad's? We were all there."

DJ sat back in her chair in relief. "Thanks, Robert."

As the conversation turned to other things, DJ regaled them with the tales of Elusive. She brought out her drawings and made the boys giggle at the baby peeking out from her mother's tail.

"These are about your best yet," Gran said, holding the pencil drawings up for better light. "She sure is a sweetheart."

"Yeah, and I finally got her to come to me." DJ told that story, then went on about the possible flood, the gorgeous yard, riding Lord Byron, taking lessons from Jackie, and what great food they had.

Lindy jerked up a restraining hand. "Enough already. DJ, you're not letting anyone else get a word in edgewise." Her look shouted "be quiet!"

"Oh, sorry." DJ slumped back. She watched her mother for any sign of relenting. She still had so much to tell. Wasn't she interested? The boys leaned against her knees.

"DJ, tell us more stories," one pleaded, the other nodding.

"How about we kids go in the other room and let the grown-ups talk all they want?" She didn't even try to keep the sarcastic bite out of her words. DJ looked up to catch a questioning look from Robert. Gran just shook her head.

Letting the boys pull her to her feet, DJ and her escorts left the room. They settled in the family room, all three in Joe's big recliner. DJ told them again about the filly, this time making it more of a story. "The Adventures of Elusive, Ellie for Short." Whenever she asked, "And do you know what happened then?" the boys gave her another idea, and off the story would go again. Then she drew pictures to illustrate the story and let the boys color them.

By the time they were ready to leave, DJ had pretty much forgotten about her hurt feelings, but when they got home, she knew for certain her mother hadn't.

"I didn't appreciate your sassy remark," Lindy said before DJ went up the stairs. "I also think you should have called me to say you'd had an accident."

"Sorry." DJ knew if she said anything more, another smart remark might explode into the air. Why would she want to call when her mother probably would have ordered her to come home at once?

"Brad at least should have had the courtesy to call."

"But, Mom—"

"No buts." Lindy took another tack. "Is your homework done?"

DJ shook her head. "I forgot to take it with me. It's not Brad's fault."

"Well, someone in this family has to be responsible."

Sorry didn't seem to be cutting it, so DJ chose not to say it again. "Good night, Mother. I'll try to do better." She stomped on the first step of the stairs but changed her footing fast. She would not get into a fight and ruin the entire weekend.

But the old "not fairs" raged in DJ's head, keeping her from falling asleep. Here she had been so excited about her visit and all the neat things that happened, and her mother got into a hissy fit. All Lindy could think of was homework and who was responsible. Who was her mother to say that? Until the last year, she'd hardly ever asked about homework—and never about the Academy. Gran had done all the asking, just like Gran had done everything around the house. Lindy hadn't done much of anything but work, go to school, come home, and study. She hardly took a minute in her loaded schedule for her daughter.

DJ flipped over on her other side. Let God see if He could figure this one out—she sure couldn't. But the Bible verses she'd memorized in Sunday school started a parade through her wide-awake mind. *Honor your father and your mother, so that you may live long in the land the LORD your God is giving you. . . . Love one another. . . . Rejoice in the Lord always. Again I will say, rejoice!*

DJ flipped from side to side with each verse. Finally, she sat up in bed and rubbed her eyes. "God, I need to get to sleep so I can get up early to study. I didn't yell at my mother this time—I thought I did pretty well. Anyway, you know I'm trying to control my mouth and my temper. What gives?" She waited, her arms crossed on her raised knees and her good cheek resting on her wrist.

A soft tap at her door made her think, for just an instant, God had arrived to answer her.

"Come in."

Lindy poked her head in and, seeing DJ sitting up, entered the room. "I heard you tossing around. Can't sleep, either?"

Enough light from the streetlights entered the windows that DJ could see her mother's shape but not her expression. At least the tone of voice sounded comforting. She hung on to Lindy's last word. "Either?"

"Yeah, I kept hearing our conversation over and over."

DJ waited. "Me too." She scooted over and patted the bed beside her. "You can sit down if you want."

Lindy sat, one knee up on the bed, so she was partly facing DJ. "That bandage on your face scared me half to pieces."

"Mom, it's no big deal."

"If you had to have stitches, it's going to leave a scar. That *is* a big deal to me."

"The doctor said it would disappear with time. We'll hardly be able to see it."

"The thought of a scar on your face doesn't bother you?"

"Not a whole lot, but then I haven't seen it yet. Jackie changed the bandage. She said a scar like this would have been a badge of honor back in the days of sword fights."

"Great. So my daughter walks down the aisle at my wedding looking like she's been in a duel."

DJ snorted. She could tell from the tone that her mother was poking fun of the idea. "Does it really bother you?"

"Not really. Not as much as the fact that you got hurt and neither Gran nor I were with you. Besides, you can cover the scar up with makeup if you like."

"Mom, you and Gran can't be with me all of my life." Still, her mother's words warmed DJ's insides.

"I know. But cut me some slack, okay? I'm just learning about this mom stuff."

DJ thought a bit. "You know, I see Joe more than Gran nowadays. I miss her, especially in the mornings."

"Funny, she said the same thing the other day." Lindy turned and patted DJ's hands on her knees. "You think you can sleep now?"

"Mm-hmm." DJ could feel her eyelids getting heavy.

"Me too." Lindy stood and leaned over to kiss DJ's cheek. "Mom reminded me that you have a very forgiving heart. I'm glad you do. Sometimes I think you are more grown-up than I am."

"Huh?" *Great, that was an intelligent, mature answer. Try again.*

"Only in some ways, of course."

"Night, Mom. I love you."

"Thank you, Darla Jean Randall." Lindy's voice wore a coat of tears. "Have a good day tomorrow." She sniffed as she went out the door.

DJ snuggled back down in her bed. The words "I love you" had just popped out. Had she ever before said "I love you" to her mother? Gran yes, but to her mother? Not for a few years at least.

"Thank you, heavenly Father," she whispered just before dropping off to sleep.

———

DJ explained her accident about fifty times at school the next day. Her eye was already turning black, especially underneath. "I look like a raccoon," she muttered to Amy in the washroom after lunch.

"Not really. They have two black eyes and no bandage." Amy brushed her black hair and wrapped a scrunchie around the thick, straight mass. "Did you hear what happened at the Academy this weekend?"

"How would I if you didn't tell me?" DJ turned from examining the bandage and the new zit on her chin.

"Joe might have." Amy stuffed her brush back into her backpack.

"They were too grossed out about my face to think of anything else."

"How come you told Gran not to tell your mother?"

" 'Cause I was afraid she'd freak and probably give my da—Brad—a bad time. And it wasn't his fault. I let Herndon turn out on me. When I think about it, it was probably all my own fault. My timing was off when he ticked it the first time, so then he didn't have confidence in me, and well, he turned out. I shoulda been ready."

"I wouldn't let Bridget hear me say that." Amy headed for the door. "Come on, we'll be late."

"I know—what do you think, I'm stupid or something?"

Amy raised one straight eyebrow.

"Don't answer that." As Amy headed the opposite way, DJ hollered after her, "So what happened at the Academy?"

Amy turned around, walking backward. "Tell you later."

Keeping her mind on her classes the rest of the day wasn't easy.

"So what happened?" DJ pounced with her question as soon as she and Amy met again at their locker.

"Bridget will probably introduce her to you." Amy sorted through her books to decide what to take home.

"Who? Amy Marie Yamamoto, do you want an eye to match mine?"

Amy ducked away and slung her backpack over one shoulder. "Mrs. Lamond Ellsindorf—you-can-call-me-Bunny—that's who." Amy threw a you-really-don't-want-to-know-more look over her shoulder. "To listen to her tell it, she is the most important rider on the East Coast, or was, until her husband got transferred out here to the wilds of California and she was *forced* to come with him."

They climbed into the backseat of the Yamamoto minivan. Amy's older brother, John, who after finally, as he said, turning the big one-six, had just gotten his driver's license, was driving.

"There'll be no comments from the peewee section," he growled.

"John." Mrs. Yamamoto might not be very big, but one word from her, and her children shaped up. "Hi, you two. Ignore the grouch here. DJ, whatever happened to your face?" She turned around to see better.

DJ briefly told her story again, sharing enough to be polite.

"And the wedding coming up, too. What a shame." She turned back to the front. "Now, John, you watch your speed." The implied "this time" made DJ glance curiously at Amy.

She mouthed, "He got a warning ticket." DJ covered her snort with a sneeze.

"So what about that Mrs. What's-her-name?" DJ asked when she could look at Amy without giggling.

"You'll see" was all Amy would say.

DJ was in for a flurry of questions about her new look later at the Academy. "Think I'll just wear a sign that says 'I got dumped' or something," DJ muttered to Major.

He sniffed the bandage and snorted, spraying her with a fine mist. "So you don't like the smell of bandage, huh?" She wiped her face. "Thanks a big fat lot." She leaned against his neck and hugged him, making sure her bandage didn't rub against him. The doctor had said to keep it clean and dry. So far, she'd managed.

Patches, too, gave her the once-over. Instead of snorting, he backed away.

"Oh yeah, anything to act nervous about, you'll take." She snapped a tie shank on his halter and snubbed him down to a stall bar. Patches couldn't be trusted to stand still or keep his teeth to himself while being groomed. She'd learned that the hard way, too.

Once she had him groomed and saddled, she settled in for a rough ride. "Now, you just behave yourself, and we'll get along fine."

His ears flicked back and forth, letting her know he was listening, but his attention was clearly on a flashy bay taking jumps in the middle of the covered arena.

"Make sure you stay to the outside," Bridget said as she opened the gate to the arena. "Give the jumper plenty of room." She smiled up at DJ. "I am glad you were not hurt worse. Next time, lower the jump after a refusal, then work up to the earlier height. Get your horse's confidence back and yours, too."

"Thanks." *Who blabbed?* she wondered. But when DJ felt Patches hump his back, she put all other thoughts from her mind. Arena sand wasn't one of her favorite meals. She could tell after her warm-up laps that Mrs. Johnson had been riding over the weekend because Patches suddenly figured he could do whatever he wanted. DJ thought otherwise. Their training time was nearly over before he gave up the battle.

"You know, you stubborn beast, we would both have a lot more fun if you'd do what you're told, when you're told."

The next time through, he started, stopped, cantered slow and easy, changed leads, and even backed up with only a flicking of his ears.

"He about used up all your patience?" Bridget swung the gate open to let them out.

"Tried to."

"You do well with him. Mrs. Johnson was asking if you thought he was ready for you to work with the two of them together."

"Me?"

Bridget nodded.

Doing her best to keep her cool and watch Patches at the same time, DJ asked, "What do you think?"

"Until I watched you work him today, I thought any time but . . ."

"He's not usually this much of a pain. She has to learn to make him mind is all."

"I will let her know that you will take her on as a student. She can set up a regular lesson time with you when she is ready. You will be paid double, one hour on him and one coaching them both. Any questions?"

DJ shook her head. "Not now, but later, I bet."

"Good. See you on Megs in—"

"Could you maybe give me half an hour?"

DJ could have groomed six horses in that time, her hands flew so fast. Wait until she told Amy. An adult student!

But in the car, Amy was too busy grumbling to let DJ squeeze a word in edgewise. "That . . . that witch. She thinks she owns the place and that all of us are her slaves!"

After hearing Amy out, DJ asked, "So why does Bridget let her get away with stuff like that?"

Both Joe and Amy shrugged.

"But I'll start asking around," Joe promised. "Something odd is going on here."

DJ had been home an hour before she heard the garage door open and her mother's car pull inside. The meat loaf in the oven smelled good and would be done in half an hour, along with the baked potatoes. Just a few minutes before, DJ had checked everything to make sure nothing was out of place. The house looked good, the dinner smelled better, and DJ had washed and changed clothes. Tonight, she and her mother would have a good evening together.

"There are two messages on the machine for you," she said while taking the plates down to set the table.

"Thanks, dear. What a day this has been!" Lindy set her briefcase on the counter and slipped off her heels.

"You want a cup of tea?"

"That sounds heavenly. Make it a raspberry zinger, okay?" She punched the code into the machine and scribbled some numbers as she listened. After dialing, she tapped a pearl-tinted fingernail on the countertop.

DJ knew that simple gesture said her mother was feeling worse than she looked. With no lipstick, smeared mascara, and her hair tousled as if she'd raked her fingers through it in frustration, she didn't look like the normally polished Lindy.

After the greeting, Lindy exploded. "What! What do you mean?" A pause. "No, that can't be."

DJ froze. Now what?

Lindy hung up the phone, eyes closed, face twisted as though she were in pain.

"Mom, what's wrong?"

"The Carillion—you know, the place we were planning to have the reception? It burned to the ground last night. Maybe this is the sign I've been afraid would happen. I just knew we'd have to call off the wedding!"

Chapter • 7

"No, Mom! You can't do that!" DJ grabbed her mother's shoulders.

Lindy shrugged her off. "I don't see any alternative. We can't find a place to house the reception this close to the date." She rubbed her forehead. "There are just too many things going wrong."

DJ stared at her mother. *What can I do? God, surely you have a place in mind for the reception. Help!* She waited, hoping for a sign, a clue, anything.

Nothing. Her mind felt as blank as the message board in front of her. At a sound, she turned from studying the blank board to her mother, who now stood with her forehead against a cupboard door, her shoulders shaking. *She's crying. Mom is crying.* DJ started forward and stopped. What could she do?

Quickly, she grabbed the box of tissues from the counter and crossed to her mother. "Here." Her voice came as gently as it did with a flighty foal. "Come on, Mom. Let's go into the other room."

"I . . . I can't h-handle any m-more." Tears streamed down Lindy's face as she pulled a tissue from the proffered box. "Robert will be so disappointed." She blew her nose and wiped her eyes, but within a heartbeat, she was more tear streaked than before. And still the tears kept on.

DJ steered her to the sofa. "Sit." When Lindy collapsed against the soft cushions, DJ took the place beside her. She set the box of tissues on her mother's lap and picked up her shaking hand.

"How about if I call Gran?"

A violent shake of the head met that suggestion. *Robert? Should I call Robert?* No, he lived too far away. *God, you're the only one near enough to help.* She rubbed her mom's shoulder and gently tucked the hair behind her ear. How many times had Gran done the same for her? Loving pats and a soothing tone meant love more than anything else did to DJ. She made herself relax and let her mother cry.

Finally, the downpour changed to a shower, then to a meandering drop. After more nose blowing and eye wiping, Lindy at last laid her hands in her lap, a clump of tissues mounded beside her. She blinked and drew in a deep breath, letting it out in a sigh.

"I really don't think I'm cut out to be a wife and a mother."

"You already *are* a mother—my mother."

"You're right. Then being a wife is the problem."

"No, a place for the reception is the problem." DJ propped her elbows on her knees. "I think Gran and Joe might have an idea where else to look. If nothing else, we can have it in the church basement. Or in the covered arena at the Academy."

"Great. I can see us all dressed up in our fancy clothes, making sure some horse doesn't eat the wedding cake."

DJ blinked. Her mother had made a joke, a good sign. "There's got to be other places to have a reception."

"You may not know this, but I called lots of other places before settling on this one. They were either too expensive or unavailable or . . ."

"Or what?"

"Or . . . I had already chosen the Carillion." Lindy rubbed her tongue over her lower lip. "I think I gave the list to Gran."

DJ could see the wheels start turning again. "You want me to call Robert for you and tell him the wedding is off?" DJ couldn't resist the urge to tease her mother even if it might prove to be the dumbest thing she'd ever done.

Lindy rolled her swollen red eyes. "Not yet anyway." She blew her nose again. "Maybe I just needed a good cry."

"M-o-t-h-e-r."

"Well, a cry sometimes releases pent-up stress and—"

The phone rang. DJ crossed to the table next to the wing chair and picked up the cordless phone. "Hi, this is DJ."

"Hi yourself." Robert's voice sounded as tired as Lindy's. "Your mom there?"

"I . . . ah, just a minute." DJ buried the phone against her shoulder. "It's Robert," she whispered. "You want to call him back?"

Lindy shook her head. "No, I'll take it." She sniffed. "Is something burning?"

"Burning? Yikes, the meat loaf!" DJ handed the phone to her mother and dashed for the kitchen. Grabbing a potholder, she pulled open the oven. Smoke billowed up in her face, making her eyes sting and a cough erupt. At least there were no flames. She opened the window above the sink, gulping in the fresh air. From here, she could hear her mother talking in the family room, her tone sounding almost normal again. DJ returned to the open oven, where the apples she'd set in a bread pan now sat in a crust of smoking burnt sugar. All the water had evaporated.

She pulled the pan from the oven and set it on another hot pad. "I guess the apples don't look too terrible if we don't eat the black stuff," she told herself as she turned off the oven and took out the meat loaf, now dark brown on the bottom. She placed the crusty baked potatoes on the counter along side of it. So much for a perfect dinner, but then this wasn't turning into a perfect night anyway.

DJ went ahead and fixed her plate, taking it to the dining room. The two place settings now looked forlorn at the end and side of the long table. She thought of the meals eaten here with Gran and Gramps and Mom long ago, and lately with Robert and the boys. The room had seemed so full of life those other times, but now the silence hovered like a ghostly presence that snuffed out sounds.

Surely Robert could talk some sense into her mother.

But where *could* they hold the reception? The next phone call had to be to Gran, that was for sure. She would come up with an answer, like always. Of course, Gran came up with answers because she always prayed about them first. God sure seemed to listen to Gran's prayers.

Did that mean He *didn't* listen to hers? DJ thoughtfully poured ketchup on her meat loaf. No, God had answered her prayers many times, too—Gran would say all the time, adding that sometimes DJ just didn't like His answers. So what was God saying now?

She heard her mother dialing the phone. From the conversation,

DJ knew her mother and Gran were talking. She picked up her plate and fork and wandered into the family room, sitting in the wing chair. Her mother nodded to her and kept on talking. A frown would have meant DJ should leave the room.

When Lindy pushed the Off button and laid down the phone, she looked over at her daughter. "You were right. We . . . *I* won't cancel the wedding. This is a challenge, not a conclusion."

DJ could feel her smile widening with every word. "Way to go, Mom. You aren't a quitter."

"No, I'm not. And neither are you." Lindy closed her eyes and shook her head. "Not that quitting didn't sound real inviting a while ago." She looked up again after studying her hands, clasped casually on her knees. "What is it that smells burnt?"

"The baked apples. The rest of the dinner is on the stove." DJ could feel her appetite coming back. "You want me to fix you a plate?"

"I think I'll go change first. I feel like a wrung-out dishrag. I'll eat later and put the food away."

"Guess that means I can get to my homework right away." DJ took her plate back to the kitchen, then looked over her shoulder. "You okay?"

"I am now—or will be. I guess we could have the reception here or over at Gran's if need be. So it would be crowded. So what?"

DJ and her mother walked up the stairs together, arms around each other's waist.

———

Several hours later when DJ turned out her light, she went to stand at the window to watch the mist rainbowing in the streetlights. Weddings, floods, fires, new fathers—what else could happen?

———

The next afternoon, DJ met the new woman at the Academy.

"Put that pole back up."

DJ turned from her teaching position at the far end of the arena where she had her three students circling to leave space for the jumper.

"I think she's talking to you," Angie Lincoln said as she trotted past DJ.

"Who?"

"That lady."

"I said, put that pole back up." The woman on the light chestnut horse flung the words over her shoulder as she cantered past and headed for another jump.

DJ signaled to the girls to keep circling and crossed the sandy space to set the rail back up on the standards. *Who does this woman think she is?* DJ swallowed the rest of the thought before she could get any more worked up than she already was. Stalking back to her class, she pasted a smile on her face.

"Okay, kids, lope now and watch your leads." DJ felt unfriendly eyes drill a stare into her back. She heard another tick, but this time, there was no thud of a falling pole. She watched her students intently, making comments as needed and cheering them on. Krissie, her blue eyes glacial, kept sending icy looks in the jumper's direction.

"Come on, kids, concentrate on your horse and what you are doing." DJ let them make another round before signaling them to join her in the center of their circle. "Okay, you did good, like you always do. Good enough to move on. Let's start working on backing up so we can begin opening gates pretty soon. I know you all plan on trail-riding, and that class calls for opening and going through a gate."

Angie raised her hand. "I already know how to back up. Want to see?"

DJ nodded.

Angie pulled back on her reins. "Back." She clucked at the same time. "Come on, back." Her horse shook his head but did as asked. Backing slowly, he angled toward the horse on his left.

"Good. Anyone else?" The other two shook their heads.

DJ had them all dismount and showed them how to hold the reins and push against their horse's shoulder, giving the back-up command at the same time. She helped each girl, reminding them all to praise their horses and pat them for doing right. After the ground work, they mounted, and again she helped each one, herself on the ground and her students in the saddle.

Sam's horse kept shaking his head and playing with his bit. He did not want to back up for anything. DJ persisted, reminding Sam, "After squeezing, you have to lean forward slightly to open the door so he can back up." The horse gave in and stepped back. DJ looked up at the grin on the girl's face.

"See, you just have to be patient."

"And stubborn." Sam, short for Samantha, leaned forward and patted her horse's neck. "Good boy."

DJ smiled up at the girl. "You did a great job of keeping your cool, kiddo."

"I'm learning." Sam tightened her reins as her horse tried to go forward. "Whoa."

When the lesson was over, DJ followed the girls to the barn to make sure they untacked their horses properly. She refused to even look at the woman still working her horse over the jumps, now with one of the other student workers adjusting the bars. Her tone held no more kindness than before. *Has the woman never learned to at least say please?*

That night, Robert and the boys arrived loaded down with boxes of Chinese food for dinner. DJ was setting the table when the phone rang. Because she was closest, Lindy answered it.

DJ looked up when her mother's voice turned extra polite. Pausing in the doorway, she waited.

"Yes, Brad, I have a moment." Lindy paused. "I see."

If only she could hear the other side of the conversation. DJ itched to run for the other phone.

"So you're saying you'd like DJ to attend a horse show with you and Jackie a week from Thursday."

DJ clenched her hands to her sides. *Oh, please, Mom, say yes.*

"I'll have to give this some thought. With the wedding coming up . . . well, how about if I get back to you tomorrow?"

DJ could feel her shoulders slump.

"DJ, we's hungry," Bobby and Billy announced as one.

She set the plates in front of each of them and reached for a carton of sweet-and-sour prawns, the boys' favorite. She tried to listen over their chatter, without success. "Shhh!" She glared at them.

Their mouths turned to Os, and they shrank back as if she'd hit them.

"DJ, was that necessary?" Robert's voice held more than a trace of anger.

Chapter • 8

DJ felt as if she'd been struck.

Two lower lips quivered as the Double Bs looked first to their father and then back to DJ.

"I'm sorry, guys." She hunkered down between the two of them and wrapped an arm around each boy. "Please forgive me?"

With four arms strangling her neck, DJ fought back the hot moisture burning behind her eyes.

"I forgive you." The blue eyes on the right said more than the words.

"Me too." The one on the left wriggled in his chair. " 'Cause we loves you."

The words rang in DJ's mind long after the boys had left and Robert had given her a hug that said the same.

Is that what would make this family possible? Was there enough love for Brad and Jackie, too?

When she told her grandmother her worries the next afternoon after her stint at the Academy, DJ just shook her head. "Just like you all these years, Gran. How come something so simple as being a family is so hard to live out?"

Gran stroked DJ's hair as DJ leaned against her grandmother's knee. "It is so simple to love, yet sometimes we get in the way of it. Mostly because we want our own way, I guess. Remember, simple and easy aren't the same."

"I want Mom to let me go to the horse show with Brad and Jackie. It would be so cool to see her compete, and Lord Byron is an awesome horse." DJ sat still for a few moments. "Did Robert tell you that I hollered at the boys?"

"No."

"I hurt their feelings, so he yelled at me, and that hurt *my* feelings." She sighed, a deep sigh that started way down and worked its way up. "What a mess. And all because I wanted to hear what Mom was saying to Brad." She turned to give her grandmother one of those I-blew-it half grins. "Of course, listening in would have been eavesdropping, and how many times have you warned me against that?"

Gran put gentle hands on both sides of DJ's face and kissed her forehead from above. "More than once, my dear, more than once."

"More than once what?" Joe ambled into the room, his glasses pushed up on his forehead. "You seen my book, Mel? I can't find it anywhere."

"Which one?"

"The one about training a roping horse. I wanted to show DJ a picture in it." He looked over the room.

"Did you check the bookshelf?"

He shrugged and winked at DJ. "Now, why didn't I think of that?"

DJ and Gran laughed together as he left the room. When he called to report he'd found the book, they laughed again.

When Lindy came to pick up DJ later, she accepted the offered cup of coffee and took a place at the table. "So, Mother, what did you find?"

"How does the Oak House sound?"

"Really?" Lindy set her coffee down with a thump. "That's perfect. Even closer to the church and—"

"And it costs less, if you can believe it. I know for a fact their food is better than the Carillion's, too."

"And it *is* bigger." Lindy reached a hand across to her mother. "I can't believe it."

DJ felt like she was at a tennis match, swiveling her head between the two. "So God did good, huh?"

Lindy looked at her daughter, then slowly nodded her head. "Yes, He did."

DJ and Gran shared a secret smile. Lindy was coming around.

When Brad called later that evening, DJ answered the phone. "Looks like Major's leg is finally okay," she said when he asked about her horse. "I get to ride him for a brief warm-up tomorrow, then add more time each day. One of these days, the rain will let up for more than a couple of hours at a time and we'll get to use the jumping arena again."

"Speaking of jumping, have you heard of a woman named Mrs. Lamond Ellsindorf? Most people call her Bunny."

"Yes, I think so. Why?"

DJ went on to tell him about the woman's rudeness and how all the Academy kids already hated her. "She never says please or thank you. Just orders us around like we're her slaves."

"Hmm. That doesn't sound like the woman we met. I'll ask Jackie and let you know when I pick you up a week from tomorrow. You'll be ready, right?"

"You mean I get to go?"

"That's what your mother said when she called me today. She didn't tell you?"

"Nope, we were talking about the new reception place. Guess she forgot."

"You'll need some dressy casual clothes, like a blazer or a good sweater."

"Sure." She mentally inventoried her clothes closet. She'd outgrown the one outfit she kept for special events. "I'll be ready. Thanks, Da— Brad." She hung up, wondering at her slip of the tongue. Was she really beginning to think of him as Dad?

Later, after an hour at her books, DJ got a black cherry soda from the refrigerator and sat down beside her mother on the sofa. "Thanks for letting me go to the horse show."

"You're welcome. Robert and I agree that it will be a good experience for you."

DJ figured she owed Robert a big thank-you. She picked at the cuticle on her thumb, then took a swallow of the soda. *How can I ask for another favor?* "When do we go pick up the dresses for the wedding?"

"I don't know. I should call, I guess." Lindy looked up from reading the paper. "Why?"

"Well, I need some nice clothes for the trip."

Lindy looked at her daughter thoughtfully. "Yes, you do. It's time you began to develop a style of your own."

"I don't need a whole wardrobe." DJ started to say something else, then thought the better of it. "I . . . I thought maybe a tailored jacket of some kind or something. Mine are all for the show-ring."

Lindy folded the newspaper and placed it on the table. "Let's go see what you have that might work and make a list of what you need."

DJ groaned to herself. *Leave it to my mother to make a production out of it. All I want is a blazer.* But by the time they'd finished, she was almost looking forward to the shopping trip. Almost.

Thursday poured its way into the Bay Area. Water sheeted the whole street, not just the gutters and drains, when Mrs. Yamamoto drove the kids to school. At times, the windshield wipers couldn't clear the glass fast enough, and they were nearly late, the traffic was moving so slow.

The low places between the buildings looked like miniature lakes as the students slogged from building to building. The outside lockers gave the rain another chance at the kids. DJ kept all her books in her backpack so she didn't have to stand and fight with her combination.

"What a yucky day!" She bailed into the van as soon as Amy shoved open the back door. John was already in the front seat, a frown on his face because he wasn't getting to drive.

"Just don't ask again, John," Mrs. Yamamoto cautioned. "Hi, girls. DJ, Joe called to say he and some of the other retired police were going up north of here to help fill sandbags. He wants you to take care of Ranger for him."

"Sure."

"Can you be ready in half an hour? I can't think that anyone will ride in weather like this."

"All right." DJ looked at Amy, who hadn't said a word so far. "What's wrong? You sick?"

Amy nodded. "I think I'm going to throw up." She suddenly sat up very straight. "Mom! Quick, stop the car!"

In spite of the rain, Amy hung her head out the van door and heaved. When she finally sat back in the seat, DJ handed her a napkin. "You look terrible."

"Thanks." Amy leaned her head back and closed her eyes.

"You going to make it home now?" Mrs. Yamamoto turned to check on her daughter. "Looks like you'll have another horse to take care of, DJ. Unless John—"

"No time. I have to be at Dad's. It's my day to work."

"No problem. I'll do it." DJ put her hand on Amy's shoulder. "You cold?"

"F-fr-freezing." Amy wrapped both arms around her middle. "I knew I shoulda called home earlier, but . . . well . . ."

Her last words disappeared on the wind as DJ threw open the door and bailed out. The wild wind tried to blow her back in, but she slammed the door shut and headed for the front door, digging in her pocket for the key. Why hadn't she thought to get it out earlier? A branch had blown off the oak tree in the front yard, flattening the snowball bush beside it.

Even standing under the porch roof, DJ was battered by the wind, which blew rain down her neck. The downspouts sounded like waterfalls, and the heavy drops hammered the glass, sheeting the windows in their rush downward. DJ huddled deeper in her slicker until she finally inserted the key in the lock.

The house felt damp and empty, as if lonely huddling against the storm. DJ picked up the phone to call Gran, realizing that the power was off since the light on the answering machine glowed neither green nor red. At least the kitchen phone still worked.

"Hi. Mrs. Yamamoto is taking me to the Academy, but Amy is sick. Could you please pick me up afterward?"

"Sure will. You have power over there?"

"Nope."

"I'm afraid we're in the same boat, but I have the fireplace going so we can roast hot dogs for dinner. Leave a note for your mother. On second thought, you get ready, and I'll call. Bring your stuff to spend the night if the power doesn't come back on."

———————

DJ did her chores and Amy's, too. Because of the rain driving in from the west, the horses stabled in the open stalls were drenched in spite of the roof. Water ran down the aisle to where one of the men had trenched it off to the sides before it could run into the barn. Since so many people couldn't make it to the Academy, it was already growing dark outside by the time the stalls were cleaned and the horses fed and groomed. Due to the power outage, Bridget had closed the ring, so no one was riding.

DJ and Tony Andrada stood back from the door, watching the rain sheet across the parking area.

"This is about as bad as the hurricanes where I came from." Tony shook his head. "If I never see one of those suckers again, it'll be too soon. And here I thought California had good weather."

DJ rubbed her cold hands together. She should have brought gloves, but whoever heard of wearing gloves because of cold California weather? She did have riding gloves, but she only wore them when she had to.

"You had a chance to help the Queen yet?" DJ asked Tony. Mrs. Ellsindorf had earned her nickname.

"I stay out of her way. Seems to work."

"Lucky you!" Just then Gran drove in and parked right in front of the door. "See ya." DJ dashed outside again, duffel and backpack in hand. The wind slammed the car door shut for her, barely missing her leg.

"I can't imagine what it's like for those people helping sandbag." Gran peered through the brief clearing made by the wipers. "You better be praying for your grandfather and his crew up there while I drive us home."

"You heard from him?"

"Nope." They nearly had to shout to be heard above the rain, the heater, and the wipers.

DJ sent her prayers heavenward, including one for her mother and every other unlucky person on the roads.

As they drove past Robert's new house, DJ glanced over—just in time to see a chunk of the roof lift off and roll across the yard.

Chapter • 9

"Gran, stop! The roof!"

"I'm not stopping here. I'm getting us home and in the house as fast as I can. We'll call Robert when we get there." They both ducked instinctively as a branch, broken off a tree just ahead, sailed straight at them, then slid across the roof.

DJ gripped the door handle. *What is happening at the barns? I know Gran won't go back tonight. God, please, keep Major safe. And help us to get home safely, too. We have only a little way to go now.*

As Gran turned the station wagon into her driveway, they heard a loud crack. Straight ahead, the pine tree behind the garage crashed forward, splintering one side of the garage as it fell. Electric wires leaped and fluttered, coming to rest across the driveway.

"Two more seconds, and we'd have been right there." Gran pointed to where the lines lay. The garage settled into a tilt that made it look like a toy a child had bashed. "Thank you, heavenly Father, for keeping us safe. And for taking our power away earlier."

"Amen." DJ breathed the word. Her heart still felt as if it would leap right out of her chest and flutter to the ground like the wires had. She peered out, the falling darkness more pronounced without streetlights. "You think you still have a phone?"

Gran turned off the ignition. "Possibly. Those lines are buried underground. Joe kept saying he wanted to trench and bury our electric lines, too, but somehow we didn't get to it."

"Not like you guys haven't been busy or anything." DJ shot her grandmother a look of love. Gran's face gleamed stark white in the reflection from the headlights, and her normally strong hands shook as she flicked off the interior light.

"The car could have been in the garage. *We* could have been in the garage, just getting out. Oh, DJ, I am so grateful." Tears formed at the edges of her eyes. "God is so good to us." Gran brushed the drops away. "Let's head for the house. You wait a minute until I get the door unlocked."

"How about if I unlock the door and you wait?"

Gran snorted. "I don't think so. My hand will quit shaking enough to insert the key."

DJ held hers up. "Then you're in better shape than me." They held up matching hands, hands that trembled in spite of their best efforts to keep them still.

"The rest of me feels just the same." Gran tucked her purse under her arm. "Time to get our evening shower." She shoved open the car door, fighting the wind that howled against it. When she stepped free, the door slammed on its own.

DJ waited until Gran got to the door, then bolted from the car. Running to the house was like leaning into a solid wall—an invisible wall that nearly dropped her on her face when it huffed, then blew her backward. If, as Tony had said, this storm felt almost like a hurricane, DJ had no desire to research the difference.

Once inside, the howling wind was muted enough by the snug house that DJ and Gran could at least talk in normal voices.

"I'm in the kitchen," Gran called. The flare of a just-lit kerosene lamp warmed the way for DJ. "Looks like we're going to have to play pioneers," Gran said as she lit another. "I can remember my mother talking about lamplight when she was a girl and how it was more flattering."

DJ knew Gran had grown up in the South on a farm. She and Gramps had moved to California after he had been stationed there during his term in the navy. One of Gran's sisters still lived on the home place, as they called it, but she refused to visit California. Scared to death of earthquakes, Gran always said with a laugh. At one time, the barn on the home place had been destroyed by a tornado, but only

Gran saw the humor in that. As for DJ, she didn't have a whole lot of patience for or interest in her Southern relatives. It was hard to care about people you'd never met.

She shucked off her slicker and shook her head, wet hair whipping her stinging cheeks.

"Land, child, get in the shower while we still have hot water. You take one bathroom, and I'll take the other."

"The fire needs more wood first," DJ said. "Maybe I better bring in a stack before I dry off."

"Good idea. We can set it by the back door to dry. If you dig down a layer or two, it shouldn't be so wet. Joe has it covered, but nothing will stay dry in driving rain like this." Gran glanced at the clock, grimaced, and checked her watch. "I sure wish he were home. What must it be like up on the river?"

DJ shuddered. Surely they had ordered the workers into buildings to protect them. She pulled her wet slicker back on and headed for the back door. The wind tore at the door, but DJ managed to get it open. The storm door was another matter. The wind grabbed it and slammed it against the wall so hard, the glass shattered and the aluminum frame bent.

"Don't worry about that!" Gran hollered over the wind. "Hand the wood to me and I'll stack it. Careful!"

Within a few minutes, the laundry room took on a new purpose. Instead of being used to wash and dry clothes, wood was stacked everywhere—on the floor, the dryer, the washer, and in the deep double sink. They moved the last loads right into the family room and stacked them on papers out of the way along one wall.

Gran answered the phone as DJ returned with one last load.

"I don't know how bad it was," she was saying when DJ entered the kitchen. "DJ is the one who saw the roof go. I didn't dare take my eyes off the road."

DJ hung up both their slickers in the laundry room and left her boots there, too. Her jeans felt like she'd gone swimming in them.

"Robert says thanks for letting him know about the roof but that there's nothing to be done until the storm abates. They've closed all the bridges across the Bay, so he's stuck in the city. He said he wouldn't ask his local crew to come over, either." She trailed a finger across her chin, then shook her head. "I know worrying about Joe won't help a bit but . . ." She reached out to rub DJ's shoulder.

"You always say to put people in the Lord's hands and leave them there."

"I'm tryin', darlin'. You have no idea how hard I'm tryin'."

The deepening of her grandmother's Southern accent told DJ how upset her grandmother was. Wishing she could do more, she wrapped both arms around Gran's shoulders and hugged. The two rocked together, sharing comfort in the lamplight, an oasis in the midst of the storm.

Lindy called later to say she was fine. She and a bunch of co-workers were holed up at the office, where they still had power. The cafe on the first floor of the building was doing gangbuster business, trying to feed all the stranded. She had no idea when she'd be home.

DJ and Gran went back to their cozy picnic in front of the fireplace. When the phone rang again, they looked at each other, hope blazoned across their faces. Tears spurted as soon as Gran heard the deep voice on the line.

"Oh, darlin', I was so worried about you." Gran wiped her nose on the back of her hand, making DJ laugh. She handed her grandmother a box of tissues. "No, we're fine—warm and dry, thanks to the fireplace. We haven't had power for hours. You're the one who we've been worried about." She nodded while he talked.

"Tell him I love him," DJ said. Gran nodded again.

After hanging up, Gran relaxed against the padded chair, her arms around her knees. She took the crispy marshmallow off the fork that DJ extended. "Perfect. They moved the volunteers to a school until the storm calms down enough for travel to be safe. Right now there are too many falling trees by the river, so only emergency vehicles are out on the roads." The phone rang again.

"Why, Brad, thank you for calling. Yes, we're fine. DJ and I are piggin' out on hot dogs and marshmallows in front of a fire. That's right, no power. Sure, here she is." Gran handed DJ the phone.

"Hi. How are things up your way?" DJ inquired.

"The levee is holding, so we're safe so far. The other rivers are much worse than the Petaluma. All the horses are in the barns or loose in the arena. Of course, the power's out, but that's not the important thing right now. With my luck, that mare will foal tonight."

"Really?"

"No, I don't think so. She promised to wait for you."

"I hope so." She told him where the others were stranded. "A pine tree fell on Gran's garage, and a chunk of the roof blew off the house Robert is remodeling, but we're okay. I've never been out in such a storm in my life." When she hung up, she put another marshmallow on her fork. "Burned or brown?"

"Brown, as in dark." Gran fluffed her hair and stretched back against the chair. "How come I feel like it's the middle of the night?"

"Got me." DJ blew on the marshmallow she'd gotten too close to the fire. "Guess this one is mine." She drew off the outer coating and returned the gooey rest to the fire. "You want me to get out the sleeping bags?"

"No, I think our beds will be warm enough. I'll just come out and put more wood in the fire once in a while." They both listened, suddenly aware of the quiet. "The wind has died down. Thank you, God."

DJ nibbled on the marshmallow as she went to look out the window. Rain still sluiced down, but at least the roar of water and wind was gone. She thought about asking Gran if they could drive over to the Academy but knew the answer without wasting her breath. If only she'd thought to call Bridget before it got so late. Wouldn't the academy owner call them if something was wrong?

The rain had stopped during the night, and the clouds had blown away. The sun rose again as if the horrible storm was a thing of everyone's imagination. Much to DJ's disgust, they had school as usual since the power came back on during the night, too.

After helping her feed and water the horses, Gran drove DJ to school in the morning. Amy was still home sick. *I can tell this is going to be a really great day*, DJ grumbled to herself. *If I'd known Amy was sick, I could at least have fed Josh.* Other than mushy stalls, the Academy had weathered the storm all right, certainly better than Gran's garage.

DJ had a hard time keeping her mind on her classes. She would rather have been home helping Gran clean up the branches from the fallen tree. *Wait till Joe and Robert see the mess—they'll have a fit.*

Her afternoon went to pot when her algebra teacher called for a quiz. DJ took out paper and pencil, making sure she had a good eraser. She'd done the homework, but still . . . a quiz today?

"I hate algebra," she muttered before the teacher called for silence. The guy across the aisle muttered with her. She looked up at the problems on the board. *If x=3* . . .

She could feel her head begin to fuzz up, so she forced her mind to concentrate on the numbers and letters on the board. But when the teacher called time and said to hand your paper to the person behind you, she knew there were at least two wrong out of the ten. She hadn't even gotten to them.

She ended up with four wrong and barely a passing grade. If her mother found out, she might say no to the horse show. Granted, her total grade at the end of the quarter wouldn't be totally dependent on four mistakes, but this hadn't been the first time she'd blown a quiz.

When she school day finally ended, DJ slunked into the rear seat of the Yamamoto van. John was driving again, whistling and tapping the steering wheel, waiting for her.

"Will you take care of Josh tonight, DJ?" he asked. "I need to get to work right away."

"Sure." She turned to Mrs. Yamamoto. "How's Amy?"

"It turns out she has bronchitis on top of a flu bug, so it'll be a few days before she can come back to school. I took her to the doctor this morning. The antibiotics he prescribed will help soon."

"Is she coughing her head off?"

"Sure is. And not having power yesterday didn't help. She was so cold we brought her down to sleep by the fireplace."

"I'll ride my bike to the Academy," DJ said when she got out of the car and waved. "Tell Amy I'll call her later."

As John backed out the driveway, she had a brainstorm—maybe John would help her with algebra. He was a numbers genius. Computer genius, too.

She went into the house, still thinking about algebra. Probably there was a computer program that could help her understand this stuff. She stacked the few dishes in the dishwasher, threw a load of her things in the wash, and headed for the Academy. Her mother had been home to change clothes but hadn't even left a message. Now what was going on?

―――――――

No classes today, read the sign posted on the duties board. And here she'd just been able to ride Major again. Did that mean she couldn't work Patches, either? DJ checked in Bridget's office, but no one was there. The arena stood empty.

The place felt about as deserted as her own home. Where was everyone?

DJ went into the barn knowing she had to take care of at least three horses. Dirty stalls called to her. She got some carrots out of the refrigerator and, breaking them into small pieces, filled her pockets. Retrieving the wheelbarrow and manure fork, she waved to Hilary Jones, who was grooming her horse in the other aisle, and made her way to Major's stall.

Major leaned against the stall bars, stretching to greet her. His nose quivered in a soundless nicker, his ears nearly touching at the tips.

"Hi, fella, you had a lonely day without a visit from GJ?" She fed him a carrot and tickled the whisker brush on his upper lip. Ranger stuck his head out over the bars of his stall and tossed his head, demanding a treat, too.

"Hey, stuff it, kid. I'll get to you in a minute."

Ranger nickered again, even more demanding this time, including a stamp of one front foot.

"What a spoiled brat you are." She gave Major another treat and rubbed up behind his ears. "You should give him lessons in manners, you know." Major rubbed his forehead against the front of her jacket and nosed her pockets for more carrot. "Be back in a minute."

She gave him a pat and walked the few steps to Ranger's gate. "Now, see here."

Ranger tossed his head, his forelock and mane flopping with the action.

DJ gave him a carrot chunk and scratched his cheek while he chewed. "Does Joe give you whatever you want? You seem like a hopeless case." Ranger snuffled her hands, then her pockets. "Oh, so you know where we keep the stuff, do you?" She gave him another treat and stepped back, her hands on her hips. "That rain sure soaked your bedding. I better bring in tons of shavings or you'll be standing in the mud."

She tied Major in the aisle and began forking the wet and dirty shaving and straw mixture into the wheelbarrow. Only minutes passed before she removed her Windbreaker and hung it over a bar. She'd become spoiled herself with Joe cleaning the stalls weekday mornings. She wiped the sweat from her forehead and trundled the barrow to dump, refill, and dump again. When she was down to bare, wet ground, she headed for the shavings pile and dumped several loads on the bare floor of the stall. She made it plenty deep before spreading a layer of straw on top of that.

If it ever rained like that again, she could hang plastic on the outside wall to keep the rain from soaking the dirt in the stall. She decided to mention it to Bridget when they had time.

She brought Major back into his stall and began on Ranger's. On a trek to the ramp where they dumped the dirty bedding, she heard Bridget's voice coming from the stalls on the opposite side of the area. "At least someone is here," she told Ranger when he nickered for another treat.

When both horses had clean stalls, she refilled the water buckets and hung hay in each net before doing the same for Amy's horse. After putting the wheelbarrow and things away, she picked up the grooming bucket and, starting with Josh, groomed all three horses.

She found Bridget up on the roof with a hammer and nails. One of the stable workers was with her on the roof, and another was handing up sheets of corrugated fiberglass roofing to be nailed in place.

"If you want extra work, you can help." Bridget finished nailing off a section, then stood and kneaded the middle of her back with her fists.

DJ wanted to ask why *she* was up there but kept her mouth closed. "I'm not much of a help with a hammer, but if you have other stuff to do, I can maybe handle that."

"I would rather you not ride in the arena today since some of the roofing is loose and could come down." Bridget helped slide the next roofing panel in place. "So if your stalls are clean and the horses cared for, that is all for the day." She smiled down at DJ. "Thank you for the offer to help, but I think we have it under control."

"See you." DJ turned to go and saw Mrs. Ellsindorf coming their way. The woman's face was permanently carved into a frowning glare. She passed without an acknowledgment of any kind, as though DJ wasn't even on the same planet with her, let alone the same aisle.

Well, hello to you, too—and I hope you have a nice day. DJ saw Hilary coming toward her, shaking her head.

"We sure get some interesting people around here." Hilary set the wheelbarrow down and took the fork to load shavings.

"Interesting—is that what you call her?"

"Well, not quite, but you've got to at least try to be polite, you know."

"That's what Gran says, too." DJ shook her head. "But why is she so mad all the time?"

"I imagine not being able to ride in the arena ticked her off today. I wish she'd ride in the morning so we didn't have to make way for her. Guess no one told her the afternoons are left to us kids." Hilary forked the shavings as she talked.

"Maybe she has a job or something." DJ looked out to where Bridget had come off the roof to talk with the woman.

"Maybe." Hilary's tone said she didn't believe it for a second.

"Well, see ya." DJ headed back to Major's stall to check his leg before she left. Even if he didn't need the ice packs anymore, a rubbing with liniment wouldn't hurt.

After she'd parked her bike in the garage, she shucked her boots at the bootjack by the back door and entered the kitchen. The blinking light on the answering machine caught her attention, and she pushed the Play button.

"DJ, Robert and the boys are coming out around five so we can go over to the house and inspect the damage. Could you take care of Bobby and Billy for a while? Robert said he'd bring dinner." DJ nodded as she waited for the next message.

"DJ, Joe called to ask if you would take care of Ranger for him. He said he'd be home later tonight and he'll do tomorrow as usual. I had hoped to catch you before you left. Call me if there's a problem."

"Already done, Gran," DJ said as she poked the rewind switch. She went upstairs to change into clean clothes, then checked to make sure things were picked up. Since all seemed to be in order, she took the cordless phone and a can of soda to Gran's old chair, where she sat with both legs over one arm while she dialed Amy.

"She's taking a bath," Mrs. Yamamoto said after answering. "Can she call you back?"

"Sure." DJ hung up and dialed Gran's number. After reassuring her grandmother that the horses were cared for, DJ asked, "You want me to come over tomorrow and help clean up the mess around there?"

"No thanks, darlin'. Joe says we have to let the insurance adjuster see the damage first so we can turn in our claim. We'll probably make up a work party this weekend. Do you want to go shopping tonight for your jacket and things?"

"Can't. I've got the Double Bs while Mom and Robert inspect the damage to the house and figure out what to do. How about tomorrow night?"

"We'll see. Y'all want to come here for dinner?"

"Thanks, but Robert is bringing it." DJ went on to tell her the news of the day, making a joke out of the sour look on Mrs. Ellsindorf's face. "I think she practices looking mad and bad."

"She must be a terribly unhappy person."

"Now, don't you getting any ideas." DJ swung her feet and let them thud against the chair. "She's not my problem, and I don't have to like her."

"Seems to me like she needs a lot of prayer."

DJ sighed. "Why did I ever bring her up? Gran, you pray for her if you want to, but I'd rather you prayed for me to do better in algebra. Why do I need to learn the stuff?"

After hanging up, DJ headed back upstairs to start her homework. She had a book report due the next week and hadn't begun to read the book yet. She flopped down on her bed on her stomach, Jennie McGrady Mystery in hand. She began reading as she munched on an apple, her feet scissoring the air. Soon, she was so caught up in the book she didn't even know her mother had come home until Lindy stuck her head in the door.

"Hi, DJ, doing your homework?"

"Yup. Gotta get ahead." DJ rolled over enough to see her mother. "You look beat."

"Thanks. Even though they put us up at the hotel last night, I didn't get much sleep with that storm raging outside. Then I had an appointment at eight, so I just changed clothes here and left again. I sure wish I had time to crash for a bit. . . ." She checked her watch. "If they arrive before I get out of the shower, you entertain them, okay?"

DJ nodded and went back to her book.

The fried chicken and fixings Robert brought disappeared in record time. He and Lindy left DJ and the boys to clean up. "You guys mind DJ now."

"We will." They wore their cherub look. "Bye, Daddy."

DJ played Go Fish with them for a while, then said, "Look, guys, I'd love to keep playing, but I have a ton of homework to do for Monday, and it won't get done unless I start on it now. How about I set you up with crayons and some paper for coloring while I study?"

" 'Kay. Then will you play horsie?"

DJ groaned. "I guess so. But first you have to be quiet." She led the way up the stairs to her room and set them on the floor with their crayons and papers. Back on her bed, she returned to the world of Jennie McGrady.

"Daddy's here!" The shout jolted her back to her own room.

Papers flew as the boys leaped to their feet and bolted out the door.

DJ blinked as she surveyed the scattered mess. Her blue notebook lay on the floor next to her drawing pad. Pages of each mixed with the paper she'd given the boys for drawing. Her heart thudded—one of them had colored on one of her pictures of the foal!

Her mood darkening, she rummaged through the papers. They'd used others of her drawings for coloring, too, and her algebra papers now wore colored streaks, wavy lines, and circles.

"Bobby and Billy!" DJ hit the stairs running, fury flaming red before her eyes.

Chapter • 10

"Hey, DJ, you don't have to yell at them like that." Robert looked up from hugging his boys.

"But they colored on my drawings!" DJ thrust the messy sheets at him. "Look."

"DJ, don't talk like that to Robert!" Lindy turned from hanging up her coat. "What is the matter with you?"

"They ruined my drawings of the filly—the ones Gran said are the best I've ever done."

Robert took the sheets of drawing paper from her hand, glancing from them down at the Double Bs, who wore expressions of total confusion mixed in with sorrow and a bit of fear. Lindy crossed to investigate the damage, too.

"DJ said to color so she could study." One twin thrust out his lower lip.

"We was quiet." A tear bobbled on a set of long eyelashes.

"Can you do the drawings over, DJ?" Robert asked quietly.

"That isn't the point here!" Lindy huffed. "Darla Jean Randall, *you* were the one in charge. That makes *you* responsible if something goes wrong. After all, you agreed to watch the boys." Lindy advanced on her daughter.

DJ clamped her teeth together and glared at her mother.

"Didn't you?"

What could DJ do but nod? *But why couldn't the Bs keep to the stuff I gave them to do?* "They still shouldn't have gotten into my drawings." She crossed her arms over her chest. Maybe if she squeezed hard enough, she could keep the ugliness inside.

Rotten, nosy little brats. All that hard work gone to waste. And she'd thought to frame one for Brad. At least *he* cared about her drawings. He loved them.

She glared again at the twins, steeling herself against their tears.

"I'm talking to you, Darla Jean."

"I hear you. What do you want me to do, fall on my knees and apologize? They"—she stabbed her finger at the boys—"should apologize to me." She jabbed her chest with the same finger.

"DJ, don't talk to your mother that way." Robert cut into their growing fight.

"Stay out of this, Robert. This is between me and DJ." Lindy flashed him a look that would send most people scrambling.

"Now, honey." Robert dropped his voice and tried to sound soothing.

As if that isn't the oldest trick in the book. It won't work with her, either. DJ felt her jaw go even more rigid—if that were possible.

By now, both boys were sobbing. At the sight of them, DJ felt tears gather behind her own eyes. She squinted at her mother. "It wasn't my fault! You always think everything is my fault and that I never do things right. I'm never home on time, I'm—"

"That's enough!" Robert thundered, cutting the air with his hand as though separating the chaotic group.

Four sets of eyes stared at him.

Two pairs of small arms clung to his thighs.

Lindy stood there, her mouth open.

DJ spun around to head back up the stairs.

"Sit down!" Robert's words snapped DJ around like a whip. She parked herself on the bottom step, but when she tried to lean back as if she didn't care what he said, her body wouldn't lean. Instead, her arms wrapped around her knees, and she hid her face in the comfort of her worn jeans.

She heard the soft *woosh* of air from the pillows of the sofa as someone sank into it. Her mother was following Robert's instructions, too.

The boys sniffled, followed by another *woosh* from the sofa. Robert this time? She peeked beyond the safety of her arms. Robert now had one arm around her mother, but Lindy was sitting as stiffly as her daughter. The boys had divided, one sticking with Robert, the other with Lindy.

Only DJ was alone.

The carpet from the stairs to the sofa looked about five hundred miles wide.

She shut her eyes against the sight and ordered herself not to cry. *Don't you dare!* She wanted to plug her ears against the voice that whispered inside her head, *It* was *your fault, you know.*

What would Gran say when she heard about this latest mess?

"Now, I know we're all uptight, what with the wedding coming and the storm, but fighting isn't going to solve anything. It never does." Robert's voice was firm.

Maybe not, but it makes me feel better, DJ argued.

Yeah, right, it does.

Her nose itched, and she needed a tissue. Her throat filled, and her eyes burned. *I'm not going to cry.* DJ's nose began to drip.

God, you know I hate it when I get mad like this. I might as well have beat those two little guys up like I wanted to. Look at them. DJ sneaked another peek. Her mother looked like someone had sucker-punched her, her face was so white and pinched, and there were black blotches under her eyes. Was she tired, or had her mascara smeared?

Lindy rubbed both her eyes and her forehead. "I agree. This family has to learn to talk out problems without getting into a fight."

But we're not a family—not yet!

DJ could hear footsteps coming closer. One sniff, then another, told her it was the Double Bs.

A small hand came to rest on her arm. "DJ, please. We's sorry."

Another hung on her other arm. "Please, DJ? We won't ever touch your stuff again. Ever. We promise."

Much against her will, DJ wrapped an arm around each of them. "I'm sorry, too, guys. I shoulda been watching you like I was supposed to."

"You should have put your things away, too. This wouldn't have happened then," Lindy said, her voice as tired as her face.

Instead of answering her mother, DJ hugged the boys. *As usual, everything is my fault.*

"Look, I'm sorry I'm not perfect like—" One look at Robert's face and DJ snapped her mouth shut. She waited again. "Mom, Robert, I'm sorry. Please forgive me?"

When Robert nodded and smiled at her, she looked to the boys, who stood, sober as sticks, by her knees. "You too?"

They threw their arms around her neck. "We love you, DJ."

"I love you guys, too." She squeezed them back, feeling the anger drain right out of her head and down and out through her toes. She took in a deep breath. "Don't worry, guys, I'll draw the pictures again. Fiddle, maybe they'll come out even better the second time. Besides, you didn't ruin them all."

But later, after Robert and the boys had left, DJ realized her mother hadn't said she'd forgiven her yet. In fact, she hadn't said anything to DJ since. What was going on now?

Should I go in and talk to Mom, or should I wait for her to come to me? Maybe I should just skip the whole thing. DJ chose the latter and, after gathering up her things for the morning and cleaning up the mess the boys had left, climbed into bed and prayed. She snuggled down to get warm. How come Gran hadn't called to say Joe was home? How come DJ's life was always such a disaster?

A note on the message board greeted her in the morning. *Please forgive me, DJ. I was too tired to think last night. I forgave you immediately and didn't realize I hadn't said anything until much later. Tell Gran to call me at the office after one. I have a few things to take care of. Love, Mom.*

DJ read the words again. Now her heart felt just like the sun bursting through the clouds. A new day had come. She called Gran before running out the door, and Joe answered.

"Hi, kid. Sorry we didn't call last night, but it got to be so late."

"Are you okay?" DJ wrapped the cord around her finger.

"Other than feeling like I was run over by a fleet of eighteen-wheelers, I'll make it. That sandbag stuff is for younger guys. Look, I'll take care of the horses today if you'll do it tomorrow. I'm going back up with the guys to help clean up now that the river is down again."

"You want some help?"

"Sure, if your mom doesn't mind. They can use every able pair of hands we can get."

"I'll ask around the Academy today to see if others want to come."

DJ heard a horn honk. "My ride's here. See ya tonight."

By the end of the day, DJ had rounded up seven kids to help with the cleanup. They agreed to meet at the school at 8:00 a.m. on Sunday, bringing lunches and drinks for themselves. DJ reminded everyone to bring gloves and rain gear in case another storm struck.

"My dad can take a bunch in the van," Tony Andrada offered. "I'll ask him and call you if it doesn't work out."

When they drove up to the front of the school in the morning, the group had grown. Whole families were there besides the high school kids. Joe had everyone assigned a ride and the troop on the road within half an hour.

"Boy, you sure know how to get a group going." DJ looked at him with pride.

"They teach you crowd control at the police academy." Joe, driving the lead car, checked the rearview mirror. "Anyway, it was you who started the thing rolling. Any time I want something done from now on, I know who to call."

"DJ's always been one to fight for the underdog," Gran said. "I know Robert and Lindy would be here, too, if there wasn't so much to do before the wedding and so little time to do it in. Of course, losing part of the roof to that new addition sure didn't help anything."

"Yeah, now we're going to have to live in our cramped house longer." DJ shook her head. "How can two five-year-old boys take up so much room? They aren't very big."

"Boys always take up more room than girls," Hilary said from the seat next to DJ. "Our house felt empty when my big brother went off to college."

DJ couldn't believe her eyes when they drove up Highway 29. Half of the vineyards were still underwater, the knobby grape vines looking like grotesque arms reaching above the water's surface.

Joe talked on his cell phone for a few minutes, then directed the caravan into a housing development that bordered the Napa River. Mud covered everything, filling the streets and yards. The flood's high-water mark had crept two feet up on the walls of the houses.

"Pee-uw." DJ wanted to hold her nose. "How come floods smell so bad?"

"Well, the sewer lines and septic tanks were flooded, for one thing, plus some barnyards and—"

"I get the picture." DJ looked longingly at the many boxes of food in the back of the Explorer. "You guys must have been making sand-wiches all night."

"Close. You watch, though, they'll disappear fast."

A man with a Day-Glo orange vest came to the door before they could climb out. "Hi, Joe, see ya brought the troops."

"Sure did. How you want them deployed?"

Frank Smith introduced himself, then gave everyone instructions and handed out shovels and rakes to the empty-handed. They all set to work, some inside the houses, and some out. DJ helped tear up carpets, scrape away mud, scrub inside and outside walls, and rake the worst of the mess off people's yards. Soon, a huge, brown worm of dirt grew in the middle of the street, waiting for the loaders and trucks to haul it away.

Gran carried the boxes of food and bottles of water and soda to one spot, and Frank announced that homeowners were welcome to come help themselves. The food disappeared as Joe had promised. Shoveling mud was mighty hungry work.

"My arms are killing me," DJ moaned to Hilary. The two of them and John Yamamoto had been a team all day.

John shook his head. "I'm sure glad we live on a hill. Mom has always wanted to live near a river, but there's not a chance she'll get her way now."

"I've got aches where I didn't know I had muscles." Hilary dumped another scoop into the wheelbarrow. "At least we get to go home to hot showers. All these people can't." She gestured at the houses around them. "Those that have water have to boil it before they can use it."

DJ looked down at her clothes, caked solid with mud. "For once, my mom will be right when she says I stink!"

Instead of going shopping that night, DJ fell asleep in the bathtub. She'd taken a shower first to wash the mud off, then soaked her aching muscles. Her mother helped her into bed.

"What a mess," DJ mumbled as she drifted off to sleep.

At school Monday, DJ wasn't the only one walking like a frozen zombie. Others who'd helped wore the same half-open eyes and winced whenever they sat down or stood up. It was especially difficult to keep her eyes open during the film in history.

"DJ." The gentle voice and the tap on the shoulder seemed to come from far away.

"Huh?" Her cheek felt smashed, and her eyes hot.

"DJ, I think you should wake up now. The bell is about to ring." Ms. Fisher smiled down at her.

DJ felt like crawling under the desk or melting into a puddle and sliming out the door. How long had she been asleep?

"Way to go." The boy in the desk behind her poked her in the back. The bell rang, and the race for the door was on.

DJ couldn't look the teacher or anyone else in the eye. She'd never fallen asleep in class before. What would her mother say? Surely one time wasn't concern enough for the teacher to send a note home with her.

"DJ." Ms. Fisher called her name.

"Yes?" DJ studied the tip of her fingernail.

"Don't feel so bad. I thought the movie was boring, too. Besides, I heard what you did yesterday. From what the other teachers have been saying, you're not the only one who's fallen asleep in class today."

"Thanks, but I still feel like an idiot."

"Just get some extra rest tonight. Good thing there are people like you in this world who care about others. I'm proud of you."

It was amazing how awake DJ felt after the compliment—even algebra went well.

At the Academy, she worked with Patches for her usual hour, carefully keeping to the outer edge of the ring. The jumps had been set up again, and Mrs. Ellsindorf had enlisted one of the stable hands to manage the standards and bars for her. DJ wanted to watch but knew that taking her attention off Patches would be a mistake.

"I should have put you out on the hot walker," she muttered after another session of crow-hopping. Patches flicked his ear back and forth, taking in the action in the middle of the ring, the conversations at the barns, and anything else going on within eye or earshot.

"Give it up!" The mischievous horse had rounded his spine and tried to get his head down for the umpteenth time.

DJ forced him to stand for a full three minutes until he finally let out his breath. From then on, he behaved perfectly.

"Patches, you old clown, what is your family going to do with you? What will it take for you to behave all the time, not just when you are ready?" He kept the steady lope in his line three feet from the walls and rails.

"You handle him so well," Mrs. Johnson said with a smile. "It's a pleasure to watch you two."

"How long have you been standing there?"

"Not long."

Good, then she didn't see her horse acting like a bronco. "When will you be starting your lessons with me?"

"Whenever you say. I'm ready anytime now." Mrs. Johnson reached over the bar to rub Patches' neck. "I know all I have to do is learn to make him mind me." She looked up at DJ. "And I'm counting on you to show me how. You're doing so well with Andrew that I know we'll do fine, too."

DJ felt a warm spot in her middle at the compliments. "Andrew is the one who's working hard, you know."

"I know. Say, I'll take Patches back and put him away, if you like. I know you have a lesson coming up with Bridget." She swung open the gate, giving a merry wave to Mrs. Ellsindorf at the same time.

Patches shot straight up in the air.

Chapter • 11

"Knock it off, Patches." DJ threw her weight forward and smacked the rearing horse between the ears.

Patches dropped to his feet and shook his head.

"DJ, I'm so sorry! That was all my fault." Mrs. Johnson had the fence rails in a death grip.

"No problem. Wait here. We'll be right back." DJ signaled the horse to a jog and took him around the arena, calling him every kind of name she could think of. Patches never even flicked an ear, his head low. If a horse could be embarrassed, he certainly acted that way.

"You are the greatest actor I ever met." DJ's voice had gone from scolding to teasing. She stopped him back at the gate.

"Is he all right?" Mrs. Johnson swung the gate open very carefully.

"Patches looks for things to spook at. In fact, you should have named him Spook." DJ swung off the horse and walked beside his owner. "You just have to watch him every single moment. Lots of horses settle down more as they get older." She rubbed Patches' nose. "I'm sure he will, too."

DJ hoped and prayed she was right. Otherwise, how could the Johnson family ever go trail-riding together like they wanted?

After the pounding Patches had given her, riding Megs for her own lesson felt like sitting on a padded cushion. DJ concentrated on every aspect of her body position and movement, as well as that of her horse, keeping Megs on the bit and bending around the leg like Jackie had taught her. When Bridget signaled her to the side to talk, DJ actually looked forward to it.

"You did well, *ma petite.*"

"Merci."

Bridget smiled up at her. "You are learning quickly. Now to transfer that learning to Major."

"I know. At least I know what 'right' feels like now. I can see what you mean about both horse and rider becoming better athletes through dressage."

"Riding Lord Byron did not make you want to concentrate on dressage?"

On Saturday, DJ had told Bridget all about her fantastic rides. DJ shook her head. "There's just nothing like being airborne. Even Lord Byron didn't leave the ground."

"Spoken like a true jumper. Ah, well, we have plenty of work ahead. Next week, you should be able to work with Major again. Do not rush him, though. Build up the strength in that leg slowly so it does not become a recurring problem."

"I will." DJ thought a moment. "How slowly do you mean?"

"A very wise question." Bridget laid out a plan for the next two weeks, patted Megs on the shoulder, and turned to answer a request from another rider.

After putting Megs away, DJ fed Major, Ranger, and Josh, scooped out some droppings, and jumped on her bike to head home. With Joe working on cleanup at home and Amy still on the sick list, she felt as if a chunk of her world was missing. She wished she dared stop by Amy's, but a phone call would have to do. Her mother might already be home, and tonight they were finally going to pick up the wedding dresses and shop for something for DJ to wear at the horse show.

"Mom, I'm home," DJ yelled up the stairs, hearing the sound of running water. When there was no answer, she took the steps two at a time and tapped on the door to her mother's bathroom. "I'm home," she repeated.

"Good. Can you be ready to leave in half an hour?" Lindy called back.

"I'll hurry."

She made it in twenty-nine minutes flat.

———————

"The dresses are beautiful," Gran said later at the restaurant. "I'm glad I didn't try to make them myself."

"You would have made them beautifully, too." Lindy looked up from reading her menu.

"Oh, I know, but they wouldn't have been ready by now, and my book illustrations wouldn't have been done for my deadline, either."

"And you'd have been a basket case." Lindy smiled. "Let alone me. Things are bad enough as they are."

"Bad how?" DJ asked.

"Bad as in so crazy I can't keep up." Lindy raised her hands palm up. "You know, this is the first time in weeks I haven't had somewhere else I had to be or something to do as soon as I get home."

"So everything is set for the wedding, then."

"Out of the mouths of babes." Gran's eyes held a twinkle that said she wholeheartedly agreed.

"Not that I'm a babe."

"No, not a babe of either kind," Lindy said. "And thank God, too."

DJ looked from her mother to her grandmother, then broke out in laughter. Her mother had tickled her funny bone.

"I don't see what's so funny." Lindy looked puzzled.

Gran shrugged and shook her head. The twinkle in her eyes said *she* got the joke.

So her mother hadn't meant to be funny. DJ took a long swallow from her soda. Oh well, at least she knew her mother had a sense of humor somewhere in there, even though she claimed she couldn't remember the punch line of a joke if she were paid to.

———————

Somehow they managed to find just the right clothes for DJ—and without her having to try on fifty different things, which she disliked doing even more than algebra. The navy bomber jacket looked good with tan pants, jeans, or even a skirt—if DJ had owned one. With a couple of new turtlenecks and a V-neck sweater, along with some clothes she already owned, DJ could mix and match to go anywhere.

When her mother insisted on buying her some chunky-heeled dress boots, DJ didn't argue. A small purse with a long, thin shoulder strap would take the place of her backpack.

"Thanks, Mom, Gran," DJ said for the umpteenth time.

"You're welcome." Lindy looked up in the rearview mirror to catch DJ's eye. "I still think we should have gotten you the robe and pj's."

"I don't need them."

"Sure you do. In fact, I think I'll pick them up after work tomorrow. Do have enough underwear?"

"M-o-t-h-e-r."

"She's not going to the moon and back," Gran said with a chuckle. When Lindy started to say something, Gran continued. "This just shows you are really a mother at heart after all, dear. I wonder how many times I told you to be sure to have clean underwear—no holes—"

"Just in case I had an accident and had to go to the emergency room," Lindy and DJ finished the words together.

The warm glow remained inside DJ's heart as she put her new things away and got ready for bed. Shopping hadn't been so bad after all.

"Thanks, God, today was super. And thanks that Amy gets to come back to school tomorrow—I've sure missed her. Please help all the people who've been flooded and thanks for keeping Joe safe, as well as Brad and Jackie and all their horses." She fell asleep still giving thanks.

DJ and Amy talked nonstop on the way to school in the morning, through lunch, and on the way home. They still hadn't gotten caught up when it was time to leave for the Academy. Since the sun and clouds were in a contest for first place, they rode their bikes for a change, but pumping up the hill set Amy to coughing.

"You sure you shouldn't go home and rest? I can take care of Josh another day or two." DJ paused to wait until Amy caught her breath.

"No way! I've been in jail too long already. I was about to call you to come bust me out." The talking made her cough again. "This will go away some year—the doctor said so."

"Okay, but—"

"No buts. Get your legs moving, we've got horses waiting for us!"

That night, Brad called to tell her that Jackie had left that morning with Lord Byron and a friend's horse in the trailer. The two women were driving and wanted to get to the showgrounds a couple of days early to get acclimated.

"You and I will be flying. We have an early flight on Friday out of San Francisco, so how about if I pick you up Thursday evening about six or six-thirty? Traffic should have let up by then."

DJ felt a shiver run up her back. She was finally going to see what a top-level dressage show was like! " 'Kay. I'll be ready. See ya."

When the phone rang again, it was Robert. DJ expected the call to be for her mother, but he said he wanted to speak with her first.

"What's up?" DJ leaned against the counter, one elbow propped on the top.

"How about you and I go out to dinner tomorrow night and then by the house? I have some questions about how you want your room done."

"Done?"

"You know—colors, carpet, things like that. We can put in book-shelves, too, so you have storage space for your art supplies."

"Oh."

"That okay?"

"Ah . . . sure. What time?" *But what do I know about decorating a room?* It would help if she didn't sound like a yo-yo brain when they talked.

They finished making their plans with Robert saying he'd set it up with her mother.

DJ snagged a can of soda from the fridge, dug in the drawer for an apple, bumped the door shut with her foot, then wandered upstairs to her room. She stared at the posters of horses on her walls—horses jumping, playing, racing; mares and foals in the field; horses in stalls. A large picture of Major held the place of honor. Her own drawings took up lots of space, too. But it was the intertwined Olympic rings over the head of a bay horse, front feet tucked close to his chest as he cleared a brick wall, that brought her to a stop. Only on television had she seen horses and riders of this caliber. Maybe one day Brad would take her to one of the big jumping shows. She might see one of *her* heroes there.

Visions of her jumping with a horse that looked surprisingly like Lord Byron sent her off to sleep.

"So where would you like to go for dinner?" Robert asked once they were in the car.

DJ started to say, "I don't know," then stopped herself. "What would *you* like?"

"Not pizza."

DJ agreed. That was the Bs' favorite meal in all the world, besides fried chicken and hamburgers. "You want ribs?"

"Not tonight. Chinese?"

DJ thought a moment. She always liked Chinese food. "Honey-walnut prawns?"

"You've got it. You want to choose which restaurant?"

"The one down on Contra Costa, across from Taco Bell." DJ fastened her seat belt. "We haven't been there in a long time."

While they were waiting for their dinner to be served, Robert opened a folder and laid some fabric, paint, and carpet samples on the table. "Have you been thinking of what you'd like in your room?"

"Honest, I'm clueless."

"Okay, I'll ask questions, and you answer." At her nod, he began. "Entertainment center?"

"For what?"

"Don't you have a television or stereo? What about a VCR?" When she shook her head at all of the above, he stared at her. "I thought all teenagers had those things."

"Not this one. I have a small boom box, but it's broken. I use the one downstairs."

At his puzzled look, she drew in a breath. "I know I'm strange, but I like it quiet when I study and even more so when I draw. I get so lost in what I'm doing, I don't need noise."

"Well, you've relieved my mind on one account, that's for sure." He grinned at her questioning look. "I was afraid my hearing would go due to loud music."

"Not mine."

"Do you have any books?"

"Mostly on horses and drawing, but I do have some novels, too."

"Computer?"

"I wish."

Their food came, but Robert kept on asking questions while they ate. "What about storage for your art supplies and a drafting table?"

"Really?"

"Sure. We'll include shelves and drawers for a computer in your work area, too, since I think you should have one."

"Have you talked with Mom about all this?"

"No. Why?" He stopped with a prawn halfway to his mouth. "It's your room."

When she just stared at him, he set down his chopsticks. "What? Do I have some sauce on my chin?"

She shook her head. "I think I better pinch myself to see if I'm dreaming."

"I thought maybe we should tile the area around the drafting table so you can put an easel there if you'd like, too. Gran suggested that. She said that someday you might do more than pencil drawings. You'll have a place to work at her home, as well, because she's going to add studio space when they rebuild the garage."

"She is?" DJ got the feeling they'd been doing a lot of talking without her knowledge.

"Yes, they'll be adding a potter's wheel and kiln then, too. Gran thought that would be something all the grandchildren could enjoy." He smiled again. "You want that last prawn?"

When DJ shook her head, he popped it in his mouth, along with the last walnut. "They can box the leftovers."

"What leftovers?" DJ teased.

Once at the new house, DJ and Robert made their way upstairs to the original master bedroom, which was slotted to become DJ's new room.

"I thought maybe we'd add a window over here—floor length, if you like—and this area would work for your art supplies and desk. What do you think?"

Walking in front of her, he pointed to the closet. "We'll put all the space-saving goodies in there—you know, shelves, drawers, and that kind of thing, And then," he indicated an entire wall, "this would look great done in floor-to-ceiling shelves for books and art and trophies."

Dazed, DJ followed Robert into the large bathroom. "We can do both a shower and a tub in here, if you want. I thought maybe you'd like a tub with jets to help work out your sore muscles. Lindy says the hot tub outside will be enough but—"

"Whoa, Robert!" DJ held up a hand. "If we were talking about a barn, I would have good ideas about what to do, but this . . . this is kinda much. I like everything you've suggested. How can I choose?"

"DJ." He turned and rested a hand on her shoulder. "You don't have to choose one thing over another unless you want to. The basic structure is what's important right now, like the new window or adding more closet space. The new tub would have to go in now, too, of course. Gran said she'd help you pick out colors, but we could ask a decorator to pitch in if you'd rather." He stood back, waiting.

DJ sucked in a deep breath. "I'd love to have big windows, but the closet is fine. I'll leave it to you to decide on the tub. I'm a shower person unless my muscles are really yelling. Everything else sounds wonderful." She paused to sort through it all.

"I'm not sure what colors offhand." She thought hard. "Maybe different shades of blue, with sand and—"

"I get the picture. If we could find wood in a deep, blood bay shade, how would that be?"

"Perfect." She glanced up at him out of the corner of her eye. "I've always liked gray, too—as in dappled. And Lippizaner white can't be beat."

Robert clasped an arm around her shoulders. "You've got your head on straight, DJ, that's for sure. And when we get to building the barn, you can help draw up the blueprints."

DJ took one last look at the room before turning out the light. *Wait till Amy hears about this!*

They were nearly back to her house when Robert said, "You know, I have a favor to ask."

"What?"

"Can you be extra patient with your mother in the next week or so? She's pretty uptight about the wedding and all."

"Who isn't?" The words just slipped out. "Sorry."

"I know, we all are. There's just so much to be done yet." He clicked on his turn signal. "I want all of us to be relaxed and ready to enjoy the wedding—no fights, no tempers. Maybe I'm dreaming, but I'm giving everyone this speech, including me. If we all cut each other some slack, we'll do all right."

"I'll try." DJ shook her head. "Cancel that. I'll do it."

Robert parked the car in the driveway and turned off the lights. "I know you will."

When they got out, they had to run to the house to keep from getting wet. The rain had returned.

Chapter • 12

"Thanks, Lindy, for letting DJ come with us. I'll have her home early Sunday night."

"I appreciate that." Lindy turned to DJ. "Now, you call if there's any change of plans."

DJ nodded and gave her mother a hug. "See you." She tried to act nonchalant, but keeping the excitement down was like trying to stop the rain. She'd be flying to a big-time horse show in the morning!

Brad picked up her duffel bag and held the door open for her. Feeling like the queen bee herself, DJ headed for the Land Rover. The rain had changed from a light mist to a sheeting blanket.

The drive to the farm passed with the kind of conversation two people have who are devoted to the same pastime. Neither one could ever talk horses too much. The heavy rain made it impossible to see the water-covered lowlands of the Napa Valley, the Sonoma Valley, and then the Petaluma, but Brad told her about them all.

When they stepped out of the car, DJ could hear the river that flowed between the levees at the low end of the fields.

"Let's take your things in and get some rain gear, then I need to check that mare. You can come if you want."

"Sure I do. Do you think she'll foal tonight?"

"I hope not—but then I thought she would foal last week some time. You never can tell for sure."

Brad unlocked the door and motioned DJ inside. "I have a lantern down at the barn. I hate to turn on all the lights and wake the horses up." He carried her bag to her room. "There's plenty of rain gear by the door, so you needn't unpack yours. Jackie called today and said it's really nice down south. Wish some of that sun would make its way back up here."

DJ draped her wet Windbreaker over the chair and followed her father back down the hall. Thanks to the drumming rain, even the house felt damp. She rubbed her arms. Good thing she had a sweater on.

The rain sounded even louder on the roof of the horse barn. Brad flicked the switch on a battery-operated lantern hanging right inside the doorway, and a soft glow spread a circle around them. The lights from the Land Rover automatically shut off as Brad slid the barn door closed.

A horse nickered from somewhere in the dimness. Straw rustled under restless hooves. Both foaling stalls were occupied. In one the mare stood placidly in the corner, opening her eyes just enough to acknowledge the two humans before going back to dozing. In the other, the heavy-sided mare paced and rocked from one foot to another.

"Uh-oh." Brad handed DJ the lantern. He opened the stall door and motioned her to step inside with him.

From the books she'd read, DJ knew that restlessness could be an indication of beginning or first-stage labor in a mare.

The mare's tail twitched, and she reached past her shoulder to nip at her ribs, a sign of pain. She paced and shifted, then paced and shifted again.

"I'll be right back, old girl." Brad patted the mare one more time and left the stall. "You ever wrapped a horse's tail?"

"For shows."

"This isn't much different—just not as fancy." Brad went to the tack room and returned with a roll of white wrap. "Here, I'll start and then you can do it. Set the lantern on the shelf there."

He wrapped the first couple of rounds, starting at the top of the tail, then handed DJ the roll. "Go most of the way down with this. It keeps her tail from tangling in the birth sac."

DJ tested the tightness and continued wrapping. "How many foals has she had?"

"Ten or so, I think. She's an old hand at it, anyway, so I don't expect any trouble." He repositioned the camera monitor in the corner so it could view the entire stall. "This way I can check on her without coming down to the barn. Stupid thing is, I let Ramone have the night off because he'll be here full time when we're down at the show." He stroked the mare's sweaty neck, talking to her in a soothing voice.

Watching him, DJ knew where she got her horse sense.

"Did you always love horses like this?" she asked softly.

"I've always liked them, but I think the love grew as I got older. My hope of owning a horse-breeding and showing ranch was just a dream for many years. I had to become established as an attorney first. Then I met Jackie at a horse show, and we put our dreams together." As he spoke, he walked around the mare, keeping a gentle hand on her at all times. He checked her udder. "Couldn't you wait a couple more days, old girl?"

She snorted, then bent her front legs and collapsed with a grunt on her side.

"Good. If you're going to do this, let's get it over with." Brad knelt beside her, continuing to stroke her neck.

The mare surged to her feet and began the rocking and pacing motion again. But within a few minutes, she quieted down, relaxed, and began to doze.

"Now what?"

"The contractions have stopped for who knows how long. Could be an hour, could be twenty-four. Some mares refuse to have their foal while a human is anywhere around, but I've been with Soda here for the last four, so I know that's not the case."

"I read once that wild horses could stop the birthing if danger threatened."

"Not just wild ones. That's why we set up the monitoring system. A thermostat keeps it the perfect temperature in here, too. Neither too cold nor too hot is good for the foal."

"I didn't know it could be so complicated."

"Yeah, well, when foals are worth thousands of dollars, you can't be too careful." Brad checked his watch. "It's nearly nine. Morning is going to come awfully early, so maybe you should hit the sack."

"And miss this?"

"No, you won't miss anything. I'll keep checking her, and if she goes into stage-two labor, I'll wake you."

"Promise?"

"Promise."

"If it comes on fast, I may miss it." DJ glanced over her shoulder at the mare, who now looked as if nothing had happened. She opened her eyes and exhaled a heavy breath as they left the large, loose box stall, but even her ears didn't twitch.

"You want anything to eat or drink?" Brad asked when they reached the kitchen. He pointed to the TV in the corner, which showed the mare sound asleep in her stall. "I'm having hot chocolate."

"That sounds good." DJ pulled out a bar stool and turned so she could watch the screen.

"I have another screen in my bedroom. I can set it to wake me however often I want so I can check on her. Of course, it would be better to have a man down there at the barn, but I think we still have a couple of hours or more to go."

After finishing the cocoa, DJ headed for bed, certain she'd never go to sleep. She was not only going to a horse show in the morning, she was going to watch a foal come into the world! She whispered her thank-yous and blessings into the stillness of the dark room. Without streetlights like at home, the dark here was really dark, even with the blinds left wide open. "And please, God, take care of Soda and her baby."

———

A tree branch brushed against the window, startling DJ from the doze she was sure would never come. She took in a deep breath and pulled the covers up over her ears. Why had a dumb tree branch startled her?

"DJ," Brad's voice floated out of the darkness sometime later, "it looks like we're going to have a foal tonight." Her father touched her shoulder.

"Okay."

"I'll meet you in the kitchen." He left the room.

"Okay."

DJ blinked hard, trying to get her eyes to stay open as she hopped from the bed and into her clothes. She added a long-sleeved turtleneck under the sweat shirt and heavy socks to keep her feet warm inside her boots. Slicking her hair back and wrapping a scrunchie around it as she walked, she got to the kitchen as Brad hung up the phone.

"Ramone is on his way. He said the river is rising fast. Apparently, there was more rain to the north of us than we had here. They're sand-bagging the levee upriver." He shook his head. "If the water overflows, we could be in a world of trouble."

"You think it could?"

"I doubt it, but stranger things have happened. For now, first things first. Soda doesn't look like she's waiting on us."

DJ glanced at the monitor screen. The mare was rising to her feet again.

The roar of the river was muted by the barn walls. Soda had lain down again but heaved herself back up when they entered the stall.

"Move very slowly around her from now on," Brad cautioned. "The calmer we are, the easier it will be for her." He circled the mare. "No sign of the sac yet. It might still be a while."

DJ stroked Soda's neck and smoothed her cheek. The mare seemed to accept her there, though her restlessness continued.

When the water broke, Brad breathed a sigh of relief. "Soon now."

Fifteen minutes passed.

To DJ, it seemed like two days. She listened as her father softly explained all that was happening with the mare and unborn foal.

"You want to interfere as little as possible," he said. "God set this process in motion, and it works better when you leave it alone—unless you're sure there's trouble. And I'm thinking more and more that's what we're in here."

"Are you going to call the vet?"

"Not yet, but it's a real possibility."

She and Brad both sat in a corner of the stall. Another ten minutes dragged by. The mare was down, then up, back down on one side, then the other.

"Something is definitely wrong. Now that she's up, I'm going to check to see if the foal is in the right position." He took off his jacket and pulled a long, sterile rubber glove from the bucket he'd brought from the tack room. "Hold her head for me, please."

DJ watched as he carefully inserted his hand into the birth canal. The mare flinched but stood still. "What is it?"

"I can't find the other foot." He reached farther. "It's bent back at the knee." A contraction clamped around his arm, making him wince.

"You okay?"

"Better than this baby here." He gritted his teeth. "I've got to get that leg straightened out. That's what's slowing her down." He closed his eyes as another contraction squeezed off the circulation all the way to his shoulder. "Okay, girl, now as you relax, let me find that hoof."

Please, God, help him. DJ kept on stroking the horse and pleading for help at the same time.

"Got it." He grunted again. "You have to be careful that you don't injure either the foal or the sac it's in. The mare, either, for that matter." Brad sighed with relief. "There."

DJ sent a thank-you heavenward as her father withdrew his hand. Pulling the glove off, he came to stand beside her. The mare groaned and lay back down.

"She's on the right side now. And that little one is ready to join us."

They both hunkered down at the rear of the mare. The protruding sac had grown in size.

"You should see the front hooves any minute now." He kept a steady hand on the mare's haunches. "Come on, girl, I don't want to have to pull it."

DJ bit her lip in delight. Two tiny hooves, still covered by the white sac, inched out. Another contraction, and she could see the knees. On the next, the foal's head, nose pressed to the legs, appeared.

"Okay, girl, keep it coming. Right now, DJ, is a crucial moment. Too long at this point, and the baby could have breathing problems because its cord is being pinched."

While his voice was soft and even, DJ could hear the concern. Never had she realized how many things could go wrong.

With a mighty contraction on the mare's part, the foal, still totally covered by the white sac, slipped out onto the straw.

And didn't move.

Brad knelt beside the still form, ripped the sack away from the foal's head, and with a clump of straw, wiped out the tiny nostrils. Still no movement.

"It's not breathing. DJ, call the vet." He motioned to the cell phone in a holder in the corner. He gave her the number to punch in, then pinched the foal's lower nostril closed and blew into the upper nostril.

DJ's fingers were shaking so hard, she could hardly dial. She watched her father breathe in and blow out in a steady rhythm. He stopped to compress the foal's ribs.

The phone rang in her ear. *Please, God, please.* An answering machine kicked on. "Dr. Benton is out on a call right now. Please leave your number, and as soon as he can, he will check for messages and return your call."

"I got an answering machine."

"Leave our number. He'll call from his mobile phone as soon as he's back in his truck."

DJ did as she was told. At that moment, the foal's ribs rose and fell—the most beautiful sight DJ had seen in her whole life. The baby was breathing! It would live now. She set the phone down.

The foal pulled back against Brad's grip and began thrashing its feet.

Brad cleaned the remainder of the sack away and stepped back. "Thank God for His mercies."

"I did . . . I do." DJ could feel tears burning behind her eyes. *Don't cry now*, she scolded herself.

"Pretty amazing, isn't it?" Brad draped an arm across her shoulders and squeezed her to him. "Nearly makes me cry every time I see it."

DJ sniffed. "Good, then I don't feel like such an idiot."

"Seeing a miracle in action should make anyone cry. We're not out of the woods with this one yet, but at least we're on the right path."

Brad took a thick towel out of the bucket. "You want to rub her down?"

"The mare?"

"No, the foal. Soda will be on her feet in a while to start pushing this one to get up and begin nursing."

Brad collected the sac when the afterbirth came and put them both in a plastic bag.

"Why do you keep those?"

"If there's a problem, much can be learned from this. For instance, if there's an infection, it could tell us what kind and if all the afterbirth is out—if it isn't, the mare could get an infection, too. Also, it tells us if there was any problem for the foal before birth, such as a rip in the membranes or poor circulation."

"Oh."

The phone beeped, and Brad answered it. "We have a filly here, but she's weak because she was a long time coming. I had to go in and straighten a front leg, and she couldn't start breathing without help. Yes, I think we'll be okay. I'll let you know if things change."

But while the baby tried, an hour later she still didn't have her feet under her. Even DJ could tell the foal was getting tired.

Soda whuffled to her foal, licking her and pushing sometimes with her nose. But the foal lay quietly after another major effort to stand.

"Look, Soda is dripping milk."

"She's losing her colostrum. We might have to tube-feed this one, so I'd better see if we can save some of that." Brad brought a plastic jar back from the tack room. "I have some frozen from another mare if we need it."

He said it so matter-of-factly that DJ nearly missed the point. The filly might not be able to nurse—and if it didn't eat, it would die. Her stomach clenched as though someone had tied a rope around it and jerked.

The sound of an automobile outside the barn captured their attention.

"Good, Ramone is here. He's a better milker than I am."

"Sorry I took so long. One road was flooded, so I had to go back around." Ramone took in the situation at a glance. "Trouble, eh?"

"Could you do the honors?" Brad handed him the jar. "Don't take too much in case she makes it up on her own and can nurse."

Brad took a clipboard off a nail and checked his watch, where he'd clicked the Stop button when the foal fully emerged. "Born at 3:15, needed assistance with . . ." he mumbled as he wrote, then looked down at DJ, who sat in the corner watching the mare and foal. "Keep praying."

"I am."

He clicked another button on his watch. "Uh-oh. We should be leaving for the airport right about now."

Ramone broke in. "Like I said, the main road's closed. You should have left earlier." He capped the jar and set it on the shelf. "Sorry I got here so late."

"It wouldn't have made any difference. I wouldn't have left. We'll just have to take a later flight."

Relief made DJ's shoulders slump. She didn't want to leave the foal right now, no matter how much she wanted to see Jackie compete.

———————

By daylight, even with help, the foal had neither stood on her own nor been able to nurse. Brad called the vet again.

Chapter • 13

"How about if I trailer a load of the horses up to the Carsons?"

Brad looked up at his foreman. "Something telling you that's what we should be doing?"

Ramone nodded. "Juan and I can do that. I really think we should get them all out of here." He took off his hat and scrubbed his dark hair smooth before putting it back on. "I've never seen the river so high—not since they built the levee. You always say it's better to be safe than sorry."

"It would take a Noah-type flood to reach the house."

"Sure, but the barns aren't up that high."

DJ watched the conversation ping-pong back and forth. Brad had insisted they come up to the house to eat. While she was hungry enough to devour the scrambled eggs he made, all she could think of was the foal. She had to stand and suck to nurse. Nothing major, unless she was too weak already.

A thought made her catch her breath. She choked on the toast in her mouth.

"You all right?" Brad leaned toward her.

DJ waved him away, then coughed, choked, and coughed again. A glass of water appeared in front of her. She took a clear breath, swallowed a couple of gulps, and breathed deeply.

"I'm fine. Guess it went down the wrong spout." She could feel the heat in her face from both the coughing fit and embarrassment. She looked at her father. "You don't think something is wrong with the foal's lungs or anything, do you?"

"The thought's crossed my mind. This one seems to have had a couple of strikes against her before she even got here." He folded his arms on the table and leaned toward her. "DJ, sometimes these things happen. Maybe her lungs didn't develop quite right, or her heart. If that's the case, then the biggest favor we can do for her is put her down. We can't let her suffer."

DJ could feel the tears welling as fast as Brad was talking. *Put her down before she even has a chance to live? That's not fair! You've got to give her a chance.* She didn't dare say a word because then her tears would stream like the rain on the windows.

A car horn honked.

"Benton's here," Ramone said, checking out the window by the front door.

Brad looked over at DJ. "We'll know more after the vet examines her. Then we'll feed her using a stomach tube to see if that helps get her on her feet. I'll give her every chance, Deej. She's worth the time and effort."

The new nickname made DJ smile as she slid her arms into the brown jacket her father had loaned her. *Deej, huh?*

Back in the barn, nothing had changed. The mare hadn't given up on encouraging her foal, but the little one still lay flat out in the straw. DJ took a moment to thank God the foal was still breathing as she watched the vet, who, after donning a coverall and boots that had been rinsed in disinfectant, knelt beside the foal. He listened to her heart and lungs, belly sounds, then looked up the nostrils and in her mouth, eyes, and ears.

"Everything sounds normal," he said, rising to his feet. "She's just weak. Let's get some milk in her via the tube and see if that doesn't help. We should get her nursing on a false teat until she can stand on her own."

"False teat?" DJ looked to her father.

"A special nipple on a bottle that acts more like the real thing. Could you halter the mare and tie her to that bar, please?"

DJ did as he asked. In the meantime, Brad retrieved the milk from the refrigerator in the tack room and, after warming it in the microwave, returned to the stall.

By then, Dr. Benton had worked the rubber tubing up through the foal's nose and down its throat. Ramone held her while Brad slowly poured the colostrum into the cupped end of the tube.

"I'm going to take a blood sample to see if we're fighting any infections," the vet said as he located a vein in the foal's neck and pulled a syringe full of dark fluid. "Let her be for a while, then assist her once she struggles to her feet." He smiled at DJ. "Brad knows all of this, but repeating it never hurts, and I knew you'd want to know what's going on."

"Thanks." DJ left off stroking the mare and sank down behind the foal. She smoothed the fuzzy mane and brushed straw from the now dry coat. The foal raised her head and tried gathering her legs under her to be more upright. DJ inched closer to let the foal use her knees as a brace. With her legs folded under her, the baby rested her nose on the straw, still breathing heavily from the exertion.

Brad untied the mare but held the end of the rope. "She doesn't seem to mind you at all." The mare sniffed DJ's hair, then nudged her baby.

"Give her a minute, girl," DJ whispered.

"I've got another call to make," Dr. Benton said. "Call me if there's any change for the worse. Keep up the good work, DJ. I can tell you get along with horses like your dad does."

———

But an hour later, no matter how much DJ and the mare coaxed the foal, she could not get to her feet. DJ could hear the men loading horses into the long trailer outside. Matadorian was the first, followed by the better blooded show horses, until they had ten loaded. She heard the truck drive off, and Brad returned to the stall.

"DJ, I've set our tickets for the six o'clock flight. That means we need to leave here by three."

"You mean leave her like this?"

"Juan will take care of her. He's great with the foals."

"But . . . but I can't just leave her."

The mare nickered at the rise in DJ's voice and shifted from one foot to another.

DJ tried to calm down and forced her voice to a lower note. "Please."

"You've been up most of the night. Will you want to shower before we go?" Brad shrugged at the pleading look on her face. "What can I say, Deej? Jackie needs me with her, and the farm needs me here. The reality is sometimes I have to be gone—that's why I hire extremely capable people."

Ramone slid open the door and, trying to keep his voice low, stammered, "Bad news. The levee broke less than a mile upriver. Water is pouring into our side of the valley."

"I see. Well, there go our lower fields, but the water shouldn't pose a problem up this far. The house and barns will be fine."

"But if you don't leave right now, the road will be closed."

"I can't leave with something like this going on. Besides, that would leave you all alone. Juan won't be able to return with the truck." He turned back to the foaling stall. "Well, DJ, you got your wish. We aren't going anywhere." He closed his eyes. "Oh no. I better get you out of here. Your mother will have that proverbial cow for certain if she hears you're caught in a flood."

"No way—I'm not leaving." DJ got to her feet, nearly collapsing on the foot that had gone to sleep.

The mare laid her ears back. The foal struggled to rise, too, her thin legs scrambling but refusing to work together. She collapsed again, flat out, flanks heaving.

"Sorry to pull rank, but you have to go. And it has to be *now*, so I can get back."

"Where will you take her?" Ramone asked.

"To . . . ah, to the Lodesly place. I'll call them now. Her mother can pick her up there." He dialed but when the answering machine came on, he hit the cancel button. Another call had the same result.

DJ stood with her arms crossed, trying to keep the fury inside. He needed her here and instead he was trying to find someone else to keep her. He was right that Mom would be mad, but it wasn't as if they had planned this. "Mom will understand this was an emergency."

Brad handed her the phone. "The others have probably either left or are outside trying to salvage things from the flood. Their homes are on hills like this one, so their houses should be safe. At this point, it looks like we have no choice but for you to stay."

"Do you want me to call my mother?"

"Oh." Brad reached for the phone. "I'll do it." But when he dialed, the answering machine clicked on there, too. As he left a message, DJ shook her head.

"She's at work. Why not wait and tell her later when I can talk with her?"

"Too late, I've left the message." Brad pressed the Off button again.

Suddenly, the barn turned dark as the dim barn lights flickered out. Rain-streaked windows let in what little outdoor light remained.

"We've got to keep it warm enough for the foal in here, so let's get the generator going. Ramone, you start that, and I'll go up to the house and turn off the switches. DJ, why don't you call your grandmother so she doesn't worry."

"Okay."

This time when the phone rang, there was someone to pick it up.

"DJ, are you all right?" Gran's voice carried the love of years through the wire.

"We're fine, Gran, but we haven't left for Los Angeles yet—or rather now we won't."

"What's happening?"

"Well, the mare foaled during the night, and the baby has some problems, so we've been working with her. And we just got word that the levee broke and . . . no, Gran, we'll be okay. Brad says the house and barns are high enough on the hill that we're in no danger—we're just stuck here. No, by the time you could get here, the roads will be flooded. Don't worry, I'm safe." She almost mentioned them relocating some of the horses, but she thought the better of it.

"Oh, and, Gran, please pray for this filly. She just hasn't got the strength to stand, and if she can't stand, she can't nurse. I'll be feeding her from the bottle."

After promising to keep them posted and saying good-bye, DJ set the phone back in its cradle. Now if only she could get the foal to stand.

One of the Bible verses Gran had given DJ when she wanted to quit chewing her fingernails came floating through her mind. *Not by might nor by power, but by my Spirit, says the Lord.* She hummed the tune it was set to as she approached the stall again.

The mare turned from pulling hay out of the sling and pricked her ears. DJ heard a chugging sound, and the lights flickered and came back on.

"See, that's what God means about His Spirit," she confided to the mare. "With His Spirit, there is light and heat. God's power is stronger than even that crazy river." The more DJ said the words, the more she believed them herself. They were safe from the flood, but what about the weak foal? Surely God meant for His Spirit to take care of all His living creatures.

DJ let herself back into the stall and eased next to the mare, stroking her neck and watching the foal sleep. "God, you've brought us this far. Thanks for that. Now please give this filly the strength to stand and nurse so she can grow right and healthy. She is so little and weak." DJ sniffed and wished she had a handkerchief. "Please help us again."

She leaned against the mare, inhaling the scent of horse. She could hear the mare in the next stall, groaning as she lay down. Was she going into labor, too? Down the aisle, the remaining horses ate or dozed, the contented sounds of a normal barn. From outside, she could hear the river.

The door squeaked open, and Ramone entered, followed by Brad.

"You can see the river," Ramone was saying.

"I know, but it won't climb this high." Brad leaned over the stall and handed DJ a zipped plastic bag. "You might want to wash your hands first, but I figured if you were as hungry as I am, your stomach rumbling might scare the old girl here." He nodded toward the mare.

"Thanks." DJ grinned and slumped down the stall wall, crossing her legs to sit more comfortably. Rubbing her hands mostly clean on her thighs, she pulled half the sandwich from the bag and attacked.

"We could go sit on the chairs in my office—I have the coffee machine on, and I know there are sodas in the refrigerator."

"I'm fine. How long before we feed her again?"

"Any time Ramone wants to milk the mare. I have powdered substitute to mix, too, but the more colostrum we can get in her, the better."

"Did you check on the fields?" DJ looked up to see Ramone standing beside her father.

"I did. I just hope there's plenty of good fertilizer in that mud because it will be a while before our grass can push up through it."

"It's only mud?" DJ asked around a bite of ham and cheese.

"Nope, there's a lot of water, too. You can actually watch it rising up the slope. I sure am glad I didn't put the buildings down on the flat when we built. Was tempted to at the time."

Suddenly, the roar of helicopter blades seemed to hang right over the barn. "The river has flooded, and the water will continue to rise," the voice echoed above. "Please evacuate. If you need help, wave something white."

Brad went out in the driving rain and waved them off. Even though the sound of the blades disappeared, the rain drumming on the roof and cascading through the downspouts made enough noise to make talking softly difficult.

DJ could feel herself slipping into her own world, a place where the sun shone and foals danced across a fenced pasture. A place where Major rolled in knee-deep grass and then took her jumping over the fences. She fought to keep her eyes open.

Ramone entered the stall. "Would you please hold Soda while I see if I can get some more milk for the little one?"

"Sure." DJ yawned when she stood up to take hold of Soda, who twitched her tail and shifted her front feet, but stood still for the most part. "Will you put a tube down the filly again?"

"No, this time we'll use the bottle. You'll do well with her, I know."

When Ramone returned, he had the artificial teat connected to a squarish plastic bottle. "Just see if you can get her to suck on it. She'll probably fight you if you try to open her jaws, but she'll get the hang of it eventually."

DJ looked from the bottle to the foal. Why did this seem like it could be difficult? Surely the baby was hungry enough now to take about anything.

But it didn't work that way. When DJ held the nipple against the foal's lips, she shook her head. Then DJ held the baby's head and tried to force the nipple in, but the struggle wasn't worth it. As the foal fought DJ, the mare grew more restless, finally laying her ears back.

"Don't worry about Soda. She's tied up." Ramone lowered himself down beside DJ. "Try wetting your fingers with the milk and rubbing it on her lips."

DJ did, but the foal would have none of it.

Once more she tried, this time by pressing down on the lower jawbone and inserting the nipple from the side. Nada.

Pleading, coaxing, dribbling the milk in the cup of the lower lip— nothing worked. Only her jeans grew wet from all the milk that bypassed the baby's throat.

"She's stubborn, that one." Brad returned from making some more phone calls. "Why don't you call it a day? You look about done in."

"What are you going to do?"

"Ramone and I are going to move the equipment out of the office and the tack room and store it all upstairs. Just in case."

"Just in case what?"

"Just in case the water does indeed get up to the barn. I didn't think it could happen but . . ."

DJ went to stand at the door. Sure enough. It looked like the house and barns were on an island surrounded by dirty brown water all the way around—and coming closer.

Chapter • 14

"Have you ever filled sandbags?" Brad asked in a teasing tone.

DJ noticed the smile never quite reached his eyes. "No, but I did clean up a flood site last weekend over in Napa."

"Well, let's hope and pray it doesn't come to that." Brad turned back to Ramone. "But better safe than sorry, right?"

Ramone fingered his gray-flecked mustache. "We'd better get started—we have a lot of doors in this barn. And we'd better begin with the well house."

"You're right. If that generator gets flooded, we won't have any clean water. Boiling water for this many horses will be almost impossible." Brad visibly relaxed his shoulders.

A jingle played in DJ's head. *Water, water, everywhere—and not a drop to drink.*

"Back to the barn," Brad picked up his train of thought. "What if we laid down plastic and set straw bales on top of it? Do you think that might hold?"

Ramone nodded. "Don't know why not."

"It would be faster than bagging. Besides, what are we going to use for sandbags?"

"I have some in my truck." Ramone motioned outside. "Kept them there just in case it flooded down at my mother's house. Since I can't get to her anyway, we can use them here."

"We could cut squares of plastic, dump sand on them, and tie them." DJ leaned against the wall of the box stall. "Or we could make tubes and tie them at both ends." She thought of all the presents she had wrapped both ways.

"Okay. You try feeding the foal again, and Ramone and I'll get started."

The phone beeped, and Brad answered it. "Sorry, Jackie, it looks like we're stuck here. No, we're safe, but there's a chance it could get wet in the barn. I know, I never thought it could happen, either, but the water's already within a couple of feet of the pump house. No, coming home won't help—you couldn't get here even if you tried. At least I know you're safer where you are." He hung up and looked at DJ.

"Deej, how about filling every container you can find with water while we have it? I wish we'd brought the stock tank up from the lower field. Hindsight is always wonderful, of course."

"Sure. Do you want me to go up to the house and fill the tubs? That's what we do at home."

"Yes, and there are some plastic jugs in the pantry. Put drinking water in those."

DJ stepped outside. Sure enough, their island had shrunk. Now water covered the long drive out to the county road. She ran up the rise to the house to do as her father had asked.

Without power for heat, the house already felt cold and damp. She turned on the water in the two tubs, filled the jugs, and pulled out all the kettles to fill, too. In spite of her father's reassuring words, she felt like a rock had taken up residence in her stomach. While the floodwater wasn't moving fast, its steady lapping up the rise reminded her that they had no control over the river.

On her way back down to the barn, she looked up at the sky, drizzling now instead of a downpour. "God, please stop the storm. I know you can do it. Please." She put buckets under every spigot and turned them on, hauling the water to the tubs she found for the arena. With everything full, she returned to the barn.

Back inside, an occasional hoof thudded against a wall and nervous nickers rippled from stall to stall as the horses let their fear be known. The sound of the river so close was very different from what they were used to.

DJ heated the bottle for the foal in the microwave and took deep breaths to calm herself. She knew panic never helped anyone, but knowing and doing were two separate things. This was like getting ready to go in the show-ring, only worse.

The filly lay sleeping.

"Ah, little one, please don't sleep your life away." DJ entered the stall, petting and talking to the mare first before approaching the foal. Head up, the foal watched her with wide, dark eyes.

"Come on, you've got to get used to me. Surely we can be friends by now." Were the filly's eyes brighter? Perkier? Or was it wishful thinking?

DJ shook her head at the thoughts that careened through her mind and knelt by the foal. "Do you want me to squirt this in your mouth or what?" Her singsong monologue at least worked to calm the mare. The filly thrashed around, trying to get her feet under her so she could run. DJ sat without moving until the baby's panic let up.

"Now that you have that over with, let's try some of this good stuff." She tickled the filly's lips with the nipple, but the foal turned her head away. "I know you should be standing to nurse from your mother, but that doesn't seem possible right now."

The mare nudged her foal and whickered deep in her throat. "See, mind your mother, you silly thing. Either get up and get going or drink to become strong enough to get up and get going."

DJ even tried prying open the foal's jaws and forcing in the nipple, but the baby's thrashing made the mare nervous. "I wonder if we could make a sling to hold you up." DJ wet the nipple with the mare's milk again.

"Give it up for now, DJ." Brad appeared at the door. "We need your help with sandbagging."

"The pump's shot." Ramone, soaked to his waist, entered at a run.

"Get some dry clothes on, man, so you don't catch your death. We'll be filling more bags."

The horses corralled in the arena stayed in a group at the far end as they shoveled sand up from the arena floor, rolled the tubes, and tied the ends. Ramone pushed the full wheelbarrow out to the barn doors and slung the bags in place. Brad and DJ tried desperately to keep up with the filling.

After an hour, DJ's arms and shoulders felt six inches longer—and all six inches ached.

Still the water level kept rising.

They scooped, tied, and hauled faster. The helicopter flew over again, the loud voice of an emergency relief worker asking if they wanted help getting out. As before, Brad turned down the offer.

Water crept into the arena, turning the sand to mud. The horses now galloped from one end to the other, whinnying their fear.

One by one, water seeped into the stalls under the doors that hadn't been bagged or set with straw bales. However, the front and rear doors stayed dry, thanks to the bags already in place.

The team worked on, bagging and hauling, sweat running down their faces, their muscles screaming for relief.

Once all the doors had a double layer of bags in place, they stopped. Dark came early and, with it, an increase in rainfall. Ramone swept out what water had seeped in and threw down fresh straw to replace that which was soaked in the stalls.

Meanwhile, DJ and Brad hung slings of hay from the arena walls and refilled the tubs of water. As the buckets emptied, Brad set them under the downspouts from the barn roof.

"No sense wasting what clean water God sends us." He dug his fists into his back and stretched aching muscles. DJ did the same.

Never in her life had she been so tired. Every muscle in her body had cramped at one time or another in the last hours. Her feet felt like they weighed forty pounds each, and her hands hung heavy by her sides. *Good thing they're attached,* she thought, trying to lift them to take her wet gloves off.

"Come on, let's go make some dinner. There's nothing more to be done right now." Brad led the way out to Ramone's pickup truck, splashing through the water that sheeted the concrete pad. The radio spilled out flood information on the way to the house.

"The Santa Rosa area should get some relief by midnight tonight as the river crests at an anticipated twenty-five feet above flood stage. The actual crest will depend on the rainfall we receive in the next hours."

"Twenty-five feet! Last I heard we were at twenty-two. Three more feet." Brad thumped the steering wheel with the heel of his hand.

"We have to get the horses out of the barn." Ramone slumped against the door, looking as exhausted as DJ felt.

"If we let them loose, they'll all come toward the house. There's no way the water will go that high."

"What about the foal?" DJ asked.

Brad thought a moment while parking. "We'll move the mare and foal into the garage—the other one, too. With our luck, she'll drop her foal tonight." They climbed from the truck and hobbled wearily toward the door.

Brad turned on the battery-powered lamps he had set out in the kitchen. "Good thing we have a gas stove. DJ, dig under that counter, will you? The old coffeepot should be under there somewhere."

While she was searching, Brad hunted in the freezer section of the refrigerator. "I know Jackie left us some frozen soups. We better use as much frozen food as we can in case the power is off for a couple of days." He handed Ramone the sandwich fixings and took the plastic pouches of soup to the stove. Plopping them into a pan of water, he turned on the heat.

Before long, they sat down to vegetable soup and ham-and-cheese sandwiches. DJ even drank a cup of coffee well laced with hot chocolate mix.

They ate without talking, as if they hadn't seen food in a week. "Just put your things in the sink," Brad instructed.

"Ramone, we'll haul up straw first for DJ to put out in the garage while you and I bring up some of those aluminum fence panels. All those mares need to do is bang into some of the stuff on the shelves and they'll go right through the roof."

He hesitated a moment. "On second thought, Ramone, you get the straw while DJ and I move the stuff from the garage into the house. That'll give us more space. We'll worry about the fence panels once that's done."

DJ felt herself sinking down into the chair. Her head jerked, and she blinked. *No time to sleep now.* She picked up her dishes and carried them to the sink. Amazing—she'd never fallen asleep that fast in her entire life.

Ramone dumped off the bales of straw and went to pick up the panels while Brad and DJ moved storage boxes, Christmas decorations, gardening supplies, and other stuff into the house, stacking it down the hall and in the living room. She drove the lawnmower out, and Brad backed out Jackie's car.

"Okay, let's put the panels up here." He indicated the separation between the garage doors. "That way the mares will each have an entire bay." While the men fastened the fence panels, DJ spread the straw good and deep.

Back down in the barn twenty minutes later, Brad brought out blankets for each of the mares and one for the foal. "DJ, if you lead Soda, I'll carry the foal. Ramone, you bring Hannah."

They buckled the blankets around the mares and added leads with chains to loop over their noses. "Just in case we need more control," Brad said, noticing DJ's reluctance.

"Now, let's get this little one on her feet so I can pick her up."

DJ held the mare while Ramone got the baby into an almost standing position so Brad could slip one arm around her rump and another around her chest. For some reason, the filly stopped struggling, and they started the long parade up to the house. Halfway there, Brad paused to catch his breath.

"You want to trade?" Ramone asked.

Brad shook his head. "I'll make it. Let's not take a chance."

DJ lead Soda into one section of the garage and loosened the lead so the mare could investigate the surroundings. She checked on her baby first, then nosed at the aluminum panels. She took a place right beside the foal, standing guard in the strange place. With Hannah moving around in the other pen, Soda kept her body between the foal and the other horse.

"You watch them, and we'll start hauling hay. We need to get enough up here to feed everyone for at least a couple of days." Brad climbed back in the truck and waved at DJ as he and Ramone returned to the barn.

DJ shivered in the wind that blew in the open garage doors. If she was cold, what about the foal?

With bales of hay and straw stacked outside the aluminum panels to provide insulation and inside the garage to keep dry, Brad and Ramone held the mares while DJ punched the button to close the garage doors. Soda rolled her eyes at the sound of the motor and the sight of the lowering doors, but Brad kept her calm with a firm hand and his soothing voice.

"Why don't you warm the bottle up in a pan of water on the stove,

DJ? If the filly won't drink it this time, we're going to have to tube-feed her again. I hate to have to do that in case something goes wrong."

"How about if I bring up some more panels and we fence off the front of the house so we can let the other horses loose?" Ramone suggested.

"Sounds like a good idea. I'd hate for all of Jackie's shrubs and flowers to get eaten and trampled, but it's a small price to pay compared to losing any horses. With the panels, we can have it both ways."

DJ took the bottle into the kitchen and set it to warm in a pan full of water. Her eyes felt so full of sand, she could barely see the numbers on the dial.

The gas lit with a bit of a pop, and she held her hands to the heat. She'd never known the meaning of bone weary before now. She had blisters on her hands from shoveling, and her muscles felt like liquid.

Never had the thought of a soak in a hot tub of water been so appealing. But getting food in that foal was far more important right now. DJ shook herself awake and tested the milk by dribbling some on her skin. Back to the battle.

With the doors closed, the garage had warmed some. She heard the truck drive back up the hill, then the sound of metal posts being driven into the ground. With each *kathunk* of the heavy iron sleeve that slammed down on the top of the post, she saw the mare flinch. It felt as if they were driving the posts right into DJ's skull.

And no matter what she tried, the foal refused to drink.

DJ sank down by the battery-powered lamp in the corner of the stall. "God, what can I do? This baby is getting weaker, and she could get really sick with all the weather problems we've been having. Please, please help me. Help us. Thanks for your protection from the flooding. We'd sure be grateful if you ended the storm now." She rested her head on her knees, her arms wrapped around her legs.

Soda came over and nosed DJ's hair, then whuffled and nudged her baby. The foal managed to get up on her brisket with her legs tucked under her.

"Come on, baby, all the way."

The pounding outside stopped.

DJ heard no more.

"DJ. Darla Jean."

"Huh?"

"You better get to bed." Brad knelt in front of his daughter.

"I . . . I can't. Got to feed the foal." She blinked her eyes and yawned wide enough to crack her jaw.

"Ramone and I will tube-feed her."

"No, let's try holding her up in a sling first. You guys hold her, and I'll see if I can't get her to nurse on her mother. She's gotten used to us handling her, so maybe she won't fight this time."

"I think you need to go to bed."

"Please, Dad."

At the look on his face, DJ realized what she had said. Where had the "Dad" come from? Was that really what she wanted to call him? It must be since it had just come out.

"Please."

"All right. One more try."

DJ struggled to her feet. "How are the rest of the horses?"

"Fine. We threw out hay, so they aren't exploring much right now. The generator at the barn drowned out. If I'd had time, I'd have brought it up to the house. I still might." He rubbed his forehead and his face. "Only so much you can do, I guess."

"I'll get a sheet to use for a sling, okay?"

"Yeah, fine. Ramone, come help us in here, will you?" When there was no answer, he stuck his head out the side door and called again.

Now what? DJ wondered as she took a flashlight to go in search of a sheet for a sling. *Please, there can't be one more thing to go wrong.*

Chapter • 15

Ramone—where is Ramone?

DJ tried not to think about the missing Ramone as she dug in the linen closet for an old sheet. Nothing looked remotely old in the beam of the flashlight. She finally found a stack of plain, white flat sheets down on the bottom shelf. Taking two for good measure, she headed back to the garage. Only the horses were there.

Setting the sheets on a stack of straw bales, she stepped outside, her flashlight in hand. "Brad?" The sound of her voice sent horses trotting away. They were more spooked than she was. And at this point, that was saying something. DJ shivered. "Dad?" She raised her voice.

More snorts, followed by the sound of hooves *schlupping* away.

What could have happened to them?

DJ walked toward the truck, which was parked off to the side to keep the drive clear. Both men were sitting inside. She breathed a sigh of relief. But why hadn't they answered her?

The truck was running—the drone of the idling engine told her that. Feeling as if she'd learned she was the only human left alive on the planet, DJ forced herself to go toward the vehicle.

Hand trembling, she opened the door.

Rumbling snores nearly drowned out the drone of the engine. They were both sound asleep!

DJ nibbled on her lip. Between the foaling and the flood, the two had gone for nearly two days without sleep. Should she let them sleep? But the filly needed feeding.

"Dad?" Calling him that was getting easier.

DJ waited and noticed something felt different. She looked up, and her face stayed dry. It wasn't raining!

"Dad, it quit raining!" She touched his shoulder.

He jerked as though she'd poked him with a cattle prod set on full force.

"Wha-what is it?" He peered at her, eyes owl round and blinking. "DJ, are you all right? Wha-what happened?"

"You fell asleep."

Brad let his head fall against the back of the seat. "I came to find Ramone, and he was asleep. So I thought I'd just sit in the warm cab for a minute or two before I woke him up." He scrubbed his face with both hands. "We need to feed the foal."

"Yes, we do, but guess what else is up?"

He looked at her as if answering would take too much effort.

"It quit raining!"

"Thank you, heavenly Father."

Brad's heartfelt praise brought him out of the truck, hands raised palm up.

DJ wasn't sure whether he was praising God or testing for rain, but his next words clued her in.

"No more rain. Thank you, God!"

She guessed it was both.

At his shout, Ramone jerked upright. "What's happening?"

Brad pointed toward the sky.

Ramone climbed stiffly from the truck. "How long have I been asleep? I didn't mean to do that—fall asleep, I mean."

"No problem, Ramone. Look!" Brad pointed upward again.

"The rain stopped! Look, there's even a star up there. I was beginning to think they had all disappeared forever." Ramone thumped a hand on the hood of the truck, the noise spooking the curious horses that had gathered around them.

"Well, that's one of many major prayers answered. Now, how about the foal?"

Brad turned to Ramone. "DJ thinks we should try a sling. It might make sense now that the filly has been handled so much. If Soda will cooperate, too. . . ."

"Whatever. I'm game."

The three entered the garage, and DJ picked up the sheets. "I hope these are okay to use."

"Deej, honey, anything is okay to use at this point. Everything but us and the horses are replaceable." He took the sheets. "And you and Ramone are more important than thousands of horses—hands down."

The glow around DJ's heart radiated clear to her fingertips.

The men stroked Soda first, then approached the filly. She raised her head and appeared to be studying them. But when she didn't thrash her legs, DJ began to wonder if she was too weak to fight.

They folded the sheet the long way and slid it under the foal's belly. On three, they gently hoisted her into the air, letting her feet touch the ground. The foal scrambled for a moment but quieted again. Head up, she looked toward her mother.

"Oh, wow." DJ led Soda over to the trio. "Come on, old girl, let's make this count." *Please, God, please*, marched through her mind as DJ guided the filly toward her mother's udder.

"Please, God, let this work," she heard Brad murmur behind her.

DJ stroked the filly's head, crouching down so she could see what she was doing.

The filly started to pull away, bobbing her head and bumping the mare's flank.

"Easy, now, little one, you can do this." *Please.*

"If you can, Deej, squirt a little milk on her muzzle."

DJ aimed a teat toward the filly and squeezed. She missed.

The men moved the filly an inch or two closer.

Bump, nudge, bump. DJ pulled another stream of milk from the mare. It hit the baby's muzzle and dripped down over her lips. A pink tongue peeked out and licked the milk.

DJ held her breath.

One more bump, and the filly found the teat. She wrapped her tongue around it, pulling it into her mouth.

She began to nurse.

DJ swabbed away the tears. "She's doing it," she whispered around a throat so tight, she could hardly swallow.

"I know," Brad's voice came, reverent as a prayer. "Thank you, Father, for big favors."

"Amen to that." Ramone's voice resounded with the same awe as Brad's and DJ's.

When the foal dropped her head a good time later, the men lowered her to the straw. She sighed and lay flat out on her side.

"You earned a good rest, little one. Sleep well." Brad got up from his knees. "And speaking of sleep, I vote we all do that. Ramone, I'll pull the Murphy bed in the rec room down for you. Sorry I can't offer anyone a hot shower, but warm covers will have to do."

They trooped into the house, jerking off their boots at the bootjack by the back door. DJ moved woodenly to her room, where she stripped off her filthy clothes with her eyes already half shut. She struggled into her sweats and, sitting on the side of the bed, pulled heavy socks over her freezing feet. She hung her head and sat there, as if frozen.

"Deej, getting into the bed before going to sleep would have been a good idea."

She felt her father lift her legs and swing them up on the bed. She tried to say thank-you when he pulled the covers over her, but the effort was too great.

When she woke, weak sunlight cast a square on the hardwood floor. "The filly! She should have been fed again long ago." DJ threw back the covers and leaped into her clothes, hitting the floor running. Without waiting to put on her boots, she opened the door to the garage.

The filly stood at her mother's side, head up and under the flank, nursing on her own, her brush of a tail flicking from side to side.

DJ glanced at her watch. Nearly noon—she'd slept for hours. "Why didn't they wake me?" she muttered as she shoved her feet into her boots and pulled them on. Snagging a jacket off the peg, she stepped outside.

The clouds looked like old dishcloths, tightly wrung and tattered. But the sun managed to find the holes between them and beam its warmth down onto the soaked earth. Horses nickered, and a pair of crows flew overhead, their caws sounding more like a song of rejoicing than a threat of doom.

A line of broken sticks and grasses lay in a mud coat that showed the highest reach of the flooded river. Now the water lapped a good foot below that mark.

DJ looked down to the barns. Water still stood well up the walls, the gray mud line above showing how far the water had already receded.

DJ drew in a deep breath of fresh air—and wished she hadn't. After working on the cleanup last weekend, she knew the smell would only get worse. Small breaths would serve her better until her nose decided to ignore the stink.

"So, everyone, where's my dad?"

"Right behind you." Brad draped an arm around her shoulders. "I'd still be sleeping if the phone hadn't rang. Your mother called to see how we are. All in all, I think she is handling this fairly well. When I said you were still sleeping, she said for you to call her back. Then I found your room empty."

"I should have called her before I went to bed."

"At 3:00 a.m.?"

"Was that what time it was?"

"Mm-hmm." Brad stretched his arms above his head and yawned. His arm thumped back on her shoulders.

"Did you see the foal nursing?"

"Yup. I checked on them around six, and she was up then."

"You coulda told me."

"What? And wake the sleeping beauty? Even I've got more sense than that."

She dug an elbow into his ribs, but not too hard.

They heard a click and a buzz behind them. The spotlight between the garage doors went on.

"Power, we've got power!" Brad spun her in a circle, then wrapped her in a bear hug. "Come on, daughter, we're going to have a *real* breakfast."

Ramone came to the door. "You have a phone call, boss."

"Thanks. How about you and DJ feed and water the horses while I make breakfast?"

Ramone nodded to where a couple of the loose horses were drinking from the dirty floodwater. "You told them that plan yet?"

"Well, at least water the two mares from the water in the bathtubs."

The other foal was born late that Saturday night. Once again, Brad woke DJ in time. An hour later, he said, "This is what a normal foaling is like—the mare does all the work, and I cheer her on."

DJ looked over to where both Soda and her baby lay sleeping. "I'll take this kind of delivery any day. But that baby over there sure stole a piece of my heart."

"Yeah, I know. I kind of think she should be yours." At the look on her face, he put up his hands. "You earned her, you know. I might have ended up putting her down just because I didn't have time for her with all the other stuff going on."

"Dad!"

"Well, you never know. What do you think would be a good name for her?"

"Soda's Storm Clouds. I'd call her Stormy for short."

"Sounds like a winner to me." Brad shook his head. "I think I'm going to keep you on retainer as horse namer."

"Did . . . did you mean it about her being mine?" DJ was almost afraid to ask. Surely he'd been joking.

"Yes, I did. I mean I do. You'll be on her registration papers as the legal owner."

"Wow! That's so . . . I—it's just awesome." DJ turned and gave him a two-arm, rib-crunching hug as hard as her sore arms could squeeze. "Thank you. A gazillion times over, thank you!"

"Once is enough. If you squeeze my aching ribs again, I'll have to scream. And I doubt it's cool for a father to scream because of his daughter's hugs."

DJ grinned and leaned into the warmth of his side.

Chapter · 16

"I'm really glad you're home . . . and safe."

"Me too." DJ looked up from her history book. "Come on in, Mom. I'm almost done."

Lindy sat down on the edge of the bed. "It felt like you were gone forever. And listening to the news about the water rising . . . DJ, all I could do was pray."

DJ leaned back in her chair and crossed one ankle over her other knee. "You were praying for me?"

"Yes, almost continually. As were Gran and Joe and Amy and Robert and Bobby and Billy—"

"God answered, right?"

Lindy nodded. "I've decided something."

DJ caught her breath. *Now what?* But her mother's face didn't wear gloom and doom. "What?"

"I've decided I'm going to make prayer a regular part of my life. I know Mom says we aren't supposed to bargain with God, but I told Him that if He would bring you safely home, I would put Him at the center of my life."

DJ felt like fireworks had just exploded, sending sparkles cascading in her mind.

"Now, I'm not exactly sure what I agreed to, but I intend to live up to it."

"Gran and I've been praying for you about this for a long time." The words tumbled out. DJ knew if she said much more, she would either explode and bounce off the walls or fall apart in tears. "Have you told Robert?"

Lindy nodded. "And my mother."

"So you believe Jesus is God's son?"

"I've believed that since I was a teenager but . . ."

DJ waited for the rest of the sentence. When none came, she leaned forward. "But?"

"But I let life take over and thought I could handle it all myself." Lindy shook her head. "Silly, huh?"

DJ got up and crossed to the bed, sitting down beside her mother. "Mom, this is the best present you could ever give me."

Lindy looked up, one side of her mouth quirked in a mini smile. "Even better than an Arabian filly of your own?"

DJ scrunched her eyes as if she was trying hard to make up her mind. "Yup, even better than Stormy." Her grin said she was teasing.

With a gentle and loving hand, Lindy smoothed a lock of hair back from DJ's cheek. "Brad was so proud of you—said he couldn't have made it through without your help. I am, too. I know what a level-headed, responsible kid you are."

"Most of the time," DJ joked.

"Most of the time, yes—and what more can a parent ask for?" She hugged her daughter close. "Guess what?" she whispered in DJ's ear. "Six more days till the wedding! I think I'm going to have a nervous breakdown."

"Not with your level-headed, responsible daughter on your tail, you won't."

The two laughed and hugged again.

"If what they say about a bad dress rehearsal being good for the actual performance holds true, then this wedding will go like a dream," Lindy said when DJ came down the stairs on Saturday morning.

"Last night wasn't *that* bad." DJ smiled at her mother, sitting in Gran's wing chair with her Bible on her lap. "You look good like that."

"Like what?"

"Reading like Gran in her chair."

Lindy nodded. "It just feels right to sit here to read my Bible. Must be all those prayers that were offered up from this very place."

DJ came over and sat beside her mother's feet, leaning against Lindy's knee. "It feels good, too."

Lindy stroked down the entire length of her daughter's hair. "You have such beautiful hair, DJ. How about if I style it for you for the wedding?"

"Okay by me. Are you going to have your hair done?"

"No, Robert asked me to wear it like I always do, so that's what I'm doing. I want this wedding to be a celebration that everyone will enjoy, not a fancy show."

Three hours later, all dressed in their wedding finery, Gran, Lindy, and DJ waited in the narthex of the church. All the guests had been seated, and the organ played a medley of hymns.

"These shoes pinch my feet," DJ muttered for Gran's ears only. DJ smoothed a hand down the front of her high-necked dusty rose satin dress. The sleeves, puffed at the top and fitted from elbow to wrist, made her feel like she had stepped out of the pages of an earlier time. The toe-length skirt swished, playing a melody of its own with every move she made. If princesses felt like this, DJ figured she could handle the role. She sniffed the miniature roses and carnations in her nosegay. They smelled almost but not quite as good as a horse.

"You look lovely, darlin'. You can take the shoes off after it's over. I brought your white sandals just in case," Gran whispered back.

"Leave it to you to be prepared." DJ turned to her mother. "Mom, you look fantabulous. Are you as happy as you look?"

Lindy nodded. "You know those butterflies you talk about before a show class?" DJ nodded. "How do you get them to fly in formation?"

DJ chuckled. "I concentrate on my horse until I enter the ring. Once I'm there, they fly together like they're supposed to. Works every time."

"Okay." Lindy took a deep breath and let it all out. "Here we go. Let's enter the ring!"

At a signal from the usher, the organist began the "Wedding March," and the doors swung open.

DJ listened for the beat and started out on her left foot like she'd been told. She held her bouquet of red carnations and white lilies in front of her and rubbed the ring she wore on her thumb. The ring that Lindy would place on Robert's finger.

She glided down the aisle, smiling at Brad and Jackie in one row, and the Yamamoto family in another. Amy gave her a thumbs-up signal.

When DJ reached the front, she smiled up at Robert; at Joe, who was best man; then down at Bobby and Billy. She winked at them, and they clapped their hands over their mouths to keep from giggling.

DJ turned and watched Gran and Lindy start through the door. While the shoulder-length veil hid her mother's face, she seemed to be lit from within with a glow that turned the simple cream-colored satin dress to radiant shimmers. Beside her, Gran beamed at everyone as their march down the aisle began. Everyone stood in honor of the bride.

DJ felt like cheering and crying all at once. She wanted to jump and shout, "Hey, that beautiful woman in satin is my mother—and the other one is my grandmother."

When the completed party was at the front, DJ moved to stand beside her mother and Gran so the three of them faced the altar. The minister asked, "Who gives this woman to this man?"

Gran and DJ replied together, "We do."

"Us too," the twins added with serious faces.

DJ, Lindy, and Gran hugged each other, barely able to keep from laughing. Then Robert gently took Lindy's hand and brought her forward. DJ took her place next to her mother, and Gran moved in next to her.

Feeling someone tug on her skirt, DJ looked down into the smiling faces of the twins, one on each side.

"Are you our sister yet?" Billy—or was it Bobby?—asked in his idea of a whisper. Those at the back of the church could hear it as well as those chuckling in the front.

DJ shook her head. "Soon."

The verses were read, the soloist sang, and the vows given in strong voices.

"Is she our mother yet?" Another dual whisper.

"Soon." DJ pulled the ring off her thumb and handed it to her mother. At least her part of the ceremony was done. The rings were exchanged and prayers said. As Robert kissed his bride, Bobby and Billy grinned at each other, clapped their hands, and threw themselves at Lindy's skirts. "Now we's a family!"

Laughter rippled through the room, and Robert and Lindy hugged both the boys and DJ.

"They're right, you know," Robert said for all the guests to hear. "We *are* a family now, praise God." To the applause of their family and friends, he tucked Lindy's hand in his arm and said, "Follow us, kids." The five of them, trailed by a laughing Gran and Joe, marched back down the aisle.

"Can we eat now?" one of the boys asked.

"I want cake," stated the other.

"Soon," DJ answered again. "Very soon."

They stepped out into the bright sun, and DJ raised her face to the warm rays. The storm clouds had passed, and they were headed into a bright new day—as a family.